PENGUIN BOOKS

GOTHIC TALES OF TERROR

*Volume One*
*Classic Horror Stories from Great Britain*

Peter Haining was born in England in 1940. He
began his career as a journalist, went on to become
Features Editor of a London magazine, and is now
Editorial Director of one of England's largest publishing houses. He has been an avid student of the
macabre and the occult for many years. Books to
his credit include *The Gentlewomen of Evil*, *The
Witchcraft Reader*, *The Wild Night Company*, and
*The Clans of Darkness*.

# GOTHIC TALES OF TERROR

## VOLUME ONE
### CLASSIC HORROR STORIES FROM
### GREAT BRITAIN

*Edited by Peter Haining*

PENGUIN BOOKS INC
BALTIMORE . MARYLAND

Penguin Books Inc., 7110 Ambassador Road, Baltimore, Maryland 21207, U.S.A.

—

First Published in the United States by Taplinger Publishing Co., Inc. 1972
Published in Penguin Books 1973
Reprinted 1974

—

Selection and original material copyright © Peter Haining, 1972

—

Printed in Great Britain

Yet tales of terror are her dear delight,
All in the wintry storm to read at night.

GEORGE CRABBE
(1784–1832)

# Contents

# *Acknowledgements*

In the compiling of a collection such as this a great many books containing source material have been consulted – the most important of these are acknowledged in the text – but I must further note my indebtedness to the pioneer work in the Gothic genre which was carried out by the late Montague Summers and related in his two superb works, *The Gothic Quest* and *A Gothic Bibliography*. Without their cataloguing and detailing of so much material my task would have been immeasurably more difficult, perhaps even impossible.

Libraries and their staffs have naturally played an important role in the locating of rare books, pamphlets and magazines and I would like to record my thanks to those anonymous people who worked tirelessly and with abounding enthusiasm at the British Museum, London, the London Library and the University of London. Also a special word of gratitude to Mr A. H. Wesencraft, the curator of the Harry Price Library in London whose personal knowledge has always been so generously imparted.

Finally my thanks go to the several private collectors who so graciously allowed me access to their valuable libraries but do not wish to be named here; Ken Chapman for his invaluable aid in locating much rare material; and to Richard Taplinger, my American publisher, who so eagerly supported this project when it was no more than an idea – I trust his faith has to some measure been justified by the completed work.

PETER HAINING

# Introduction

Again, all hail! if tales like thine may please,
St Luke alone can vanquish the disease.
Even Satan's self with thee might dread to dwell,
And in thy skull discern a deeper hell!

> From a poem by Lord Byron
> applauding the skill of Matthew Lewis,
> author of *The Monk*

To the average reader the term 'Gothic Novel' probably conjures up pictures of dust-laden, mouldering volumes full of archaic prose and stories of old fashioned deeds of daring. As a literary milestone it has few chroniclers and even fewer supporters; of its greatest products a mere handful are still remembered by title alone and such has been the uncaring hand of fate on its shelves that today only the world's greatest libraries can boast anything like a comprehensive coverage of its heyday.

Yet what was the Gothic Novel? And if it has, or had, any value, why should we trouble to remember it today?

For a period of seventy-five years (1765–1840) it was perhaps the most widely read and enjoyed form of popular literature in Britain and much of Europe. The most important novels in the genre were sold by the thousands, translated avidly and plagiarized to an astonishing degree. The interest in these books ranged through all stratas of society from the poorest members of the serving class struggling over each word to the intelligent and educated gentry – 'all were alive to the solemn and terrible graces of the appalling spectre', according to Dr Nathan Drake. This eighteenth century literary pundit who lived during the great vogue of the novel underlined the point further in his *Literary Hours* (1798) when he wrote, 'Of all the various kinds of superstition which have in any age influenced the human mind, none appear to have operated with so much effect as the Gothic ... even the most enlightened mind, the mind free from all taint of superstition, involuntarily acknowledges its power.'

The Gothic 'Influence' did not cease after this period, either. For evolving from these works have come the ghost and horror novels and stories which are now so keenly read around the world. Its influence, too, has directly and indirectly, inspired many subsequent important writers of the macabre, including E. F. Benson, M. R. James, Lord Dunsany, Bram Stoker, H. P. Lovecraft and many more. The transition, we can see, came through a gradual merging of the outright Gothic tale – as we shall define it in a minute – with other forms of expression as the novel itself came to include the whole range of human experience. Today, the 'tale of terror' is told for its own sake, but in continuance of the great tradition still satisfies that very human desire for new sensations without running any actual danger.

So, therefore, should we in our enjoyment of a good modern horror story forget its beginnings? Allow, in the words of Montague Summers, the greatest advocate and single most important scholar on the genre, all the original authors and their stories to pass 'scrip and scrippage to that phantom limbo "where things destroyed are swept to things unborn"?' Mark no popular memorial to the genius of Horace Walpole, Ann Radcliffe, Matthew Lewis, Charles Maturin; the skill of William Beckford, Francis ,Lathom, Harrison Ainsworth, Lord Lytton and Thomas Peckett Prest; even the anonymous hands of a veritable army of Gothic writers? Should all these – and their compatriots in Europe and indeed America – have no record save in learned treatises or in the minds of scholars?

The very fact that this book exists is part of the answer; the rest remains with your appreciation of what it contains. For me, the Gothic story is what it has always been, a marvellous escape from reality, an exciting journey through distant lands and strange experiences, a brush with the unknown, a footstep in the dark, a fluttering pulse and an evening's sheer entertainment.

If it had never been, I passionately believe, we should all have been the poorer.

*

What, though, *is* the Gothic tale? Dr Johnston defined it as 'a fiction, a tale of wild adventure of love and war' while William Lyon Phelps in *The Beginnings of the English Romantic Movement* (1893) said it was 'synonymous with the barbarous, the lawless and the tawdry'. Nearer to my own heart is Theodore Watts-Dunton's claim that it brought a 'renaissance of wonder' to English Literature.

The Gothic novel developed as a result of a genuine impulse felt among people of the late eighteenth century for freedom, for escape from the drab realities of life. Those who had, had to excess, and those who did not eked out bitter and miserable lives with little incentive and less hope. There was unrest everywhere, the threat of war hovered in the air continually and the future looked unrelentingly bleak. In literature both prose and poetry were straightjacketed in formality and even the most passionate reader was wearying of the endless social portraits and domestic scenes. A change, indeed, was long overdue.

What happened has been crystallized by Montague Summers in his definitive study of the genre, *The Gothic Quest*. He wrote, 'The Gothic romantic movement which arose did not merely open up new and lovelier vistas of literature, but, as was inevitable, the whole of human life ... in the ruined abbeys and frowning castles, in the haunted galleries and feudal halls, the pathless forests and lonely landscapes we recognize a revolt against the heavy materialism, the dullness and drab actuality of Hanoverian days.'

The writers of these stories, then, offered their readers a 'romantic retreat from the sordid ugliness of their surroundings' – the surroundings we can still see so vividly depicted in the paintings of Hogarth. They provided the wherewithal to stir the emotions of fear and pity. Their methods for achieving these ends were simple and straightforward as Eino Railo has shown in his study *The Haunted Castle* (1927):

1. By dealing with supernatural events as such, i.e. without argument or explanation.
2. By dealing with them in such a manner that they only appear to be supernatural and are capable of being satisfactorily explained.
3. By dealing with them in a manner which permits 'scientific' explanation.
4. By dealing realistically with horrors of which the worst reach into abnormality.

Within this context we find four distinctive kinds of Gothic tale, all covered by the one term and frequently intermingled. The earliest, and most basic form, was the romantic tale with haunted castle, tyrant master, oppressed maiden, knightly hero and the spectre figure 'to fill the viewer's mind with dread'. The intervention of the one on the lives of the others was to be the resolution of the story. To this framework was shortly added the elements of terror in the form of demonic beings and supernatural entities who usually acted with malevolence and cunning for a variety of purposes. In turn came the historical Gothic tale which drew on old legends and superstitions and finally, and of less importance, the Oriental tale which in the main relied heavily on the works such as *The Arabian Nights*.

These, then, were the facets of the Gothic tale which we find developing after the publication in 1765 of the work which can justifiably be called the originator of the genre, Horace Walpole's *The Castle of Otranto*.

That the authors were alive to their readers' desire for escape is well evidenced by how many of the tales are set in southern climes, *The Castle of Otranto*, for instance, in Italy, Mrs Radcliffe's *The Romance of the Forest* in France, and Matthew Lewis's *The Monk* in Spain. Even those novels which did not wander as far afield made the most of the black and mysterious reaches of Germany – which could have been on the other side of the moon for all the chances the average reader had of ever being able to visit them.

One cannot help noticing, too, the tremendous pace of the

stories, how the reader is hurled wildly from one incident to the next, how ghost piles upon ghost and blood, gore and death pour from the pages in a veritable flood. This was story-telling of a kind the public had never experienced before. It gripped their interest immediately and never allowed them to cease turning the pages. In the light of this it is perhaps not surprising to find that many of the stories were themselves written at great speed: Walpole, for instance, wrote *The Castle of Otranto* in less than two months, Lewis composed *The Monk* in ten weeks and the amazing William Beckford took a matter of days to complete *Vathek*. Perhaps the other claims of complete works having been written overnight should be treated with some scepticism, but such was the public demand at the height of the vogue, and the author's desire to communicate action and drama at great speed, that one can well believe that every writer, like Matthew Lewis was 'horribly bit by the rage of writing'.

The way in which the Gothic tales of terror and romance were published often differed from the norm, too. While the major works of Walpole, Radcliffe, Lewis, Maturin, etc. were produced in three and four volume sets, beautifully bound and embossed, the bulk appeared in cheaper editions or chapbooks which sold at anything from one penny to a shilling. In this way, of course, the publishers could hope to attract even the lowliest citizen and to ensure that no one could be in any doubt about the contents, each publication would carry a string of blood-curdling titles and sub-titles and be full of grim woodcuts and engravings liberally daubed in yellow, red, green and blue.

'To readers of the time,' Edith Birkhead has commented in her admirable study, *The Tale of Terror* (1921), 'a blue book meant not a dirty book or a pamphlet filled with statistics but a sixpenny shocker.'

Today these books – in many ways the fore-runners of paperbacks – are of the utmost rarity, but the reader with the time and inclination could spend a fascinating few hours in the British Museum perusing the library's extensive collection. In his reverie he would doubtless become aware, as I did, of the vast number of different publishers who put out these works, some to prosper and eventually turn their backs on such a beginning and become 'respectable', others to fall by the wayside in the cut-throat race of keeping up with the public taste. (One of the more successful of these men, according to legend, did so well at one period that he was frequently to be seen driving around London in a gold carriage complete with footmen in matching cockades!)

The major part of the market for the Gothic *romances* seems quite clearly to have been women – women of all classes from the meanest bawd to ladies of the nobility. That some of them occasionally had their sensibilities 'upset' by the stories seems quite likely, and indeed there is on record in Ireland one amusing account of a gentlewoman who, discussing a certain volume with her bookseller retorted, 'A shocking bad book to be sure, sir; but I have carefully looked through every page and underscored all the naughty passages and cautioned my young ladies what they are to skip without reading!'

In the case of pure Gothic *terror*, the indications are that men and women alike enthused over these, although William Blake in his 'Fair Elenor' (1783) makes us wonder if it wasn't perhaps true, in the final analysis, that the ladies had the stronger stomachs for horror? For as he says:

> She thinks of bones
> And grinning skulls and corruptible death
> Wrapped in his shroud; and now fancies she hears
> Deep sighs and sees pale, sickly ghosts gliding.

*

That, briefly then, was the world of the Gothic terror-romance. To the reading public it gave a new form of literary entertainment that has endured in a constantly changing form to the present day. But what, you might ask, of this collection? How does it enlarge on what I have discussed?

Obviously the republication of the great novels in the genre is something that can only come from demand and approaches to publishers; what I have attempted to do here is to trace the development of the genre through the *short tales of terror* written by its greatest exponents. In bringing these together I hope I have provided not only entertainment with the stories themselves, but also an insight into the people and times which began the evolvement towards today's most widely read type of short story, the ghost or horror tale.

The scope of my work has been as ambitious as sources and publishing economics will allow. The material ranges from Walpole to Edgar Allan Poe (who perhaps more than any other writer bridged the gap between the old Gothic tale and the modern horror story) and takes in Britain, the important centres of Europe, and America. In all I have selected some sixty stories to do justice to my theme,* but if I indicate that these are less than a tenth of all the tales I collected, you will have some idea of the wealth of material available.

The format I have adopted has its drawbacks, of course. Because only short stories were admissible, students of literature will probably notice that there are a number of important names missing – these are the men and women who had neither the time nor inclination to tackle such work and therefore, sadly, can be offered no place here. Sometimes, too, the reader will find what he may well consider a minor story by one of the major writers: this has been done deliberately as certain Gothic short stories do occasionally find their way into modern anthologies and I wanted wherever humanly possible to use only material that had been out of print for a century or more. Poetry, also, should perhaps have found a place in these pages as it was closely allied to the short story during the development of the genre, but a line had to be drawn somewhere and perhaps at a later date one might return to the subject to trace this influence in a further volume.

Finally, a caution. While every possible care has been taken to ensure accuracy and reliable accreditation of all the stories herein, the field is one in which errors (often deliberately created by unscrupulous publishers) abound, and I apologize now for

---

* *Editor's note* The work is being published in two volumes and consequently the stories are equally divided between each book.

any mistakes which may unwittingly have occurred. Still, be that as it may, I feel confident, that, in the words of Edith Birkhead, 'Here, indeed, may those who will and dare, sup full with horrors.'

PETER HAINING

London – New York
March 1970
January 1971

Pale Terror trembling guards the fountain's head,
And rouses Fancy on her wakeful bed;
From realms of viewless spirits tears the veil,
And there reveals the unutterable tale.

MATTHEW LEWIS

# Maddalena

*or*

## The Fate of the Florentines

## Horace Walpole

### (1717–1797)

'Visions, you know, have always been my pasture; and so far from growing old enough to quarrel with their emptiness, I almost think there is no wisdom comparable to that of exchanging what is called the realities of life for dreams. Old castles, old pictures, old histories, and the babble of old people, make one live back into centuries that cannot disappoint one. One holds fast and surely what is past.' So wrote Horace Walpole,* 4th Earl of Orford, dilettante, Member of Parliament, printer, architect and justifiably acclaimed 'Father of the Gothic Novel'. To this man we owe, in the words of Montague Summers, 'nothing less than a revolution in public taste – his romance. *The Castle of Otranto*, caused the ghost story as we know it today'.

Horace Walpole was the third son of the distinguished English statesman, Sir Robert Walpole (1676–1745), and although he was initially to follow in his father's footsteps as a politician, he formed an early delight in literature and was to make his mark on history in this sphere of activity. An extravagant and colourful personality (he frequently dressed in outlandish frills, silks and buckles), he soon became bored with Parliamentary life and in 1747 bought a coachman's cottage in Twickenham which he re-designed into the famous Gothic 'castle' at Strawberry Hill. This strange, brooding building undoubtedly gave Walpole macabre inspiration and soon 'The Abbot of Strawberry' (as he once signed himself) was busy writing: his masterwork, *The Castle of Otranto*, resulting in the autumn of 1764.

Fearing that the book might receive the same kind of public ridi-

*In a letter to his friend George Montague, 5 January 1766.

cule to which his 'castle' had been subjected, Walpole published it on Christmas Eve as a 'story translated from the Italian by William Marshal, gent'. However, its immediate acclaim caused him to admit to the authorship and confide to certain friends that it was also partly the result of a dream in which he had been in an ancient castle and 'seen a gigantic hand in armour' approach him.

Despite the immense success of *The Castle of Otranto*, which has continued to be read and appreciated ever since – Walpole was to write only one other Gothic novel, *The Mysterious Mother* (1768) and retell a handful of supernatural legends which were later included in his *Unpublished Tales*. (It is from this book that the following 'Italian Legend' is taken.) Nonetheless, he had achieved as scholars put it, 'a notable landmark in the history of English taste and English literature'. The Gothic novel had arrived.

THERE has always been to my mind a something hallowed and mysterious – a strange shadowy hue which seems not of this world, cast over the period of the history of Europe, generally designated 'the dark ages'. The minds of the nations seemed then to have sunk beneath the terrible and undermining convulsions which they had undergone (ere the barbarian banners were triumphantly unfurled, and waved over the conquests of the Hun, the Vandal, and the Goth,) into a long, dark, dismal night of heavy and restless slumber. Their greatest efforts, inconsiderable though always daring, resembled the misdirected starts of a troubled rest. Their intelligence seems to have been as a dream to themselves, and is ever so now to us. Yet then there was the soul of bold enterprise and watchful prowess; the mailed knight and lady fair – the castle, the warden, and the armed retainers – the sternest encounters relieved by the brightness of soft eyes, and the stoniest hearts refined and purified beneath the tender influence of women's love. Then too there was the name of Petrarch and his Laura, the wild and flashing light of Ariosto's muse, and the shadowy, unearthly inspiration of the patriot poet Dante. All, and much more than all this, is circled in our eyes within a halo which shades to softer loveliness, while it does not obscure those days of old romance; elating the mind to a fond enthusiasm for its brighter, while it steeps it into a willing forgetfulness of its darker and more repugnant shapes.

I remember hearing, some years ago, in the neighbourhood of Pisa, a legend of those dark yet fondly recollected times. I tell it, because it is of them, and this must be its only merit.

Everyone knows, or at least ought to know the wretched condition to which the city of Pisa was reduced about the end of the fifteenth century. Then it was that this little state almost fell a victim to the ambition, or causeless vengeance, of the Florentines; and but for a spark of high independence, her only and best inheritance of the great republic, which still lingered among the petty communities of Italy, together with a fixed and rooted hatred towards the invaders of her liberty, she would have been swept from her existence as a nation and a people.

Just on the eve of the breaking out of that concealed and bitter enmity which had long rankled in the bosoms of the two states, Florentines were to be seen in the streets of Pisa, and some of France upon the liberties of Naples had roused their animosity to its full and reckless strength, their inhabitants lived in a sort of society together, restrained and suspicious it is true, yet not without the traces of apparent friendship at least. Many Florentines were to be seen in the streets of Pisa, and some Pisans in the streets of Florence. Still the collisions, when they happened to come into collision, were far from friendly. Each scowled on the other, as if he would have given way at once to open enmity; but both were equally afraid to begin the attack. The heart's wish of the one was to have spit in the face of the other, and cry 'villain'; but somehow or other there existed for several years a sort of courtesy and restraint on both sides, which prevented this generally taking place, though sometimes it did occur.

As always happens in cases of this kind, the fair sex were sure to catch up and perpetuate the spirit of their lords. Withered matrons and spinster ladies had their national 'likes and dislikes', and along with these their feuds and bitter hostilities. In spite of all this, however, there were often little love affairs between the youth of the two cities, genial and fond, though at times burning into madness, the same as love has always appeared and now appears under the sun of Italy:

Where fiercest passion riots unconfined,
And in its madness fires the softest mind.

About this time there lived in Pisa a rich Florentine merchant, by name Jacopo. He had retired many years from trade, living quietly and contentedly on his gains. Pisa had become his place of residence, not so much from choice as from the strong associations with which it was connected in his mind – reminiscences of his early love, which his business-life and business-habits had all been unable to efface. Pisa had been the birthplace of his wife, and the first scene of the first and fondest affection he had ever known. There too the curtain had dropped, and left him widowed in heart and life. It was to him therefore as the enchanter's palace of light and darkness, which he would gladly have avoided, but which he found it impossible to tear himself from. He clung to it, as the spirit of an injured maid is said, in the old legends, to linger round the scene of her ruin. Those who have had the links of earliest and consequently most powerful love snapt asunder ere well united, alone know the feelings which still through life attach themselves to the scene of its first raptures, even though its original brightness may afterwards have been dimmed by becoming the scene of its bitterest desolation.

His wife died little more than a year after they had been united, leaving Jacopo a daughter. On this solitary pledge of his wedded love, all his attention had been lavished, and no expense spared; so that when Maddalena attained the age of womanhood there was scarcely a more accomplished, and not a more beautiful and gentle maiden to be found in the whole of Pisa. She was the image of her mother in figure, mind, and temper; and this had bound, if possible, more closely the ties of paternal affection. Jacopo, in the warmth of his love had never allowed her to leave his sight, or at least to be far from him. She was seldom to be met with in the public places, to which, in those days, the youth of her age so generally resorted. The lists, the dance, and the marriage feast were seldom graced by her presence; and even when she did make her appearance there, it was more as a spectator than a partaker in their gaieties; for Jacopo, though he lived in that dissolute age, knew and dreaded the danger to which youth and beauty are exposed to in their communion with the world.

Under the protection and guidance of this fatherly solicitude, Maddalena had arrived at the age of seventeen, and her heart was still her own. Many of the richest nobles of Pisa had made proposals for her hand, which Jacopo had deemed it prudent to refuse. Nay, scarce was there a finger in all Pisa that could touch the lute, which was not, some night, or other of the year, sweeping its chords beneath her latticed window. She used to smile as she heard the serenades to her own beauty, at times admiring the musicians skill, and sometimes blushing as she heard herself, in the same stanza compared to the rose, the lily, and the morning star.

One night in December – it was a cold and silent night, and the moon was up, which steeped, as it were, the pure white marble of Pisa in her own still purer and whiter light – Maddalena sat alone in her panelled chamber, in anxious expectation of the return of her father, who had been absent for some hours. The moonlight, streaming through the casement at which she sat, fell full and bright on the picture of an old crusader, giving a shadowy and unusual look to the countenance. This, together with the wild imagery of one of the Provençal ballads she had been reading, deeply embued her mind with a melancholy and tender feeling. She threw down the ballad -- she gazed on the bold and rugged outlines of the warrior's face – she attempted again to read – she desisted – and her eyes were riveted on the dark contour of the warrior's countenance, made more striking by the moonlight which rested upon it. Her mind could not settle. The hour and the scene altogether had wrought her up into that feverish feeling of romance which all young hearts have known, and they the most who have held least intercourse with the world.

While she continued in this state, half in pleasure, half in pain, the tones of a lute, in a slow and solemn Italian air, softly arose from below the casement at which she sat. At first the musician's fingers seemed scarcely to touch the chords. A single note was only now and then heard, like the distant murmur of a stream in the desert; then it gradually rose, and rose, and swelled into deeper softness, till the music at length burst into all the voluptuousness of perfect melody. Love could not have fixed upon a better hour to insinuate himself into the most impenetrable heart. A maid alone and in moonlight, with her senses floating on the lovely sounds of music, and her heart steeped in romantic feeling, rather woos than shuns his approaches; and we need scarcely inform our readers of either sex that so it was with Maddalena. — While the stranger sung in a clear and manly voice the words of a plaintive canzonetta, she drew back the casement, and half afraid, yet anxious to catch a glimpse of the musician, she leant herself timidly over it. The minstrel's eyes were fixed intently on the spot where she was; and when he saw her gently open the lattice, the notes of his lute seemed to swell into greater rapture, continuing on the air even after the musician had ceased. Maddalena could perceive, standing in a shadow of the moonlight, occasioned by a projecting part of the building, a young cavalier, wrapt in a loose cloak, and underneath it and across his breast one of those old fashioned lutes which we may see every day represented in the prints of the wandering Troubadours. The youth sighed, looked fondly, knelt, and talked of love. She spoke not, but she listened.

We write not for the stupid elf, squire, or dame, who has yet to be told that love needs but a beginning; or who cannot guess, till they have it staring them out of countenance in black and white, that Borgiano (for so the youth was called) and Maddalena were lovers before a week had past. It is time, however, to inform our readers that the youth was of Florentine extraction; that he had come to Pisa to avail himself of her schools, which had even then obtained great celebrity throughout Europe; and that he was in the middle of his studies when the incident which we have related took place.

Love, more perhaps in Italy than in any other country, has

always had free liberty to run its own course. Plant it but in two bosoms, and they are sure, in spite of the keenest vigilance, to have their meetings, their sighs, and their oaths. Jacopo knew no more of what was going on between his daughter and Borgiano than the nightingale which sat and sang above the bower, the scene of their earliest and only interview. Women, if the truth must be told, were then the same as they are now; daughters, in love matters, cheated their grey-haired fathers, and wives not infrequently their fatherly husbands.

Jacopo had been invited one evening to the house of the nobles, where several of the principal men of Pisa were assembled. Meali Lanfranchi, one of these, had paid court to the old gentleman, and completely cheated him out of his affection. A proposal was made by him for the hand of Maddalena, which was readily enough agreed to by Jacopo, who saw no reason, nor did he rack his brain for any, why he should not unite himself in the person of his daughter with the first of the Pisan nobility. Meali was a branch of the Lanfranchi family, one of the oldest and most powerful in the state. He had lived but little in his native place, and having newly returned to it after a long absence, he was, of course, the theme of much and general observation. His faults were either altogether unknown, or glossed over in the novelty of his return; and whether it was that Jacopo was dazzled with his rank, or captivated by his address, it was agreed before they parted that an interview should take place on the following day. Lanfranchi, satisfied with the progress he had made, went exulting to his palace, and Jacopo, musing and chuckling all the way over the elevation which he fondly anticipated for his daughter. He found her in a thoughtful mood, and waiting his return.

Borgiano had that evening made a more open avowal of his love than he had hitherto done. He had sworn his plighted faith, and had entreated a return from her; but however pleasing the request might be, it had distressed Maddalena. It was true she loved him, yet she had scarcely ever dared to own it to herself. With the strange caprice of every maiden who loves for the first time, she had dwelt with fond delight on her affection, and everything connected with it, when alone, and when it was seen only in the lights and shadows which fancy chose to bestow. Yet when her lover made the avowal, which she could not but expect, she was strangely disconcerted, and even depressed in spirits. In this state Jacopo found her on his arrival at home.

'Maddalena,' he said, patting her at the same time under the chin, 'what would you say, Maddalena, if you were now to become a wife?'

'A wife, father?'

'Aye, a wife, Maddalena; and a wife to the first noble in Pisa. What think you of that, my girl?'

'I think, father; I only think I would rather be your child than wife to the first noble in all the world.'

'Well, well, Maddalena, your affection is not unreturned, and I like you not the worse for this coyness; 'tis your sex's best failing. But we shall talk more of it tomorrow, when your lover comes. And then, my girl, when he is here, there will be soft words and stolen glances. You will be gay as a lark in a May morning, and your lover – but good night, good night,' he said, suddenly stopping when he saw that his daughter took little heed of the rhapsody he was pouring upon her ears; and imprinting a paternal kiss upon her cheek, which had flushed into a burning crimson when she heard him talk of the morrow and a lover, he left her to herself.

Next morning Lanfranchi, punctual to a moment, was at the house of his new friend Jacopo, who of course received him with the kindest welcome. – Maddalena stood with her arm leant upon the lattice, her eye turned to the broad expanse of field and vineyard, gradually lessening perspectively till they joined in with the blue towering Appenines in the distance: and, strange for a female in the immediate presence of an avowed lover to whom she had no heart to give, she looked all unconcern. But it was only the appearance of a command, and not a real mastery which she possessed over her feelings. And Lanfranchi, though a man of the world, and little accustomed to lay any restraint upon his inclinations, felt confused under the composed look and commanding beauty of Maddalena. She ventured to cast but one glance on her professed suitor. He was a man apparently about thirty years of age, with a keen grey eye, whose expression, though subdued at present, seemed rather of command than of entreaty, and suited well with the dark and overshadowing mass of his eyebrows. A green silk doublet, bespangled with gold, hung down from his shoulder, and in his hand he bore a round cap of the same colour, which was ornamented with an eagle's feather.

When Jacopo, in order to give him an opportunity of declaring himself, had left the apartment, Lanfranchi changed immediately his former awkwardness and want of confidence for the manner and freedom of a man who had only to speak in order to be obeyed. Gazing on Maddalena with the licentious look of a professed libertine, he seized her by the hand, and poured forth a torrent of vows and protestations. The maid gave a sort of involuntary shudder, and started back, but Lanfranchi still pressing his suit, attempted to put his arm around her waist.

'Is this the manner, Sir, you repay my father's kindness, by insult to his daughter?' she said and she accompanied these words with a look of offended dignity, which for a moment confused Lanfranchi, and ere he could recover from his surprise, she left the apartment.

Jacopo, as he entered the room, smiling, smirking, and looking sufficiently wise, found Lanfranchi standing as if a spell had hardened every limb of him to stone. But whatever the old man's thoughts were, he determined to remain silent on the subject till the other should inform him of what had passed. Lanfranchi, however, bade him adieu, without adverting even to the object of his visit, but not without many invitations from Jacopo to return on the morrow. The morrow came, and so did Lanfranchi; but Maddalena remained inflexible in never leaving her apartment as long as his visits lasted. She was convinced that her father would never force her into a marriage so much against her inclination. All this time (what will not love effect?) Borgiano and the maiden had their stolen interviews, and surely not the less delightful that they were stolen. Often, when all were at rest, and the moon threw her faint light across their path, they wandered in the garden, which sloped beautifully down to the banks of the river. There daybreak often found them, and that hour – the loveliest hour of all – when the sun rises from behind the Appenines, like a new-born spirit starting from the mountain tops, and his freshened beams rest on the glittering rocks of Carrara and the white marble buildings of Pisa, or float on the green waves of the far-rolling Tuscan sea – that hour was the least beloved by them, for it told of parting.

Matters were in this situation when the report of the invasion of Charles the Eighth of France, who had already entered the Italian frontier, spread consternation far and wide throughout the whole land. Some beheld in this wild and ambitious scheme, the foreboding clouds of that ruin and desolation which, a month or two afterwards, it spread over the fairest cities in Italy. Others, who with reason or from imagination looked upon their wretchedness as already beyond the possibility of being increased, turned to the Gallic invader as to a saving angel, and flocked to do him homage.

The gradual and ambitious encroachments made upon the territories of Pisa by the Florentines, had, previously to Charles's invasion, kindled into a flame those sparks of enmity which had so long lain smothered in the bosoms of the two states. Pisa had now taken the alarm, but as yet ventured upon no act of open hostility. She lay like a tigress in her den, determined to avoid any offensive measures on her part, but resolved to offer the firmest resistance to any assault upon her liberty. She knew that her ill-disciplined and worse organized army formed but a feeble barrier against the regular condottiere of Florence. This consciousness of her own weakness, more, perhaps, than any other consideration, served to continue, so long, her sullen and unwilling forebearance.

To her inhabitants in such a state of mind, Providence seemed to have interposed in directing Charles's march across the Alps. Scarcely, therefore, had he quitted Lucca on his way to this city, when its inhabitants gathered around him, pouring forth the most tumultuous expressions of their joy, and hailing him as the saviour of their country. The wavering and deceitful policy of this monarch, whose good deeds seldom went farther than the promise, was not wanting on the present occasion. He met the ardent solicitations of the Pisans, and gave them the assurance of his protection. This favourable reply raised them from the lowest despondency into the wildest exultation. Regarding it as their emancipation from slavery, they broke forth into the utmost excesses; every badge which distinguished the Florentines throughout the city was demolished: and it might well be said, that the matin bell of liberty to the one state pealed a death note on the ear of the other.

Jacopo was within the sphere of this persecution, but on account of his age, and the influence he possessed with many of the nobles, he was allowed two days to deliberate whether he should leave the city unmolested, or brave the fury of the populace, by remaining within its walls. Lanfranchi had all along continued his suit to Maddalena, with as little success as he had at first commenced it; though his addresses had assumed a more determined tone, and he demanded her union with him, more as if he were condescending on his part than she granting a favour on hers.

On the night after Charles had made his entrance into Pisa, Lanfranchi came to the house of Jacopo. He was dressed out as a reveller, and indeed from his eye and gait, it was evident he had lately risen from a company of Bacchanals. The old man, attended by his daughter, sat in an apartment the farthest from the street, (for not a Florentine dared to be seen), whose dark hangings and sombre tapestry gave a melancholy hue to the faces of its inmates, and contrasted strangely with the gay colours of Lanfranchi's dress. As the old man rose to receive him, his guest seemed to cast upon them both the eye of a serpent, which already has its prey within its power; – pityless, remorseless, determined, – his look was like that of one, whose word carried life or death. Jacopo seemed almost to tremble under his scowl, and the heart of Maddalena almost leapt from its seat as her eye met his.

'Cheer up, good father,' said Lanfranchi in a merry tone –

'Nay, look not so dull, man, ne'er a dog in all Pisa dares to bite when I say hold; and the boldest hand in the city shall not touch a single hair of that white head of thine if I say no.'

The old man remained silent.

'Rouse thee, man, or I shall think thee coward if thou quakest so. As father of my bride, I pledge my word you shall be safe were you ten Florentines, aye, by the holy virgin, were you ten thousand Florentines.'

At this last sentence, the tears burst forth from Maddalena's eyes.

'What! weeping and groans on a bridal eve? Throw them away, my pretty ladybird, we shall have no clouds over our honeymoon:' continued Lanfranchi in the same tone – and advancing to where Maddalena was sitting, he attempted to put his arm round her neck but she repelled him – 'Desist, sir; for though you were hateful to me in your prosperity you are doubly so in our distress.'

Lanfranchi burst into a scornful laugh – 'How pretty the fair thing looks in a passion; by my faith she might enact tragedy.'

Jacopo's blood was fired within him, at this last insult.

'Villain!' cried the old man, – 'dost thou think to trample upon us in our misery; and triumph over us in our misfortunes? She shall never be yours.'

'Villain – ha – villain; I think that was the word you used. Why you miserable dotard – villain, forsooth – a gentleman can't make love to your daughter, and tell her how beautiful she is, but you must call him – villain! Hark you, old man, you have been drinking freely, and I pardon you; besides, there's not a Florentine now in the city that does not hate us Pisans. I tell you plainly, your daughter shall be mine tomorrow!'

'Never! never!' exclaimed Maddalena.

'Hush! peace! my pretty prattler. By tomorrow's night she shall be mine, old man, or death may chance to you, and worse perhaps to her.'

'Holy virgin!' said Maddalena, kneeling before a small image of the Madonna, 'shield his grey hairs – save, oh save my father; let not him die for the misfortune of his daughter.'

A pretty enough orison, and prettily told,' said Lanfranchi, scornfully; 'but even that will scarcely save you.'

Maddalena still knelt; her hands were clasped over her face, down which her tears fell heavy and fast.

Lanfranchi looked upon her more with the eye of wild licentious appetite than of love; more of keen-searching mockery than of pity.

'Pray on,' he said, 'aye, pray loud, and well too; it may be the last prayer your father can partake in.'

'Have you no pity?' exclaimed Maddalena, seizing at the same time, with both hands, the corner of his doublet; 'Spare him — stain not your hands with his blood. — I am your victim, slay but me, heaven will pardon you the murder.'

'That may be all in good time, thou prattler,' Lanfranchi replied, in a deep calm tone of voice; and tearing his doublet from her hands, he left the house.

When he was gone, the father and the daughter remained silent. The old man's thoughts of himself and his own safety were drowned in one resistless and prevailing feeling of horror for the wretch who had just left them. He thought but of the villain that interview had disclosed; to whom, but a day before, he would have given his daughter in preference to any other. Maddalena's emotions were not so easily concentrated in one point. The man whom she had always before regarded with indifference; as one whom, as she could not love, she could easily cast off; now appeared to her in all the colours of a demon, crying aloud for her father's blood and her destruction. But wretched and pitiable as was her present condition, she attempted to comfort her father, who had sunk upon his knees in a state of terrible bewilderment. The old man rose as she addressed him; he had no heart to speak. His dim eye, on which a tear swam, like a cloud of vapour hanging over a dying light, the last of a deserted hall, told more than his tongue could utter. 'Good night, Maddalena, good night, and heaven be your protector;' said Jacopo as he embraced his daughter. 'God have mercy,' answered Maddalena, as he left the apartment.

When the maiden was left alone, and her mind was distracted

between the thoughts which tempested within her breast; then, indeed, she felt the anguish of a horror-haunted spirit. – When she thought of her approaching doom, and her own miserable situation, she fancied the cup of her grief was full. But when she recurred to Borgiano, and thought of their love and their misfortunes, her spirit died within her. Then she reverted to the horrors threatened to her by Lanfranchi, and an icy coldness crept around her heart, like one who stands on the outermost verge of a tottering precipice, chained to the spot without the power of escaping. And was there really no way of saving themselves? she thought, and at last resolved to go to the house of a Pisan lady, at a short distance, and consult with her on the likeliest means of escape.

She seated herself at the latticed window; her eyes rested, but all unconscious of its beauties, on the splendid night scene which lay stretched before her. The moon shone over the vine rows, the palaces, and hanging tower of Pisa, resting on the calm, clear wave which almost slumbered on the shore close by; for the sea had not then, as it has now, like a capricious mistress, abandoned this delightful city; while the nightingale, seated on top branch of an olive tree, seemed to 'tune its sad heart to music.' But these had no pleasure for Maddalena's mind. Her mind rolled unobserving over the beauties of the one, and her ear was not attuned to the melody of the other. She had remained in this situation but a short time, when the figure of a man appeared below the window at which she sat. It was Borgiano. He beckoned her to speak; but ere she could undo the casement, he had fled, and immediately a crowd of Pisans ran shouting up the same path he had taken. When the confusion was past, and all was again silent, Maddalena, wrapping herself in one of those long folding mantles, so common a part of the ladies' dress in the fifteenth and sixteenth centuries, glided with light and anxious steps along the gallery leading from her apartment into the street. Even in that hour of darkness, (for it was already far past midnight), the ways were crowded with groups of Pisans, and resounded with the burst of their boisterous revelry. With trembling step and fearful heart, she hurried past the assemblages of riotous nobility and drunken rabble, which in every corner stopped her passage; and, luckily no one attempted to interrupt her, till she arrived in safety at the top of the avenue, from which she had a view of Lanfranchi's palace. She raised the hood and veil which hid her face, retiring at the same time beneath a portico at one corner of the street. While she stood here, looking down upon the palace below, which shone with a thousand coloured lights, and from which she heard the sounds of Wassail, and the dull loud notes of music, an individual in a loose riding cloak, with a mask over his face, approached her. Maddalena drew forward her veil, but the stranger had already recognized her. 'You are a Florentine, and daughter of the rich Jacopo;' he said, in a low voice.

'May I ask,' replied Maddalena, 'who the stranger is that takes an interest in my fate?' – as she spoke, she again walked on.

'Stay!' said the other, seizing her by the arm 'are you mad thus to run heedless to your own destruction? Fly! another hour in this city! the death hounds are abroad; and woe to every Florentine that shall then be found in Pisa. These are not the words of a man who has any interest in you or in anyone more than common humanity.' The maid knew not what to say, or what course to follow. She had no reason to distrust the stranger; yet at that moment she was little inclined to place confidence in anyone. While she remained in this uncertainty, several individuals, clad in bright armour, issued from the palace, and entered the avenue, at the top of which Maddalena and the stranger stood.

'Haste with me, maiden,' he said anxiously, 'or all is lost.'

She remained mute and motionless; she had not the power to move. This last adventure had completely worn out her already exhausted spirits. In the meantime the stranger raised her up in his arms, and hastened with her down a narrow passage, leading from that part of the city to its suburbs. They had scarcely entered in, when the voices of those they had already seen, were heard distinctly as they passed along the avenue.

'Now for the old Florentine, Jacopo!' said one.

'Take him,' said another, 'flesh, blood, bones, and all: give me his coffers, my staunch hearts, and you may hack, and hew, and divide his anatomy amongst you.'

'Coffers!' interrupted a third, 'curse the old dotard and his gold; give me but —'

'What?' said a gruff voice.

'The sweet little jewel that decks his casket.'

'A mere lapidary; shut his mouth!' said, or rather bellowed the same rough voice, and a hoarse laugh ran through the whole party.

'Aye, laugh on,' said the other, 'but this bright jewel shall be mine; this lady rose-bud; this daughter of the Florentine.'

'Bah;' said he of the gruff voice, 'the girl shall be mine; I've sworn it on my sword: and whoso makes me break my oath, must break its blade too.'

The sound of their voices gradually dying away as they passed on, their conversation was no longer audible. The stranger, in the meantime, hurried on with Maddalena, sometimes supporting her in his arms, at other times assisting her as she walked almost unconsciously along the path he conducted her. At length they reached an old massy ruin, the solitary remnant of a former age, where were already assembled a crowd of Florentines. Amongst them there were several females, many with their clothes loosely thrown about them, some bearing in their arms half naked children, and all of them in tears. When Maddalena and her conductor arrived, they were just upon the point of setting forth upon their journey. She was mounted on a quiet pony, along side of which the stranger rode; leading it by the reins, and at the same time assisting the maiden to retain her seat. With several other ladies, apparently of distinction, she was placed in the troop of armed horsemen; all the time unconscious of where she was, or of the part she was acting. Thus prepared, the party rode on at a sharp pace in the direction of Florence.

They chose, for greater security, a lonely and sequestered road along the banks of the river Arno. The rapid motion with which she was hurried forward, somewhat brought Maddalena to herself. 'My father! where is my father?' were the first words she uttered.

'Fear not, he is safe,' said the person who conducted her. There was no time for further conversation on either side, for as they turned up a road which led round a little bend formed by the river, they were met by a party of armed Pisans. 'Pisans!' ran in whispers round the whole of the one party. 'Arm, arm my brave hearts!' shouted the other. In a moment or two all was in an uproar – the men on either side attacked, and were attacked, while the clash of their arms was mingled with the screams of the women.

The stroke of a halbert, aimed at her conductor, slightly grazed the shoulder of Maddalena; and slight as the blow was, it was sufficient in her enfeebled state to fell her to the ground. This encounter ended as encounters generally did at that time, especially in Italy, where more blows were given than blood spilt, and more booty taken than lives lost. In the present instance, as each Pisan struck his adversary to the ground, he took from him what most pleased his fancy, and then galloped off, leaving his companions to provide for themselves. Maddalena became the prize of one of these, not, however, before her conductor, who persisted in defending her, was fell to the earth by a mortal wound. In falling, the mask dropped from his face, and revealed to Maddalena the features of a faithful domestic, who had lived in her father's family several years before. She was hurried again towards the city with even more rapidity than she had left it. When again within its walls, she was led to one of the prisons, where many Florentines had that night been shut up. As they passed along the damp gallery, a dismal groan arose from the floor of the passage which conducted to her cell. The light of a torch, which was carried by one of the attendants, discovered the body of a man apparently in the writhings of death, stretched across her path. As she passed him, the dying man took firm hold of Maddalena's foot with his hand. The others attempted to disengage his grip, but it was clenched in a death grasp. Maddalena still possessed her senses enough to be able to discover the mangled form of the expiring wretch who held her to the spot, and to see the dark clotted blood in which he weltered. At the sight she staggered where she stood, and uttering one of those wild hysteric screams, which anyone who has once heard a woman utter can never forget, she fell senseless to the ground. A Pisan of the party severed the hand and arm from the body; for a while it still clung to her foot, as the others carried her within the cell; where, laying her on a stone bench which ran along the wall, they left her in a death-like stupor, to live or die.

Charles the Eighth, though fond in the extreme of all the pomp and display of chivalry, possessed few of the milder and more refined shades of character, which, in its early existence, distinguished that splendid institution. A species of absurd vanity often drowned in him even the common feelings, which are seldom altogether extinguished in any breast, imparting to some parts of his character a dismal hue of tyranny and oppression, while it stamped others with an appearance of weakness and imbecility. In spite of all this, he was not devoid, when freed from this his worst and greatest failing, of the seeds of a more elevated mind, which, had it never felt the contagion of despotic royalty and its power, might have ripened into better fruit than it ever bore in him His best virtue was, perhaps, a strong commiseration for the miseries of which his ambition was the cause, and a consequent desire of repairing them.

A feeling of this sort came over him when he was informed of the outrages committed on the Florentines; and next morning, forgetting the pleasures to which he was naturally so prone, he rode through the streets of Pisa, attended by a party of armed knights, commanding the prisoners to be immediately released. Among the number of miserable prisons which the monarch visited in person, was the one into which Maddalena had been thrown the evening before. Accompanied by two knights of his retinue, he entered the cell where she sat, or rather lay, on the stone bench which was formed out of the body of the wall. The lower part of her garment was soaked in blood, her face was as pale as ashes, and her eyes being closed, it seemed as if she was in sound untroubled sleep.

'A pretty chaffinch this,' whispered one of his attendants in the ear of the king; 'is't not a shame to see so pretty a bird in so rascally a cage?'

'By my knighthood, 'tis,' replied the monarch in an equally low tone of voice.

'Methinks these white lips,' replied the other, 'would grow redder beneath a kiss – shall I taste them out of courtesy to your majesty?'

'Out upon thee for a recreant knight! – can I not taste them, think ye, myself?'

As he spoke, the monarch leaning forward imprinted a kiss on Maddalena's cheek. She started up, and looked wildly round her – her large blue eyes were dim, but even then not without expression.

'Ha! there's blood upon thee!' the poor girl exclaimed; 'see – there, you have murdered Jacopo – go wash thyself – thou hast too gay a look!'

The monarch spoke some words of comfort to her, taking her at the same time by the hand.

'Let me see thee,' said Maddalena, in a hollow disconnected voice, and looking closely into his face. 'I'faith, a sprightly executioner to kill an old man and then his daughter. There's an old song – but I've forgot it now: I used to sing it long ago, and Borgiano liked it – no, no, I don't mean Borgiano – Jacopo liked it, but – they're all dead! all dead!

> With crimson drops his grey hairs dripp'd,
>   For they murdered the good old man!
> The knights they danced, the ladies tripp'd,
>   As they murdered the poor old man!
> Then sadly sing, heigh ho! sweetheart!
>   They've murdered the poor old man.'

'A sad song for so lovely a songstress!' said one of the attendants to the monarch.

'Some love-go-mad girl,' said the other, 'some Florent –'

'Hush!' interrupted the king, 'this is no subject for ribald mirth.'

'Mirth!' said the broken-spirited girl, casting her body at the same time into a sort of capricious bend, and smiling; 'mirth, my love-a-lady – aye, there shall be mirth, and laughter, and smiles, when this poor heart shall have broken utterly. We shall sing, and be happy, and free from care, when all of us meet again, Jacopo, Borgiano, and I. Nay, look not so dull – your bride is not dead. Hark! there she sings, light o' heart – she is beckoning you. – Go!'

Less, probably, than those of any other man of his day, had Charles's feelings been exposed to the appeals of human misery. The pitiable condition of this wretched girl roused his deepest commiseration; and 'albeit unused to the melting mood,' he turned away from the melancholy spectacle, and fairly wept.

'Nay, weep not for me,' she said in a more connected tone than she had hitherto used; 'all, all are gone who loved me, or whom I loved – and I must weep when I would often sing.'

She spoke in such a note of settled sorrow, and such a look of placid composure still seemed to float over her destitution, that the monarch could not command his feelings enough to speak. While he stood thus mute and pitying, his eyes intently fixed on the still beautiful face and form of the unfortunate maniac, Jacopo rushed into the apartment. He ran to his daughter, but she started wildly back from his embrace.

'Do you not know your father?' said the old man; 'I am your father – speak to me Maddalena!' – 'You! you cannot be my father,' exclaimed the girl, 'his hair was as white as snow, and yours is red with blood! look how the blood drips from it – my old father's blood and Borgiano's.'

'My child! my child!' the old man cried in an agony of heart.

'This is indeed too much for him to bear!' said the monarch, supporting at the same time Jacopo, whose inward feeling had completely overpowered his strength. Maddalena came up to him as he lay fainting in the arms of the king.

'Sad heart, he has lost his father too; perhaps they have murdered his lady-love, as they did my Borgiano. We shall weep together over our misfortunes; aye, and sing to ease our hearts.'

By the order of the monarch, the still insensible Jacopo was borne out of the apartment. From this state of lethargy he never totally recovered, lingering on in the same miserable condition for several days till at length he expired. Once only, immediately before his death, when his soul, as it were, found a resting place between light and darkness, he recovered for a moment to a sense of his afflictions. In this brief period, he had called frequently on the name of his daughter, and accused Lanfranchi as the murderer of himself and her.

Charles himself assisted in conveying Maddalena from her dungeon; and, save that her cheek was pale, and her eye was at one time moveless, and at another rolled wildly, she was still as beautiful as ever. A weeping fit, which had succeeded in the capriciousness of her mind's disorder, the wilder ebullitions of the moment before, had tamed her look into that state of meaningless quiescence, the most distressful condition in which anyone can witness a fellow creature, especially as it was in the present instance, in the case of a beautiful young woman.

As they were slowly conducting her along, they were met at the prison-door by Borgiano, who having been freed along with the other Florentines, took the earliest opportunity of inquiring after the fate of Maddalena.

We shall not attempt to describe their meeting. Even he was unrecognized. All may imagine, though none can adequately describe the utter loneliness of heart, the agony and the despair which fell upon Borgiano, as he saw his fondest hopes blighted; and when he beheld the face upon which in happier hours he had delighted to gaze, now causelessly brightening into a smile, and now clouded with a tear, giving him the maddening assurance that her mind was gone for ever.

In the retirement to which she was conducted, her frenzy gradually subsided from its first turbulence, and at times she had even a dim recollection of the miseries which had befallen her. But these intervals were always brief, and she again, after a few minutes' apparent coherence relapsed into the dull sombre melancholy, which ever marks the victims of her distemper. Borgiano, though he strove when she was gay, to assume in her presence a gaiety which his heart knew not, was in secret tormented with a thousand passions. Pity, and love, and sorrow

at times melted his very heart within him; at others, a sort of un-
directed rage swept away every softer feeling: till at length his
whole soul settled in a burning and wreckless desire of vengeance, and Lanfranchi was its object. He had been present
when Jacopo had uttered his last words. They had sunk deep
into his heart at the time, and weighed heavily on his recollection now. Till at last he waited only for a fitting opportunity to
hurl destruction on the head of a wretch whom the lips of a
dying man had cursed.

As he walked one evening moody and melancholy along a
quiet and retired quarter of the Lang' darno, he met with the
object of his hate; swords were mutually drawn; and however
Lanfranchi might have the advantage of his adversary in skill,
Borgiano pressed upon him so furiously, that he rushed within
his guard, and stabbed him to the heart. The weapon broke as
the dying man staggered to the ground; and sheathing the remainder of his sword, the Florentine retired hastily from the
spot. A crowd was speedily gathered to the scene. At first the
name of Lanfranchi was on the lips of everyone; but when
'Florence' was decyphered in the faint light on the fragment of
the weapon, which someone had extracted, still reeking and
warm with blood, the sorrow of the people burst forth into
tumultuous rage. 'Some accursed Florentine!' passed from man
to man. – 'Down with the Florentine curs!' was next their cry;
and when their minds were more settled, and they knew their
own object, a search was commenced in the house of every
Florentine family within the city. Borgiano, with that infatuation which seems ever to haunt men when engaged in the most
desperate enterprises, had carried home with him the handle of
the blade. It was stained with blood – the fragment corresponded with it exactly. These were damning proofs of guilt to the
minds of the outrageous populace, to whom even more super-
ficial evidence would have sufficed to convict any Florentine in
their present ebullition of fury. They hurried him before judges
who were not less prejudiced against him than his accusers; and
as in those days proceedings against a criminal were brief in
proportion as they were unjust; – his trial was concluded ere
it was well begun. Death by the wheel was the sentence.

Maddalena, even in her lowliness and retirement, could distinguish the name of Borgiano uttered in curses fom Pisan tongues from every corner of the city. Roused by this into a state of excitement, restless, yet without an object, she escaped into the street; her dress in careless disarray, her hair untied, and her eye fixed in the wildness of unsettled thought. She wandered on through the people, an object of pity to some, of derision to others. She came, whether by instinct or chance, to the very spot where the whole circumstance of death was going on. Already had Borgiano's slow and terrible death been begun. He had endured the agonies of their most refined torture without gratifying their cruelty by uttering a single groan; and even the executioners, in spite of their hatred to his race, began almost to pity him, when they beheld one so young surrendering his life without a murmur.

Maddalena saw and recognized Borgiano as his limbs were writhing on the wheel. She rushed into the middle of the crowd – most of whom made way for her, as if unconsciously; others she tore aside, till she stood on the very spot where Borgiano was expiring on the rack; his eyes were then almost closed for ever – another turn of the wheel, and life was fled. Had Maddalena really recognized in him the companion of her moonlight wandering, the gentle wooer, whom even in her madness her soul had ceaselessly clung to? – For a while she stood motionless, as if gazing on the terrific sight before her, then fell to the ground stiff and moveless. Her heart had leapt for ever from its seat; and there she lay a cold and lifeless corpse, within a foot or two of Borgiano's mangled remains.

They were buried in the same grave by the kindness, or it may have been, by the derision of the Pisans. It was immediately under the hanging tower; and upon it some friend had placed a slab of polished marble, upon which the words 'Borgiano and Maddalena' were engraved. At the beginning of the last century it was still to be seen, though the ground had then gradually risen around it, and it was in some degree hid beneath a profusion of luxuriant wild flowers. Now it is completely lost to the sight, and no record remains to tell of their ill-fated love.

# Sir Bertrand

## Mrs Anne Letitia Barbauld

### (1773)

Amazing as it may seem in hindsight, it was to be a decade before
the next really significant Gothic novel after Walpole's *The Castle
of Otranto* appeared. This was *The Champion of Virtue* (retitled
*The Old English Baron: A Gothic Story* on its second edition) by
Clara Reeve which was published in 1777 at Colchester in Essex. (It is
an interesting point that the book should have been issued not from
London but from 'the oldest recorded town in Britain' still complete
with ancient fortifications and chambers.)

In the interim period there had indeed been numerous poor imitations of Walpole's masterpiece, and some other motley works, but
just one 'fragment' is worthy of our attention here, this next
item, *Sir Bertrand*. Some authorities have attributed this story –
undoubtedly intended as part of a much longer work – to Miss
Reeve, but enquiries show conclusively that it was the work of Anne
Letitia Aikin, the wife of a clergyman Reverend Rochemont Bar-
bauld. It was first published in a collection of stories in 1773 and
prefaced by an essay 'On the Pleasure Derived from Objects of
Terror'. In the *Letters of Horace Walpole* we learn that this Miss
Aikin had visited the master at Strawberry Hill because of the deep
impression his book had had on her. 'She desired to see the Castle of
Otranto and I let her see all the antiquities of it', he wrote. Later
he read the young woman's story and noted, 'It was excellent. Miss
Aikin flattered me even by stooping to tread in my eccentric steps.'
This was an opinion he never changed, even in later life when,
sickened by 'all these pale shadows of my story' he delivered a
scathing attack on the Gothic genre in general, and *The Old English
Baron* in particular.

In *Sir Bertrand*, Miss Aikin demonstrates a grasp of the principles of the Gothic terror-romance which doubly underline the misfortune that she did not go on further with the projected novel -- completed, it might well have changed the pattern of the developing genre. Certainly, though, she is well entitled to the praise of Edith Birkhead who wrote, 'She seems to have realized the limitations of Walpole's marvellous machinery, and to have attempted to explore the regions of the fearful unknown ... She is a pioneer in the art of freezing the blood.'

SIR BERTRAND turned his steed towards the wolds, hoping to cross these dreary moors before the curfew. But ere he had proceeded half his journey, he was bewildered by the different tracks; and not being able, as far as the eye could reach, to espy any object but the brown heath surrounding him, he was at length quite uncertain which way he should direct his course. Night overtook him in this situation. It was one of those nights when the moon gives a faint glimmering of light through the thick black clouds of a louring sky. Now and then she emerged in full splendour from her veil, and then instantly retired behind it, having just served to give the forlorn Sir Bertrand a wide extended prospect over the desolate waste. Hope and native courage awhile urged him to push forwards, but at length the increasing darkness and fatigue of body and mind overcame him; he dreaded moving from the ground he stood on, for fear of unknown pits and bogs; and alighting from his horse in despair, he threw himself on the ground. He had not long continued in that posture when the sullen toll of a distant bell struck his ears— he started up, and turning towards the sound, discerned a dim twinkling light. Instantly he seized his horse's bridle, and with cautious steps advanced towards it. After a painful march he was stopped by a moated ditch surrounding the place from whence the light proceeded; and by a momentary glimpse of moonlight he had a full view of a large antique mansion, with turrets at the corners, and an ample porch in the centre. The injuries of time were strongly marked on everything about it. The roof in various places was fallen in, the battlements were half demolished, and the windows broken and dismantled. A drawbridge, with a ruinous gateway at each end, led to the court before the building. He entered; and instantly the light, which proceeded from a window in one of the turrets, glided along and vanished; at the same moment the moon sunk beneath a black cloud, and the night was darker than ever. All was silent. – Sir Bertrand fastened his steed under a shed, and approaching the house, traversed its whole front with light and slow footsteps. – All was still as death. – He looked in at the lower windows, but could not distinguish a single obpect through the imprenetrable gloom. After a short parley with himself, he entered the porch, and seizing a massy iron knocker at the gate, lifted it up, and, hesitating, at length struck a loud stroke. – The noise resounded through the whole mansion with hollow echoes. – All was still again – he repeated the strokes more boldly and loudly – another interval ensued – a third time he knocked, and a third time all was still. He then fell back to some distance, that he might discern whether any light could be seen in the whole front. It again appeared in the same place, and quickly glided away as before – at the same instant a deep sullen toll sounded from the turret. Sir Bertrand's heart made a fearful stop – he was awhile motionless; then terror impelled him to make some hasty steps towards his steed – but shame stopped his flight; and urged by honour and a resistless desire of finishing the adventure, he returned to the porch; and working up his soul to a full steadiness of resolution, he drew forth his sword with one hand, and with the other lifted up the latch of the gate. The heavy door, creaking upon its hinges, reluctantly yielded to his hand – he applied his shoulder to it, and forced it open – he quitted it, and stepped forward – the door instantly shut with a thundering clap. Sir Bertrand's blood was chilled – he turned back to find the door, and it was long ere his trembling hands could seize it: but his utmost strength could not open it again. After several ineffectual attempts, he looked behind him, and beheld, across a hall, upon a large staircase, a pale bluish flame which cast a dismal gleam of light around. He again summoned forth his courage, and advanced, towards it. It retired. He came to the foot of the stairs, and after a moment's deliberation ascended. He went slowly up, the flame retiring before him, till he came to a wide gallery. The flame proceeded along it, and he followed in silent horror, treading lightly, for the echoes of his footsteps startled him. It led him to the foot of another staircase, and then vanished. At the same instant another toll sounded from the turret – Sir Bertrand felt it strike upon his heart. He was now in total darkness, and with his arms extended, began to ascend the second staircase. A dead cold hand met his left hand, and firmly grasped it, drawing him forcibly forwards – he endeavoured to disengage himself, but could not – he made a furious blow with his sword, and instantly a loud shriek pierced his ears, and the dead hand was left powerless with his. – He dropped it, and rushed forward with a desperate valour. The stairs were narrow and winding, and interrupted by frequent breaches, and loose fragments of stone. The staircase grew narrower and narrower, and at length terminated in a low iron gate. Sir Bertrand pushed it open – it led to an intricate winding passage, just large enough to admit a person upon his hands and knees. A faint glimmering of light served to show the nature of the place. Sir Bertrand entered. A deep hollow groan resounded from a distance through the vault. He went forwards, and proceeding beyond the first turning, he discerned the same blue flame which had before conducted him. He followed it. The vault at length suddenly opened into a lofty gallery, in the midst of which a figure appeared, completely armed, thrusting forwards the bloody stump of an arm with a terrible frown and menacing gesture, and brandishing a sword in his hand. Sir Bertrand undauntedly sprang forwards, and aimed a fierce blow at the figure; it instantly vanished, letting fall a massy iron key. The flame now rested upon a pair of ample folding-doors at the end of the gallery. Sir Bertrand went up to it, and applied the key to a brazen lock – with difficulty he turned the bolt – instantly the doors flew open, and discovered a large apartment, at the end of which was a coffin rested upon a bier, with a taper burning upon each side of it. Along the room on both sides were gigantic statues of black marble, attired in the Moorish habit, and holding enormous sabres in their right hands. Each of them reared his arm, and advanced one leg forwards, as the knight entered; at the same moment the lid of the coffin flew open, and the bell tolled. The flame still glided forwards, and Sir Bertrand resolutely followed, till he arrived within six paces of the coffin. Suddenly, a lady in a shroud and black veil rose up in it, and stretched out her arms towards him; at the same time the statues clashed their sabres and advanced. Sir Bertrand flew to the lady and clasped her in his arms – she threw up her veil and kissed his lips; and instantly the whole building shook as with an earthquake, and fell asunder with a horrible crash. Sir Bertrand was thrown into a sudden trance, and on recovering, found himself seated on a velvet sofa, in the most magnificent room he had ever seen, lighted with innumerable tapers, in lustres of pure crystal. A sumptuous banquet was set in the middle. The doors opening to soft music, a lady of incomparable beauty, attired with amazing splendour, entered, surrounded by a troop of gay nymphs more fair than the Graces. She advanced to the knight, and falling on her knees thanked him as her deliverer. The nymphs placed a garland of laurel upon his head, and the lady led him by the hand to the banquet, and sat beside him. The nymphs placed themselves at the table, and a numerous train of servants entering, served up the feast, delicious music playing all the time. Sir Bertrand could not speak for astonishment – he could only return their honours by courteous looks and gestures.

# The Haunted Chamber

## Mrs Ann Radcliffe
## (1764–1823)

As Miss Clara Reeve, the next great name in the Gothic genre after Walpole, published no short stories admissible for this collection,* we now pass on to the celebrated figure of Mrs Radcliffe. With the close of the eighteenth century we find that the enthusiasm which had greeted the work of the two main pioneers had now reached the proportions of a real demand for more such novels and stories. But for the appearance of Mrs Radcliffe and her work, however, there are serious grounds for contention that the genre might have swiftly faded into obscurity if not disappeared completely; for during her most constructive years she completely overshadowed her contemporaries and most other Gothic tales were either dreadfully bad or pitiful copies.

Still today something of an illusive character, Mrs Radcliffe is probably most widely known through the references to her in Jane Austen's *Northanger Abbey*. Despite the fact that she is much noted in passing in the letters and memoirs of her contemporaries, biographical details are scarce and the titles of her books and their publication are often the only record of her passing years. The wife of a weekly newspaper editor, she lived either quietly at home writing or travelling abroad, observing and recording. She undoubtedly read a great deal from old chronicles and contemporary works and the publication of an undistinguished historical novel with Gothic undertones, *The Recess* by Sophia Lee in 1785 is believed to have caught her interest and prompted her to take up her own pen in a similar venture. In quick succession followed, *A Sicilian*

---

* Miss Reeve did write one short supernatural tale, 'Castle Connor – An Irish Story', but this was unfortunately lost on a coach journey in May 1787 and never recovered.

*Romance* (1790), *The Romance of the Forest* (1791) and her greatest achievement, *The Mysteries of Udolpho* in 1794. The books won her an immediate and devoted following and were to influence writers such as Byron, Shelley, Charlotte Brontë and, in particular, two Gothic writers-to-be, Matthew Lewis and Charles Maturin.

The following episode from *The Mysteries of Udolpho* has been described by William Hazlitt in *The English Novelists* as 'the greatest treat which Mrs Radcliffe's pen has provided for the lovers of the marvellous and the terrible'. Her other great admirer, Sir Walter Scott, also prefaced the story thus: 'The best and most admired specimen of her art is the mysterious disappearance of Ludovico, after having undertaken to watch for a night in a haunted apartment; and the mind of the reader is finely wound up for some strange catastrophe, by the admirable ghost story which he is represented as perusing to amuse his solitude, as the scene closes upon him.'

THE count gave orders for the north apartments to be opened and prepared for the reception of Ludovico; but Dorothee, remembering what she had lately witnessed there, feared to obey; and not one of the other servants daring to venture thither, the rooms remained shut up till the time when Ludovico was to retire thither for the night, an hour for which the whole household waited with the greatest impatience.

After supper, Ludovico, by the order of the count, attended him in his closet, where they remained alone for near half an hour, and on leaving which his lord delivered to him a sword.

'It has seen service in mortal quarrels,' said the count, jocosely; 'you will use it honourably no doubt in a spiritual one. Tomorrow let me hear that there is not one ghost remaining in the château.'

Ludovico received it with a respectful bow. 'You shall be obeyed, my lord,' said he; 'I will engage that no spectre shall disturb the peace of the château after this night.'

They now returned to the supper-room, where the count's guests awaited to accompany him and Ludovico to the north apartments; and Dorothee, being summoned for the keys, delivered them to Ludovico, who then led the way, followed by most of the inhabitants of the château. Having reached the back staircase, several of the servants shrunk back and refused to go further, but the rest followed him to the top of the staircase, where a broad landing-place allowed them to flock round him, while he applied the key to the door, during which they watched him with as much eager curiosity as if he had been performing some magical rite.

Ludovico, unaccustomed to the lock, could not turn it, and Dorothee, who had lingered far behind, was called forward, under whose hand the door opened slowly, and her eye glancing within the dusky chamber, she uttered a sudden shriek and retreated. At this signal of alarm the greater part of the crowd hurried down, and the count, Henri, and Ludovico were left alone to pursue the inquiry, who instantly rushed into the apartment, Ludovico with a drawn sword, which he had just time to draw from the scabbard, the count with a lamp in his hand, and Henri carrying a basket containing provision for the courageous adventurer.

Having looked hastily round the first room, where nothing appeared to justify alarm, they passed on to the second; and here too all being quiet, they proceeded to a third in a more tempered step. The count had now leisure to smile at the discomposure into which he had been surprised, and to ask Ludovico in which room he designed to pass the night.

'There are several chambers beyond these, your excellenza,' said Ludovico, pointing to a door, 'and in one of them is a bed, they say. I will pass the night there; and when I am weary of watching, I can lie down.'

'Good,' said the count; 'let us go on. You see, these rooms show nothing but damp walls and decaying furniture. I have been so much occupied since I came to the château, that I have not looked into them till now. Remember, Ludovico, to tell the housekeeper tomorrow to throw open these windows. The damask hangings are dropping to pieces; I will have them taken down, and this antique furniture removed.'

'Dear sir,' said Henri, 'here is an armchair so massy with gilding, that it resembles one of the state chairs in the Louvre more than anything else.'

'Yes,' said the count, stopping a moment to survey it, 'there is a history belonging to that chair, but I have not time to tell it; let us pass on. This suite runs to a greater extent than I imagined; it is many years since I was in them. But where is the bedroom you speak of, Ludovico? These are only ante-chambers to the great drawing-room. I remember them in their splendour.'

'The bed, my lord,' replied Ludovico, 'they told me was in a room that opens beyond the saloon and terminates the suite.'

'O, here is the saloon,' said the count, as they entered the spacious apartment in which Emily and Dorothee had rested. He here stood for a moment, surveying the reliques of faded grandeur which it exhibited, the sumptuous tapestry, the long and low sofas of velvet with frames heavily carved and gilded, the floor inlaid with small squares of fine marble, and covered in the centre with a piece of rich tapestry work, the casements of painted glass, and the large Venetian mirrors of a size and quality such as that period France could not make, which reflected on every side the spacious apartment. These had also formerly reflected a gay and brilliant scene, for this had been the state room of the château, and here the marchioness had held the assemblies that made part of the festivities of her nuptials. If the wand of a magician could have recalled the vanished groups – many of them vanished even from the earth! – that once had passed over these polished mirrors, what a varied and contrasted picture would they have exhibited with the present! Now, instead of a blaze of lights, and a splendid and busy crowd, they reflected only the rays of the one glimmering lamp which the count held up, and which scarcely served to show the three forlorn figures that stood surveying the room, and the spacious and dusky walls around them.

'Ah!' said the count to Henri, awaking from his deep reverie, 'how the scene is changed since last I saw it! I was a young man then, and the marchioness was alive and in her bloom; many other persons were here too, who are now no more. There stood the orchestra, here we tripped in many a sprightly maze – the walls echoing to the dance. Now they resound only one feeble voice, and even that will, ere long, be heard no more. My son, remember that I was once as young as yourself, and that you must pass away like those who have preceded you – like those who, as they sung and danced in this most gay apartment, forgot that years are made up of moments, and that every step they took carried them nearer to their graves. But such reflections are useless – I had almost said criminal – unless they teach us to prepare for eternity, since otherwise they cloud our present happiness without guiding us to a future one. But enough of this – let us go on.'

Ludovico now opened the door of the bedroom, and the count, as he entered, was struck with the funeral appearance which the dark arras gave to it. He approached the bed with an emotion of solemnity, and, perceiving it to be covered with a pall of black velvet, paused. 'What can this mean?' said he, as he gazed upon it.

'I have heard, my lord,' said Ludovico, as he stood at the feet, looking within the canopied curtains, 'that the Lady Marchioness de Villeroi died in this chamber, and remained here till she was removed to be buried; and this perhaps, signor, may account for the pall.'

The count made no reply, but stood for a few moments engaged in thought, and evidently much affected. Then, turning to Ludovico, he asked him with a serious air, whether he thought his courage would support him through the night. 'If you doubt this,' added the count, 'do not be ashamed to own it; I will release you from your engagement without exposing you to the triumphs of your fellow-servants.' Ludovico paused; pride and something very like fear seemed struggling in his breast: pride, however, was victorious; – he blushed, and his hesitation ceased.

'No, my lord,' said he, 'I will go through with what I have begun; and I am grateful for your consideration. On that hearth I will make a fire; and with the good cheer in this basket, I doubt not I shall do well.'

'Be it so,' said the count: 'but how will you beguile the tediousness of the night, if you do not sleep?'

'When I am weary, my lord,' replied Ludovico, 'I shall not fear to sleep; in the meanwhile, I have a book that will entertain me.'

'Well,' said the count, 'I hope nothing will disturb you; but if you should be seriously alarmed in the night, come to my apartment. I have too much confidence in your good sense and courage to believe you will be alarmed on slight grounds, or suffer the gloom of this chamber, or its remote situation, to overcome you with ideal terrors. Tomorrow I shall have to thank you for an important service; these rooms shall then be thrown open, and my people will then be convinced of their error. Good night, Ludovico; let me see you early in the morning, and remember what I lately said to you.'

'I will, my lord. Good night to your excellenza – let me attend you with the light.'

He lighted the count and Henri through the chambers to the outer door. On the landing-place stood a lamp, which one of the affrighted servants had left; and Henri, as he took it up, again bade Ludovico 'good night', who, having respectfully returned the wish, closed the door upon them and fastened it. Then, as he retired to the bedchamber, he examined the rooms through which he passed with more minuteness than he had done before; for he apprehended that some person might have concealed himself in them for the purpose of frightening him. No one, however, but himself was in these chambers; and leaving open the doors through which he passed, he came again to the great drawing-room, whose spaciousness and silent gloom somewhat startled him. For a moment he stood looking back through the long suite of rooms he had just quitted; and as he turned, perceiving a light and his own figure reflected in one of the large mirrors, he started. Other objects, too, were seen obscurely on its dark surface, but he paused not to examine them, and returned hastily into the bedroom, as he surveyed which, he observed the door of the Oriel, and opened it. All within was still. On looking round, his eye was caught by the portrait of the deceased marchioness, upon which he gazed for a considerable time with great attention and some surprise; and then, having examined the closet, he returned into the bedroom, where he kindled a wood fire, the bright blaze of which revived his spirit which had begun to yield to the gloom and silence of the place; for gusts of wind alone broke at intervals this silence. He now drew a small table and a chair near the fire, took a bottle of wine and some cold provision out of his basket, and regaled himself. When he had finished his repast he laid his sword upon the table, and not feeling disposed to sleep, drew from his pocket the book he had spoken of. It was a volume of old Provençal tales. Having stirred the fire into a brighter blaze, trimmed his lamp, and drawn his chair upon the hearth, he began to read; and his attention was soon wholly occupied by the scenes which the page disclosed.

The count, meanwhile, had returned to the supper-room, whither those of the party who had attended him to the north apartment had retreated upon hearing Dorothee's scream, and who were now earnest in their inquiries concerning those chambers. The count rallied his guests on their precipitate retreat, and on the superstitious inclinations which had occasioned it; and this led to the question, whether the spirit, after it has quitted the body, is ever permitted to revisit the earth; and if it is, whether it was possible for spirits to become visible to the sense? The baron was of opinion, that the first was probable, and the last was possible; and he endeavoured to justify this opinion by respectable authorities, both ancient and modern, which he quoted. The count, however, was decidedly against him; and a long conversation ensued, in which the usual arguments on these subjects were on both sides brought forward with skill and discussed with candour, but without converting either party to the opinion of his opponent. The effect of their conversation on their auditors was various. Though the count had much the superiority of the baron in point of argument, he had fewer adherents; for that love, so natural to the human mind, of whatever is able to distend its faculties with wonder and astonishment, attached the majority of the company to the side of the baron; and though many of the count's propositions were unanswerable, his opponents were inclined to believe this the consequence of their own want of knowledge on so abstracted a subject, rather than that arguments did not exist which were forcible enough to conquer him.

Blanche was pale with attention, till the ridicule in her father's glance called a blush upon her countenance, and she then endeavoured to forget the superstitious tales she had been told in the convent. Meanwhile, Emily had been listening with deep attention to the discussion of what was to her a very interesting question; and remembering the appearance she had seen in the apartment of the late marchioness, she was frequently chilled with awe. Several times she was on the point of mentioning what she had seen, but the fear of giving pain to the count, and the dread of his ridicule, restrained her; and awaiting in anxious expectation the event of Ludovico's intrepidity, she determined that her future silence should depend upon it.

When the party had separated for the night, and the count retired to his dressing-room, the remembrance of the desolate scenes he had so lately witnessed in his own mansion deeply affected him, but at length he was aroused from his reverie and his silence. 'What music is that I hear?' said he suddenly to his valet. 'Who plays at this late hour?'

The man made no reply; and the count continued to listen, and then added, 'That is no common musician; he touches the instrument with a delicate hand. Who is it, Pierre?'

'My lord!' said the man, hesitatingly.

'Who plays that instrument?' repeated the count.

'Does not your lordship know, then?' said the valet.

'What mean you?' said the count, somewhat sternly.

'Nothing, my lord, I mean nothing,' rejoined the man submissively; 'only – that music – goes about the house at midnight often, and I thought your lordship might have heard it before.'

'Music goes about the house at midnight! Poor fellow! Does nobody dance to the music, too?'

'It is not in the château, I believe, my lord. The sounds come from the woods, they say, though they seem so very near; but then a spirit can do anything.'

'Ah, poor fellow!' said the count, 'I perceive you are as silly as the rest of them; tomorrow you will be convinced of your ridiculous error. But, hark! what noise is that?'

'Oh, my lord! that is the voice we often hear with music.'

'Often!' said the count; 'how often, pray? It is a very fine one.'

'Why, my lord, I myself have not heard it more than two or three times; but there are those who have lived here longer, that have heard it often enough.'

'What a swell was that!' exclaimed the count, as he still listened; 'and now, what a dying cadence! This is surely something more than mortal.'

'That is what they say, my lord,' said the valet; 'they say it is nothing mortal that utters it; and if I might say my thoughts —'

'Peace!' said the count; and he listened till the strain died away.

'This is strange,' said he, as he returned from the window. 'Close the casements, Pierre.'

Pierre obeyed, and the count soon after dismissed him, but did not so soon lose the remembrance of the music, which long vibrated in his fancy in tones of melting sweetness, while surprise and perplexity engaged his thoughts.

Ludovico, meanwhile, in his remote chamber, heard now and then the faint echo of a closing door as the family retired to rest; and then the hall-clock, at a great distance, struck twelve. 'It is midnight,' said he, and he looked suspiciously round the spacious chamber. The fire on the hearth was now nearly expiring, for his attention having been engaged by the book before him, he had forgotten everything besides; but he soon added fresh wood, not because he was cold, though the night was stormy, but because he was cheerless; and having again trimmed the lamp, he poured out a glass of wine, drew his chair nearer to the crackling blaze, tried to be deaf to the wind that howled mournfully at the casements, endeavoured to abstract his mind from the melancholy that was stealing upon him, and again took up his book. It had been lent to him by Dorothee, who had formerly picked it up in an obscure corner of the marquis's library;

and who, having opened it, and perceived some of the marvels it related, had carefully preserved it for her own entertainment, its condition giving her some excuse for detaining it from its proper station. The damp corner into which it had fallen, had caused the cover to be so disfigured and mouldy, and the leaves to be so discoloured with spots, that it was not without difficulty the letters could be traced. The fictions of the Provençal writers, whether drawn fom the Arabian legends brought by the Saracens into Spain, or recounting the chivalric exploits performed by crusaders whom the troubadours accompanied to the East, were generally splendid, and always marvellous both in scenery and incident; and it is not wonderful that Dorothee and Ludovico should be fascinated by inventions which had captivated the careless imagination in every rank of society in a former age. Some of the tales, however, in the book now before Ludovico were of simple structure, and exhibited nothing of the magnificent machinery and heroic manners which usually characterized the fables of the twelfth century, and of this description was the one he now happened to open; which in its original style was of great length, but may be thus shortly related. The reader will perceive it is strongly tinctured with the superstition of the times.

### THE PROVENÇAL TALE

There lived, in the province of Bretagne, a noble baron, famous for his magnificence and courtly hospitalities. His castle was graced with ladies of exquisite beauty, and thronged with illustrious knights; for the honour he paid to feats of chivalry invited the brave of distant countries to enter his lists, and his court was more splendid than those of many princes. Eight minstrels were retained in his service, who used to sing to their harps romantic fictions taken from the Arabians, or adventures of chivalry that befell knights during the crusades, or the martial deeds of the baron, their lord; while he, surrounded by his knights and ladies, banqueted in the great hall of the castle, where the costly tapestry that adorned the walls with pictured exploits of his ancestors, the casements of painted glass enriched with armorial bearings, the gorgeous banners that waved along the roof, the sumptuous canopies, the profusion of gold and silver that glittered on the sideboards, the numerous dishes that covered the tables, the number and gay liveries of the attendants, with the chivalric and splendid attire of the guests, united to form a scene of magnificence such as we may not hope to see in these degenerate days.

Of the baron the following adventure is related: – One night, having retired late from the banquet to his chamber, and dismissed his attendants, he was surprised by the appearance of a stranger of a noble air, but of a sorrowful and dejected countenance. Believing that this person had been secreted in the apartment, since it appeared impossible he could have lately passed the ante-room unobserved by the pages in waiting, who would have prevented this intrusion on their lord, the baron, calling loudly for his people, drew his sword, which he had not yet taken from his side, and stood upon his defence. The stranger, slowly advancing, told him that there was nothing to fear; that he came with no hostile intent, but to communicate to him a terrible secret, which it was necessary for him to know.

The baron, appeased by the courteous manner of the stranger, after surveying him for some time in silence, returned his sword into the scabbard, and desired him to explain the means by which he had obtained access to the chamber, and the purpose of this extraordinary visit.

Without answering either of these inquiries, the stranger said that he could not then explain himself, but that, if the baron would follow him to the edge of the forest, at a short distance from the castle walls, he would there convince him that he had something of importance to disclose.

This proposal again alarmed the baron, who would scarcely believe that the stranger meant to draw him to so solitary a spot at this hour of the night without harbouring a design against his life, and he refused to go; observing at the same time, that if the stranger's purpose was an honourable one, he would not persist in refusing to reveal the occasion of his visit in the apartment where they stood.

While he spoke this, he viewed the stranger still more attentively than before, but observed no change in his countenance, nor any symptom that might intimate a consciousness of evil design. He was habited like a knight, was of a tall and majestic stature, and of dignified and courteous manners. Still, however, he refused to communicate the substance of his errand in any place but that he had mentioned; and at the same time gave hints concerning the secret he would disclose, that awakened a degree of solemn curiosity in the baron, which at length induced him to consent to the stranger on certain conditions.

'Sir knight,' said he, 'I will attend you to the forest, and will take with me only four of my people, who shall witness our conference.'

To this, however, the knight objected.

'What I would disclose,' said he with solemnity, 'is to you alone. There are only three living persons to whom the circumstance is known: it is of more consequence to you and your house than I shall now explain. In future years you will look back to this night with satisfaction or repentance, accordingly as you now determine. As you would hereafter prosper, follow me; I pledge you the honour of a knight that no evil shall befall you. If you are contented to dare futurity, remain in your chamber, and I will depart as I came.'

'Sir knight,' replied the baron; 'how is it possible that my future peace can depend upon my present determination?'

'That is not now to be told,' said the stranger; 'I have explained myself to the utmost. It is late: if you follow me it must be quickly; you will do well to consider the alternative.'

The baron mused, and, as he looked upon the knight, he perceived his countenance assume a singular solemnity.

(Here Ludovico thought he heard a noise, and he threw a glance round the chamber, and then held up the lamp to assist his observation; but not perceiving anything to confirm his alarm, he took up the book again, and pursued the story.)

The baron paced his apartment for some time in silence, impressed by the words of the stranger, whose extraordinary request he feared to grant, and feared also to refuse. At length he said, 'Sir knight, you are utterly unknown to me; tell me, yourself, is it reasonable that I should trust myself alone with a stranger, at this hour, in the solitary forest? Tell me, at least, who you are, and who assisted to secrete you in this chamber.'

The knight frowned at these words, and was a moment silent; then, with a countenance somewhat stern, he said, 'I am an English knight; I am called Sir Bevys of Lancaster, and my deeds are not unknown at the holy city, whence I was returning to my native land, when I was benighted in the forest.'

'You name is not unknown to fame,' said the baron; 'I have heard of it.' (The knight looked haughtily.) 'But why, since my castle is known to entertain all true knights, did not your herald announce you? Why did you not appear at the banquet, where your presence would have been welcomed, instead of hiding yourself in my castle, and stealing to my chamber at midnight?'

The stranger frowned, and turned away in silence; but the baron repeated the questions.

'I come not,' said the knight, 'to answer inquiries, but to reveal facts. If you would know more, follow me; and again I pledge the honour of a knight that you shall return in safety. Be quick in your determination – I must be gone.'

After some farther hesitation, the baron determined to follow the stranger, and to see the result of his extraordinary request; he therefore again drew forth his sword, and, taking up a lamp, bade the knight lead on. The latter obeyed; and opening the door of the chamber, they passed into the ante-room, where the baron, surprised to find all his pages asleep, stopped, and with hasty violence was going to reprimand them for their carelessness, when the knight waved his hand, and looked so expressively at the baron, that the latter restrained his resentment, and passed on.

The knight, having descended a staircase, opened a secret door, which the baron had believed was only known to himself; and proceeding through several narrow and winding passages, came at length to a small gate that opened beyond the walls of the castle. Perceiving that these secret passages were so well known to a stranger, the baron felt inclined to turn back from an adventure that appeared to partake of treachery as well as danger. Then, considering that he was armed, and observing the courteous and noble air of his conductor, his courage returned, he blushed that it had failed him for a moment, and he resolved to trace the mystery to its source.

He now found himself on the healthy platform, before the great gates of his castle, where, on looking up, he perceived lights glimmering in the different casements of the guests, who were retiring to sleep; and while he shivered in the blast, and looked on the dark and desolate scene around him, he thought of the comforts of his warm chamber, rendered cheerful by the blaze of wood, and felt, for a moment, the full contrast of his present situation.

(Here Ludovico paused a moment, and, looking at his own fire, gave it a brightening stir.)

The wind was strong, and the baron watched his lamp with anxiety, expecting every moment, to see it extinguished; but though the flame wavered, it did not expire, and he still followed the stranger, who often sighed as he went, but did not speak.

When they reached the borders of the forest, the knight turned and raised his head, as if he meant to address the baron, but then closing his lips, in silence he walked on.

As they entered beneath the dark and spreading boughs, the baron, affected by the solemnity of the scene, hesitated whether to proceed, and demanded how much farther they were to go. The knight replied only by a gesture, and the baron, with hesitating steps and a suspicious eye, followed through an obscure and intricate path, till, having proceeded a considerable way, he again demanded whither they were going, and refused to proceed unless he was informed.

As he said this, he looked at his own sword and at the knight alternately, who shook his head, and whose dejected countenance disarmed the baron, for a moment, of suspicion.

'A little farther is the place whither I would lead you,' said the stranger; 'no evil shall befall you – I have sworn it on the honour of a knight.'

The baron, reassured, again followed in silence, and they soon arrived at a deep recess of the forest, where the dark and lofty chestnuts entirely excluded the sky, and which was so overgrown with underwood that they proceeded with difficulty. The knight sighed deeply as he passed, and sometimes paused; and having at length reached a spot where the trees crowded into a knot, he turned, and with a terrific look, pointing to the ground, the baron saw there the body of a man, stretched at its length, and weltering in blood; a ghastly wound was on the forehead, and death appeared already to have contracted the features.

The baron, on perceiving the spectacle, started in horror, looked at the knight for explanation, and was then going to raise the body, and examine if there were any remains of life; but the stranger, waving his hand, fixed upon him a look so earnest and mournful, as not only much surprised him, but made him desist.

But what were the baron's emotions when, on holding the lamp near the features of the corpse, he discovered the exact resemblance of the stranger his conductor, to whom he now looked up in astonishment and inquiry! As he gazed he perceived the countenance of the knight change and begin to fade, till his whole form gradually vanished from his astonished sense! While the baron stood, fixed to the spot, a voice was heard to utter these words:

(Ludovico started, and laid down the book for he thought he heard a voice in the chamber, and he looked towards the bed, where, however, he saw only the dark curtain and the pall. He listened, scarcely daring to draw his breath, but heard only the distant roaring of the sea in the storm, and the blast that rushed by the casements; when, concluding that he had been deceived by its sighings, he took up his book to finish his story.)

While the baron stood, fixed to the spot, a voice was heard to utter these words:

'The body of Sir Bevys of Lancaster, a noble knight of England, lies before you. He was this night waylaid and murdered, as he journeyed from the holy city towards his native land. Respect the honour of knighthood, and the law of humanity; inter the body in christian ground, and cause his murderers to be punished. As ye observe or neglect this, shall peace and happiness, or war and misery, light upon you and your house for ever!'

The baron, when he recovered from the awe and astonishment into which this adventure had thrown him, returned to his castle, whither he caused the body of Sir Bevys to be removed; and on the following day it was interred, with the honours of knighthood, in the chapel of the castle, attended by all the noble knights and ladies who graced the court of Baron de Brunne.

Ludovico, having finished this story, laid aside the book, for he felt drowsy; and after putting more wood on the fire, and taking another glass of wine, he reposed himself in the armchair on the hearth. In his dream he still beheld the chamber where the rally was, and once or twice started from imperfect slumbers, imagining he saw a man's face looking over the high back of his armchair. This idea had so strongly impressed him, that, when he raised his eyes, he almost expected to meet other eyes fixed upon his own; and he quitted his seat, and looked behind the chair before he felt perfectly convinced that no person was there.

Thus closed the hour.

The count, who had slept little during the night, rose early, and, anxious to speak with Ludovico, went to the north apartment; but the outer door having been fastened on the preceding night, he was obliged to knock loudly for admittance. Neither the knocking nor his voice was heard: he renewed his calls more loudly than before; after which a total silence ensued; and the count, finding all his efforts to be heard ineffectual, at length began to fear that some accident had befallen Ludovico, whom terror of an imaginary being might have deprived of his senses. He therefore left the door with an intention of summoning his servants to force it open, some of whom he now heard moving in the lower part of the château.

To the count's inquiries whether they had seen or heard anything of Ludovico, they replied, in affright, that not one of them had ventured on the north side of the château since the preceding night.

'He sleeps soundly, then,' said the count, 'and is at such a distance from the outer door, which is fastened, that to gain admittance to the chambers it will be necessary to force it. Bring an instrument, and follow me.'

The servants stood mute and dejected, and it was not till nearly all the household were assembled, that the count's orders were obeyed. In the meantime, Dorothee was telling of a door that opened from a gallery leading from the great staircase into the last ante-room of the saloon, and this being much nearer to the bedchamber, it appeared probable that Ludovico might be easily awakened by an attempt to open it. Thither, therefore, the count went; but his voice was as ineffectual at this door as it had proved at the remoter one; and now, seriously interested for Ludovico, he was himself going to strike upon the door with the instrument, when he observed its singular beauty, and withheld the blow. It appeared on the first glance to be of ebony, so dark and close was its grain, and so high its polish; but it proved to be only of larch wood, of the growth of Provence, then famous for its forests of larch. The beauty of its polished hue, and of its delicate carvings, determined the count to spare this door, and he returned to that leading from the back staircase, which being at length forced, he entered the first ante-room, followed by Henri and a few of the most courageous of his servants, the rest waiting the event of the inquiry on the stairs and landing-place.

All was silence in the chambers through which the count passed, and, having reached the saloon, he called loudly upon Ludovico; after which, still receiving no answer, he threw open the door of the bedroom, and entered.

The profound stillness within confirmed his apprehensions for Ludovico, for not even the breathings of a person in sleep were heard; and his uncertainty was not soon terminated, since the shutters being all closed, the chamber was too dark for any object to be distinguished in it.

The count bade a servant open them, who, as he crossed the

room to do so, stumbled over something, and fell to the floor, when his cry occasioned such a panic among the few of his fellows who had ventured thus far, that they instantly fled, and the count and Henri were left to finish the adventure.

Henri then sprang across the room, and, opening a window-shutter, they perceived that the man had fallen over a chair near the hearth, in which Ludovico had been sitting; – for he sat there no longer, nor could anywhere be seen by the imperfect light that was admitted into the apartment. The count, seriously alarmed, now opened other shutters, that he might be enabled to examine farther; and Ludovico not yet appearing, he stood for a moment suspended in astonishment, and scarcely trusting his senses, till his eyes glancing on the bed, he advanced to examine whether he was there asleep. No person, however, was in it; and he proceeded to the Oriel, where everything remained as on the preceding night; but Ludovico was nowhere to be found.

The count now checked his amazement, considering that Ludovico might have left the chambers during the night, overcome by the terrors which their lonely desolation and the recollected reports concerning them had inspired. Yet, if this had been the fact, the man would naturally have sought society, and his fellow-servants had all declared they had not seen him; the door of the outer room also had been found fastened, with the key on the inside; it was impossible, therefore, for him to have passed through that; and all the outer doors of this suite were found, on examination, to be bolted and locked, with the keys also within them. The count, being then compelled to believe that the lad had escaped through the casements, next examined them; but such as opened wide enough to admit the body of a man were found to be carefully secured either by iron bars or by shutters, and no vestige appeared of any person having attempted to pass them; neither was it probable that Ludovico would have incurred the risk of breaking his neck by leaping from a window, when he might have walked safely through a door.

The count's amazement did not admit of words; but he returned once more to examine the bedroom, where was no appearance of disorder, except that occasioned by the late over-throw of the chair, near which had stood a small table; and on this Ludovico's sword, his lamp, the book he had been reading, and the remains of his flask of wine, still remained. At the foot of the table, too, was the basket, with some fragments of provision and wood.

Henri and the servant now uttered their astonishment without reserve, and though the count said little, there was a seriousness in his manner that expressed much. It appeared that Ludovico must have quitted these rooms by some concealed passage, for the count could not believe that any supernatural means had occasioned this event; yet, if there was any such passage, it seemed inexplicable why he should retreat through it; and it was equally surprising, that not even the smallest vestige should appear by which his progress could be traced. In the rooms, everything remained as much in order as if he had just walked out by the common way.

The count himself assisted in lifting the arras with which the bedchamber, saloon, and one of the ante-rooms were hung, that he might discover if any door had been concealed behind it; but after a laborious search, none was found; and he at length quitted the apartments, having secured the door of the last antechamber the key of which he took into his own possession. He then gave orders that strict search should be made for Ludovico, not only in the château, but in the neighbourhood, and retiring with Henri to his closet, they remained there in conversation for a considerable time; and whatever was the subject of it, Henri from this hour lost much of his vivacity; and his manners were particularly grave and reserved, whenever the topic, which now agitated the count's family with wonder and alarm, was introduced.*

* The château had been inhabited before the count came into its possession. He was not aware that the apparently outward walls contained a series of passages and staircases, which led to unknown vaults underground, and, therefore, he never thought of looking for a door in those parts of the chamber which he supposed to be next to the air. In these was a communication with the room. The château (for we are not here in Udolpho) was on the sea-shore in Languedoc; its vaults had become the store-house of pirates, who did their best to keep up the supernatural delusions that hindered people from searching the premises; and these pirates had carried Ludovico away.

# The Abbey of Clunedale

## Dr Nathan Drake
## (1766–1836)

A perhaps less-noted figure than Mrs Radcliffe who was to make his own special contribution to the Gothic genre at this time was Dr Nathan Drake who published a continuing journal of essays and stories entitled *Literary Hours* from 1798 to 1804. Dr Drake can certainly be regarded as one of the most important literary commentators of the period and his reviews of contemporary work show a deep interest and careful study of the supernatural story.

In the first edition of his work, the doctor began examining the public taste for Gothic stories and pronounced sharply 'It has been too much the fashion among critical writers to condemn the introduction of supernatural agency although it is perfectly consonant with the common feelings of mankind. I may venture, I think, to predict that if at any time these romantic legends be totally laid aside, our national literature will degenerate into mere morality, criticism and satire.' Strong words indeed, but Dr Drake was prepared to press his point in controversy and was also not afraid of being himself the butt of these critics by appending his own efforts in the story-form – each constructed to illustrate the various types of supernatural and preternatural agency.

The man himself was almost a walking advertisement for the tales he so vaunted: stylish in dress, refined in manners and courtly in speech. Apart from his writing he practised as a physician first at Sudbury in Suffolk and afterwards at Hadleigh. In later life his views on trends in public taste were eagerly sought by publishers and booksellers and editions of his *Literary Hours* ran through a number of impressions.

Of the Gothic tales which Dr Drake himself wrote, perhaps the one to best show his underlying purpose and also his own narrative skill is *The Abbey of Clunedale*. By his own admission the story is 'an attempt at the "explained supernatural" in the style of Mrs Radcliffe'.

THE last rays of the setting sun yet lingered on the mountains which surrounded the district of —; when Edward de Courtenay, after two fatiguing campaigns on the plains of Flanders, in one of which the gallant Sidney fell, re-entered his native village towards the end of August, 1587. He had lost his father a few months before his departure for the Continent, a loss which had occasioned him the most severe affliction, and had induced him thus early in life to seek, amid the din of arms, and the splendour of military parade, a pause from painful recollection. Time, however, though it had mitigated the first poignant emotions of grief, had not subdued the tender feelings of regret and sorrow, and the well-known objects of his early childhood and his opening youth, associated as they were with the salutary precepts and fond affection of the best of parents, awakened in his mind a train of melancholy yet soothing thoughts, as with slow and pausing steps he moved along the venerable avenue of trees, which led to his paternal mansion. Twilight had by this time wrapt every object in a veil of pleasing obscurity; all was hushed in the softest repose, and the massiness of the foliage under which he passed, and the magnitude and solitary grandeur of his Gothic halls impressed the imagination of Edward with deep sensations of solemnity and awe. Two grey-headed servants, who had lived for near half a century in the family, received their young master at the gate, and whilst the tears trickled down their withered cheeks, expressed with artless simplicity their joy, and blessed the return of the son of their ancient benefactor.

After some affectionate inquiries concerning the neighbouring villagers, and the families of these old men, Edward expressed his intention of walking to the Abbey of Clunedale, which lay about a mile distant from the house; his filial affection, the pensive retrospect of events endeared to memory, the sweetness and tranquillity of the evening, and that enthusiasm so congenial to the best emotions of the heart, gave birth to the wish of lingering a few moments over the turf which covered the remains of his beloved parent. Scarce however, had he intimated this resolution, when the ghastly paleness which overspread the countenances of his domestics, and the dismay that sat upon their features, assured him that something extraordinary was connected with the determination he had adopted, and, upon inquiry, his terrified servants informed him, though with some confusion and reluctance, that, for some months past, they and the country round had been alarmed by strange sights and noises at the Abbey, and that no one durst approach the place after sunset. Edward, smiling at the superstitious fears of his attendants, which he attributed solely to their ignorance and their love for the marvellous, assured them he entertained no apprehension for the event, and that he hoped shortly to convince them that their alarm was altogether unfounded. Saying this, he turned into the great avenue, and striking off to the left, soon reached the river, on whose winding banks a pathway led to the Abbey.

This venerable structure had been surrendered to the rapacity of Henry the Eighth in 1540, and having been partly unroofed during the same year, had experienced a rapid decay. It continued, however, along with the sacred ground adjoining to it, to be a depository of the dead, and part of the family of the Courtenays had for some centuries reposed in vaults built on the outside of the great west entrance of the church. In a spot adjacent to this ancient cemetery lay also the remains of the father of Edward, and hither filial piety was now conducting the young warrior as the gathering shades of evening dropped their deep grey tints on all around.

The solemn stillness of the air, the tremulous and uncertain light through which every object appeared, the soothing murmur of the water, whose distant track could be discovered only by the white vapour which hovered on its surface, together with the sedate and sweeping movement of the melancholy owl as it sailed slowly and conspicuously down the valley, had all a natural tendency to induce a state of mind more than usually susceptible of awful impressions. Over Edward, predisposed to serious reflection by the sacred purport of his visit, they exerted a powerful dominion, and he entered the precincts of the Abbey in deep meditation on the possibility of the reappearance of the departed.

The view of the Abbey, too, dismantled and falling fast to decay, presented an image of departed greatness admirably calculated to awaken recollections of the mutability and transient nature of all human possessions. Its fine Gothic windows and arches streaming with ivy, were only just perceptible through the dusk, as Edward reached the consecrated ground; where, kneeling down at the tomb of his father, he remained for some time absorbed in the tender indulgence of sorrow. Having closed, however, his pious petitions for the soul of the deceased, he was rising from the hallowed mould, and about to retrace his pathway homewards, when a dim light glimmering from amidst the ruins arrested his attention. Greatly astonished at a phenomenon so singular, and suddenly calling to remembrance the ghastly appearance and fearful reports made by his servants, he stood for some moments riveted to the spot, with his eyes fixed on the light, which still continued to gleam steadily though faintly from the same quarter. Determined however to ascertain from what cause it proceeded, and almost ashamed of the childish apprehensions he had betrayed, he cautiously, and without making the least noise, approached the west entrance of the church; here the light however appeared to issue from the choir, which being at a considerable distance, and towards the other end of the building, he glided along its exterior, and passing the refectory and chapter-house, re-entered the church by the south portal near the choir. With footsteps light as air he moved along the damp and mouldering pavement, whilst pale rays gleaming from afar faintly glanced on the shafts of some pillars seen in distant perspective down the great aisle. Having now entered the choir, he could distinctly perceive the place from whence the light proceeded, and, on approaching still nearer, dimly distinguished a human form kneeling opposite to it. Not an accent, however, reached his ear, and, except the rustling noise occasioned by the flight of some night-birds along remote parts of the ruin, a deep and awful silence prevailed.

The curiosity of Courtenay being now strongly excited, though mingled with some degree of apprehension and wonder, he determined to ascertain, if possible, who the stranger was, and from what motives he visited, at so unusual an hour, a place so solitary and deserted; passing therefore noiseless along one of the side aisles separated from the choir by a kind of elegant latticework, he at length stood parallel with the spot where the figure was situated, and had a perfect side view of the object of his search. It appeared to be a middle-aged man, who was kneeling on a white-marble slab, near the great altar, and before a small niche in the screen which divides the choir from the east end of the church; in the niche were placed a lamp and a crucifix; and he had round him a coarse black garment bound with a leathern girdle, but no covering on his head; and, as the light gleamed upon his features, Edward was shocked at the despair that seemed fixed in their expression: his hands were clasped together, his eyes turned towards heaven, and heavy and convulsive sighs at intervals escaped from his bosom, whilst the breeze of night, lifting at times his disordered hair, added peculiar wildness to a countenance which, though elegantly moulded, was of ghastly paleness, and had a sterness and severity in its aspect, and every now and then displayed such an acute sense of conscious guilt, as chilled the beholder, and almost suppressed the rising emotions of pity. Edward, who had impatiently witnessed this extraordinary scene, was about to address the unhappy man, when groans as from a spirit in torture, and which seemed to rend the very bosom from which they issued, prevented his intention, and he beheld the miserable stranger prostrate in agony on the marble. In a few minutes, however, he arose, and drawing from beneath his garment an unsheathed sword, held it stretched in his hands towards heaven, whilst his countenance assumed still deeper marks of horror, and his eyes glared with the lightning of frenzy. At this instant, when, apprehensive for the event, Edward deemed it highly necessary to interfere, and was stepping forward with that view, his purpose was suddenly arrested by the sound of distant music, which stealing along the remote parts of the Abbey in notes that breathed a soothing and delicious harmony, seemed the work of enchantment, or to arise from the viewless harps of spirits of the blest. Over the agitated soul of the stranger it appeared to diffuse the balm of peace; his features became less rigid and stern, his eyes assumed a milder expression, he crossed his arms in meek submission on his bosom, and as the tones, now swelling with the richest melody of heaven, now tremulously dying away in accents of the most ravishing sweetness, approached still nearer, the tears started in his eyes, and coursing down his cheeks bathed the deadly instrument yet gleaming in his grasp; this, however, with a heavy sigh he now placed in the niche, and bowing gently forward seemed to pray devoutly: the convulsions which had shaken his frame ceased; tranquillity sat upon his brow, whilst, in strains that melted into holy rapture every harsh emotion, the same celestial music still passed along the air, and filled the compass of the Abbey.

Courtenay, whose every faculty had been nearly absorbed through the influence of this unseen minstrelsy, had yet witnessed, with sincere pleasure, the favourable change in the mind and countenance of the stranger, who still knelt before the lamp, by whose pale light he beheld a perfect resignation tranquillize those features which a few minutes before had been distorted by the struggles of remorse; for such had been the soothing and salutary effects of harmony in allaying the perturbations of a wounded and self-accusing spirit, that hope now cheered the bosom so recently the mansion of despair.

Whilst Edward, in sacred regard to the noblest feelings of humanity, forbore to interrupt the progress of emotions so friendly to virtue and contrition, the music, which had gradually, and with many a dying close, breathed fainter and fainter on the ear, now, in tones that whispered peace and mercy, and which sounded sweet as the accents of departed saints, melted into air, and deep silence again pervaded the Abbey. This, however, continued not long, for in a few moments was heard the echo of light footsteps, and presently Courtenay, by the glimmering of the lamp, indistinctly beheld some object which, gliding rapidly up the choir, moved towards the spot where the stranger was yet kneeling. His astonishment was increased when, on its approaching nearer, he could perceive the form of a young and elegant woman. She was clothed perfectly in white, except where the vest was bound by a black zone, and over her shoulders flowed negligently a profusion of light brown hair. A smile of the most winning sweetness played upon her features, though the dewy lustre of her eye, and the tears that lingered on her cheek, revealed the struggles of the heart. The stranger, who had risen at her approach, embraced her with the most affectionate emotion; they were both silent, however, and both now kneeling on the marble slab employed some time in prayer. Nothing ever appeared to Courtenay more interesting than the countenance of this beautiful young woman, thus lighted up by all the sensibility of acute feeling; her eyes bathed in tears, and lifted towards heaven, beamed forth an expression truly angelic, whilst the exquisite delicacy of her complexion and features, over which the expensive graces had diffused their most fascinating charms, together with the simplicity and energy of her devotion as with clasped hands and trembling lips she implored the assistance of the Divine Spirit, formed a picture worthy of the canvas of Raphael.

Edward now saw before him the cause of those rumours and fears which had been circulated with so much industry in the neighbourhood, for, since the appearance of this amiable young woman, he had been perfectly convinced that the music to which he had lately listened with so much rapture, had its origin with her. In a still night these sounds might be heard to some distance, and, together with the glimmering of the light, would occasion no small alarm to the peasant who should happen at that time to be passing near the Abbey, and whose apprehensions, thus excited, might easily create some imaginary being, the offspring of ignorance and terror; or perhaps some pilgrim, more daring than the rest, had penetrated the interior of the ruin, and had probably beheld one of the very striking figures now present to his eyes. This, without further inquiry, he had deemed, what indeed would, at first, be the surmise of any spectator, some vision of another world, and had thus strengthened the superstition of the country, and protected the seclusion of the strangers.

As these reflections were passing through his mind, the interesting objects which had given them birth had risen from their kneeling posture, and after interchanging looks of mingled gratitude and delight, were arm in arm retiring from the sacred marble, when Edward, whose eagerness to discover the motives of the elder stranger's conduct had been greatly augmented since the appearance of his fair companion, determined, if possible to trace them to the place of their abode. Entering the choir, therefore, by one of the lateral doors, he followed them with slow and silent footsteps, preserving such a distance as, he thought, might prevent the lamp from revealing his person. He had pursued them in this manner unobserved through the choir, but upon their suddenly turning at an acute angle to enter the cloisters, the light streaming faintly on his figure discovered him to the younger stranger, who, uttering a loud shriek, leaned trembling on the arm of her friend.

Courtenay now immediately rushing forward endeavoured to allay their apprehensions, by informing them of his name and place of residence, and the motives which had, at this time of night, led him to visit the Abbey: he told them that, filial piety having drawn him to the tomb of his father, he had very unexpectedly perceived a light in the interior of the building; which strongly exciting his curiosity, and corroborating the reports of the country, he had endeavoured to ascertain its cause, and in so doing had discovered the attitude and employment of the elder stranger, who, together with his fair attendant, rather increasing than mitigating his astonishment, he had attempted, by following them at a distance, to ascertain their abode, it being his intention, at some future period to solicit an explanation of what he had now witnessed.

Whilst Edward was yet speaking, a ghastly paleness overspread the countenance of the elder stranger; it was momentary, however; for soon resuming his tranquility, he addressed

Courtenay in a low but firm tone of voice. 'I am sorry, Sir,' said he, 'to have occasioned, by my partial residence here, so much apprehension among the inhabitants of your village; but as I have reasons for wishing concealment, at least for a time, I have thought it necessary, though acquainted with their fears, not to undeceive them. But with you I know already I can have no motives for disguise; for, though from great change of feature, brought on by deep sorrow, and great change of apparel, I have hitherto escaped your recognition, you will find by-and-by that we were formerly better acquainted. In the mean time I will conduct you to the spot we inhabit, where, should you wish for an explanation of the extraordinary scenes you have been a spectator of this night, the recital, though it will cost me many struggles, shall be given you, and I do this, strange as it may now sound to you, actuated by the recollection of past friendship.' Having said thus, he and his beautiful partner, who had listened with almost as much surprise as Edward to an address so unexpected, moved slowly on, and Courtenay, occupied in fruitless conjecture, followed in silence.

They passed along a large portion of the cloisters, whose perspective, as seen by the dreary light of the lamp, had a singularly awful effect, and then, ascending some steps, entered what is termed the Dormitory, and which was carried over this part of the Abbey to a considerable distance. Here, in two small chambers, where the roof remained sufficiently entire, were a couple of beds, and a small quantity of neat furniture, and here the stranger pausing, invited Edward to enter. 'These rooms,' observed he, 'are my occasional habitation for at least twice-a-week during the night: but before I commence the melancholy narrative of my crimes and sufferings, I will endeavour to recall your recollection to your companion in arms upon the Continent; for this purpose I will retire for a few minutes and put on the dress I usually come hither in, the habit you now see upon me being merely assumed after reaching this place as best suited to the situation of my mind, to the penitence and humiliation that await me here.' His tone of speaking, as he thus addressed Courtenay, was perceivably altered, being much more open and

full than before, and brought to Edward's ear a voice he had
been accustomed to, though he could not at the moment appropriate it to any individual of his acquaintance. During his absence, his amiable companion, who had not perfectly recovered
from the alarm into which she had been thrown by Courtenay's
intrusion, sat silent and reserved, until Edward, observing some
manuscript-music in the room, ventured to inquire if the exquisite performance he had listened to with so much delight in the
Abbey had not originated with her. A deep sigh at this question
escaped her bosom, and her eyes filled with tears, whilst in
tremulous accents she replied, that, owing to the great relief and
support her brother experienced from music, she always accompanied him to this place, and that it was a source of the purest
happiness to her to be thus able, through the medium of her
harp and voice, to alleviate and soothe his sorrows. For this purpose the instrument was left at the Abbey, and was placed in
that part of the ruin where its tones were best heard, and produced the most pleasing effect. At this instant the door opening,
the stranger entered clothed in a mourning military undress, and
bearing a taper in his hand; he placed himself, the light gleaming steadily on his countenance, opposite Courtenay, who involuntarily started at his appearance. 'Do you not remember,' he
exclaimed, 'the officer who was wounded by your side at the
battle of Zutphen' – 'My God!' cried Edward, 'can it be Clifford?' – 'The same, my friend, the same,' he replied; 'though
action has anticipated on his features the characters of age. You
behold, Courtenay, the most unfortunate, the most miserable of
men – but let me not pain my sweet Caroline by the recital of
facts which have already wounded almost to dissolution her
tender heart – we will walk, my friend, into the Abbey; its awe-
ful gloom will better suit the dreadful tale I have to unfold.'
Saying this, and promising his sister to return in a few minutes,
they descended into the cloisters, and from thence through the
choir into the body of the church.

The tranquility of the night, and the light and refreshing
breeze that yet lingered amid the ruin, and swept through its
long withdrawing aisles, were unavailing to mitigate the

agitation of Clifford, as with trembling footsteps he passed along the choir. 'Oh, my friend,' he exclaimed, 'the spirits of those I have injured hover near us! Beneath that marble slab, my Courtenay, on which you saw me kneel with so much horror and remorse, repose the relics of a beloved wife, of the most amiable of her sex, and who owes her death (God of mercy register not the deed!) to the wild suggestions of my jealous frenzy.' Whilst thus speaking, they hurried rapidly forwards towards the western part of the Abbey; and here Clifford, resuming more composure, proceeded in his narrative. 'You may probably recollect about a twelve-month ago my obtaining leave of the Earl of Leicester to visit England; I came, my friend, upon a fatal errand. I had learnt, through the medium of an officious relation, that my wife, my beloved Matilda, of whose affection and accomplishments you have frequently heard me speak with rapture, had attached herself to a young man who had visited in the neighbourhood of my estate at C—n, but that she had lately removed for the summer months to a small house and farm I possess within a mile or two of this Abbey, and that here likewise she continued to receive the attentions of the young stranger. Fired by representations such as these, and racked with cureless jealousy, I returned to England in disguise, and found the report of my relation the theme of common conversation in the county. It was on the evening of a fine summer's day that I reached the hamlet of G—, and with a trembling hand and palpitating heart knocked at my own door. The servant informed me that Matilda had walked towards the Abbey. I immediately took the same route: the sun had set; and the grey tinting of evening had wrapt every object in uniform repose; the moon however was rising, and in a short time silvered parts of the ruin and its neighbouring trees. I placed myself in the shadow of one of the buttresses, and had not waited long ere Matilda, my beautiful Matilda, appeared, leaning on the arm of the stranger. You may conceive the extreme agitation of my soul at a spectacle like this; unhappily, revenge was, at the instant, the predominating emotion, and rushing forward with my sword, I called upon the villain, as I then thought him, to defend himself. — Shocked by the suddenness of the attack, and the wild impetuosity of my manner, Matilda fell insensible on the earth, and only recovered recollection at the moment when my sword had pierced the bosom of the stranger, though whose guard I had broken in the first fury of the assault. With shrieks of agony and despair she sprang towards the murdered youth, and falling on his body exclaimed, "My brother, my dear, dear brother!"

'Had all nature fallen in dissolution around me, my astonishment and horror could not have been greater than what I felt from these words. The very marrow froze in my bones, and I stood fixed to the ground an image of despair and guilt. Meantime the life-blood of the unhappy Walsingham ebbed fast away, and he expired at my feet, and in the arms of his beloved sister, who, at this event, perhaps fortunately for us both, relapsed into a state of insensibility. My own emotions, on recovering from the stupor into which I had been thrown, were those I believe of frenzy, nor can I now dwell upon them with safety, nor without a partial dereliction of intellect. Suffice it to say, that I had sufficient presence of mind left to apply for assistance at the nearest cottage, and that the hapless victims of my folly were at length conveyed to the habitation of Matilda. Another dreadful scene awaited her, the recognition of her husband as the murderer of her brother – this, through the attention of my friends, for I myself was incapable of acting with rationality, was for some time postponed; it came at length, however, through the agonies of my remorse and contrition, to her knowledge, and two months have scarce elapsed since I placed her by the side of her poor brother, who, at the fatal moment of our rencounter, had not been many months returned from the Indies, and was in person a perfect stranger to your friend. Beneath that marble slab they rest, my Courtenay, and ere this, I believe, and through the medium of my own lawless hand, I should have partaken of their grave, had not my beloved sister, my amiable and gentle Caroline, stepped in, like an angel, between her brother and destruction.

'Singular as it may appear, the greatest satisfaction I now receive, is from frequent visits to the tomb of Matilda and her brother; there, over the relics of those I have injured, to implore the mercy of an offended Deity; such, however, are the agonies I suffer from the recollection of my crime, that even this resource would be denied me were it not for the intervention of the powers of music; partial I have ever been to this enchanting art, and I am indebted to it for the mitigation and repression of feelings that would otherwise exhaust my shattered frame. You have witnessed the severe struggles of remorse which at times agitate this afflicted heart, you have likewise seen the soothing and salutary effects of harmony. My Caroline's voice and harp have thus repeatedly lulled to repose the fever of a wounded spirit, the workings nearly of despair. A state of mind friendly to devotion, and no longer at war with itself, is usually the effect of her sweet and pathetic strains; it is then I think myself forgiven; it is then I seem to hear the gentle accents of my Matilda in concert with the heavenly tones; they whisper of eternal pace, and sensations of unutterable pleasure steal through every nerve.

'When such is the result, when peace and piety are the offspring of the act, you will not wonder at my visits to this melancholy ruin; soon as the shades of evening have spread their friendly covert, twice a-week we hasten hither from our cottage; a scene, similar to what you have been a spectator of tonight, takes place, and we retire to rest in the little rooms which we have rendered habitable in the dormitory. In the morning very early we quit the house of penitence and prayer; and such is the dread which the occasional glimmering of lights and the sounds of distant music have given birth to in the country, that none but our servant, who is faithful to the secret, dare approach near the place; we have consequently hitherto, save by yourself, remained undiscovered, and even unsuspected.

'Such, my friend, is the history of my crimes and sufferings, and such the causes of the phenomena you have beheld tonight, — but see, Courtenay, my lovely Caroline, she to whom under heaven I am indebted for any portion of tranquillity I yet enjoy, is approaching to meet us. I can discern her by the whiteness of her robes gliding down yon distant aisle.'

Caroline had become apprehensive for her brother, and had stolen from the dormitory with the view of checking a conversation which she was afraid would prove too affecting for his spirits. Edward beheld her, as she drew near, rather as a being from the regions of the blest, the messenger of peace and virtue, than as partaking of the frailties of humanity. If the beauties of her person had before interested him in her favour, her conduct towards the unhappy Clifford had given him the fullest conviction of the purity and goodness of her heart, of the strength and energy of her mind; and from this moment he determined, if possible, to secure an interest in a bosom so fraught with all that could exalt and decorate the lot of life.

He was now compelled, however, though greatly reluctant, to take leave of his friends for the night, and hasten to remove the extreme alarm into which his servants had been thrown by his unexpected detention. They had approached, as near as their fears would permit them, to the Abbey, for to enter its precincts was a deed they thought too daring for man, and had there exerted all their strength, though in vain, in repeatedly calling him by his name. It was therefore with a joy little short of madness they again beheld their master, who, as soon as these symptoms of rapture had subsided, had great difficulty in repressing their curiosity, which was on full stretch for information from another world.

It may here perhaps be necessary to add, that time, and the soothing attentions of his beloved sister, restored at length to perfect peace, and to the almost certain hope of pardon from the Deity, the hitherto agitated mind of Clifford. — I can also add, that time saw the union of Caroline and Edward, and that with them, at the hospitable mansion of the Courtenays, Clifford passed the remainder of his days.

# The Anaconda

## Matthew Gregory Lewis
## (1775–1818)

No name figures larger in the history of Gothic literature than that of Matthew Lewis, indeed it has become almost synonymous with the genre, representing in many minds both the best and the worst that it has to offer. According to Eino Railo, Lewis introduced 'terror-romantic-realism' to the story form by way of 'a series of themes calculated in themselves, when presented in all their fearful nakedness, to evoke a sensation of terror'.

To the point in time when Lewis burst on the scene with his sensational novel, *The Monk* (1796), the Gothic genre had merely exploited haunted castles, tyrants, demure maidens in peril and their manly saviours; the new master introduced endless blood and gore, the dead alive, human corruption, degeneracy and – in general – 'rioted in horrors to an extent hardly to be found elsewhere'.

Matthew Gregory Lewis, the son of a leading British statesman, spent his childhood at Stanstead Hall in Essex, a large, rambling house reputedly haunted and certainly sinister and gloomy at the best of times. Against this kind of background it is hardly surprising that the young man should form an interest in the supernatural and this was heightened in 1792–1793 when he visited the fashionable German spa at Weimer, met Goethe, and was introduced to the blood-curdling Schauerromane, then much in vogue with the country's readers. Returning to England, he swiftly composed *The Monk*, a tale of a young friar lured into devilry and lust, which on its publication created a furore throughout England. The critics ranged in their opinions from declaring it a work of genius to one of blasphemy and obscenity. The Society for the Suppression of Vice was so outraged by the novel that they succeeded in having it seized by the authorities and in the ensuing lawsuit, Lewis was ordered to remove all references to the Bible and delete a number of highly sensual passages 'before the minds and bodies of the people be corrupted'. In fact, three editions of the work had already been printed and sold out, so these 'corrections' could not be effected until the fourth printing; and this time Lewis – or 'Monk' Lewis as he was now being widely called – was the Literary Lion of England.

The effect of *The Monk* on literature, and indeed on public taste, was instantaneous: a flood of imitations and tales of diablerie poured on to the market. The Gothic terror-romance was undoubtedly here to stay!

Lewis wrote several other novels and a number of short stories, but all were tempered with a desire he felt to avoid further scandal. *The Anaconda* – 'a horrible East Indian tale', to quote Montague Summers – is taken from his collection, *Romantic Tales*, published in 1808, and again demonstrates that Lewis was continually prepared to range far in his search for strange locations and extraordinary characters.

In 1817 Lewis went to seek rest and solitude on the family sugar plantations in Jamaica, but returning in the spring of the following year he contracted fever and after several days of suffering died on 14 May 1818. As is the custom at sea, his body was committed to the waves almost immediately – the actual ceremony giving rise to an incident which might well have sprung from the pages of one of his own books. According to the account of a fellow passenger, as the coffin – which was shrouded in a canvas sack – passed into the water, it failed to sink and the wind inflated the sackcloth, causing the cortege to sail slowly off into the morning haze. 'The supernatural quality of this vision,' says one report, 'greatly alarmed the crew and passengers, for it seemed a last recognition by fate of Lewis's position as the great creator of spectral effects.'

'The Lord in heaven forbid!' exclaimed the old man, while every limb was convulsed with horror, the blood forsook his cheeks, and he clasped his hands in agony: 'but the thing is impossible!' he resumed, after a few moments passed in reflection, 'absolutely impossible! What! Everard? a boy, whose childhood was passed under my own roof, under my very eye? whose manners are so mild, who was ever so gentle, so grateful, so kind; whose heart I know as well as I do my own. Bless my

soul, sister Milman, what a fright you have given me! But it's
no great matter now, for, when I reflect upon this history of
yours, I see clearly that the thing is quite impossible, and so
there's an end of it.'

'Now was there ever anything so provoking! Brother,
brother, let me tell you, that at your time of life it is quite a
shame to suffer yourself to be so blinded by prejudice. His childhood was passed under your roof, forsooth! but where did he
pass his youth, I should be glad to know? why, among tigers
and alligators that swallow up poor dear little children at a
mouthful, and great ugly black-a-moor monsters, who eat nothing but human flesh, heaven bless us! and where's the great
wonder, that living in such graceless company Everard should
have picked up some of their bloody tricks? Nay, brother, to
tell you a bit of my mind, for my own part I always suspected,
that there was something awkward in the manner by which he
came by such a sight of money; though, to be sure, I never imagined that the business was half so bad as it proves to be.'

'Proves to be, sister! proves to be, indeed! Let me remind you
that you have proved nothing, though God knows you have asserted enough to make every hair on my head stand on end:
and as to his fortune, I make no doubt that Everard can give as
satisfactory an account of his making it, as the honestest man
within the bills of mortality.'

'I should be glad to know then, why he so obstinately refuses
to give any account at all? It's above a year since he returned
from the East Indies, and yet there isn't a human being a bit
better informed on the subject than we were on the first day of
his landing; though I'm sure it's not for want of asking, for
many and many a good hour have I passed in pumping, and
pumping, and yet here do I sit at this moment no whit the
wiser! He always puts on such a solemn look, and takes the
first opportunity of turning the conversation to something else:
nay, the other day, when I wouldn't be fobbed off with a
cock-and-a-bull story about heaven knows what, and put the
question home to him in so many words, — "By what means
did you, Everard Brooke, get so much money?" He turned his

back plump upon me, and stalked out of the room; which was no great proof of his good-breeding, you'll say; but mercy upon us! good-breeding isn't what the gentleman values himself upon, for it was but last Friday that he bounced out of the room to call Towser off, who was barking at a little dirty beggar-boy, though he saw that I had dropped my teaspoon, and was obliged to stoop for it myself! a great bear! but indeed I expected nothing better from a man who has lived so long among Hottentots.'

'Well, sister! I dare say that he ought to have stopped to pick up your teaspoon; though to be sure I can't find in my heart to blame him very much for having gone first to rescue the beggar-boy, being afraid that I should have committed exactly the same fault myself. But you know I never pretended to good-breeding, and in all matters of politeness, sister Milman, I must give way to your better judgement and experience. However, I cannot be equally submissive respecting the material point; and in spite of all that you have advanced I must still maintain my opinion, that Everard came by his money honestly, whatever you may have heard to the contrary.'

'Then why won't he let a body know how he came by it? Let me tell you, brother, that when a man has anything good to tell of himself, he isn't so fond of holding his tongue; nay, for that matter, to hold one's tongue at all isn't natural, and I warrant you, whoever does so has some good reason at bottom for submitting to such a disagreeable restraint, if one could but get him to own it: and so think the Williamsons, and the Joneses, and my cousin Dickins, and all the family of the Burnabys: for I am not of so uncommunicative a temper as your darling Everard, Heaven be praised for it! No; if I get a bit of information, I am too generous to keep it to myself, and have no peace, till all my neighbours are as well informed as I am. So this morning, I no sooner got possession of this bloody story, than I ordered my chariot, and drove round the village to communicate it to all our friends and relations. To be sure, they were mightily shocked at the account, as who wouldn't be? But they confessed, that they always expected to find something wrong at the bottom of this mystery, and they think it a mercy that I should have discovered the truth, before things were gone too far between Everard and your daughter Jessy.'

'And so you have been carrying this fine story all round the village? I protest now, sister Jane, it seems to me, that you have been giving yourself a great deal of very unnecessary trouble; and if, after all, your assertions should prove to be unfounded, I know not what recompence you can make poor Everard for this attempt to blast his character. The most innocent circumstances may be so construed as to wear an awkward appearance: there are always enough ill-natured people in the world ready to spread about scandalous reports, and Everard has too much merit not to have excited plenty of enemies; and here you have just now picked up a strange, unaccountable, rigmarole tale from one of these, and –'

'From one of his enemies,' exclaimed Mrs Milman, fanning herself violently; 'very fine truly! when I heard the whole story with these ears of mine from the mouth of his own little coffee-coloured barbarian! Yes, to be sure! Mirza is a violent enemy of Mr Everard's, that cannot be denied!'

The old merchant's face underwent a considerable change at hearing these last sentences; he looked distressed, and rubbed his forehead for some moments in evident anxiety.

'Mirza!' he repeated after a pause; 'sister Jane, recollect yourself; this is no trifling matter! are you quite sure that Mirza asserts the truth of the story which I have just heard you relate?'

'I tell you, brother, for the second time, that I heard him tell it with my own ears! not indeed all at once, for the wicked little heathen knew too well how little it was to his master's credit that the fact should get abroad. Ah! he is a cunning hand, I promise you! But I went round about, and round about, and wormed and wormed, and kept beating the bush, till I got it all out of him. I confess I was obliged to promise faithfully that his master should never know a syllable about it, for he said that it would give him pain to hear it mentioned, as to be sure well it may; but, when I found what a horrible secret it was, I had a great deal too much conscience to keep my promise, and lost no time in making the monster's guilt known to the whole neighbourhood.'

'Well, well sister! I won't pretend to say that you did wrong, and I doubt not you acted from the best motives; but yet I can't help wishing that you had acted otherwise! This Everard – poor, dear, wicked fellow – he was once so good, so affectionate; I would have betted all I have in the world, that it wasn't in his nature to kill so much as a fly; and to murder a woman – a woman too that he had promised to marry!'

'Aye! and to murder her in such a shocking manner too! First to shoot at her from behind a hedge, and when he found the poor creature was only wounded, to have the heart to run up to her, and actually beat her brains out with a club! Why, Mirza said, that he verily believed that she was above half an hour dying.'

'I never heard of anything so horrible.'

'But what is worst, he wasn't contented with destroying the poor girl's body; he had previously ruined her precious soul! It seems that her name was Nancy O'Connor; an Irish family, I suppose. I once knew an Irish officer of that name myself. I was but a girl then, and danced with him at the Hackney Assembly, and a mighty genteel comely-looking man he was, though he had but one eye; but that's neither here nor there. Well, as I was telling you, this Nancy was either the daughter or the wife of a rich planter, with whom Everard lived as clerk, or factor, or something of that kind. Well! and so this poor girl fell in love with Everard, and he on his side was wonderfully attentive to Nancy; for Mirza says, that he passed whole days and nights in watching her, and ogling her, so that she actually could hardly stir without his knowing it; till at last he worked himself so totally into her good graces, and got such an influence over her mind, that (knowing his patron to have made a will entirely in Nancy's favour) he persuaded her to poison poor Mr O'Connor, in order that she might share his wealth with her abominable lover.'

'Poison her father! monstrous!'

'Her father, or her husband, for (as I said before) I am not

certain which; but I should rather suppose it was her father, for
it seems the poor deceived old man made it his dying request to
her, that she should make Everard her husband as soon as ever
the funeral was over: so you may judge how artfully the hypo-
crite must have played his cards! Well! now it was supposed
that Everard would immediately have made Nancy Mrs Brooke:
the settlements were all drawn up; the clothes were bought; the
wedding-day was fixed: when, lo and behold, what do you
think the ungrateful monster did? He persuaded the poor
young creature to dispose of all her property; and when it was
converted into money, and jewels, and such-like, he enticed her
into a wood, where he robbed and murdered her in the manner
which you have just heard; and then, getting on board a vessel
with his plunder in all haste, he managed to escape from Ceylon, before the officers of justice had time to discover what was
become of him! The only thing which surprises me is, that he
should have brought away Mirza with him; but as the young
heathen was then quite a child, I suppose his master thought it
probable that he knew nothing of this bloody business, or would
certainly forget it during the voyage. And now, brother, what
have you to say in behalf of your fine Mr Everard? Ah! how
often have I told you, over and over again, I was certain that
something bad would come out against him all in good time!
But you were obstinate; you still let him come dangling about
your house, and keep hankering and hankering after your
daughter Jessy; and now you may think yourself well off if the
girl's heart isn't fixed upon having the vagabond, and getting her
brains knocked out in her turn, like poor Miss Nancy O'Connor.'

Partial as the old man was to Everard, he could not but feel
his faith in him a good deal shaken by this long string of horrible circumstances, and by the positive manner in which they
were advanced. And now flocked in one after another the
Joneses, and the Williamsons, and all the family of the Burnabys, with their wondering, and their blessing themselves, and
their exclamations, and their pity for poor Miss O'Connor, and
their having long suspected nothing better. The good old man
listened in silence, and sighed, while they assailed him thus on

all sides; but though he could not venture to contradict them, he could not find it in his heart to join in their censures of the man whom he had so long esteemed, and whom he still loved so tenderly. But when at length cousin Dickins made his appearance, (a man of great importance in this family, for he was rich, a bachelor, advanced in years, and Jessy's godfather), and announced his thorough belief in Mrs Milman's story, it was no longer in old Elmwood's power to remain neutral in the business. He declared his submission to cousin Dickins' better judgement, and his intention of declining any further communication with Mr Brooke; for he no longer dared to call him by the familiar and affectionate appellation of Everard.

This declaration was received with great satisfaction by all present, and the resolution was pronounced *nem. con.* to be extremely judicious: the delinquent was at this time in London, whither he had repaired (as it was suspected) for the purpose of ascertaining the exact state of his property, in order that on his return he might lay it before Elmwood, accompanied by a formal demand of his daughter's hand. This absence was thought very fortunate by the company, as it afforded the best opportunity for putting Jessy upon her guard; and it was determined to summon her without loss of time, make known to her the true character of the man with whom she had so imprudently been suffered to associate, and insist upon her making a solemn promise in full convocation, that she would from that moment give up all communication with him.

Jessy made her appearance. Alas! the fate of her heart had been long decided. As she listened to the strange and horrible tale, she sometimes coloured with indignation against the accusers, and then again her cheeks grew pale through fear lest the accusation should prove well founded. The charge was concluded; the promise was demanded; yet still Jessy spoke not, but sat absorbed in terror and grief. In vain was her lover's guilt repeated; in vain was she called upon to declare her abhorrence of him; still Jessy only answered with her tears. Her friendly relations turned up the white of their eyes at her blindness and delusion: Mrs Milman was loud in exclaiming against the obstinacy and wrong-headedness of young people, who would fancy themselves wiser than their parents; and the formidable cousin Dickins, assuming one of his most severe and dignified looks, insisted upon her giving an immediate answer.

Terrified almost out of her senses at this formal address, the trembling Jessy now contrived to sob out 'a hope that her aunt had been mistaken, that Everard would still be able to prove his innocence.' – 'Innocence!' so impossible a supposition was of itself sufficient to set the whole assembly in an uproar: the Williamsons, the Joneses, Cousin Dickins, and all the family of the Burnabys, gave tongue at once; and above a dozen voices were still busy in affixing the least flattering epithets possible to the name of Everard, when the door opened, and Everard himself stood before them. He was just returned fom London, and had hastened to assure himself of Jessy's welfare. In the next moment you might have heard a pin drop. The debate had been carried on in too loud a tone to permit his being ignorant of the nature of their disclosure; but, at all events, the evident and universal embarrassment which his presence created, left him no doubt that himself had been brought upon the carpet, and that in a manner by no means to his credit. His sun-burnt cheek glowed with indignation, as he gazed round the circle, and requested to know the meaning of those appellations by which, while ascending the stairs, he had heard himself described.

The question being general, no person thought it necessary to take it to himself. Each looked towards his neighbour, as if he expected the answer to come from thence, and consequently all continued silent. Everard now found it needful to particularize and turning to Cousin Dickins (whose voice had been supereminently loud) he demanded of him the desired explanation.

'Why, really, sir,' stammered out Cousin Dickins, adjusting his neckcloth, in order to conceal his embarrassment; 'really, Mr Everard – as to what was said – I can only say – that I said nothing – that is to say, not that I quite said nothing – though, to say truth, it was almost as good as nothing – for it was nothing from my own knowledge – I only repeated – I only observed – that, if what Mrs Milman said was true –'

'Mrs Milman?' interrupted Everard, 'that's enough; now then we get a step nearer to the source of the business. Will you then, madam, have the goodness to explain your reason for applying such approbrious epithets to the name of Everard Brooke — a name which, I am bold to say, deserves them as little as that of any person in this society. I wait for your reply, madam.'

'Well, sir, and by my faith you shall have it,' answered Mrs Milman, who by this time had recovered herself, and was now resolved to carry the business through with flying colours, by assuming a double quantity of assurance. 'You shall have it, never fear! And if it turns out that your name is really as good as any one's in the company, and that you really did not poison the old gentleman, and beat Miss Nancy's brains out, why then so much the better for you, that's all, and there's no harm done.'

'Poison the old gentleman? Beat out Miss Nancy's brains? What Miss Nancy? What old gentleman? Why, in the name of Heaven, Mrs Milman, where did you pick up this farrago of nonsense?'

'I pick up, indeed! Let me tell you, sir, that I never picked up anything, or anybody in my life; and that if you talk of picking up, you are the much more likely person to pick up of the two. And now I'm about it, I'll let you into another piece of my mind. It's extremely rude in you to call my conversation a *farrago of nonsense*; but truly it's no wonder, for I'm not the first lady that you have treated with rudeness, Heaven knows! and more's the pity — Miss Nancy for that.'

'Miss Nancy again!' exclaimed Everard, 'and who the devil then is Miss Nancy?'

'What then you don't know Miss Nancy? No; never heard of Miss Nancy O'Connor, I warrant?'

'No, madam; I never did.'

'Well, come, now, that is a good one! To beat a lady's brains out, and then to cut her acquaintance, and pretend you know nothing about her, is the finest piece of modern good-breeding that I ever heard of! Nay, indeed, I never expected much good breeding from you, sir, ever since that affair of the teaspoon. But one thing I can tell you; your little copper-coloured Hottentot, Mirza, sings a very different song from you on this occasion; for I had the whole story from his own lips.'

'From Mirza's? impossible!'

'It's not mighty polite in you to contradict one so plump, sir, but no matter for that, I repeat it; Mirza told me himself that you had poisoned a gentleman, and beat his daughter's brains out; and now so much for that, and butter to fish. Nay, if you don't choose to believe me, call the boy hither, and ask him; I desire no better, and I see him playing in the garden at this moment.'

'And it shall be done instantly!' cried Everard, at the same time throwing up the window – 'Mirza! Mirza!'

Mirza was soon in the room.

'Pray, Mirza, what is the meaning –' began Everard, but Mrs Milman immediately interrupted him.

'Silence, if you please, sir; I'll examine the boy myself. Come here, Mirza; well, and how d'ye do, my dear? Pray, Mirza, what was that pretty story you told me this morning about poisoning somebody, and killing somebody with a club, and –'

'Oh! Missy, Missy!' cried Mirza, 'you no say dat! Massa tell me no talk – Massa grieve – Massa angry.'

'No, no, child; he'll not be angry. He wants to hear how prettily you tell the story, and so you must tell it all; mustn't he, Mr Brooke?' Everard gave a sign of assent. 'You know, Mirza, it was all about how your master made his fortune; well, and so, Mirza, (upon my word, you're a very nice lad, and there's six-pence for you), well, and so you say, Mirza, and so you say, my dear, that your master killed her in a wood! what? did he kill her quite?'

'Iss, quite! She quite dead! Massa beat brains out wid great club!'

'I, Mirza?' exclaimed Everard; 'did I?'

'Iss, dad you did, Massa! and God him bless you for it!'

'Bless him for it!' whispered Mrs Milman to Cousin Dick-ins, 'there's fine morality! the wicked little heathen! but you'll hear more presently!' then turning again to the boy; 'well but, Mirza, you told me something too about poisoning – what,

I suppose, before your master killed Miss Anne O'Connor.'

'Conda! Conda!' interrupted the boy.

'Condor, was it?' repeated Mrs Milman: 'well, well, Connor or Condor, the name makes no great difference. Well, Mirza, and so you say, that this Anne O'Condor, instigated by your master, I suppose.'

'Oh! my massa! my massa!' shrieked Mirza in a tone of agony, at the same time pointing to Everard; who, pale as death, and with a countenance expressing the most painful agitation, rushed to a table on which stood a decanter of water, of which he hastily swallowed a draught; though so violently did his hands shake that the goblet was carried to his lips with difficulty.

'Forgive my leaving you so abruptly,' said he, in a faltering voice; 'I will return in a few minutes;' and he hastily quitted the apartment, followed by Mirza.

Now then his guilt was past doubting! Mrs Milman spread out her petticoats, fanned herself with an air of triumph, and began a sermon upon the wonderful effects of conscience. Surprise had checked the course of Jessy's tears; the blood had deserted her lips and cheeks, and she sat motionless, looking like a marble statue. The good old Elmwood felt in his own the wound which his darling's heart had just received; but he had nothing to offer for her relief, except a fond pressure of her hand, and a sigh of compassion. The rest of the company shrugged up their shoulders at the depravity of human nature, and nodded their head significantly at one another, as if they had been so many Chinese josses. Suddenly the door opened; and Mrs Milman was still in the full flow of her eloquence when Everard re-entered the room, to all appearance perfectly recovered from his late disorder.

'Mrs Milman,' said he, 'I am now master of the whole of this business. Your ignorance of circumstances peculiar to the East, the singularity of my adventures, and the broken English in which you heard them related, have led you into a most extraordinary mistake. I cannot clear it up, without subjecting myself to the most agonizing recollections, and rending open afresh those wounds, which, it's true, are scarred over, but which are too deep and too deadly to be ever thoroughly healed. If, therefore, the opinion of the world were alone concerned, that opinion which is so little necessary to my own happiness, I should leave you in your error, rather than subject myself to the pain of an explanation. But I see in this circle two persons, one of whom possesses too dear an interest in my affections to permit my leaving a single thorn in her gentle bosom which I have it in my power to remove; while the paternal kindness which the other showed to me while I was still a boy, demands that I should convince him that it was not shown to one unworthy. To calm their feelings, I will sacrifice my own; and, much as I shall suffer while making the recital, the recital of my adventures shall still be made. Be attentive then, and everything shall be explained.'

Curiosity now became the predominant expression – Elmwood breathed freer, held up his head higher than before, and shook his daughter's hand affectionately; a roseate blush stole over the lovely fair face of Jessy, while a look of silent gratitude thanked her father; the rest of the company drew their chairs closer together, and prepared to listen with all their ears.

Everard seated himself, and thus began.

You are already aware that my fortune was made in the island of Ceylon. It was there that I was so lucky as to find employment in the house of a man whose virtues rendered him as much the object of universal esteem, as the favours which he conferred upon me entitled him to my peculiar gratitude. I was engaged by him as his secretary, but all other names were soon forgotten by us both in that of friends. He was an Englishman as well as myself, and perhaps this had no slight influence in producing so strict an intimacy between us. A variety of untoward circumstances had compelled him to abandon his native land, and sail in pursuit of fortune to the East. His toil had not been vain: the capricious goddess, who fled from him with such disdain in Europe, now showered her favours upon his head with the most unwearied profusion. He had consumed but a few years in Ceylon, and was already rich and possessed of a distinguished situation. It seemed as if fortune was at length resolved to convince the world, that she was not always blind; for, had she searched the whole island through, she would have found it difficult to bestow wealth and honour upon a wiser or a better man. But, of all his treasures, that which he counted most precious, that for which he thanked Heaven's bounty at every moment of his existence, and with every pulsation of his heart, was a wife who united all the beauty and graces of her sex with all the firmness and judgement of ours. One only blessing was denied them: Louisa was not a mother.

My friend and patron (his name was Seafield) possessed a villa at a small distance from Columbo. The place, it's true, was of no great extent, but it united, in their fullest perfection, all those charms which render Nature in that climate so irresistible an enchantress. This was Seafield's most beloved residence, and hither he hastened whenever the duties of his station permitted his absenting himself for a few days from Colombo: in particular, there was a small circular pavilion designed by his own hand, and raised under his own inspection, to which he was particularly partial, and in which he was accustomed to pass the greatest portion of his time. It stood some few hundred yards from the dwelling-house, and was situated on a small eminence, whence the prospect over land and sea was of a description rich, varied, and extensive. Around it towered a thick circle of palm trees, resembling a colonnade: their leafy fans formed a second cupola above the roof; and, while they prevented a single sunbeam from piercing through the coolness of their embowering shades, their tall and slender stems permitted not the eye to lose one of the innumerable charms afforded by the surrounding landscape.

This delightful spot happened to be the residence of Seafield's whole family, when accidental business of importance required Louisa's presence at Columbo. Conscious that her husband considered everyday as lost which he was compelled to pass at a distance from his beloved retreat, she positively refused his attendance, but accepting me as her escort she departed for the city. Diligence and impatience to return home enabled her to dispatch her affairs in less time than she had expected them to occupy; and in the very first moment that she found herself once more at liberty, she ordered the palanquins to be prepared, and her slaves to hold themselves in readiness for departing. Our journey was performed by night, for the double purpose of reaching home the sooner, and of escaping the ardour of the noonday sun. We arrived an hour after daybreak, yet Seafield was already abroad.

'As usual, he ascended the hill to enjoy the beauty of the rising-sun.' Thus said Zadi, Seafield's old and attached domestic; in whose favour his master made an exception to his general opinion, that, in all their transactions with Europeans, the natives of this island were totally devoid of gratitude, honesty, and good faith.

'We shall find him in the pavilion, then?' said Louisa.

'Not an hour ago I left him writing,' was the answer.

'We will go thither and surprise him,' she said, addressing herself to me. 'Wait here while I change my dress; a few moments will suffice for my toilet, and I shall expect to find you here when I return.'

In the meanwhile, I remained leaning against one of the columns which supported the small portico by which the door was sheltered. From hence I enjoyed an uninterrupted view of the hill and its pavilion, which, surrounded by its light and beautiful garland of palm trees, attracted the sight irresistibly. While my eye dwelt with satisfaction on their broad sheltering heads, I fancied that I could discover a large excrescence upon the stem of one of them, extremely unusual in those trees, which in general rear themselves perpendicularly towards the sky, regular and straight as the pillars of a colonnade. It resembled a large branch, extending from one stem to its neighbour; and what puzzled me more in this appearance, was, that it seemed occasionally to be waved backwards and forwards, though the breathing of the sea-gale was so gentle, that it scarcely moved the leaves on the neighbouring branches. I made a variety of guesses to account for this phenomenon, but every thing which my memory or my imagination could suggest, seemed inadequate to solve this difficulty entirely to my satisfaction.

I was still puzzling myself with conjectures, when Zadi drew near me with some slight refreshments. I pointed to the branch, whose apparent motion had excited so much of my attention, and inquired, whether he could at all account for the strong effect produced upon it by the sea-breeze, while the slighter boughs were so gently agitated. He immediately turned himself towards the palm trees; but no sooner did his eye rest upon the spot in question, than the silver basket with its contents dropped from his hands, the paleness of death spread itself over his swarthy countenance; he caught at one of the columns, to save himself from falling on the ground; and, while his eyes expressed the deepest horror and consternation, he pronounced with difficulty – 'The Anaconda! – That is the Anaconda! We are undone!'

What could have produced an effect so sudden and so violent upon a man, whom I well knew to inherit from nature the most determined courage, and most remarkable self-possession, was to me absolutely incomprehensible. But though I was ignorant of its cause, the sight of his extreme alarm was almost sufficient to shake my own presence of mind. I saw that he was on the point of sinking on the earth, overpowered by his emotions. I sprang towards him, and caught him in my arms.

'For the love of heaven,' I exclaimed, 'compose yourself, old man! Tell me what terrifies you thus. What mean you by the anaconda? What can occasion these complaints, and this alarm?'

He endeavoured to recover himself; he strove to speak, but in vain; and, before I could understand the accents of his stammering tongue, Louisa joined us, and without observing the slave's agitation put her arm within mine, and advanced towards the pavilion. This action seemed to restore to Zadi the lost powers of his body and mind. With a loud cry he threw himself on his knees before us, and in words interrupted by sobs, and accompanied by tears, he forbade our crossing the threshold.

'Your first step without these walls,' he exclaimed, 'leads to inevitable destruction. Every door must be bolted; every window must be barred. This mansion must resemble a sepulchre, where nothing living is to be found.'

And, while he spoke, he hastily closed and locked the folding-doors, through which we had a prospect of the pavilion. Louisa observed his singular behaviour, and the agitation of his countenance, with looks which expressed the most lively astonishment.

'Are you distracted, Zadi?' she asked, after a few moments. 'What mean these tears, and these expressions so alarming? And why do you forbid our going to your master?'

'You're going to –? Almighty God! My master! He is yonder! Oh! he is lost! – he is lost beyond the power of saving!'

'He is lost, say you? Answer me, old man! What mean you? What fear you? Oh! how my heart beats with terror!'

Her frame trembled with anxiety, while she gazed with wide-stretched eyes upon the messenger of evil tidings, and pressed my arm with a convulsive grasp.

'Recollect yourself, my good Zadi!' said I; 'what is this anaconda, which you speak of with such terror? I have seen nothing except the branch of a palm tree, which the wind moved backwards and forwards, singularly enough, it's true, but still there was nothing in it alarming.'

'Not alarming?' repeated the Indian, wringing his hands; 'not alarming? The Lord have mercy on me, miserable old man! Ah! Mr Everard, that branch of the palm tree! Alas! alas! It is no branch! It is a snake! a terrible snake! We call it an anaconda and its kind is in size the most enormous, in nature the most fierce, and in appetite the most ravenous, of any to be found through all Ceylon! See! see!' he continued, approaching one of the windows, 'see how the monster plays among the branches! It always twines and twists itself into those folds, and knots, and circles, when it prepares to dart itself upon the ground, like lightning, to seize its prey! Oh! my master! my poor dear master! He never can escape! Nothing can save him!'

Half of this alarming explanation was more than enough to

throw the wretched Louisa into a state of distraction. Her features were so distorted by terror, that she was scarcely to be known for the same woman, her eyes stretched almost to breaking, and her hands folded together with as strong a grasp as if she meant them never to be again separated, she exclaimed, in a voice so hollow and so expressive of suffocation that it pierced her hearers to the very heart. 'My husband! – my beloved! Oh! help me to save him, good, good men! Forsake him not! Oh! forsake him not!'

But at this moment the wife required assistance not less than the husband. Overpowered by her sensations, she fainted in my arms; Zadi flew to summon her female attendants; and I bore the pale insensible Louisa back to her own apartment, though Zadi's dreadful narrative had almost deprived me of animation myself.

Our endeavours to re-kindle the extinguished flame of life were at length successful. Her eyes opened; she cast around her a look of apprehension.

'Oh! why are you still here?' said she to me in a feeble voice 'Is his life then of so little consequence? Fly to his succour! Rescue him, or let me die! In preserving him, you will preserve me if he perishes, I am lost!'

'He lives! he lives! heaven be thanked! he still lives!' thus shouted the faithful Zadi, as he rushed into Louisa's apartment. His anxious vigilance had induced him to examine every part of the mansion, and ascertain with his own eyes that it was perfectly secure against danger. He now returned out of breath from the balcony, whence he had discovered to his great satisfaction, that his view was unimpeded over the whole pavilion. He remarked, that the door and all the windows (as far as the power of vision extended) were closely fastened; and hence he very reasonably concluded, that his master had been aware of the enemy's approach in full time to take every necessary precaution for his safety.

'Hear you that, my dear lady?' I exclaimed, while I took Louisa's hand; surely, this intelligence is a one sufficient to restore your strength and tranquillity. We had nothing to apprehend for Seafield, except his being surprised by the monster while unprepared. But you see that he has had time to shut out the danger: he has now nothing to do but to remain quietly within his retreat, and the snake will either not discover his being so near, or at any rate will be able to break through the bulwarks which separate them. The whole business therefore is a disagreeable blockade for an hour, or perhaps less; at the end of which the anaconda will grow weary of waiting for its prey, and be retiring to seek it in some other quarter, will release our friend, and then we shall be quit for the fright.'

The satisfaction with which I thus endeavoured to reassure the agonized heart of Louisa, was thoroughly established in my own. But Zadi, whose own feelings were too much agitated by his master's situation to permit his attending to those of others, hastened with too little consideration to destroy the hope, which I so fondly indulged, and with which I strove to soothe the afflicted wife.

'Oh! no, no, no!' he exclaimed; 'we must not reckon upon the snake's leaving us so soon! When the anaconda has once chosen a group of trees for her abode, and is seen to sport among their branches, in the manner in which we saw her amusing herself, she will remain there for whole days and weeks watching patiently for her prey, till every chance of success fails her, and absolute famine compels her to emigrate: but her capacity of existing without food is almost inconceivable, and till she removes of her own free will, no human power is able to drive her from her retreat.'

'Almighty Powers!' stammered out the trembling Louisa, 'then he is lost indeed! Even should those slight barriers be sufficient to protect him from the monster's fury, he must still at last fall a prey to the assaults of hunger!'

My frowning looks easily made the old man aware of the imprudence which he had just committed: but the mischief was irreparable. Every thing, which his imagination could suggest to soften the effect produced by his ill-judged confession, was unable to blunt the arrow, which had carried with it into the heart of his mistress the poison of despair.

'But after all,' said I, 'why are we to take it for granted that our friend is actually exposed to this urgent danger? By your own account, Zadi, above an hour had elapsed between your leaving your master in the pavilion, and your discovery of the Anaconda; and what then can be more likely than the day being so delightful, he should have gone out to walk, and have quitted the pavilion before the snake's approach?'

'Angel of comfort!' exclaimed Louisa, while she seized my hand, and pressed it to her lips; 'blessed, ever blessed be you for that suggestion! Why should it not be, as you suppose? Why should not his absence have rescued him?'

'Ah! dear heaven!' sighed the old man, and shook his head; 'the doors closed, the windows all fastened –'

'Prove nothing,' I interrupted him; 'when did Seafield ever leave his favourite retreat without taking those precautions? Perhaps, at this very moment that we are trembling for his safety, he is at the distance of miles from the place of danger! Perhaps, nothing more is requisite for his full security than that we should take the precaution of warning him in time, lest he should return to the dangerous pavilion instead of coming straight to the house. Come, come, Zadi; let us hasten to find him! Summon together all the male domestics, as well as our palanquin-bearers; let us divide them into small parties and send them into every path, by which it is possible for Seafield to regain the hill.'

'Yes, hasten! hasten!' cried Louisa; 'the thought that you may come too late, pierces me to the very soul: yet on his having already quitted the pavilion hangs my whole, my only hope! Hasten, friends! oh! hasten to find him!'

Her eagerness would not suffer us to remain a moment. We consigned her to the care of her female attendants. We then collected the male inhabitants of the house together with all speed, and having armed them in the best manner that time would permit, we approached in different quarters as near the fatal hill, as the protecting shelter of trees and branches would allow us, without running the risk of being discovered by the anaconda. Zadi remained with me.

On our way, I endeavoured to compose my thoughts, and to make myself master of every particular respecting the danger, to which the friend of my heart was exposed. My own alarm, and Louisa's presence, had hitherto prevented my obtaining a thorough knowledge of the nature of Seafield's situation, and what he had to apprehend: but, now that I was alone with him, I lost no time before I questioned Zadi.

'You see, old man,' said I, 'how your fatal outcry, "an anaconda," has palsied every soul through excess of terror. Now your imprudence will have been most unpardonable, should it turn out that you spoke without being quite certain of the fact, or if you should be found through your own natural timidity to have exaggerated the danger. Recollect yourself, therefore, and then answer me calmly and frankly. Are you positive, that what you saw was really an anaconda; and in the dreadful account which you have just given of her, have you not in some degree overstepped the limits of truth?'

'Sir,' answered the good old man, 'though it were the last word which I have to utter in this world, I should still repeat my former assertions. Why, the very name of this creature is enough to make every native of this island feel the blood freeze in his veins! and that I have not deceived myself, is, alas! but too certain. I have already seen the anaconda twice at no greater distance than now; though never one of such a monstrous length and thickness as that which is at present before us. This country would speedily become a wilderness, if fortunately these reptiles were not very rarely met with; for in general they remain concealed within the recesses of the deepest woods; there clinging round the branches of some gigantic tree, they remain waiting with inexhaustible patience for an opportunity of darting down upon their prey, the first man or animal who is unlucky enough to pass beneath them. How it happens, that this snake should have advanced so far into the open country, is what I can least comprehend: but as the rainy season is but just over, it is most probable, that she has been swept away by the irresistible violence of some of the mountain-torrents.'

During this conversation we had continued to advance under

favour of the thick-woven underwood, till we were scarcely more than a hundred paces distant from the monster. We could now examine it with the most perfect distinctness, and the eye was able to take in at once the whole extent of its gigantic structure. It was a sight calculated to excite in equal degrees our horror and our admiration: it united the most singular and brilliant beauty with everything that could impress the beholder with apprehension; and, though while gazing upon it I felt that every limb shuddered involuntarily, I was still compelled to own, that never had I witnessed an exhibition more fascinating or more gratifying to the eye.

The anaconda was still employed in twisting itself in a thousand coils among the palm-branches with such restless activity, with rapidity so inconceivable, that it was frequently impossible for the sight to follow her movements. At one moment, she fastened herself by the end of her tail to the very summit of the loftiest tree, and, stretched out at her whole length, swung backwards and forwards like the pendulum of a clock, so that her head almost seemed to graze the earth beneath her; then in another, before the eye was aware of her intention, she totally disappeared among the leafy canopies. Now she slid down the stem, winding herself round and round it; and now again only the extremity of her tail remained twisted round the root, while she stretched out her body upon the grass, and with elevated head and high-arching neck described a large or a small circle, as her capricious pleasure prompted.

These latter movements gave us an opportunity to discriminate with more exactness (during a few seconds at a time) the singular richness and beauty of her tints. The long slender body was covered with a network of glittering scales, girdling it round with rings above rings, and effectually securing it against every attack. The head was of a yellowish green, and marked in the middle of the skull with a large dark spot, from whence small stripes of pale yellow were drawn down to the jaws. A broad circle of the same colour went round the throat like a necklace, on either side of which were two olive-coloured patches, in shape resembling shields. Along the back ran a chain of black waves with sharp-pointed edges, from whence on both sides narrow flesh-coloured rings and broad bands of the brightest yellow (alternately and in the most regular order) descended in zigzag fashion towards the silver-white stomach, where they lost themselves imperceptibly : but what served more than all to dazzle the eye with the brilliance of variegated colouring, were innumerable spots of a rich and vivid reddish-purple, sprinkled without order over the whole surface of the upper skin ; for with the animal's slightest movement all these points, and spots, and contrasts of variegated hues, melted together in the sunbeams, and formed one universal blaze composed of all the colours of the rainbow.

Much as I admired the splendour of its garment, not less did I wonder at the enormous thickness of this terrific creature, which did not yield in bulk to that of a man of moderate size. Yet by comparing its thickness with its length, Zadi was decidedly of opinion, that the anaconda must have been greatly reduced by a fast of unusually long duration. But the tranquillity of our observations was suddenly disturbed by perceiving, that she desisted abruptly from her airy gambols, and remained motionless at the foot of the palm-tree with her head elevated and turned towards the pavilion, as if in the act of listening !

At that moment, oh ! God ! with what violence did my heart beat against my bosom ! If (as from every circumstance appeared but too probable) my friend was really shut up within the pavilion, it was beyond a doubt, that the monster had discovered his being so near her, and was now on the point of making a serious attack ! We could see distinctly the shape of her hideous head and the flames of her great piercing eyeballs, reflected from the glass windows, whose shutters had been closed from within. But the sight of her own terrors seemed to scare even the snake herself, for she instantly recoiled; and then laying herself down close to the threshold of the circular pavilion, she encompassed it entirely, as if she was determined to secure her destined victim irrevocably, by enclosing him within the impassable limits of her magic ring.

Deeply penetrated with the sense of that danger by which my

friend was menaced, I forgot my own, and seizing my gun placed it to my shoulder; the ball whistled through the air: I was an excellent marksman, and was certain that I had pointed my piece exactly at the monster's head: and yet, whether too great anxiety made my hand shake, or that the animal at that very moment made some slight change in her attitude, I know not, but it is at least certain, that not the slightest shrinking gave me reason to believe, that she felt herself at all injured. In the meanwhile, Zadi had seized my arm, and drawn me forcibly ino a deeper part of the thicket.

'Ah! Mr Everard!' sighed he; 'I was well aware, that the anaconda can set all our firearms at defiance. Her scaly hide renders her invulnerable, except when one is quite close to her; and all that you have done is to put your own safety in danger, without advancing a single step nearer to my master's relief.'

However, it did not appear, that our enemy had paid much attention to my assault upon her. On the contrary, she only busied herself in renewing her attempts to gain an entrance through the pavilion's windows: till at length, seemingly wearied with her unavailing efforts, she retired slowly, and concealed herself under the verdant umbrella of the palm-trees. We also had discovered our former lurking place; though we were now more irresolute than ever, as to the means most proper to be adopted towards the rescue of my friend.

While we stood thus with our eyes fixed immoveably upon the pavilion, we observed the door to be slightly agitated. After a minute, the lock was gently drawn back; slowly, and with the utmost caution, did the door expand about the breadth of half a foot, and out sprang the little Psyche, a beautiful Italian greyhound, Seafield's favourite play-fellow and inseparable companion. As if conscious of her danger, she rushed down the hill with her utmost swiftness; but with still greater swiftness did the anaconda in one monstrous spring dart rattling down from its airy covert. The poor little animal was seized: we could just hear a short half-suppressed cry, which marked its dying agony; for the dreadful jawbone moved but twice, or thrice, and lo! the dog's chine was broken, and every bone in its body splintered.

The snake then dragged her prey to the foot of the palm-tree, (for in order to produce the proper exertion of strength, it seemed necessary for her to have the stem or strong branch of some tree to cling to), where she stretched herself out upon the grass at her ease, and began with her black tongue to separate the flesh from the bones of the crushed little animal.

The distress, occasioned in my mind by this sight, in itself so painful and disgusting, was converted into agony by the reflections to which it gave birth, after the first moments of horror and surprise were passed! That fact was now confirmed, which till this moment (in order to preserve at least a gleam of comfort however faint) I had obstinately refused to believe. Seafield then was actually in the pavilion! The discharge of my musket had in all probability made him aware, that his friends were at no great distance. No one but he could have unclosed the door so cautiously, in order to leave his little favourite at liberty to quit their common shelter; and Zadi was positive, that he had observed a riband fastened round the neck of the animal, to which something white appeared to be attached, in form resembling a letter. It was then a message to *us*! a cry for assistance! a sacred injunction, that we should not abandon him in this season of his utmost need! What agony of soul must he have endured. What agony of soul must he even at that moment be enduring! To what a pitch of desperation must his mind have been worked up, before his trembling hand could have resolved to draw back the bolt, which was the only barrier between himself and annihilation! How bitter a pang must it have given his tender benevolent heart, when he drove out his fond and faithful companion, and exposed her to such danger! and then flattering himself (as no doubt he did) that the little animal's speed would surely enable her to escape. Oh! what a cruel wound must Psyche's expiring half-heard cry have given to his feelings! These reflections, or at least others nearly similar to them, almost deprived poor Zadi of his senses altogether.

'Oh! powers of mercy!' he exclaimed repeatedly; 'what did his letter mean to tell us? That at this moment he is struggling with despair? Alas! alas! we know it, we feel it! and yet here we stand inactive, without counsel, without resolution, without hope!'

'Patience! patience!' said I, interrupting him: 'it is evident, that our waiting here is of no advantage. Let us return home, and endeavour to find means of giving some more effectual assistance than our tears.'

We found the domestics returned from their unavailing expedition, and the greatest part of them assembled in the courtyard, whose lofty walls afforded them a secure refuge: being all natives of Ceylon, they were well acquainted with the nature and pursuits of the anaconda, either from their own experience, or from hearsay: but, almost deprived of the power of thought by their terrors, no one was able to point out any means for attacking her with success. I immediately despatched two of them to Columbo, to explain our situation, and demand assistance. I also desired, that medical aid might be sent to Louisa, and that if they could possibly find one, they should bring back with them a speaking trumpet. I then repaired to poor Louisa, and endeavoured to comfort her heart with a faint gleam of hope, which my own was incapable of admitting. I failed in the attempt; she was a prey to the most abject despair: nor was I more successful in my endeavours to persuade her to withdraw from this scene of horror, and accompany my messengers to Columbo; a measure which was advisable both on account of her own security, and because her absence would leave us at liberty to bestow our undivided attention upon her husband. But finding her resolved not to remove from the scene of Seafield's danger, I returned to the courtyard, where the dejected domestics were still lamenting over the situation of their master, and expatiating on the dreadful properties of the anaconda.

'Friends!' I exclaimed, 'there is not one among us all to whom the master of this house has not been a benefactor! Now that he is threatened with destruction, now is the time for us to show our gratitude for his kindness! Come then; let every one follow me, who loves his lord, and who bears an honest heart in his bosom. Let us despise the danger of the attack and set forward in a full body to deliver him by force! We are armed; in numbers, in reflection, in skill, the advantage is on our side. The bolder that we rush upon our enemy, the less dreadful will she appear to us. My life for it, she will be alarmed at the attack, will fly before us, and thus we shall enjoy the inestimable pleasure of rescuing our friend from death. Now then! let all who are of my opinion show themselves to be men, and range themselves on this side of the court.'

Alas! Zadi was the only one who obeyed this invitation: the rest, poor timid wretches (in number between twenty and thirty), stood there trembling, gazing upon each other with doubtful looks, and whispering together, as if desirous of discovering an excuse for the cowardice of each in the ignominy of his neighbour. After a few minutes, one of them, whom the rest had appointed to be spokesman, advanced towards me, and stammered out their general assurance: 'that to attack the famished snake with force would be nothing better than absolute madness.'

This hope disappointed, I next resolved to try, what effect of terror might be produced upon the monster by the united shouts and outcries of so considerable a body, assisted by the general and repeated discharge of our fire-arms. Our preparations were soon made; Louisa was apprised of the clamour which was going to be made: and, in truth, we raised an uproar so loud and so well sustained, that it seemed almost capable of waking the sleepers in the grave. From all the casements we discharged at the same moment our muskets provided with a double charge, and a hail of bullets rattled about the head of the gigantic snake, who afforded us a fair aim. Yet still she continued to play her gambols quietly among the trees; nay, she did not give any sign by which we could judge, that she was sensible of our attack. After a few moments spent in this manner with no better effect, we found that our provision of ammunition was exhausted: besides, we were ourselves too much fatigued to continue any longer an attempt, which afforded us so little prospect of producing any advantage.

By this time the day was drawing rapidly to its close. By dint of turning the painful subject frequently in my mind, and mak-

ing every possible conjecture, one means of scaring the anaconda had suggested itself, which appeared to me well worthy of
attention; but in order to put it in execution the darkness of the
night was necessary. I had often read in books of travels, what
powerful aid had been derived from fire against the attacks of
wild beasts, and how lions and tigers had often forgotten their
thirst of blood, and betaken themselves to flight, like the most
timid animals, when scared by a fire-brand whirled round, or
the blaze of a flaming heap of straw. Armed with such weapons,
I was determined, as soon as night should be set in, to approach
the anaconda, and put her courage to the proof, even though
the faithful Zadi should be the only one of sufficient courage to
assist me in my venturous design.

The night arrived: an awful stillness reigned all around us;
our enemy, however, still was watchful; for from time to time
we could hear her rustling among the branches. I passed the
twilight in endeavouring to comfort Louisa with the prospect of
a serious attack to be made upon the snake the next day, from
which (as I assured her) much better success might be expected;
but I judged it prudent to conceal from her our nightly enterprise, the effect of which appeared even to myself too uncertain
to make me venture to ground upon it any promise of advantage. Besides, her exhausted strength made it absolutely necessary, that she should pass some moments in tranquillity; a state,
which seemed to me absolutely incompatible with the tumults
of expectation, which the knowledge of our proposed adventure
would naturally excite in her bosom.

At length a sign given by Zadi made me aware, that all our
preparations were completed. Louisa was reclining on a couch
with her eyes closed, and seemed to have fallen into a kind of
lethargy. I stole softly from the apartment, and was on the point
of quitting the house, when a means suggested itself to me of
communicating my design to my friend, even before the arrival
of the speaking trumpet, which I expected the next day from
Columbo. I recollected, that I had lately taught Seafield a common European trick of combination, by which two persons
separated from each other (having first agreed upon their

measures) could convey their sentiments without the help of words: a certain number of blows, corresponding with the number of the place which each letter of the four and twenty holds in the alphabet, enabled the striker to form words and sentences, by which the hearer without other communication was made aware of the steps, which without his knowledge it had been settled for him to take. This trifle had but lately served us to puzzle Louisa, and pass away an idle evening hour; and I flattered myself with the possibility, that it might still exist in Seafield's remembrance. At any rate, I resolved to make the trial without loss of time, and the stillness of the night seemed to afford me the most favourable opportunity for executing my plan with success.

A thin smooth board, well calculated for reverberating sounds, and a strong hammer were easily procured. With these I hastened to the balcony, and began by striking as many blows as the alphabet required, (that is, one to A, two to B, twenty-four to Z, &c.) till I had gone through it regularly. I trusted that this orderly manner of proceeding would awaken his attention; and having completed the alphabet, I told him (in the same manner) if he comprehended my meaning, to strike three blows within the pavilion, as loud as he possibly could. Oh! heavenly powers! I had not long to wait! it was not long before three faint sounds informed me, that I was understood, and never did music seem so sweet to my ear! I hurried to tell Louisa, that I had found a means of communicating with her husband, and that I was going to command him to be of good cheer in her name and for her sake. A silent melancholy smile, a convulsive pressure of my hand, were my reward; and I now hastened again to the balcony to assure the poor prisoner, that I was labouring for his relief; that Louisa was well, and begged him to be patient and composed; and that I requested him to keep up his spirits, and resist the attacks of despair, since he might depend upon it, that I would rescue him, or perish in the attempt. I concluded by desiring him to assure me, that he would confide in the activity of my friendship, by repeating his former signal: I now suffered my hammer to rest – I listened – again, more audibly than before, did I hear the three wished-for blows given from within the pavilion, and I now hastened to prosecute my nightly plan with fresh spirits and renovated ardour.

Excited by Zadi's remonstrances, about a dozen of the bravest among the domestics and palanquin-bearers were assembled with torches in their hands in the courtyard. My design was, to steal as near the hill as the underwood would permit, under favour of the darkness, and only guided by a single dark lanthorn. When we could approach no further without hazard, we were to light our torches as fast as possible, and whirling them round and round, to rush towards the pavilion with loud shouts, in order that our attack might be accompanied by all the terrors and advantage of surprise.

Zadi, to whose care the guiding lanthorn was confided, went foremost; I followed close upon his footsteps, and thus with extreme caution and in profound silence did we press through bushes and brambles, till we arrived above half as near again to the pavilion, as the position which we had occupied during the day. The anaconda now lay right before us, quiet and unsuspecting; nor could we have wished for a better opportunity for executing our plan with every probability of success. We now turned to our companions. – But, just Heaven! who can express our astonishment and vexation, and how did our heart sicken at perceiving, that the faithless cowards had shrunk from the danger now that it was so near at hand, and had profited by the darkness to steal away one by one! I was alone with Zadi: we concluded with justice, that for only two persons to make the attempt must be unavailing, and the old man flattered himself, that he should be able to shame his comrades into a resumption of their more manly resolutions. I had but little hopes of his success; yet no choice was left me but to follow him and endeavour to give double strength to his persuasions and reproaches.

Both were employed in vain: their terrors had subdued all sense of shame completely. They called us madmen for wishing to expose ourselves to the fury of the famished anaconda; and, instead of promising any future assistance, they declared, that they would only wait for daybreak to secure themselves by flight

from a danger so imminent. In the meanwhile Zadi was busy in
fastening several torches together in pairs.

'Come, sir!' he cried to me: 'let us lose no more precious
time in endeavouring to inspire these heartless knaves with
courage! Let us leave the cowards, and try whether perhaps the
glare of these torches, doubled as you see them, may not of
themselves be sufficient to dazzle and scare away the monster.
At the worst we can but perish with our dear master, and it is
better to die than not perform our duty!'

I obeyed him: we hastened back to the pavilion. Already were
we on the point of ascending the hill, when I felt my arm seized
by someone with a convulsive grasp. I turned hastily round: a
thin figure, breathless through speed and anxiety, and whose
white garments fluttered in the breeze of night, stood beside me.
It was Louisa! Our dispute with the slaves had not passed so
quietly, but that our voices had reached the ear of Seafield's sor-
rowing wife, whose sore anguish of heart permitted not slumber
to approach. She questioned her attendants; by artful inter-
rogatories she contrived to draw from them the peculiar nature
of the enterprise on which we were engaged. She feigned to
sleep: and, as soon as her women were thrown off their guard,
she stole from her apartment, seized a torch, and followed us,
determined to share with us the danger and its reward.

My whole resolution failed me, when I recognized the new-
comer, and when she made known in a few short expressive
words her desperate resolution. In a low voice I conjured her to
return to the mansion-house; I protested, that her presence robbed our arms of strength and our hearts of courage; and I asked
her, whether it was not enough agony for us to tremble for an
existence so dear as Seafield's, without being obliged to risk the
loss of another life equally precious?

'My life for his!' was the only reply which she gave to my
remonstrances; 'my life for his! — What shall I rest my hands
idly before me, while strangers are active in his defence? Shall
I have to blame myself during the remnant of my existence for
having done nothing for him in the time of his extreme need —
*Nothing*? Shall my husband actually be rescued by his friends,

while his careless wife has not even *attempted* to preserve him?
— No, Everard, no! my life for his! my life for his!'

I listened with admiration to the overflowings of this noble
heart! How to resist her vehemence I knew not! I was compelled to give way to her, and yet was conscious that her presence
must entirely destroy every chance of our success. It would have
been madness to venture in her company to that extreme point
of danger, to which Zadi and myself had before not scrupled to
advance. The anaconda too appeared at this moment to be more
restless than formerly: doubtless the sound of our footsteps, and
our whispering dispute, must already have betrayed our being
in the neighbourhood. Nevertheless, we hastily kindled our fire-
brands, one of which we held in each hand, and as we whirled
them rapidly backwards and forwards we went forth shouts and
shrieks with all our strength; the dead stillness of all around us
rendered our outcries doubly dreadful.

A rushing sound among the tops of the palm-trees, as if
branch by branch they were forcibly snapped asunder, was the
answer given to our challenge. It was the anaconda (whether
excited by fear or by anger, I will not pretend to decide) who
darted herself from tree to tree with tremendous leaps, while the
slender stems were bent and shaken by her burthen. At the same
time we were alarmed by a loud hissing, so piercingly sharp,
that it seemed close at our ears, and her eyes, blazing with their
own vindictive fires, shot lightnings through the gloom of night.

In truth, this appearance was in every respect so dreadful, that
it required no ordinary courage to witness it without agitation.
I cannot deny, that while gazing on it I felt my hair stand on
end and my blood run cold; and I observed that Zadi strove to
keep his teeth closed together, in order to prevent me from hearing them chatter. I turned with apprehension to Louisa. Alas!
there lay the wretched wife on the earth deprived of consciousness. This sight was sufficient to banish every other consideration. I threw away my torches hastily, clasped the unfortunate in
my arms, and with Zadi's help bore her with all speed back to
the mansion-house; prosperous in this alone, we then retired
unpursued by the anaconda. Here, after a long interval of

insensibility, we at length succeeded in recalling Louisa's flying spirits. She revived; but it was only to dwell upon the midnight scene, from which we were just returned, and which her inflamed imagination painted in colours, if possible, still more dreadful that the reality. She called without ceasing upon her husband and upon me: and since it was out of my power to give more active assistance elsewhere, it would have been barbarous in me to leave her, without endeavouring by soothing and persuasion to dissipate the gloomy ideas by which her heated brain was distracted.

Thus passed away the remainder of the night, which left us even with less hope and resolution than we possessed when it arrived. The melancholy morning at length dawned; but the sun was scarcely risen when Zadi rushed into the apartment. His eyes sparkled, and the beating of his heart almost choked his words before he was able to give them utterance.

'Oh! Mr Everard!' he exclaimed, 'my master – my dear master! He has still hope! He has still courage! He endeavours to communicate with us! We shall soon know how matters go with him – what he wishes to be done – what he expects us to do. Yes! yes! we *will* soon know it!'

It was some time before he was sufficiently calm to explain to me the cause of this emotion. At length I learned, that in examining the pavilion he had just discovered a sheet of paper thrust through the crevice of the door, and which, apparently detained by one of its corners, fluttered loosely in the air, unable to effect its escape. Doubtless it was a letter, which Seafield hoped some favourable gust of wind would carry within our reach, but which he had not sufficiently disengaged from its narrow passage. As to reading the contents, even if the distance had permitted it, Zadi was not possessed of the knowledge requisite. He therefore had hastened in all diligence to communicate to me this discovery, from which I also derived some hope, though fainter than that which filled the bosom of the faithful Zadi.

We hurried to the hill, approached still nearer than we had ventured to do hitherto, and, with the assistance of an excellent telescope, I endeavoured to decipher the characters traced upon the important paper. Alas! that there actually *were* characters traced on it, was all that I could distinguish; for the light paper fluttered continually in the wind, and was never suffered to rest for two seconds together. My inexhaustible patience, my un-wearied exertions, long struggled against the evident impossibil-ity of success: I gained nothing by them except the conviction, that to prosecute the attempt further would only be to throw away a greater portion of my time. Zadi, in breathless silence, and his eyes fixed on my face unalterably, watched my every movement.

'Then you give up the point?' said he at length, while a livid paleness overspread his dark countenance, and such a trembling seized him, that I could see his every limb shaking; 'well, then, there is no more to be said! Let us return to the house, and take courage: I will fetch you the paper.'

'Old man!' I exclaimed, startling at this unexpected assur-ance, 'What say you? Your good intention is worthy of your good heart; but you would make an unavailing sacrifice to your fidelity; you may bring destruction on yourself, but you never will bring the paper from thence. To do that is out of any mortal power!'

'May be so! may be so!' repeated the Indian; 'but at least the trial shall be made. It seems, as if my master's voice cried to me, that his safety depended on that paper; and should I be worthy to belong to him, if I were deaf to my master's cry? By the God of my fathers, I will either come back to you with that paper, or never will come back again.'

And with every word that he spoke, his tone became stronger, his step firmer, and the fire of resolution illuminated his large dark eyes.

During this contention we reached the courtyard; in silence, and absorbed in himself, did this unequalled servant make the necessary preparations for his undertaking. His plan was to con-ceal his whole person, from head to foot, under a covering of boughs and cocoa-leaves, resembling as much as possible the broken branches with which the snake's gambols or indignation had strewn the hill all around her. Under this verdant shield, he flattered himself that he should be able to creep gradually to the pavilion door, unperceived by the anaconda.

'I have been accustomed,' said he, 'to this kind of work from my earliest infancy. In my time I was reckoned an expert elephant-hunter, and by means of this artifice have frequently made those enormous animals my prize.'

But a few minutes were past, and already was Zadi accoutred in this singular disguise. He provided himself with no weapons except his dagger. He obstinately refused to suffer me to accompany him, assuring me that I should only put my own life in danger, without being able to afford him the least assistance. He was so positive, that I was obliged to give up the point: but I was at least determined to accompany the noble-minded fellow with my eyes, as well as with my fervent prayers and wishes. From the balcony of the mansion-house I had an extensive and unimpeded view over the surrounding objects; and from hence I saw Zadi set forward on his perilous adventure, taking through precaution a wide circuit, in order to reach the hill itself.

With equal prudence he made his approach on that side, where the pavilion would screen him from the enemy's observation. From time to time I lost sight of him among the underwood; even when he was before my eyes I occasionally doubted whether it was he indeed, so cautiously and so artfully did he make his approach, creeping on his hands and knees, sometimes remaining without stirring, sometimes stealing forwards with a movement so imperceptible, that it almost eluded the keenness of sight. He was a living example to me of the discretion, assiduity, and skill, which the savage employs in laying his ambuscades, and stealing upon his unsuspecting enemy.

And now favoured by the long grass and fragments of boughs, with which the ground was covered, had Zadi by a thousand serpentine movements reached the wall of the pavilion. My heart beat violently, as I saw on one side the anaconda, as yet, it is true, suspecting nothing, but still dreadful from her appearance, and exhibiting every moment awful proofs of her strength, by the powerful leaps with which she darted herself from bough to bough; and, on the other hand, separated from her by the distance of ten yards at most, I beheld a poor, infirm, and aged man, whose force consisted only in his courage and his discretion.

Zadi in the mean while remained so tranquil and so motionless in his present position near the pavilion-door, that the monster could not fail of being deceived by so unsuspicious an appearance. The Indian's eye was fixed immoveably upon the snake, and followed all her twistings and windings with incessant application, while she swung herself with unwearied activity backwards and forwards, now here, now there, now above, now below; till, at the very moment when she shot herself over him in a bound of prodigious extent, I suddenly saw the invaluable paper disappear from its place, without being able to perceive the means by which it was brought into the power of the successful lurker.

I clasped my hands in ecstasy, and poured out my thanks to God from the very bottom of my heart. But all was not yet done. It required no less caution and dexterity to retire than to approach; and never did I offer up more fervent vows than at the moment when the animated thicket began to set itself in motion. Slower than the hour-hand of a dial, now moving forwards, now backwards, now right, now left, it stole itself down the hill. Still it went on, and on, and lower, and lower, till, with inexpressible delight, I saw it almost at the very foot of the hill; and now at length I began to draw my breath without pain. 'The noble fellow is safe,' said I to myself. At that moment, whether joy at the successful issue of his attempt had deprived him of part of his former caution, or whether some accidental derangement of the sheltering branches discovered enough to excite the reptile's suspicion, at that moment I saw the anaconda dart from above, and in the quickness of thought she reached the bottom of the hill, and enveloped the unfortunate in her folds! A piercing shriek of horror burst from me! I felt all my blood conceal itself within my veins!

Yet even in this dreadful situation wonderful was the presence of mind which Zadi still preserved; wonderful was the courage, the activity, and the skill, with which he defended himself against the monster. Grasping his dagger with firm and steady hand, he struck it with repeated blows between the impenetrable scales of his enemy, sought out with inconceivable address the most tender parts to strike, and at length succeeded in giving her so deep and so well-placed a wound, that it must needs have worked her up to the most extreme pitch of pain and fury; for suddenly I beheld him only girdled by a single fold of the anaconda's tail, with which (in the same manner that one who has unexpectedly grasped a nettle, throws it away) she hurled the poor wretch into the air far away, till I lost him among the surrounding bushes. As for the snake, she hastily regained her former hiding-place, where she lay quiet and concealed for some time before she resumed her usual sports; though when she did resume them, it was evidently with less sprightliness than before.

My agony is not to be described! Nothing was to be seen of the unfortunate Indian. What was become of him? Had he been killed by the violence of the fall? Or was he at that moment struggling in the pangs of death? His preservation I considered as beyond the limits of possibility; and yet it seemed to me inhuman and ungrateful quite to abandon him to his fate, without having first exhausted every possible means of assisting him. Irresistibly carried away by these sentiments, I rushed from the balcony, and hastened towards the hill by the same course which he had pursued himself, and which I could easily track by the depression of the dewy grass. Towards that side, also, had he been thrown by the anaconda, and it was probable that the thicket might shelter me, till I could reach the spot where he lay dying. In the eagerness of this hope, I totally overlooked the extreme risk of an undertaking, the very idea of which but four-and-twenty hours sooner would have made me shudder through every limb. So true is it, that violent emotions communicate a force to the mind, which enables it to rise above itself, and gives it courage to encounter danger and even death without the shrinking of a single nerve.

Suddenly my attention was arrested by a faint murmur! It came from a thicket at no great distance: I listened again! Oh heavens! it was the voice of Zadi. I lost not a moment in hastening to the place; he heard me; he opened his eye-lids, which seemed already closed in eternal sleep, recognized me as I raised him in my arms, and a faint smile stole over his countenance, as he stretched out his hand to me with difficulty.

'Take it,' he said; 'God be thanked, that I am able to reward your kindness so well; – even in the monster's grasp, I still kept fast hold of it: Oh, take it, take it!'

It was the paper which he had purchased so dearly, and which the faithful creature extended towards me.

'Read it!' he continued; 'lose no time! before I am deprived of my senses again – and for ever – at least let me have the satisfaction to know – what my master wished me to do! – alas! alas! now you will be left alone to assist him!'

'And assist him I will, doubt it not, thou noble heart,' I replied, while I strove to raise him from the ground; 'but my first assistance must be given to yourself.'

It was in vain that he conjured me to leave him to his fate, and only think of effecting his master's rescue. Without heeding him I managed to lift him upon my shoulders, and tottering beneath his weight I endeavoured to effect our escape from the dangerous vicinity of the pavilion. With difficulty I succeeded in regaining the open ground. Fortunately some of the other domestics saw us from the house, and hastened to relieve me from my wretched burthen. Assisted by them, I at length saw Zadi safely deposited on a sofa in the mansion-house; he was again on the point of losing all sensibility; but, a cordial of powerful virtue being administered without delay, his strength was restored sufficiently to preserve him from a relapse.

It's true, none of his limbs were fractured, but he was dreadfully bruised by his fall; his breast and ribs had been almost crushed together by the close-drawn folds of the serpent; he was totally unable to move so much as a finger, and his condition was such as would have excited pity even in the most insensible nature. As for me, I almost sunk beneath this addition to that general calamity, which seemed to increase with every succeeding moment. I was now a single man, to whose hand

Providence had committed the lives of three afflicted creatures!
Never did mortal pray to heaven with more fervour or more unaffected zeal, that I did while imploring the Divine grace to
assist me in fulfilling a mission so sacred and so difficult.

But as for Zadi, he seemed to have already forgotten himself,
his past dangers, and present pains. He implored me to waste no
more time in striving to mitigate his sufferings, and assured me,
that the letter of his dear afflicted master would be the best balsam for all his wounds. I compliance with his earnest entreaties,
I prepared to peruse the paper: but the tears gushed into my
eyes on recognizing the well-known handwriting, and it was
with difficulty that I deciphered the following words:

'Oh! I understand you well, my friends, my beloved-ones!
your voices, still more your unremitting and desperate exertions
to relieve me – all convince me, that you are near me; that you
feel for me; that you spare no labour to effect my rescue! Alas!
you will labour in vain! Death has already enveloped me in his
dark circle; there is no escape; I have already bidden farewell to
life; I cannot long survive in this atmosphere, corrupted as it is
by the pestilential vapours, constantly exhaling from the monster's jaws. I die resigned; but do not embitter this last and
heavy hour by the apprehension, lest your exertions in my behalf should be the means of involving you in my danger. By all
that is sacred and dear, I conjure you, abandon me to my unhappy fate; fly! oh! fly far from hence: it is my last, my only,
my most earnest request!

'Everard! Oh! Everard, my poor wife! Do not abandon my
Louisa!'

A cold shuddering ran through my bones: the poisonous air
robbed us even of our last wretched hope, that the anaconda
might at length retire wearied out with her vain expectations,
and leave my friend at liberty to quit his retreat. But now it was
evident from his letter that, long ere this could happen, Seafield
would be no more! immediate help must save him, or none!
Zadi sobbed aloud: it was an addition to my own grief to think,
that I had been obliged to give a fresh pang to his faithful
bosom, and it wrung me to the very soul, when I saw him give

way openly to this burst of sorrow. Suddenly he uttered a shriek so loud, that it startled all who heard him.

'No! no!' he exclaimed in the most violent agitation – 'No! no he shall not bid farewell to life for ever! there are still means. Oh! wretch that I am! curses, eternal curses on my old head, that I did not think of it till now, and now it comes too late! I might have saved him! I might have saved him! Had I but thought of it sooner my master would have been safe at this moment! now it is too late! he must die, and 'tis my heedlessness which kills him!'

'For mercy sake,' I cried, 'explain yourself, old man! You see that our messengers are not returned from Columbo – every moment that we lose is inestimable! If you really do know any means of rescue, tell it, discover it! Delay not an instant! Speak! To what means do you allude?'

'It is too late! it is too late;' he repeated; 'no one but myself could have carried it through; and here I lie, without the power to move a limb, and no one else will undertake a task so desperate!'

'The means! the means!' I exclaimed again, almost frantic with agitation.

'Well, then!' he resumed, his words frequently interrupted with groans; 'the anaconda is, as I told you formerly, the most voracious animal in nature. She is invincible while stimulated by hunger, but she can be overcome by a very child as soon as she has satiated herself with food; then she loses the flexibility of her joints, and instead of her restless activity she seems plunged in a benumbing torpor, and remains unable to move, overpowered by the burthen of her immoderate meal.'

'Excellent dear old man!' said I, in rapture at the ray of hope with which his words inspired me; 'is what you say certain? Could we but satiate this anaconda –'

'My master were rescued!' he replied: 'but to effect this requires the risk of a life; and who will venture that? Oh! were but these old limbs as they were two hours ago. Could I but remove the mountain load which weighs upon my chest, and prevents my breathing.'

'Oh! if I am but right in my guess!' I interrupted the old man; 'you would have driven her prey to the anaconda?'

'The whole herd! the whole herd!' shouted Zadi; and he sank back exhausted by the violence of his emotions. 'This thought,' he continued in a low voice after the pause of a moment, 'this thought suggested itself to my recollection long ago; but, wretch that I was, I believed its execution to be impracticable – the plague, which lately prevailed here among the cattle, has occasioned them to be removed from this part of the country, and they are gone too far to be recalled in time to afford the required assistance. In despair, therefore, I banished this scheme from my thoughts; but now that I am rendered unable to put it in execution, I remember.'

'What? what?' I inquired, almost breathless with anxiety.

'You know well Van Derkel, the rich Hollander, whose estate joins this? He is the most positive man breathing, and having once declared our fears of the plague to be groundless, he refused out of pure obstinacy to suffer his cattle to accompany those of his neighbours; they remain on his estate at this moment; an herd might easily be procured, and then – but it is too late, now it is too late! none but his faithful servant would dare –'

'What?' said I, interrupting him; 'will not his faithful friend?'

Zadi's looks met mine; they burned with new fire, while he confessed that on me alone now rested his only hope. The flames in his eyes seemed to have communicated themselves to my heart; and the blessings with which he loaded me, and the effusions of gratitude to Heaven and to me which he poured forth, confirmed the resolution which I had already adopted.

'Be of good comfort, friend!' said I, as I turned to leave him; 'the man whom you sought is found! I will tread that path which no other will tread, and I now leave you for the purpose of seeking it.'

Zadi's eyes were now filled with tears of joy.

'May the God of my fathers bless you!' he said, raising his eye to heaven; 'now then I can die contented; now then the hour of my master's deliverance will strike at last.'

I lost no time in hastening to Van Derkel's. I offered his herdsman the whole sum in my possession, if he would assist me in driving the beasts under the palm-trees: but he shuddered at the proposal, and rejected my proffered gold. I was not yet discouraged. By his master's authority I promised him freedom, provided he would but venture so far as to advance with the herd to the extremity of the little grove, which on the north-side separated the hill from the open country. He hesitated; again I pressed him; and at length he stammered out his consent, but in a voice so faint, and with a look of such irresolution, as convinced me, that I could place little dependence upon his promised help.

However, I at least neglected none of the means, which might contribute to our mutual safety: I caused the slaves to prepare with all diligence a couple of machines similar to those under which Zadi had performed his hazardous undertaking. Covered with these, we began to drive the cattle slowly before us; and as the general agitation had caused them to be totally neglected by their keepers, during their confinement in a place which afforded no herbage for their nourishment, hunger made them more obedient than we should probably have otherwise found them; and thus did we advance towards the hill, though the little resolution of my companion evidently grew still less with every step which we took forwards. To encourage him, I bade him observe the tranquillity of the anaconda, who had gradually withdrawn herself into her green shelter, so that we might almost have doubted her being really there.

'That is the very thing which alarms me!' answered the trembling slave; 'I am sure that she has already discovered, and now lurks concealed among the leaves, in order that she may make her prey more secure. Now then, not one step further will I advance; what I have already ventured is enough to merit liberty; but at all events I had rather pass the rest of my days in fetters, than purchase my freedom by advancing a single foot beyond this spot!'

And with these words he hurried away. However, I was the less disturbed at his forsaking me, when I perceived, that without him I could manage to drive the cattle forwards, and that no natural instinct made them aware of the neighbourhood of their enemy. It was not long before we arrived at the hill-foot. I was now obliged to leave the animals to their own guidance, feeling themselves no longer annoyed by my goad they gave way to the impulse of hunger, and dispersing themselves carelessly began to feed upon the welcome herbage; but how great was my joy at perceiving the bull separate himself from the rest of the herd and begin to ascend the hill. We arrived near the group of palm-trees; everything was hushed and tranquil; not a sound was to be heard except the noise of the scattered branches, as the bull trampled them beneath his feet: the anaconda seemed to have disappeared altogether.

But on a sudden a loud and rattling rush was heard among the palms, and with a single spring the snake darted down like a thunder-clap and twisted herself with her whole body round her devoted victim. Before the animal was yet aware of his danger, he already felt his dewlap enclosed between the wide-expanded jaws of the monster, and her teeth struck into it deeply. Roaring aloud he endeavoured to fly, and succeeded in dragging his tormentor a few yards away with him; but instantly she coiled herself round him in three or four wide folds, and drew these knots so close together, that the entangled beast was incapable of moving, and remained as if rooted to the place, already struggling with the terrors and pangs of death. The first noise of this extraordinary contest had been sufficient to put the remaining cattle to flight.

Unequal as was the strife, still it was not over instantly. The noble beast wanted not spirit to defend himself, nor was his strength easily exhausted. Now he rolled himself on the ground, and endeavoured to crush the enemy with his weight; now he swelled every nerve and exerted the power of every muscle, to burst the fetters in which his limbs were enveloped; he shook himself violently; he stamped, he bit, he roared, he pawed up the earth, he foamed at the mouth, and then dashed himself on the ground again with convulsive struggles. But with every moment the anaconda's teeth imprinted on his flesh new wounds; with every moment she drew her folds tighter and tighter; till, after struggling for a full quarter of an hour, I at length saw the poor animal stretched out at full length and breathless, totally deprived of motion and of life.

Now then I expected to see the anaconda gratify the hunger by which she had so long been tormented: but I was ignorant, that it is not the custom of this animal to divide its prey, but to swallow it at one enormous morsel. The size of the murdered bull made this impossible without much preparation; and I now learned, from the snake's proceedings, the necessity which there was for her always remaining in the neighbourhood of some large tree.

She again seized the bull with her teeth, and dragged it to the foot of the stoutest palm. Here she endeavoured to place it upright, leaning against the trunk. Having effected this, she enveloped the tree and the carcase together in one great fold, and continued to draw this closer, till she had broken every individual bone in her victim's body into a thousand pieces, and had actually reduced it into a shapeless mass of flesh. She was still occupied in this manner, when I hastened back to the mansion-house to rejoice Louisa and Zadi with the assurance of my success.

The roaring of the bull had already prepared the latter for my tidings. He limped to meet me at the door in spite of his bodily agonies, and overpowered me with thanks and benedictions. He also informed me, that the expected succours from Columbo were at length arrived, and that a physician had accompanied them. I immediately requested to see the latter, and commissioned him to impart the good news of Seafield's approaching deliverance to Louisa, with such precautions as might prevent her enfeebled constitution from suffering through excess of joy. I also recommended Zadi to his care, and then hastened back to complete my work; Zadi having assured me, that it was absolutely necessary to watch for the moment, when the anaconda should have swallowed her prey, and be enervated and overcome by the torpor of indigestion.

'You will be in no want of assistants,' he added; 'my fellow-servants are all ready to accompany you, not only because I have succeeded in convincing them that all danger is now at an end, but because among the natives of Ceylon the flesh of the anaconda is looked upon as most delicious food.'

In fact, on entering the courtyard I found the whole body of domestics, women and children as well as men, prepared for the attack with clubs, hatchets, and every sort of weapon, which had offered itself to their hands. The party from Columbo were well provided with ammunition; and we now all set joyfully forwards for the hill, though, on approaching it, we judged it as well still to use some little precaution.

I advanced beyond the rest. The anaconda had by this time entirely covered the carcase with her slime, and was in the very act of gorging this monstrous morsel. This task was not accomplished without violent efforts: a full hour elapsed before she had quite finished her dreadful meal; at length the carcase was entirely swallowed, and she stretched herself out at full length in the grass, with her stomach distended to the most astonishing dimensions. Every trace of her former liveliness and activity had disappeared! Her immoderate appetite had now yielded her up, impotent and defenceless, a prey even to the least formidable foe.

I hasten to conclude this long and painful tragedy. I discharged my musket at the monster at a moderate distance. This time the ball struck her close by her eye. She felt herself wounded: her body swelled with spite and venom, and every stripe of her variegated skin shone with more brilliant and vivid colours. But as to revenging herself upon her assailant, of that she was now totally incapable. She made one vain attempt to regain her old retreat among the boughs of the palm-trees, but sank down again upon the grass motionless and helpless. The report of my musket was the signal agreed upon to give notice to the expectant crowd, that they might approach without danger. Everyone now rushed towards the snake with loud shouting and clamours of joy. We all at once attacked her, and she soon expired under a thousand blows; but I did not wait to witness this catastrophe. A dearer interest occupied my mind: I hastened with all speed to the pavilion, and knocked loudly at the door, which was fastened within.

'Seafield! my friend!' I exclaimed; ''tis I! 'tis Everard! Open open! I bring you life and liberty.'

A minute passed – another – and still I listened in vain for an answer. Had fatigue overpowered him? Was he asleep, that he answered not? I knocked again; I spoke a second time, and louder; I listened so attentively that I could have distinguished the humming of a gnat within the pavilion. Heaven and earth! was it possible that after all I had come too late? The thought was distraction! I snatched an axe from one of the slaves, and after a few blows the pavilion door flew open.

I rushed into the room, and looked eagerly round for my friend – I found him! Oh! Heaven! his eyes were closed, his cheeks pale; every feature in his noble countenance so changed, that he was scarcely to be recognized! He lay extended in his armchair, and the noise of our entrance seemed to rouse him from a long stupor. He saw me; a faint smile played round his wan lips, while he attempted to stretch out his hand to me, but it sank down again from weakness: I threw my arms round him and pressed him to my heart in an agony of joy.

'You are safe!' I endeavoured to say; but the attempt to repress my gushing tears choked my voice, and the sounds were unintelligible.

'Yes!' said he with difficulty, 'this is being a friend indeed! But tell me! Louisa –?'

'She lives, and expects you,' I replied; 'come, come! my friend; rouse yourself! Make an effort, and shake off this lethargy! Look upon your danger as no more than a frightful dream, and awake to the real happiness which awaits you!'

'It waits not for me!' he answered faintly: 'I have received my death-warrant in this chamber. My minutes are counted! Louisa – Oh! bear me to Louisa!'

The chamber was hot and close even to suffocation. We removed him with all speed into the open air, four of the slaves bearing him as he sat in his armchair; but as we conveyed him down the hill we took care to turn his face away from the spot where lay the breathless but still horrible anaconda. The purer atmosphere seemed immediately to produce a beneficial effect upon the sufferer; and his strength was still further recruited by a few drops of a cordial, with which I had taken care to provide myself, and which I administered with the utmost caution.

On our arrival at the mansion-house, we found that Zadi's attention had already provided everything which his master could possibly need. His bed was prepared; every kind of refreshment was in readiness, and the physician was waiting to afford his much-required assistance. But we soon found that the most effectual medicine for Seafield would be the sight of Louisa; and as the physician was of opinion, that the lady was more likely to suffer from anxiety to see her husband, than from the agitation of the interview, my friend was indulged in his wish, and we supported him to the chamber, where his wife so anxiously was expecting his approach.

I will not attempt to describe this interview, nor that which afterwards took place between Seafield and the faithful Zadi; the feeling heart of itself will fill up this chasm; yet I cannot omit mentioning, that it was not till I had explained to my friend the whole extent of his obligations to that faithful Indian, and till the repeated orders of his master compelled him to appear before him, that Zadi indulged his ardent wish to throw himself at the feet of his beloved lord. And why then did he deprive himself so long of a pleasure which he desired so earnestly? The noble fellow was unwilling to assist his master by showing him how much and how severely he had suffered for his sake! I cannot tell you how much both the re-united couple and myself were affected by this uncommon mark of delicacy and consideration.

Oh! how happily and how swiftly fled away the first days which succeeded the deliverance of my friend: alas! those first days were the only ones destined to pass happily. It was soon but too evident, that Seafield's sufferings in that fatal pavilion had injured his constitution irreparably. With every succeeding day his strength visibly decreased, and the blighted flower bowed itself still nearer to the ground. His malady defied the power of medicine; he seemed to perish away before our eyes; and the physician was at length compelled to acknowledge that all the powers of art were insufficient to sustain any longer Seafield's exhausted frame. Not the unsatisfied demands of nature; not the hunger which gnawed his entrails, nor the burning thirst which dried up his palate; not the agonies of his mind, and his painful wrestling against despair: none of these had affected him so fatally. — No; it was the pestiferous breath exhaling from the jaws of the anaconda, which had penetrated into Seafield's close and sultry prison; and whose force, concentrated and increased by confinement, had fallen upon his constitution like a baleful mildew, and planted the seeds of dissolution in the very marrow of his life.

What Louisa and myself endured, while watching his slow but constantly progressive journey to the tomb, no words can utter. He gave Zadi and his three sons their freedom, and made over to him a small estate near Columbo, fully sufficient to secure the comfort of the good old man for the remainder of his existence. During the last days of his illness he frequently reminded me of the letter which he had written in the pavilion, and of which Zadi had obtained possession at such extreme risk; this paper he frequently charged me to consider as his dying testament; he as frequently repeated the same thing to his wife, while she wept by his bedside. His last words were like his letter, 'Forsake not my poor Louisa!' His last action was to place her hand in mine — he sank back a corpse on his pillow, and Louisa fell lifeless at my feet.

Yet she saw him once more; she insisted on pressing her lips once again to his. I trembled for the convulsive agonies which her delicate frame would undergo during this last and most painful scene: yet was I still more alarmed, when I witnessed the composure of her affliction. She held his hand in hers; she spoke not one word; she heaved not one sigh; not a single tear escaped from her burning eyes. She stood long motionless by his bedside; she bent down, and pressed her colourless lips upon his closed lids; and then slowly and silently she withdrew to her widowed chamber.

I chose for Seafield's sepulchre the place which he had always loved best, and where he had suffered the most; his tomb was raised in the fatal pavilion. Zadi and myself laid our friend in the earth; we should have thought his coffin profaned, had we suffered any other hands to touch it. Seafield and his sufferings slept in the grave: his less fortunate friends still lived to lament him.

My benefactor had left his property jointly to Louisa and myself; and his wishes respecting us had been expressed too clearly to be misunderstood. Louisa was among the loveliest of her sex; but I should have counted it profanation, had my heart suffered itself to harbour one thought of her less pure than is offered at the shrine of some enfranchised saint. I loved not Louisa; no, I adored her. Alas! it was not long before she became a saint indeed.

She complained not, but she sorrowed; she suffered, but it was in silence. In vain did she forbid her lips to confess the progress which grief made in her constitution: her emaciated form sufficiently betrayed it. A few melancholy weeks had elapsed since the death of my friend, when one morning her terrified women informed me, that she was not in her apartment, nor apparently had been in bed all night. My heart instructed me well where to seek the unfortunate. I flew to the pavilion; she was stretched on the marble stone, which covered her husband. In the agony of grief she had burst a blood vessel, and her limbs were already cold; her countenance was calm, and a faint smile seemed to play round her lips: it was the only smile which I had seen there since Seafield's death. She was deposited in the same grave with her husband; for myself, I was unable to sustain the weight of grief imposed upon me by this second calamity, and a long and dangerous illness was the consequence of my mental sufferings.

The skill of my physician saved my life; and no sooner was I able to quit the house, than I resolved to withdraw from a land rendered hateful to me by such bitter recollections. In consequence of Louisa's decease, the whole of Seafield's property by his will devolved to me — I endeavoured to prevail on Zadi to accept some part of it, but he declared that his master's liberality had gone beyond his utmost wishes.

'Yet one request,' said he, 'I will venture to make. My two eldest sons are grown up and able to take care of themselves; but the third is young, and I feel that my death can be at no great distance. His brothers may treat him ill, or at least may neglect him; but condescend to take him into your care, let him be your servant, and I shall not have a wish in this world left unaccomplished. Under the protection of an honest man, my boy cannot fail to become an honest man himself.'

Mirza (for that was the lad's name, the same who is now with me) was in the room, and joined his entreaties to his father's with such earnestness, that I could not refuse their request. I soon after left Ceylon, followed by Zadi's blessings; the good old man is still alive, and by a third hand I hear from him frequently; but the letters which he dictates embrace but two topics, anxiety for the welfare of his son, and regret for the loss of his beloved master.

'You are now informed,' continued Everard after a moment's pause, addressing himself to the whole society, 'you are now informed by what means I acquired my fortune. It was the gift of gratitude: but never can I recollect the dreadful service which I rendered Seafield (and, alas! which I rendered him in vain!) without feeling my frame convulsed with horror, and my mind tortured by the most painful recollections. It is this which has ever made me unwilling to discourse on the means by which I became possessed of my wealth. Yet I cannot but think it somewhat hard, that mere silence should be construed into positive guilt; and that I should be treated as if convicted of the most atrocious crimes, because I have not thought it necessary to make public my private life, and to rend open anew the wounds of my heart for the gratification of idle and impertinent curiosity.'

Everard was silent; so were all around him. Confusion blushed on every cheek, except on Jessy's, whose tender heart had been deeply affected by the mournful story, and whose mild blue eyes still floated in tears, though every now and then a smile beamed through them in approbation of her lover's conduct. Her father at length mustered up his courage, and broke through this embarrassing silence.

'My dear good Everard,' said he, 'I know not how to excuse my friends here for telling me so many slanders of you, not myself for having been credulous enough to believe them. In truth, there is but one person in the room, whose lips are worthy to convey to you our apology: there then, let them make it,' – and with these words he placed the blushing Jessy in Everard's arms.

And Jessy's lips wisely expressed the apology in a kiss; and Everard acknowledged, while he pressed her to his bosom as his bride, that the apology was not only sufficient, but a reward in full for the sufferings which he had experienced through the vicissitudes of his whole past life!

# The Monk of Horror

*or*

## The Conclave of Corpses

## Anonymous
## (1798)

As I intimated in the previous introduction, Matthew Lewis's *The Monk* spawned a host of imitations both in England and Europe. Some publishers did little more than openly plagiarize the original work, while others created similar tales of evil and perversion and then brazenly labelled them as being 'by the author of *The Monk*'.

Montague Summers has studied many of these copies and forgeries at some length in his splendid work, *The Gothic Quest*, and it is hardly surprising to learn that very few of them are still extant today. Without exception they lacked the originality and skilful daring of Lewis's work and were in the main hastily composed and atrociously illustrated and printed. However, as the first great outpouring of Gothic *terror* – albeit imitative – the stories should be marked in this collection and I have endeavoured to select a tale which is both reflective, a little unusual and with some literary merit. *The Monk of Horror* appeared in an anonymous little chapbook illustrated with red and yellow woodcuts and boldly entitled, *Tales of the Crypt – in the style of The Monk* (1798).

SOME three hundred years since, when the convent of Kreutzberg was in its glory, one of the monks who dwelt therein, wishing to ascertain something of the hereafter of those whose bodies lay all undecayed in the cemetery, visited it alone in the dead of night for the purpose of prosecuting his inquiries on that fearful subject. As he opened the trap-door of the vault a light burst from below; but deeming it to be only the lamp of the sacristan, the monk drew back and awaited his departure concealed behind the high altar. The sacristan emerged not, however, from the opening; and the monk, tired of waiting, approached, and finally descended the rugged steps which led into the dreary depths. No sooner had he set foot on the lower-most stair, than the well-known scene underwent a complete transformation in his eyes. He had long been accustomed to visit the vault, and whenever the sacristan went thither, he was almost sure to be with him. He therefore knew every part of it as well as he did the interior of his own narrow cell, and the arrangement of its contents was perfectly familiar to his eyes. What, then, was his horror to perceive that this arrangement, which even but that morning had come under his observation as usual, was altogether altered, and a new and wonderful one substituted in its stead.

A dim lurid light pervaded the desolate abode of darkness, and it just sufficed to give to his view a sight of the most singular description.

On each side of him the dead but imperishable bodies of the long-buried brothers of the convent sat erect in their lidless coffins, their cold, starry eyes glaring at him with lifeless rigidity, their withered fingers locked together on their breasts, their stiffened limbs motionless and still. It was a sight to petrify the stoutest heart; and the monk's quailed before it, though he was a philosopher, and a sceptic to boot. At the upper end of the vault, at a rude table formed of a decayed coffin, or something which once served the same purpose, sat three monks. They were the oldest corpses in the charnel-house, for the inquisitive brother knew their faces well; and the cadaverous hue of their cheeks seemed still more cadaverous in the dim light shed upon them, while their hollow eyes gave forth what looked to him like flashes of flame. A large book lay open before one of them, and the others bent over the rotten table as if in intense pain, or in deep and fixed attention. No word was said; no sound was heard; the vault was as silent as the grave, its awful tenants still as statues.

Fain would the curious monk have receded from this horrible place; fain would he have retraced his steps and sought again his cell, fain would he have shut his eyes to the fearful scene; but he could not stir from the spot, he felt rooted there; and though he once succeeded in turning his eyes to the entrance of the vault, to his infinite surprise and dismay he could not discover where it lay, nor perceive any possible means of exit. He stood thus for some time. At length the aged monk at the table beckoned him to advance. With slow tottering steps he made his way to the group, and at length stood in front of the table, while the other monks raised their heads and glanced at him with fixed, lifeless looks that froze the current of his blood. He knew not what to do; his senses were fast forsaking him; Heaven seemed to have deserted him for his incredulity. In this moment of doubt and fear he bethought him of a prayer, and as he proceeded he felt himself becoming possessed of a confidence he had before unknown. He looked on the book before him. It was a large volume, bound in black, and clasped with bands of gold, with fastenings of the same metal. It was inscribed at the top of each page.

'*Liber Obedientiae.*'

He could read no further. He then looked, first in the eyes of him before whom it lay open, and then in those of his fellows. He finally glanced around the vault on the corpses who filled every visible coffin in its dark and spacious womb. Speech came to him, and resolution to use it. He addressed himself to the awful beings in whose presence he stood, in the words of one having authority with them.

'*Pax vobis,*' 'twas thus he spake – 'Peace be to ye.'

'*Hic nulla pax,*' replied an aged monk, in a hollow, tremulous tone, bearing his breast the while – 'Here is no peace.'

He pointed to his bosom as he spoke, and the monk, casting his eye upon it, beheld his heart within surrounded by living fire, which seemed to feed on it but not consume it. He turned away in affright, but ceased not to prosecute his inquiries.

'*Pax vobis, in nomine Domini,*' he spake again – 'Peace be to ye, in the name of the Lord.'

'*Hic non pax,*' the hollow and heartrending tones of the ancient monk who sat at the right of the table were heard to answer.

On glancing at the bared bosom of this hapless being also the same sight was exhibited – the heart surrounded by a devouring flame, but still remaining fresh and unconsumed under its operation. Once more the monk turned away and addressed the aged man in the centre.

'*Pax vobis, in nomine Domini,*' he proceeded.

At these words the being to whom they were addressed raised his head, put forward his hand, and closing the book with a loud clap, said –

'Speak on. It is yours to ask, and mine to answer.'

The monk felt reassured, and his courage rose with the occasion.

'Who are ye?' he inquired; 'who may ye be?'

'We know not!' was the answer, 'alas! we know not!'

'We know not, we know not!' echoed in melancholy tones the denizens of the vault.

'What do ye here?' pursued the querist.

'We await the last day, the day of the last judgement! Alas for us! woe! woe!'

'Woe! woe!' resounded on all sides.

The monk was appalled, but still he proceeded.

'What did ye to deserve such doom as this? What may your crime be that deserves such dole and sorrow?'

As he asked the question the earth shook under him, and a crowd of skeletons uprose from a range of graves which yawned suddenly at his feet.

'These are our victims,' answered the old monk. 'They suffered at our hands. We suffer now, while they are at peace; and we shall suffer.'

'For how long?' asked the monk.

'For ever and ever!' was the answer.

'For ever and ever, for ever and ever!' died along the vault.

'May God have mercy on us!' was all the monk could exclaim.

The skeletons vanished, the graves closing over them. The aged men disappeared from his view, the bodies fell back in their coffins, the light fled, and the den of death was once more enveloped in its usual darkness.

On the monk's revival he found himself lying at the foot of the altar. The grey dawn of a spring morning was visible, and he was fain to retire to his cell as secretly as he could, for fear he should be discovered.

From thenceforth he eschewed vain philosophy, says the legend, and, devoting his time to the pursuit of true knowledge, and the extension of the power, greatness, and glory of the Church, died in the odour of sanctity, and was buried in that holy vault, where his body is still visible.

# The Nymph of the Fountain

## William Beckford

## (1759–1844)

Another figure in the history of the Gothic genre to whom some authorities attach almost as much importance as Matthew Lewis is William Beckford, author of the great Oriental terror novel, *Vathek*, which added a new dimension to the literature on its publication in 1787. Although tales from the East had been popular in Europe from 1704 (with the first translation of *The Arabian Nights*), it was Beckford and his *History of the Caliph Vathek* which gave it both widespread importance and a part in the terror-romance school.

William Thomas Beckford, the son of a former Lord Mayor of London, achieved fame as a literary prodigy at the tender age of seventeen when his first work, a witty and scholarly study of art, *Memoirs of Extraordinary Painters*, was published. Immensely wealthy, flamboyant and self-indulgent, Beckford travelled restlessly, argued fervently and ruined what promised to be a successful career in politics through scandal and intrigue. Like Horace Walpole, Beckford dreamed of his own personal castle and in 1796 realized this by building Fonthill Abbey which had a central tower some 300 feet tall! Unfortunately this edifice collapsed – but its owner's only regret was that he had not been present to see it fall.

The novel *Vathek* with its story of the Caliph's terrifying search for the secrets of the Universe, was written by Beckford in the calmer days of his youth and it is a measure of his talent that it was composed entirely in French. (The first English translation was actually a pirate version and appeared both without the author's approval and labelled as 'translation from the Arabic'.) Beckford had doubtlessly read those Oriental novels which were in circulation at the time and to their fantasy and colour added the violent patterns and genius of his own imagination. As Edith Birkhead has written, 'Beckford's life and character contained elements as grotesque and fantastic as his romance. He revelled in golden glories and his schemes were as grandeous and ambitious as those of an Eastern caliph.'

The Beckford papers contain the manuscripts of a number of dark tales which the author worked on at various periods of his life, but of all his compositions the following tale which he adapted and reworked from a German legend seems to me to contain some of the finest elements of storytelling and Gothic horror. In the absence of an Oriental story from his pen it makes an ideal substitute. The probable date of publication was 1791.

AT the distance of three miles from Blackpool in Swabia, there was situated a strong freebooter's hold: it was occupied by a valiant knight, named Siegfried. He was the flower of the freebooting errantry, the scourge of the confederate towns, and the terror of all merchants and carriers, who ventured along the high roads, without purchasing his passport. The moment his vizor was down, his cuirass fixed, his sword girt about his loins, and his golden spurs tinkled at his heels, his heart was steeled to rapine and bloodshed. In conformity with the prejudices of the age, he accounted pillage and plunder among the distinguished privileges of the noblesse: so he fell, from time to time, without mercy, upon the defenceless traders and country people; and being himself muscular and stout, he acknowledged no law but the right of the stronger. At the alarm, 'Siegfried is abroad! Siegfried is at hand!' all Swabia was seized with consternation; the peasants flocked into the fortified towns, and the watchmen upon the towers blew their horns aloud, to give warning of the danger.

But at home, when he had doffed his armour, this dread freebooter became gentle as a lamb, hospitable as an Arab, the kindest of masters, and the fondest of husbands. His wife was a soft, amiable lady, a perfect pattern of virtue and good conduct. She loved her husband with the most inviolable attachment, and superintended her household with unremitting diligence. When

Siegfried sallied forth in quest of adventures, it was not her custom to sit at the lattice, looking out for admirers, but she set her
hand to the wheel, and drew out the flax to a thread so fine, that
Arachne herself, the Lydian spinstress, need not have been
ashamed to own it. She had brought her husband two daughters, whom she assiduously instructed in the lessons of piety and
virtue. In her monastic retirement nothing disturbed her peace
of mind, except the unjust means by which her husband acquired his wealth. In her heart she abhorred this privilege of
robbery, and she received no satisfaction from his presents of
costly stuffs, interwoven with gold and silver. 'Of what use is
all this to me, bedewed as it is with the tears of the wronged?'
would she say to herself, as she threw it into her coffer, where it
was suffered to lie without further notice. She found some relief
to these melancholy reflections in administering consolation to
the captives, who had fallen into Siegfried's clutches: and numbers from time to time were released in consequence of her me-
diation; and she never failed to furnish privately with a small
sum to bear their expenses home.

At the foot of the eminence on which the castle was seated, a
plentiful spring arose within a kind of natural grotto, and immediately concealed itself among the tangled thickets. The
fountain-head, according to tradition, was inhabited by a nymph
of the family of the Naiads, though, instead of that sort of Gre-
cian appellation, she passed here under the name of the Nicksy.
If report spoke true, she had sometimes been seen, on the eve of
important occurrences, in the castle. Whenever, during her husband's absence, the noble lady wanted to breathe the fresh air
beyond the gloomy walls of the mansion, or steal out to exercise
her charity in secret, it was her custom to repair to this fountain.
This spot was her favourite retreat. At the grotto she appointed
to meet the poor, whom the porter had refused admittance; and
here she not only distributed among them the remnants of her
table on set days, but also made them considerable presents of
money.

Once, when Siegfried had sallied forth with his troop, to way-
lay the merchants coming from Augspurg fair, he tarried abroad

beyond the time he had fixed for his return. His affectionate lady, alarmed at the unprecedented delay, apprehended nothing less than that he had been slain in the encounter, or at least had fallen into the enemy's hand. Hope and fear wrestled in her bosom for several days. She would often call out to the dwarf that kept watch upon the battlements: 'Look out, Hansel, towards the wood, and see what makes such a rustling among the trees. – Hark! I hear a trampling of horses in the valley! – What raises yonder cloud of dust? – Dost thou espy thy master hastening home?' Hansel mournfully replied, 'There is nothing stirring in the wood – I hear no trampling of horses in the valley – I see no clouds of dust rising – there is no nodding of plumes afar off.' She repeated these inquiries incessantly, till the evening star began to twinkle, and the full moon peeped over the eastern hills. Being no longer able to endure her apartment, she threw her cloak over her shoulders, and stole out at the private door towards the grove of beeches, that she might pursue her melancholy ideas without interruption, beside her favourite fountain. Her eye was dissolved in tears, and her moans harmonized with the melting murmurs of the rivulet, as it lost itself among the thick grass.

As she approached the grotto, it seemed as if an airy phantom hovered just within the entrance; but she was too deeply absorbed in sorrow to pay much attention to the vision; and a transitory idea, that it was some illusion of the moonlight, passed half unperceived across her imagination. But on a nearer approach a figure in white was distinctly seen to move, and to beckon her into the grove. An involuntary horror fell upon the mournful lady, but she did not fly back; she only stopped short to take a more distinct view. The report concerning the inhabitant of the spring, that circulated in the neighbourhood, had not failed to reach her ears, and she now recognized the phantom in white for the nymph of the fountain. She concluded that the apparition denoted some important family event: and her husband being uppermost in her thoughts, she instantly began to tear her raven locks, and set up a loud lamentation, 'Alas, unhappy day! Ah, Siegfried, Siegfried, thou art no more! – Woe is me, thou art cold and stiff! – Thou hast made me a widow, and thy poor children are become orphans!'

While she lamented in this manner, wringing her hands and beating her bosom, a gentle voice was heard to proceed from the grotto: 'Be not afflicted Matilda; I do not come to announce bad tidings: approach without fear; I am only a friend that wishes to converse with you.' The appearance and address of the Naiad were so little alarming, that the noble lady did not hesitate to comply with the invitation. As she stepped into the grotto, the inhabitant took her kindly by the hand, kissed her forehead, seated herself close beside her, and spake: 'Welcome to my habitation, beloved mortal, whose heart is pure as the water of my fountain: therefore the invisible powers are all propitious to thee. As for me, the only favour I can confer upon thee is to disclose the fortunes of thy life. Thy husband is safe: ere the morning cock crows thou shalt fold him in thy arms. Do not be apprehensive of mourning for thy husband, the spring of thy life shall be dried up before his. But thou must first bear a daughter in an eventful hour. The balance of her fate is equally posed between happiness and misery. The stars are not unpropitious, but an unfriendly gleam threatens to rob her of a mother's fostering care.'

The tender-hearted Matilda was greatly affected, when she heard that her daughter was to become an infant orphan. She was unable to suppress her maternal tears. The Naiad, deeply touched by her sorrow, endeavoured to compose her mind: 'Be not afflicted beyond measure; when thou art no longer able to tend thy infant, I will myself discharge a mother's office, on condition, however, that I am chosen for one of her godmothers, that I may have some interest in the babe. Be careful at the same time that the child, provided thou wilt entrust her to me, brings me back safe the baptismal gift which I shall leave with her.' This was no offer to be rejected: to ratify the treaty, the Naiad took a smooth pebble out of the rivulet, and gave it to Matilda; charging her, at the proper season, to send one of her damsels to throw it onto the fountainhead, when she would consider it as a summons to attend the ceremony. The matron promised that her injunction should be punctually observed, laid all these things up in her heart, and returned to the castle. Her Naiad patroness stepped into the water, and vanished.

Not long afterwards the dwarf blew a merry blast with his horn from the watchtower; and Siegfried, with his horsemen and a rich booty, entered the courtyard. Before a year had expired, the virtuous lady communicated to her lord a discovery, which raised in his mind the pleasing expectation of the arrival of an heir male. It cost Matilda much reflection, before she could contrive how to manage about the Nymph of the Fountain, for many reasons restrained her from communicating the adventure at the grove to her husband. About the same time it happened that Siegfried received a message of mortal defiance from a knight whom he had offended at a feast. He lost no time in equipping himself and his squires, and when, according to his custom, he came to bid his wife farewell, just before he mounted, she eagerly inquired into the nature of his design; and when, instead of satisfying her, he affectionately reproved her for her unusual and ill-timed curiosity, she covered her face and wept bitterly. Her tears melted the knight's generous heart nevertheless he tore himself away, and, without showing any signs of sympathy, rode briskly to the place of rendezvous, where, after a severe conflict, he dismounted his adversary, and returned in triumph.

His faithful spouse received him with open arms: and by endearing conversation, and all the artillery of female address, strove to extort a communication of his late adventure. But he constantly barricaded every avenue to his heart by the bolt of insensibility, and all her artifices were unavailing. Finding that she still persisted in her purpose, he endeavoured to abash her by raillery; — 'Good grandmother Eve, thy daughters have not degenerated: prying curiosity has continued to be the portion of woman to the present day; not one but would have longed for the forbidden fruit.' 'I beg your pardon, my dear husband,' replied the artful dame; 'you are too partial to the ladies; there is not a man existing who has not received his lawful portion of mother Eve's inheritance; the whole difference consists in this, the loving wife neither has, nor is permitted to have a secret from her husband. Could I find it in my heart to conceal anything from you, I would risk a great wager that you would never be at rest till you had drawn the secret from me.' 'And I assure you, upon my honour,' replied he, 'that your secret would never give me a moment's uneasiness – nay, you may make the trial, I give you my full consent.' This was just the point to which Matilda desired to bring her husband: 'Well then,' said she, 'you know, my dear, that my time is fast approaching. You shall allow me to choose one of the godmothers. I design this office for a dear friend, whom I have locked up in my heart, but with whom you are altogether unacquainted. I only desire that you will never press me to tell who she is, whence she comes, nor where she lives. If you promise this, and keep steady to the obligation, I will consent to lose the wager, and willingly own that the firmness of imperial man has a right to triumph over the frailty of our sex.' Siegfried, without scruple, engaged his honour to forbear all inquiry; and Matilda secretly rejoiced at the success of her stratagem.

In a few weeks she presented her husband with a daughter. The father would much rather have taken a boy into his arms; he nevertheless rode about in high spirits to invite his friends and neighbours to the christening. They all appeared on the appointed day; and when the lady heard the rolling of carriages, the neighing of horses, and the hum of a large company, she called to her one of her trusty maids, and charged her, 'Take this pebble; go and throw it behind you, without saying a word, into the fountain in the grotto: be careful to do exactly as I have directed you.' The maid punctually obeyed the injunction; and before she returned, an unknown lady stepped into the apartment where the company was assembled, and made her obeisance very gracefully to the knights and dames. When the child was brought out, and the priest had gone up to the font, the highest place fell to the stranger, every one respectfully making way for her. Her beauty, and the gracefulness of her demeanour attracted every eye; and above all the splendour of her dress, which consisted of a flowing gown of azure blue silk, with cuffs turned up with white satin; she was, moreover, as heavily laden with pearls and jewels as my Lady of Loretto on her transparent veil, which flowed in easy folds from the crown of the head, over her shoulders, down to her heels: and the tip of the veil was dripping wet, as if it had been drawn through water.

The unknown lady, by her unexpected appearance, had so disarranged the groupe, that they forgot to ask for instructions about the child's name; so the priest christened it Matilda, after its mother. After the ceremony, little Matilda was carried back to her mother, and the ladies followed in order to congratulate the new-made mother, and bestow upon their god-daughter the accustomed baptismal boon. At sight of the stranger Matilda betrayed some emotion. She probably felt a mixture of pleasure and surprise, at the punctuality shewn by the Naiad in the performance of her engagement. She cast a stolen glance at her husband, who replied by a smile, which none of the bystanders could decypher, and afterwards affected to take no notice of the stranger. The presents now engaged all the mother's attention: a shower of gold was poured upon the nursling from the liberal hands of its sponsors. Last of all, the unknown lady came forward with her boon, and much disappointed the expectations of her associates. They looked for a present of inestimable value from so splendid a personage, especially when they saw her produce, and unfold with great care and method, a silk case, which, as it turned out, contained nothing but a musk-ball, and that not the precious drug, but an imitation, turned in box-wood. – This she laid very gravely upon the cradle, and gave the mother a friendly kiss upon the forehead, and then quitted the apartment.

So paltry a present occasioned a loud whisper through the room, and a laugh of scorn succeeded. Several shrewd remarks and sly allusions – for the festivity of a christening has in all ages been remarkable for its effect in brightening the wit – entertained the guests at the expense of the fair stranger. But, as the knight and his lady observed a mysterious silence upon the subject, both the curious and voluble were obliged to rest satisfied with distant conjectures. No more was seen of the stranger, nor could anyone tell which way she had vanished. Siegfried was secretly tormented to know who the lady with the dripping veil, for so, for want of a better name, was she entitled, might be. His tongue, however, was bound by the dread of falling into a woman's weakness, and by the inviolable sanctity of his knightly word. Nevertheless, in the moment of matrimonial confidence, the question, 'Tell me now, my dear, who was the lady with the dripping veil,' often was ready to bolt. He expected one day or other a full gratification of his curiosity by dint of cunning or caresses, firmly relying on that property of the female heart, in consequence of which it is as little able to keep a secret as a sieve of holding water. For this time, however, he was mistaken in his calculation. Matilda kept the bridle on her tongue, and laid up the riddle in her heart with no less care than the musk-ball in her casket of jewels.

Ere the infant had outgrown the leading-strings, the nymph's prophecy respecting her affectionate mother was fulfilled; she was taken ill, and died so suddenly, that she had not even time to think of the musk-ball, much less could she dispose of it for the advantage of little Matilda, according to the directions of her patroness. Siegfried was unfortunately absent at a tournament at Augspurg, and was on his way homeward as this melancholy event happened, with his heart bounding for joy, on account of a prize he had received from the hands of the Emperor Frederick himself. As soon as the dwarf on the watchtower was aware of his lord's approach, he blew his horn, as usual, to announce his arrival to the people in the castle; but he did not blow a cheerful note, as on former occasions. The mournful blast smote the knight's heart sore, and raised up sad apprehensions in his breast: 'Alas!' he cries, 'do you hear those doleful sounds? It is more ungrateful to my ears than the screech-owl's screaming. Hansel proclaims nothing good: I fear it is a death's blast.' The squires were all dumb with apprehension, they looked their master sorrowfully in the face; at last one took up the word, and spake, 'There goes a single raven croaking to our left hand — Heaven defend us! for I am afraid there is a corpse in the house.' The knight upon this clapped spurs to his horse, and galloped over the heath till the sparks flew amain. The drawbridge fell; he cast an eager look into the courtyard, where he beheld the symbol of a dead body set out before the door; it consisted of a lantern crowned with a flag of crape, and with a light; moreover all the window-shutters were closed. At the same instant he heard the lamentation of the household, for they had just placed Matilda's coffin on the bier. At the head sat the two elder daughters, all covered with crape and frize. They were silently shedding showers of tears over their departed mother. The youngest was seated at the foot; she was as yet incapable of feeling her loss, and so she was employed in stripping, with childish unconcern, the flowers that were strewed over the dead body. This melancholy spectacle was too much for Siegfried's firmness: he began to sob and lament aloud, fell upon the ice-cold corpse, bedewed the wan cheeks with his tears, pressed with his quivering lips against the pale mouth, and gave himself up, without reserve, to the bitterness of sorrow. Having laid up his armour in the armoury, he drew his hat deep over his eyes, put on a black mourning cloak, and took his place beside the bier, brooding over his affliction; and at length conferred on his deceased wife the last honours of a solemn funeral.

It has been remarked by a certain great wit, that the most violent feelings are always the shortest in their duration. Accordingly the knight, bowed as he had been to the ground, felt the load of sorrow grow lighter by degrees, and in a short time entertained serious thoughts of repairing his loss by a second wife. The lot of his choice fell upon a brisk young damsel, the very antitype of the gentle Matilda. The household of course soon put on a different form. The new lady delighted in pomp and parade; her extravagance knew no bounds, and she comported herself haughtily towards the domestics; she held banquets and carousals without number; her fruitfulness peopled the house with a numerous progeny. The daughters of the first marriage were disregarded, and they very soon were put out of sight and out of mind. The two elder sisters were placed in a religious establishment in Germany. Little Matilda was banished to a remote corner of the house, and placed under the superintendance of a nurse, that she might no more intrude upon her stepmother's notice. As this vain woman was utterly averse to all household affairs, her want of economy rose to such a pitch, that the revenues arising from club-law were inadequate to the expenses, although the knight stretched his privilege to the utmost. My lady found herself frequently under the necessity of despoiling the repositories of her predecessor. She was obliged to barter away the rich stuffs, or surrender them on pawn to the Jews. Happening one day to be in great household distress, she rummaged every drawer and coffer for valuables; in her search, she stumbled upon a private compartment in an old escrutoire, and, to her great joy, among other articles, fell upon Matilda's casket of jewels. Her greedy eye devoured the sparkling diamond rings, the ear-pendants, bracelets, necklaces, lockets, and the whole trinkets besides. She took an accurate inventory of the whole stock, examined article by article, and calculated in idea, how much this glorious windfall would produce. Among other rarities she was aware of the wooden musk-ball; she tried to unscrew it, but it was swelled by the damp. She then poised it on her hand, but finding it as light as a hollow nut, she concluded it was an empty ring-case, and tossed it as if worthless lumber out at the window.

Little Matilda happened to be playing on the grass-plot immediately below. Seeing a round body roll along the turf, she grasped with a child's eagerness at the new plaything; nor was she a whit less delighted at this, than her mother-in-law at the other prize. It afforded her amusement for several days; she was so fond of it, that she would not part with it out of her own hands. One sultry summer's noon, the nurse carried her charge to the grotto for coolness; the child, after a while, asked for her afternoon's cake; but the nurse had forgotten to bring it, and did not chuse to be at the trouble of going back quite to the house: so, to keep the little one quiet, she went among the bushes to pluck a handful of blackberries. The child meanwhile played with the musk-ball, rolling it before her and running after it: once she rolled it a little too far, and the child's joy, in the strictest sense, tumbled into the water. Immediately a female, fresh as the morning, beautiful as an angel, and smiling like one of the Graces, appeared in view. The child started, for at first she supposed it was her stepmother, in whose way she never came without a beating or a scolding. But the Nymph accosted her in the most engaging terms: 'Be not afraid, my little dear, I am thy godmamma: come to me: look, here is thy plaything that fell into the water.' The sight of this enticed the child towards her: the Nymph took her up in her arms, pressed her gently to her bosom, kissed her affectionately, and bedewed her face with tears. 'Poor little orphan,' said she, 'I have promised to be instead of a mother to thee, and I will keep my word. Come often here to see me. Thou wilt always find me in this grotto upon throwing a pebble into the fountainhead. Keep thy musk-ball with the utmost care: be sure, never play with it any more, lest thou lose it; for some time or other, it will fulfil three of thy wishes. When thou art grown a little older, I will tell thee more. At present thou wouldst not understand me.' She gave her much good advice besides, suitable to her tender age, and, above all things, enjoined her silence. Soon afterwards the nurse returned, and the Nymph was gone.

Matilda was a sensible, intelligent child; and she had reflection enough to hold her tongue on the subject of godmamma Nicksy. At her return to the castle, she asked for needle and thread, which she used for the purpose of sewing the musk-ball in the lower tuck of her frock. All her thoughts are now turned towards the fountain. Whenever the weather permitted, she proposed a walk there: her superintendant could deny nothing to the coaxing little maid; and, as she seemed to inherit this predilection, the grotto having always been the favourite retreat of her mother, she gratified her wishes so much the more cheerfully. Matilda always contrived some pretext for sending away the nurse; no sooner was her back fairly turned, than she dropped a pebble into the spring, which instantly procured her the company of her indulgent godmother. In a few revolutions of the year, the little orphan attained the age of puberty: her charms disclosed themselves as the bud of a rose opens its hundred leaves, opens in modest dignity amid the many-coloured race of vulgar flowers. She blossomed indeed but in the kitchen-garden; for she lived unnoticed among the servants, she was never suffered to appear at her stepmother's voluptuous banquets, but was confined to her chamber, where she employed herself in needle-work; and at the close of the day found, in the society of the Nymph of the Fountain, ample compensation for the noisy pleasures of which she was deprived. The Naiad was not only her companion and confidante, but likewise her instructress in every female accomplishment; and she was studious to form her exactly after the pattern of her virtuous mother.

One day the Nymph redoubled her tenderness: she clasped the charming Matilda in her arms, reclined her head upon her shoulder, and displayed so much melancholy fondness, that the young lady could not refrain from letting fall some sympathizing tears upon her hand, as she pressed it in silence against her lips. The Naiad appeared still more afflicted at this correspondence of feeling; 'Alas! my child,' said she, in a mournful voice, 'thou weepest, and knowest not wherefore; but thy tears are ominous of thy fate. A sad revolution awaits yon fortress upon the hill. Ere the mower whets his scythe, or the west wind whistles over the stubble of the wheat field, all shall be desolate and forlorn. When the maidens of the castle go forth, at the hour of twilight, to fetch water from my spring, and return with empty pitchers, then remember that the calamity is at hand. Preserve carefully the musk-ball, which will fulfil three of the wishes, but do not squander away this privilege heedlessly. Fare thee well; we meet no more at this spot.' She then instructed her ward in another magic property of the ball, which might be serviceable in time of need. At length her tears and sobs stifled her voice, and she was no more seen. One evening, about the season of corn harvest, the maids that went out for water returned pale and affrighted, with their pitchers empty; their teeth chattered, and every limb quivered as if they were shaken by the shivering fit of an ague. 'The lady in white,' they reported, 'is sitting beside the well, uttering deep sighs, and wringing her hands in great affliction.' Of this evil omen most of the squires armour-bearers made mock, declaring it to be all illusion and women's prate. Curiosity, however, carried several out to examine whether the report was true or false. They saw the same apparition; nevertheless they mustered up courage to approach the fountain, but as they came near the phantom was gone. Many interpretations were attempted, but no one fell upon the true import of the sign; Matilda alone was privy to it; but she held her peace, in compliance with the strenuous injunction of the Naiad. She repaired, dejected, to her chamber, where she sat alone, in fearful expectation of the things that were to come to pass.

Siegfried of Blackpool had degenerated by this time into a mere woman's tool: he could never satisfy his spend thrift wife with enough of robbery and plunder. When he was not abroad waylaying travellers, she prepared a feast, invited a number of bacchanalian comrades, and kept him in a continued fit of intoxication, that he might not perceive the decay of his household. When there was a want of money or provisions, Jacob Fugger's broad-wheeled wagons, or the rich bales of the Venetians, afforded a never failing resource. Outraged at these continual depredations, the general congress of the Swabian alliance determined upon Siegfried's destruction, since remonstrances and admonitions were of no avail. Before he would believe they were in right earnest, the banners of the confederates were displayed before his castle-gate, and nothing was left him but the resolution to sell his life as dear as possible. The guns shattered the bastions: on both sides the cross-bowmen did their utmost; it hailed bolts and arrows: a shaft, discharged in a luckless moment, when Siegfried's protecting angel had stepped aside, pierced his vizor, and lodged deep in his brain. Great dismay fell upon his party at the loss of their undaunted leader: the cowardly hoisted a white flag; the courageous tore it down again from the tower: the enemy, concluding, from these appearances, that discord and confusion prevailed within the fort, seized the opportunity for making the assault; they clambered over the walls, carried the gates, let down the drawbridge, and smote every living thing that came in the way with the edge of their sword: they did not spare even the extravagant wife, the author of the calamity, nor her helpless children, for the allies were as much exasperated against the freebooting nobility, as the French mob against their feudal seigneurs, since the fall of despotism. The castle was ransacked, then set on fire and levelled with the ground, so that not one stone was left on another.

During the alarm of the siege, Matilda barricaded the door of her apartment in the best manner she was able, and took post at her little window in the roof of her house; and having observed the issue of the affair from this advantageous station, and finding that bolts and bars were not likely to afford her any farther security, she put on her veil, and then turned her musk-ball thrice round, at the same time repeating the words her friend the Naiad had taught her:

> Behind me, night, before me, day,
> That none behold my secret way.

She now came down stairs in perfect confidence, and passed unperceived through the confusion of slaughter. She did not quit her paternal residence without deep sorrow of heart, which was much aggravated by her being utterly at a loss which way to take. She hastened from the scene of carnage and desolation, till her delicate feet absolutely refused to serve her any longer. The falling of night, together with extreme weariness, constrained her to take up her lodging at the foot of an oak, in the open fields. As soon as she had seated herself on the cold turf, her tears began to flow, and she made no attempt to restrain them. She turned aside her head to take a farewell view, and to breathe her last blessing on the place where she had passed the years of her childhood. As she lifted her eyes, behold the sky appeared all blood-red: from this sign she concluded that the residence of her forefathers had become a prey to the flames. She turned away her face from this horrid spectacle, heartily wishing for the hour when the sparkling stars should grow dim, and the dawn peep from the east. Ere the morning dew had settled in big round tears on the grass, she proceeded on her wandering pilgrimage. She arrived betimes at her village, where a compassionate housewife took her in, and recruited her strength with a slice of bread and a bowl of milk. With this woman she bartered her clothes in exchange for meaner apparel, and then joined a company of carriers on their way to Augspurg. In her forlorn situation, she had no other resource than to seek a place in some family : but, as it was not the season for hiring servants, it was a long time before she could find employment.

Count Conrad of Swabeck, a knight of the order of knights templars, chancellor and champion of the diocese of Augspurg, had a palace in that city, where he usually resided in winter. During his absence Gertrude, the housekeeper, bore sovereign sway in the mansion. Gertrude, like many other worthy persons of her sex and calling, had engrafted the failing of an inexorable scold upon the virtue of unremitting industry. Her failing was so much more notorious throughout the city, than her virtue, that few servants offered their services, and none had been able to stay out their time with her. She raised such an alarm, wherever she moved, that the maids dreaded the rattling of her keys as much as children do hobgoblins. Saucepans and heads suffered alike for her ill-humours; when no projectiles were within reach, she would wield her bunch of keys in her brawny arm, and beat the sides and shoulders of her subalterns black and blue. Every description of an ill-conditioned woman was summed up with, 'in short, she is as bad as Gertrude, the Count's housekeeper.' One day she had administered her office of correction so rigorously, that all the household decamped with one consent: it was at this conjuncture that the gentle Matilda approached to offer her services. But she had taken care to conceal her elegant shape, by fastening a large lump on her left shoulder as if she had been crooked; her beautiful auburn hair was covered with a large coarse cap; and she had anointed her face and hands, in imitation of the gipsies, with juice of walnut husks. Mother Gertrude, who, on hearing the bell ring, poked her head out at the window, was no sooner aware of the singular figure at the door, than she exclaimed, in her shrill tone, 'Go, get about your business, hussy : there is nothing for great idle girls, like you, here; such sluts should be in the house of correction !' After this salutation she hastily shut the window.

Matilda was not to be so easily repulsed. She rang till the Megara's head was a second time protruded from the casement, for the purpose of retorting upon this insolence of perseverance a torrent of abuse. But before she could unfold her toothless jaws, the young lady had declared her business. – 'Who art thou?' demanded the head from above, 'Whence dost thou come? And what canst thou do?' – The supposed gipsy answered:

> 'I am an orphan, Matilda by name:
> I'm a stout girl and nimble,
> An manage the thimble;
> Can spin, card, and knit,
> And handle the spit;
> I can stew, bake, and brew;
> Am honest and true,
> And here to serve you.'

The housekeeper, softened by the whimsical recitative of all these important qualifications, opened her door to the nut brown virgin, and gave her a shilling in earnest, as kitchen-maid. The new hireling plied her business so diligently, that Gertrude, for want of practice, lost her dexterity at hurling saucepans at a mark. She still, however, retained her morose and querulous humour; and was sure to find fault with everything. Nevertheless her subaltern, by avoiding all contradiction, by gentleness and patience, saved herself many effusions of ill-humour.

About the falling of the first snow, the housekeeper had the whole mansion swept and scoured, the cobwebs brushed, the windows washed, the floors sanded, the shutters opened, and every thing put in readiness for the reception of her lord, who soon afterwards made his appearance, followed by a long train of servants, a troop of horses, and a loud cry of hounds. The arrival of the Templar raised little curiosity in Matilda; her work in the kitchen had grown so upon her hands, that she had not a moment to gape after him. One morning, as she was drawing water at the well, he accidentally passed by her, and his appearance kindled sensations in her bosom to which it had hitherto been an entire stranger. She beheld a young man, whose beauty exceeded the fairest of her dreams. The sparkling of his eye, the good-humour that lightened up his features, his flowing hair, half concealed by the plumes that over-shadowed his soldier's hat, his firm step, and the grace of his whole demeanour, acted so powerfully on her heart, that the blood moved with increasing velocity along her veins. She now, for the first time, felt the degraded station to which an untoward fate had reduced her, and this sentiment was a heavier load than the large pitcher. She returned, deeply musing to the kitchen, and, for the first time since she had begun to exercise her culinary functions, over-salted all the soup, an oversight which drew down upon her a severe reprimand from the housekeeper. The handsome knight hovered before her imagination day and night: she was continually longing to see him; and whenever she heard the sound of his spurs, as he crossed the courtyard, she was sure to discover a want of water in the kitchen, and ran with the pitcher in her hand to the well; though the stately cavalier never once condescended to bestow a glance upon her.

Count Conrad seemed to exist merely for the purpose of pleasure. He attended every banquet and rejoicing in the city, which, from its commerce with the Venetians, was become rich and luxurious. One day there was a tilting-match at the ring: the next a tournament; the third a mayor's feast. Nor was there any scarcity of dances at the town hall, and in every street. Here the noblemen toyed and frolicked with the citizens' daughters; occasionally presenting them with gold rings and silken stuffs. By carnival-time this tumult of dissipation had arisen to its highest pitch, but Matilda had no share in the festivity: she sat all day in the smoky kitchen, and wept till her pining eyes became sore, constantly bewailing the caprice of fortune, which heaps a profusion of the joy of life over her favourites, while from others she greedily snatches every instant of cheerfulness. Her heart was heavy she knew not why; for she had no suspicion that love had taken up his abode there. This restless inmate, who throws every house where he lodges into confusion, whispered everyday a thousand romantic schemes into her head, and every night busied her fancy with bewitching dreams. She was now walking arm in arm with the Templar in a delicious garden: now she was immured in the sanctuary of the cloister; the Count was standing at the grate, longing to converse with her, but the strict abbess would not grant permission: sometimes he was leading her out to open a festive dance. These enchanting dreams were very often suddenly cut short by the jingling of Mother Gertrude's bunch of keys, with which it was her custom to rouse the sleeping household betimes. However the ideas spun by imagination during the night, served to amuse her thoughts by day.

Love knows no dangers; the enamoured Matilda formed project after project, till at last she fell upon a scheme to realize the fondest of her dreams. She had still her godmother the Naiad's musk-ball safe: she had never felt any desire to open it, and make an essay of its power to gratify her wishes. She now resolved to try the experiment. The citizens of Augspurg had, about this time, prepared a sumptuous banquet, in compliment to the Emperor Frederic, on the birth of his son, Prince Maximilian. The rejoicings were to continue three days. Innumerable nobles and prelates were invited. Each day there was a tournament, and a rich prize for the victor: each evening the most beautiful damsels danced with the knights till break of day. Count Conrad did not fail to attend these festivities; each time he was the favourite of the matrons and virgins. No one, indeed, could hope to share his lawful love, for he was Templar; nevertheless he was the object of all their good wishes – he was so handsome, and danced so charmingly.

Matilda had come to the resolution of sallying forth in quest of adventures, on this occasion. After she had arranged the kitchen, and everything was quiet in the house, she retired to her bedchamber, and, washing away the tawny varnish with sweet-scented soap, called the lilies and roses of her complexion into new bloom. She then took the musk-ball into her hand, and wished for a new gown, as rich and elegant as fancy could form, with all its appurtenances. On screwing off the top, a piece of silk issued out, expanding itself, and rustling all the while, as if a stream of water was gushing on her lap. On examination it proved a full dress, fitted up with every little article: the gown fitted as exactly as if it had been cast on her body. – While she was putting it on, she felt that internal exultation, which girls always experience when they adorn themselves for the sake of the other sex, and spread out their dangerous meshes. Her vanity was fully gratified, as she took a survey of her dress, and she was perfectly content with herself. Accordingly she did not defer a moment longer the execution of her stratagem. She thrice whirled round the magic ball, saying,

> In sleep profound,
> Each eye be drown'd.

Instantly a deep slumber fell upon all the household, not excepting the vigilant housekeeper and the Janus at the door. Matilda glided in a moment out of the house, passed unseen along the streets, and stepped into the ballroom with the air of one of the Graces. The charming new figure raised great admiration among the company; and along the lofty gallery which encircled the ballroom there arose a general whisper. Some admired the elegance of the stranger's person, others the fashion of her dress, others inquired who she was, and whence she came; but on these points no one could satisfy his neighbour's curiosity. Among the noble knights, who crowded to take a peep at the unknown damsel, the Templar was far from hindmost. He was by no means a woman hater; and, though an exact connoisseur in the sex, he thought he had never seen a sweeter person nor a more happy countenance. He approached, and engaged her to dance. She modestly presented her hand, and danced with enchanting elegance. Her nimble feet scarce touched the floor, and the ease and gracefulness of her movements set every eye in rapture. Count Conrad paid his heart for his partner. He no more quitted the fair dancer. He said as many fine things and pushed his suit with as much zeal and earnestness, as the most enamoured of our heroes of romance, for whom the world becomes too narrow a stage, the moment they are goaded on by malicious Cupid. Matilda was as little mistress of her own heart: she conquered, and was vanquished in her turn. Her first essay in love was crowned with success equal to her fondest wishes. It was not in her power to keep the sympathy of her feelings concealed beneath the cloak of female reserve. The enraptured knight soon perceived that he was no hopeless lover; his chief anxiety arose from his entire ignorance of his charming partner; and how to prosecute his suit, unless he could discover where she lived. But on this subject all inquiries were in vain: she eluded every question, and after all his efforts he could only obtain a promise that she would make her appearance at the next night's ball. He thought to outwit her, in case she should forfeit her word, by posting all his servants to watch her home, for he supposed her to be of Augspurg, while the company, from his unremitting attention, concluded she was a lady of the Count's acquaintance.

The dawn had already peeped, before she could find an opportunity of slipping away from the knight, and quitting the room. But no sooner had she passed the door, than she turned her musk-ball thrice round, and repeated the spell:

> Behind me, night, before me, day,
> That none behold my secret way.

By these means she got to her chamber, in spite of the Baron's sentinels, who did not catch a glimpse of her, though they were hovering in every street. No sooner had she shut the door behind her, than she locked up the silken apparel safe in her box, put on her greasy cook's dress, and resumed her ordinary occupations. The old housekeeper, who had been rattling up the rest of the servants with her bunch of keys, finding Matilda stirring so early, bestowed an ungracious compliment on her diligence.

Never had any day appeared so tedious to the knight as that which succeeded the ball. Every hour seemed a week: his heart was in perpetual agitation between longing impatience and apprehension, lest the inscrutable beauty should fail in her engagement, for Suspicion, the train-bearer of Love, allowed his thoughts as little repose as the wind did the flag that was flying on the tower. At the approach of evening he equipped himself for the ball, with greater magnificence than the preceding day; the three golden rings the ancient badge of nobility, all beset with diamonds, sparkled in the front of his dress. He was the

first at the rendezvous of pleasure, where, having stationed himself so as to command the entrance, he scrutinized everyone who
came in with the keen eyes of an eagle, expecting, with all the
eagerness of impatience, the arrival of his dulcinea. The evening
star was already advanced high in the horizon, before the young
lady could find time to retire to her chamber, and consider what
she should do: whether she should extort a second wish from
the musk-ball, or reserve it for some more important occurrence
of life. The faithful counsellor, Reason, advised the latter; but
Love enjoined the former with such impetuosity, that Reason
was quite silenced, and soon withdrew altogether. Matilda
wished for a dress of rose-coloured satin, most sumptuously be-
decked with jewels. The complaisant musk-ball exerted its
powers: the apparel exceeded the lady's expectation; she performed, in high spirits, the rites of the toilette, and, by the help
of the talisman, arrived at the spot where she was so ardently expected, without having been beheld by mortal eye. She appeared
far more charming than before. The heart of Conrad bounded
for joy at the first glimpse of her person. A power, as irresistible
as the central attraction of the globe, hurried him towards her
through the vortex of dancers; and as he had now almost given
up all hopes of seeing her again, he was unable to breathe forth
the effusions of his gladness. In order to gain time to recover
himself, and to hide his confusion, he led her out to dance,
when every couple immediately made way for the charming
pair. The beautiful stranger, hand in hand with the noble
knight, floated along, light as the goddess of spring upon the
pinion of Zephyr.

At the conclusion of the dance, Count Conrad conducted his
partner into the contiguous apartment, under the pretext of offering her some refreshment. Here, in the tone of a well-bred
courtier, he said a thousand flattering things, as he had done the
day before; but the cold language of politeness insensibly kindling into the language of the heart terminated in a passionate
and earnest declaration of love. Matilda hearkened with bash-
ful gladness: her beating heart and glowing cheeks betrayed
her inward emotions; and when she was pressed for a verbal

declaration, she modestly said: 'I am not displeased, noble knight, with what you have expressed of affection both today and before: I am unwilling to believe that your purpose is to deceive me by false insinuations. But how can I participate of the wedded love of a Templar, who must have taken the vow of perpetual celibacy. Solve me this paradox, or you will find that you might as well have uttered your smooth language to the winds: therefore explain without disguise how we may be united according to the rites of holy mother church, that so our marriage may abide in the sight of God and man.'

The knight answered seriously and without guile: 'You speak as becomes a discreet and virtuous maiden; I will therefore solve your difficulty without fraud or deceit, and satisfy your question. You must know that at the time of my reception into the order my brother William, the heir of the family was alive. Since his decease I have obtained a dispensation from my vow, as the last remaining branch of the house, and am at liberty to quit the profession of knighthood whenever I please. But never till the moment I saw you, has almighty love taken possession of my heart: from that instant I felt an entire change within my bosom; and I finally persuaded that you, and no other, are allotted me by Heaven as my wedded bride. If therefore you do not refuse me your hand, nothing from this moment forwards but death shall part us.' 'Consider well what you propose,' replied Matilda, 'lest repentance overtake you. Those who marry in haste, have commonly leisure to repent. I am an entire stranger: you know nothing of my rank or station; whether I am your equal in birth and dignity, or whether a borrowed lustre dazzles your eyes. It is unbecoming a man of your rank to promise anything lightly: but a nobleman's engagements should be held inviolable.' Here Count Conrad eagerly seized her hand, pressed it close to his heart, and in the warmth of his affection exclaimed, 'Yes, I pledge my knightly honour, and engage my soul's salvation, were you the meanest man's daughter, and but a pure and undefiled virgin, I will receive you for my wedded wife, and raise you to high honour.'

On this he pulled a diamond ring from his finger, and gave it her as the pledge of his truth; and took in return the first kiss from her chaste untasted lips, and thus proceeded: 'That you may entertain no suspicion of my purpose, I invite you three days hence to my house, where I will appoint my friends, – knights, nobles, and prelates, – to be witness to our union.'

Matilda resisted this proposal with all her might: she was not satisfied at the galloping rate at which the knight's love proceeded; but determined to prove the constancy of his affection. He did not cease to press her to consent, but she said neither no or yes. The company did not break up before the dawn of day. Matilda vanished; and the knight, who had not enjoyed one wink of sleep, summoned the vigilant housekeeper betimes, and gave her orders to prepare a sumptuous feast.

As the dread skeleton figure with the scythe traverses palaces and cottages, mowing down whatever falls in his way, so old Gertrude, having her inexorable fist armed with the slaughtering knife, paced through the poultry-yard and hen-pens, dispensing life and death among the domestic fowls. The unsuspecting tenants of the court fell by dozens before her burnished blade, flapped their wings in agony for the last time, and hens, doves, and stupid capons, yielded up their lives in heaps. Matilda had so many fowls to pluck, draw, and skewer, that she was obliged to give up her night's rest: yet she did not grudge her labour, well knowing that the banquet was all on her account. The hour approached; the cheerful host flew to receive every guest as he arrived, and every time the knocker sounded, he imagined the beautiful stranger was at the door: but when it was opened, some reverend prelate's paunch, matron's gravity, or solemn office-bearer's visage, strutted in. Though the guests were assembled, the server lingered long before he served up the dishes. Sir Conrad still waited for the charming bride; but at last, when she did not appear, he was reluctantly obliged to give the signal for dinner. When the guests were seated, there appeared one cover too much; but no one could guess who it was that had dishonoured the knight's invitation. The founder of the feast lost his cheerfulness by perceptible gradations, and in spite of all his exertions it was not in his power to enliven his guests with the spirit of mirth. The leaven of spleen soon soured the sweet cake of social joy, and in the banqueting room there prevailed a silence as dead as at a funeral feast. The musicians who had been summoned for the evening ball, were discharged; and for this time the banquet ended without one tuneful sound, in the house that had always before been the mansion of joy.

The disconcerted guests stole away at an unusually early hour: the knight longed for the solitude of his bedchamber; he was impatient for an opportunity to ruminate at liberty on the fickleness of love. While his reflections were engaged by the melancholy subject, he tossed and tumbled to and fro on his bed: with the most intense exertion of thought, he could not determine what conclusion to draw from the absence of his mistress. The blood boiled in his veins; and ere he had closed an eye, the sun peeped in through his curtains. The servants found their master in a violent paroxysm of fever, wrestling with wild fancies. This discovery threw the whole family into the most violent consternation: the men of medicine tripped up and down stairs, exhibited solemn faces, and wrote recipes by the yard: in the apothecary's shop the mortars were all set going as if they had been chiming for morning prayer. But not one of the physicians fell upon the herb Eye-balm, which alone allays longing in love; as to their balsams of life, and essence of pearls, the patient rejected them all; he would hearken to no plan of diet, he conjured the leeches not to plague him, but to allow the sand of his hour-glass to run out quietly, without hastening its pace, by shaking with their officious hands.

For seven long days did secret chagrin gnaw Count Conrad's heart; the roses of his cheeks were all withered; the fire of his eyes was extinguished; the breath of life was suspended between his lips, like a thin morning mist in the valleys, which the slightest gust of wind is capable of dissipating altogether. Matilda had perfect intelligence of everything that was going forward within doors. It was not either from caprice or prudery that she had declined the knight's invitation. It cost her a hard conflict between head and heart — reason and inclination, before she could firmly resolve not to hearken to the call of her beloved. But on the one hand she was desirous of proving the constancy of her fiery suitor, and she hesitated on the other to extort its last wish from the musk-ball: for she considered that a new dress was necessary to the bride; and her godmother had charged her not to lavish away her wishes thoughtlessly. Nevertheless, on the feast day she felt very heavy at heart, retired to a corner, and wept bitterly. The Count's illness, of which she easily divined the cause, gave her still a greater concern; and when she heard of his extreme danger, she was quite inconsolable.

The seventh day, according to the prognostication of the physicians, was to determine for life or death. We may easily conjecture that Matilda voted in favour of her beloved; that she might be instrumental in his recovery was a very probable conjecture, only she could not devise any method of bringing forward her services. However, among the thousand talents which love imparts or unfolds, that of invention is included. In the morning Matilda waited as usual, upon the housekeeper, to receive her instructions respecting the bill of fare. But old Gertrude was in too deep tribulation to be capable of arranging the simplest matter, much less could she regulate the important affair of dinner. Big tears rolled down her leathern cheeks: 'Ah! Matilda,' she sobbed, 'our good master will not live out the day.' These were gloomy tidings: the young lady was ready to sink for sorrow; she soon, however, recovered her spirits, and said, 'Do not despair of our lord's life, he will not die, but recover; this night I have dreamed a good dream.' Old Gertrude was a living repository of dreams: she hunted out every dream of the servants and whenever she could seize one, imagined an interpretation that depended on herself only to fulfil; for the most agreeable dreams in her system boded nothing but squabbles and scolding. 'Let me hear thy dream, that I may interpret it,' said she. – 'I thought,' replied Matilda, 'that I was at home with my mother, she took me aside, and taught me how to prepare a broth from nine sorts of herbs, which cures all sickness, if you do but take three spoonfuls. Prepare this broth for thy master, and he will not die, but get better from the hour he shall eat of it.' Gertrude, much struck at the relation of this dream refraining for the present from all allegorical interpretations. – 'Thy dream,' said she, 'is too extraordinary to have come by chance. Go, this instant, and make ready thy broth, and I will try if I cannot prevail on our lord to taste it.'

Sir Conrad lay feeble, motionless, and immersed in meditations upon his departure hence: he was desirous of receiving the sacrament of extreme unction. In this situation Gertrude entered into his chamber, and by the suppleness of her tongue soon turned aside his thoughts from the contemplation of the four last things. In order to deliver himself from the torment of her well-meant loquacity, he was fain to promise whatever she desired. Meanwhile Matilda prepared an excellent restorative soup, with all sorts of garden herbs and costly spices, and when she had dished it, she dropped the diamond ring, given her by the knight as a pledge of constancy, into the basin, and then bade the servant to carry it up.

The patient so much dreaded the housekeeper's boisterous eloquence, which still echoed in his ears, that he constrained himself to swallow a couple of spoonfuls. In stirring his mess to the bottom he felt a hard body, which could have no business there. He fished it out with the spoon, and beheld, to his astonishment, his own diamond ring. His eye immediately beamed life and youthful fire; his pale, deathly countenance cleared up: to the great satisfaction of Gertrude, and the servants in waiting, he emptied the whole basin, with visible signs of a good appetite. They all ascribed this happy change to the soup for the knight had taken care to keep his ring concealed from the bystanders. He now turned to Gertrude, and inquired, 'Who prepared this good soup for me, that restores my strength, and calls me back to life?' The motherly dame wished the reviving patient to keep himself still, and by no means to exert himself in speaking, she therefore replied, 'Do not give yourself any concern, good sir knight, about the person who prepared the soup: God be praised that it has had the good effect for which all of us prayed!' This evasion was not likely to satisfy the Count: he gravely insisted on an answer to his question, when the housekeeper gave him this information: 'There is a young gipsy servant in the kitchen, she understands the virtues of every herb and plant, it was she who prepared the soup that has done you so much good.' 'Bring her to me this moment,' resumed the knight, 'that I may thank and recompense her for the life she has saved.' 'Pardon me, I beseech you, Sir,' returned Gertrude, 'but the very sight of her would make you ill again. She is as ugly as a toad; her clothes are black and greasy; her hands and face are bedaubed with soot and ashes.' 'Do as I order you,' concluded the Count, 'and let me hear no longer demurs.' Old Gertrude obeyed in silence: she summoned Matilda quickly from the kitchen, and threw over her shoulders her own veil, which she wore at mass, and ushered her, thus caparisoned, into the sick chamber. The knight gave orders that everyone should retire, and shut the door close. He then addressed the gipsy, 'You must acknowledge freely, my girl, how you came by the ring I found in the basin in which my breakfast was served up.' 'Noble knight,' replied the damsel, 'I received the ring out of your own hands: you presented it to me the second evening we danced together at the public rejoicings, it was when you vowed eternal love and constancy to me. – Look now, and say whether my figure or station deserves that on my account you should sink into an early grave. In compassion for the condition to which you were reduced, I could no longer suffer you to remain in such a mistake.'

Count Conrad's weak stomach was not prepared for so strong an antidote to love; he surveyed her some moments in astonishment, and paused. But his imagination soon presented the idea of his charming partner, with whom he by no means reconcile the contrast before his eyes. He naturally conceived a suspicion, that his amour had been betrayed, and his friends were practising a pious fraud to extricate him. Still, however, the genuine ring was proof positive that the beautiful stranger was some way or other concerned in the plot. He therefore determined to cross-examine and convict her out of her own mouth: 'If you are indeed,' said he, 'the lovely maiden to whom I devoted my heart, be assured that I am ready to fulfil my engagement; but take care how you attempt to impose upon me. Reassume but the form under which you appeared two successive nights at the ballroom; make your body taper and straight like a young pine; strip off your scaly skin, like the snake; and like the cameleon change your colour; and the words which I uttered when I delivered this ring to you shall be sacred and inviolable. But if you cannot perform these requisitions, I shall cause you to be corrected for a vile impostor and a thief, unless you satisfy me how you gained possession of this ring.' — 'Alas!' replied Matilda, sighing, 'if it be only the glare of beauty that has dazzled your eyes, woe be to me when time or chance shall rob me of these transient charms; when age shall have spoiled this tender shape, and bowed me down to the ground; when the roses and lilies shall fade, and this sleek skin become shrivelled! When the borrowed form, under which I now appear, shall, as some time it will, belong to me, what will become of your vows and promises?'

Sir Conrad was staggered at this speech, which seemed much too considerate for a kitchen wench. 'Know,' he replied, 'that beauty captivates the heart of man, but virtue alone can retain in the soft bandage of love.' — 'Be it so,' returned the damsel in disguise; 'I go to fulfil your requisitions: the decision of my fate shall be left to your own heart.'

Sir Conrad fluctuated between hope and the dread of a new deception: he called old Gertrude to him, and gave her strict orders: — 'Attend this girl to her chamber, and wait at the door while she puts on her clean clothes. Be sure you do not stir till she comes out.' Old Gertrude took her prisoner under charge, without being able to guess the intention of her lord's injunctions. As they were going upstairs, she inquired, 'If thou hast any fine clothes, why dost thou never shew them to me? But if thou has no change, follow me to my chamber, and I will lend thee what thou needest.' Here upon she went through the whole inventory of her old fashioned wardrobe, by the help of which she had made conquests half a century ago. As she reckoned them up, article by article, a gleam of recollection of past days darted upon her mind. Matilda took little notice of her catalogue: she only asked for a bit of soap and a handful of bran, took up a wash-hand basin, entered her attic, and shut the door, while the new-appointed duenna watched on the outside with all the punctuality that had been recommended to her.

The knight, big with expectation, quitted his bed, put on his most elegant suit, and betook himself to his drawing-room, there to abide the final issue of his love adventure. His impatience made the time seem long, and under his uncertainty he paced quickly up and down the room. Just as the finger of the Italian clock on the Augspurg town hall pointed to eighteen o'clock, the hour of midday, the folding doors flew open of a sudden; the train of a silk negligee rustled along the antichamber: Matilda, arrayed like a bride, and beautiful as the Goddess of Love, stepped into the room. Sir Conrad exclaimed, in the transport of a lover intoxicated with joy, 'Goddess or mortal! whichsoever you may be, behold me prostrate at your feet, ready to renew the vows I have already made, and to confirm them by the most solemn oaths, provided you do not disdain to receive this hand and heart.'

The lady modestly raised the suppliant knight: 'Gently, sir knight, I pray: do not be too rash with your vows; you behold me here in my right shape, but in all other respects I am an utter stranger to you. Many a man has been deceived by a smooth face. You have still the ring on your finger.' Sir Conrad instantly drew it off, and it sparkled on his partner's hand, and she resigned herself to the knight. 'Hence-forward,' she said, 'you are the beloved of my heart. I have no longer any secret for you. I am the daughter of Siegfried the Strong, that stout and honourable knight, whose misfortunes, doubtless, are well know to you. I escaped with difficulty from the downfall of my father's house; and under your roof, though in mean estate, have I found safety and protection.' She proceeded to relate the whole of her story, without even suppressing the mystery of the muskball. Count Conrad, utterly forgetting that he had just been sick to death, invited, for the following day, all the guests who had been driven away by his dejection, before whom he solemnly espoused his bride; and when the server had served up dinner, and counted round, he found that there was no cover too much.

The knight now relinquished the order, and celebrated the marriage with great magnificence. But amid all these important transactions, old Gertrude was totally inactive. The day she kept watch at Matilda's chamber-door, so great was the consternation with which she was seized, at seeing a lady in sumptuous apparel come forth, that she tumbled backward off her seat, dislocated her hip-bone, and limped all her life afterwards.

The new-married couple spent their honeymoon in Augspurg, in mutual happiness and innocent enjoyments, like the first human pair in the garden of Eden. The youthful bride, penetrated by the tender passion, would often recline on her husband's bosom, and pour out the artless dictates of her pure affection. One day, with the most endearing affection, she inquired, 'If you have any latent wish in your breast, impart it to me; I will adopt it, and you shall instantly be gratified. For my own part, the possession of you has left me without anything further to desire; so I shall willingly excuse the musk-ball the wish which is still in reserve.' Count Conrad clasped his affectionate bride fondly in his arms, and firmly protested that he had nothing further to ask for upon earth, except the continuance of their mutual felicity. The musk-ball, therefore, lost all its value in the eyes of its fair possessor, nor had she any motive for preserving it, except a grateful remembrance of her benefactress.

Count Conrad's mother was still living. She passed her widowhood in retirement, at the family seat at Swabeck. Her dutiful daughter-in-law had for some time longed, out of pure filial affection, to beg her blessing, and thank her for the noble son whom she had borne. But the Count always found some pretext for declining the visit; he now proposed, instead, a summer excursion to an estate that had lately fallen to him, and bordered upon the grounds belonging to Siegfried's demolished fortress. Matilda consented with great eagerness. She rejoiced at the idea of revisiting the spot where she had spent her early youth. She explored the ruins of her father's residence; dropped a duteous tear over the ashes of her parents; walked to the Naiad's fountain, and hoped her presence would induce the Nymph to manifest herself. Many a pebble dropped into the spring-head, without the desired effect. Even the musk-ball floated on the surface like an empty bubble, and Matilda herself was fain to be at the trouble of fishing it out again. No Nicksy rose to view, although another christening was at hand; for the lady was on the point of bestowing on her Count one of the blessings of wedlock. She brought forth a boy beautiful as Cupid; and the joy of the parents was so extravagant, that they had almost stifled him with kindness. The mother would never part with him from her arms. She herself watched every breath of the little innocent, although the Count had hired a discreet nurse to attend the infant. But the third night, while all within the castle were buried in profound sleep, after a day of tumultuous rejoicing, and a light slumber had fallen upon the watchful mother, on awaking she found the child vanished out of her arms. She called out in a voice of surprise and terror, 'Nurse! where have you laid my babe?' 'Noble lady,' replied the nurse, 'the dear infant lies in your arms.' The bed and bedchamber were strictly searched, but nothing could be found, except a few spots of blood upon the floor. The nurse, on perceiving this, uttered a loud scream, 'God and all his holy saints have mercy on us! – the Great Griffin has been here, and carried off the child.' The lady pined for the loss of her child, till she became pale and emaciated, and Sir Conrad was inconsolable. Though the belief in the Great Griffin did not weigh a single grain of mustard in his mind, yet, as he could not explain the accident in any plausible manner, he allowed the nurse's prattle free range, and applied himself to comfort his afflicted wife; and she, out of deference to him, who hated all sadness, forced a cheerful countenance.

Time, the assuager of grief, closed by degrees the wound of the mother's heart, and love made up her loss by a second son. Boundless joy for the new heir reigned throughout the palace. The Count feasted with all his neighbours for a whole day's journey round about; the bowl of congratulation passed incessantly from hand to hand; from the lord and his guests to the porter at the door, all drank to the health of the young Count. The anxious mother would not part with the boy; and she resisted the influence of sleep as long as ever her strength would permit. When at last she was not longer able to refuse the call of nature, she took the golden chain from her neck, slung it round the infant's body, and fastened the other end on her own arm: she then crossed herself and the child, that the Great Griffin might have no power to hurt it, and soon after was overtaken by an irresistible slumber. She awoke at the first ray of morning, but – horrible to tell! the sweet babe had vanished out of her arms. In the first alarm she called as before, 'Nurse! where have you laid my infant?' and nurse replied, 'Noble lady, the babe lies in your arms.' Matilda examined the golden chain that was wrapped round her arm; she found that one of the links had been cut through by a pair of sharp scissors, and swooned away at the discovery. The nurse raised an alarm in the house; and Count Conrad, upon hearing what had befallen his lady, drew his knightly sword in a transport of rage and indignation, firmly resolved to inflict condign punishment on the nurse.

'Wretched woman!' he exclaimed in a voice of thunder, 'did I not give thee strict charge to watch all night, and never once to turn aside thine eye from the infant, that when the monster came to rob the sleeping mother, thou mightest raise the house by thy outcries, and scare the Great Griffin away? But thou shalt now sleep an everlasting sleep.'

The woman fell down on her knees before him: 'Yes, my noble lord, I entreat you, as you hope for mercy hereafter, to slay me this instant, that I may carry to the grave the horrid deed mine eyes have seen this night: and which neither rewards nor punishments shall extort from me.' – The Count paused: 'What deed,' he asked, 'have thine eyes beheld this night, too horrid for thy tongue to tell? Better confess, as becomes a faithful servant, than have thy secrets extorted from thee by the rack.' 'Alas!' replied the woman, 'what does your ill-fortune instigate you to force from me! Better the fatal secret were buried with me in the cold ground.' The Count, whose curiosity was only raised the more by suspense, took the woman aside into a private apartment, and by threats and promises forced from her a discovery, which he would fain have been saved the pain of making. 'Your lady, since I must needs disclose it, is a vile sorceress; but she doats without reserve upon you, insomuch that she does not spare even the fruit of her own body to procure the means of preserving your love, and her own beauty unperishable. At the dead of night, when everything was hushed in repose, she feigned herself asleep, and I, without well knowing why, did the same. Not long afterwards she called me by my name, but I took no notice of her proceedings, and feigned to be sound asleep. Supposing me fast asleep, she raised herself upright in her bed, took the infant, and pressing it to her bosom, kissed it fondly, and lisped these words, which I distinctly overheard, "Child of bone, be transformed in to a charm to secure me thy father's love. Now, thou little innocent, go to thy brother, and then I will prepare, from nine sorts of herbs and thy bones, a potent draught, which will perpetuate my beauty and thy father's fondness." – Having said this, she drew a diamond needle out of her hair, forced it through the infant's heart, held the poor innocent out to bleed, and when it had ceased struggling laid it upon the bed before her, took out her musk-ball, and muttered a few words to herself. As she unscrewed the cover, a magic flame blazed forth, and consumed the body in a few moments. She carefully gathered the bones and ashes into a box, which she pushed under the bed. She then, as if suddenly awaking, cried out, "Nurse! what have you done with my babe?" and I replied, shuddering for fear of her sorcery, "Noble lady, the infant lies in your arms." Thereupon she began to shew signs of bitter sorrow, and I ran out of the room, under pretence of calling assistance. – These are the particulars of the horrid deed, which you have forced me to disclose. I am ready to ratify the truth of my words, by suffering the ordeal of carrying a red-hot bar of iron in my naked hands thrice up and down the courtyard.'

Sir Conrad stood as still as though he had been petrified; and it was a long time before he could utter a word. – When he had a little collected himself, he said: 'What occasion is there for the fiery trial? The stamp of truth is impressed on your words; I feel and fully believe that all is as you say. Keep the horrid secret close pent up in your heart. Intrust it to no mortal, not even to the priest when you confess. I will purchase a dispensation from the bishop of Augspurg, so that this sin shall not be imputed to you in this world, nor in that which is to come. I will go in to the hyena with a feigned countenance; and while I embrace her, and speak comfort to her, be sure to draw the box with the dead bones from under the bed, and deliver it secretly to me.'

He stepped into his wife's chamber with the air of a man firm though deeply touched. His lady received him with the eye where no guilt was depicted, though her soul was wounded to death. She did not speak, but her countenance resembled an angel's; the first glance extinguished her husband's rage and madness, for his heart was enflamed by these furious passions. Compassion softened the spirit of vengeance; he clasped the unhappy mother to his bosom, and she moistened his garment with the tears of her affliction. He spoke kind and consoling words to her, but was all the while impatient to quit the scene of abomination. Meantime the nurse had taken care punctually to perform what she was ordered respecting the delivery of the horrid reservoir of bones. It cost his heart a hard struggle before he could determine the fate of the supposed sorceress. He at length resolved to get rid of her privately, and without drawing the notice of mankind towards his domestic grievances. He mounted his steed, and rode away towards Augspurg, after he had given his seneschal these orders, – 'When the Countess, according to the custom of the country, leaves her chamber at the expiration of nine days, for the purpose of bathing, bolt the door on the outside, and let the fires be raised as high as possible, that she may sink under the vehemence of the heat, and come no more out alive.' – The seneschal, who, in common with the whole household, adored his kind and tender-hearted lady, heard these orders with the utmost sorrow and concern. But nevertheless he was afraid to open his lips in opposition to the knight, on account of the positive manner in which he spoke. On the ninth day Matilda gave orders for heating the bath. Her husband, she thought, would not abide long at Augspurg; and she wished, before his return, to eradicate every vestige of her late misfortunes. On entering the bathing-room she observed the air quiver from heat, and she made an effort to retreat, but a vigorous arm forced her irresistibly forwards, and she instantly heard some one without bolt and bar the door. She cried out for help in vain – nobody heard; the fuel was now piled high, and the fire raised, till the furnace glowed like a potter's furnace.

It was not difficult to divine the meaning of all these circumstances. The Countess resigned herself to her fate; only the odious suspicion, which she apprehended had fallen upon her, afflicted her soul much more than her disgraceful death. She took advantage of the last moments of recollection, and drawing a silver pin out of her hair, inscribed these words on the whited wall of the apartment, 'Fare thee well, my Conrad! I die a willing but innocent victim, in consequence of thy commands.' She then threw herself down upon a couch, as her last agonies were approaching. Nature, however, on the approach of the evil hour, will make an involuntary struggle against her dissolution. In the anguish occasioned by the suffocating heat, as the unhappy sufferer tossed and tumbled on the couch, the musk-ball, which she had constantly carried about her, fell to the ground. She snatched it eagerly up, and cried aloud, 'O godmother Naiad, if it be in thy power, deliver me from a dishonourable death, and vindicate my innocence!' She screwed off the top, and the same instant a thick mist arose out of the musk-ball, and diffusing itself through the whole apartment, refreshed the Countess, so that she no longer felt any oppression. The watery vapours from the grotto in the rock had either absorbed the heat, or the kind godmother, in virtue of the antipathy of Naiads to the fiery element, had vanquished her natural enemy. The cloud collected itself into a visible form; and Matilda, whose apprehensions for her life had now vanished, beheld, to her unspeakable joy, the Nymph of the Fountain clasping the new-born infant to her bosom, and holding the elder boy with her right hand.

'Hail, my beloved Matilda!' exclaimed the Naiad: 'happy

was it for thee that thou didst not so heedlessly lavish the third wish of thy musk-ball as the two former. Behold here the two living witnesses of thy innocence; they will enable thee to triumph over the black calumny under which thou hadst nearly sunk. The inauspicious star that threatened thy life, now rapidly verges of its decline; henceforward the musk-ball will fulfil no more of thy wishes; but nothing further remains for thee to desire; I will unfold the riddle of thy fate; – know, that the mother of thy husband is the author of all thy calamity. The marriage of her son proved a dagger to the heart of that proud woman; who imagined he had stained the honour of his house by taking a kitchen-wench to his bed. She breathed nothing but curses and execrations against him, and would no longer acknowledge him for the offspring of her womb. All her thoughts were bent on contrivances and plots to destroy thee, although the vigilance of thy husband had hitherto frustrated her malicious designs. She, however at last succeeded to elude his vigilance by means of a fawning, hypocritical nurse. She induced this woman, by the most liberal promises, to take thy first-born out of thy arms, whilst asleep, and cast it, like a whelp into the water. Fortunately she chose my spring-head for her wicked purpose; and I received the boy in my arms, and have ever since nursed him as his mother. In the same manner did she undesignedly commit to my charge the second son of my dear Matilda. It was this vile deceitful nurse who became thy accuser. She persuaded the Count that thou wert a sorceress, that a magic flame had issued from the musk-ball – thou shouldst have kept thy secret better – in which thou hadst consumed thy children in order to prepare a love potion from the remains. She delivered into his hands a box full of the bones of doves and fowls, which he took for the remains of his children, and, in consequence of this mistake, gave orders to stifle thee in the bath. Spurred on by penitence, and an eager desire to countermand this cruel sentence, though he still holds thee guilty, he is now on his return from Augspurg; and in one short hour thou wilt recline, with thy honour vindicated, on his bosom.' The Nymph, having uttered these words, stooped to kiss the Countess's forehead. She then, without waiting for any reply, involved herself in her veil of mist, and was no more seen.

Meanwhile the Count's servants were exerting their utmost efforts to revive the extinguished fire. They thought they could hear the sound of human voices within, whence they concluded that the Countess was still alive. But all their stirring and blowing were ineffectual. The wood would no more take fire than if they had put on a charge of snow-balls. Not long afterwards Count Conrad rode up full speed, and eagerly inquired how it fared with his lady. The servants informed him that they had heated the room right hot, but that the fire went suddenly out, and they supposed that the Countess was yet alive. This intelligence rejoiced his heart. He dismounted, knocked at the door, and called out through the keyhole, 'Art thou alive, Matilda?' And the Countess, hearing her husband's voice, replied, 'Yes, my dear lord, I am alive, and my children are also alive.' Overjoyed at this answer, the impatient Count bade his servants break open the door, the key not being at hand, he rushing into the bathing-room, fell down at the feet of his injured lady, bedewed her unpolluted hands with the tears of repentance, led her and the charming pledges of her innocence and love out of the dreary place of execution to her own apartment, and heard from her own mouth the true account of these transactions. Enraged at the foul calumny and the shameful sacrifice of his infants, he issued orders to apprehend and shut up the treacherous nurse in the bath – The fire now burned kindly, – the chimney roared, – the flames played aloft in the air, – and soon stewed out the diabolical woman's black soul.

# The Black Spider

## Anonymous

### (*circa* 1798)

Although many Gothic tales appeared bearing the authors or authoress's name (or at least a very clear indication as to who the writer was), a great many more were published anonymously and this has made attribution in later years no easy task.

We can be reasonably sure that many of these 'faceless authors' were the hacks who abounded in London at this period, turning their pens to whatever was required by publishers and producing in the main work that was eminently forgettable. According to Montague Summers the aim of these writers was 'first to give his narrative as exciting a title as possible and secondly to cram into his limited space as many shocking, mysterious and horrid incidents as possible. Another less savoury aspect of their 'craft' was the abridging and copying of the major novels (which often ran to three and four volumes) into single chap-books, these then being sold for a few pence. All the most important books in the genre suffered from this kind of plagiarism and in the worst instances nothing more than the names of the key characters and the titles were changed before republication !

The main market for these pirate editions was, of course, the less-educated people and the young, both of whom were immediately attracted by their cheapness and the gaudy prints which graced their pages. The occasional original story or novel did certainly appear and among the vast amount of dross a jewel or two may be found: such I believe is *The Black Spider*, which appeared in a sixpenny book of tales published by William M'Kenny about 1798. In several respects the story and the book were the forerunners of the paperback anthologies of ghost and horror stories which are now so popular in many countries.

AMONG the numerous and appalling lessons, which the vices of mankind in times gone by, read to the coevals of later years, the adventures of Rodolpho de Burkart are not the least awful. Possessed of more than ordinary intellectual powers, a capacious memory and impetuous application soon carried him through the dull routine, which the acquisition of rudimental knowledge imposes on youth; and released him from those trammels, which the uninformed mind is necessarily subjected to, in the first stages of instruction.

When thus master of the usual branches of learning, he was placed, at a comparatively early age, in one of the numerous universities, which have rendered Germany so famous. Here unfortunately, his young and aspiring mind received a wrong bias, from the instructions of a crazy professor, who entailed on his unfortunate pupil, all the follies of which he was himself the dupe, and wore out his faculties in an incessant application to studies which were worse than useless.

Among these were Alchemy; an abberation of the chemical art, which its mad professors dignified into a science, and pursued with far greater zeal, than they devoted to the useful operations of chemistry. The professor, to whose care Rodolpho was committed, was a votary of this science, the principles of which are, that there is a universal solvent capable of decomposing every substance, but the precious metal gold, into which it converts the baser metals; in addition to these properties, it has the miraculous power of conferring perpetual youth and immortality on its possessors.

The professor was not a noviciate in the science. He possessed a commodious laboratory, in which he had long practised all the fooleries of his art, and scraped crucibles, and blew furnaces, with unwearied industry. Into this sanctum sanctorum, he now introduced his pupil, infected with the falses of Alchemy, and master of much figurative nonsense, which its unfortunate devotees imagined to contain the principles of the art. In this chamber of science Rodolpho soon commenced his labours, and he too, scraped crucibles, and blew furnaces, from morning till night, with the most laudable patience and industry. Among the numerous experiments tried by the learned professor, or perhaps more properly speaking among those he tried to try, the following two merit our particular attention. First, a plate of gold on which was painted, eyes, nose, and mouth, to typify its representative character of the sun, was immured in a sand bath, there to remain in a rich glow, until the sun had performed his annual course. Three hundred and sixty five nights blowing, of course, caused a great consumption of charcoal, and produced nothing, save much sweat from the experimentalist. – In a mattross elevated over a spirit lamp – a green liquid, compounded of many salts, was to undergo a slow evaporation, till a pillicle announced its powers sufficiently concentrated. It was easy enough to evaporate to a pillicle, but the mischief was, that this phenomenon should not take place, till the silver moon had described her orbit, and nothing but a month's slow boiling would do; 'neither more nor less,' as Portia says to Shylock. This experiment, although tried with great success by the professor and his pupil, never entirely succeeded, owing to the extreme difficulty of adjusting the heat, so as to effect the given degree of concentration in the proper ratio of time; however the professor and his pupil boiled eggs remarkably well. These grand experiments, it may be supposed, were not the only ones which occupied their time and attention: innumerable retorts, receivers, and mattrosses were continually boiling, bursting, and breaking, around the experimentalists, and an ugly urchin, who was permitted to sweep out the laboratory, derived an handsome independence, and 'cut a swell' at the fruit stalls, by the sale of the broken glass.

After two years of slavery had been passed by the pupil in the laboratory, nearly three thousand retorts, receivers, and mattrosses were reduced to atoms; and much good, genuine gold dissolved, melted, and lost, the professor, who, like his pupil, was assiduously blowing a charcoal furnace, suddenly relaxed his labours – the bellows ceased to blow, the red glow of the charcoal gave place to occasional scintillations, and the professor in an invoking attitude, with impassioned but reverend utterance, addressed his Saint, thus : – 'Shade of Cornelius Agrippa ! how my shirt sticks to my back ! '

The professor had scarce uttered these words, when the bursting of a large retort of liquor, intended to become Aqua mirabilis, put an end to his apostrophe, and so grievously scalded both him and his pupil, as to render immediate pharmaceutical aid necessary.

Rodolpho was placed under the care of a learned professor of phlebottomy, who after administering much external plaster, physicked, blistered, purged and bolussed his patient till he had reduced him to the common standard of humanity; and cured of his enthusiasm for this science, Rodolpho gave up the search for Elixir Vitae.

Rodolpho during the confinement of his sick chamber, perused many medical and anatomical treaties, and on his return to convalescence, attended the lectures of the worthy professor under whose care he had been placed. The lecture room was amply supplied with proper objects for illustration of the science. Skeletons shewed the fabric, muscular, and other dissections, the superstratum and construction of the human body, and nature thus exhibited to the pupil, convinced him that we are 'wonderfully and fearfully made'. Rodolpho felt this on his entry – it struck a chill to his heart – his frame was unnerved, and he would have fallen to the ground, had not his conductors supported him – this feeling soon wore off, and he surveyed and inspected the dissections without emotion – in a week he had acquired firmness to take up the dissecting knife, and mangle the 'subjects', and could smile at the miserable conceits and jests of the elder students, as they jocosely discussed whether a corpse under examination, had more adipose membrane than muscular fibre, or whether the pia mater was larger than the dura mater; and in a fortnight he had become a 'regular carver', and could cut up the heart of a man, and cut a joke at the same time.

During his pupilage to the Alchemistic professor, Rodolpho had studied electricity and galvanism, which had both been resorted to in the search after the philosopher's stone, and in his few hours of occasional relaxation had sometimes amused himself by making a calf's head look foolish, or a dead frog dance to the tune of his galvanic battery. He now experimented on the subjects for dissection, and could make a corpse raise an arm or a leg, open and shut its eyes or mouth at will.

The new buried corpse of a young female which had been stolen from a neighbouring cemetery, was, on its way to the Anatomical Theatre, deposited in the apartment of Rodolpho, with a view to its removal at a more convenient season, and this he considered a good opportunity of ascertaining the utmost power of his galvanic battery – indeed he had sometimes almost entertained the belief that the mere muscular motion first caused by the application of galvanism, might by its continued action, be converted into more than involuntary agitation, and that, when muscular action had been sufficiently excited, it would cause the heart to beat, the lungs to inflate, the blood to flow; and then thought he reanimation must ensue. All was prepared, and he gradually applied the powers of his battery to the corpse before him – it caused at first a sort of tremor of the whole body, – then muscular action commenced – Rodolpho turned to increase the strength of the battery – he thought he heard a sigh – he stood aghast and motionless till he was sure he heard a moan, and then the corpse before him half uplifted its head, and raised its arm – it started half upright – opened its eyes – gazed wildly – and sunk again. Rodolpho now knew what nature had revived, and he immediately procured assistance and conveyed the body to the Infirmary attached to the university.

At this juncture a summons from the father of Rodolpho suddenly arrived, requiring the immediate presence of his son – he was at the point of death; our hero arrived at his paternal home in time to receive his father's blessing and last instructions. After the burial, and when the first violent emotions of grief had subsided, he began to investigate into his father's affairs, naturally anxious to ascertain what he was heir to, and found that he must in a great measure depend on his good spirits to feed and clothe him.

Rodolpho's thoughts had been so much engaged by the circumstances of his sudden recall from college and his father's death with its attendant cares and duties, as to wholly banish all recollection of his last galvanic experiment, when he received a letter from the professor of anatomy, informing him that the corpse he had recalled to life had been completely restored to health – that she was the daughter of Baron von Stickmeheart, that having fallen into a lethargic state she had been supposed dead, and too hastily buried. This letter enclosed another from the Baron, expressing in high terms his thanks for the restoration of his child, and closing with a pressing invitation to his château.

The events that followed are such as are familiar to every reader of romance, and we shall not dilate either upon them, or upon the beauty of Leonora, for that was the name of the resuscitated lady; sufficient to say that Rodolpho immediately accepted the invitation – was hospitably entertained by the father – fell in love with the daughter – and after exchanging eternal vows of constancy and affection with the fair Leonora, was kicked out of doors for his presumption. – Baron Von Stickmeheart although he felt grateful for Rodolpho's services, feeling equal contempt for his poverty.

Rodolpho lingered many a long and weary day, near the spot where his beloved Leonora resided, but the Baron was too cautious in his measures to give the lovers an opportunity of again meeting.

In his lurkings round the château, he more than once encountered the noble lord who, confident that he had by his precautions secured his daughter from all access, good humouredly rallied our hero on his fruitless endeavours to catch a glance of his mistress, and advised him to give up the idle pursuit in which he was engaged, and apply himself to some other, by which he might acquire sufficient wealth to rank himself equal to the lady he aspired to.

Rodolpho listened to these admonitions with a long face and heavy heart – his alchemistic labours had taught him patience, but he knew too well that if he must be rich before his union with Leonora could take place, many a year of hope deferred and

lingering expectation must be passed, ere he could count gold
enough to buy his bride. At length, finding no relaxation in the
baron's precautionary measures, and more than all convinced by
the baron's friendly conduct towards him in other points where
his daughter was not concerned, Rodolpho resolved to return
homeward and adopt the course recommended to him. Before
however he quitted the locality so dear to him, he visited every
spot that could remind him of his Leonora – every rustic arbour
where they had sat, and enjoyed the converse sweet that none
but lovers know. – When every stump of tree on which Leonora
had rested, had received his benediction, he felt that he must depart and with a heavy sigh looked towards the path he must take
to return, when he recollected that one object, which was associated with the idea of his mistress, had been neglected, in this,
his farewell perambulation. There stood not far from the
château of the baron, a noble fir-tree, which reared on high its
lofty head, and spread its branches wide around: this was an
object which had often excited the admiration of the lovers in
the walks together. He surveyed it now with peculiar attention
and regard, and sighing deeply as he viewed it, thought how
many years would perhaps elapse, ere he might again behold
either that, or Leonora. He threw himself on the turf and reclined beneath its branches, and in a melancholy stupor, forgot
awhile his sorrow. But thought was not idle, his busy brain in
wild succession, let loose ideas which mocked the sober understanding. In imagination he again commenced his alchemistic
labours – again scraped crucibles and bellows blew – again
watched over the slow boiling of Aqua mirabilis – a female of
exquisite beauty appeared to rise from the boiling compound,
gradually expanding to the stature of humanity. – She held in
her right hand a golden sceptre headed by a transparent globe
which contained a fluid of golden hue – she held it forth to
Rodolpho, but as he seemed to rise to receive it – a retort burst
with loud detonation, and the spectrum vanished. The climax
of fancy past, reason resumed her sway, and Rodolpho awoke.

He had at first reclined himself beneath the branches of the
fir-tree to shade him from the rays of a setting sun – while the

sky shone in glorious splendour. The noble fern now sheltered him from the rain which fell in torrents – the sky was dark and obscured – the wind rushed in by stormy blasts, while the lightning flashed vividly, followed by loud peals of thunder. The storm was succeeded by a gloomy calm, and the sky, disburdened by the falling of the rain, glared with a bluish light. As Rodolpho lay half asleep beneath the tree, he saw strange shapes flitting around him, and then quite awake with terror, he sat up motionless and breathless to observe them. They became more numerous and regular in their motions, and after capering about individually, took hands, and forming a ring, danced round the fern. Rodolpho lay in a state more likely to be imagined than described, and the cold perspiration bedewed his face and limbs, as he listened to a doggrel chorus, raised by the hellish figurants.

### CHORUS OF IMPS

Here we are! – Here we are!
  Above in the sky, below on the earth,
We have come from the land of night afar,
  Where the sun never gleams, where the darkness
        has birth.

The mighty wheel of a hundred years
  Has turned on its axis since last we met,
And now we have come to calm your fears,
  But must depart, ere the sun be set.

And we must reside in the land of gloom,
  'Midst thunder, fire, and pain,
Till this century's past, and another has come,
  And then we'll revisit the earth again.

Here we are! – Here we are!
  From North and South, from East and West,
To know how you do and how you fare,
  We must obey the high behest.
      And dance about
      The fir so stout,
Where you are confined and can't come out!

But we must away — we must away,
For the sun sinks fast and we cannot stay;
And the storm comes on and the rain comes fast,
And we must away, ere the day be passed.

We'll once more dance around the fern,
Then away we go, then away we go,
We know you're safe and we must say so;
We'll once more dance around the fern,
Ere we sink below to the fires that burn,
And as nothing has happened our sport to mar,
We'll bid you good-bye with a loud Ha! Ha! Ha!

At the conclusion of the chorus, the elves disappeared. This ballet of the devils had a good effect upon Rodolpho; it took off his thoughts from Leonora, and fully occupied his mind. He was about to depart from the forest when a hollow deep toned voice addressed him thus: — 'Stranger! happy and fortunate; whom fate has led upon this spot — speak, what wouldst thou? Once in a hundred years 'tis mine to grant whatever can be asked for. The hour is passing fast which gives that power. — Speak! stranger! speak! and lose not the golden opportunity thou hast attained.' — Rodolpho, startled and bewildered by surprise, was unable to answer; the previous exhibition of the Devil's pantomime had prepared him against much alarm at any strange object he might see in crossing the forest, but he never dreamt of holding conference with anything supernatural. The voice again addressed him — 'Speak! stranger! speak — why dost thou hesitate? — But once in a hundred years I offer — the hour is passing, which once past, leaves me dumb for another century — speak! what wouldst? — power — honour — fame — knowledge — these are mine to grant.' Rodolpho had half a mind to sneak off quietly without reply, but knowing riches, power, honour, fame and knowledge were not everyday bargains, he screwed up his courage to the sticking place, rejoined, 'Mysterious being! — who art thou? — hast thou, indeed, the power, and will to grant thus largely?' — 'Doubt not,' replied the voice, 'speak, ask, and thy wish is granted.'

Rodolpho had read the history of the Devil and Doctor Faustus, so he replied 'You offer well, but grant ye these great gifts without condition?' – 'Without condition! without condition!' rejoined the voice. 'Thou hast but one single task to perform for all that I can give thee – I want no bond of blood nor penalty of soul.' 'What is it that I must do to merit such a recompense,' asked Rodolpho eagerly. 'Set me free!' replied the mysterious voice; 'on a level with yon eye, upon this fir tree you may discern a knotty peg – pull but that out, and I am free. Immured within this fern for many a century past have I pined in misery. – But once in an hundred years have I the power of speech – but once in an hundred years the chance of liberation – that hour is passing – hesitate not, or I am dumb and powerless for another century.' 'What power,' asked Rodolpho, 'has confined thee thus? – what crime has thou committed to merit such a doom?' 'An evil power confines me thus! No crime have I committed to merit such a doom – haste thee stranger – deliver me, and lose not the golden opportunity, – if riches, power, honour, fame and knowledge please thee not, ask something else – or hast thou not a mistress whom these gifts might grace?'

The imprisoned spirit had now hit the right nail on the head, and stood some chance of liberation. Our hero thought only of his beloved, and hesitated no longer, but pulled out the peg, when out crawled a black spider which swelled to an enormous size as it descended the tree. Rodolpho, who expected to see a 'dainty Ariel' spring from confinement, singing 'merrily, merrily, shall I live now, under the blossom that hangs on the bough,' drew back with astonishment as he viewed the reptile before him. 'Nay, startle not, friend,' said the same voice as before – 'I shall not wear this livery long!' and as it spoke, the spider gradually assumed a human form, and said, 'Thanks for your kindness; but words alone are nothing – now for deeds – first then, behold your Leonora.' And Leonora rushed into Rodolpho's arms. The lovers were too overjoyed at thus meeting again, to notice what was passing around them, and on their relapse into ordinary human feelings, Rodolpho found that the demon had quietly walked off. He thought this a dirty trick of

the imp, that after making such proud offers and liberal promises, he should sneak off without so much as a 'good-bye', or
'good morning', he however concealed his chagrin from
Leonora, and in her sweet society, forgot both the demon, and
his pie-crust promises. He inquired to what fortunate accident
were they indebted for their happy meeting, and found that
Baron Von Stickmeheart, having overgorged himself with Sal-
magunda, had been obliged to relax in his strict discipline, as he
required the assistance of his daughter for the administration of
the comforts of his sick chamber, and that Leonora, having left
the precincts of her father's château to enjoy the evening breeze,
felt herself drawn as if by an irresistible impulse, to the spot
where they had met. He also found that she had not seen the
spider demon, and knew nothing either of him or his braggart
offers. The evening was now pretty far advanced, and having
conducted Leonora to as near the château as prudence permitted, he returned to his lodging for the night.

Rodolpho on his awakening in the morning, had so confused
a recollection of the occurrences of the preceding day, that after
a long self confabulation, he set down the whole as a dream – he
thought, as well he might, that he had a distinct recollection of
pulling out the peg, and liberating the demon – and of his previous tempting offers – but then, the total absence of any evidence of their fulfilment, convinced him that the whole could be
nothing more than a dream.

These ruminations passed in his mind, as he lay awake in his
bed, with his eyes under his nightcap; but when he pulled off
that elegant article of night attire, new subjects of astonishment
presented themselves. He found himself lying on a sumptuous
bed in a chamber, very different from that he had retired to rest
in. This last excitation of astonishment quite bewildered him,
and he was amazed indeed. When he had a little come to himself, he scrambled out of bed, and began capering and vaulting
about the room, to convince himself that he was really awake;
during his gymnastic exercises, a valet whose appearance showed
he belonged to the establishment of a nobleman of consequence,
entered the chamber, and stood bowing before him. – Rodolpho

stared at him for several minutes, quite lost in amazement, when the ill-suppressed tittering of the valet, a little recalled him to his senses. On viewing him more composedly, Rodolpho thought he had seen him before, and was a little calmed by the idea that now rushed into his head, that he must be in the château of the Baron Von Stickmeheart, and after several vain efforts to speak, he articulated 'Who are you!' 'I have the honour to be your lordship's gentleman,' replied the valet, bowing very low. Rodolpho was all abroad again, and he chattered rather than said – 'My lordship's gentleman! and who am I then?' 'Your lordship knows, your lordship has the honour to be the Count Von Attenburg,' answered the valet. Rodolpho turned from him and threw himself on the bed. As his agitation calmed, he thought of Abon Hassan, the Duke and the Devil, and Kit Sly, then his mind reverted back to the imprisoned spirit in the fern, and the more he thought, the firmer was his conviction that the occurrences of the previous day were indeed reality – yet he was afraid to open his eyes, lest he should find himself again deceived. He was anxious to ascertain what the fact was, but he dared not – he made efforts to open his eyes, and himself resisted those efforts; at length he summoned up sufficient courage to set about the solution of the question another way – he began with hastily feeling the bed furniture! It certainly was a different bed from that he recollected retiring in – he could not remember seeing such a great tassel as he felt in his hand belonging to the curtains, but still he was not sufficiently encouraged to open his eyes, and he resolved to try another experiment before he resorted to that desperate measure – with great joy he recollected that the bed he had laid himself down on, was rather too short for him, and that he had poked his feet out at the bottom when he wished to lay straight – again he jumped into bed and stretched himself at length, and to his great satisfaction, found that his feet could not reach the bottom of the bed by near a foot – this gave him courage – he opened his eyes, and the bed was still sumptuous, the bedchamber still magnificent, and the grinning valet was still grinning and bowing at his side.

Rodolpho, now fortune was buckled on his back, felt highly offended at the familiar manner in which the valet conducted himself, and with an assumption of dignity suitable to the proud fortune he had reached, asked the 'stupid booby', as he condescendingly designated him, what he was grinning and sniggering at. This interrogation silenced the rascal's giggling, and he submissively asked if his lordship had any commands for him. 'None at present,' replied Rodolpho, 'I shall this morning dress without assistance, but attend within call;' as Rodolpho spoke, he recollected he did not know his valet's name, so he said, 'Ah! fellow! what name do I generally call you by?' – 'Your lordship,' replied the valet, 'generally calls me Brushat, but sometimes – the Spider Demon!' – While he spoke, his countenance changed, and Rodolpho recognized the same features as he saw when the gigantic spider assumed a human form. ''Tis as I suspected then,' said Rodolpho, without evincing much emotion, 'and half the mystery's explained, but how, and by what means am I thus metamorphosed into the Count Von Attenburg, and as I suppose master of a fortune suited to my rank?' 'The Count Von Attenburg,' replied the demon, 'last night breathed his last in that bed,' pointing to the one in which Rodolpho had slept, – 'and you have succeeded to his honours.' 'By what means?' rejoined Rodolpho. 'By the agency of my power,' replied the demon. 'But if I cannot boast a legal title, what is to ensure my possession?' again interrogated Rodolpho, (who had now equipped himself in a splendid suit of blue and gold); 'instant detection must take place, unless you have provided some expedient to render the deception infallible.' – 'I have done so,' said the demon, drawing aside a curtain. 'See ye that portrait of the late Count Von Attenburg – 'twas finished but a few days since – and now,' continued the demon, drawing aside another curtain from before a splendid mirror, 'behold the present Count Von Attenburg! – what say ye of detection now?' Rodolpho looked at himself in the glass, and saw that he was habited exactly as the figure. 'This is mere disguise, mere stage trick,' said he, 'a change of dress will not maintain me in the station I have thus usurped.' 'Look again,' replied the demon, 'and your fears will be at rest.' Rodolpho did look again, and started back with horror as he discovered that he had no merely changed his dress, but his countenance also, and found the portrait and his own reflection in the glass were exactly similar. 'Demon!' exclaimed he, 'instantly restore me to my former person and estate, and leave me for ever!' 'No! no!' replied the demon, 'we part not so soon, my friendship is not of such brief continuance.' 'Demon of hell! deceitful tempter!' again exclaimed Rodolpho, 'withdraw thee from my sight and trouble me no more.' The demon after a loud laugh of scorn and bitterness, vanished.

Our hero, much relieved by his departure, paced the chamber in gloomy mood, debating within himself how he should act in this strange dilemma – he looked and looked again in the glass, but his former features were not restored to him, and after waiting in anxious expectation several hours, he still found his countenance, and that of the picture, the same. He now felt internal qualms of a somewhat unpleasant nature, from going without his breakfast, and hunger compelled him to pull the bell rope – his summons was answered by Brushat. Rodolpho, who had indulged the hope that the evil spirit had departed from him forever, shuddered as he recognized him. 'What is your lordship's pleasure?' inquired Brushat. Rodolpho was too much agitated to answer, and Brushat continued, 'Will not your lordship take breakfast; 'tis much later than your lordship usually takes your morning refreshment.' Rodolpho answered him by an affirmative inclination of the head, and Brushat led the way. After descending a handsome painted staircase, they entered a splendid hall, where an excellent breakfast was set out. It is well known that a starved tiger is as gentle as a lamb, Rodolpho, now he had got the wind in his stomach, was very mild and tractable, and treated Brushat with as much civility, as, considering their relative situations of lord and slave, could be expected. While partaking of the very excellent breakfast aforesaid, his agitation of mind subsided, and by the time he had satiated his appetite, he was quite resigned to his fate. He was much gratified by observing that Brushat shewed no signs of his satanic origin, and appeared quite an ordinary valet. Rodolpho thought he could not employ the time, between breakfast and dinner, better than by going over, and inspecting his new mansion; so having signified his intention to Brushat, the latter led the way. The hall they were in, opened by folding doors into another still more elegant and spacious, which led to a library and picture gallery. Rodolpho after surveying the interior of his château, walked over the grounds attached to it, and found everything very much to his satisfaction. In crossing a bridge over an artificial waterfall, he discerned a handsome château in the background, and inquiring of his attendant to whom it belonged, received answer, that it was the château of Baron Von Stickmeheart. This information recalled to his mind his love for Leonora, whom he had forgotten in his turmoil of soul and novelty of situation. He thought of her with varied emotions of pleasure and pain, he was delighted to think that his present good fortune, that is to say, his rank and wealth, removed the only obstacle which appeared to their union; but this feeling merged into sensations of a less pleasing character, as he recollected he was not only changed in estate, but in person also. He sighed to think that this circumstance might prove a greater obstacle to his happiness than the former, and returning to the château in a pensive mood, he retired to the library to indulge in his melancholy feelings. He took up, looked at, and threw down the books almost unconscious of what he was doing – he tried to read, but they were all Greek to him now. Rodolpho, who was well acquainted with many languages, and thought he knew the characters at least of almost all, was astonished, after a most attentive and careful examination of one volume, to find that he could not decipher in what language it was. He strained his eyes in painful efforts to discover a resemblance to characters he knew, but these were totally different to all he had ever before seen, they eluded all detection of their meaning, and to use a common expression, and double negative, he could neither make head nor tail of it; he let the book fall in despair, and this simple circumstance revealed to him the secret – he had taken up the book topsy turvy, and begun at the wrong end. As he had already bestowed so much time on the volume, he resolved now to see what it was, he found it to be a collection of romantic legends, and as he glanced over its pages, thought of the days when he considered those marvellous narrations, but as the creations of imagination – as mere fiction; but now his own adventures, gave them a character and importance of a much higher grade, and compelled a credence of their wondrous relations. This idea brought no comfort with it; in all the 'Legends of the Wild' he had ever read, he knew that the supernaturals had always most woefully the advantage over the naturals, and that they generally ended in smoke. As he turned over its pages, an illustration attached to one of the legends, caught his eye – the subject was a spectre barber shaving a terrified mortal, who had much rather been well tarred, and shaved with a piece of iron hoop, by the jolly dogs of Neptune, in latitude 0°, though the spectre barber shaved gratis.

'Ah!' said Rodolpho to himself, 'had I been but shaved by a spectre barber, though he had shaved my head clean, yet the effluxion of a short period of time would have at once restored to me both happiness and a good head of hair! But thus changed as I am in form and feature, my growth in the favour of my mistress, will be much slower than that of my beard!'

Brushat now entered the library, he came to announce the arrival of Baron Von Stickmeheart, who was on friendly, not to say intimate terms of acquaintance with the Count Von Attenburg, and who was of course quite ignorant of the extraordinary change that had taken place.

Rodolpho hastened to receive the baron, who had been ushered into the state drawing-room. He was greeted by a friendly shake of the hand, and the usual exchange of courteous inquiries having been made, and the state of the weather properly ascertained, and sufficiently commented upon; 'how d'ye do's', 'fine day', 'rather cloudy though', and similar interjections gave way to conversation of a more connected and interesting nature. 'He's gone,' said the Baron, seizing the Count's hand, 'he's gone off; and the girl will soon forget him.'

The Count, who had but assumed the form of the last

possessor of the title, without inheriting his memory and mind, was quite in the dark as to whom 'he's gone' could apply, and could not divine who he could be: he had however the presence of mind to say, 'Indeed! how fortunate.' 'Fortunate indeed,' returned the Baron, 'Leonora will now receive your attentions with less reserve, than when her head was full of Professor de Burkart.' The hero of our tale now discovered that he himself was the person alluded to by the baron, and was well pleased to find that though as Rodolpho de Burkart he was despised and avoided, yet that as the Count Von Attenburg, he was a welcomed and encouraged suitor at Château Stickmeheart. After having invited the Count to dine with him and Leonora, the Baron took his leave. — Rodolpho arrived at Château Stickmeheart, full an hour before the appointed time, and an hour and a half before he was wanted; the cook dreaded dinner being called for before everything was ready: the baron had retired to his chamber, to take a little repose after his morning's walk, as it was one of his maxims of health, never to dine in a state of fatigue: and to Leonora any visitor would have been an unwelcome one. Rodolpho was too well-bred to disturb the Baron's repose, and learning, on inquiry after the lady Leonora, that she was walking in the grounds attached to the château, he went in quest of her. He ranged the grounds over and over again, without meeting with Leonora, and then thinking she might perhaps of ventured beyond the precincts of her father's château, he left the enclosed lands, and sought for her in the surrounding wilds, but found her not; he penetrated deeper into the forest, and on arriving at the spot, where stood the fir tree before mentioned, there discovered the object of his search. Leonora had been much disappointed, by finding on inquiry at the cottage, where Rodolpho had slept, on the night of their last interview, that he had departed thence before daybreak, without any previous intimation of his intention to its inmates; and had been led to visit that spot, by a vague hope that she might here meet Rodolpho. Here then the lovers again met, but with very different feelings to those they experienced on their former interview. Leonora who had been 'sitting like patience on a monument' at the foot of the fern, was much disconcerted being discovered there, by him, whom she only knew as the Count Von Attenburg, while Rodolpho felt equal confusion. He had intended to communicate to Leonora, all the strange circumstances that had occurred previously to, and since their last meeting: but his tongue clove to the roof of his mouth, when he would speak, and he felt a secret dread of revealing them. Thus compelled to sustain a false character, he greeted Leonora with cold formality, and mere commonplace conversation passed between them, as he led her homewards. Leonora paid the count the attention due to his rank and station, but was otherwise very reserved in her carriage towards him. The baron did all he could to bring about a better understanding between them, but all his efforts were abortive, and he only preserved the equanimity of his temper, by the consideration, that time's miraculous power would subdue the obstinacy of his daughter: and the baron was quite correct in his notion. Time's miraculous power works wonders, and a year's effluxion placed the count on a very different footing at Château Stickmeheart. No tidings of Rodolpho reached Leonora; the Count was so constant a visitor, that habit removed the irksomeness and repugnance she formerly felt at his presence: till at length his visits became very agreeable. Some of our fair readers may deem this change in the sentiments of our heroine, very inconsistent with the idea they have been led to entertain of her character, but we beg they will bear in mind, that there was a great similarity between Rodolpho, in his former and his present estate, he was changed but in outward circumstances; the man was still the same. Rodolpho often resolved to cut short his courtship by the avowal of his real character, but never could summon sufficient courage to do so; he seemed restrained from the disclosure, by an inward dread that something fatal would attend the revelation of the mystery that enveloped him. One day when Leonora was particularly gracious, he determined to overcome this repugnance, and own himself Rodolpho. He fell at her feet in a very graceful attitude, but as he raised his eyes to meet those of his mistress, was horror-struck at beholding the Spider Demon standing before him, with his finger on his lip; the usual mute sign of imposing silence.

This unexpected and ill-timed visitation of the Spider Demon, struck Rodolpho with horror, he endeavoured to account for his agitation, by attributing it to sudden indisposition, and immediately left Château Stickmeheart. When he arrived at his own château he directed Brushat to attend him in the library. Rodolpho, who always felt 'tremor cordis' when that mysterious being was present, had never, since their colloquy, when he first discovered his elevation to the Peerage, held further conference with the demon, but endeavoured to consider him, as what he appeared to be, an ordinary valet. He was now resolved to come to an explanation with the demon, and demand the reason of the warning given him so mal apropos. He was astonished to find, on interrogating Brushat, that he pretended total ignorance of any of the mysterious circumstances before related, and Brushat was equally astonished at the strange, and to him, unintelligible inquiries of his lordship, who was now compelled to solve this fresh difficulty by supposition that the demon had assumed the form of the domestic. Though disappointed in one respect, he was greatly pleased at discovering that the demon was not so constantly before him as he had imagined. At the present moment, however, the demon was wanted, and Rodolpho began cogitating how he could summon him before him. I can call him from the vasty deep, thought Rodolpho; but I must take my chance whether he will come or not, when I do call him. Rodolpho considered that the best and most likely method to produce a satisfactory result, would be an invocation in the chamber, where the demon had formerly appeared to him. He proceeded there accordingly, and thus invoked him:

> Spirit of the demon tree,
> Whom I released from misery,
> Where e're thou art, obey my call
> And hither come, before night fall.

No demon however appeared, and Rodolpho was obliged to exercise his poetic genius, in the composition of another verse:

Demon Spider of the tree,
Thy compact thou has soon forgot:
In keeping word and faith with me,
Methinks the most exact you're not.

The demon now stood before him. 'Oh! ho!' said he, 'now I am wanted; the last time you scared me from you with maledictions.' 'And I am like to do so again,' said Rodolpho; 'I had not called thee now, hadst thou not come uncalled for. Why was I cursed with thy hideous silent visitation, this very day, in an hour too sacred, to love and beauty?' 'That was a friendly warning to thee,' answered the demon, 'had not my appearance prevented thee, like another Sampson, thou hadst revealed to thy Delilah, where thy strength lay, and met destruction. Shouldst thou ever communicate the secret of thy metamorphoses to mortal ear, that moment thy existence ends.'

Rodolpho heard the communication in silence, he had no heart to reply; and the demon, having waited as long as good-breeding required, disappeared. His wonted elasticity of mind soon threw off the apathy created by the demon's warning, and Rodolpho again visited Château Stickmeheart. In a short time his assiduities overcame the weak barrier which Leonora's faint recollection of Rodolpho in his former estate opposed to their union, and to the great joy of Baron Von Stickmeheart, the noble houses of Von Stickmeheart and Von Attenburg were united in the persons of Rodolpho and Leonora. The marriage festival was kept with every 'pomp and circumstance', suited to the exalted rank of the parties; the festivities commenced under the most auspicious expectations, but after a week of happiness and pleasure had been passed, amidst the varied scenes of enjoyment, which château Attenburg presented at this period, an event happened which melted every fair one into grief, and struck every manly breast with horror. While Rodolpho and his bride sat surrounded by their friends, under a tented canopy in the gardens, a sudden outcry was heard from another part, and a horror-struck domestic rushed forward, to communicate the harrowing intelligence, that the Baron Von Stickmeheart had been murdered. The fair Leonora and the majority of the ladies present, of course fainted, and while they were being conveyed to the château, Rodolpho and the rest, repaired to the scene of murder. The baron lay weltering in his gore, and a group of domestics stood on one side, with the murderer in their custody. After the first emotions of horror, excited by the appalling spectacle, had subsided, a general cry issued from all, of 'Who is the murderer?' The domestics, in whose custody he was, reluctantly produced the assassin. The gaze of all was in an instant on the miscreant, and to their great astonishment, he was recognized as the confidential valet of the count, as Brushat! The assembled guests, who were nearly all connected by the ties of consanguinity to the deceased, loudly invocated justice on the murderer, and immediately called upon Rudolpho, instead of restoring to the common dilatory course of preceeding, to sit in his baronial hall of justice, according to the feudal law, and there pronounce judgement on the murderer. The count, who had always found Brushat a faithful and attached domestic, was reluctant to adopt the hasty procedure recommended: and his reluctance increased, as he formed the opinion that this scene of horror, arose from the machinations of the Demon; and that he had again assumed the form of Brushat, with a much more fell purpose than on the former occasion. He had resolved to resign the supposed assassin to the ordinary course of law, when one of the guests, more loud in his outcries than the rest, cautioned Rodolpho how he refused the general call for justice, and stated to him that there was already a murmuring among them, that Rodolpho must be in some way connected with the commission of the black deed, as it had been perpetrated by his own confidential domestic. Thus assailed, Rodolpho was compelled to yield to the united voice of the guests. The long unused baronial hall of justice, was hastily prepared, and the reluctant judge ascended his tribunal. Baron Pratterpace, whom we have before mentioned, as the foremost of the vengeance-calling throng, came forward as the accuser, and advocate of justice; he narrated what he imagined to be the circumstances of the case, with great forensic eloquence. He dilated on the atrocity of the crime committed, and argued that as the prisoner was the confidential servant of Rodolpho, and the latter, the son-in-law of the murdered victim to cupidity or hatred, that the prisoner must be considered as if he were the assassin of his master, and visited with the usual rigidity, and extreme of punishment, awarded in such cases. He was particular in dwelling on the fact of the murderer being the confidential servant of Rodolpho, in order that by thus influencing the mind of the count, with the impression that his own safety called for the sacrifice of Brushat, the latter might have no chance of escape. Baron Pratterpace, being one of those impetuous prejudiced men, who, having once formed an opinion, never suffer themselves to be convinced of their error, but pursue the delusion to the end, had determined that Brushat was the murderer, and he had also determined that he should suffer execution for his offence. These feelings caused the acrimony of heart with which he pursued the prisoner 'to the death', and it would have excessively mortified him, had Brushat been, even by the clearest proofs, declared innocent. As it was, however, he was not doomed to experience a disappointment: the prisoner could offer no defence, save protestations of innocence, which were rendered nugatory by the reluctant evidence of the prisoner's fellow domestics. No one but Rodolpho could doubt the guilt of the prisoner, but he, with the gloomy suspicion of the truth rankling in his breast, felt a conviction of his innocence. The accuser loudly called for judgement, and the judge, unable to resist the current of his opinion and offered proffer, pronounced Brushat the murderer. The assembled throng did not wait for sentence to be passed, but as Rodolpho sunk back in his seat, overcome by his emotions, they dragged the prisoner to instant execution. Rodolpho, who, for a few minutes, had been lost in his feelings, started up as he heard the shout raised on the termination of Brushat's mundane existence: and perceived the demon standing before him, with his finger on his lip as in his last uncalled for visitation: after a loud burst of hideous laughter, the demon vanished, leaving Rodolpho in that state of mind, to which, since his first interview with the demon, he was too much accustomed. Time's mellowing hand, which had already done much for Rodolpho, gradually erased from his recollection, this unfortunate transaction,

but by the period of its removal, another cause of irritation
of a different description arose. The coffers of château Attenburg were exhausted – the count, whose thoughts were divided
between his love for Leonora, and the bewildering mysteries
which surrounded him, of course paid no attention to household economy, but trusted the entire management of his estate
to Brushat, in whose hands he found it. So long as he considered Brushat to be the demon in human guise, he knew that
he had no power to oppose the demon's will, and when awakened from that delusion, he felt no disposition to change his
household arrangements. Brushat was in one sense faithful to
his trust, he did not by private peculation defraud his master,
but he suffered him to live on a scale of magnificence his estate
could not maintain; and which gradually ate up his property.
Rodopho, on discovering the situation he was in, knew he had
no alternative, but either to sink to his former obscurity, or else
again invoke the aid of the Spider Demon. He would himself
gladly have retired from his splendid deception, but he could
not involve in his degradation the wife of his bosom, and who
was now shortly to become the mother of his child. Still he delayed the effort from day to day, till the birth of a son and the
newly awakened feelings of a father, gave him courage to put in
execution the measures necessary to secure the future welfare of
his offspring. He accordingly entered the chamber of the
demon conference, which had been abandoned as a sleeping
apartment, and used as a mere lumber room. His invocation
now, was as follows:

> Spider demon of the tree,
>  A curse yourself! – a curse to me,
> Hither come where e're you be,
> And rescue me from misery.
>
> Deceitful tempter! braggart imp!
> Hast thou forgot the years of old,
> When in the fir-tree thou didst limp,
> Ere I released thee from thy hold?

'What now?' said the demon, standing at the count's elbow.
'For what purpose am I again summoned by Rodolpho de

Burkart!' 'When I released thee from the fir tree,' returned the count, 'didst thou not promise to perform whate'er I asked for?' 'And did not I keep my word,' answered the demon, 'did not I create thee Count Von Attenburg – did not I invest thee too, with riches – and with accruing revenues to support that high estate? If you have wasted patrimony with prodigal expenditures – blame not me. I promised but one gift; not a continuity of favours. However, I am not ungrateful, nor unmindful of your services; what is it that you ask for now?' 'To restore my broken fortunes, that I may still maintain my credit, and leave a fair name and inheritance to my child;' was the count's reply. 'On one condition will I perform your wish,' rejoined the demon. 'Name it,' said the count. 'Within a cottage near your lordship's domain,' said the demon, 'a few days since a new-born infant saw the light – 'tis the child of poverty and obscurity – 'tis the sure heir of misery – think'ye not 'twere kind to release its spirit from the bonds of clay that fetter it, and let it float a cherubim to heaven? Grasp but its throat tight, and the thing is done! This perform, and I will restore your broken fortunes.' Rodolpho heard the proposal with mingled emotions of horror, and something like joy; his fortunes were desperate – he had nerved himself up for the worst – but he shuddered at the thoughts of committing murder to retrieve himself – still he had not the courage at once to reject the demon's temptation. The demon, observing Rodolpho's hesitation, knew that he had half accomplished his hellish work, and continued – 'What say ye! Hesitate not too long, or your fortunes may be irretrievable – let your credit be once blasted, and no power, human or demoniac, can restore you.' 'But what a price must I pay for the bubble reputation;' exclaimed Rodolpho, 'murder a sleeping infant – never.' 'You forget,' said the demon, ''twill not be the first murder your lordship has committed!' 'What mean ye?' demanded the count. The demon replied, 'Did not your lordship murder Brushat – your faithful Brushat? I murdered the baron, and you knew it too well, yet you suffered the innocent Brushat to die upon the scaffold as his murderer – nay, yourself condemned him, with a firm conviction of his innocence. Was not that murder, think'ye!' 'Demon, forbear,' exclaimed Rodolpho, 'forbear to upbraid me with the guilt your own machinations have plunged me in. Would that I could retrace my steps to the point where first I listened to your tempting offers – but I am too sure your victim – ye have led me on step by step in guilt, that now my callous heart shudders not at the thoughts of committing infanticide. Lead me – lead me to the cottage of murder – and then we part I trust for ever.' 'Your lordship,' said the demon, 'need not go so far – the child of death is here.' – As he spoke, the demon threw off a mantle from his side, and exposed to view an infant sleeping in his arms; Rodolpho was staggered, but he nerved himself up with desperate energy, and without looking at it, grasped the infant's throat, when a loud burst of laughter from the demon announced the consummation of his crime. 'Now,' said the demon, 'you will find the coffers of Von Attenburg refilled – its mortgages redeemed;' and the demon disappeared. Rodolpho remained in the chamber several hours, in a gloomy and bewildering reverie: on his quitting it, he was amazed to find a general expression of grief on the countenances of his attendants, they seemed to avoid him as he passed: when he reached the chamber of Leonora, he found its expression more violent. She was surrounded by her weeping attendants, who were engaged in restoring her from a fainting fit, Rodolpho hastily demanded the cause of grief; he was answered by bursts of tears, and mute pointings to the cradle of his child; a cold sweat came over Rodolpho, he immediately surmised the fatal cause of sorrow – in wild despair he gazed on the infant – its throat was black from the grasp of strangulation, and it lay dead before him. In wild frenzy, he cursed himself and the deceitful demon who had betrayed him. 'Cursed demon of the tree;' he exclaimed, 'thou hast now indeed made a victim of Rodolpho de Burkart.' As he spoke he fell in the agonies of despair and death – a loud burst of demon laughter was heard – the hideous black spider appeared as after it had descended from the fir tree, and from it arose the demon, who laughed loudly as he exclaimed, 'How like ye the web the Black Spider weaves – another fly I've caught;' and disappeared.

# The Water Spectre

## Francis Lathom

## (1777–1832)

'In many ways Francis Lathom is one of the most interesting and one of the most typical secondary figures among the whole school of the Gothic novelists.' (Montague Summers, *The Gothic Quest*.)

Now that we have considered the major writers responsible for the evolution of the Gothic novel in England, we can turn, as the eighteenth century dissolves into the nineteenth, to one or two of those lesser, but nonetheless important, figures who also helped in the development of this unique form of literature. And, as Montague Summers indicates, who is there more interesting to begin with than Francis Lathom?

The illegitimate son of an English peer, Lathom was deeply interested in the theatre from an early age and while still in his teens wrote a comedy, 'All in A Bustle', which was performed at the Norwich Theatre in 1795. The Gothic genre had also caught his attention by this time and his first novel was *The Castle of Ollanda,* which, while it featured a haunted castle, presented logical explanations for all the mysteries. *The Midnight Bell* which followed in 1798 actually established his name in the genre and in time was accorded the accolade of mention in the list of such books in *Northanger Abbey*.

Still only twenty-one, Lathom did not, however, allow success to lure him away from his first love, the theatre, and at the start of the new century we find him busy on several comedies for the Norwich Theatre. A third Gothic novel, *Mystery*, appeared in 1800 and firmly placed him among the leading writers of his day. From this point his life is somewhat shrouded in mystery, too, and although he certainly abandoned the theatre some years later to live in semi-retirement in Scotland and continue writing, the claims that a homo-

sexual love affair brought about this change have never been fully
substantiated. Further works did flow from his pen and he became
known as something of an eccentric on the Aberdeenshire farm at
Bogdavic where he lived, earning the nick-name, 'Boggie's Lord'.

In later life he travelled in Europe and America but not surprisingly continued to set much of his work in the Scotland which
had become so dear to him. He died in May 1832 and was buried in
the churchyard at Fyvie. Today his novels remain almost completely
unread and his once great popularity among 'common readers' forgotten. The story which follows demonstrates Lathom's knowledge
of Scottish supernatural lore and his swift piling of horror upon
horror. *The Water Spectre* was probably written about 1809.

MUCHARDUS, the usurping Thane of Dungivan, had murdered
Roderic the late owner of that title, whom he had treacherously
invited to an entertainment in a castle that he possessed on the
banks of the Clyde. As soon as the banquet was nearly concluded, Roderic arose, courteously took leave of his entertainer
and his guests, and descended the stairs. But he was not allowed
to quit Boswell Castle. His faithful followers had been previously dispatched, and buried in one of the vaults beneath the
edifice. To one of these, which was formed into a kind of dungeon, the hapless Roderic was forcibly dragged, and fastened to
the stone wall by an iron chain.

Three days and nights did the unfortunate Roderic remain in
this wretched lodging; his bed the cold ground, with oaten cake
and water for food; and this vile treatment he received from one
on whom he had heaped innumerable favours, and honoured
with his confidence.

On the fourth night of Roderic's dreadful confinement, Muchardus entered his dungeon; in one hand he carried a written
paper, in the other a dagger; the man who had always brought
Roderic's food, carried a torch before the recreant lord. Roderic
surveyed his foe with silent indignation.

After a pause of a few minutes, Muchardus presented to the
Thane the paper which he had brought, and desired him to
peruse it with attention. He did so, and found it to be drawn up

as a will, by which he bequeathed to his treacherous friend all his vast possessions, and the Thaneship of Dungivan.

'For what vile purpose have you brought me this infamous scroll?' demanded the Thane.

'By signing that paper,' replied Muchardus, 'you will preserve your existence. Liberty, 'tis true, I cannot grant you, consistent with my own designs and safety; yet you shall be secreted in the best apartment my castle affords; and every wish you can form, that will not tend to a discovery of your still being an inhabitant of this world, shall be attended to with the most scrupulous exactness.'

The Thane's eyes darted fire at this disclosure of the premeditated villainy of Muchardus, and he tore the paper to atoms.

The enraged Muchardus flew towards his victim, and repeatedly plunged his dagger in his breast, till, with a heavy groan, he fell, and expired at the feet of his murderer.

Muchardus then left the dungeon, and returned to his own apartment, where he employed one of his emissaries, whom he had sworn to secrecy, to draw up another paper of the same purport as that which the Thane had destroyed. Muchardus had several papers in his possession, which had been written by Roderic, and to most of them his signature was affixed. This they copied with great exactness, and then prepared to reap the fruits of their wicked design.

The corpse of the murdered Thane was taken ere the dawn of day, and flung into a briery dell, where it was left, having been previously stript of every article of value.

The absence of the Thane and his attendants from the Castle of Dungivan, had caused a very serious alarm to his vassals and adherents, who had made many successless researches in the mountains, and inquired at every habitation, if they could give any tidings of their lord; but no one had seen the Thane since the day he went to Boswell Castle.

Some days after the murder had been committed, the body of the Thane was found in the dell, by some huntsmen, who were led to the spot by the sagacity of their hounds. The marks of violence on his person, and his being despoiled of the property about it, which was known to have been of great value on that fatal day, as he had arrayed himself most sumptuously, and put on a variety of ornaments to honour the banquet of Muchardus, led the persons interested in the discovery, to conjecture that his attendants had murdered him, and made off with the booty. And as their bodies could no where be found, the report strengthened every day. Nor was Muchardus in the least suspected of the murder.

That chief having proceeded so far with a success equal to his most sanguine wishes, hastened to put the finishing blow to his manoeuvres. He carried the forged will to be placed in a drawer in one of the chambers where he was sure it would not be overlooked. It was accordingly found by persons empowered to search for the papers of the deceased. Muchardus was accordingly declared sole heir of the late Thane of Dungivan: not much to the surprise of any person, as the great intimacy between him and Roderick had been so apparent; yet they greatly regretted the change, as the tyrannical disposition of Muchardus was too well known, and often experienced by those whom fortune had placed under him.

Muchardus (now Thane of Dungivan) had attained the height of his ambition; yet his pillow was strewed with mental thorns. Ah! how unlike the prosperity of the good man! Conscience, from whose reproaches we cannot flee, perpetually reminded him of his crimes, and made him shudder with apprehension, lest retributive vengeance should overtake his guilty head.

The late Thane married, in early youth, a most beauteous lady, the heiress of a neighbouring chieftain. With her he fondly hoped for many years of happiness: but his hopes were vain; the peerless Matilda expired in giving birth to her first born, the lovely Donald; the traitor Muchardus being one of the sponsors that answered for his faith at the font.

Two years passed on, and the widowed Thane still indulged his grief, undiminished by the lapse of time. Muchardus artfully endeavoured to learn the sentiments of his friend, as far as regarded his re-engaging in matrimonial ties. To his great, though concealed satisfaction, he heard from Dungivan, that he had solemnly vowed never to take a second bride, but to cherish a tender remembrance of his Matilda, and pray for a reunion with her in those realms of bliss where the pangs of separation should be unknown.

Muchardus had for some time past viewed the possessions of Dungivan with a coveting eye; and he thought it feasible to obtain the Thaneship by the murder of the father and son, as they had no near relatives to make a claim. After much deliberation, he concluded that it would be most prudent to remove the child first from this world; as, in case of the death of the Thane preceding that of Donald, the latter might be placed out of his reach.

Annie, the young woman who nursed the little Lord, was walking on the banks of the Clyde, when she was seized by four men masked and armed, who tore Donald from her arms. Two of them ran off with the child; and the other two bound Annie to a tree, and then followed their companions.

The length of time that his son was absent alarmed the Thane, and he sent some of the domestics to search for Annie and her charge, and require their immediate return.

They soon discovered the nurse, and heard her dismal story. They led her back to the castle in an agony of grief, and acquainted the Thane with the tidings. He tore his hair, and rent his garments; nor would he listen to the consolations that Muchardus seemed so eager to administer.

Various conjectures were formed who could be the perpetrator of such a deed; but no one, upon mature reflection, appeared feasible.

The Thane had not, to his knowledge, an enemy existing; for his demeanour had been goodwill to all; nor did he conceive how any person, as he had no immediate heir, could be benefitted by the death or removal of his son. Alas! he clasped to his bosom as a chosen friend, his deadly foe, the cause of all his sorrow: for it was Muchardus that had employed ruffians to seize young Donald.

Allan, the man who was trusted with the management of

this vile plot, was ordered by his employer, to take the child and precipitate him into the Clyde as soon as he had got rid of the men who were joined with him in the enterprise.

Allan took the young Lord to his cottage, where he intended to secrete him till the surrounding objects were enveloped in the gloom of night, and then execute the horrid design which he had pledged his faith to commit. When he entered his humble habitation, he found Jannette, his wife, bitterly lamenting over the corpse of her son, their only child. When Allan departed in the morning, he had left the young Ambrose playing before the door of the cottage, with the rose of health glowing on his cheeks. A few hours after, death had seized his victim; and on the father's return, he found himself bereft of his only hope. Nor did he fail to attribute this calamity as the vengeance of an offended God. He felt what it was to lose a child: and he pitied the sufferings that the Thane must endure. – 'They are more than my own,' ejaculated the now penitent Allan, 'I know the end of mine; but the poor Lord is uncertain what is the fate of his at this moment.'

'But tomorrow,' continued Allan, after a pause, in which he recollected the injunctions of his employer, 'tomorrow thy corpse will, perhaps, be discovered floating in the Clyde, and his apprehensions will be confirmed by a horrid reality.'

'You will not, surely, murder this sweet babe,' exclaimed Jannette in agony, and clasped the young Donald to her breast.

'I must,' said Allan; 'I have sworn. Behold the price of my villainy;' emptying the contents of a wellfilled purse on the table; 'and I am to have as much more when Lord Muchardus is convinced that the deed is executed.'

'I will not part with him,' said Jannette, 'he shall supply the place of my child. You have been very wicked, Allan; but you are not yet a murderer. The children are nearly of a size; nor are their features much different; only the heir of Dungivan is so beautifully fair, and our Ambrose is nearly olive; yet that will not be when the poor babe has lain in the water.'

'What mean you?' said Allan, who instantly comprehended and applauded the plan which she had in part expressed.

Jannette gave the young Donald some food; and exchanging his apparel for some belonging to her own deceased baby, she lulled him asleep; and placing him in the cradle of his predecessor, she began to prepare her design.

She dressed her lifeless infant in the costly robes which had been worn by the heir of Dungivan, placing also the ornaments of that nobleman about the little corpse; only reserving a gold chain, with a small miniature of the Thane attached to it, and which hanging loosely round the neck, might well be supposed to have dropt off in the water. As soon as it was dark, Allan went and flung the child into the river Clyde, accompanying the act with many heartfelt tears and sorrowful lamentations.

Jannette, most fortunately for their plan, had not mentioned to any of the neighbouring cottagers the death of her Ambrose. Under the pretence of the child's being afflicted with a contagious disease, she contrived to keep him in the upper chamber of her cottage, from which she so completely excluded the light, that, if anyone entered by chance, it was impossible to discover the deceit that had been practised.

The body of the infant was not discovered till the third day, when it was brought on shore by some young men who had been out in a boat fishing. It was soon recognized by the dress to be the young Lord Donald, (for the features were not now discernible), and was conveyed to the Castle of Dungivan. The Thane was overwhelmed with despair; he ordered a sumptuous funeral, and then immured himself in a solitary apartment of the north tower.

Allan waited on Muchardus to claim his promised reward, which he gave him, with much praise for his adroitness in performing his commands. Allan then repaired to Jannette, and gathering together what they wished to convey with them, left the cottage at the dead of night, and procured a conveyance to Perth, from whence they meant to travel to some remote part of Scotland, where they might dwell in safety, for they were not without fear of Muchardus, as they supposed that he would devise schemes to annihilate all those who were acquainted with his atrocities. Nor were their conjectures ill-founded;

Muchardus rested not till he had removed those whose aid he had purchased with his gold; and he felt great disappointment on discovering that Allan had escaped with safety.

To murder the Thane was the next purpose of Muchardus; but while he was deliberating on the best means to facilitate his design with safety to his own person, Dungivan was suddenly ordered to attend his monarch to England, where he was going to ratify some agreement he had entered into with the monarch of that kingdom; and the schemes of his treacherous friend were at that time defeated.

After passing some time in England, the Thane of Dungivan joined the Crusaders, and repaired to the Holy Land, where he performed wonders with his single arm against infidels. He passed sixteen years in foreign countries ere he revisited his native place, which he did with a determination to domesticate there in peace for the remainder of his days.

He was yet in the prime of his age; and his valour had made him an object of esteem and admiration. All the neighbouring nobility gave splendid entertainments in honour of his return. – Among the rest, Muchardus, with whom he had instantly renewed the friendship of their youth, was not slow in preparing the banquet, and planning the death of his unsuspecting guest.

The manner in which Muchardus obtained his ill-acquired grandeur has already been described; but he was not happy. To divert his thoughts from dwelling on the past events of his life, which were not of a nature to bear retrospection, he resolved to marry. There was an heiress of great property, who had been consigned to his guardianship by her deceased father. The beauty of Lady Catharine fascinated his senses, while her accumulating wealth held out a lure to his avarice, and fondness for ostentatious parade. Muchardus was still handsome; few men were more indebted to nature for the gifts she had so lavishly bestowed on him. His countenance was formed to command: but the tyrannical passions and habits he had for many years imbibed, sometimes spread over his features a fierceness almost terrific. Lady Catharine beheld him with a fixed aversion. Two years she had resided at Dungivan, and had witnessed enough of his disposition to make her shrink with terror, and daily deplore the infatuation by which her parent was blinded, when he chose the Thane during her minority.

At this period, Caledonia was much governed by the influence of the Weird Sisters. From the birth of young Donald, they had resolved to protect him, and work his weal, and the woe of his father's murderer.

Allan had long since lost his Jannette. He beheld Donald with the most fervent affection. The noble and heroic mind of the youth often called forth his wonder and admiration. A native dignity, that adorned his soul, was not subdued by present poverty, or the small expectations he had of acquiring any worldly wealth. Allan could not subdue the regret that constantly arose when Donald met his view; he wished to see him fill the place in society which was his right; but his fears, and the improbability of his tale being believed, made him bury the secret in his bosom.

He had been very successful in the tilling of a small farm, which he had purchased with part of the money which Muchhardus had given him as a reward for the supposed murder of the child. All the savings which arose from this source were hoarded for Donald; for he had always retained that appellation from the time of his protectors leaving the precincts of Dungivan. The youth was now in his twentieth year, and the above-mentioned savings Allan was debating with himself how he could best lay out for the benefit of Donald, when he received an intimation from one of the Weird Sisters, that he was to return with his young charge to the banks of the Clyde. Allan disposed of his farm, and obeyed the commands he had received; and he was once more settled in a cottage among the mountains of Dungivan; and heard with horror of the murder of the late Thane, which, from the proofs he had already had of the villainy of the present one, he was not slow in attributing to him.

Time had silvered over the head of Allan, and so altered his person, that no one recognized him as Allan, under the name he thought it now expedient with his own safety to assume.

According to the instructions he had received from the Weird Sisters, he repaired to all the neighbouring Thanes, and made an avowal of the transaction in which he had been engaged with respect to the heir of Dungivan, and the way he was preserved by Jannette's interposition.

A particular mark, which Allan asserted to be on the back of Donald's neck, was well known to several of the nobles, who had heard it remarked while the heir was yet in his infancy; this, and several other convincing circumstances, placed his identity beyond a doubt: but none of them were willing to make an enemy of the fierce Muchardus, whose power and undaunted exploits had effectually awed the neighbouring chieftains from interfering in his concerns. Nor could all the endeavours of the aged Allan raise the hapless youth one friend to assert his rights, and the poor old man soon expired under the pressure of the regret that he experienced.

Donald was ignorant of these applications, and the purport of them; for Allan had never disclosed to him the nobleness of his birth. He knew his lofty spirit would not suffer him to sink into silent obscurity while an usurper enjoyed his domains. And what could his single arm effect against his deadliest foe, who would inevitably hurl him to destruction?

Though none of the chieftains would engage in the cause of the orphan, yet their converse on the subject was not carried on so secretly, but that it reached the ears of Muchardus, and gave him the most dire apprehensions; though he openly derided the report as a most absurd imposture.

Anxious to know if he should possess his guilty honours unmolested, and win the love of the beauteous Lady Catharine, he resolved to seek the Weird Sisters. For this purpose he left Dungivan Castle, attended by Sandy, the only domestic he took with him, and repaired to a forest near the cave of Fingal, where the mysterious Sisters were said to resort, and perform their midnight orgies.

When he approached the spot, he directed Sandy to wait his return at the foot of a large tree, which he pointed out to his notice. He then proceeded fearfully on. The soul of the Thane was appalled; the wind rose to a tremendous height; the thunder rolled over his head, and the blue lightning flashed in his face – terror-struck, he resolved to give up his design of visiting the Sisters; but he had lost the path which led back to the castle, and he wandered he knew not whither. Now and then he beheld a faint light, which he hoped proceeded from the cave of some anchorite, where he could obtain shelter.

He soon came to a rock, in the hollow of which was a door partly open, whence issued a pale gleam of light. The door flew back at his touch, and he entered a misty cavern; the light increased to a supernatural brightness, and in a few moments the Weird Sisters appeared, and saluted him with a discordant voice.

> 'Hail! We know what brought thee here.
> Wicked chieftain, shake with fear,
> The assassin shuns his downy bed:
> Can he shun the restless dead?
> No, while in the forest drear,
> Roderic, rise, and meet him here!
> And the wounds he gave display.
> Remorse be his by night and day.'

The mysterious Sisters then severally requested what he sought to know. 'Ask!' – 'Require!' – 'Demand!' – exclaimed the Weird Beings.

Muchardus inquired if he should perish by an avenging sword.

The first Sister replied, 'that no human power should harm Muchardus.'

He then demanded who was next to enjoy the domains of Dungivan.

The second Sister answered, 'that the lawful heir of the murdered Roderic, and his bride, Lady Catharine, the peerless rose of the Clyde, would succeed him.'

Muchardus's heart appeared to die within him at these words; and it was not till the third Sister again repeated the question, of what he sought to know, that he recovered sufficiently to ask how many years of his existence still remained.

The bearded sister would not give an explicit answer to this important question; but remarked to him, that he had once seen the apparition of the murdered Roderic.

Muchardus, while his frame trembled with horror at the recollection of the appalling scene he had witnessed in one of the galleries of the castle, faintly replied in the affirmative.

'Mark me then,' said the witch; 'you will not survive the third appearance of the dreadful spectre.'

The sisters then vanished from his view: and Muchardus, affrighted at the gloom (for the witches had left him in total darkness), was going to quit the cave with precipitation, when the murdered Roderic stood before him, and intercepted his progress.

Muchardus gazed on the hairy form with the greatest agony, till a chilling sweat bedewed his forehead; his limbs failed him, and he fell senseless on the floor of the cave.

In this situation he was found by Sandy, who alarmed by the Thane's long absence, ventured from his leafy shelter, as soon as the storm had abated, to seek him; in which charitable design he succeeded with some difficulty, and was much terrified with meeting the Weird Sisters in his path, who maliciously diverted themselves with exciting his fears, and then suffered him to proceed.

He found his master just recovering from a death-like swoon. He assisted him to rise; and Muchardus, having glanced his eye around, and, to his great relief, perceiving no spectre, exerted himself to leave the horrid cave; and was led by Sandy to the Castle, where he retired to his splendid couch the most miserable of human beings.

Donald, since the death of Allan, his supposed parent, had remained in his cottage, as he had not yet met with the opportunity he coveted of embracing a military life.

In his solitary walks about the mountains, he frequently met Lady Catharine, and her attendant, Moggy Cameron. A fervent passion for the noble fair one took possession of his bosom; and he reasoned with himself in vain against its increasing influence; for Love, that leveller of rank, was constantly inspiring him with hope.

Lady Catharine was not insensible to the attentions of Donald; and she often breathed forth a secret prayer that he had been of equal birth with herself.

Near five weeks had elapsed since their first casual meeting, when one morning the Lady Catharine being with some of her attendants on the Clyde, in a small sailing-boat, a sudden gust of wind upset it; and the fair lady was precipitated into the water, Donald, who had been walking on the banks for some time, and surveying the lovely Catharine with delight, as the vessel slowly glided along, immediately saw her danger, and plunged into the stream to snatch her from impending death. He happily succeeded in bearing his lovely burthen safe to the shore, and led her till they arrived at the castle gates, where he abruptly left her, ere she could express her thanks for the service he had rendered so opportunely.

From this auspicious day, gratitude, united to love, created for Donald a strong interest in her heart: yet prudence bade her avoid him; there was no prospect that the prejudices which her friends would entertain against such a suitor, could be overcome, and she resolved to spare him and herself, if possible from the pangs of a hopeless passion.

Donald no longer met her in his walks; he felt the change in her behaviour most severely, and became a votary of sorrow and despair, courting the influence of these passions in the still hours of the night, wandering among precipices and dreary forests. Chance led him to the cave where Muchardus had obtained an audience with the Weird Sisters, about an hour after that Thane had quitted it. The Sisters again appeared. Instead of cringing to them with the abject servility of Dungivan's usurping lord, he demanded with some sternness, what they wanted with him. But his asperity was soon transformed into profound respect, when they expressed their solicitude for his weal, and claimed his attention to what they had to impart.

The eldest of the Weird Sisters then gave a concise account of the crimes of the present Thane, and informed Donald that he was at that time plotting his destruction; being in dread of his revenge, and his gaining the affections of Lady Catharine.

The Weird Sisters then joined in admonishing him as to his future conduct; and one of them delivered to Donald a white silk flag, on which were woven some mysterious characters. This, she told him, would once, and once only, be of singular service to him in extreme danger, and that being the case, she exhorted him not to try its efficacy till all other resources had failed, and his own exertions proved abortive.

Donald took a courteous leave of the bounteous Sisters; and repaired to his cottage in a far different frame of mind from that he had ever experienced before. His birth was noble – worthy of Lady Catharine; and he felt that it was possible for time and perseverance to bestow on him a happiness which the preceding day he had regarded as unattainable.

The next day he was informed by a person who had a sincere regard for his safety that the Thane had discovered him to be the lawful heir of the domain, and had privately suborned persons to assassinate him, not assigning the true reason for that horrid design, but charging him with the attempt to seduce Lady Catharine from her duty, by persuading her to leave the castle of her guardian, and share a beggar's fate. – That lady, the informant added, was now strictly confined within the circle of her own apartments, and forced to listen to the hateful addresses of the Thane.

Donald on receiving this intimation, thought it most prudent to leave his present habitation, and repair to the court of King Malcolm, and submit the cause to him. In searching the papers of the deceased Allan, he discovered a written attestation of the deceit he had practised to save the infant's life, describing some particular marks of fruit he had on his body, together with the chain he wore round his neck, which was now fastened to the paper.

These proofs were very consoling to Donald, and made him commence his journey with more alacrity; and by the noon of the day on which he set out, he had travelled many miles. The heat of the midday sun greatly incommoded him, and he grew faint and weary.

A neat cottage presented itself to view, and he knocked at the door to request admittance, that he might rest till the cool of the evening. This the loquacious hostess denied him; and during his expostulations with her on the subject, she unguardedly betrayed to his knowledge, that her inhospitable refusal was owing to her having sheltered Lady Catharine, who had escaped from the Castle to her humble roof, she having been led hither by her attendant, Moggy Cameron, who was daughter to the cottager.

Donald had betrayed so much emotion during the recital, that the good dame, alarmed at the consequences that might ensue from her communicating so much to a stranger, entered the dwelling, and closed the door.

Donald, hurt at her manner, and disappointed at not obtaining an interview with Lady Catharine, to whom he wished to impart the intelligence he had received from the Weird Sisters, and worn out by fatigue, fainted at the door of the cottage. The noise he made in falling, brought its inmates to his relief; and Lady Catharine instantly recognized her faithful Donald. He soon revived; and the fair one had just listened with pleasing surprise to his narrative, when a party of Muchardus's soldiers, who had been sent in pursuit of the fugitives, arrived, and conveyed the lovers to the Castle, where Donald was confined in a dungeon, and Sandy, having interfered in the behalf of the young lord, was also made a prisoner; and guards were set over them; but, by a successful strategem of Moggy, who intoxicated their keepers, and procured the keys, they were liberated, and quitted the Castle walls.

By the direction of Moggy, they repaired to an isolated building about two miles from Dungiven; and in less than an hour they were joined by Lady Catharine and her attendants, they having escaped from the spies which Muchardus had set round them, by means of a subterraneous winding, which led from the stairs of the north tower to a grotto that terminated one of the avenues of the Castle grounds.

They proceeded in their flight for two days unmolested when, alas! they were again taken in the toils, and the Thane in person headed the pursuers.

As soon as they arrived at the Castle, Muchardus ordered some of his followers to take young Donald to the cave of Fingal (a long subterraneous passage cut through a rock, and filled with a branch of the river), in a boat, and destroy him. In vain Catharine knelt, and besought him to avert the sentence; he was inexorable; and the fair one, frantic with despair, rushed out of the Castle ere the Thane had time to intercept her progress. Sandy, who had attentively watched her, followed, and by her directions procured a boat, and repaired with her to the cave of Fingal. They arrived there first; and securing the boat in one of the inlets, Lady Catharine hid herself behind a projection of the rock, to watch the actions of the Thane, who soon arrived in a boat only, attended by the man who handled the oars. Contrary to the expectations of Catharine, Muchardus suspected her being in the cave, and soon discovered her hiding place, from which he dragged her into his boat, just at the instant that the one in which Donald and his intended assassins were sitting, entered the place pitched on for the scene of his destruction.

Catharine, in her struggles to get from the Thane fell into the water, and would have perished, but for the activity of Sandy, who succeeded in replacing her in the boat which had conveyed her hither, while Donald, who was a confined spectator of the accident, was almost senseless with despair.

The Thane now offered to grant Donald his life, if he would renounce his presumptuous claim and the hand of Lady Catharine; but the youth rejected the proposal with the scorn it merited. A secret impulse made Muchardus wish to save the youth's life, if he could consistent with his own terms; and he vowed to release him, and provide for his future weal, if Lady Catharine would instantly become his bride, and resign all thought of Donald. She gave an heroic refusal; and the enraged Thane ordered the assassins to strangle their victim. Struggles were of no avail; the youth remembered the injunctions of the Weird Sisters, and waved the flag three times in the air. The Spectre of his Sire arose in the midst of the water, and pronounced the doom of his vile murderer, who sank with the boat and perished.

Donald was instantly conveyed with Lady Catharine back to the Castle, where the most lively transports of joy took place among the domestics at receiving the son of Roderic for their lord; for they had groaned under the tyranny of Muchardus.

Donald found no difficulty in getting his title acknowledged by his sovereign; and his union with the fair Catharine was productive of the utmost felicity to themselves and their offspring.

# Secrets of Cabalism

*or*

*Ravenstone and Alice of Huntingdon*

## William Child Green
## (Dates unknown)

Another man in the same mould as Francis Lathom was William Child Green, described by one contemporary report as 'the favourite of the circulating libraries'. These institutions which made popular literature inexpensively available to the ordinary people and, secretly, not a few of the gentry, thrived in most towns and cities of Britain and had a voracious appetite for all the thrilling and romantic reading material which publishers could supply them. And, although he wrote a mere eight Gothic novels, such was the storytelling ability of William Green that his productions were seized upon by footman and scullery maid alike throughout the length and breadth of the country.

Of the man we know very little except that he lived in Walworth, London, and was a frequent guest at the best literary and social circles of the time. In conversation he apparently admitted to having been influenced by Mrs Radcliffe and Matthew Lewis, but this seems to have been more in terms of absorbing the popular aspects of their writing rather than slavishly copying their plots and ideas as others did. Among his most successful works were *The Maniac of the Desert* (1821) and *The Prophecy of Duncannon* (1824) both based on actual events.

Green, in fact, was a keen student of history and an avid collector of old legends and folk tales, and this penchant can be seen to good effect in the following story which was published anonymously in a Christmas annual, circa 1819. It was undoubtedly written before he had begun work on any of his novels and despite its imperfections, shows several new methods of evoking Gothic terror which we have not encountered before in these pages.

ON the evening of the 29th of June, 1555, in one of the narrow streets near the Poultry Compter, in London, a dark square-built ruffian, in a thrum cap and leathern jerkin, suddenly sprung forth from his hiding-place, and struck his dagger with all his force against the breast of a man passing by. 'By my holidam,' said the man, 'that would have craved no thanks if my coat-hardy had been thinner – but thou shalt have a jape (a fool's mark) for thy leman to know thee by,' – and flourishing a short gisarme, or double-pointed weapon, in his left hand, with his right, on which he seemed to wear an iron glove, he stamped a sufficient mark on the assassin's face, and vanished in a moment.

'Why, thou Lozel!' said another ruffian, starting from beneath a penthouse, 'wast playing at barley-break with a wooden knife? Thou wilt hardly earn twenty pounds this bout.'

'A plague on his cloak, Coniers! – he must have had a gambason under it. – Thou mayest earn the coin thyself; – thou hast gotten a gold ring and twenty shillings in part payment.'

Get thee gone to thy needle and baudekin again, like a woman's tailor as thou art! Thou hast struck a wrong man, and he has taken away thy nose that he may swear to the right one. – That last quart of huff-cap made froth of thy brains.'

'My basilard is sharp enough for thee, I warrant,' muttered his disappointed companion, as he drew his tough hyke or cloak over his bruises, and slunk into a darker alley. Meanwhile, the subject of their discourse and of their villany strode with increased haste towards the Compter-prison, and inquired for the condemned prisoner, John Bradford. The keeper knew Bishop Gardiner's secretary, and admitted him without hesitation, hoping that he brought terms of grace to the pious man, whose meek demeanour in the prison had won love from all about him. The secretary found him on his knees, as his custom was, eating his square meal in that humble posture, and meditating with his hat drawn over his face. He rose to receive his visitors and his tall slender person, held gracefully erect, aided a countenance which derived from a faint bloom and a beard of rich brown, an expression of youthful beauty such as a painter would not have deemed unworthy the great giver of the creed for which he suffered. Gardiner's secretary uncovered his head, and, bending it humbly, kissed his hand with tears. 'Be of good comfort, brother,' said Bradford, – 'I have done nothing in this realm except in godly quietness, unless at Paul's Cross, where I bestirred myself to save him who is now Bishop of Bath, when his rash sermon provoked the multitude.'

'Ah, Bradford! Bradford!' replied his visitor, 'thou didst save him who will now burn thee. Had it not been for thee, I had run him through with my sword that day!' Bradford started back, and looked earnestly, – 'I know thy voice now, and I remember that voice said those same words in my ear when the turmoil was at Paul's Cross. For what comest thou now? A man of blood is no fit company for a sinner going to die.'

'Not while I live, my most dear tutor; I am Rufford of Edlesburgh.'

The old man threw his arms about his neck, and hung on it for an instant. 'It is twelve years since I saw thee, and my heart grieved when I heard a voice like thine in the fierce riot at Paul's Cross. Art thou here bodily, or, do I only dream? There is a rumour abroad, that thy old enemy, Coniers, slew thee at Huntingdon last year.'

'He meant well, John Bradford, but I had a thick hilted pourpoint and a tough leathern cap; I have met his minions more than once, and they know what print my hand leaves. Enough of this – I am not in England now as Giles Rufford; I shall do thee better service as what I seem.'

'Seeming never was good service,' said the divine: 'what hast thou to do with me, who am in God's hands?'

'He makes medicines of asps and vipers,' answered his pupil; 'I shall serve him if I save his minister, though it be by subtlety. I have crept into Gardiner's favour by my skill in strange tongues and Hebrew secrets, therefore I am now his secretary: and I have an ally in the very chamber of our queen-mistress.'

'That woman is not unwise or unmerciful,' replied Bradford, 'in things that touch not her faith; but I will be helped by no unfair practice on her. Mercy with God's mercy will be welcome, but I am readier to die than to be his forsworn servant.'

'Master, there can be no evil in gathering the fruit Providence has ripened for us. Gardiner was Wolsey's disciple once, and hath more heathen learning in him than Catholic zeal. There is a leaven left of his old studies which will work us good. He believes in the cabalism of the Jews, and reads strange books from Padua and Antwerp, which tell him of lucky and lucky days. He shall be made to think tomorrow full of evil omens, and his superstition shall shake his cruelty.'

'Thou art but a green youth still,' rejoined Bradford, 'if thou knowest not that cruelty is superstition's child. Take heed that his heathenish witchcraft doth not shake both thy wit and thy safety. For though I sleep but little, and have few dreams of earthly things, there came, as I think, a vision raised by no holy art, into my prison last night. And it had such a touch of heaven's beauty in its face, and such rare music in its voice, that it well nigh tempted me to believe its promise. But I remembered my frailty, and was safe.'

The secretary's eyes shone brightly, and half a smile opened his lips. But he lowered both his eyes and his voice as he replied, 'What did this fair vision promise?'

'Safety and release, if I would trust her, and be pledged to obey her.' – There was a long pause before the young man spoke again. – 'Do you not remember, my foster-father, the wild laurel that grew near my birthplace? An astrologer at Pisa told me it should not wither till the day of my death. And it seems to me, when I walked under its shade, that the leaves made strange music, as if a spirit had touched them. It is greener and richer than its neighbours, and the fountain that flows near its root has, as men believe, a rare power of healing –

the dreams that visit me when I sleep near it are always the visitings of a courteous and lovely spirit. What if the legends of Greece and Syria speak truth? May we not both have guardian spirits that choose earthly shapes?'

'My son,' replied Bradford, 'those thoughts are the diamond-drops that lie on the young roses of life; but the Sun of Truth and Reason should disperse them. Man has one guardian, and he needs no more unless he forgets that One. Thou wast called in thy youth the silken pleader, because thy words were like fine threads spun into a rich tissue. Be wary lest they entangle thee, and become a snare instead of a banner fit to guide Christians. I am a blighted tree marked for the fire, and thou canst not save me by searing the freshness of thy young laurel for my sake.'

'I will shame the astrologer tomorrow,' said the pupil; 'and therefore I must make this hour brief. She who rules the queen's secrets has had a bribe to make Mary merciful. There is hope of a birth at court, and death ought not to be busy. Fare-ye-well! but do not distrust that fair apparition if it should open these prison-doors tomorrow.' — So saying, the young man departed without heeding Bradford's monitory gesture.

Stephen Gardiner, Bishop of Winchester, and High Chancellor by Mary's favour, sat that night alone and thoughtful in his closet. He had been the chief commissioner appointed to preside at Bradford's trial: and though he had eagerly urged his colleagues to condemn him, he secretly abhorred the time-serving cruelty of Bishop Bonner and the cowardice of Bourne, who had not dared to save the life of the benefactor but had begged to save his own. 'You have tarried late,' said Gardiner, as his secretary entered — 'the stars are waning, and their intelligence will be imperfect.'

'I traced it before midnight,' replied the secretary, 'but I needed the help of your lordship's science.'

'It is strange,' said the patron, leaning thoughtfully on one of Roger Bacon's volumes, 'that men in every age and climate, and of every creed, have this appetite for an useless knowledge — and it would be stranger, if both profane and sacred history did not shew us that such knowledge had been sometimes granted, though in vain. – What is that paper in thy hand?'

'It is a clumsy calculation, my lord, of this night's aspect. I learned in Araby, as your lordship knows, some small guesses at Chaldean astrology; but I deem the characters and engraven signs of the Hermetic men more powerful in arresting the intelligent bodies in the heavens. They were the symbols used by Pythagoras and Zoroaster, and their great master Apollonius.'

'Ignatius Loyola and Athanasius Kircher did not disdain them,' replied the Bishop, crossing himself – 'But what was the fruit of thy calculation?'

'Nothing,' answered his secretary humbly – 'nothing at least not already known to one more able than myself. The first of July is a day of evil omen, and the last day of June has a doubtful influence. My intelligence says, if life be taken on that day, a mitre will be among ashes.'

'Ha! and the heretics will think it if Bradford dies, for they are wont to say, he is worthier of a bishopric than we of a parish priesthood. Thou hast not yet told all.'

'My lord, I see the rest dimly. – There are symbols of a falling star and a flame quenched in blood. They tell of a gorgeous funeral soon.'

Gardiner was silent several minutes before he raised his head. 'Thou knowest, Ravenstone, that I was like the Jesuit Loyola, a student of earthly things, and a servant in profane wars before I took the cross. Therefore I sinned not when I learned as he did. And thou knowest he thought much of heathen and Egyptian conjuration; but that is not my secret. Plato and Socrates had their attendant demons. I have seen, it may be, such a one in a dream last night. Methought there stood by me in an oratory a woman of queen-like beauty and strange beauty. She shewed me, as it were beyond a mist, a green tree growing near a fountain, and the star that shone on that fountain was the brightest in the sky; but presently the tree grew wide and broad, and the light of the star set behind it. Then I saw in my cathedral at Winchester my own effigies on a tomb, but all the inscription was effaced and broken except the date, and I read "the first day of July" – Is it not strange, Raven-stone, that a dream should so well tally with thy planetary reck-oning? Yet I was once told by a witch-woman, that the Bishop of Winchester should read out Queen Mary's funeral sermon.'

'So he may, my lord,' said the secretary, who called himself Ravenstone, 'but there may be a White Bishop of Winchester.'

'Ah! I trow thy meaning – White is a shrewd churchman, and looks for my place. Hearken to me, then – I have a thought that evil is gathering against me tonight; to profit by a dream, I will go privily from London within this hour, and abide in secret at Winchester till the ides of June are past. But take thou my signet-ring, and put my seal and countersign to Bradford's death-warrant when it comes from court.'

'Does my lord think it will be sent?' said the secretary calmly – 'They say the queen's bedchamber-woman has told her, she will be the mother of no living thing if she harms ought that has life.'

'Tush – that woman is a crafty giglet, but we need such helps when a queen reigns. It was well done, Ravenstone, to promise her Giles Rufford's lands. Since the man is dead, and his heir murdered him, we will make Alice of Huntingdon his heiress.'

Not a muscle in the pretended Ravenstone's face changed, and his deep black eye was steady as he replied – 'It will be well done, my lord, if she is faithful. At what hour is John Bradford to die?'

'Bid the marshal of the prison have a care of him till four o'clock tomorrow morning, for he is a gay and glorious talker; and so was his namesake, mad John of Munster, even among red hot irons. Look to the warrant, Ravenstone, and see it speedily sent to Newgate. That done – nay, come nearer – I would speak in thine ear. There is a coffer in my private cham-ber which I have left unlocked. Attach my signet-ring to the silver chain, and let me know what thou shalt hear; but let this be done in the very noon of night, when no eye nor ear but thine can reach it.'

Ravenstone promised, and his hand trembled with joy as he received the ring. It was already almost midnight, and Gardiner, as he stole out of his house, stopped to look at the moon's rainbow, then deemed a rare and awful omen. 'Alice of Huntingdon is busy,' said he, with a ghastly smile, 'but the dead man's land will be free enough for the blue-eyed witch – she cannot buy a husband without it.' – And stealing a look at Ravenstone, the Chancellor-bishop departed.

'I am a fool,' said young Ravenstone to himself, 'and worse than a fool, to heed how this wanton giglet may be made fit for a knave's bribe, – and yet that this dull bigot, this surly and selfish drone, should have such glimpses of a poet's paradise, is a wonder worth envying. I have heard and seen men in love with Platonic superstition under the hot skies of Spain, where the air seems as if it was the breathing of kind spirits and the waters are bright enough for the dwelling; but here in this foggy island – in this old man's dark head and iron heart! I will see what familiar demon stoops to hold converse with such a sorcerer.'

And young Ravenstone locked himself in his chamber, not ill-pleased that his better purpose would serve as covert and gilding for his secret passion to pry into his patron's mystery. He arrayed his person in the apparel he had provided to equip him as Gardiner's representative; and while he threw it over the close purpoint and tunic which fitted his comely figure, he smiled in scorn as he remembered the ugliness and decrepitude he meant to counterfeit. At the eleventh hour, when the darkness of the narrow streets, interrupted only by a few lanterns swinging above his head, made his passage safe, he admitted himself into the Bishop's house by a private postern, of which he kept a master-key. By the same key's help he entered the chamber, and ringing his patron's silver bell, gave notice to the page in waiting that his presence was needful. When this confidential servant entered, he was not surprised to see, as he supposed, the bishop seated behind his leathern screen muffled in his huge rochet or lawn garment, as if he had privately returned from council, according to his custom. 'Hath no messenger arrived from the court?' said the counterfeit prelate. 'None, my lord, for the queen, they say is sore sick.' – 'Tarry not an instant if one cometh, and see that the marshal of the compter be waiting here to take warrant, and execute it at his peril before day-break.' The page retired; and Ravenstone, alone, saw the coffer standing on its solitary pedestal near him. It was unlocked, and he found within it only a deep silver bowl with a chain poised exactly in its centre. Ravenstone was no stranger to the mode of divination practised with such instruments. What could he risk by suspending the signet-ring as Gardiner had requested? His curiosity prevailed, and the ring when attached to the silver chain vibrated of itself, and struck the sides of the bowl three times distinctly. He listened eagerly to its clear and deep sound, expecting some response, and when he looked up, Alice of Huntingdon stood by his side.

This woman had a queen-like stature, to which the height of her volupure, or veil, twisted in large white folds like an Asiatic turban, gave increased majesty. Her supertunic, of a thick stuff, in those days called Stammel, hung from her shoulders with that ample flow which distinguishes the drapery of a Dian in ancient sculpture. 'You summoned me,' she said, 'and I attend you.'

Ravenstone, though he believed himself sporting with the superstition of Gardiner as with a tool, felt startled by her sudden appearance; and a thrill of the same superstitious awe he had mocked in his patron, passed through his own blood. But he recollected his purpose and his disguise; and still keeping the cowering attitude which befitted the bishop, he replied, 'Where is thy skill in divination if thou knowest not what I need?'

'I have studied thy ruling planet,' said Alice of Huntingdon, 'and as thy wishes are without number, so they are without a place in thy destiny. But I have read the signs of Mary Tudor's, and I know which of her high officers will lose his staff this night.'

'Knowest thou the marks of his visage, Alice?' asked the counterfeit bishop, bending down his head, and drawing his hood still farther over it.

'Hear them,' replied Alice: 'a swarthy colour, hanging look, frowning brows, eyes an inch within his head, hooked nose, wide nostrils, ever snuffing the wind, a sparrow-mouth, great hands, long talons rather than nails on his feet, which make him shuffle in his gait as in his actions – these are the marks of his visage and his shape; none can tell his wit, for it has all shapes. Dost thou know this portrait, my Lord of Winchester?'

'Full well, woman,' answered Ravenstone, 'and his trust is in a witch whose blue eyes shame heaven for lending its colour to hypocrisy; and her flattery has made boys think the tree she loved and the fountain she smiled on became holy. And now she serves two masters, one blinded by his folly, the other by his age.'

Ravenstone, as he spoke, dropped the rochet-hood from his shoulders, and shaking back his long jet-black hair, stood before her in the firmness and grace of his youthful figure. Alice did not shrink or recede a step. She laughed, but it was a laugh so musical, and aided by a glance of such sweet mirth, that Ravenstone relaxed the stern grasp he had laid upon her mantle. 'The warrant, Alice! It is midnight, and the marshal waits – where is the warrant for John Bradford's release?'

'It is in my hand,' she said, 'and needs only thy sign and seal; here is the handwriting of our queen.'

Ravenstone snatched the parchment, but did not rashly sign without unfolding it. 'Thou art deceived, Alice, or willing to deceive; this is a marriage contract, investing thee with the lands of Giles Rufford as thy dowry.'

'And to whom,' asked she, smiling, 'does my queen-mistress licence me to give it by her own manual sign?'

Ravenstone looked again, and saw his name entered, and himself described as the husband chosen for her maid of honour by Queen Mary. 'Has she also signed,' he said, the reprieve of John Bradford?'

'It is in my hand, and now in thy sight Henry Ravenstone; but the seal that will save thy friend may not be placed till thou hast given sign and seal to this contract. Choose! –'

The warrant for Bradford's liberation was spread before him, and her other hand held the contract of espousals. He smiled as he met the gaze of her keen blue eyes, and wrote the name of Henry Ravenstone in the blank left for it. She added her own without removing those keen eyes from his; and placing the parchment in her gipsire, suffered him to take the warrant of his friend's release. It was full and clear, but when he turned to seek the chancellor's signet-ring, the coffer had closed upon it. 'Blame thyself, Ravenstone!' said Alice of Huntingdon; 'thou hast laughed at the tales of imps and fairies, yet thou hadst woman's weakness enough to pry into that coffer and expect a miracle. As if thy master had not wit sufficient to devise a safe place for his ring, which thy curiosity placed there more than thy obedience! Didst thou think I came into this chamber like a sylph or an elfin, without hearing the stroke on the silver bowl which gave notice thou wast here? Truly, Ravenstone, man's vanity is the only witch that governs him.'

'Beautiful demon! when the crafty churchman who tutors thy cunning has no need of it, will thy master, the great Prince of Fire, save thee from the stake?'

'My trust in myself,' she answered; and throwing her cloak and wimple on the ground, she loosened her bright hair till it fell to her feet, and waving round her uncovered shoulders, and amongst the thin blue silk that clung to her shape, like wreaths of gold. Her eyes, large and brilliant as the wild leopard's, shone with such imperial beauty as almost to create the triumph they demanded. 'Be no rebel to my power, Ravenstone, for it is thy safety. Gardiner has ordered Bradford's death without appeal, and feigned his dream of danger to decoy thee here! But I have earned a fair estate by serving him, and thou mayest share it with me.' 'Thy wages are not yet paid, Alice!' he replied, grinding his teeth. 'That fair estate is mine, and that contract can avail thee nothing without my will – Henry Ravenstone is a name as false as thy promise to save Bradford.' Alice paused an instant, then laughing shrilly, clapped her hands thrice. In that instant the chamber was filled with armed men, who surrounded and struck down their victim notwithstanding his desperate defence. 'This is not the bishop!' one of the men exclaimed, 'this is not Stephen of Winchester; we shall not be paid for this.' 'He is Giles Rufford of Huntingdon,' answered his companion, the ruffian Coniers, 'and I am already paid.' Alice would have escaped had not the length of her dishevelled hair enabled her treacherous accomplices to seize it. They twined it round her throat to stifle her cries, making her boasted beauty the instrument of her destruction. She was dragged to Newgate on a charge of sorcery, and executed the next morning by John Bradford's side, in male attire, lest her rare loveliness should excite compassion. He knew her, and looking at the laurel-stems mingled with the faggots, said, as if conscious of his young friend's death – 'Alas! the green tree has perished for my sake!' – It was indeed his favourite laurel, which had been hewn down with cruel malice for this purpose. The people, just even in their superstitions to a good man's memory, still believe the earth remains parched and barren where John Bradford perished on the first of July 1555; and his heart, which escaped the flames, like his fellow martyr's, Archbishop Cranmer's, was embalmed and wrapped in laurel-leaves. His memory is sanctified by the religion honoured, while Alice of Huntingdon's sunk among dust and ashes, as a worthy emblem of the Cabalism she practised.

# The Unknown!

or

## The Knight of the Blood-Red Plume

## 'Anne of Swansea'
## (Mrs Julia Anne Curtis)
## (1764–1838)

Not a few of the authors of Gothic novels seem to have been
'characters' in their own right – flamboyant, outrageous, and frequently the topic of public conversation. This seems to have applied
to women as well as men and in Mrs Julia Anne Curtis, or 'Anne of
Swansea' as she was known, we have an almost typical example.

This lady's early life seems to have passed without too much incident, but after a bigamous first marriage and then being swiftly
made a widow by her second husband, she achieved considerable
notoriety by attempting to poison herself in Westminster Abbey. Her
sister, the famous actress Sarah Siddons, then made arrangements
for her to live in Swansea and it was here that for a time she became
the mistress of the actor Edmund Kean, actually writing a drama for
him in 1809.

There was no containing her love of flamboyance, however, and
she was soon a renowned local figure carousing around the city and
proclaiming herself as the youngest sister of Mrs Siddons. When
news of this behaviour reached the actress she endeavoured to contain the scandal by offering Mrs Curtis an annual sum of £20 a year
'on condition that she permanently resides not less than one hundred and fifty miles from London'.

This act of disapproval may well have had the desired effect, for
the lady then turned to writing in earnest – her first work appearing
to considerable praise in Welsh journals and then in volume form
through a leading London publisher. Her *Sicilian Mysteries* (1812)

and *Deeds of the Olden Times* (1826) were among the most popular books of their respective years. The following legend which has been authoritatively attributed to Mrs Curtis concerns the ruined castle of Rhuddlan which stands on the River Clwyd in Flintshire and is the subject of a number of supernatural tales.

'– STAY, pilgrim; whither wendst thou?'

'– Cold is the north wind that plays around the mountains – heart-chilling the snow that's wafted across the moor – still bleaker blows the blast, cutting, keen, and freezing, as the grey mist of evening falls upon the vales; – frozen is the path that winds through yon forest; upon the leafless trees hangs the winters' hoary frost – and cheerless the bosom of him doom'd to wander along the lone path in such a night as this.'

'– Turn thee, pilgrim! and bend thy step to Rhuddlan's ruined walls, where thou mayst, undisturbed, waste the gloomy night, and take the morning to enjoy the road.'

'– Pious hermit! knowst thou not, from dusky eve until return of morn, that tortured spirits in yon castle rove? E'en now, the blood runs chill in my veins, while I do think on what I've seen. Such groans have met my ears – such sights my eyes – and screams and riotous laughs mingled with the winds that whistled through the broken arches of the courts – e'en now, the sweat of terror dews my brow, and languid beats my heart.'

'– Say, didst thou penetrate the hall?'

'– I did; and, on the hearth, some dried leaves to warm my shivering frame. I spread my wallet's fare upon the ground – with joyful heart, began to merry make – but angry spirits broke upon my glee, and fearful noises hailed my livid cheek. Instantly I dropped upon my trembling knee, and told my beads; but the screams increased – a ray of flame shot through the room, and before me stood a warrior in complete armour clad – his casque was down, and above his brow there waved a blood-red plume. No word he spake, but looked upon me with earnestness; his eye was as the sloe, black – as the basilisk's fascinating – his cheek was wan and deathlike. I would have fled, but my feet seemed chained to the ground, and my heart feared to beat against my bosom. At this moment I heard a female voice, that loudly sounded in the hall. – "I come, Erilda," cried the red-plumed knight; and instantly vanished. Again were the screams repeated; and showers of blood fell upon the marble flooring on which I stood. – My veins were filled with icicles from my heart; but, rendered desperate by fear, in the midst of the most horrible howlings, I flew; and the expiring embers of my fire casting a faint light, guided me along the courts through which I darted with the rapidity of lightning. Venerable hermit, again I dare not trust myself in Rhuddlan's walls. I have opposed my bosom to the Saxon's sword, and never trembled; I have braved dangers for my country, and was never known to tremble; – but I dare not face the spirits of the angry Clwyd.'

The hermit smiled.

'– Thou seest yon rock, which, threatening, hangs above the river – which, rippling along, now laves against its broken sides. In the bosom of that rock, I dwell. Peace is its inmate. My cell is humble, but hospitable; and in its lap the weary pilgrim has often found repose. Rest thou with me this night to share it, friend, and eke my frugal meal.'

'– Holy father with joy I follow you; hunger and fatigue sore oppress me; and my wearied limbs almost refuse their wonted office.'

The venerable hermit conducted the wearied pilgrim to his cell, which was clean – his meal was wholesome. The pilgrim ate of the frugal repast; and a crystal water, springing from the rock, was the beverage on which the man of piety regaled. This was proferred in a rudely carved wooden bowl to his guest, who drank, and felt relieved. He now drew his stool near the hearth, on which the faggot blazed; and the hermit, to beguile the moments, and remove the fear which occupied his companion's breast, thus related of the Knight of the Blood-red Plume and the fair Erilda.

High on the walls of Rhuddlan waved the black flag of death – loud the bell of the neighbouring priory tolled the solemn knell, which every vale re-echoed round, and the sad response floated to the ear through every passing gale. – The monks, in solemn voice, sung a mass for the everlasting repose of the deceased – a thousand tapers illumined the chapel – and bounteously was the dole distributed to the surrounding poor. The evening blast was keen – the grey mist circled the mountain's craggy brow – and thin flakes of snow beat in the traveller's face, while cold and shivering airs wafted his cloak aside. Sir Rhyswick the Hardy heard, as he advanced, the echo of the distant bell; and spurring his mettled steed, with heart harbouring many fears, pursued his course fleetly through the forest.

'Use speed, Sir Knight!' cried a voice in his ear. 'Egberta dies!'

Rhyswick turned pale.

'Egberta's bosom's cold;' continued the voice, 'and vain will be your sighs.'

The Knight in dismay checked his horse, and inclined his head to whence he thought the sound proceeded; but nothing met his eye; all was vacant before him, and only the quivering bough, fanned by the breeze, was heard. Rather alarmed, he set spurs to the sides of his steed – still the snow was drifted in his face. Night was now ushered to the heavens, and it was with difficulty he could maintain the path that branched through the forest. The web-winged bat brushed by his ear in her circular flight; and the ominous screech-owl, straining her throat, proclaimed the dissolution of the deceased.

Sir Rhyswick heaved a sigh; a melancholy thought stole across his brain, and, arriving at the banks of the Clwyd, he beheld, with trembling, the many tapers in the priory of Rhuddlan, and heard more distinctly the solemn bell.

'Egberta is no more,' cried the voice that had before accosted him; 'Egberta is in Heaven.'

The Knight turned round; but, beholding no one, and agonized by the prediction, again he roused his steed, and flew, pale and breathless to the castle. He blew the loud horn suspended at the gate of Twr Silod, the strong tower which stands upon the banks of the river: and the loud blast echoing in the courts, aroused the ominous bird that had alighted on its battlements, who, flapping her heavy wings, resumed her flight, uttering a wild, discordant scream. The portal was opened to receive him; and Sir Rhyswick entered through a long range of vassals, habited in mournful weeds.

'Is the prediction true, then?' he exclaimed: and, rushing to the apartment of Egberta, found her cold and breathless. The colour that once adorned her cheek was faded – her eyes were shrouded – and her lips became more pale, from which the last breath had so lately issued. A serene smile mantled her countenance – her locks were carefully bound in rose-bands – her corpse was prepared for the earth – and two monks sat on each side of her, offering up their holy prayers for her repose. Sir Rhyswick, overcome by this unexpected sight, with a groan, fainted upon the couch. Some servants that had attended him from the hall, conveyed him in a state of insensibility to his chamber; and, the next day, the virtuous Egberta was deposited in the chapel of the castle. Maidens strewed the path with flowers, along which their sainted lady was borne; and some monks from the neighbouring priory sung a solemn dirge over her – bare-headed and with their arms crossed upon their bosoms. The fair Erilda with her own hands decked the person of her mother with flowers; and those flowers were moist with a daughter's tears. A requiem, chaunted by the monks, and in which the maiden joined, closed the ceremony; and Erilda, with oppressed heart, returned to the castle.

Sir Rhyswick, whose grief would not permit him to attend the funeral rites, pressed the affectionate girl to his bosom; and they sought mutual consolation in each other.

Rhyswick the Hardy was the friend and favourite of his prince; he had fought in all the wars of his country, since the first moment he could hurl the spear – victory had always attended his arms; but now, his beard was silvered with age – peace was restored to the land, and he had hoped, at Rhuddlan, in the bosom of his Egberta, to pass away his few remaining years. Bliddyn ap Cynvyn had united in himself by conquest, the sovereignty of Gwynedd, or North Wales, with Powys: and thus had terminated a war that had long threatened destruction to either nation. With pleasure did Wales observe her implac-

able enemy, the English, struggling to overcome a foreign foe –
bloody were the battles fought with William of Normandy, sur-
named the Bastard; and, with secret satisfaction, did Bliddyn
ap Cynvyn, a silent spectator, see either army reduced and weakened in the sanguinary contest. Sir Rhyswick had by his beloved
Egberta, (from whose fond arms the war had often torn him,
and who, in his last absence, being attacked by a sudden and
violent illness, in a few days expired), one only daughter. To
Erilda he now looked forward for future happiness. She was
beautiful as the morn – roseate health sat upon her smiling
cheek – meekness and charity in her lustre-beaming eye – her
teeth were as so many snowdrops, regularly even – her breath,
like the dewed rose-bud, of glowing fragrance – a dimple revelled playfully near her mouth – and the rich ringlets of her
yellow hair floated carelessly on her fine curved shoulders. Upon
her snowy breasts she wore a ruby cross, suspended by a gold
chain – and down her taper limbs the dazzling folds of her
white garments flowed. Erilda was not more beautiful in person than in mind; for, as lovely a bosom as ever nature formed,
encased a heart enrich with every virtue. She was the subject of
universal admiration; all tongues were lavish in her praise, and
many suitors came to ask her hand: but, though extremely sensitive, no one, as yet, claimed an interest in her heart: the warm
shaft of love had not pierced her glowing veins; and gay and
affable to all – reserved to few – she preserved that freedom
which the lover cannot retain. The loss of her mother imparted
a melancholy to her cheek, that rendered her far more lovely.
Sir Rhyswick indulged in grief, and the castle was one scene of
mourning. On the brow of the rock, that o'erlooks the angry
Clwyd, which rolls beneath, the poorer vassals and dependents
of Rhuddlan, every evening came to receive the bounty of their
young mistress. It was these excavations in the rock that echoed
the soft plaintive notes of her melodious harp. – On this rock
she sung, and the spirits of the murmuring river were charmed,
as they lay in their oozy bed, with the soft pleasing strains – the
billows ceased to roll in admiration, and Zephyrus drew back
his head, in mute attention to the rapturous lay.

Once, when the return of twilight was announced in the heavens, by the rich crimson streaks and blushing gold that occupied the vast expanse of sky, and Erilda accompanied with her voice the trembling harp, a warrior Knight, mounted on a barbed steed, in sable armour clad, with a Blood-red Plume waving on his brow, approached the spot from whence the sound proceeded. Erilda, on hearing the advance of horses' feet, turned hastily around; and, with modest courtesy, welcomed the Knight, who had thus obtruded on her privacy. There was something in his gait and appearance that struck her with awe; and the unknown, dismounting from his steed, occupied a seat beside her. Again she struck upon the trembling chords, with fearful hand. The stranger sighed, as he gazed upon her; and, when her eye met his, she withdrew it, blushing, on the ground. The shade of night approached, and misty fogs obscured the starry sky.

'Sir Knight,' she cried, with a courteous smile, while an unusual palpitation thrilled through her heart, of admiration mingled with fear, 'Rhuddlan's hospitable walls are ready to receive you; and no warrior passes her warlike towers, without partaking and acknowledging the munificence of Rhyswick the Hardy.'

'Fair lady!' replied the unknown, 'the hospitality of the gallant chieftain, so famed, is not unknown to me; but I must onward on my journey, nor taste the bounty which all admire.'

'Sir Knight! this is not courteous.'

'Lady, adieu! it must not be: I live in hopes that we shall meet again.'

Saying this, he pressed her hand to his lips, and mounting his steed, flew with the rapidity of the winds along the shadowed plain that stood before her. His horse, so fleet, seemed to skim along the ground: and in an instant he was borne from her sight.

Erilda was astonished; there was a wildness in the jet black eye of the unknown, that, while it fascinated, alarmed her – a beautiful colour tinged his cheek; but not of that nature to which she was accustomed. His locks were black and sleek – his figure was noble and commanding — his voice, though harmony itself, still conveyed a hollow sound that was not pleasing. In short, his whole appearance, while it charmed to admiration, filled her with a kind of tremor; and she returned to the palace of Rhuddlan, charmed, and at the same time awed, with the martial appearance of the stranger.

'What majesty in his countenance!' exclaimed she to herself. — 'What nobleness in his demeanour! And, ah! what melancholy seems to occupy his soul, that dims the sparkling lustre of his jet black eye, and clouds those animating features, otherwise beaming with cheerfulness. Surely such dejection is not natural in him? No, no; some hidden secret preys upon his heart; perhaps love, which, as I have heard bards relate, feeds upon the roseate hue of health — gives languor to the eye — paleness to the cheek — and despoils the heart of its manhood — that reduces firmness to trepidity — and poisons the noble mind with weaknesses that are engendered by timidity.'

Erilda sighed. — Sir Rhyswick met her as she was seeking her chamber; the good old man bore the resemblance of his grief upon his fretted cheek; but he endeavoured to be cheerful; and, with an assumed smile, he conducted her to the supper-hall.

Erilda vainly attempted to be gay, but variety of thought occupied her brain; the soul-inspiring song of the family bard charmed not her ear, who, at the board, when the gay goblet circulated at the tables, raised high his tuneful voice to the sublimest pitch, in commemoration of deeds of other days, and sung of triumph, and of glorious war.

Erilda, whose heart was affected by another subject, was not moved with the sweet sounds of the trembling harp, nor participated that emotion which the song of patriotism inspired in the breasts of the auditors. Had the theme been love, the air been plaintive as the ring dove's tender tale, Erilda's soul had wasted in the strain, and owned the power of music, when in melody with her feelings. Affectionately imprinting a kiss upon the bearded cheek of Sir Rhyswick, attended by her page, she bade adieu to the knight; and, retiring to her couch, attempted to lull those wild and troubled thoughts that agitated and oppressed her; but the blood-plumed knight, in her slumbers, stood before her: his graceful form – his pensive, melancholy countenance, she pictured to herself: and sighs of regret, when she awoke, and found the unreal image vanished, stole from her heaving breast.

With the first dawn of morning, Erilda arose, and flew to the monastery of Rhuddlan, to offer up her daily prayers. The holy father confessor gave her absolution, on a declaration of her errors; and again she sought the much-loved spot, where she had met the unknown. She looked towards the path he had taken the preceding evening, he no longer occupied it; and, seating herself upon the rock, she played an air, soft and melodious as the strains of Philomel; but, dissatisfied with her execution, she turned the instrument aside; her voice, she conceived, wanted its usual sweetness – the harp was out of tune – and her fingers, lingering upon the strings, damped the swelling note.

Erilda sighed, and sighed so deep, that the echo, from the excavated rocks, returned them to her ear. – At length the tear glistened in her eye.

'Why, why am I thus concerned for a wandering unknown, whom chance, perhaps, conducted to this spot for a first, and only time? Who, ere now, is leagues distant from my sighs, and who does not entertain one thought of me? Away, hope, thou delusive image, from my bosom – I never shall behold him more – my heart must harbour no such sighs.'

Saying this, with the firmness of resolution, she turned her step towards the castle. Sir Rhyswick was preparing for the chase; the hounds and hawks were abroad – all was noise and confusion – and Erilda consented to make one of the throng. Buckling on her breast the mantle of green, and slinging across her shoulder the bow and arrow quiver, mounted on a cream-backed palfrey, she joined them.

The adjacent forest echoed back the huntsmen's loud horns, and the affrighted deer pricked up their ears to the well-known blast. The yell of the dogs sounded in the deep glens –

the loud halloo succeeded — and nimbly o'er the bogs and marshes bounded the fleet object of their sport. It was noon when Sir Rhyswick ordered his vassals to strike their tents upon the plain; and, after refreshing them with a rich repast, again they repaired to renew the chase; the ripe mead, in a golden goblet, was presented to the fair Erilda, who, in the midst of her damsels, looked like the goddess of the wood — and Sir Rhyswick drank from the hirlas horn the soul-reviving cwrrw. Soon again was the panting deer pursued up craggy cliffs — through streams and valleys — over the heath — across the moor — and through the mazy forest. Erilda startled a speckled doe from the bosom of a dark glen; and drawing her arrow to the head, in the silver bow, pierced her in the breast. Though wounded the animal made good her flight, and darted away like lightning.

The heroic huntress fleetly pursued; while the horns and hounds echoed from another part of the plain. Long did the doe maintain her speed, and kept in sight, with the arrow in her breast, until the pale-faced moon appeared, emerging from a cloud, and silvering the glassy lake. At length, the wounded animal dropped, and instantly expired.

Erilda dismounted her steed; and now, she first discovered herself to be absent from her train, and at an hour when angry demons ride upon the air and mutter mischief. Cold winds wafted her brown hair aside; and fast descended the grey mist of evening. In vain Erilda listened to catch the halloo of the huntsmen. No longer the horn sounded in the vale — all was drear and silent, save the hollow murmuring of the wind, forcing its passage, sighing though the trees. Almost fainting with fear, she leaned upon her bow: she endeavoured to blow the horn that was suspended at her breast, but it fell from her grasp, and the bow shrunk from her hand. At length, summoning more fortitude, she remounted her steed; and not knowing what road to take, gave her horse the reins, trusting herself to the protection of her household spirit. — Away flew the impatient steed through the forest — over hill and dale: the turf trembled beneath his hoofs, and the white foam frothed at his extended nostrils. On a sudden, the bell of a neighbouring monastery sounded in the gale, and blazing torches were seen waving through different parts of a wood that lay before her. 'Hilli, oh ho!' cried the huntress, with hope animating her bosom; 'Hilli, oh ho!' but her voice returned responsive to her ear, and the flaming brands disappeared. Still she pursued the path, and fleetly flew the cream-backed palfrey on which she rode – now again the huntsman's horn was heard winding at a great distance, and now the approaching clank of horses' hoofs convinced her that the attendants of the chieftain, her father, were in pursuit of her. Erilda, checking her steed, awaited their coming up with her; but those in pursuit took a different route; and the sounds dying away, as the attendants receded, all was again hushed. At length, weary of suspense, she proceeded; and, turning the angle of a jutting rock that bulged in the fertile Clwyd, she observed a horseman slowly parading its banks. Pensive was his face – his right hand rested on a battleaxe – his left held the reins of a nut-brown courser – his soul seemed occupied by melancholy – his brain to be distracted by tormenting thoughts. – Erilda advanced towards him, and fixing her blue eyes upon his cheek, to her astonishment recognized the stranger Knight of the Blood-red Plume. His vizor was up, and melancholy tinged his whole countenance – a sigh, half suppressed, trembled on his lips – despondency seemed to depress his heart, that shed a transitory gloom over every feature, and preyed upon that energy of mind, which his interesting eye betrayed as certainly possessing. Erilda, unable to curb her impetuous steed, who reared upon his hind legs, and snorted in rage, called to the Knight, who, wrapped in thought, observed her not.

'Good stranger,' cried the daughter of haughty Rhuddlan's chieftain, 'I throw myself under your protection; conduct the strayed Erilda to Rhuddlan's hall, and the blessings of a distracted parent shall be yours.'

'Divine daughter of the first of chieftains,' replied the Knight, eagerly grasping his horse's reins; 'I am subject to your commands – my life shall be to your service.'

Erilda, smiling, gave him her hand, which he pressed respectfully to his lips: and, proceeding, the lofty turrets of Rhuddlan appeared in view. The pale moon, shedding her rays on its dark battlements, reflected them to the Clwyd, which in soft billows rippled beneath the mount on which it stood. Numberless torches were seen glaring in the hands of the disconsolate attendants of the chieftain, who, in the agony of grief, dispersed them round the country in search of her. All was bustle; and, no sooner did she appear among them, than loud shouts rent the air, and they flew to bear the welcome tidings to Sir Rhyswick. The stranger Knight conducted her across the courts; and the fond father, impatient to clasp her to his arms, hastened towards her. Erilda fell upon his bosom; and the tear of joy dropped from the old man's beard upon her shoulder. The Knight, in his turn, received the caresses of the venerable chieftain, who, boundless in his joy, would have lavished on him empires, had he had them to command.

'Tell me, Sir Knight,' cried Rhyswick, 'to whom am I indebted for the restoration of Erilda to my aged arms? Let me fall upon my knees at his feet, and bless him.'

'Hospitable chieftain, my name is Wertwrold, a forlorn and suffering wanderer; the world contains no home to shelter me — no friend to welcome me; but, though sorrows oppress my heart, I am ever ready to give joy to others, — Erilda is once more yours,' he added with a sigh, and bowing his head, was about to depart.

'Nay, stranger, this night you must share that joy which you have imparted to our breast, and make Rhuddlan your residence.'

'Your pardon,' cried the Knight, 'my envious fortune denies that I should taste of pleasure — I must away, ere the stars fade on the horizon.'

'Wertwrold,' returned Erilda, 'the maid whom you have protected entreats your stay — upon her knee entreats it: do not dispirit our festivity by your departure. Come, let me conduct you to marble-hall.'

The Knight, overpowered by their entreaties, at length

yielded; and Erilda taking him by the hand, introduced him to the festive board, where sat the harpers, tuning their strings, awaiting the approach of the chieftain and his guests. Wertwrold appeared struck with the dazzling splendour of the hall that had regaled princes: rich crimson tapestry hung down the walls in festoons fringed with gold, between pillars of the fairest marble, disposed at equal distances, supporting cornices of polished silver; the carved ceiling displayed emblematical devices of war and of the chase; in one part, Diana was painted with her bow; in another, Caractacus engaging the Romans.

Erilda conducted the Knight to a cedar stool, covered with crimson, and edged with gold, at the table, on which were profusely scattered carved goblets, sumptuously embossed, and flowing with ripe mead. The harpers, during the repast, raised their voices in praise of the ancestors of Rhyswick, and regularly traced his descent, in bardic song; describing each great feat his fathers had performed. And now, the midnight bell sounding, dissipated their mirth – the bards were dismissed – and Wertwrold was led to a couch by one of the attendants, after saluting the fair hand of Erilda, which she offered to him, in token of her favour. The morning dawned unusually splendid – the early dew sparkled on the grass blade – and the effulgent sun rising, tinted the horizon with his gay beams – gentle was the air that played around the mountains – sweet and odoriferous was the scented gale – the river Clwyd timidly flowing, fearful lest it should interrupt the calmness that prevailed, was scarcely seen to move – and Erilda, whose troubled thoughts the preceding evening had denied her rest, hastened to the delightful rock where she first beheld the stranger, Wertwrold; there to indulge in sighs, and those thoughts that, while they pained, pleased. The solitary spot afforded her an opportunity to indulge in the melancholy of her mind; here she could sit and gaze with pensive eye upon the calm waters, as they laved against the shore, and involve her brain in a chaos of bewildering reflection, unobserved by anyone. Erilda never knew till now what it was to love – never knew till now what sighs the absence of him or her we love creates – and now she felt the pains, was unable to sustain them. The Red-plumed Knight was master of her heart and of her fate; violent was the passion that raged in her bosom, threatening to consume her by a slow lingering fire; for it appeared impossible the passion could be gratified. Seated upon an arm of the rock that overhangs the Clwyd, tears flowing down her lovely cheeks, agitated by similar thoughts, and overcome by weight of her emotions, weary, not having tasted of repose the preceding night, she sunk into a slumber, her head reclined upon her lily arm.

Wertwrold left the castle to taste of the refreshing air, ere the Baron descended from his chamber, or the loud bell summoned them to breakfast. His feet, as if by instinct, led him to the spot where first Erilda had attracted his notice. How much was he astonished to behold the lovely maiden in a sweet sleep! He stood awhile to observe her, and the tenderest sensation thrilled through his whole soul; her auburn locks played carelessly upon her temples, and her blue eyes were shrouded with long dark lashes; the tint of the carnation was displayed upon her cheek – a perfect ruby colour were her lips – the white rose leaf, through which runs the blue enamelled vein, was not more fair than her forehead, or more sweet than her breath – the soft air that played around her, wafted the thin gauze aside that shadowed her snowy bosom, and revealed beauties, which monarchs, on beholding, would have languished to enjoy. – Wertwrold, transported in the ecstasy of passion, dropped upon his knee, and imprinted a kiss upon her cheek.

Erilda, at this moment, awoke; and the Knight, conscious of the crime he had committed, drew back, abashed and trembling. Erilda was alike confused, and Wertwrold, seizing this opportunity, clasped hold of her hand with fervour, and pressing it between his, exclaimed, 'Lovely Erilda, pardon the presumption which your beauty has inspired – if 'tis a crime to adore you, then am I most criminal; but I bow to my fate – doomed to be unhappy, I willingly resign myself the victim of cruel fortune.'

'Say, Sir Knight,' cried the embarrassed Erilda, lending her hand to raise him from the ground, 'why are you thus persecuted? Repose your sorrows in my bosom; indeed, you will find in me one much interested for you. – Erilda, from her heart pities you.'

'And does Erilda pity me?' he returned, rising, and assuming a seat by her side. 'Oh, welcome, ye sorrows! for, henceforward, mingled with your bitter tears, ye convey a pleasure in the thought, that she whom all the world adores, feels for my sufferings: the scalding tear shall no longer flow without its balm – the arrow of anguish, while it wounds, shall on its poison-tipped point, convey a healing balsam to my soul.'

'But say, Sir Knight – why is your fate involved in mystery? Lend me your confidence – make me mistress of your secret – my bosom shall be its prison-house; and so tenacious will I be in retaining it, that even to myself I will not dare to whisper it.'

'Oh, lady, could I burst the fetters that chain my tongue to secrecy, I should enjoy a luxury in my grief; but, no, it is forbid – you behold in me a houseless wanderer, against whom the vengeance of Heaven is imprecated, doomed, for a term, to be a solitary inhabitant of the earth – with no settled home to shelter me – no friend to console me – no one to whom I can confide my sorrows.'

'Well!' cried Erilda, with impatience.

'Lady, I dare reveal no more – the cause must remain unknown.'

Erilda could scarce conceal her agitation. 'And when,' with a tremulous voice, she added, 'will the term expire, that frees you of your misery?'

'Then – when a virgin shall be found, of noble birth, and honour speckless as the mountain's dazzling snow, whose beauty shall be the theme of courts and palaces – whose virtue shall be the admiration of those, whom, with parent bounty she has fostered – whose hand shall be urged by knights of rank and enterprise – who shall withstand the temptation of wealth and power, equipage and title – who shall sincerely love me for myself alone, and brave all dangers, to arrive at the haven of my arms.'

Erilda turned pale; the colour on her cheek flew, and her

whole frame became agitated. At this moment the loud bell of the castle tolled the breakfast hour, and endeavouring to re-assume her wonted spirits, 'Come,' she cried gaily, 'we have wasted much time in idle talk.'

Wertwrold lent her his arm, and they proceeded to Rhuddlan. The young Knight at their earnest solicitation, consented to remain at the castle a few days, and various sports were devised to amuse him: nothing was spared to make him forget his griefs. But, in the midst of splendid gaiety, Wertwrold was still himself — melancholy still clouded his brow, and stole the roseate colour of his cheek.

On the second evening, as the last rays of the sun were reflected upon the lakes, and the misty crown of twilight circled the mountain's peak, Erilda, whose bosom was tortured by the love she bore the unhappy Wertwrold, strayed in the garden adjoining the castle. The day had been rather sultry, and, attended by her little foot page, she made towards the fountain, with an intent to bathe. She had already unloosed her hair, when she observed, extended upon the yellow sands, Wertwrold; he was in a sound sleep — and, approaching with tremulous step, she hung over him with an eye brimful of tears.

'Unhappy Knight!' she cried. — 'Where shall be found the maid who can assuage the anguish of thy bosom, and restore to its former peace? — Where shall that maid be found, speckless as thou hast described, who will renounce every pretension for thee? Alas! alas! let me not buoy myself up with faint hopes — Wertwrold shall yet be happy, but Erilda will be for ever miserable. Yes, yes, some more happy maid than thou, Erilda, will gain the heart of Wertwrold, and tear the bond asunder that dates his misery.'

Faster flowed her tears — her agony became more acute — and, clasping her hands together, she sunk down by his side — her eyes were pensive, fixed on his, that were shrouded in sleep; and wrapped in ecstasy, she watched every breath that swelled his bosom, and escaped his lips. How beautiful did he appear, as he lay reclined upon the ground — what a dew sparkled on his lips — what a colour revelled upon his cheeks; his jet black

hair, on which the water-drop, from bathing, glistened, clus-
tered in silky curls around his head. He had laid aside his armour, and the true shape and mouldings of his manly limbs were
visible; his neck and bosom were bare – they were of the most
masculine beauty.

'Ah, Erilda!' exclaimed he in his slumbers, 'you alone can
liberate my anguished heart – you alone can restore the smile to
my fretted cheek – but you do not love me.'

'Hear it, Heavens!' cried the enraptured maid; 'Oh, Wertwrold!' and fainted upon his bosom.

The Knight awoke from the violence of her fall, and he
gazed upon her in astonishment. – 'Erilda!' he exclaimed, and
bathing her temples with cold water, she soon revived; her
her wild eyes were timidly revealed to the light – and as soon as
she discovered herself in the arms of Wertwrold, she gave a
faint scream, and broke from his embrace. 'Erilda!' cried the
Knight with fervour, 'my fate is in your hands – do with me
as you please – you alone can avert my cruel destiny. From this
moment, I cease to hope or to despair.'

Erilda was in an agony insupportable – tears choked her utterance, and pressing his hand between her's, she flew to conceal her anguish in another part of the garden. They met at the
supper board, but she, feigning indisposition, begged leave to
retire; and full early did the Baron and his guests press the
downy pillow.

In her chamber Erilda indulged her sighs: Sir Rhyswick had
chosen the heir apparent of Wales for her future lord, and she
well knew it was in vain to contest his choice. The chieftain
loved the happiness of his child, but the love of aggrandisement
he cherished in his bosom; and he looked forward with fond delight to the time when Erilda might, with the partner of her
pleasures, share the thrones of Gwynedd and Powys. A few
days was to see the young Prince at Rhuddlan – preparations
were making for his reception – Sir Rhyswick with pleasure beheld the nuptial day advancing – but Erilda viewed its approach with agony. The night was far advanced, ere her
troubled thoughts were invaded by sleep, yet still maintaining

their empire, they conjured up visions to the closed eyes. Erilda dreamed, that her father, over-powered by his affection for her, and her entreaties, yielded his consent to her union with Wertwrold, and placed her hand in his. Transported with joy, she threw her arms round her lover's neck; at this junction awaking, she found the Knight clasped in her embrace. Recoiling with horror from his arms, and recovering her senses, that were at first bewildered, 'Away,' she cried in a tone of terror : 'perfidious Knight, leave me; your conduct calls for my indignation. Oh, Wertwrold! was it possible for me to imagine you would thus repay the hospitality you have here experienced, by invading, in the midnight hour, the chamber of the defenceless? — Begone,' she added, with a contemptuous frown, 'ere I call my attendants, and expose the serpent who repays the favour of Rhuddlan's lord with abusing his confidence.'

'Yet hear me, Erilda,' returned the Knight, 'ere I am gone for ever; I came but to gaze my last farewell on that lovely countenance that dooms me to everlasting misery : my neighing steed now waits at the castle gate, and I must bid these much loved haunts adieu for ever. Farewell, Erilda — irresistible fate leads me hence — and, oh! sometimes give a thought on him who, added to his agonies, harbours for you a fruitless passion!'

Wertwrold paused.

'For ever!' exclaimed Erilda; 'Oh, Wertwrold!'

'Could my absence,' continued the Knight, 'create one pang in your breast, though grateful would the knowledge be to my heart, still it would inflict a wound, Erilda, urging my brain to distraction, when I paused on your unhappiness. — Which ever way I turn, misery attends me — endless sorrow is my bitter portion : that I am indifferent to Erilda creates another pang.'

'Oh, Wertwrold!' cried the maid; and, sinking on his bosom, 'I am yours, and yours alone.'

'Do not my ears deceive me,' cried the enraptured Knight; 'does Erilda really love me — will she renounce the world for me?'

'The world!'

'Yes,' returned Wertwrold, 'and then shall my felicity

dawn: Erilda must renounce everything to be mine — to share with me those transports which virtuous love creates.'

'You speak in mystery.'

'Erilda must, with heroic fortitude, overcome every obstacle to our union — must place implicit confidence in my faith — and sacrifice everything for me. The firm mind can stand, unshaken, on the stupendous rock, and smile upon the gulf beneath that threatens to devour — so must the woman who would gain my arms.'

'Wertwrold!'

'Take this ring, Erilda, it is a charmed one: which, when breathed upon, brings me to your presence: use it as you need me, and I fly, in obedience to your command, though at the extremity of the world.'

'Yet stay; you leave me in doubt.'

'Erilda must use her own discretion, I have not power to direct her. Farewell,' he cried; and pressing her to his bosom, instantly retired, leaving her lost in wonder and amazement.

For a time she could scarcely believe her senses — everything appeared as a dream before her eyes — but she possessed the charming ring — and the deluding thought vanished, that told her the preceding scene was the mere fabrication of her imagination.

At breakfast time she met Sir Rhyswick, who was not a little surprised and angered with the abrupt departure of his guest.

Erilda endeavoured to plead his cause — urging that business of the utmost import demanded his immediate attendance, and that to her he apologized.

The generous chieftain was well satisfied with the excuse, although he had hoped Wertwrold, in whose favour he was much interested, should have been present at the solemnization of Erilda's nuptials, which the fourth day was to see performed, according to a message which he had received from the young Prince, who, impatient to call Erilda his bride, thus early appointed the day.

Sir Rhyswick, with joy expressed in his countenance, imparted the news to his daughter, who, falling upon her knees —

her cheeks bathed in tears – and grasping his hand, entreated him, as he considered her happiness, to forego his intentions.

'How?' cried the astonished Baron.

'I shall never know happiness with a man whom my heart will not acknowledge for its lord,' returned the afflicted Erilda: 'Oh! as you love my peace of mind, send back the prince – Erilda cannot be the bride of Morven – another object has enchained her heart.'

'How?' exclaimed the indignant Baron; 'Does Erilda reject the heir to the throne of Wales?'

'It would be criminal to my hand, when another possesses my heart. Oh, my father! the happy Morven will find one more worthy of being his bride – one more closely in conjunction with his soul – who will return his fond affection with affection.'

'Erilda,' cried the venerable chieftain with firmness, 'I seek not to know him whom your heart has chosen. If you value my affection, Morven must be your future lord; if not, your father is lost to you for ever.' Thus saying, he retired, leaving the distracted maid overwhelmed with grief.

Sir Rhyswick would not see her the rest of the day: and a messenger in the evening coming to her chamber, bid her prepare on the morrow to receive Morven, who was expected at the castle, attended by a numerous retinue.

Erilda, in an agony of distraction, threw herself upon the couch; her tears more plenteously flowed to her relief, and eased those labouring sighs that swelled her agitated bosom. She, casting her eyes upon the magic ring that encircled her finger; pressed it to her lips, and her warm breath sullying the ruby that sparkled upon it, instantly the Blood-red Knight stood before her.

'I come,' he cried, 'at your command, from the bosom of the vasty deep, to serve the mistress of my heart.'

Wertwrold took a seat by her side – Erilda hung her head upon his shoulder; her cheek was pale with weeping – her eyes languid and heavy.

'Oh, Wertwrold!' she exclaimed, 'this must be our last

meeting; the son of Cynvyn claims Erilda's hand, and even now is on the road to Rhuddlan, to lead her to the bridal altar.'

'And will Erilda yield her honour, then, at the sordid entreaties of avarice and pride? Will she prostitute herself, embittering the remainder of her days to gratify another's passion?'

'Wertwrold! you –'

'Oh, lady! the fond affection glowing in my bosom has heaped a world of ruin in my heart – I see the gulf yawning at my feet – I see what tortures are preparing for me, and fly to meet my doom. – It Erilda is who hurls me to destruction – it is Erilda who mocks my sighs, and points me to the spot where angry demons wait to glut them on my blood. But these inflictions I can brave – for, she I love proves false – she who deceitfully sighed, "I am yours, and yours alone."'

'You amaze and terrify me: what tortures what inflictions are those you dread? Oh, Wertwrold! do not keep me in suspense – tell me who, or what are you.'

'Who I am, lady, must remain a secret – what I am, my warm sighs, my great affliction have revealed – your lover. Oh, Erilda! I am man, with half his fortitude – man, with all his weaknesses: love animates and distracts my bosom; and she whom I wed, must wed me for myself alone.'

'Fond Wertwrold! I question you no more – and oh! how shall I convince you that my heart is yours – doomed as I am to misery and Morven.'

She fixed her languishing eyes upon his countenance – Wertwrold paused.

Erilda's chamber looked into the castle garden; the woodbine and honeysuckle climbed above her window, and a rose-tree entwined itself with the odorous branches of the honeysuckle – some sprigs hung pendant near the sashes of the casement, where the flower blowed and scented the air with its refreshing sweets.

Wertwrold eagerly slipped a spray that boasted a full blown flower and a ripening bud, which he presented to Erilda.

'Look you,' he cried; 'look on these flowers – the beauty of the one withers, while the other ripens. Here we see a rich bloom upon the cheek of youth; what a glowing fragrance does its breath impart! how sweet is the dew that hangs upon the expanding leaf! how rich! how luxuriant! how captivating to the senses! Would it not be cruel to pluck this early bud, ere it hath tasted of that dew which now sparkles on its lip – and, at the moment when it is about to enjoy those sweets which are prepared for early life? – Lady, this new plucked bud, in an hour shall perish – life shall fly its newly created bosom – the hand of man hath deprived it of its succours, and, ere it ceased to charm, it dies, unpitied, unrespected.' Then turning to the other – 'This full-blown rose, whose shrivelled leaf betrays a speedy dissolution, having tasted of all the pleasures life affords, and enjoyed them in their full sense, prepares to die. The morning sun, instead of cheering, shall wither its juiceless fibres – the flavour of its breath is fled – and the falling dew animates it not – the airs are cold and freezing that play around it – and plucked, it would not perish sooner than were it left to wither upon the spray.'

'I do not understand you.'

'Lady, if one of these flowers must be torn from the branch of life, which would you sacrifice?'

'The full-blown.'

'Then live, Erilda – live to enjoy the tide of pleasure and of happiness.'

'Wertwrold, your words convey a horrible meaning; my soul shudders at the thought.'

'What thought, Erilda? – I ask you but to live – is the thought mercenary? I ask you but to taste of those pleasures, which he for whom you would sacrifice your happiness and person, cannot enjoy. Sir Rhyswick has nearly numbered his years – and dissolution betrays its approach upon his cheek: his infirm limbs – his shrivelled form – his silvery beard – and aged eye, like the full-blown rose, confirms a speedy termination of his life.'

Erilda fainted upon his bosom – his arms encircled her waist – hers were entwined round his neck: the colour of returning life soon crimsoned her cheek: her lips were pressed to his; the kiss was exchanged that imparted a mutual glow to the heart, and filled it with voluptuous thoughts.

'Erilda is mine, eternally,' cried the Knight.

'I am yours, for ever,' sighed the maid with half fainting voice.

'Tomorrow she will leave Rhuddlan for my arms?'

'Tomorrow, I am yours.'

They parted – each transported with the warmth of passion; and the ensuing eve was to see Erilda preparing her flight from her paternal home.

The next morning, Morven and his numerous retinue were heard upon their march across the mountain: the martial clang of their warlike instruments was heard at a great distance; and some messengers preceding, brought the early news of his approach and presents for the bride. The castle gates were thrown open to receive them – white flags waved upon the walls, that were thronged with armed soldiers, who owned Rhuddlan's powerful lord for their chieftain; and bards and harpers raised high their voices in praise of the fair Erilda.

Morven entered the castle, amidst the acclamations of the generous people, who loudly testified their joy at his approach, and whose loud shouts rent the air. Sir Rhyswick received him with every demonstration of pleasure, and instantly conducted him to the presence of his daughter.

Erilda, habited in robes of virgin white, that flowed adown her taper limbs, in the midst of her maidens, welcomed him with a smile. She looked beautiful – her cheeks were flushed with the ripe tincture of the rose – her blue eyes beamed with expression – her hair was tastefully disposed upon her forehead – and silver beads flowed down her fine-shaped bosom.

Morven saluted her with affability. For a while the young Prince was transfixed with wonder and admiration; her beauty far exceeded, in his estimation, the report that had reached his ear; and he looked with impatience for the moment that was to make her his bride.

The day was spent in merry pastimes; but Erilda was depressed with fears; she trembled at the promise she had made to Wertwrold, and more than once resolved to break it. The evening fast approached, and she grew more and more alarmed; at length the last rays of the declining sun were reflected upon the lake – the tinkling bell of the goat-herds caught her ear – the much dreaded time was arrived – her heart fluttered in her bosom – and wild and unknowing what she did, she sought the harbour where she had promised to meet the unknown.

Werthold was already there; with eagerness he clasped her to his bosom – with unallayed passion pressed her lips to his.

'Oh, Erilda!' he sighed, 'do I hold you in my arms, and shall my present bliss be equalled by the future? Come,' he continued, 'let us hasten our departure; a coracle waits us on the Clwyd, to waft us to the opposite shore.'

'Werthold!' exclaimed the affrighted maid; 'I dare not – do not tempt me – I must remain – and – be the bride of Morven.'

'Perjured Erilda! false fleeting woman – is this your truth – is this your constancy? Then farewell for ever.'

'Yet stay,' she cried, 'one moment: Oh, Wertwrold! do not leave me a prey to my own thoughts.'

'Will Erilda be mine?'

'Yes, yes.'

'Voluntarily mine?'

'Oh, yes!' exclaimed the maid, unconscious of what she said, observing lights at the further end of the walk, and fearful lest they should discover her with the unknown.

'Erilda will fly her paternal roof for Wertwrold?'

'Yes, yes.'

'Regardless of a father's tears and remonstrances?'

'I am Wertwrold's, and Wertwrold's alone!' she exclaimed, more alarmed by the nearer approach of the lights; 'and no power on earth shall separate me from his arms.'

The Knight of the Blood-red Plume smiled – it was the smile of satisfaction; and he placed in her hand a dagger.

'Use it,' he cried, 'in self-defence alone. Where is Sir Rhyswick?'

At this moment, a number of torches were seen flaming down the walks – Sir Rhyswick was at the head of a party of servants, whose countenances were expressive of fear.

'See!' cried Erilda, 'they bend their steps this way; we shall be discovered.'

'Take this dagger,' returned the Knight, thrusting it into her hand.

'How am I to use it?' exclaimed the maid in terror.

'Sir Rhyswick advances; 'tis him alone we have to fear. – Plunge it in his bosom.'

'In the bosom of my father?' cried she, with horror. 'Wertwrold – Merciful heavens! do not my ears deceive me? Horror! Horror! In the bosom of my father! – Away, monster.'

'Come to my arms, Erilda,' exclaimed the Knight, 'I have proved your virtue, and you are doubly dear to me.' He pressed the trembling maid to his bosom.

At this moment, Sir Rhyswick entered the arbour.

'This way – this way!' cried Wertwrold: and hurrying through a small outlet, that led to the river; footsteps pursued them. Still Erilda held the dagger in her hand, and the pale moonbeams silvering the path, betrayed the shadow of a person in pursuit, wrapped in a long cloak.

'We are betrayed,' cried Wertwrold; 'our pursuer must die.'

'I see the coracle; it is at shore,' said Erilda. And, at this moment, some one seized her white robe behind.

'Plunge your dagger in his heart,' cried Wertwrold.

'Hold your impious hand!' returned a hollow voice.

'Strike!' demanded the Knight.

'Stay, murderess!' uttered the voice.

'Our safety pleads for his death,' rejoined Wertwrold.

The hand of the pursuer now clasped Erilda's shoulder; who, disentangling herself and rendered frantic, turned hastily round, and plunged the dagger in her assailant's breast.

The wounded man dropped upon the ground. 'Cruel Erilda!' escaped his lips, and he instantly expired.

'Hence God-abandoned murderers;' muttered the voice that had before arrested the arm of Erilda. 'Fly to meet thy doom.'

'Hark!' cried the maid; 'heard you nothing? — What voice was that?'

Terror sat on her brow — her lips were pale with fear — her eyes looked wild and fiery.

'I heard nothing but the winds sighing along the strand.'

'Do you hear nothing,' exclaimed she. 'Merciful God! What have I done — "Murderess!" — Oh, let me look on him I have slain.'

She approached the corpse, spite of the entreaties of Wertwrold; and discovered, wrapped in a long cloak, the bleeding body of Sir Rhyswick! A crimson stream flowed from the fresh-made wound — his eyes were filmed and closed in death — his cheek was wan — his mouth wide and distended.

'Oh, God! my father!' exclaimed Erilda, — 'Murdered by my hands!' And fell fainting upon his bleeding breast.

Wertwrold endeavoured to recall her to recollection; but, for a long time, vain were his attempts. At length, recovering, 'Leave me,' she cried; 'leave me to die with my murdered father. — Away! Anguish gnaws my breast. — Abandoned by Heaven, leave me to die, and receive the punishment of my guilt.'

'You rave, Erilda! — See, the vassals of the Baron draw near! — Hark now their voices are heard — their torches gleam in the walks; we shall be discovered, Erilda, let me arouse you from this torpor — let us fly, Erilda, and save ourselves from an ignominious death.'

'Away!' cried the distracted maid; 'I am a wretch unfit to live — more unfit to die: yet I will expiate the foul offence by submitting to those tortures that await me — which exceed not the agonies of my own bosom. Oh! my much loved father!' she exclaimed, 'your daughter — your own daughter, is your murderer.'

She fell upon his bosom; and still the Blood-plumed Knight urged her to fly.

'Erilda!' he returned, 'what false notions occupy your breast! Rather by penitence expiate the crime: the foul offence is not to be atoned by death. Heaven in its wrath has doomed your soul to everlasting torments; live then, and, by penitence, seek to appease its vengeance.'

'What mercy can the wretched murderer of her parent hope for? – Leave me, Wertwrold; distraction rages through my brain. – I am lost – for ever lost – God-abandoned – doomed to everlasting torments.'

'Oh, Erilda! think on your spotless fame to be blasted by the scandalizing tongue of futurity – think on the curses each peasant slave will mutter on her who was once her country's boast; the name of Erilda shall be shuddered at by those who judge not of the motive but the act – children shall be rocked to their slumbers with the frightful relation of her guilt, and she shall live for ever in the detestation and abhorrence even of the criminal. – The pilgrim shall hear and tremble at her tale – the monk shall cross himself, and tell his beads, when he passes Rhuddlan's blood-stained towers – all nature shall be shocked with her enormities; and not a pitying sigh shall be heaved to her memory. Come, Erilda, let us fly; penitence shall soon restore peace to your bosom, and your crime shall be forgotten.'

'Oh, no! I will remain and sigh out my last breath on the cold bosom of my father.'

'See, Erilda, the torches advance, Prince Morven is at their head; this way he bends his steps – he has his eye upon us – Distraction! – we are lost.'

'Ah! Morven! comes he hither to witness my shame?' exclaimed the maid; 'I cannot stand the inquiring glance of his penetrating eye.'

'Then hasten to the coracle, Erilda, which now awaits us on the shore. – Haste, Erilda, hear you not their voices? – They approach – they are at our heels.'

At this moment, a number of voices exclaimed, 'This way!'

'Oh, hide me – hide me from them; they come – they come;' cried Erilda. And clasping the hand of Wertwrold, she flew to the strand where the coracle was anchored.

The footsteps approached; and numberless torches lined the strand. Sir Rhyswick was discovered by the vassals of Rhuddlan, wrapped up in his cloak, and bathed in his blood. His heart was cold in his bosom – no signs of life animated his cheek, that was pale and deathlike. His silvery beard was distained and clotted with gore; – the last breath had issued from his mouth.

Morven had the corpse borne to the castle, where it lay in state for three days; when it was deposited in the earth, and five-hundred masses were sung for his eternal repose.

In the meantime, the despairing Erilda having set her foot on board the vessel, was borne over the thin wave with the rapidity of lightning. Torches still lined the stand; and their glaring light was reflected to the opposite shore, breaking through the horrible darkness that clouded the earth.

'Vain is your flight, murderess!' whispered a voice in the breeze. – 'Mountains cannot conceal your guilt, or cover you from the wrath of the great avenger. – To the furthermost corner of the world, the retributive sword of justice shall pursue you.'

'Hark!' cried Erilda, clinging to the bosom of her seducer, while horror distorted her countenance. 'Hark; heard you not a voice? Oh, heard you not a voice? Oh, Wertwrold! – hide me – hide me.'

She buried her face in her cloak, while the warrior Knight maintained a contemptuous silence; at length, gazing upon her with satisfaction, he exclaimed:

'And is Erilda mine – do I now press her in my arms – do I now hold her to my heart, beyond the power of man to tear her from me? Why, this, indeed, is triumph – she is mine, voluntarily mine – she has fled her paternal roof for me, an unknown – she has rejected Morven, the heir apparent to the crown of Wales, who came to her with a heart full of love, and proffered the wealth of his country at her feet, to share her smiles, for me an unknown! She has renounced her claim to virtue, embraced infamy for a spotless name, has preferred the blast of scandal to the mild breath of praise, and all this for me, an UNKNOWN!'

A horrible smile, as he concluded, played upon his cheek. – Erilda started from his bosom.

'Wertwrold?' she exclaimed; – 'Do you upbraid me?'

'Enamoured beauty, no! To ME, this guilt is pleasure: had you deluged the world in a sea of blood, or brought another chaos on the earth – Wertwrold would have smiled.'

'For Heaven's sake,' cried the almost expiring criminal; 'tell me, who are you?'

'*The Warrior Knight of the Blood-red Plume*: but,' he continued, 'Erilda is beyond the reach of mercy – is inevitably mine – and I will reveal myself in all my glowing colours. I am an agent of the great infernal – my residence is in the bosom of the Clwyd – my occupation is to aggravate the crimes on earth, and be the great instigator of war and rapine: in my bosom spring those seeds of faction, which I scatter in the breasts of princes, urging them to raise the sword against each other's life, and plunge each other's nation in a torrent of destructive war: but this had ceased – Morven's father had restored Wales to prosperity and peace – and I, in the bosom of my native stream, was doomed to sleep and brood new broils, in painful inactivity. While thus my mind was occupied with thought, an incubus approached my oozy bed, and breathed Erilda's fame into my ear: I was aroused with the sweet image my fancy drew; and, on beholding the enchanting object, found her sweeter than my imagination had painted her – and, from that moment, I resolved to make her mine. I heard of her many virtues – of her piety – and what a feeling heart she boasted; this news instructed me what shape to assume; and the Warrior Knight of the Blood-red Plume answered every purpose. Erilda was easily ensnared: she pitied me, because she thought me unfortunate – pity instantly begat love – love the glowing fire of all-consuming passion. I had no power to deceive, but speciously –'

'Monster!' exclaimed the frantic wretch, 'you were all deception.'

'There Erilda wrongs me,' cried the fiend; 'she deceived herself – she thought me what her heart hoped I was – I did not need much art to gain her – she readily entered into all my views – embraced my projects as fast as they were uttered.'

Erilda threw herself upon her knees.

'Nay, prayer is vain,' continued the fiend; 'you are lost to

Heaven – you scrupled to commit an immediate murder, yet planned a lingering death for the parent who had nurtured you – you would not stab, but preferred planting daggers in your father's bosom. – Murderess! you bid him who gave you life, live for a time in agony, to reflect on his daughter's infamy.'

Erilda shrunk with horror and affright from the hideous monster, who now resumed his original shape, amidst the yell of demons, who rose from the sandy deep, upon the curling wave, to greet their chief. The eyes of the sanguinary fiend, emitting a sulphureous flame, were fixed upon the pale countenance of the guilty maid, whom he grasped round the waist in malignant triumph. Green scales covered his body; from his mouth and nostrils he breathed the white frothen waters – and various animals, fostered by the liquid element, trailed their pestiferous slime across his carcase. In his right hand he held a trident, which he raised on high to plunge in the bosom of his victim, who, screaming, burst from his embrace, and falling upon her knees, implored of Heaven protection. Loud thunders shook the sky – terrific lightning flashed in her eyes – and the furious winds bursting through the mountains, swelled the agitated river beyond its bounds. The fiend, with malignant yell, pursued Erilda – the trident entered her bosom – and crimson torrents of her virgin blood gushed from the yawning wound – in agony she fell – the demon, twining his hand in her fair locks, hurled her to the deep, and, sated with triumph, vanished with his coracle.

Long time did the white-browed waves bear up Erilda: in her last moments, she beheld the pale spectre of Sir Rhyswick, who advanced upon the rolling waters, that seemed to shrink from his feet, placing his fore-finger to the deep wound in his breast. More dreadful were her screams – and billow succeeding billow, bore her near the shore. Struggling for life, she clung to a loose rock to save herself, which yielding to her grasp, came rolling down, and crashed her to pieces.

The hermit paused. –

Since then has Rhuddlan's castle been the seat of anarchy. – Monarchs, indeed, have made it their residence; but, each night, Erilda's screams are heard, and the Warrior of the Blood-red Plume is seen pursuing her through the ruined courts.

Such is the tale of Rhuddlan's ruined towers. Pilgrim, go thy way, stop not within its blasted walls, foul fiends ride upon the misty air, and the demons of the angry Clwyd claim it as their right.

# The Dance of the Dead

## Anonymous

### (*circa* 1810)

Ever since the publication of *The Monk*, tales of raising the dead had become highly popular among readers and a leaf through any catalogue of the period reveals titles like *The Animated Skeleton* (1798), *The Sepulchral Summons* (1804) and *The Midnight Groan; Invoking an Exposure of the Horrible Secrets of the Nocturnal Assembly* (1808).

Not surprisingly because Germany had the reputation of being the most witch-plagued nation in the world, a great many of these tales of necromancy and resurrection are set there; the Hartz Mountains being particularly popular. Like so much of the secondary Gothic material there is great repetition of character and plot in this area, and the researcher is almost inclined to abandon the quest for something representative yet fresh. The few stories which I have encountered that do succeed are almost all based on some old legend, and such is the case with *The Dance of the Dead*, fleshed out by the anonymous author from a Silesian folk tale. Readers will quickly note the similarity between it and the famous children's fairy tale of the *Pied Piper of Hamlin*.

MANY a century back, if the old German Chronicle may be credited, an aged wandering bagpiper settled at Neisse, a small town in Silesia. He lived quietly and honestly, and at first played his tunes in secret for his own amusement; but it was not long, as his neighbours delighted in listening to him, and would often in the calm of a warm midsummer evening gather round his door, whilst he called forth the cheering sounds of harmony, before Master Willibald became acquainted both with old and young, was flattered and caressed and lived in content and prosperity.

The gallant beaux of the place, who had near his door first beheld those lovely creatures, for whose sake they had written so much bad poetry, and lost so much more valuable time, were his constant customers for melting songs, while they drowned the softer passages with the depth of their sighs. The old citizens invited him at their solemn dinner-parties; and no bride would have deemed her wedding-feast to be completely celebrated, had not Master Willibald played the bridal dance of his own composition. For this very purpose he had invented a most tender melody, which united gaiety and gravity, playful ideas and melancholy feelings, forming a true emblem of the matrimonial life. A feeble trace of this tune is still to be found in what is called the old German 'Grandfather's Dance', which, as far down as the time of our parents, was an important requisite of a wedding feast, and is even heard now and then in our days. As often as Master Willibald played this tune, the prudest spinster would not refuse to dance, the stooping matron moved again her time-stiffened joints, and the grey-haired grandfather danced it merrily with the blooming offspring of his children. This dance seemed really to restore youth to the old, and this was the cause of its being called, at first in jest, and afterwards generally, the 'Grandfather's Dance'.

A young painter, of the name of Wido, lived with Master Willibald; he was thought to be the son, or the foster-son, of the musician. The effect of the old man's art on this youth was lost. He remained silent and mournful at the most mirth inspiring tunes Willibald played to him; and at the balls to which he was often invited, he rarely mingled with the gay: but would retire into a corner, and fix his eyes on the loveliest fair one that graced the room, neither daring to address, nor to offer her his hand. Her father, the mayor of the town, was a proud and haughty man, who would have thought his dignity lessened, had an unknown limner cast his eye upon his daughter. But the beautiful Emma was not of her father's opinion: for the young girl loved with all the ardour of a first and secret passion, the backward, though handsome youth. Often when she perceived the expressive eyes of Wido endeavouring to catch unobservedly her glances, she would abate her liveliness, and allow the youth of her heart to have the undisturbed view of her beautiful and variable features. She easily read afterwards, in his brightening face, the eloquent gratitude of his heart; and although she turned blushingly away, the fire on her cheeks, and the sparkling in her eyes, kindled new flames of love and hope in her lover's bosom.

Master Willibald had for a long time promised to assist the love-sick youth in obtaining his soul's dearest object. Sometimes he intended, like the wizards of yore, to torment the mayor with an enchanted dance, and compel him by exhaustion to grant everything; sometimes, like a second Orpheus, he proposed to carry away, by the power of his harmony, the sweet bride from the Tartarian abode of her father. But Wido always had objections: he never would allow the parent of his fair one to be harmed by the slightest offence, and hoped to win him by perseverance and complacency.

Willibald told him, 'Thou art an idiot, if thou hopest to win, by an open and honourable sentiment, like thy love, the approbation of a rich and proud old fool. He will not surrender without some of the plagues of Egypt are put in force against him. When once Emma is thine, and he no more can change what has happened, then you wilt find him friendly and kind. I blame myself for having promised to do nothing against thy will, but death acquits every debt, and still I shall help thee in my own way.'

Poor Wido was not the only one on the path of whose life the mayor strewed thorns and briars. The whole town had very little affection for their chief, and delighted to oppose him at every opportunity; for he was harsh and cruel, and punished severely the citizens for trifling and innocent mirth, unless they purchased pardon by the means of heavy penalties and bribes.

After the yearly wine-fair in the month of January, he was in the habit of obliging them to pay all their earnings into his treasury, to make amends for their past merriments. One day the tyrant of Neisse had put their patience to too hard a trial, and broken the last tie of obedience, from his oppressed townsmen. The malcontents had created a riot, and filled their persecutor with deadly fear; for they threatened nothing less than to set fire to his house, and to burn him, together with all the riches he had gathered by oppressing them.

At this critical moment, Wido went to Master Willibald, and said to him, 'Now, my old friend, is the time when you may help me with your art, as you frequently have offered to do. If your music be really so powerful as you say it is, go then and deliver the mayor, by softening the enraged mob. As a reward he certainly will grant you any thing you may request. Speak then a word for me and my love, and demand my beloved Emma as the price of your assistance.' The bag-piper laughed at this speech, and replied, 'We must satisfy the follies of children, in order to prevent them crying.' And so he took his bagpipe and walked slowly down to the town-house-square, where the rioters, armed with pikes, lances, and lighted torches, were laying waste the mansion of the worshipful head of the town.

Master Willibald placed himself near a pillar, and began to play his 'Grandfather's Dance'. Scarcely were the first notes of this favourite tune heard, when the rage-distorted countenances became smiling and cheerful, the frowning brows lost their dark expression, pikes and torches fell out of the threatening fists, and the enraged assailants moved about marking with their steps the measure of the music. At last, the whole multitude began to dance, and the square, that was lately the scene of riot and confusion, bore now the appearance of a gay dancing assembly. The piper, with his magic bag-pipe, led on through the streets, all the people danced behind him, and each citizen returned jumping to his home, which shortly before he had left with very different feelings.

The mayor, saved from this imminent danger, knew not how to express his gratitude; he promised to Master Willibald every thing he might demand, even were it half his property. But the bag-piper replied, smiling, saying his expectations were not so lofty, and that for himself he wanted no temporal goods what-

ever; but since his lordship, the mayor, had pledged his word
to grant to him in every thing he might demand, so he beseeched
him, with due respect, to grant fair Emma's hand for his Wido.
But the haughty mayor was highly displeased at this proposal. He made every possible excuse; and as Master Willibald
repeatedly reminded him of his promise, he did, what the des-
pots of those dark times were in the habit of doing, and which
those of our enlightened days still practise, he declared his dignity offended; pronounced Master Willibald to be a disturber
of the peace, an enemy of the public security, and allowed him
to forget in a prison the promise of his lord, the mayor. Not
satisfied herewith, he accused him of witchcraft, caused him to
be tried by pretending he was the very bag-piper and rat-catcher
of Hamlin, who was, at that time, and is still in so bad a repute
in the German provinces, for having carried off by his infernal
art all the children of that ill-fated town. 'The only difference,'
said the wise mayor, between the two cases, was, that at Hamlin
only the children had been made to dance to his pipe, but here
young and old seemed under the same magical influence. By
such artful delusions, the mayor turned every merciful heart
from the prisoner. The dread of necromancy, and the example
of the children of Hamlin, worked so strongly, that sheriffs and
clerks were writing day and night. The secretary calculated already the expense of the funeral-pile; the sexton petitioned for
a new rope to toll the dead-bell for the poor sinner; the carpen-
ters prepared scaffolds for the spectators of the expected execution; and the judges rehearsed the grand scene, which they
prepared to play at the condemnation of the famous bag-piping
rat-catcher. But although justice was sharp, Master Willibald
was still sharper: for as he once had laughed very heartily over
the important preparations for his end, he now laid himself
down upon his straw and died!

Shortly before his death, he sent for his beloved Wido, and
addressed him for the last time. — 'Young man,' said he, 'thou
seest, that in thy way of viewing mankind and the world I can
render thee no assistance. I am tired of the whims thy folly obliged me to perform. Thou hast now acquired experience

enough fully to comprehend, that nobody should calculate, or at least ground, his designs on the goodness of human nature, even if he himself should be too good to lose entirely his belief in the goodness of others. I, for my own part, would not rely upon the fulfilment of my last request to thee, if thine own interest would not induce thee to its performance. When I am dead, be careful to see that my old bag-pipe is buried with me. To detain it would be of no use to thee, but it may be the cause of thy happiness, if it is laid underground with me.' Wido promised to observe strictly the last commands of his old friend, who shortly after closed his eyes. Scarcely had the report of Master Willibald's sudden death spread, when old and young came to ascertain the truth. The mayor was more pleased with this turn of the affair than any other; for the indifference with which the prisoner had received the news of his approaching promotion to the funeral-pile, induced his worship to suppose, the old bag-piper might some fine day be found invisible in his prison, or rather be found not there at all; or the cunning wizard, being at the stake, might have caused a wisp of straw to burn instead of his person, to the eternal shame of the court of Neisse. He therefore ordered the corpse to be buried as speedily as possible, as no sentence to burn the body had yet been pronounced. An unhallowed corner of the churchyard, close to the wall, was the place assigned for poor Willibald's resting-place. The jailor, as the lawful heir of the deceased prisoner, having examined his property, asked what should become of the bag-pipe, as a corpus delicti.

Wido, who was present, was on the point to make his request, when the mayor, full of zeal, thus pronounced his sentence: 'To avoid every possible mischief, this wicked, worthless tool shall be buried together with its master.' So they put it into the coffin at the side of the corpse, and early in the morning pipe and piper were carried away and buried. But strange things happened in the following night. The watchmen on the tower were looking out, according to the custom of the age, to give the alarm in case of fire in the surrounding country, when about midnight, they saw, by the light of the moon, Master Willibald rising out of his tomb near the church-yard wall. He held his bag-pipe under his arm, and leaning against a high tomb-stone, upon which the moon shed her brightest rays, he began to blow, and fingered the pipes, just as he was accustomed to do when he was alive.

Whilst the watchmen, astonished at this sight, gazed wisely on one another, many other graves opened; their skeleton-inhabitants peeped out with their bare skulls, looked about, nodded to the measure, rose afterwards wholly out of their coffins, and moved their rattling limbs into a nimble dance. At the church-windows, and the gates of the vaults, other empty eye-holes stared on the dancing place: the withered arms began to shake the iron gates, till locks and bolts sprung off, and out came the skeletons, eager to mingle in the dance of the dead. Now the light dancers stilted about, over the hillocks and tomb-stones, and whirled around in a merry waltz, that the shrouds waved in the wind about the fleshless limbs, until the church-clock struck twelve, when all the dancers, great and small, returned to their narrow cells; the player took his bag-pipe under his arm, and likewise returned to his vacant coffin. Long before the dawn of the day, the watchman awoke the mayor, and made him, with trembling lips and knocking knees, the awful report of the horrid night-scene. He enjoined strict secrecy on them, and promised to watch with them the following night on the tower. Nevertheless, the news soon spread through the town, and at the close of the evening, all the surrounding windows and roofs were lined with virtuosi and cognoscenti of the old dark arts, who all before hand were engaged in discussions on the possibility or impossibility of the events they expected to witness before midnight.

The bag-piper was not behind his time. At the first sound of the bell announcing the eleventh hour, he rose slowly, leaned against the tomb-stone, and began his tune. The ball guests seemed to have been waiting for the music; for at the very first notes they rushed forth out of the graves and vaults, through grass hills and heavy stones. Corpses and skeletons, shrouded and bare, tall and small, men and women, all running to and

fro, dancing and turning, wheeling and whirling round the
player, quicker or more slow according to the measure he
played, till the clock tolled the hour of midnight. Then dancers
and piper withdrew again to rest. The living spectators, at their
windows and on their roofs, now confessed, that 'there are
more things in heaven and earth than are dreamt of in our
philosophy.' The mayor had no sooner retired from the tower,
than he ordered the painter to be cast into prison that very night,
hoping to learn from his examination, or perhaps by putting
him to the torture, how the magic nuisance of his foster-father
might be removed.

Wido did not fail to remind the mayor of his ingratitude
towards Master Willibald, and maintained that the deceased
troubled the town, bereft the dead of their rest, and the living of
their sleep, only because he had received, instead of the promised reward for the liberation of the mayor, a scornful refusal,
and moreover had been thrown into prison most unjustly, and
buried in a degrading manner. This speech made a very deep
impression upon the minds of the magistrates; they instantly
ordered the body of Master Willibald to be taken out of his
tomb, and laid in a more respectable place. The sexton, to show
his perception of the occasion, took the bag-pipe out of the coffin, and hung it over his bed. For he reasoned thus: if the enchanting or enchanted musician could not help following his
profession even in the tomb, he at least would not be able to
play to the dancers without his instrument. But at night, after
the clock had struck eleven, he heard distinctly a knock at his
door; and when he opened it, with the expectation of some
deadly and lucrative accident requiring his skill, he beheld the
buried Master Willibald in propria persona. 'My bag-pipe,' said
he, very composedly, and passing by the trembling sexton, he
took it from the wall where it was hung up: then he returned
to his tomb-stone, and began to blow. The guests, invited by
the tune, came like the preceding night, and were preparing
for their midnight dance in the church-yard. But this time the
musician began to march forward and proceeded with his
numerous and ghastly suite through the gate of the church-

yard to the town, and led his nightly parade through all the
streets, till the clock struck twelve, when all returned again to
their dark abodes.

The inhabitants of Neisse now began to fear, lest the awful
night wanderers might shortly enter their own houses. Some
of the chief magistrates earnestly entreated the mayor to lay the
charm, by making good his word to the bag-piper. But the
mayor would not listen to it; he even pretended that Wido
shared in the infernal arts of the old rat-catcher, and added,
'The dauber deserves rather the funeral-pile than the bridal-
bed.' But in the following night the dancing spectres came
again into the town, and although no music was heard, yet it
was easily seen by their emotions, that the dancers went through
the figure of the 'Grandfather's Dance'. This night they behaved much worse than before. For they stopped at the house
wherein a betrothed damsel lived, and here they turned in a
wild whirling dance round a shadow, which resembled perfectly the spinster, in whose honour they moved the nightly
bridal-dance. Next day the whole town was filled with mourning; for all the damsels whose shadows were seen dancing with
the spectres, had died suddenly. The same thing happened again
the following night. The dancing skeletons turned before the
houses, and wherever they had been, there was, next morning,
a dead bride lying on the bier.

The citizens were determined no longer to expose their
daughters and mistresses to such an imminent danger. They
threatened the mayor to carry Emma away by force and to lead
her to Wido, unless the mayor would permit their union to be
celebrated before the beginning of the night. The choice was a
difficult one, for the mayor disliked the one just as much as the
other; but as he found himself in the uncommon situation,
where a man may choose with perfect freedom, he, as a free
being, declared freely his Emma to be Wido's bride.

Long before the spectre-hour the guests sat at the wedding-
table. The first stroke of the bell sounded, and immediately the
favourite tune of the well-known bridal-dance was heard. The
guests, frightened to death, and fearing the spell might still

continue to work, hastened to the windows, and beheld the bag-piper, followed by a long row of figures in white shrouds, moving to the wedding-house. He remained at the door and played; but the procession went on slowly, and proceeded even to the festive hall. Here the strange pale guests rubbed their eyes, and looked about them full of astonishment, like sleep walkers just awakened. The wedding guests fled behind the chairs and tables; but soon the cheeks of the phantoms began to colour, their white lips became blooming like young rose-buds; they gazed at each other full of wonder and joy, and well-known voices called friendly names. They were soon known as revived corpses, now blooming in all the brightness of youth and health: and who should they be but the brides whose sudden death had filled the whole town with mourning, and who, now recovered from their enchanted slumber, had been led by Master Willibald with his magic pipe, out of their graves to the merry wedding-feast. The wonderful old man blew a last and cheerful farewell tune, and disappeared. He was never seen again.

Wido was of the opinion the bag-piper was none other than the famous Spirit of the Silesian Mountains. The younger painter met him once when he travelled through the hills, and acquired (he never knew how) his favour. He promised the youth to assist him in his love-suit, and he kept his word, although after his own jesting fashion.

Wido remained all his life-time a favourite with the Spirit of the Mountains. He grew rich, and became celebrated. His dear Emma brought him every year a handsome child, his pictures were sought after even in Italy and England; and the 'Dance of the Dead', of which Basil, Antwerp, Dresden, Lubeck, and many other places boast, are only copies or imitations of Wido's original painting, which he had executed in memory of the real 'Dance of the Dead at Neisse'! But, alas! this picture is lost, and no collector of paintings has yet been able to discover it, for the gratification of the cognoscenti, and the benefit of the history of art.

# Leixlip Castle

## Charles Maturin

## (1780–1824)

After Matthew Lewis, Charles Robert Maturin stands as probably the most famous Gothic horror novelist – indeed the title (if not the contents) of his *Melmoth the Wanderer* is familiar to even the most casual reader of macabre literature. Yet for all this fame, Maturin's works are incredibly scarce and few exist outside the shelves of the world's major libraries.

The son of exiled French Protestants who settled in Ireland, Maturin became a curate at St Peter's Church, Dublin, and although he carried out his duties with care and devotion found the impulse to write demanding more and more of his attention. Despite being shy and introspective as a youth, maturity brought a complete change in his character and he was soon to be seen dressed in the latest fashions and mingling with the society crowds.

The Reverend Maturin's first published novel was *The Fatal Revenge* (1807) which appeared under the name of Jasper Denis Murphy – but such was its immediate popularity (Sir Walter Scott was just one of many cities who singled it out for special praise) that the young curate owned up to the authorship. Success followed success and as Maturin's fame grew so did the stories of his outlandish behaviour. *The Gentlemen's Magazine*, for one, devoted several pages in the spring of 1825 to recounting his idiosyncracies and noted that he preferred writing in a room full of noisy people, his own mouth covered with a paste of flour and water to prevent him from joining in the conversation! He also apparently often wore a red wafer on his forehead to show he was in the process of composition, made his wife wear rouge though she naturally had a high colour and occasionally went fishing dressed in a blue coat and silk stockings!

For all this, Maturin was undoubtedly a man of real literary talent and his contributions to the Gothic genre 'touched genius' according to Montague Summers. The highpoint of his career was certainly *Melmoth the Wanderer*, the tale of a man doomed to immortal life, which appeared in 1820. Critics called it a 'memory haunting book' and Balzac was so moved by it that he wrote a sequel, *Melmoth Reconcilié à L'Eglise* in 1835. As far as can be ascertained, *Leixlip Castle* is the only short story Maturin wrote and it appeared in a collection of stories, *The Literary Souvenir or Cabinet of Poetry and Romance*, edited and published by a friend in 1825. It is, in my estimation, a fitting tribute to the man of whom Amédée Pichot wrote, 'were it not for his occasional extravagancies, Maturin must be accounted the most sublime genius English Literature could ever boast'.

THE incidents of the following tale are not merely *founded* on fact, they are facts themselves, which occurred at no very distant period in my own family. The marriage of the parties, their sudden and mysterious separation, and their total alienation from each other until the last period of their mortal existence, are all *facts*. I cannot vouch for the truth of the supernatural solution given to all these mysteries; but I must still consider the story as a fine specimen of Gothic horrors, and can never forget the impression it made on me when I heard it related for the first time among many other thrilling traditions of the same description.
                                                              – C.R.M.

The tranquillity of the Catholics of Ireland during the disturbed periods of 1715 and 1745, was most commendable, and somewhat extraordinary; to enter into an analysis of their probable motives, is not at all the object of the writer of this tale, as it is pleasanter to state the fact of their honour, than at this distance of time to assign dubious and unsatisfactory reasons for it. Many of them, however, showed a kind of secret disgust at the existing state of affairs, by quitting their family residences and wandering about like persons who were uncertain of their homes, or possibly expecting better from some near and fortunate contingency.

Among the rest was a Jacobite Baronet, who, sick of his un-congenial situation in a Whig neighbourhood, in the north – where he heard of nothing but the heroic defence of London-derry; the barbarities of the French generals; and the resistless exhortations of the godly Mr Walker, a Presbyterian clergyman, to whom the citizens gave the title of 'Evangelist'; – quitted his paternal residence, and about the year 1720 hired the Castle of Leixlip for three years (it was then the property of the Con-nollys, who let it to triennial tenants); and removed thither with his family, which consisted of three daughters – their mother having long been dead.

The Castle of Leixlip, at that period, possessed a character of romantic beauty and feudal grandeur, such as few buildings in Ireland can claim, and which is now, alas, totally effaced by the destruction of its noble woods; on the destroyers of which the writer would wish 'a minstrel's malison were said'. – Leixlip, though about seven miles from Dublin, has all the sequestered and picturesque character that imagination could ascribe to a landscape a hundred miles from, not only the metropolis but an inhabited town. After driving a dull mile (an Irish mile) in passing from Lucan to Leixlip, the road – hedged up on one side of the high wall that bounds the demesne of the Veseys, and on the other by low enclosures, over whose rugged tops you have no view at all – at once opens on Leixlip Bridge, at almost a right angle, and displays a luxury of landscape on which the eye that has seen it even in childhood dwells with delighted recollection. – Leixlip Bridge, a rude but solid structure, pro-jects from a high bank of the Liffey, and slopes rapidly to the opposite side, which there lies remarkably low. To the right the plantations of the Vesey's demesne – no longer obscured by walls – almost mingle their dark woods in its stream, with the opposite ones of Marshfield and St Catherine's. The river is scarcely visible, overshadowed as it is by the deep, rich and bending foliage of the trees. To the left it bursts out in all the brilliancy of light, washes the garden steps of the houses of Leixlip, wanders round the low walls of its churchyard, plays with the pleasure-boat moored under the arches on which the summer-house of the Castle is raised, and then loses itself among the rich woods that once skirted those grounds to its very brink. The contrast on the other side, with the luxuriant walks, scattered shrubberies, temples seated on pinnacles, and thickets that conceal from you the sight of the river until you are on its banks, that mark the character of the grounds which are now the property of Colonel Marly, is peculiarly striking.

Visible above the highest roofs of the town, though a quarter of a mile distant from them, are the ruins of Confy Castle, a right good old predatory tower of the stirring times when blood was shed like water; and as you pass the bridge you catch a glimpse of the waterfall (or salmon-leap, as it is called) on whose noon-day lustre, or moon-light beauty, probably the rough livers of that age when Confy Castle was 'a tower of strength', never glanced an eye or cast a thought, as they clattered in their harness over Leixlip Bridge, or waded through the stream before that convenience was in existence.

Whether the solitude in which he lived contributed to tranquillize Sir Redmond Blaney's feelings, or whether they had begun to rust from want of collision with those of others, it is impossible to say, but certain it is, that the good Baronet began gradually to lose his tenacity in political matters; and except when a Jacobite friend came to dine with him, and drink with many a significant 'nod and beck and smile', the King over the water – or the parish-priest (good man) spoke of the hopes of better times, and the final success of the *right* cause, and the old religion – or a Jacobite servant was heard in the solitude of the large mansion whistling 'Charlie is my darling', to which Sir Redmond involuntarily responded in a deep bass voice, somewhat the worse for wear, and marked with more emphasis than good discretion – except, as I have said, on such occasions, the Baronet's politics, like his life, seemed passing away without notice or effort. Domestic calamities, too, pressed sorely on the old gentleman: of his three daughters, the youngest, Jane, had disappeared in so extraordinary a manner in her childhood, that though it is but a wild, remote family tradition, I cannot help relating it: –

The girl was of uncommon beauty and intelligence, and was suffered to wander about the neighbourhood of the castle with the daughter of a servant, who was also called Jane, as a *nom de caresse*. One evening Jane Blaney and her young companion went far and deep into the woods; their absence created no uneasiness at the time, as these excursions were by no means unusual, till her playfellow returned home alone and weeping, at a very late hour. Her account was, that, in passing through a lane at some distance from the castle, an old woman, in the *Fingallian* dress, (a red petticoat and a long green jacket), suddenly started out of a thicket, and took Jane Blaney by the arm: she had in her hand two rushes, one of which she threw over her shoulder, and giving the other to the child, motioned to her to do the same. Her young companion, terrified at what she saw, was running away, when Jane Blaney called after her – 'Good-bye, good-bye, it is a long time before you will see me again.' The girl said they then disappeared, and she found her way home as she could. An indefatigable search was immediately commenced – woods were traversed, thickets were explored, ponds were drained – all in vain. The pursuit and the hope were at length given up. Ten years afterwards, the housekeeper of Sir Redmond, having remembered that she left the key of a closet where sweetmeats were kept, on the kitchen-table, returned to fetch it. As she approached the door, she heard a childish voice murmuring – 'Cold – cold – cold how long it is since I have felt a fire !' – She advanced, and saw, to her amazement, Jane Blaney, shrunk to half her usual size, and covered with rags, crouching over the embers of the fire. The housekeeper flew in terror from the spot, and roused the servants, but the vision had fled. The child was reported to have been seen several times afterwards, as diminutive in form, as though she had not grown an inch since she was ten years of age, and always crouching over a fire, whether in the turret-room or kitchen, complaining of cold and hunger, and apparently covered with rags. Her existence is still said to be protracted under these dismal circumstances, so unlike those of Lucy Gray in Wordsworth's beautiful ballad:

> Yet some will say, that to this day
>    She is a living child –
> That they have met sweet Lucy Gray
>    Upon the lonely wild;
> O'er rough and smooth she trips along,
>    And never looks behind;
> And hums a solitary song
>    That whistles in the wind.

The fate of the eldest daughter was more melancholy, though less extraordinary; she was addressed by a gentleman of competent fortune and unexceptionable character: he was a Catholic, moreover; and Sir Redmond Blaney signed the marriage articles, in full satisfaction of the security of his daughter's soul, as well as of her jointure. The marriage was celebrated at the Castle of Leixlip; and, after the bride and bridegroom had retired, the guests still remained drinking to their future happiness, when suddenly, to the great alarm of Sir Redmond and his friends, loud and piercing cries were heard to issue from the part of the castle in which the bridal chamber was situated.

Some of the more courageous hurried up stairs; it was too late – the wretched bridegroom had burst, on that fatal night, into a sudden and most horrible paroxysm of insanity. The mangled form of the unfortunate and expiring lady bore attestation to the mortal virulence with which the disease had operated on the wretched husband, who died a victim to it himself after the involuntary murder of his bride. The bodies were interred, as soon as decency would permit, and the story hushed up.

Sir Redmond's hopes of Jane's recovery were diminishing every day, though he still continued to listen to every wild tale told by the domestics; and all his care was supposed to be now directed towards his only surviving daughter. Anne, living in solitude, and partaking only of the very limited education of Irish females of that period, was left very much to the servants, among whom she increased her taste for superstitious and supernatural horrors, to a degree that had a most disastrous effect on her future life.

Among the numerous menials of the Castle, there was one 'withered crone', who had been nurse to the late Lady Blaney's mother, and whose memory was a complete *Thesaurus terrorum*. The mysterious fate of Jane first encouraged her sister to listen to the wild tales of this hag, who avouched, that at one time she saw the fugitive standing before the portrait of her late mother in one of the apartments of the Castle, and muttering to herself – 'Woe's me, woe's me! how little my mother thought her wee Jane would ever come to be what she is!' But as Anne grew older she began more 'seriously to incline' to the hag's promises that she could show her her future bridegroom, on the performance of certain ceremonies, which she at first revolted from as horrible and impious; but, finally, at the repeated instigation of the old woman, consented to act a part in. The period fixed upon for the performance of these unhallowed rites, was now approaching – it was near the 31st of October – the eventful night, when such ceremonies were, and still are supposed, in the North of Ireland, to be most potent in their effects. All day long the Crone took care to lower the mind of the young lady to the proper key of submissive and trembling credulity, by every horrible story she could relate; and she told them with frightful and supernatural energy. This woman was called *Collogue* by the family, a name equivalent to Gossip in England, or Cummer in Scotland (though her real name was Bridget Dease); and she verified the name, by the exercise of an unwearied loquacity, an indefatigable memory, and a rage for communicating and inflicting terror, that spared no victim in the household, from the groom, whom she sent shivering to his rug, to the Lady of the Castle, over whom she felt she held unbounded sway.

The 31st of October arrived – the Castle was perfectly quiet before eleven o'clock; half an hour afterwards, the Collogue and Anne Blaney were seen gliding along a passage that led to what is called King John's Tower, where it is said that monarch received the homage of the Irish princes as Lord of Ireland, and which, at all events, is the most ancient part of the structure. The Collogue opened a small door with a key which she had secreted about her, and urged the young lady to hurry on. Anne advanced to the postern, and stood there irresolute and trembling like a timid swimmer on the bank of an unknown stream. It was a dark autumnal evening; a heavy wind sighed among the woods of the Castle, and bowed the branches of the lower trees almost to the waves of the Liffey, which, swelled by recent rains, struggled and roared amid the stones that obstructed its channel. The steep descent from the Castle lay before her, with its dark avenue of elms; a few lights still burned in the little village of Leixlip – but from the lateness of the hour it was probable they would soon be extinguished.

The lady lingered – 'And must I go alone?' said she, foreseeing that the terrors of her fearful journey could be aggravated by her more fearful purpose.

'Ye must, or all will be spoiled,' said the hag, shading the miserable light, that did not extend its influence above six inches on the path of the victim. 'Ye must go alone – and I will watch for you here, dear, till you come back, and then see what will come to you at twelve o'clock.'

The unfortunate girl paused. 'Oh! Collogue, Collogue, if you would but come with me. Oh! Collogue, come with me, if it be but to the bottom of the castlehill.'

'If I went with you, dear, we should never reach the top of it alive again, for there are them near that would tear us both in pieces.'

'Oh! Collogue, Collogue – let me turn back then, and go to my own room – I have advanced too far, and I have done too much.'

'And that's what you have, dear, and so you must go further, and do more still, unless, when you return to your own room, you would see the likeness of *some one* instead of a handsome young bridegroom.'

The young lady looked about her for a moment, terror and wild hope trembling at her heart – then, with a sudden impulse of supernatural courage, she darted like a bird from the terrace of the Castle, the fluttering of her white garments was seen for a few moments, and then the hag who had been shading the flickering light with her hand, bolted the postern, and, placing the candle before a glazed loophole, sat down on a stone seat in the recess of the tower, to watch the event of the spell. It was an hour before the young lady returned; when her face was as pale, and her eyes as fixed, as those of a dead body, but she held in her grasp *a dripping garment*, a proof that her errand had been performed. She flung it into her companion's hands, and then stood panting and gazing wildly about her as if she knew not where she was. The hag herself grew terrified at the insane and breathless state of her victim, and hurried her to her chamber; but here the preparations for the terrible ceremonies of the night were the first objects that struck her, and, shivering at the sight, she covered her eyes with her hands, and stood immovably fixed in the middle of the room.

It needed all the hag's persuasions (aided even by mysterious menaces), combined with the returning faculties and reviving curiosity of the poor girl, to prevail on her to go through the remaining business of the night. At length she said, as if in desperation, 'I *will* go through with it: but be in the next room; and if what I dread should happen, I will ring my father's little silver bell which I have secured for the night – and as you have a soul to be saved, Collogue, come to me at its first sound.'

The hag promised, gave her last instructions with eager and jealous minuteness, and then retired to her own room, which was adjacent to that of the young lady. Her candle had burned out, but she stirred up the embers of her turf fire, and sat nodding over them, and smoothing the pallet from time to time, but resolved not to lie down while there was a chance of a sound from the lady's room, for which she herself, withered as her feelings were, waited with a mingled feeling of anxiety and terror.

It was now long past midnight, and all was silent as the grave throughout the Castle. The hag dozed over the embers till her head touched her knees, then started up as the sound of the bell seemed to tinkle in her ears, then dozed again, and again started as the bell appeared to tinkle more distinctly – suddenly she was roused, not by the bell, but by the most piercing and horrible cries from the neighbouring chamber. The Crone, aghast for the first time, at the possible consequences of the mischief she might have occasioned, hastened to the room. Anne was in convulsions, and the hag was compelled reluctantly to call up the housekeeper (removing meanwhile the implements of the ceremony), and assist in applying all the specifics known at that day, burnt feathers, etc., to restore her. When they had at length succeeded, the housekeeper was dismissed, the door was bolted, and the Collogue was left alone with Anne; the subject of their conference might have been guessed at, but was not known until many years afterwards; but Anne that night held in her hand, in the shape of a weapon with the use of which neither of them was acquainted, an evidence that her chamber had been visited by a being of no earthly form.

This evidence the hag importuned her to destroy, or to remove, but she persisted with fatal tenacity in keeping it. She locked it up, however, immediately, and seemed to think she had acquired a right, since she had grappled so fearfully with the mysteries of futurity, to know all the secrets of which that weapon might yet lead to the disclosure. But from that night it was observed that her character, her manner, and even her countenance, became altered. She grew stern and solitary, shrunk at the sight of her former associates, and imperatively forbade the slightest allusion to the circumstances which had occasioned this mysterious change.

It was a few days subsequent to this event that Anne, who after dinner had left the Chaplain reading the life of St Francis Xavier to Sir Redmond, and retired to her own room to work, and, perhaps, to muse, was surprised to hear the bell at the outer gate ring loudy and repeatedly – a sound she had never heard since her first residence in the Castle; for the few guests who resorted there came and departed as noiselessly as humble visitors at the house of a great man generally do. Straightway there rode up the avenue of elms, which we have already mentioned, a stately gentleman, followed by four servants, all mounted, the two former having pistols in their holsters, and the two latter carrying saddle-bags before them: though it was the first week

in November, the dinner hour being one o'clock, Anne had light
enough to notice all these circumstances. The arrival of the
stranger seemed to cause much, though not unwelcome tumult
in the Castle; orders were loudly and hastily given for the accommodation of the servants and horses – steps were heard
traversing the numerous passages for a full hour – then all was
still; and it was said that Sir Redmond had locked with his own
hand the door of the room where he and the stranger sat, and
desired that no one should dare to approach it. About two hours
afterwards, a female servant came with orders from her master,
to have a plentiful supper ready by eight o'clock, at which he
desired the presence of his daughter. The family establishment
was on a handsome scale for an Irish house, and Anne had only
to descend to the kitchen to order the roasted chickens to be well
strewed with brown sugar according to the unrefined fashion
of the day, to inspect the mixing of the bowl of sago with its
allowance of a bottle of port wine and a large handful of the
richest spices, and to order particularly that the pease pudding
should have a huge lump of cold salt butter stuck in its centre;
and then, her household cares being over, to retire to her room
and array herself in a robe of white damask for the occasion.
At eight o'clock she was summoned to the supper-room. She
came in, according to the fashion of the times, with the first
dish; but as she passed through the ante-room, where the servants were holding lights and bearing the dishes, her sleeve was
twitched, and the ghastly face of the Collogue pushed close to
hers; while she muttered 'Did not I say *he would come for
you*, dear?' Anne's blood ran cold, but she advanced, saluted
her father and the stranger with two low and distinct rever-
ences, and then took her place at the table. Her feelings of awe
and perhaps terror at the whisper of her associate, were not
diminished by the appearance of the stranger; there was a singular and mute solemnity in his manner during the meal. He
ate nothing. Sir Redmond appeared constrained, gloomy and
thoughtful. At length, starting, he said (without naming the
stranger's name), 'You will drink my daughter's health?' The
stranger intimated his willingness to have that honour, but

absently filled his glass with water; Anne put a few drops of wine into hers, and bowed towards him. At that moment, for the first time since they had met, she beheld his face – it was pale as that of a corpse. The deadly whiteness of his cheeks and lips, the hollow and distant sound of his voice, and the strange lustre of his large dark moveless eyes, strongly fixed on her, made her pause and even tremble as she raised the glass to her lips; she set it down, and then with another silent reverence retired to her chamber.

There she found Bridget Dease, busy in collecting the turf that burned on the hearth, for there was no grate in the apartment. 'Why are you here?' she said, impatiently.

The hag turned on her, with a ghastly grin of congratulation, 'Did not I tell you that *he* would come for you?'

'I believe he has,' said the unfortunate girl, sinking into the huge wicker chair by her bedside; 'for never did I see mortal with such a look.'

'But is not he a fine stately gentleman?' pursued the hag.

'He looks as if he were not of this world,' said Anne.

'Of this world, or of the next,' said the hag, raising her bony fore-finger, 'mark my words – so sure as the – (here she repeated some of the horrible formularies of the 31st of October) – so sure he will be your bridegroom.'

'Then I shall be the bride of a corpse,' said Anne; 'for he I saw tonight is no living man.'

A fortnight elapsed, and whether Anne became reconciled to the features she had thought so ghastly, by the discovery that they were the handsomest she had ever beheld – and that the voice, whose sound at first was so strange and unearthly, was subdued into a tone of plaintive softness when addressing her – or whether it is impossible for two young persons with unoccupied hearts to meet in the country, and meet often, to gaze silently on the same stream, wander under the same trees, and listen together to the wind that waves the branches, without experiencing an assimilation of feeling rapidly succeeding an assimilation of taste; – or whether it was from all these causes combined, but in less than a month Anne heard the declaration of the stranger's passion with many a blush, though without a sigh. He now avowed his name and rank. He stated himself to be a Scottish Baronet, of the name of Sir Richard Maxwell; family misfortunes had driven him from his country, and for ever precluded the possibility of his return: he had transferred his property to Ireland, and purposed to fix his residence there for life. Such was his statement. The courtship of those days was brief and simple. Anne became the wife of Sir Richard, and, I believe, they resided with her father till his death, when they removed to their estate in the North. There they remained for several years, in tranquillity and happiness, and had a numerous family. Sir Richard's conduct was marked by but two peculiarities: he not only shunned the intercourse, but the sight of any of his countrymen, and, if he happened to hear that a Scotsman had arrived in the neighbouring town, he shut himself up till assured of the stranger's departure. The other was his custom of retiring to his own chamber, and remaining invisible to his family on the anniversary of the 31st October. The lady, who had her own associations connected with that period, only questioned him once on the subject of this seclusion, and was then solemnly and even sternly enjoined never to repeat her inquiry. Matters stood thus, somewhat mysteriously, but not unhappily, when on a sudden, without any cause assigned or assignable, Sir Richard and Lady Maxwell parted, and never more met in this world, nor was she ever permitted to see one of her children to her dying hour. He continued to live at the family mansion, and she fixed her residence with a distant relative in a remote part of the country. So total was the disunion, that the name of either was never heard to pass the other's lips, from the moment of separation until that of dissolution.

Lady Maxwell survived Sir Richard forty years, living to the great age of ninety-six; and, according to a promise, previously given, disclosed to a descendent with whom she had lived, the following extraordinary circumstances.

She said that on the night of the 31st of October, about seventy-five years before, at the instigation of her ill-advising attendant, she had washed one of her garments in a place where four streams met, and peformed other unhallowed ceremonies under the direction of the Collogue, in the expectation that her future husband would appear to her in her chamber at twelve o'clock that night. The critical moment arrived, but with it no lover-like form. A vision of indescribable horror approached her bed, and flinging at her an iron weapon of a shape and construction unknown to her, bade her 'recognize her future husband by *that*.' The terrors of this visit soon deprived her of her senses; but on her recovery, she persisted, as has been said, in keeping the fearful pledge of the reality of the vision, which, on examination, appeared to be incrusted with blood. It remained concealed in the inmost drawer of her cabinet till the morning of the separation. On that morning, Sir Richard Maxwell rose before daylight to join a hunting party – he wanted a knife for some accidental purpose, and, missing his own, called to Lady Maxwell, who was still in bed, to lend him one. The lady, who was half asleep, answered, that in such a drawer of her cabinet he would find one. He went, however, to another, and the next moment she was fully awakened by seeing her husband present the terrible weapon to her throat, and threaten her with instant death unless she disclosed how she came by it. She supplicated for life, and then, in an agony of horror and contrition, told the tale of that eventful night. He gazed at her for a moment with a countenance which rage, hatred, and despair converted, as she avowed, into a living likeness of the demon-visage she had once beheld (so singularly was the fated resemblance fulfilled), and then exclaiming, 'You won me by the devil's aid, but you shall not keep me long,' left her – to meet no more in this world. Her husband's secret was not unknown to the lady, though the means by which she became possessed of it were wholly unwarrantable. Her curiosity had been strongly excited by her husband's aversion to his countrymen, and it was so stimulated by the arrival of a Scottish gentleman in the neighbourhood some time before, who professed himself formerly acquainted with Sir Richard, and spoke mysteriously of the causes that drove him from his country – that she contrived to procure an interview with him under a feigned name, and obtained from him the knowledge of circumstances which embittered her after-life to its latest hour. His story was this:

Sir Richard Maxwell was at deadly feud with a younger brother; a family feast was proposed to reconcile them, and as the use of knives and forks was then unknown in the Highlands, the company met armed with their dirks for the purpose of carving. They drank deeply; the feast, instead of harmonizing, began to inflame their spirits; the topics of old strife were renewed; hands, that at first touched their weapons in defiance, drew them at last in fury, and in the fray, Sir Richard mortally wounded his brother. His life was with difficulty saved from the vengeance of the clan, and he was hurried towards the sea-coast, near which the house stood, and concealed there till a vessel could be procured to convey him to Ireland. He embarked *on the night of the 31st of October*, and while he was traversing the deck in unutterable agony of spirit, his hand accidentally touched the dirk which he had unconsciously worn ever since the fatal night. He drew it, and, praying 'that the guilt of his brother's blood might be as far from his soul, as he could fling that weapon from his body,' sent it with all his strength into the air. This instrument he found secreted in the lady's cabinet, and whether he really believed her to have become possessed of it by supernatural means, or whether he feared his wife was a secret witness of his crime, has not been ascertained, but the result was what I have stated.

The reparation took place on the discovery: — for the rest,

> I know not how the truth may be,
> I tell the Tale as 'twas told to me.

# The Vampyre

## John William Polidori
## (1795–1821)

The 'gathering' which brought Lord Byron, Percy Shelley, his
wife, Mary, and Dr John Polidori to the shores of Lake Geneva in
June 1816 and resulted in the most famous of all horror novels,
*Frankenstein*, is now part of literary history. Confined in their
Mansion or Campagne Chapuis by two weeks of torrential rain, the
Shelleys had invited their new neighbour, Lord Byron and his companion, to join them and there began a joint reading of a collection
of German ghost stories, *Fantasmagoriana*. So stimulated were they
all by the tales, that it was agreed each should try and produce a
similar item for the entertainment of the company. The three men
set to work almost immediately, but for Mary Shelley inspiration
was hard to come by and it was not until several nights later that her
mind was fired by a nightmare in which a 'pale student of unhallowed arts created the awful phantom of a man'. From this experience came *Frankenstein*.

The first to complete his allotted task was Dr Polidori, the secretary and travelling compaion to Byron who, with his tale, *The
Vampyre*, introduced the legendary blood-sucking creature of the
night to English literature. John William Polidori was twenty-one
at the time of the gathering and although he had been taken into
the English poet's service on good recommendation, it was not long
before these two men of different temperaments were quarrelling
fiercely. Indeed, before the summer was out they parted (Byron
having become exasperated by the 'eternal nonsense, emptiness, ill-
humour and vanity of that young man') and Polidori returned to
England where he set up a medical practice in Norwich. His contact
with the literati, however, nagged at his ambitions and he decided
to move to London and attempt to earn fame for himself in this

sphere. Sadly, his talent without the inspiration of such as Byron and Shelley around him was limited and eventually he committed suicide after his books failed and he fell heavily into debt through gambling.

The story of the initial publication of *The Vampyre* is also interesting in that it was first ascribed to Lord Byron and appeared as being by him (in 1819) despite vehement protests by both Polidori and Byron himself who wrote to the publisher, 'I am not the author, and never heard of the work in question until now.' After further effort Polidori was able to establish his authorship of the piece (and with it his sole claim to literary remembrance) although he did admit that he had made use of suggestions provided by his late employer who planned a not dissimilar tale. Here it is, then, and afterwards we shall examine examples of Gothic writing by each of the other members of that remarkable quartet . . .


IT happened that in the midst of the dissipations attendant upon a London winter, there appeared at the various parties of the leaders of the *ton* a nobleman, more remarkable for his singularities, than his rank. He gazed upon the mirth around him, as if he could not participate therein. Apparently, the light laughter of the fair only attracted his attention, that he might by a look quell it, and throw fear into those breasts where thoughtlessness reigned. Those who felt this sensation of awe, could not explain whence it arose: some attributed it to the dead grey eye, which, fixing upon the object's face, did not seem to penetrate, and at one glance to pierce through to the inward workings of the heart; but fell upon the cheek with a leaden ray that weighed upon the skin it could not pass. His peculiarities caused him to be invited to every house; all wished to see him, and those who had been accustomed to violent excitement, and now felt the weight of *ennui*, were pleased at having something in their presence capable of engaging their attention. In spite of the deadly hue of his face, which never gained a warmer tint, either from the blush of modesty, or from the strong emotion of passion, though its form and outline were beautiful, many of the female hunters after notoriety attempted to win his attentions, and gain, at least, some marks of what they might term affection: Lady Mercer, who had been the mockery of every monster shewn in drawing-rooms since her marriage, threw herself in his way, and did all but put on the dress of a mountebank, to attract his notice – though in vain – when she stood before him: though his eyes were apparently fixed upon hers, still it seemed as if they were unperceived; – even her un-appalled impudence was baffled, and she left the field. But though the common adultress could not influence even the guidance of his eyes, it was not that the female sex was indifferent to him: yet such was the apparent caution with which he spoke to the virtuous wife and innocent daughter, that few knew he ever addressed himself to females. He had, however, the reputation of a winning tongue; and whether it was that it even overcame the dread of his singular character, or that they were moved by his apparent hatred of vice, he was as often among those females who form the boast of their sex from their domestic virtues, as among those who sully it by their vices.

About the same time, there came to London a young gentleman of the name of Aubrey: he was an orphan left with an only sister in the possession of great wealth, by parents who died while he was yet in childhood. Left also to himself by guardians, who thought it their duty merely to take care of his fortune, while they relinquished the more important charge of his mind to the care of mercenary subalterns, he cultivated more his imagination than his judgment. He had, hence, that high romantic feeling of honour and candour, which daily ruins so many milliners' apprentices. He believed all to sympathize with virtue, and thought that vice was thrown in by Providence merely for the picturesque effect of the scene, as we see in romances: he thought that the misery of a cottage merely consisted in the vesting of clothes, which were as warm, but which were better adapted to the painter's eye by their irregular folds and various coloured patches. He thought, in fine, that the dreams of poets were the realities of life. He was handsome, frank, and rich: for these reasons, upon his entering into the gay circles, many mothers surrounded him, striving which should describe with least truth their languishing or romping favourites: the daughters at the same time, by their brightening countenances when he approached, and by their sparkling eyes, when he opened his lips, soon led him into false notions of his talents and his merit. Attached as he was to the romance of his solitary hours, he was startled at finding, that, except in the tallow and wax candles that flickered, not from the presence of a ghost, but from want of snuffing, there was no foundation in real life for any of that congeries of pleasing pictures and descriptions contained in those volumes, from which he had formed his study. Finding, however, some compensation in his gratified vanity, he was about to relinquish his dreams, when the extraordinary being we have above described, crossed him in his career.

He watched him; and the very impossibility of forming an idea of the character of a man entirely absorbed in himself, who gave few other signs of his observation of external objects, than the tacit assent to their existence, implied by the avoidance of their contact, allowing his imagination to picture everything that flattered its propensity to extravagant ideas, he soon formed this object into the hero of a romance, and determined to observe the offspring of his fancy, rather than the person before him. He became acquainted with him, paid him attentions, and so far advanced upon his notice, that his presence was always recognized. He gradually learnt that Lord Ruthven's affairs were embarrassed, and soon found, from the notes of preparation in — Street, that he was about to travel. Desirous of gaining some information respecting this singular character, who, till now, had only whetted his curiosity, he hinted to his guardians, that it was time for him to perform the tour, which for many generations has been thought necessary to enable the young to take some rapid steps in the career of vice towards putting themselves upon an equality with the aged, and not allowing them to appear as if fallen from the skies, whenever scandalous intrigues are mentioned as the subjects of pleasantry or of praise, according to the degree of skill shewn in carrying them on. They consented: and Aubrey immediately mentioning his intentions to Lord Ruthven, was surprised to receive from him a proposal to join him. Flattered by such a mark of esteem from him, who, apparently, had nothing in common with other men, he gladly accepted it, and in a few days they had passed the circling waters.

Hitherto, Aubrey had had no opportunity of studying Lord Ruthven's character, and now he found, that, though many more of his actions were exposed to his view, the results offered different conclusions from the apparent motives to his conduct. His companion was profuse in his liberality – the idle, the vagabond, and the beggar, received from his hand more than enough to relieve their immediate wants. But Aubrey could not avoid remarking, that it was not upon the virtuous, reduced to indigence by the misfortunes attendant even upon virtue, that he bestowed his alms – these were sent from the door with hardly suppressed sneers; but when the profligate came to ask something, not to relieve his wants, but to allow him to wallow in his lust, or to sink him still deeper in his iniquity, he was sent away with rich charity. This was, however, attributed by him to the greater importunity of the vicious, which generally prevails over the retiring bashfulness of the virtuous indigent. There was one circumstance about the charity of his Lordship, which was still more impressed upon his mind: all those upon whom it was bestowed, inevitably found that there was a curse upon it, for they were all either led to the scaffold, or sunk to the lowest and the most abject misery. At Brussels and other towns through which they passed, Aubrey was surprised at the apparent eagerness with which his companion sought for the centres of all fashionable vice; there he entered into all the spirit of the faro table: he betted, and always gambled with success, except where the known sharper was his antagonist, and then he lost even more than he gained; but it was always with the same unchanging face, with which he generally watched the society around: it was not, however so when he encountered the rash youthful novice, or the luckless father of a numerous family; then his very wish seemed fortune's law – this apparent abstractedness of mind was laid aside, and his eyes sparkled with more fire than that of the cat whilst dallying with the half-dead mouse. In every town, he left the formerly affluent youth, torn from the circle he adorned, cursing, in the solitude of a dungeon, the fate that had drawn him within the reach of this fiend; whilst many a father sat frantic, amidst the speaking looks of mute hungry children, without a single farthing of his late immense wealth, wherewith to buy even sufficient to satisfy their present craving. Yet he took no money from the gambling table; but immediately lost, to the ruiner of many, the last gilder he had just snatched from the convulsive grasp of the innocent: this might but be the result of a certain degree of knowledge, which was not, however, capable of combating the cunning of the more experienced. Aubrey often wished to represent this to his friend, and beg him to resign that charity and pleasure which proved the ruin of all, and did not tend to his own profit; but he delayed it – for each day he hoped his friend would give him some opportunity of speaking frankly and openly to him; however, this never occurred. Lord Ruthven in his carriage, and amidst the various wild and rich scenes of nature, was always the same: his eye spoke less than his lip; and though Aubrey was near the object of his curiosity, he obtained no greater gratification from it than the constant excitement of vainly wishing to break that mystery, which to his exalted imagination began to assume the appearance of something supernatural.

They soon arrived at Rome, and Aubrey for a time lost sight of his companion; he left him in daily attendance upon the morning circle of an Italian countess, whilst he went in search of the memorials of another almost deserted city. Whilst he was thus engaged, letters arrived from England, which he opened with eager impatience; the first was from his sister, breathing nothing but affection; the others were from his guardians. The latter astonished him; if it had before entered into his imagination that there was an evil power resident in his companion, these seemed to give him almost sufficient reason for the belief. His guardians insisted upon his immediately leaving his friend, and urged, that his character was dreadfully vicious, for that the possession of irresistible powers of seduction, rendered his licentious habits more dangerous to society. It had been discovered, that his contempt for the adultress had not originated in hatred of her character; but that he had required, to enhance his gratification, that his victim, the partner of his guilt, should be hurled from the pinnacle of unsullied virtue, down to the lowest abyss of infamy and degradation: in fine, that all those females whom he had sought, apparently on account of their virtue, had, since his departure, thrown even the mask aside, and had not scrupled to expose the whole deformity of their vices to the public gaze.

Aubrey determined upon leaving one, whose character had not yet shown a single bright point on which to rest the eye. He resolved to invent some plausible pretext for abandoning him altogether, purposing, in the mean while, to watch him more closely, and to let no slight circumstances pass by unnoticed. He entered into the same circle, and soon perceived, that his Lordship was endeavouring to work upon the inexperience of the daughter of the lady whose house he chiefly frequented. In Italy, it is seldom that an unmarried female is met with in society; he was therefore obliged to carry on his plans in secret; but Aubrey's eye followed him in all his windings, and soon discovered that an assignation had been appointed, which would most likely end in the ruin of an innocent, though thoughtless girl. Losing no time, he entered the apartment of Lord Ruthven, and abruptly asked him his intentions with respect to the lady, informing him at the same time that he was aware of his being about to meet her that very night. Lord Ruthven answered, that his intentions were such as he supposed all would have upon such an occasion; and upon being pressed whether he intended to marry her, merely laughed. Aubrey retired; and, immediately writing a note, to say, that from that moment he must decline accompanying his Lordship in the remainder of their proposed tour, he ordered his servant to seek other apartments, and calling upon the mother of the lady, informed her of all he knew, not only with regard to her daughter, but also concerning the character of his Lordship. The assignation was prevented. Lord Ruthven next day merely sent his servant to notify his complete assent to a separation; but did not hint any suspicion of his plans having been foiled by Aubrey's interposition.

Having left Rome, Aubrey directed his steps towards Greece,

and crossing the Peninsula, soon found himself at Athens. He then fixed his residence in the house of a Greek; and soon occupied himself in tracing the faded records of ancient glory upon monuments that apparently, ashamed of chronicling the deeds of freemen only before slaves, had hidden themselves beneath the sheltering soil or many coloured lichen. Under the same roof as himself, existed a being, so beautiful and delicate, that she might have formed the model for a painter, wishing to portray on canvas the promised hope of the faithful in Mahomet's paradise, save that her eyes spoke too much mind for anyone to think she could belong to those who had no souls. As she danced upon the plain, or tripped along the mountain's side, one would have thought the gazelle a poor type of her beauties; for who would have exchanged her eye, apparently the eye of animated nature, for that sleepy luxurious look of the animal suited but to the taste of an epicure. The light step of Ianthe often accompanied Aubrey in his search after antiquities, and often would the unconscious girl, engaged in the pursuit of a Kashmere butterfly, show the whole beauty of her form, floating as it were upon the wind, to the eager gaze of him, who forgot the letters he had just decyphered upon an almost effaced tablet, in the contemplation of her sylph-like figure. Often would her tresses falling, as she flitted around, exhibit in the sun's ray such delicately brilliant and swiftly fading hues, as might well excuse the forgetfulness of the antiquary, who let escape from his mind the very object he had before thought of vital importance to the proper interpretation of a passage in Pausanias. But why attempt to describe charms which all feel, but none can appreciate? – It was innocence, youth, and beauty, unaffected by crowded drawing-rooms and stifling balls. Whilst he drew those remains of which he wished to preserve a memorial for his future hours, she would stand by, and watch the magic effects of his pencil, in tracing the scenes of her native place; she would then describe to him the circling dance upon the open plain, would paint to him in all the glowing colours of youthful memory, the marriage pomp she remembered viewing in her infancy; and then, turning to subjects that had evidently made a greater impression upon her mind, would tell him all the supernatural tales of her nurse. Her earnestness and apparent belief of what she narrated, excited the interest even of Aubrey; and often as she told him the tale of the living vampyre, who had passed years amidst his friends, and dearest ties, forced every year, by feeding upon the life of a lovely female to prolong his existence for the ensuing months, his blood would run cold, whilst he attempted to laugh her out of such idle and horrible fantasies; but Ianthe cited to him the names of old men, who had at last detected one living among themselves, after several of their near relatives and children had been found marked with the stamp of the fiend's appetite; and when she found him so incredulous, she begged of him to believe her, for it had been remarked, that those who had dared to question their existence, always had some proof given, which obliged them, with grief and heartbreaking, to confess it was true. She detailed to him the traditional appearance of these monsters, and his horror was increased, by hearing a pretty accurate description of Lord Ruthven; he, however, still persisted in persuading her, that there could be no truth in her fears, though at the same time he wondered at the many coincidences which had all tended to excite a belief in the supernatural power of Lord Ruthven.

Aubrey began to attach himself more and more to Ianthe; her innocence, so contrasted with all the affected virtues of the women among whom he had sought for his vision of romance, won his heart; and while he ridiculed the idea of a young man of English habits, marrying an uneducated Greek girl, still he found himself more and more attached to the almost fairy form before him. He would tear himself at times from her, and, forming a plan for some antiquarian research, he would depart, determined not to return until his object was attained; but he always found it impossible to fix his attention upon the ruins around him, whilst in his mind he retained an image that seemed alone the rightful possessor of his thoughts. Ianthe was unconscious of his love, and was ever the same frank infantile being he had first known. She always seemed to part from him with reluctance; but it was because she had no longer any one with whom she could visit her favourite haunts, whilst her guardian was occupied in sketching or uncovering some fragment which had yet escaped the destructive hand of time. She had appealed to her parents on the subject of Vampyres, and they both, with several present, affirmed their existence, pale with horror at the very name. Soon after, Aubrey determined to proceed upon one of his excursions, which was to detain him for a few hours; when they heard the name of the place, they all at once begged of him not to return at night, as he must necessarily pass through a wood, where no Greek would ever remain, after the day had closed, upon any consideration. They described it as the resort of the vampyres in their nocturnal orgies, and denounced the most heavy evils as impending upon him who dared to cross their path. Aubrey made light of their representations, and tried to laugh them out of the idea; but when he saw them shudder at his daring thus to mock a superior, infernal power, the very name of which apparently made their blood freeze, he was silent.

Next morning Aubrey set off upon his excursion unattended; he was surprised to observe the melancholy face of his host, and was concerned to find that his words, mocking the belief of those horrible fiends, had inspired them with such terror. When he was about to depart, Ianthe came to the side of his horse, and earnestly begged of him to return, ere night allowed the power of these beings to be put in action; – he promised. He was, however, so occupied in his research, that he did not perceive that day-light would soon end, and that in the horizon there was one of those specks which, in the warmer climates, so rapidly gather into a tremendous mass, and pour all their rage upon the devoted country. – He at last, however, mounted his horse, determined to make up by speed for his delay: but it was too late. Twilight, in these southern climates, is almost unknown; immediately the sun sets, night begins: and ere he had advanced far, the power of the storm was above – its echoing thunders had scarcely an interval of rest; – its thick heavy rain forced its way through the canopying foliage, whilst the blue forked lightning seemed to fall and radiate at his very feet. Suddenly his horse took fright, and he was carried with dreadful rapidity through the entangled forest. The animal at last, through fatigue, stopped, and he found, by the glare of lightning, that he was in the neighbourhood of a hovel that hardly lifted itself up from the masses of dead leaves and brushwood which surrounded it. Dismounting, he approached, hoping to find someone to guide him to the town, or at least trusting to obtain shelter from the pelting of the storm. As he approached, the thunders, for a moment silent, allowed him to hear the dreadful shrieks of a woman mingling with the stifled, exultant mockery of a laugh, continued in one almost unbroken sound; – he was startled: but, roused by the thunder which again rolled over his head, he, with a sudden effort, forced open the door of the hut. He found himself in utter darkness: the sound, however, guided him. He was apparently unperceived; for, though he called, still the sounds continued, and no notice was taken of him. He found himself in contact with some one, whom he immediately seized; when a voice cried, 'Again baffled!' to which a loud laugh succeeded; and he felt himself grappled by one whose strength seemed superhuman: determined to sell his life as dearly as he could, he struggled; but it was in vain: he was lifted from his feet and hurled with enormous force against the ground: – his enemy threw himself upon him, and kneeling upon his breast, had placed his hands upon his throat – when the glare of many torches penetrating through the hole that gave light in the day, disturbed him; – he instantly rose, and, leaving his prey, rushed through the door, and in a moment the crashing of the branches, as he broke through the wood, was no longer heard. The storm was now still; and Aubrey, incapable of moving, was soon heard by those without. They entered; the light of their torches fell upon the mud walls, and the thatch loaded one very individual straw with heavy flakes of soot. At the desire of Aubrey they searched for her who had attracted him by her cries; he was again left in darkness; but what was his horror, when the light of the torches once more burst upon him, to perceive the airy form of his fair conductress brought in a lifeless corpse. He shut his eyes, hoping that it was but a vision arising from his disturbed imagination; but he again saw the same form, when he unclosed them, stretched by his side.

There was no colour upon her cheek, not even upon her lip; yet there was a stillness about her face that seemed almost as attaching as the life that once dwelt there: upon her neck and breast was blood, and upon her throat were the marks of teeth having opened the vein: to this the men pointed, crying, simultaneously struck with horror, 'A Vampyre! a Vampyre!' A litter was quickly formed, and Aubrey was laid by the side of her who had lately been to him the object of so many bright and fairy visions, now fallen with the flower of life that had died within her. He knew not what his thoughts were – his mind was benumbed and seemed to shun reflection, and take refuge in vacancy; – he held almost unconsciously in his hand a naked dagger of a particular construction, which had been found in the hut. They were soon met by different parties who had been engaged in the search of her whom a mother had missed. Their lamentable cries, as they approached the city, forewarned the parents of some dreadful catastrophe. – To describe their grief would be impossible; but when they ascertained the cause of their child's death, they looked at Aubrey, and pointed to the corpse. They were inconsolable; both died broken-hearted.

Aubrey being put to bed was seized with a most violent fever, and was often delirious; in these intervals he would call upon Lord Ruthven and upon Ianthe – by some unaccountable combination he seemed to beg of his former companion to spare the being he loved. At other times he would imprecate maledictions upon his head, and curse him as her destroyer. Lord Ruthven chanced at this time to arrive at Athens, and, from whatever motive, upon hearing of the state of Aubrey, immediately placed himself in the same house, and became his constant attendant. When the latter recovered from his delirium, he was horrified and startled at the sight of him whose image he had now combined with that of a Vampyre; but Lord Ruthven, by his kind words, implying almost repentance for the fault that had caused their separation, and still more by the attention, anxiety, and care which he showed, soon reconciled him to his presence. His lordship seemed quite changed; he no longer appeared that apathetic being who had so astonished Aubrey; but as soon as his convalescence began to be rapid, he again gradually retired into the same state of mind, and Aubrey perceived no difference from the former man, except that at times he was surprised to meet his gaze fixed intently upon him, with a smile of malicious exultation playing upon his lips: he knew not why, but this smile haunted him. During the last stage of the invalid's recovery, Lord Ruthven was apparently engaged in watching the tideless waves raised by the cooling breeze, or in marking the progress of those orbs, circling, like our world, the moveless sun; – indeed, he appeared to wish to avoid the eyes of all.

Aubrey's mind, by this shock, was much weakened, and that elasticity of spirit which had once so distinguished him now seemed to have fled for ever. He was now as much a lover of solitude and silence as Lord Ruthven; but much as he wished for solitude, his mind could not find it in the neighbourhood of Athens; if he sought it amidst the ruins he had formerly frequented, Ianthe's form stood by his side; – if he sought it in the woods, her light step would appear wandering amidst the underwood, in quest of the modest violet; then suddenly turning round, would show, to his wild imagination, her pale face and wounded throat, with a meek smile upon her lips. He determined to fly scenes, every feature of which created such bitter associations in his mind. He proposed to Lord Ruthven, to whom he held himself bound by the tender care he had taken of him during his illness, that they should visit those parts of Greece neither had yet seen. They travelled in every direction, and sought every spot to which a recollection could be attached: but though they thus hastened from place to place, yet they seemed not to heed what they gazed upon. They heard much of robbers, but they gradually began to slight these reports, which they imagined were only the invention of individuals, whose interest it was to excite the generosity of those whom they defended from pretended dangers. In consequence of thus neglecting the advice of the inhabitants, on one occasion they travelled with only a few guards, more to serve as guides than as a

defence. Upon entering, however, a narrow defile, at the bottom
of which was the bed of a torrent, with large masses of rock
brought down from the neighbouring precipices, they had reason to repent their negligence; for scarcely were the whole of the
party engaged in the narrow pass, when they were startled by
the whistling of bullets close to their heads, and by the echoed
report of several guns. In an instant their guards had left them,
and, placing themselves behind rocks, had begun to fire in the
direction whence the report came. Lord Ruthven and Aubrey,
imitating their example, retired for a moment behind the sheltering turn of the defile; but ashamed of being thus detained by
a foe, who with insulting shouts bade them advance, and being
exposed to unresisting slaughter, if any of the robbers should
climb above and take them in the rear, they determined at once
to rush forwards in search of the enemy. Hardly had they lost
the shelter of the rock, when Lord Ruthven received a shot in
the shoulder, which brought him to the ground. Aubrey hastened to his assistance; and, no longer heeding the contest or his
own peril, was soon surprised by seeing the robbers' faces
around him – his guards having, upon Lord Ruthven's being
wounded, immediately thrown up their arms and surrendered.

By promises of great reward, Aubrey soon induced them to
convey his wounded friend to a neighbouring cabin; and having agreed upon a ransom, he was no more disturbed by their
presence – they being content merely to guard the entrance till
their comrade should return with the promised sum, for which
he had an order. Lord Ruthven's strength rapidly decreased; in
two days mortification ensued, and death seemed advancing
with hasty steps. His conduct and appearance had not changed;
he seemed as unconscious of pain as he had been of the objects
about him: but towards the close of the last evening, his mind
became apparently uneasy, and his eye often fixed upon Aubrey, who was induced to offer his assistance with more than
usual earnestness – 'Assist me! you may save me – you may do
more than that – I mean not my life, I heed the death of my
existence as little as that of the passing day; but you may save
my honour, your friend's honour.' – 'How? tell me how? I

would do any thing,' replied Aubrey. – 'I need but little – my life ebbs apace – I cannot explain the whole – but if you would conceal all you know of me, my honour were free from stain in the world's mouth – and if my death were unknown for some time in England – I – I but life.' – 'It shall not be known.' – 'Swear!' cried the dying man, raising himself with exultant violence, 'Swear by all your soul reveres, by all your nature fears, swear that for a year and a day you will not impart your knowledge of my crimes or death to any living being in any way, whatever may happen, or whatever you may see.' – His eyes seemed bursting from their sockets: 'I swear!' said Aubrey; he sunk laughing upon his pillow, and breathed no more.

Aubrey retired to rest, but did not sleep; the many circumstances attending his acquaintance with this man rose upon his mind, and he knew not why; when he remembered his oath a cold shivering came over him, as if from the presentiment of something horrible awaiting him. Rising early in the morning, he was about to enter the hovel in which he had left the corpse, when a robber met him, and informed him that it was no longer there, having been conveyed by himself and comrades, upon his retiring, to the pinnacle of a neighbouring mount, according to a promise they had given his lordship, that it should be exposed to the first cold ray of the moon that rose after his death. Aubrey astonished, and taking several of the men, determined to go and bury it upon the spot where it lay. But, when he had mounted to the summit he found no trace of either the corpse or the clothes, though the robbers swore they pointed out the identical rock on which they had laid the body. For a time his mind was bewildered in conjectures, but he at last returned, convinced that they had buried the corpse for the sake of the clothes.

Weary of a country in which he had met with such terrible misfortunes, and in which all apparently conspired to heighten that superstitious melancholy that had seized upon his mind, he resolved to leave it, and soon arrived at Smyrna. While waiting for a vessel to convey him to Otranto, or to Naples, he occupied himself in arranging those effects he had with him belonging to Lord Ruthven. Amongst other things there was a case containing several weapons of offence, more or less adapted to ensure the death of the victim. There were several daggers and ataghans. Whilst turning them over, and examining their curious forms, what was his surprise at finding a sheath apparently ornamented in the same style as the dagger discovered in the fatal hut; – he shuddered; – hastening to gain further proof, he found the weapon, and his horror may be imagined when he discovered that it fitted, though peculiarly shaped, the sheath he held in his hand. His eyes seemed to need no further certainty – they seemed gazing to be bound to the dagger; yet still he wished to disbelieve; but the particular form, the same varying tints upon the haft and sheath were alike in splendour on both, and left no room for doubt; there were also drops of blood on each.

He left Smyrna, and on his way home, at Rome, his first inquiries were concerning the lady he had attempted to snatch from Lord Ruthven's seductive arts. Her parents were in distress, their fortune ruined, and she had not been heard of since the departure of his lordship. Aubrey's mind became almost broken under so many repeated horrors; he was afraid that this lady had fallen a victim to the destroyer of Ianthe. He became morose and silent; and his only occupation consisted in urging the speed of the postilions, as if he were going to save the life of some one he held dear. He arrived at Calais; a breeze, which seemed obedient to his will, soon wafted him to the English shores; and he hastened to the mansion of his fathers, and there, for a moment, appeared to lose, in the embraces and caresses of his sister, all memory of the past. If she before, by her infantine caresses, had gained his affection, now that the woman began to appear, she was still more attaching as a companion.

Miss Aubrey had not that winning grace which gains the gaze and applause of the drawing-room assemblies. There was none of that light brilliancy which only exists in the heated atmosphere of a crowded apartment. Her blue eye was never lit up by the levity of the mind beneath. There was a melancholy charm about it which did not seem to arise from misfortune, but from some feeling within, that appeared to indicate a soul conscious of a brighter realm. Her step was not that light footing, which strays wher'er a butterfly or a colour may attract – it was sedate and pensive. When alone, her face was never brightened by the smile of joy; but when her brother breathed to her his affection, and would in her presence forget those griefs she knew destroyed his rest, who would have exchanged her smile for that of the voluptuary? It seemed as if those eyes, that face were then playing in the light of their own native sphere. She was yet only eighteen, and had not been presented to the world, it having been thought by her guardians more fit that her presentation should be delayed until her brother's return from the continent, when he might be her protector. It was now, therefore, resolved that the next drawing-room, which was fast approaching, should be the epoch of her entry into the 'busy scene'. Aubrey would rather have remained in the mansion of his fathers, and fed upon the melancholy which overpowered him. He could not feel interest about the frivolities of fashionable strangers, when his mind had been so torn by the events he had witnessed; but he determined to sacrifice his own comfort to the protection of his sister. They soon arrived in town, and prepared for the next day, which had been announced as a drawing-room.

The crowd was excessive – a drawing-room had not been held for a long time, and all who were anxious to bask in the smile of royalty, hastened thither. Aubrey was there with his sister. While he was standing in a corner by himself, heedless of all around him, engaged in the remembrance that the first time he had seen Lord Ruthven was in that very place – he felt himself suddenly seized by the arm, and a voice he recognized too well, sounded in his ear – 'Remember your oath.' He had hardly courage to turn, fearful of seeing a spectre that would blast him, when he perceived, at a little distance, the same figure which had attracted his notice on this spot upon his first entry into society. He gazed till his limbs almost refusing to bear their weight, he was obliged to take the arm of a friend, and forcing a passage through the crowd, he threw himself into his carriage, and was driven home. He paced the room with hurried steps, and fixed his hands upon his head, as if he were afraid his thoughts were bursting from his brain. Lord Ruthven again before him – circumstances started up in dreadful array – the dagger – his oath. – He roused himself, he could not believe it possible – the dead rise again! – He thought his imagination had conjured up the image his mind was resting upon. It was impossible that it could be real – he determined, therefore, to go again into society; for though he attempted to ask concerning Lord Ruthven, the name hung upon his lips, and he could not succeed in gaining information. He went a few nights after with his sister to the assembly of a near relation. Leaving her under the protection of a matron, he retired into a recess, and there gave himself up to his own devouring thoughts. Perceiving, at last, that many were leaving, he roused himself, and entering another room, found his sister surrounded by several, apparently in earnest conversation; he attempted to pass and get near her, when one, whom he requested to move, turned round, and revealed to him those features he most abhorred. He sprang forward, seized his sister's arm, and, with hurried step, forced her towards the street: at the door he found himself impeded by the crowd of servants who were waiting for their lords; and while he was engaged in passing them, he again heard that voice whisper close to him – 'Remember your oath!' – He did not dare to turn, but hurrying his sister, soon reached home.

Aubrey became almost distracted. If before his mind had been absorbed by one subject, how much more completely was it engrossed, now that the certainty of the monster's living again pressed upon his thoughts. His sister's attentions were now unheeded, and it was in vain that she entreated him to explain to her what had caused his abrupt conduct. He only uttered a few words, and those terrified her. The more he thought, the more he was bewildered. His oath startled him; – was he then to allow this monster to roam, bearing ruin upon his breath, amidst all he held dear, and not avert its progress? His very sister might have been touched by him. But even if he were to break his oath, and disclose his suspicions, who would believe him? He thought of employing his own hand to free the world from such a wretch; but death, he remembered, had been already mocked. For days he remained in this state; shut up in his room, he saw no one, and ate only when his sister came, who, with eyes streaming with tears, besought him, for her sake, to support nature. At last, no longer capable of bearing stillness and solitude, he left his house, roamed from street to street, anxious to fly that image which haunted him. His dress became neglected, and he wandered, as often exposed to the noon-day sun as to the midnight damps. He was no longer to be recognized; at first he returned with the evening to the house; but at last he laid him down to rest wherever fatigue overtook him. His sister, anxious for his safety, employed people to follow him; but they were soon distanced by him who fled from a pursuer swifter than any – from thought. His conduct, however, suddenly changed. Struck with the idea that he left by his absence the whole of his friends, with a fiend amongst them, of whose presence they were unconscious, he determined to enter again into society, and watch him closely, anxious to forewarn, in spite of his oath, all whom Lord Ruthven approached with intimacy. But when he entered into a room, his haggard and suspicious looks were so striking, his inward shudderings so visible, that his sister was at last obliged to beg of him to abstain from seeking, for her sake, a society which affected him so strongly. When, however, remonstrance proved unavailing, the guardians thought proper to interpose, and, fearing that his mind was becoming alienated, they thought it high time to resume again that trust which had been before imposed upon them by Aubrey's parents.

Desirous of saving him from the injuries and sufferings he had daily encountered in his wanderings, and of preventing him from exposing to the general eye those marks of what they considered folly, they engaged a physician to reside in the house, and take constant care of him. He hardly appeared to notice it, so completely was his mind absorbed by one terrible subject. His incoherence became at last so great, that he was confined to his chamber. There he would often lie for days, incapable of being roused. He had become emaciated, his eyes had attained a glassy lustre – the only sign of affection and recollection remaining displayed itself upon the entry of his sister; then he would sometimes start, and, seizing her hands, with looks that severely afflicted her, he would desire her not to touch him. 'Oh, do not touch him – if your love for me is aught, do not go near him!' When, however, she inquired to whom he referred, his only answer was, 'True! true!' and again he sank into a state, whence not even she could rouse him. This lasted many months: gradually, however, as the year was passing, his incoherences became less frequent, and his mind threw off a portion of its gloom, whilst his guardians observed, that several times in the day he would count upon his fingers a definite number, and then smile.

The time had nearly elapsed, when, upon the last day of the year, one of his guardians entering his room, began to converse with his physician upon the melancholy circumstance of Aubrey's being in so awful a situation, when his sister was going next day to be married. Instantly Aubrey's attention was attracted; he asked anxiously to whom. Glad of this mark of returning intellect, of which they feared he had been deprived, they mentioned the name of the Earl of Marsden. Thinking this was a young Earl whom he had met with in society, Aubrey seemed pleased, and astonished them still more by his expressing his intention to be present at the nuptials, and desiring to see his sister. They answered not, but in a few minutes his sister was with him. He was apparently again capable of being affected by the influence of her lovely smile; for he pressed her to his breast, and kissed her cheek, wet with tears, flowing at the thought of her brother's being once more alive to the feelings of affection. He began to speak with all his wonted warmth, and to congratulate her upon her marriage with a person so distinguished for rank and every accomplishment; when he suddenly perceived a locket upon her breast; opening it, what was his surprise at beholding the features of the monster who had so long influenced his life. He seized the portrait in a paroxysm of rage, and trampled it under foot. Upon her asking him why he thus destroyed the resemblance of her future husband, he looked as if he did not understand her; – then seizing her hands, and gazing on her with a frantic expression of countenance, he bade her swear that she would never wed this monster, for he – But he could not advance – it seemed as if that voice again bade him remember his oath – he turned suddenly round, thinking Lord Ruthven was near him but saw no one. In the meantime the guardians and physician, who had heard the whole, and thought this was but a return of his disorder, entered, and forcing him from Miss Aubrey, desired her to leave him. He fell upon his knees to them, he implored, he begged of them to delay but for one day. They, attributing this to the insanity they imagined had taken possession of his mind, endeavoured to pacify him, and retired.

Lord Ruthven had called the morning after the drawing-room, and had been refused with every one else. When he heard of Aubrey's ill health, he readily understood himself to be the cause of it; but when he learned that he was deemed insane, his exultation and pleasure could hardly be concealed from those among whom he had gained this information. He hastened to the house of his former companion, and, by constant attendance, and the pretence of great affection for the brother and interest in his fate, he gradually won the ear of Miss Aubrey. Who could resist his power? His tongue had dangers and toils to recount – could speak of himself as of an individual having no sympathy with any being on the crowded earth, save with her to whom he addressed himself – could tell how, since he knew her, his existence had begun to seem worthy of preservation, if it were merely that he might listen to her soothing accents; – in fine, he knew so well how to use the serpent's art, or such was the will of fate, that he gained her affections. The title of the elder branch falling at length to him, he obtained an important embassy, which served as an excuse for hastening the marriage (in spite of her brother's deranged state), which was to take place the very day before his departure for the continent.

Aubrey, when he was left by the physician and his guardians, attempted to bribe the servants, but in vain. He asked for pen and paper; it was given him; he wrote a letter to his sister, conjuring her, as she valued her own happiness, her own honour, and the honour of those now in the grave, who once held her in their arms as their hope and the hope of their house, to delay but for a few hours that marriage, on which he denounced the most heavy curses. The servants promised they would deliver it; but giving it to the physician, he thought it better not to harass any more the mind of Miss Aubrey by, what he considered, the ravings of a maniac. Night passed on without rest to the busy inmates of the house; and Aubrey heard, with a horror that may more easily be conceived than described, the notes of busy preparation. Morning came, and the sound of carriages broke upon his ear. Aubrey grew almost frantic. The curiosity of the servants at last overcame their vigilance, they gradually stole away, leaving him in the custody of an helpless old woman. He seized the opportunity, with one bound was out of the room, and in a moment found himself in the apartment where all were nearly assembled. Lord Ruthven was the first to perceive him: he immediately approached, and, taking his arm by force, hurried him from the room, speechless with rage. When on the staircase, Lord Ruthven whispered in his ear – 'Remember your oath, and know, if not my bride to day, your sister is dishonoured. Women are frail!' So saying, he pushed him towards his attendants, who, roused by the old woman, had come in search of him. Aubrey could no longer support himself; his rage not finding vent, had broken a blood-vessel, and he was conveyed to bed. This was not mentioned to his sister, who was not present when he entered, as the physician was afraid of agitating her. The marriage was solemnized, and the bride and bridegroom left London.

Aubrey's weakness increased; the effusion of blood produced symptoms of the near approach of death. He desired his sister's guardians might be called, and when the midnight hour had struck, he related composedly what the reader has perused – he died immediately after.

The guardians hastened to protect Miss Aubrey; but when they arrived, it was too late. Lord Ruthven had disappeared, and Aubrey's sister had glutted the thirst of a VAMPYRE!

# The Assassins

## Percy Bysshe Shelley
### (1792–1822)

The poet Shelley, we are told, did not preserve long with his intended supernatural story during the Geneva 'gathering'. On this point, Montague Summers has written, 'Both Byron and Shelley found themselves annoyed by the platitude of prose and thus although they had set out at full gallop they speedily relinquished a task which proved foreign and uncongenial.'

In the case of Shelley this is both a sad loss and perhaps a little difficult to understand as we know that from his youth he was fascinated by tales of terror and 'wandered by night in graveyards in the hope of talk with the dead' according to at least one biographer. He also dabbled with chemical experiments and pored over ancient books of magic while still in his teens. With his cousin, Thomas Medwin, he produced a romance entitled *Nightmare* in 1810 and although in later years this predilection with horror was to abate, his early influence is often apparent in his finest works.

So much has already been written on the poet's later life that no further discussion is really called for here, but perhaps one event recorded by Polidori about Shelley at Lake Geneva is apposite. His diary for 18 June reads: 'After tea, 12 o'clock, really began to talk ghosts. Lord Byron repeated some verses of Coleridge's "Christabel", of the witch's breast; when silence ensued, Shelley, suddenly shrieking, and putting his hands to his head, ran out of the room with a candle. Threw water in his face and after gave him ether. He was looking at Mrs Shelley, and suddenly thought of a woman he had heard of who had eyes instead of nipples; which, taking hold of his mind, horrified him.'

This fragment which I have selected to represent Shelley dates from 1814 and one can hardly do better in introducing it than use the words of Mary Shelley when it first appeared in a posthumous collection of the author's works. '*The Assassins* is warmed by the fire of youth. I do not know what story he had in view. The Assassins were known in the eleventh century as a horde of Mahometans living among the recesses of Lebanon – ruled over by the Old Man of the Mountain; under whose direction various murders were committed on the Crusaders, which caused the name of the people who perpetrated them to be adopted in all European languages, to designate the crime which gave them notoriety. Shelley's old favourite, the Wandering Jew, appears in the latter sections, and, with his wild and fearful introduction into the domestic circle of a peaceful family of the Assassins, the fragment concludes. It was never touched afterwards.'

I

JERUSALEM, goaded to resistance by the incessant usurpations and insolence of Rome, leagued together its discordant factions to rebel against the common enemy and tyrant. Inferior to their foe in all but the unconquerable hope of liberty, they surrounded their city with fortifications of uncommon strength, and placed in array before the temple a band rendered desperate by patriotism and religion. Even the women preferred to die, rather than survive the ruin of their country. When the Roman army approached the walls of the sacred city, its preparations, its discipline, and its numbers, evinced the conviction of its leader, that he had no common barbarians to subdue. At the approach of the Roman army, the strangers withdrew from the city.

Among the multitudes which from every nation of the East had assembled at Jerusalem, was a little congregation of Christians. They were remarkable neither for their numbers nor their importance. They contained among them neither philosophers nor poets. Acknowledging no laws but those of God, they modelled their conduct towards their fellow-men by the conclusions of their individual judgment on the practical application of these laws. And it was apparent from the simplicity and severity of their manners, that this contempt for human institutions had produced among them a character superior in singleness and sincere self-apprehension to the slavery of pagan customs and the gross delusions of antiquated superstition. Many of their opinions considerably resembled those of the sect afterwards known by the name of Gnostics. They esteemed the human understanding to be the paramount rule of human conduct; they maintained that the obscurest religious truth required for its complete elucidation no more than the strenuous application of the energies of mind. It appeared impossible to them that any doctrine could be subversive of social happiness which is not capable of being confuted by arguments derived from the nature of existing things. With the devoutest submission to the law of Christ, they united an intrepid spirit of inquiry as to the correctest mode of acting in particular instances of conduct that occur among men. Assuming the doctrines of the Messiah concerning benevolence and justice for the regulation of their actions, they could not be persuaded to acknowledge that there was apparent in the divine code any prescribed rule whereby, for its own sake, one action rather than another, as fulfilling the will of their great Master, should be preferred.

The contempt with which the magistracy and priesthood regarded this obscure community of speculators, had hitherto protected them from persecution. But they had arrived at that precise degree of eminence and prosperity which is peculiarly obnoxious to the hostility of the rich and powerful. The moment of their departure from Jerusalem was the crisis of their future destiny. Had they continued to seek a precarious refuge in a city of the Roman empire, this persecution would not have delayed to impress a new character on their opinions and their conduct; narrow views, and the illiberality of sectarian patriotism, would not have failed speedily to obliterate the magnificence and beauty of their wild and wonderful condition.

Attached from principle to peace, despising and hating the pleasures and the customs of the degenerate mass of mankind, this unostentatious community of good and happy men fled to the solitudes of Lebanon. To Arabians and enthusiasts the solemnity and grandeur of these desolate recesses possessed peculiar attractions. It well accorded with the justice of their conceptions on the relative duties of man towards his fellow in society, that they should labour in unconstrained equality to dispossess the wolf and the tiger of their empire, and establish on its ruins the dominion of intelligence and virtue. No longer would the worshippers of the God of Nature be indebted to a hundred hands for the accommodation of their simple wants. No longer would the poison of a diseased civilization embrue their very nutriment with pestilence. They would no longer owe their very existence to the vices, the fears, and the follies of mankind. Love, friendship, and philanthropy, would now be the characteristic disposers of their industry. It is for his mistress or his friend that the labourer consecrates his toil; others are mindful, but he is forgetful, of himself. 'God feeds the hungry ravens, and clothes the lilies of the fields, and yet Solomon in all his glory is not like to one of these.'

Rome was now the shadow of her former self. The light of her grandeur and loveliness had passed away. The latest and the noblest of her poets and historians had foretold in agony her approaching slavery and degradation. The ruins of the human mind, more awful and portentous than the desolation of the most solemn temples, threw a shade of gloom upon her golden palaces which the brutal vulgar could not see, but which the mighty felt with inward trepidation and despair. The ruins of Jerusalem lay defenceless and uninhabited upon the burning sands; one visited, but in the depth of solemn awe, this accursed and solitary spot. Tradition says that there was seen to linger among the scorched and shattered fragments of the temple, one being, whom he that saw dared not to call man, with clasped hands, immoveable eyes, and a visage horribly serene. Not on the will of the capricious multitude, nor the constant fluctuations of the many and the weak, depends the change of empires and religions. These are the mere insensible elements from which a subtler intelligence moulds its enduring statuary. They that direct the changes of this mortal scene breathe the decrees of their dominion from a throne of darkness and of tempest. The power of man is great.

After many days of wandering, the Assassins pitched their tents in the valley of Bethzatanai. For ages had this fertile valley lain concealed from the adventurous search of man, among mountains of everlasting snow. The men of elder days had inhabited this spot. Piles of monumental marble and fragments of columns that in their integrity almost seemed the work of some intelligence more sportive and fantastic than the gross conceptions of mortality, lay in heaps beside the lake, and were visible beneath its transparent waves. The flowering orange-tree, the balsam, and innumerable odiferous shrubs, grew wild in the desolated portals. The fountain tanks had overflowed; and, amid the luxuriant vegetation of their margin the yellow snake held its unmolested dwelling. Hither came the tiger and the bear to contend for those once domestic animals who had forgotten the secure servitude of their ancestors. No sound, when the famished beast of prey had retreated in despair from the awful desolation of this place, at whose completion he had assisted, but the shrill cry of the stork, and the flapping of his heavy wings from the capital of the solitary column, and the scream of the hungry vulture baffled of its only victim. The lore of ancient wisdom sculptured in mystic characters on the rocks. The human spirit and the human hand had been busy here to accomplish its profoundest miracles. It was a temple dedicated to the God of knowledge and of truth. The palaces of the Caliphs and the Caesars might easily surpass these ruins in magnitude and sumptuousness: but they were the designs of tyrants and the work of slaves. Piercing genius and consummate prudence had planned and executed Bethzatanai. There was deep and important meaning in every lineament of its fantastic sculpture. The unintelligible legend, once so beautiful and perfect, so full of poetry and history, spoke, even in destruction, volumes of mysterious import, and obscure significance.

But in the season of its utmost prosperity and magnificence, art might not aspire to vie with nature in the valley of Bethzatanai. All that was wonderful and lovely was collected in this deep seclusion. The fluctuating elements seemed to have been rendered everlastingly permanent in forms of wonder and delight. The mountains of Lebanon had been divided to their base to form this happy valley; on every side their icy summits darted their white pinnacles into the clear blue sky, imaging, in their grotesque outline, minarets, and ruined domes, and columns worn with time. Far below, the silver clouds rolled their bright volumes in many beautiful shapes, and fed the eternal springs that, spanning the dark chasms like a thousand radiant rainbows, leaped into the quiet vale, then, lingering in many a dark glade among the groves of cypress and of palm, lost themselves in the lake. The immensity of these precipitous mountains, with their starry pyramids of snow, excluded the sun, which overtopped not, even in its meridian, their overhanging rocks. But a more heavenly and serener light was reflected from their icy mirrors, which, piercing through the many-tinted clouds, produced lights and colours of inexhaustible variety. The herbage was perpetually verdant, and clothed the darkest recesses of the caverns and the woods.

Nature, undisturbed, had become an enchantress in these solitudes: she had collected here all that was wonderful and divine from the armoury of her omnipotence. The very winds breathed health and renovation, and the joyousness of youthful courage. Fountains of crystalline water played perpetually among the aromatic flowers, and mingled a freshness with their odour. The pine boughs became instruments of exquisite contrivance, among which every varying breeze waked music of new and more delightful melody. Meteoric shapes, more effulgent than the moonlight, hung on the wandering clouds, and mixed in discordant dance around the spiral fountains. Blue vapours assume strange lineaments under the rocks and among the ruins, lingering like ghosts with slow and solemn step. Through a dark chasm to the east, in the long perspective of a portal glittering with the unnumbered riches of the subterranean world, shone the broad moon, pouring in one yellow and unbroken stream her horizontal beams. Nearer the icy region, autumn and spring held an alternate reign. The sere leaves fell and choked the sluggish brooks; the chilling fogs hung diamonds on every spray; and in the dark cold evening the howling winds made melancholy music in the trees. Far above, shone the bright throne of winter, clear, cold, and dazzling. Sometimes there was seen the snowflakes to fall before the sinking orb of the beamless sun, like a shower of fiery sulphur. The cataracts, arrested in their course, seemed, with their transparent columns, to support the darkbrowed rocks. Sometimes the icy whirlwind scooped the powdery snow aloft, to mingle with the hissing meteors, and scatter spangles through the rare and rayless atmosphere.

Such strange scenes of chaotic confusion and harrowing sublimity, surrounding and shutting in the vale, added to the delights of its secure and voluptuous tranquillity. No spectator could have refused to believe that some spirit of great intelligence and power had hallowed these wild and beautiful solitudes to a deep and solemn mystery.

The immediate effect of such a scene, suddenly presented to the contemplation of mortal eyes, is seldom the subject of authentic record. The coldest slave of custom cannot fail to recollect some few moments in which the breath of spring or the crowding clouds of sunset, with the pale moon shining through their fleecy skirts, or the song of some lonely bird perched on the only tree of an unfrequented heath, has awakened the touch of nature. And they were Arabians who entered the valley of Bethzatanai; men who idolated nature and the God of nature; to whom love and lofty thoughts, and the apprehensions of an uncorrupted spirit, were sustenance and life. Thus securely excluded from an abhorred world, all thought of its judgment was cancelled by the rapidity of their fervid imaginations. They ceased to acknowledge, or deigned not to advert to, the distinctions with which the majority of base and vulgar minds control the longings and struggles of the soul towards its place of rest. A new and sacred fire was kindled in their hearts and sparkled in their eyes. Every gesture, every feature, the minutest action, was modelled to beneficence and beauty by the holy inspiration that had descended on their searching spirits. The epidemic transport communicated itself through every heart with the rapidity of a blast from heaven. They were already disembodied spirits; they were already the inhabitants of paradise. To live, to

breathe, to move, was itself a sensation of immeasurable transport. Every new contemplation of the condition of his nature
brought to the happy enthusiast an added measure of delight,
and impelled to every organ, where mind is united with external things, a keener and more exquisite perception of all that
they contain of lovely and divine. To love, to be beloved, suddenly became an insatiable famine of his nature, which the wide
circle of the universe, comprehending beings of such inexhaustible variety and stupendous magnitude of excellence, appeared
too narrow and confined to satiate.

Alas, that these visitings of the spirit of life should fluctuate
and pass away! That the moments when the human mind is
commensurate with all that it can conceive of excellent and powerful, should not endure with its existence and survive its most
momentous change! But the beauty of a vernal sunset with its
overhanging curtains of empurpled cloud, is rapidly dissolved,
to return at some unexpected period, and spread an alleviating
melancholy over the dark vigils of despair.

It is true the enthusiasm of overwhelming transport which
had inspired every breast among the Assassins is no more. The
necessity of daily occupation and the ordinariness of that human
life, the burthen of which it is the destiny of every human being
to bear, had smothered, not extinguished, that divine and eternal fire. Not the less indelible and permanent were the impressions communicated to all; not the more unalterably were the
features of their social character modelled and determined by its
influence.

## II

Rome had fallen. Her senate-house had become a polluted den
of thieves and liars; her solemn temples, the arena of theological
disputants, who made fire and sword the missionaries of their
inconceivable beliefs. The city of the monster Constantine, sym-
bolizing, in the consequences of its foundation, the wickedness
and weakness of his successors, feebly imagined with declining
power the substantial eminence of the Roman name. Pilgrims
of a new and mightier faith crowded to visit the lonely ruins of

Jerusalem, and weep and pray before the sepulchre of the Eternal God. The earth was filled with discord, tumult, and ruin. The spirit of disinterested virtue had armed one-half of the civilized world against the other. Monstrous and detestable creeds poisoned and blighted the domestic charities. There was no appeal to natural love, or ancient faith, from pride, superstition, and revenge.

Four centuries had passed thus, terribly characterized by the most calamitous revolutions. The Assassins, meanwhile, undisturbed by the surrounding tumult, possessed and cultivated their fertile valley. The gradual operation of their peculiar condition had matured and perfected the singularity and excellence of their character. That cause, which had ceased to act as an immediate and overpowering excitement, became the unperceived law of their lives, and sustenance of their natures. Their religious tenets had also undergone a change, corresponding with the exalted condition of their moral being. The gratitude which they owed to the benignant Spirit by which their limited intelligences had not only been created but redeemed, was less frequently adverted to, became less the topic of comment or contemplation; not, therefore, did it cease to be their presiding guardian, the guide of their inmost thoughts, the tribunal of appeal for the minutest particulars of their conduct. They learned to identify this mysterious benefactor with the delight that is bred among the solitary rocks, and has its dwelling alike in the changing colours of the clouds and the inmost recesses of the caverns. Their future also no longer existed, but in the blissful tranquillity of the present. Time was measured and created by the vices and the miseries of men, between whom and the happy nation of the Assassins, there was no analogy nor comparison. Already had their eternal peace commenced. The darkness had passed away from the open gates of death.

The practical results produced by their faith and condition upon their external conduct were singular and memorable. Excluded from the great and various community of mankind, these solitudes became to them a sacred hermitage, in which all formed, as it were, one being, divided against itself by no contending will or factious passions. Every impulse conspired to one end, and tended to a single object. Each devoted his powers to the happiness of the other. Their republic was the scene of the perpetual contentions of benevolence; not the heartless and assumed kindness of commercial man, but the genuine virtue that has a legible superscription in every feature of the countenance, and every motion of the frame. The perverseness and calamities of those who dwelt beyond the mountains that encircled their undisturbed possessions, were unknown and unimagined. Little embarrassed by the complexities of civilized society, they knew not to conceive any happiness that can be satiated without participation, or that thirsts not to reproduce and perpetually generate itself. The path of virtue and felicity was plain and unimpeded. They clearly acknowledged, in every case, that conduct to be entitled to preference which would obviously produce the greatest pleasure. They could not conceive an instance in which it would be their duty to hesitate, in causing, at whatever expense, the greatest and most unmixed delight.

Hence arose a peculiarity which only failed to germinate in uncommon and momentous consequences, because the Assassins had retired from the intercourse of mankind, over whom other motives and principles of conduct than justice and benevolence prevail. It would be a difficult matter for men of such a sincere and simple faith, to estimate the final results of their intentions, among the corrupt and slavish multitude. They would be perplexed also in their choice of the means, whereby their intentions might be fulfilled. To produce immediate pain or disorder for the sake of future benefit, is consonant, indeed, with the purest religion and philosophy, but never fails to excite invincible repugnance in the feelings of the many. Against their predilections and distastes an Assassin, accidentally the inhabitant of a civilized community, would wage unremitting hostility from principle. He would find himself compelled to adopt means which they would abhor, for the sake of an object which they could not conceive that he should propose to himself. Secure and self-enshrined in the magnificence and pre-eminence of his conceptions, spotless as the light of heaven, he would be the victim among men of calumny and persecution. Incapable of distinguishing his motives, they would rank him among the vilest and most atrocious criminals. Great, beyond all comparison with them, they would despise him in the presumption of their ignorance. Because his spirit burned with an unquenchable passion for their welfare, they would lead him, like his illustrious master, amidst scoffs, and mockery, and insult, to the remuneration of an ignominious death.

Who hesitates to destroy a venomous serpent that has crept near his sleeping friend, except the man who selfishly dreads lest the malignant reptile should turn his fury on himself? And if the poisoner has assumed a human shape, if the bane be distinguished only from the viper's venom by the excess and extent of its devastation, will the saviour and avenger here retract and pause entrenched behind the superstition of the indefeasible divinity of man? Is the human form, then, the mere badge of a prerogative for unlicensed wickedness and mischief? Can the power derived from the weakness of the oppressed, or the ignorance of the deceived, confer the right in security to tyrannize and defraud?

The subject of regular governments, and the disciple of established superstition, dares not ask this question. For the sake of the eventual benefit, he endures what he esteems a transitory evil, and the moral degradation of man disquiets not his patience. But the religion of an Assassin imposes other virtues than endurance, when his fellow-men groan under tyranny, or have become so bestial and abject that they cannot feel their chains. An Assassin believes that man is eminently man, and only then enjoys the prerogatives of his privileged condition, when his affections and his judgment pay tribute to the God of Nature. The perverse, and vile, and vicious – what were they? Shapes of some unholy vision, moulded by the spirit of Evil, which the sword of the merciful destroyer should sweep from this beautiful world. Dreamy nothings; phantasms of misery and mischief, that hold their death-like state on glittering thrones, and in the loathsome dens of poverty. No Assassin would submissively temporize with vice, and in cold charity become a pander to falsehood and desolation. His path through the wilderness of civilized society would be marked with the blood of the oppressor and the ruiner. The wretch, whom nations tremblingly adore, would expiate in his throttling grasp a thousand licensed and venerable crimes.

How many holy liars and parasites, in solemn guise, would his saviour arm drag from their luxurious couches, and plunge in the cold charnel, that the green and many-legged monsters of the slimy grave might eat off at their leisure the lineaments of rooted malignity and detested cunning. The respectable man – the smooth, smiling, polished villain, whom all the city honours; whose very trade is lies and murder; who buys his daily bread with the blood and tears of men, would feed the ravens with his limbs. The Assassin would cater nobly for the eyeless worms of earth, and the carrion fowls of heaven.

Yet here, religion and human love had imbued the manners of those solitary people with inexpressible gentleness and benignity. Courage and active virtue, and the indignation against vice, which becomes a hurrying and irresistible passion, slept like the imprisoned earthquake, or the lightning shafts that hang in the golden clouds of evening. They were innocent, but they were capable of more than innocence; for the great principles of their faith were perpetually acknowledged and adverted to; nor had they forgotten, in this uninterrupted quiet, the author of their felicity.

Four centuries had thus worn away without producing an event. Men had died, and natural tears had been shed upon their graves, in sorrow that improves the heart. Those who had been united by love had gone to death together, leaving to their friends the bequest of a most sacred grief, and of a sadness that is allied to pleasure. Babes that hung upon their mothers' breasts had become men; men had died; and many a wild luxuriant weed that overtopped the habitations of the vale, had twined its roots around their disregarded bones. Their tranquil state was like a summer sea, whose gentle undulations disturb not the reflected stars, and break not the long still line of the rainbow hues of sunrise.

## III

Where all is thus calm, the slightest circumstance is recorded and remembered. Before the sixth century had expired one incident occurred, remarkable and strange. A young man, named Albedir, wandering in the woods, was startled by the screaming of a bird of prey, and, looking up, saw blood fall, drop by drop, from among the intertwined boughs of a cedar. Having climbed the tree, he beheld a terrible and dismaying spectacle. A naked human body was impaled on the broken branch. It was maimed and mangled horribly; every limb bent and bruised into frightful distortion, and exhibiting a breathing image of the most sickening mockery of life. A monstrous snake had scented its prey from among the mountains — and above hovered a hungry vulture. From amidst this mass of desolated humanity, two eyes, black and inexpressibly brilliant, shone with an unearthly lustre. Beneath the blood-stained eye-brows their steady rays manifested the serenity of an immortal power, the collected energy of a deathless mind, spell-secured from dissolution. A bitter smile of mingled abhorrence and scorn distorted his wounded lip — he appeared calmly to observe and measure all around — self-possession had not deserted the shattered mass of life.

The youth approached the bough on which the breathing corpse was hung. As he approached, the serpent reluctantly unwreathed his glittering coils, and crept towards his dark and loathsome cave. The vulture, impatient of his meal, fled to the mountain, that re-echoed with his hoarse screams. The cedar branches creaked with their agitating weight, faintly, as the dismal wind arose. All else was deadly silent.

At length a voice issued from the mangled man. It rattled in hoarse murmurs from his throat and lungs — his words were the conclusion of some strange mysterious soliloquy. They were broken, and without apparent connection, completing wide intervals of inexpressible conceptions.

'The great tyrant is baffled, even in success. Joy! joy! to his tortured foe! Triumph to the worm whom he tramples under his feet! Ha! His suicidal hand might dare as well abolish the mighty frame of things! Delight and exultation sit before the closed fates of death! — I fear not to dwell beneath their black and ghastly shadow. Here thy power may not avail! Thou createst — 'tis mine to ruin and destroy. — I was thy slave — I am thy equal, and thy foe. — Thousands tremble before thy throne, who, at my voice, shall dare to pluck the golden crown from thine unholy head!' He ceased. The silence of noon swallowed up his words. Albedir clung tighter to the tree — he dared not for dismay remove his eyes. He remained mute in the perturbation of deep and creeping horror.

'Albedir!' said the same voice, 'Albedir! in the name of God, approach. He that suffered me to fall, watches thee; — the gentle and merciful spirits of sweet human love, delight not in agony and horror. For pity's sake approach, in the name of thy good God, approach, Albedir!' The tones were mild and clear as the responses of Aeolian music. They floated to Albedir's ear like the warm breath of June that lingers in the lawny groves, subduing all to softness. Tears of tender affection started into his eyes. It was as the voice of a beloved friend. The partner of his childhood, the brother of his soul, seemed to call for aid, and pathetically to remonstrate with delay. He resisted not the magic impulse, but advanced towards the spot, and tenderly attempted to remove the wounded man. He cautiously descended the tree with his wretched burthen, and deposited it on the ground.

A period of strange silence intervened. Awe and cold horror were slowly proceeding to the softer sensations of tumultuous pity, when again he heard the silver modulations of the same enchanting voice. 'Weep not for me, Albedir! What wretch so utterly lost, but might inhale peace and renovation from this paradise! I am wounded, and in pain; but having found a refuge in this seclusion, and a friend in you, I am worthier of envy than compassion. Bear me to your cottage secretly: I would not disturb your gentle partner by my appearance. She must love me more dearly than a brother. I must be the playmate of your children; already I regard them with a father's love. My arrival must not be regarded as a thing of mystery and wonder. What, indeed, but that men are prone to error and exaggeration, is less inexplicable, than that a stranger, wandering on Lebanon, fell from the rocks into the vale? Albedir,' he continued, and his deepening voice assumed awful solemnity, 'in return for the affection with which I cherish thee and thine, thou owest this submission.'

Albedir implicitly submitted; not even a thought had power to refuse its deference. He reassumed his burthen, and proceeded towards the cottage. He watched until Khaled should be absent, and conveyed the stranger into an apartment appropriated for the reception of those who occasionally visited their habitation. He desired that the door should be securely fastened, and that he might not be visited until the morning of the following day.

Albedir waited with impatience for the return of Khaled. The unaccustomed weight of even so transitory a secret, hung on his ingenuous and unpractised nature, like a blighting, clinging curse. The stranger's accents had lulled him to a trance of wild and delightful imagination. Hopes, so visionary and aerial, that they had assumed no denomination, had spread themselves over his intellectual frame, and, phantoms as they were, had modelled his being to their shape. Still his mind was not exempt from the visitings of disquietude and perturbation. It was a troubled stream of thought, over whose fluctuating waves unsearchable fate seemed to preside, guiding its unforeseen alternations with an inexorable hand. Albedir paced earnestly the garden of his cottage, revolving every circumstance attendant on the incident of the day. He re-imaged with intense thought the minutest recollections of the scene. In vain – he was the slave of suggestions not to be controlled. Astonishment, horror, and awe – tumultuous sympathy, and a mysterious elevation of soul, hurried away all activity of judgment, and overwhelmed, with stunning force, every attempt at deliberation or inquiry.

His reveries were interrupted at length by the return of Khaled. She entered the cottage, that scene of undisturbed repose, in the confidence that change might as soon overwhelm the eternal world, as disturb this inviolable sanctuary. She started to behold Albedir. Without preface or remark, he recounted with eager haste the occurrences of the day. Khaled's tranquil spirit could hardly keep pace with the breathless rapidity of his narration. She was bewildered with staggering wonder even to hear his confused tones, and behold his agitated countenance.


## IV

On the following morning Albedir arose at sunrise, and visited the stranger. He found him already risen, and employed in adorning the lattice of his chamber with flowers from the garden. There was something in his attitude and occupation singularly expressive of his entire familiarity with the scene. Albedir's habitation seemed to have been his accustomed home. He addressed his host in a tone of gay and affectionate welcome, such as never fails to communicate by sympathy the feelings from which it flows.

'My friend,' said he, 'the balm of the dew of our vale is sweet; or is this garden the favoured spot where the winds conspire to scatter the best odours they can find? Come, lend me your arm awhile, I feel very weak.' He motioned to walk forth, but, as if unable to proceed, rested on the seat beside the door. For a few moments they were silent, if the interchange of cheerful and happy looks is to be called silence. At last he observed a spade that rested against the wall. 'You have only one spade, brother,' said he; 'you have only one, I suppose, of any of the instruments of tillage. Your garden ground, too, occupies a certain space which it will be necessary to enlarge. This must be quickly remedied. I cannot earn my supper of tonight, nor of tomorrow; but thenceforward, I do not mean to eat the bread of idleness. I know that you would willingly perform the additional labour which my nourishment would require; I know, also, that you would feel a degree of pleasure in the fatigue arising from this employment, but I shall contest with you such pleasures as these, and such pleasures as these alone.' His eyes were somewhat wan, and the tone of his voice languid as he spoke.

As they were thus engaged, Khaled came towards them. The

stranger beckoned to her to sit beside him, and taking her hands within his own, looked attentively on her mild countenance. Khaled inquired if he had been refreshed by sleep. He replied by a laugh of careless and inoffensive glee; and placing one of her hands within Albedir's, said, 'If this be sleep, here in this odorous vale, where these sweet smiles encompass us, and the voices of those who love are heard – if these be the visions of sleep, sister, those who lie down in misery shall arise lighter than the butterflies. I came from amid the tumult of a world, how different from this! I am unexpectedly among you, in the midst of a scene such as my imagination never dared to promise. I must remain here – I must not depart.' Khaled, recovering from the admiration and astonishment caused by the stranger's words and manner, assured him of the happiness which she should feel in such an addition to her society. Albedir, too, who had been more deeply impressed than Khaled by the event of his arrival, earnestly re-assured him of the ardour of the affection with which he had inspired them. The stranger smiled gently to hear the unaccustomed fervour of sincerity which animated their address, and was rising to retire, when Khaled said, 'You have not yet seen our children, Maimuna and Abdallah. They are by the water-side, playing with their favourite snake. We have only to cross yonder little wood, and wind down a patch cut in the rock that overhangs the lake, and we shall find them beside a recess which the shore makes there, and which a chasm, as it were the rocks and woods, encloses. Do you think you could walk there?' – 'To see your children, Khaled? I think I could, with the assistance of Albedir's arm, and yours.' – So they went through the wood of ancient cypress, intermingled with the brightness of many-tinted blooms, which gleamed like stars through its romantic glens. They crossed the green meadow, and entered among the broken chasms, beautiful as they were in their investiture of odiferous shrubs. They came at last, after pursuing a path which wound though the intricacies of a little wilderness, to the borders of the lake. They stood on the rock which overhung it, from which there was a prospect of all the miracles of nature and of art which encircled and adorned its shores. The stranger gazed upon it with a countenance unchanged by any emotion, but, as it were, thoughtfully and contemplatingly. As he gazed, Khaled ardently pressed his hand, and said, in a low yet eager voice, 'Look, look, lo there!' He turned towards her, but her eyes were not on him. She looked below – her lips were parted by the feelings which possessed her soul – her breath came and went regularly but inaudibly. She leaned over the precipice, and her dark hair hanging beside her face, gave relief to its fine lineaments, animated by such love as exceeds utterance. The stranger followed her eyes, and saw that her children were in the glen below; then raising his eyes, exchanged with her affectionate looks of congratulation and delight. The boy was apparently eight years old, the girl about two years younger. The beauty of their form and countenance was something so divine and strange, as overwhelmed the senses of the beholder like a delightful dream, with insupportable ravishment. They were arrayed in a loose robe of linen, through which the exquisite proportions of their form appeared. Unconscious that they were observed, they did not relinquish the occupation in which they were engaged. They had constructed a little boat of the bark of trees, and had given it sails of interwoven feathers, and launched it on the water. They sat beside a white flat stone, on which a small snake lay coiled, and when their work was finished, they arose and called to the snake in melodious tones, so that it understood their language. For it unwreathed its shining circles and crept to the boat, into which no sooner had it entered, than the girl loosened the band which held it to the shore, and it sailed away. Then they ran round and round the little creek, clapping their hands, and melodiously pouring out wild sounds, which the snake seemed to answer by the restless glancing of his neck. At last a breath of wind came from the shore, and the boat changed its course, and was about to leave the creek, which the snake perceived and leaped into the water, and came to the little children's feet. The girl sang to it, and it leaped into her bosom, and she crossed her fair hands over it, as if to cherish it there. Then the boy answered with a song, and it glided from beneath her hands and crept towards him. While they were thus employed, Maimuna looked up, and seeing her parents on the cliff, ran to meet them up the steep path that wound round it; and Abdallah, leaving his snake, followed joyfully.

# The Dream

## Mary Wollstonecraft Shelley

## (1792–1822)

Mary Shelley, as I noted in the introduction to *The Vampyre*, achieved most from the conclave at Lake Geneva: producing her masterwork, *Frankenstein*, still today the most famous of all horror stories. The daughter of the social reformer and free thinker William Godwin (who himself wrote a notable Gothic novel in *Caleb Williams* published in 1794), Mary's own life falls very much under the shadow of her lover and eventual husband, Percy Shelley. The two had eloped while Mary was still in her teens and a great deal of their life together was spent travelling in Europe and meeting with the other great writers and poets of the time.

The creation of *Frankenstein* was not an easy one for Mary and required the inspiration of a nightmare, and the recollection of the Gothic novels of such as Mrs Radcliffe and Matthew Lewis — who, incidentally, was to visit the lakeside villa in August 1816 and delight the company with a number of true ghost stories, all recorded by Shelley in his letters. The criticism which has been levelled at *Frankenstein* of being laborious in the early chapters and overly full of minor and barely linked sub-themes is probably the fault of Percy Shelley who encouraged his wife to expand the work after he had read the first, much shorter, draft. (This apparently began at what is now Chapter Four.) Nonetheless, Mrs Shelley's aim of 'awakening thrilling horror' with the tale is undoubtedly achieved and its unique place in literature well deserved.

In hindsight there can probably be little disputing that Mary Shelley was most at home with the short story and not a few of her tales still find their way into modern anthologies. In re-examining her work, I have come across the following story which, while it may well be classed as a minor work from her pen, will almost certainly be unknown to most readers and is a fine example of the Gothic romance story dating from the hey-day of the genre. It also seems to me a most suitable selection when related to the circumstances we have discussed about the creation of *Frankenstein* . . .

THE time of the occurrence of the little legend about to be narrated, was that of the commencement of the reign of Henry IV of France, whose accession and conversion, while they brought peace to the kingdom whose throne he ascended, were inadequate to heal the deep wounds mutually inflicted by the inimical parties. Private feuds, and the memory of mortal injuries, existed between those now apparently united; and often did the hands that had clasped each other in seeming friendly greeting, involuntarily, as the grasp was released, clasp the dagger's hilt, as fitter spokesman to their passions than the words of courtesy that had just fallen from their lips. Many of the fiercer Catholics retreated to their distant provinces; and while they concealed in solitude their rankling discontent, not less keenly did they long for the day when they might show it openly.

In a large and fortified château built on a rugged steep overlooking the Loire, not far from the town of Nantes, dwelt the last of her race, and the heiress of their fortunes, the young and beautiful Countess de Villeneuve. She had spent the preceding year in complete solitude in her secluded abode; and the mourning she wore for a father and two brothers, the victims of the civil wars, was a graceful and good reason why she did not appear at court, and mingle with its festivities. But the orphan countess inherited a high name and broad lands; and it was soon signified to her that the king, her guardian, desired that she should bestow them, together with her hand, upon some noble whose birth and accomplishments should entitle him to the gift. Constance, in reply, expressed her intention of taking vows, and retiring to a convent. The king earnestly and resolutely forbade this act, believing such an idea to be the result of sensibility overwrought by sorrow, and relying on the hope that, after a time, the genial spirit of youth would break through this cloud.

A year passed, and still the countess persisted; and at last Henry, unwilling to exercise compulsion, – desirous, too, of judging for himself of the motives that led one so beautiful, young, and gifted with fortune's favours, to desire to bury herself in a cloister, – announced his intention, now that the period of her mourning was expired, of visiting her château; and if he brought not with him, the monarch said, inducement sufficient to change her design, he would yield his consent to its fulfilment.

Many a sad hour had Constance passed – many a day of tears, and many a night of restless misery. She had closed her gates against every visitant; and, like the Lady Olivia in 'Twelfth Night', vowed herself to loneliness and weeping. Mistress of herself, she easily silenced the entreaties and remonstrances of underlings, and nursed her grief as it had been the thing she loved. Yet it was too keen, too bitter, too burning, to be a favoured guest. In fact, Constance, young, ardent, and vivacious, battled with it, struggled and longed to cast it off; but all that was joyful in itself, or fair in outward show, only served to renew it; and she could best support the burden of her sorrow with patience, when, yielding to it, it oppressed but did not torture her.

Constance had left the castle to wander in the neighbouring grounds. Lofty and extensive as were the apartments of her abode, she felt pent up within their walls, beneath their fretted roofs. The spreading uplands and the antique wood, associated to her with every dear recollection of her past life, enticed her to spend hours and days beneath their leafy coverts. The motion and change eternally working, as the wind stirred among the boughs, or the journeying sun rained its beams through them, soothed and called her out of that dull sorrow which clutched her heart with so unrelenting a pang beneath her castle roof.

There was one spot on the verge of the well-wooded park, one nook of ground, whence she could discern the country extended beyond, yet which was in itself thick set with tall umbrageous trees – a spot which she had forsworn, yet whither unconsciously her steps for ever tended, and where now again, for the twentieth time that day, she had unaware found herself. She sat upon a grassy mound, and looked wistfully on the flowers she had herself planted to adorn the verdurous recess – to her the temple of memory and love. She held the letter from the king which was the parent to her of so much despair. Dejection sat upon her features, and her gentle heart asked fate why, so young, unprotected, and forsaken, she should have to struggle with this new form of wretchedness.

'I but ask,' she thought, 'to live in my father's halls – in the spot familiar to my infancy – to water with my frequent tears the graves of those I loved; and here in these woods, where such a mad dream of happiness was mine, to celebrate for ever the obsequies of Hope!'

A rustling among the boughs now met her ear – her heart beat quick – all again was still.

'Foolish girl!' she half muttered; 'dupe of thine own passionate fancy: because here we met; because seated here I have expected, and sounds like these have announced, his dear approach; so now every coney as it stirs, and every bird as it awakens silence, speaks of him. O Gaspar! – mine once – never again will this beloved spot be made glad by thee – never more!'

Again the bushes were stirred, and footsteps were heard in the brake. She rose; her heart beat high; it must be that silly Manon, with her impertinent entreaties for her to return. But the steps were firmer and slower than would be those of her waiting-woman; and now emerging from the shade, she too plainly discerned the intruder. He first impulse was to fly: – but once again to see him – to hear his voice: – once again before she placed eternal vows between them, to stand together, and find the wide chasm filled which absence had made, could not injure the dead, and would soften the fatal sorrow that made her cheek so pale.

And now he was before her, the same beloved one with whom she had exchanged vows of constancy. He, like her, seemed sad; nor could she resist the imploring glance that entreated her for one moment to remain.

'I come, lady,' said the young knight, 'without a hope to

bend your inflexible will. I come but once again to see you, and to bid you farewell before I depart for the Holy Land. I come to beseech you not to immure yourself in the dark cloister to avoid one as hateful as myself, – one you will never see more. Whether I die or live, France and I are parted for ever !'

'That were fearful, were it true,' said Constance; 'but King Henry will never so lose his favourite cavalier. The throne you helped to build, you still will guard. Nay, as I ever had power over thought of thine, go not to Palestine.'

'One word of yours could detain me – one smile – Constance' – and the youthful lover knelt before her; but her harsher purpose was recalled by the image once so dear and familiar, now so strange and so forbidden.

'Linger no longer here !' she cried. 'No smile, no word of mine will ever again be yours. Why are you here – here, where the spirits of the dead wander, and claiming these shades as their own, curse the false girl who permits their murderer to disturb their sacred repose?'

'When love was young and you were kind,' replied the knight, 'you taught me to thread the intricacies of these woods – you welcomed me to this dear spot, where once you vowed to be my own – even beneath these ancient trees.'

'A wicked sin it was,' said Constance, 'to unbar my father's doors to the son of his enemy, and dearly is it punished !'

The young knight gained courage as she spoke; yet he dared not move, lest she, who, every instant, appeared ready to take flight, should be startled from her momentary tranquillity; but he slowly replied: – 'Those were happy days, Constance, full of terror and deep joy, when evening brought me to your feet; and while hate and vengeance were as its atmosphere to yonder frowning castle, this leafy, starlit bower was the shrine of love.'

'*Happy* ? – miserable days !' echoed Constance; 'when I imagined good could arise from failing in my duty, and that disobedience would be rewarded of God. Speak not of love, Gaspar ! – a sea of blood divides us for ever ! Approach me not ! The dead and the beloved stand even now between us: their pale shadows warn me of my fault, and menace me for listening to their murderer.'

'That am not I!' exclaimed the youth. 'Behold, Constance, we are each the last of our race. Death has dealt cruelly with us, and we are alone. It was not so when first we loved – when parent, kinsman, brother, nay, my own mother breathed curses on the house of Villeneuve; and in spite of all I blessed it. I saw thee, my lovely one, and blessed it. The God of peace planted love in our hearts, and with mystery and secrecy we met during many a summer night in the moonlit dells; and when daylight was abroad, in this sweet recess we fled to avoid its scrutiny, and here, even here, where now I kneel in supplication, we both knelt and made our vows. Shall they be broken?'

Constance wept as her lover recalled the images of happy hours. 'Never,' she exclaimed, 'O never! Thou knowest, or wilt soon know, Gaspar, the faith and resolves of one who dare not be yours. Was it for us to talk of love and happiness, when war, and hate, and blood were raging around! The fleeting flowers our young hands strewed were trampled by the deadly encounter of mortal foes. By your father's hand mine died; and little boots it to know whether, as my brother swore, and you deny, your hand did or did not deal the blow that destroyed him. You fought among those by whom he died. Say no more – no other word: it is impiety towards the unreposing dead to hear you. Go, Gaspar; forget me. Under the chivalrous and gallant Henry your career may be glorious; and some fair girl will listen, as once I did, to your vows, and be made happy by them. Farewell! May the Virgin bless you! In my cell and cloister-home I will not forget the best Christian lesson – to pray for our enemies. Gaspar, farewell!'

She glided hastily from the bower: with swift steps she threaded the glade and sought the castle. Once within the seclusion of her own apartment she gave way to the burst of grief that tore her gentle bosom like a tempest; for hers was that worst sorrow which taints past joys, making remorse wait upon the memory of bliss, and linking love and fancied guilt in such fearful society as that of the tyrant when he bound a living body to a corpse. Suddenly a thought darted into her mind. At first she rejected it as puerile and superstitious; but it would not be driven away. She called hastily for her attendant. 'Manon,' she said, 'didst thou ever sleep on St Catherine's couch?'

Manon crossed herself. 'Heaven forefend! None ever did, since I was born, but two: one fell into the Loire and was drowned; the other only looked upon the narrow bed, and returned to her own home without a word. It is an awful place; and if the votary have not led a pious and good life, woe betide the hour when she rests her head on the holy stone!'

Constance crossed herself also. 'As for our lives, it is only through our Lord and the blessed saints that we can any of us hope for righteousness. I will sleep on that couch tomorrow night!'

'Dear, my lady! and the king arrives tomorrow.'

'The more need that I resolve. It cannot be that misery so intense should dwell in any heart, and no cure be found. I had hoped to be the bringer of peace to our houses; and if the good work to be for me a crown of thorns Heaven shall direct me. I will rest tomorrow night on St Catherine's bed: and if, as I have heard, the saint deigns to direct her votaries in dreams, I will be guided by her; and, believing that I act according to the dictates of Heaven, I shall feel resigned even to the worst.'

The king was on his way to Nantes from Paris, and he slept on this night at a castle but a few miles distant. Before dawn a young cavalier was introduced into his chamber. The knight had a serious, nay, a sad aspect; and all beautiful as he was in feature and limb, looked wayworn and haggard. He stood silent in Henry's presence, who, alert and gay, turned his lively blue eyes upon his guest, saying gently, 'So thou foundest her obdurate, Gaspar?'

'I found her resolved on our mutual misery. Alas! my liege, it is not, credit me, the least of my grief, that Constance sacrifices her own happiness when she destroys mine.'

'And thou believest that she will say nay to the gaillard chevalier whom we ourselves present to her?'

'Oh, my liege, think not that thought! it cannot be. My heart deeply, most deeply, thanks you for your generous condescension. But she whom her lover's voice in solitude – whose entreaties, when memory and seclusion aided the spell – could not persuade, will resist even your majesty's commands. She is bent upon entering a cloister; and I, so please you, will now take my leave: – I am henceforth a soldier of the cross.'

'Gaspar,' said the monarch, 'I know woman better than thou. It is not by submission nor tearful plaints she is to be won. The death of her relatives naturally sits heavy at the young countess's heart; and nourishing in solitude her regret and her repentance, she fancies that Heaven itself forbids your union. Let the voice of the world reach her – the voice of earthly power and earthly kindness – the one commanding, the other pleading, and both finding response in her own heart – and by my say and the Holy Cross, she will be yours. Let our plan still hold. And now to horse: the morning wears, and the sun is risen.'

The king arrived at the bishop's palace, and proceeded forthwith to mass in the cathedral. A sumptuous dinner succeeded, and it was afternoon before the monarch proceeded through the town beside the Loire to where, a little above Nantes, the Chateau Villeneuve was situated. The young countess received him at the gate. Henry looked in vain for the cheek blanched by misery, the aspect of downcast despair which he had been taught to expect. Her cheek was flushed, her manner animated, her voice scarce tremulous. 'She loves him not,' thought Henry, 'or already her heart has consented.'

A collation was prepared for the monarch; and after some little hesitation, arising from the cheerfulness of her mien, he mentioned the name of Gaspar. Constance blushed instead of turning pale, and replied very quickly, 'Tomorrow, good my liege; I ask for a respite but until tomorrow; – all will then be decided; – tomorrow I am vowed to God – or' –

She looked confused, and the king, at once surprised and pleased, said, 'Then you hate not young De Vaudemont; – you forgive him for the inimical blood that warms his veins.'

'We are taught that we should forgive, that we should love our enemies,' the countess replied, with some trepidation.

'Now, by Saint Denis, that is a right welcome answer for the novice,' said the king, laughing. 'What ho! my faithful serving-man, Don Apollo in disguise! come forward, and thank your lady for her love.'

In such disguise as had concealed him from all, the cavalier had hung behind, and viewed with infinite surprise the demeanour and calm countenance of the lady. He could not hear her words: but was this even she whom he had seen trembling and weeping the evening before? – this she whose very heart was torn by conflicting passion? – who saw the pale ghosts of parent and kinsman stand between her and the lover whom more than her life she adored? It was a riddle hard to solve. The king's call was in unison with his impatience, and he sprang forward. He was at her feet; while she, still passion-driven overwrought by the very calmness she had assumed, uttered one cry as she recognized him, and sank senseless on the floor.

All this was very unintelligible. Even when her attendants had brought her to life, another fit succeeded, and then passionate floods of tears; while the monarch, waiting in the hall, eyeing the half-eaten collation, and humming some romance in commemoration of woman's waywardness, knew not how to reply to Vaudemont's look of bitter disappointment and anxiety. At length the countess' chief attendant came with an apology: 'Her lady was ill, very ill. The next day she would throw herself at the king's feet, at once to solicit his excuse, and to disclose her purpose.'

'Tomorrow – again tomorrow! – Does tomorrow bear some charm, maiden?' said the king. 'Can you read us the riddle, pretty one? What strange tale belongs to tomorrow, that all rests on its advent?'

Manon coloured, looked down, and hesitated. But Henry was no tyro in the art of enticing ladies' attendants to disclose their ladies' council. Manon was besides frightened by the countess' scheme, on which she was still obstinately bent, so she was the more readily induced to betray it. To sleep in St Catherine's bed, to rest on a narrow ledge overhanging the deep rapid Loire, and if, as was most probable, the luckless dreamer escaped from falling into it, to take the disturbed visions that such uneasy slumber might produce for the dictate of Heaven, was a madness of which even Henry himself could scarcely deem any woman capable. But could Constance, her whose beauty was so highly intellectual, and whom he had heard perpetually praised for her strength of mind and talents, could *she* be so strangely infatuated! And can passion play such freaks with us? – like death, levelling even the aristocracy of the soul, and bringing noble and peasant, the wise and foolish, under one thraldom? It was strange – yes she must have her way. That she hesitated in her decision was much; and it was to be hoped that St Catherine would play no ill-natured part. Should it be otherwise, a purpose to be swayed by a dream might be influenced by other waking thoughts. To the more material kind of danger some safeguard should be brought.

There is no feeling more awful than that which invades a weak human heart bent upon gratifying its ungovernable impulses in contradiction to the dictates of conscience. Forbidden pleasures are said to be the most agreeable; – it may be so to rude natures, to those who love to struggle, combat, and contest; who find happiness in a fray, and joy in the conflict of passion. But softer and sweeter was the gentle spirit of Constance; and love and duty contending crushed and tortured her poor heart. To commit her conduct to the inspirations of religion, or, if it was so to be named, of superstition, was a blessed relief. The very perils that threatened her undertaking gave zest to it; – to dare for his sake was happiness; – the very difficulty of the way that led to the completion of her wishes at once gratified her love and distracted her thoughts from her despair. Or if it was decreed that she must sacrifice all, the risk of danger and of death were of trifling import in comparison with the anguish which would then be her portion for ever.

The night threatened to be stormy, the raging wind shook the casements, and the trees waved their huge shadowy arms, as giants might in fantastic dance and mortal broil. Constance and Manon, unattended, quitted the château by a postern, and began to descend the hillside. The moon had not yet risen; and though the way was familiar to both, Manon tottered and trembled; while the countess, drawing her silken cloak around her, walked with a firm step down the steep. They came to the river's side, where a small boat was moored, and one man was in waiting. Constance stepped lightly in, and then aided her fearful companion. In a few moments they were in the middle of the stream. The warm, tempestuous, animating, equinoctial wind swept over them. For the first time since her mourning, a thrill of pleasure swelled the bosom of Constance. She hailed the emotion with double joy. It cannot be, she thought, that Heaven will forbid me to love one so brave, so generous, and so good as the noble Gaspar. Another I can never love; I shall die if divided from him; and this heart, these limbs, so alive with glowing sensation, are they already predestined to an early grave? Oh no! life speaks aloud within them. I shall live to love. Do not all things love? – the winds as they whisper to the rushing waters? the waters as they kiss the flowery banks, and speed to mingle with the sea? Heaven and earth are sustained by, and live through, love; and shall Constance alone, whose heart has ever been a deep, gushing, overflowing well of true affection, be compelled to set a stone upon the fount to lock it up for ever?

These thoughts bade fair for pleasant dreams; and perhaps the countess, an adept in the blind god's lore, therefore indulged them the more readily. But as thus she was engrossed by soft emotions, Manon caught her arm: – 'Lady, look,' she cried; 'it comes – yet the oars have no sound. Now the Virgin shield us! Would we were at home!'

A dark boat glided by them. Four rowers, habited in black cloaks, pulled at oars which, as Manon said, gave no sound; another sat at the helm: like the rest, his person was veiled in a dark mantle, but he wore no cap; and though his face was turned from them, Constance recognized her lover. 'Gaspar,' she cried aloud, 'dost thou live?' – but the figure in the boat neither turned its head nor replied, and quickly it was lost in the shadowy waters.

How changed now was the fair countess' reverie! Already Heaven had begun its spell, and unearthly forms were around, as she strained her eyes through the gloom. Now she saw and now she lost view of the bark that occasioned her terror; and now it seemed that another was there, which held the spirits of the dead; and her father waved to her from shore, and her brothers frowned on her.

Meanwhile they neared the landing. Her bark was moored in a little cove, and Constance stood upon the bank. Now she trembled, and half yielded to Manon's entreaty to return; till the unwise *suivante* mentioned the king's and De Vaudemont's name, and spoke of the answer to be given tomorrow. What answer, if she turned back from her intent?

She now hurried forward up the broken ground of the bank, and then along its edge, till they came to a hill which abruptly hung over the tide. A small chapel stood near. With trembling fingers the countess drew forth the key and unlocked its door. They entered. It was dark – save that a little lamp, flickering in the wind, showed an uncertain light from before the figure of Saint Catherine. The two women knelt; they prayed; and then rising, with a cheerful accent the countess bade her attendant good-night. She unlocked a little low iron door. It opened on a narrow cavern. The roar of waters was heard beyond. 'Thou mayest not follow, my poor Manon,' said Constance, – 'nor dost thou much desire: – this adventure is for me alone.'

It was hardly fair to leave the trembling servant in the chapel alone, who had neither hope nor fear, nor love, nor grief to beguile her; but, in those days, esquires and waiting-women often played the part of subalterns in the army, gaining knocks and no fame. Besides, Manon was safe in holy ground. The countess meanwhile pursued her way groping in the dark through the narrow tortuous passage. At length what seemed light to her long darkened sense gleamed on her. She reached an open cavern in the overhanging hill's side, looking over the rushing tide beneath. She looked out upon the night. The waters of the Loire were speeding, as since that day have they ever sped – changeful, yet the same; the heavens were thickly veiled with clouds, and the wind in the trees was as mournful and ill-omened as if it rushed round a murderer's tomb. Constance shuddered a little, and looked upon her bed, – a narrow ledge of earth and a moss-grown stone bordering on the very verge of the precipice. She doffed her mantle, – such was one of the conditions of the spell; – she bowed her head, and loosened the tresses of her dark hair; she bared her feet; and thus, fully prepared for suffering to the utmost the chill influence of the cold night, she stretched herself on the narrow couch that scarce afforded room for her repose, and whence, if she moved in sleep, she must be precipitated into the cold waters below.

At first it seemed to her as if she never should sleep again. No great wonder that exposure to the blast and her perilous position should forbid her eyelids to close. At length she fell into a reverie so soft and soothing that she wished even to watch; and then by degrees her senses became confused; and now she was on St Catherine's bed – the Loire rushing beneath, and the wild wind sweeping by – and now – oh whither? – and what dreams did the saint send, to drive her to despair, or to bid her be blest for ever?

Beneath the rugged hill, upon the dark tide, another watched, who feared a thousand things, and scarce dared hope. He had meant to precede the lady on her way, but when he found that he had outstayed his time, with muffled oars and breathless haste he had shot by the bark that contained his Constance, nor even turned at her voice, fearful to incur her blame, and her commands to return. He had seen her emerge from the passage, and shuddered as she leant over the cliff. He saw her step forth, clad as she was in white, and could mark her as she lay on the ledge beetling above. What a vigil did the lovers keep! – she given up to visionary thoughts, he knowing – and the conscious-ness thrilled his bosom with strange emotion – that love, and love for him, had led her to that perilous couch; and that while dangers surrounded her in every shape, she was alive only to the small still voice that whispered to her heart the dream which was to decide their destinies. She slept perhaps – but he waked and watched; and night wore away, as now praying, now en-tranced by alternating hope and fear, he sat in his boat, his eyes fixed on the white garb of the slumberer above.

Morning – was it morning that struggled in the clouds? Would morning ever come to waken her? And had she slept? and what dreams of weal or woe had peopled her sleep? Gaspar grew impatient. He commanded his boatmen still to wait, and he sprang forward, intent on clambering the precipice. In vain they urged the danger, nay, the impossibility of the attempt; he clung to the rugged face of the hill, and found footing where it would seem no footing was. The acclivity, indeed, was not high; the dangers of St Catherine's bed arising from the likelihood that any one who slept on so narrow a couch would be precipitated into the waters beneath. Up the steep ascent Gaspar continued to toil, and at last reached the roots of a tree that grew near the summit. Aided by its branches, he made good his stand at the very extremity of the ledge, near the pillow on which lay the uncovered head of his beloved. Her hands were folded on her bosom; her dark hair fell round her throat and pillowed her cheek; her face was serene: sleep was there in all its innocence and in all its helplessness; every wilder emotion was hushed, and her bosom heaved in regular breathing. He could see her heart beat as it lifted her fair hands crossed above. No statue hewn of marble in monumental effigy was ever half so fair; and within that surpassing form dwelt a soul true, tender, self-devoted, and affectionate as ever warmed a human breast.

With what deep passion did Gaspar gaze, gathering hope from the placidity of her angel countenance! A smile wreathed her lips; and he too involuntarily smiled, as he hailed the happy omen; when suddenly her cheek was flushed, her bosom heaved, a tear stole from her dark lashes, and then a whole shower fell, as starting up she cried, 'No! – he shall not die! – I will unloose his chains! – I will save him!' Gaspar's hand was there. He caught her light form ready to fall from the perilous couch. She opened her eyes and beheld her lover, who had watched over her dream of fate, and who had saved her.

Manon also had slept well, dreaming or not, and was startled in the morning to find that she waked surrounded by a crowd. The little desolate chapel was hung with tapestry – the altar adorned with golden chalices – the priest was chanting mass to a goodly array of kneeling knights. Manon saw that King Henry was there; and she looked for another whom she found not, when the iron door of the cavern passage opened, and Gaspar de Vaudemont entered from it, leading the fair form of Constance; who, in her white robes and dark dishevelled hair, with a face in which smiles and blushes contended with deeper emotion, approached the altar, and, kneeling with her lover, pronounced the vows that united them for ever.

It was long before the happy Gaspar could win from his lady the secret of her dream. In spite of the happiness she now enjoyed, she had suffered too much not to look back even with terror to those days when she thought love a crime, and every event connected with them wore an awful aspect. 'Many a vision,' she said, 'she had that fearful night. She had seen the spirits of her father and brothers in Paradise; she had beheld Gaspar victoriously combating among the infidels; she had beheld him in King Henry's court, favoured and beloved; and she herself – now pining in a cloister, now a bride, now grateful to Heaven for the full measure of bliss presented to her, now weeping away her sad days – till suddenly she thought herself in Paynim land; and the saint herself, St Catherine, guiding her unseen through the city of the infidels. She entered a palace, and beheld the miscreants rejoicing in victory; and then, descending to the dungeons beneath, they groped their way through damp vaults, and low, mildewed passages, to one cell, darker and more frightful than the rest. On the floor lay one with soiled and tattered garments, with unkempt locks and wild, matted beard. His cheek was worn and thin; his eyes had lost their fire; his form was a mere skeleton; the chains hung loosely on the fleshless bones.'

'And was it my appearance in that attractive state and winning costume that softened the hard heart of Constance?' asked Gaspar, smiling at this painting of what would never be.

'Even so,' replied Constance; 'for my heart whispered me that this was my doing; and who could recall the life that waned in your pulses – who restore, save the destroyer? My heart never warmed to my living, happy knight as then it did to his wasted image as it lay, in the visions of night, at my feet. A veil fell from my eyes; a darkness was dispelled from before me. Methought I then knew for the first time what life and what death was. I was bid believe that to make the living happy was not to injure the dead; and I felt how wicked and how vain was that false philosophy which placed virtue and good in hatred and unkindness. You should not die; I would loosen your chains and save you, and bid you live for love. I sprung forward, and the death I deprecated for you would, in my presumption, have been mine, – then, when first I felt the real value of life, – but that your arm was there to save me, your dear voice to bid me be blest for evermore.'

# The Burial

## Lord Byron
### (1788–1824)

Just as the first story in the group of four tales by the personalities who formed the Lake Geneva 'quartet' was actually written at the time (I refer, of course, to *The Vampyre* by John Polidori), so was this final selection by Lord Byron. As we noted, he soon tired of the 'ghost story idea' and left no more than a fragment of the novel he planned. In essence it is not unlike Polidori's tale and there is little doubt that in first discussing it, Byron had sown the seed in the mind of his sometime companion.

Lord George Gordon Byron, one of the towering figures of English letters, was brought up in semi-poverty by his vulgar and stupid mother who had been deserted by her husband and succeeded to his title on the death of 'the wicked lord', his great-uncle, in 1798. Dissipation took hold of him as a young student and when his first selection of poems was published and savagely attacked in the press, he took himself off for a riotous tour of Europe. From this trip came *Childe Harold's Pilgrimage* which reversed the opinions of all those who had attacked him previously and he became an overnight sensation.

Assuming the role of a man of mystery, he became the darling of London Society and gave birth to the concept of the 'Byronic Hero'. Suspected of incest with his wife's sister, he was later forced to flee the country and in 1816 met the Shelleys in Switzerland. From then until his death his life fell into a more ordered pattern and apart from producing some of his best work (including *Don Juan* in 1819–1824) he also actively aided the Italian revolutionaries. It was while similarly engaged in helping Greek insurgents against the Turks that he died of fever in Missolonghi in 1824.

The great German macabre story writer, E. T. A. Hoffman, noted with enthusiasm that Byron had a 'remarkable knack for the weird and the horrible' while Eino Railo says the poet was 'a zealous reader of terror romanticism and had steeped himself in the atmosphere of ancient crime and decay'. How accurate both men were can certainly be seen to good effect in the fragment reproduced here. Again, as in the case of Shelley, it is to be regretted that the author never completed his work.

'IN the year 17–, having for some time determined on a journey through countries not hitherto much frequented by travellers, I set out, accompanied by a friend, whom I shall designate by the name of Augustus Darvell. He was a few years my elder, and a man of considerable fortune and ancient family: advantages which an extensive capacity prevented him alike from undervaluing or overrating. Some peculiar circumstances in his private history had rendered him to me an object of attention, of interest, and even of regard, which neither the reserve of his manners, nor occasional indications of an inquietude at times nearly approaching to alienation of mind, could extinguish.

'I was yet young in life, which I had begun early; but my intimacy with him was of a recent date: we had been educated at the same schools and university; but his progress through these had preceded mine, and he had been deeply initiated into what is called the world, while I was yet in my novitiate. While thus engaged, I heard much both of his past and present life; and, although in these accounts there were many and irreconcilable contradictions, I could still gather from the whole that he was a being of no common order, and one who, whatever pains he might take to avoid remark, would still be remarkable. I had cultivated his acquaintance subsequently, and endeavoured to obtain his friendship, but this last appeared to be unattainable; whatever affections he might have possessed seemed now, some to have been extinguished, and others to be concentred: that his feelings were acute, I had sufficient opportunities of observing; for, although he could control, he could not altogether disguise them: still he had a power of giving to one passion the appearance of another, in such a manner that it was difficult to define the nature of what was working within him; and the expressions of his features would vary so rapidly, though slightly, that it was useless to trace them to their sources. It was evident that he was a prey to some cureless disquiet; but whether it arose from ambition, love, remorse, grief, from one or all of these, or merely from a morbid temperament akin to disease, I could not discover: there were circumstances alleged which might have justified the application to each of these causes; but, as I have before said, these were so contradictory and contradicted, that none could be fixed upon with accuracy. Where there is mystery, it is generally supposed that there must also be evil: I know not how this may be, but in him there certainly was the one, though I could not ascertain the extent of the other – and felt loth, as far as regarded himself, to believe in its existence. My advances were received with sufficient coldness: but I was young, and not easily discouraged, and at length succeeded in obtaining, to a certain degree, that common-place intercourse and moderate confidence of common and everyday concerns, created and cemented by similarity of pursuit and frequency of meeting, which is called intimacy, or friendship, according to the ideas of him who uses those words to express them.

'Darvell had already travelled extensively; and to him I had applied for information with regard to the conduct of my intended journey. It was my secret wish that he might be prevailed on to accompany me; it was also a probable hope, founded upon the shadowy restlessness which I observed in him, and to which the animation which he appeared to feel on such subjects, and his apparent indifference to all by which he was more immediately surrounded, gave fresh strength. This wish I first hinted, and then expressed: his answer, though I had partly expected it, gave me all the pleasure of surprise – he consented; and, after the requisite arrangement, we commenced our voyages. After journeying through various countries of the south of Europe, our intention was turned towards the East, according to our original destination; and it was in my progress through these regions that the incident occurred upon which will turn what I may have to relate.

'The constitution of Darvell, which must from his appearance have been in early life more than usually robust, had been for some time gradually giving away, without the intervention of any apparent disease: he had neither cough nor hectic, yet he became daily more enfeebled; his habits were temperate, and he neither declined nor complained of fatigue; yet he was evidently wasting away: he became more and more silent and sleepless, and at length so seriously altered, that my alarm grew proportionate to what I conceived to be his danger.

'We had determined, on our arrival at Smyrna, on an excursion to the ruins of Ephesus and Sardis, from which I endeavoured to dissuade him in his present state of indisposition – but in vain: there appeared to be an oppression on his mind, and a solemnity in his manner, which ill corresponded with his eagerness to proceed on what I regarded as a mere party of pleasure little suited to a valetudinarian; but I opposed him no longer – and in a few days we set off together, accompanied only by a serrugee and a single janizary.

'We had passed half-way towards the remains of Ephesus, leaving behind us the more fertile environs of Smyrna, and were entering upon that wild and tenantless tract through the marshes and defiles which lead to the few huts yet lingering over the broken columns of Diana – the roofless walls of expelled Christianity, and the still more recent but complete desolation of abandoned mosques – when the sudden and rapid illness of my companion obliged us to halt at a Turkish cemetery, the turbaned tombstones of which were the sole indication that human life had ever been a sojourner in this wilderness. The only caravansera we had seen was left some hours behind us, not a vestige of a town or even cottage was within sight or hope, and this "city of the dead" appeared to be the sole refuge of my unfortunate friend, who seemed on the verge of becoming the last of its inhabitants.

'In this situation, I looked round for a place where he might most conveniently repose: – contrary to the usual aspect of Mahometan burial-grounds, the cypresses were in this few in number, and these thinly scattered over its extent; the tombstones were mostly fallen, and worn with age: – upon one of the most considerable of these, and beneath one of the most spreading trees, Darvell supported himself, in a half-reclining posture, with great difficulty. He asked for water. I had some doubts of our being able to find any, and prepared to go in search of it with hesitating despondency: but he desired me to remain; and turning to Suleiman, our janizary, who stood by us smoking with great tranquillity, he said, "Suleiman, verbana su," (*i.e.* "bring some water,") and went on describing the spot where it was to be found with great minuteness, at a small well for camels, a few hundred yards to the right: the janizary obeyed. I said to Darvell, "How did you know this?" – He replied, "From our situation; you must perceive that this place was once inhabited, and could not have been so without springs: I have also been here before."

"'To this question I received no answer. In the mean time Suleiman returned with the water, leaving the serrugee and the horses at the fountain. The quenching of his thirst had the appearance of reviving him for a moment; and I conceived hopes of his being able to proceed, or at least to return, and I urged the attempt. He was silent – and appeared to be collecting his spirits for an effort to speak. He began –

"'This is the end of my journey, and of my life; – I came here to die; but I have a request to make, a command – for such my last words must be. – You will observe it?"

"'Most certainly; but I have better hopes."

"'I have no hopes, nor wishes, but this – conceal my death from every human being."

"I hope there will be no occasion; that you will recover, and –"

"'Peace! – it must be so: promise this."

"'I do."

"'Swear it, by all that –" He here dictated an oath of great solemnity.

"'There is no occasion for this. I will observe your request; and to doubt me is –"

"'It cannot be helped, – you must swear."

'I took the oath, it appeared to relieve him. He removed a seal ring from his finger, on which were some Arabic characters, and presented it to me. He proceeded –

'"On the ninth day of the month, at noon precisely (what month you please, but this must be the day), you must fling this ring into the salt springs which run into the Bay of Eleusis; the day after at the same hour, you must repair to the ruins of the temple of Ceres, and wait one hour."

'"Why?"

'"You will see."

'"The ninth day of the month, you say?"

'"The ninth."

'As I observed that the present was the ninth day of the month, his countenance changed, and he paused. As he sat, evidently becoming more feeble, a stork, with a snake in her beak, perched upon a tombstone near us; and, without devouring her prey, appeared to be steadfastly regarding us. I know not what impelled me to drive it away, but the attempt was useless; she made a few circles in the air, and returned exactly to the same spot. Darvell pointed to it, and smiled – he spoke – I know not whether to himself or to me – but the words were only, "'Tis well!"

'"What is well? What do you mean?"

'"No matter; you must bury me here this evening, and exactly where that bird is now perched. You know the rest of my injunctions."

'He then proceeded to give me several directions as to the manner in which his death might be best concealed. After these were finished, he exclaimed, "You perceive that bird?"

'"Certainly."

'"And the serpent writhing in her beak?"

'"Doubtless: there is nothing uncommon in it; it is her natural prey. But it is odd that she does not devour it."

'He smiled in a ghastly manner, and said faintly, "It is not yet time!" As he spoke, the stork flew away. My eyes followed it for a moment – it could hardly be longer than ten might be counted. I felt Darvell's weight, as it were, increase upon my shoulder, and turning to look upon his face, perceived that he was dead!

'I was shocked with the sudden certainty which could not be mistaken – his countenance in a few minutes became nearly black. I should have attributed so rapid a change to poison, had I not been aware that he had no opportunity of receiving it unperceived. The day was declining, the body was rapidly altering, and nothing remained but to fulfil his request. With the aid of Suleiman's ataghan and my own sabre, we scooped a shallow grave upon the spot which Darvell had indicated: the earth easily gave way, having already received some Mahometan tenant. We dug deeply as the time permitted us, and throwing the dry earth upon all that remained of the singular being so lately departed, we cut a few sods of greener turf from the less withered soil around us, and laid them upon his sepulchre.

'Between astonishment and grief, I was tearless.'

# A Tale for a Chimney Corner

## Leigh Hunt
## (1784–1859)

As a friend and occasional companion of both Byron and Shelley, Leigh Hunt is a most suitable figure to be next introduced in our study of the Gothic short story. Unlike the poets, however, Hunt had no time for terror tales and roundly attacked the leading dispenser, Matthew Lewis, and his 'little Grey Men who sit munching hearts'. None the less, he felt compelled to add grist to the Gothic mill if only because 'a man who does not contribute his quota of grim story nowadays, seems hardly to be free of the republic of letters'.

James Henry Leigh Hunt is perhaps most famous for having introduced to public attention the work of his friend Shelley, and also that of Keats, in his newspaper, *The Examiner*, which he produced with his brother. The periodical also championed liberal thinking and apart from earning Hunt a prison sentence on one occasion for libelling the Prince Regent, attracted the support of the leading writers of the time including Byron, Moore and Lamb. Hunt's own writing, and his poetry in particular, was for a time widely influential and Keats admitted to having been greatly inspired by it.

Nervous of the danger his liberal views were still running him with the authorities, Hunt decided in 1821 to spend some time abroad and he was for several months a guest of Shelley in Italy (until the poet's tragic drowning) and he then joined Byron at Pisa. In 1825 he returned to England to find a more moderate climate of thinking now existing and again took up literary journalism. In the succeeding years his Hampstead home became the most noted salon of the period for writers and poets.

*A Tale for a Chimney Corner* appeared in *The Indicator* in 1819 and portrays a much more placid ghost than any we have so far encountered. Like its creator, though, it has a special place both in this book and in nineteenth-century writing.

A MAN who does not contribute his quota of grim story nowadays, seems hardly to be free of the republic of letters. He is bound to wear a death's head as part of his insignia. If he does not frighten everybody, he is nobody. If he does not shock the ladies, what can be expected of him?

We confess we think very cheaply of these stories in general. A story, merely horrible or even awful, which contains no sentiment elevating to the human heart and its hopes, is a mere appeal to the least judicious, least healthy, and least masculine of our passions – fear. They whose attention can be gravely arrested by it, are in a fit state to receive any absurdity with respect; and this is the reason why less talents are required to enforce it, than in any other species of composition. With this opinion of such things, we may be allowed to say, that we would undertake to write a dozen horrible stories in a day, all of which should make the common worshippers of power, who were not in the very healthiest condition, turn pale. We would tell of Haunting Old Women, and Knocking Ghosts, and Solitary Lean Hands, and Empusas on One Leg, and Ladies growing Longer and Longer, and Horrid Eyes meeting us through Keyholes, and Plaintive Heads, and Shrieking Statues, and shocking Anomalies of Shape, and Things which when seen drove people mad; and Indigestion knows what besides. But who would measure talents with a leg of veal or a German sausage?

Mere grimness is as easy as grinning; but it requires something to put a handsome face on a story. Narratives become of suspicious merit in proportion as they lean to Newgate-like offences, particularly of blood and wounds. A child has a reasonable respect for a Raw-head-and-bloody-bones, because all images whatsoever of pain and terror are new and fearful to his inexperienced age; but sufferings merely physical (unless sublimated like those of Philoctetes) are commonplace to a grown man. Images, to become awful to him, must be removed from the grossness of the shambles. A death's head was a respectable thing in the hands of a poring monk, or of a nun compelled to avoid the idea of life and society, or of a hermit already buried in the desert. Holbein's Dance of Death, in which every grinning skeleton leads along a man of rank, from the Pope to the gentleman, is a good Memento Mori; but there the skeletons have an air of the ludicrous and satirical. If we were threatened with them in a grave way, as spectres, we should have a right to ask how they could walk about without muscles. Thus many of the tales written by such authors as the late Mr Lewis, who wanted sentiment to give him the heart of truth, are quite puerile. When his spectral nuns go about bleeding, we think they ought in decency to have applied to some ghost of a surgeon. His little Grey Men, who sit munching hearts, are of a piece with fellows that eat cats for a wager.

Stories that give mental pain to no purpose, or to very little purpose compared with the unpleasant ideas they excite of human nature, are as gross mistakes, in their way, as these, and twenty times as pernicious; for the latter becomes ludicrous to grown people. They originate also in the same extremes, of callousness, or of morbid want of excitement, as the others. But more of these hereafter. Our business at present is with things ghastly and ghostly.

A ghost story, to be a good one, should unite, as much as possible, objects such as they are in life with a preternatural spirit. And to be a perfect one, – at least, to add to the other utility of excitement a moral utility, – they should imply some great sentiment, – something that comes out of the next world to remind us of our duties in this; or something that helps to carry on the idea of our humanity into afterlife, even when we least think we shall take it with us. When 'the buried majesty of Denmark' revisits earth to speak to his son Hamlet, he comes armed, as he used to be, in his complete steel. His visor is raised; and the same fine face is there; only, in spite of his punishing errand and his own sufferings, with

A countenance more in sorrow than in anger.

When Donne the poet, in his thoughtful eagerness to reconcile life and death, had a figure of himself painted in a shroud, and laid by his bedside in a coffin, he did a higher thing than the monks and hermits with their skulls. It was taking his humanity with him into the other world, not affecting to lower the sense of it by regarding it piecemeal or in the framework. Burns, in his 'Tam O'Shanter,' shows the dead in their coffins after the same fashion. He does not lay bare to us their skeletons or refuse, things with which we can connect no sympathy or spiritual wonder. They still are flesh and body to retain the one; yet so look and behave, inconsistent in their very consistency, as to excite the other.

> Coffins stood round like open presses,
> Which showed the dead in their last dresses:
> And by some devilish cantrip sleight,
> Each, in his cauld hand, held a light.

Reanimation is perhaps the most ghastly of all ghastly things, uniting as it does an appearance of natural interdiction from the next world, with a supernatural experience of it. Our human consciousness is jarred out of its self-possession. The extremes of habit and newness, of commonplace and astonishment, meet suddenly, without the kindly introduction of death and change; and the stranger appals us in proportion. When the account appeared the other day in the newspapers of the galvanized dead body, whose features as well as limbs underwent such contortions, that it seemed as if it were about to rise up, one almost expected to hear, for the first time, news of the other world. Perhaps the most appalling figure in Spenser is that of Maleger ('Faerie Queene,' b. ii. c. 11):

> Upon a tygre swift and fierce he rode,
> That as the winde ran underneathe his lode,
> Whiles his long legs nigh raught unto the ground:
> Full large he was of limbe, and shoulders brode,
> But of such subtile substance and unsound,
> That like a ghost he seemed, whose grave-clothes were unbound.

Mr Coleridge, in that voyage of his to the brink of all unutterable things, the 'Ancient Mariner' (which works out, however, a fine sentiment), does not set mere ghosts or hobgoblins to man the ship again, when its crew are dead; but reanimates, for awhile, the crew themselves. There is a striking fiction of this sort in Sale's *Notes upon the Koran*. Solomon dies during the building of the temple, but his body remains leaning on a staff and overlooking the workmen, as if it were alive; till a worm gnawing through the prop, he falls down. – The contrast of the appearance of humanity with something mortal or supernatural, is always the more terrible in proportion as it is complete. In the pictures of the temptations of saints and hermits, where the holy person is surrounded, teased, and enticed, with devils and fantastic shapes, the most shocking phantasm is that of the beautiful woman. To return also to the poem abovementioned. The most appalling personage in Mr Coleridge's 'Ancient Mariner' is the Spectre-woman, who is called Life-in-Death. He renders the most hideous abstraction more terrible than it could otherwise have been, by embodying it in its own reverse. 'Death' not only 'lives' in it, but the 'unutterable' becomes uttered. To see such an unearthly passage end in such earthliness, seems to turn commonplace itself into a sort of spectral doubt. The Mariner, after describing the horrible calm, and the rotting sea in which the ship was stuck, is speaking of a strange sail which he descried in the distance:

> The western wave was all a-flame,
> The day was well nigh done!
> Almost upon the western wave
> Rested the broad bright sun;
>
> When that strange ship drove suddenly
> Betwixt us and the sun.
> And straight the sun was flecked with bars,
> (Heaven's Mother send us grace!)
> As if through a dungeon-grate he peer'd,
> With broad and burning face.
>
> Alas! (thought I, and my heart beat loud)
> How fast she neers and neers!

Are those *her* sails that glance in the sun
Like restless gossamers?

Are those *her* ribs, through which the sun
Did peer as through a grate?
And is that Woman all her crew?
Is that a death? and are there two?
Is Death that Woman's mate?

Her lips were red, her looks were free,
Her locks were yellow as gold,
Her skin was as white as leprosy,
The Night-Mare Life-in-Death was she,
Who thicks man's blood with cold.

But we must come to Mr Coleridge's story with our subtlest imaginations upon us. Now let us put our knees a little nearer the fire, and tell a homelier one about Life in Death, the ground work of it is in Sandy's *Commentary upon Ovid*, and quoted from Sabinus.*

A gentleman of Bavaria, of a noble family, was so afflicted at the death of his wife, that, unable to bear the company of any other person, gave himself up to a solitary way of living. This was the more remarkable in him, as he had been a man of jovial habits, fond of his wine and visitors, and impatient of having his numerous indulgences contradicted. But in the same temper, perhaps, might be found the cause of his sorrow; for though he would be impatient with his wife, as with others, yet his love for her was one of the gentlest wills he had; and the sweet and unaffected face which she always turned upon his anger, might have been a thing more easy for him to trespass upon, while living, than to forget when dead and gone. His very angry towards her, compared with that towards others, was a relief to him. It was rather a wish to refresh himself in the balmy feeling of her patience, than to make her unhappy herself, or to punish her, as some would have done, for that virtuous contrast to his own vice.

*The Saxon Latin poet, we presume, professor of *belles-lettres* at Frankfurt. We know nothing of him, except from a biographical dictionary.

But whether he bethought himself, after her death, that this was a very selfish mode of loving; or whether, as some thought, he had wearied out her life with habits so contrary to her own; or whether, as others reported, he had put it to a fatal risk by some lordly piece of selfwill, in consequence of which she had caught a fever on the cold river during a night of festivity; he surprised even those who thought that he loved her by the extreme bitterness of his grief. The very mention of festivity, though he was patient for the first day or two, afterwards threw him into a passion or rage; but by degrees even his rage followed his other old habits. He was gentle, but ever silent. He ate and drank but sufficient to keep him alive; and used to spend the greater part of the day in the spot where his wife was buried.

He was going there one evening, in a very melancholy manner, with his eyes turned towards the earth, and had just entered the rails of the burial-ground, when he was accosted by the mild voice of somebody coming to meet him. 'It is a blessed evening, sir,' said the voice. The gentleman looked up. Nobody but himself was allowed to be in the place at that hour, and yet he saw with astonishment a young chorister approached him. He was going to express some wonder, when, he said, the modest though assured look of the boy, and the extreme beauty of his countenance, which glowed in the setting sun before him, made an irresistible addition to the singular sweetness of his voice; and he asked him with an involuntary calmness, and a gesture of respect, not what he did there, but what he wished. 'Only to wish you all good things,' answered the stranger, who had now come up, 'and to give you this letter.' The gentleman took the letter, and saw upon it, with a beating yet scarcely bewildered heart, the handwriting of his wife. He raised his eyes again to speak to the boy, but he was gone. He cast them far and near round the place, but there were no traces of a passenger. He then opened the letter, and by the divine light of the setting sun, read these words:

'To my dear husband, who sorrows for his wife –

'Otto, my husband, the soul you regret so is returned. You will know the truth of this, and be prepared with calmness to see it, by the divineness of the messenger who has passed you. You will find me sitting in the public walk, praying for you, praying that you may never more give way to those gusts of passion and those curses against others, which divided us.

'This, with a warm hand, from the living Bertha.'

Otto (for such, it seems, was the gentleman's name) went instantly, calmly, quickly, yet with a sort of benumbed being, to the public walk. He felt, but with only a half-consciousness, as if he glided without a body, but all his spirit was awake, eager, intensely conscious. It seemed to him as if there had been but two things in the world – Life and Death; and that Death was dead. All else appeared to have been a dream. He had awaked from a waking state, and found himself all eye, and spirit, and locomotion. He said to himself, once, as he went: 'This is not a dream. I will ask my great ancestors tomorrow to my new bridal feast, for they are alive.' Otto had been calm at first, but something of old and triumphant feelings seemed again to come over him. Was he again too proud and confident? Did his earthly humours prevail again, when he thought them least upon him? We shall see.

The Bavarian arrived at the public walk. It was full of people with their wives and children, enjoying the beauty of the evening. Something like common fear came over him as he went in and out among them, looking at the benches on each side. It happened that there was only one person, a lady, sitting upon them. She had her veil down, and his being underwent a fierce but short convulsion as he went near her. Something had a little baffled the calmer inspiration of the angel that had accosted him, for fear prevailed at the instant, and Otto passed on. He returned before he had reached the end of the walk, and approached the lady again. She was still sitting in the same quiet posture, only he thought she looked at him. Again he passed her. On his second return, a grave and sweet courage came upon him, and in a quiet but firm tone of inquiry, he said, 'Bertha?' – 'I thought you had forgotten me,' said that well-known and mellow voice, which he had seemed as far from ever hearing again as earth is from heaven. He took her hand, which grasped his in turn; and they walked home in silence together, the arm, which was wound within his, giving warmth for warmth.

The neighbours seemed to have a miraculous want of wonder at the lady's reappearance. Something was said about a mock funeral, and her having withdrawn from his company for awhile; but visitors came as before, and his wife returned to her household affairs. It was only remarked that she always looked pale and pensive. But she was more kind to all, even than before; and her pensiveness seemed rather the result of some great internal thought, than of unhappiness.

For a year or two the Bavarian retained the better temper which he acquired. His fortunes flourished beyond his earliest ambition; the most amiable as well as noble persons of the district were frequent visitors; and people said that to be at Otto's house must be the next thing to being in heaven. But by degrees his selfwill returned with his prosperity. He never vented impatience on his wife, but he again began to show that the disquietude it gave her to see it vented on others was a secondary thing, in his mind, to the indulgence of it. Whether it was that his grief for her loss had been rather remorse than affection, and so he held himself secure if he treated her well, or whether he was at all times rather proud of her than fond, or whatever was the cause which again set his antipathies above his sympathies, certain it was that his old habits returned upon him; not so often, indeed, but with greater violence and pride when they did. These were the only times at which his wife was observed to show any ordinary symptoms of uneasiness.

At length, one day, some strong rebuff which he had received from an alienated neighbour threw him into such a transport of rage that he gave way to the most bitter imprecations, crying with a loud voice, 'This treatment to *me* too! To *me*! To me, who if the world knew all' – At these words, his wife, who had in vain laid her hand upon his, and looked him with dreary earnestness in the face, suddenly glided from the room. He and two or three who were present were struck with a dumb horror. They said she did not walk out, nor vanish suddenly, but glided as one who could dispense with the use of feet. After a moment's pause, the others proposed to him to follow her. He made a movement of despair, but they went. There was a short passage which turned to the right into her favourite room. They knocked at the door twice or three times, and received no answer. At last one of them gently opened it, and, looking in, they saw her, as they thought, standing before a fire, which was the only light in the room. Yet she stood so far from it as rather to be in the middle of the room; only the face was towards the fire, and she seemed looking upon it. They addressed her, but received no answer. They stepped gently towards her, and still received none. The figure stood dumb and unmoved. At last, one of them went round in front, and instantly fell on the floor. The figure was without body. A hollow hood was left instead of a face. The clothes were standing upright by themselves.

That room was blocked up for ever, for the clothes, if it might be so, to moulder away. It was called the Room of the Lady's Figure. The house after the gentleman's death was long uninhabited, and at length burnt by the peasants in an insurrection. As for himself, he died about nine months after, a gentle and childlike penitent. He had never stirred from the house since, and nobody would venture to go near him but a man who had the reputation of being a reprobate. It was from this man that the particulars of the story came first. He would distribute the gentleman's alms in great abundance to any poor stranger who would accept them, for most of the neighbours held them in horror. He tried all he could to get the parents among them to let some of their little children, or a single one of them, go to see his employer. They said he even asked it one day with tears in his eyes. But they shuddered to think of it; and the matter was not mended when this profane person, in a fit of impatience, said one day that he would have a child of his own on purpose. His employer, however, died in a day or two. They did not believe a word he told them of all the Bavarian's gentleness, looking upon the latter as a sort of ogre, and upon his agent as little better, though a good-natured-looking, earnest kind of person. It was said many years after, that this man had been a friend of the Bavarian's when young, and had been deserted by him. And the young believed it, whatever the old might do.

# The Spectre Bride

## W. Harrison Ainsworth

## (1805–1882)

In company with Thomas Peckett Prest (who we shall examine later), William Harrison Ainsworth was probably the most prolific of all the Gothic writers – though it has to be admitted that some of his works are perhaps slightly outside this category. Ainsworth is notable, too, in that he set the vast majority of his novels in England, abandoning the climes of Europe that were so dear to many of his fellows. He also sought, in his own words, to present 'stories of famous folk heroes' and among his most successful must be numbered his re-telling of the legends of Robin Hood, Dick Turpin and Jack Sheppard.

William Ainsworth was born in Manchester just after the turn of the century and was a devoted reader of terror tales from his early teens. He first took up the study of law, but after marrying the daughter of a publisher found the literary world more to his liking and began writing short stories for the popular periodicals of the day. He saw his particular task quite clearly, 'Romance, if I am not mistaken, is destined shortly to undergo an important change ... the structure commenced by Horace Walpole, "Monk" Lewis, Mrs Radcliffe and Maturin, but left imperfect and inharmonious, requires now that the rubbish which choked up its approach is removed, only the hand of the skilful architect to its entire renovation and perfection.'

After a number of successful magazine appearances (of which the story here was one, being published in *Arliss's Pocket Magazine* in 1822), Ainsworth embarked on his first novel, *Rookwood* (1834) which was inspired by a visit to the old manor house at Cuckfield Place. Although not well received by the critics, the books proved popular with readers and led to over forty more works in the ensuing half century. Ainsworth was particularly fortunate in having the talented artist George Cruikshank illustrate many of his books and this man's graphic line drawings pointed up many of the most horrifying incidents.

Through his conscious determination, William Harrison Ainsworth played an important part in re-shaping the Gothic terror tale and setting it on its path to the modern horror story.

THE castle of Hernswolf, at the close of the year 1655, was the resort of fashion and gaiety. The baron of that name was the most powerful nobleman in Germany, and equally celebrated for the patriotic achievements of his sons, and the beauty of his only daughter. The estate of Hernswolf, which was situated in the centre of the Black Forest, had been given to one of his ancestors by the gratitude of the nation, and descended with other hereditary possessions to the family of the present owner. It was a castellated, gothic mansion, built according to the fashion of the times, in the grandest style of architecture, and consisted principally of dark winding corridors, and vaulted tapestry rooms, magnificent indeed in their size, but ill-suited to private comfort, from the very circumstance of their dreary magnitude. A dark grove of pine and mountain ash encompassed the castle on every side, and threw an aspect of gloom around the scene, which was seldom enlivened by the cheering sunshine of heaven.

The castle bells rung out a merry peal at the approach of a winter twilight, and the warder was stationed with his retinue on the battlements, to announce the arrival of the company who were invited to share the amusements that reigned within the walls. The Lady Clotilda, the baron's only daughter, had but just attained her seventeenth year, and a brilliant assembly was invited to celebrate the birthday. The large vaulted apartments were thrown open for the reception of the numerous guests, and the gaieties of the evening had scarcely commenced, when the clock from the dungeon tower was heard to strike with unusual solemnity, and on the instant a tall stranger, arrayed in a deep suit of black, made his appearance in the ballroom. He bowed courteously on every side, but was received by all with the strictest reserve. No one knew who he was or whence he came, but it was evident from his appearance, that he was a nobleman of the first rank, and though his introduction was accepted with distrust, he was treated by all with respect. He addressed himself particularly to the daughter of the baron, and was so intelligent in his remarks, so lively in his sallies, and so fascinating in his address, that he quickly interested the feelings of his young and sensitive auditor. In fine, after some hesitation on the part of the host, who, with the rest of the company, was unable to approach the stranger with indifference, he was requested to remain a few days at the castle, an invitation which was cheerfully accepted.

The dead of the night drew on, and when all had retired to rest, the dull heavy bell was heard swinging to and fro in the grey tower, though there was scarcely a breath to move the forest trees. Many of the guests, when they met the next morning at the breakfast table, averred that there had been sounds as of the most heavenly music, while all persisted in affirming that they had heard awful noises, proceeding as it seemed, from the apartment which the stranger at that time occupied. He soon, however, made his appearance at the breakfast circle, and when the circumstances of the preceding night were alluded to, a dark smile of unutterable meaning played round his saturnine features, and then relapsed into an expression of the deepest melancholy. He addressed his conversation principally to Clotilda, and when he talked of the different climes he had visited, of the sunny regions of Italy, where the very air breathes the fragrance of flowers, and the summer breeze sighs over a land of sweets; when he spoke to her of those delicious countries, where the smile of the day sinks into the softer beauty of the night, and the loveliness of heaven is never for an instant obscured, he drew tears of regret from the bosom of his fair auditor, and for the first time she regretted that she was yet at home.

Days rolled on, and every moment increased the fervour of the inexpressible sentiments with which the stranger had inspired her. He never discoursed of love, but he looked it in his language, in his manner, in the insinuating tones of his voice, and in the slumbering softness of his smile, and when he found that he had succeeded in inspiring her with favourable sentiments towards him, a sneer of the most diabolical meaning spoke for an instant, and died again on his dark featured countenance. When he met her in the company of her parents, he was at once respectful and submissive, and it was only when alone with her, in her rambles through the dark recesses of the forest, that he assumed the guise of the more impassioned admirer.

As he was sitting one evening with the baron in the wainscotted apartment of the library, the conversation happened to turn upon supernatural agency. The stranger remained reserved and mysterious during the discussion, but when the baron in a jocular manner denied the existence of spirits, and satirically invoked their appearance, his eyes glowed with unearthly lustre, and his form seemed to dilate to more than its natural dimensions. When the conversation had ceased, a fearful pause of a few seconds and a chorus of celestial harmony was heard pealing through the dark forest glade. All were entranced with delight, but the stranger was disturbed and gloomy; he looked at his noble host with compassion, and something like a tear swam in his dark eye. After the lapse of a few seconds, the music died gently in the distance, and all was hushed as before. The baron soon after quitted the apartment, and was followed almost immediately by the stranger. He had not long been absent, when an awful noise, as of a person in the agonies of death, was heard, and the Baron was discovered stretched dead along the corridors. His countenance was convulsed with pain, and the grip of a human hand was visible on his blackened throat. The alarm was instantly given, the castle searched in every direction, but the stranger was seen no more. The body of the baron, in the meantime, was quietly committed to the earth, and the remembrance of the dreadful transaction, recalled but as a thing that once was.

After the departure of the stranger, who had indeed fascinated her very senses, the spirits of the gentle Clotilda evidently declined. She loved to walk early and late in the walks that he had once frequented, to recall his last words; to dwell on his sweet smile; and wander to the spot where she had once discoursed with him of love. She avoided all society, and never seemed to be happy but when left alone in the solitude of her chamber. It was then that she gave vent to her affliction in tears; and the love that the pride of maiden modesty concealed in public, burst forth in the hours of privacy. So beauteous, yet so resigned was the fair mourner, that she seemed already an angel freed from the trammels of the world, and prepared to take her flight to heaven.

As she was one summer evening rambling to the sequestered spot that had been selected as her favourite residence, a slow step advanced towards her. She turned round, and to her infinite surprise discovered the stranger. He stepped gaily to her side, and commenced an animated conversation. 'You left me,' exclaimed the delighted girl; 'and I thought all happiness was fled from me for ever; but you return, and shall we not again be happy?' – 'Happy,' replied the stranger, with a scornful burst of derision, 'Can I ever be happy again – can there – but excuse the agitation, my love, and impute it to the pleasure I experience at our meeting. Oh! I have many things to tell you; aye! and many kind words to receive; is it not so, sweet one? Come, tell me truly, have you been happy in my absence? No! I see in that sunken eye, in that pallid cheek, that the poor wanderer has at least gained some slight interest in the heart of his beloved. I have roamed to other climes, I have seen other nations; I have met with other females, beautiful and accomplished, but I have met with but one angel, and she is here before me. Accept this simple offering of my affection, dearest,' continued the stranger, plucking a heath-rose from its stem; 'it is beautiful as the wild flowers that deck thy hair, and sweet as is the love I bear thee.' 'It is sweet, indeed,' replied Clotilda, 'but its sweetness must wither ere night closes around. It is beautiful, but its beauty is short-lived, as the love evinced by man. Let not this, then, be the type of thy attachment; bring me the delicate evergreen, the sweet flower that blossoms throughout the year; and I will say, as I wreathe it in my hair, "The violets have bloomed and died – the roses have flourished and decayed; but the evergreen is still young, and so is the love of my wanderer." Friend of my heart ! – you will not – cannot desert me. I live but in you; you are my hopes, my thoughts, my existence itself: and if I lose you, I lose my all – I was but a solitary wild flower in the wilderness of nature, until you transplanted me to a more genial soil; and can you now break the fond heart you first taught to glow with passion?' – 'Speak not thus,' returned the stranger, 'it rends my very soul to hear you; – leave me – forget me – avoid me for ever – or your eternal ruin must ensue. I am a thing abandoned of God and man – and did you but see the seared heart that scarcely beats within this moving mass of deformity, you would flee me, as you would an adder in your path. Here is my heart, love, feel how cold it is; there is no pulse that betrays its emotion; for all is chilled and dead as the friends I once knew.' – 'You are unhappy, love, and your poor Clotilda shall stay to succour you. Think not I can abandon you in your misfortunes. No! I will wander with thee through the wide world, and be thy servant, thy slave, if thou wilt have it so. I will shield thee from the night winds, that they blow not too roughly on thy unprotected head. I will defend thee from the tempest that howls around; and though the cold world may devote thy name to scorn – though friends may fall off, and associates wither in the grave, there shall be one fond heart who shall love thee better in thy misfortune, and cherish thee, bless thee still.' She ceased, and her blue eyes swam in tears, as she turned it glistening with affection towards the stranger. He averted his head from her gaze, and a scornful sneer of the darkest, the deadliest malice passed over his fine countenance. In an instant, the expression subsided; his fixed glassy eye resumed its unearthly chillness, and he turned once again to his companion. 'It is the hour of sunset,' he exclaimed; 'the soft, the beauteous hour, when the hearts of lovers are happy, and nature smiles in unison with their feelings; but to me it will smile no longer – ere the morrow dawns I shall be far, very far, from the house of my beloved; from the scenes where my heart is enshrined, as in a sepulchre. But must I leave thee, sweetest flower of the wilderness, to be the sport of the whirlwind, the prey of the mountain blast?' – 'No, we will not part,' replied the impassioned girl; *'where thou goest, will I go; thy home shall be my home; and thy God shall be my God,'* – 'Swear it, swear it,' resumed the stranger, wildly grasping her by the hand; 'swear to the fearful oath I shall dictate.' He then desired her to kneel, and holding his right hand in a menacing attitude towards heaven, and throwing back his dark raven locks, exclaimed in a strain of bitter imprecation with the ghastly smile of an incarnate fiend, 'May the curses of an offended God,' he cried, 'haunt thee, cling to thee for ever – in the tempest and in the calm, in the day and in the night, in sickness and in sorrow, in life and in death, shouldst thou swerve from the promise thou hast here made to be mine. May the dark spirits of the damned howl in thine ears the accursed chorus of fiends – may despair rack thy bosom with the quenchless flames of hell! May thy soul be as the lazar-house of corruption, where the ghost of departed pleasure sits enshrined, as in a grave: where the hundred-headed worm never dies – where the fire is never extinguished. May a spirit of evil lord it over thy brow, and proclaim, as thou passest by, "THIS IS THE ABANDONED OF GOD AND MAN;" may fearful spectres haunt thee in the night season; may thy dearest friends drop day by day into the grave, and curse thee with their dying breath: may all that is most horrible in human nature, more solemn than language can frame, or lips can utter, may this, and more than this, be thy eternal portion, shouldst thou violate the oath that thou has taken.' He ceased – hardly knowing what she did, the terrified girl acceded to the awful adjuration, and promised eternal fidelity to him who was henceforth to be her lord. 'Spirits of the damned, I thank thee for thine assistance,' shouted the stranger; 'I have wooed my fair bride bravely. She is mine – mine for ever. – Aye, body and soul both mine; mine in life, and mine in death. What in tears my sweet one, ere yet the honeymoon is past? Why! indeed thou hast cause for weeping: but when next we meet, we shall meet to sign the nuptial bond.' He then imprinted a cold salute on the cheek of his young bride, and softening down the unutterable horrors of his countenance, requested her to meet him at eight o'clock on the ensuing evening, in the chapel adjoining to the castle of Hernswolf. She turned round to him with a burning sigh, as if to implore protection from himself, but the stranger was gone.

On entering the castle, she was observed to be impressed with a sense of the deepest melancholy. Her relations vainly endeavoured to ascertain the cause of her uneasiness; but the tremendous oath she had sworn completely paralysed her faculties, and she was fearful of betraying herself by even the slightest intonation of her voice, or the least variable expression of her countenance. When the evening was concluded, the family retired to rest; but Clotilda, who was unable to take repose, from the restlessness of her disposition, requested to remain alone in the library that adjoined her apartment.

All was now deep midnight; every domestic had long since retired to rest, and the only sound that could be distinguished was the sullen howl of the ban-dog as he bayed the waning moon. Clotilda remained in the library in an attitude of deep meditation. The lamp that burnt on the table, where she sat, was dying away, and the lower end of the apartment was already more than half obscured. The clock from the northern angle of the castle tolled out the hour of twelve, and the sound echoed dismally in the solemn stillness of the night. Suddenly the oaken door at the farther end of the room was gently lifted on its latch, and a bloodless figure, apparelled in the habiliments of the grave, advanced slowly up the apartment. No sound heralded its approach, as it moved with noiseless steps to the table where the lady was stationed. She did not at first perceive it, till she felt a death-cold hand fast grasped in her own, and heard a solemn voice whisper in her ear, 'Clotilda.' She looked up, a dark figure was standing beside her; she endeavoured to scream, but her voice was unequal to the exertion; her eye was fixed, as if by magic, on the form, which slowly removed the garb that concealed its countenance, and disclosed the livid eyes and skeleton shape of her father. It seemed to gaze on her with pity and regret, and mournfully exclaimed – 'Clotilda, the dresses and the servants are ready, the church bell has tolled, and the priest is at the altar, but where is the affianced bride? There is room for her in the grave, and tomorrow shall she be with me.' –

'Tomorrow?' faltered out the distracted girl; 'the spirits of hell shall have registered it, and tomorow must the bond be cancelled.' The figure ceased – slowly retired, and was soon lost in the obscurity of distance.

The morning – evening – arrived; and already as the hall clock struck eight, Clotilda was on her road to the chapel. It was a dark, gloomy night, thick masses of dun clouds sailed across the firmament, and the roar of the winter wind echoed awfully through the forest trees. She reached the appointed place; a figure was in waiting for her – it advanced – and discovered the features of the stranger. 'Why! this is well, my bride,' he exclaimed, with a sneer; 'and well will I repay thy fondness. Follow me.' They proceeded together in silence through the winding avenues of the chapel, until they reached the adjoining cemetery. Here they paused for an instant; and the stranger, in a softened tone, said, 'But one hour more, and the struggle will be over. And yet this heart of incarnate malice can feel, when it devotes so young, so pure a spirit to the grave. But it must – it must be,' he proceeded, as the memory of her past love rushed on her mind; 'for the fiend whom I obey has so willed it. Poor girl, I am leading thee indeed to our nuptials; but the priest will be death, thy parents the mouldering skeletons that rot in heaps around; and the witnesses our union, the lazy worms that revel on the carious bones of the dead. Come, my young bride, the priest is impatient for his victim.' As they proceeded, a dim blue light moved swiftly before them, and displayed at the extremity of the churchyard the portals of a vault. It was open, and they entered it in silence. The hollow wind came rushing through the gloomy abode of the dead; and on every side were piled the mouldering remnants of coffins, which dropped piece by piece upon the damp earth. Every step they took was on a dead body; and the bleached bones rattled horribly beneath their feet. In the centre of the vault rose a heap of unburied skeletons, whereon was seated a figure too awful even for the darkest imagination to conceive. As they approached it, the hollow vault rung with a hellish peal of laughter; and every mouldering corpse seemed endued with unearthly life. The stranger paused, and as he grasped his victim in his hand, one sigh burst from his heart – one tear glistened in his eye. It was but for an instant; the figure frowned awfully at his vacillation, and waved his gaunt hand.

The stranger advanced; he made certain mystic circles in the air, uttered unearthly words, and paused in excess of terror. On a sudden he raised his voice and wildly exclaimed – 'Spouse of the spirit of darkness, a few moments are yet thine; that thou may'st know to whom thou hast consigned thyself. I am the undying spirit of the wretch who curst his Saviour on the cross. He looked at me in the closing hour of his existence, and that look hath not yet passed away, for I am curst above all on earth. I am eternally condemned to hell! and must cater for my master's taste 'till the world is parched as is a scroll, and the heavens and the earth have passed away. I am he of whom thou may'st have read, and of whose feats thou may'st have heard. A million souls has my master condemned me to ensnare, and then my penance is accomplished, and I may know the repose of the grave. Thou art the thousandth soul that I have damned. I saw thee in thine hour of purity, and I marked thee at once for my home. Thy father did I murder for his temerity, and permitted to warn thee of thy fate; and myself have I beguiled for thy simplicity. Ha! the spell works bravely, and thou shall soon see, my sweet one, to whom thou hast linked thine undying fortunes, for as long as the seasons shall move on their course of nature – as long as the lightning shall flash, and the thunders roll, thy penance shall be eternal. Look below! and see to what thou art destined.' She looked, the vault split in a thousand different directions; the earth yawned asunder; and the roar of mighty waters was heard. A living ocean of molten fire glowed in the abyss beneath her, and blending with the shrieks of the damned, and the triumphant shouts of the fiends, rendered horror more horrible than imagination. Ten millions of souls were writhing in the fiery flames, and as the boiling billows dashed them against the blackened rocks of adamant, they cursed with the blasphemies of despair; and each curse echoed in thunder across the wave. The stranger rushed towards his victim. For an instant he held her over the burning vista, looked fondly in her face, and wept as he were a child. This was but the impulse of a moment; again he grasped her in his arms, dashed her from him with fury; and as her last parting glance was cast in kindness on his face, shouted aloud, 'not mine is the crime, but the religion that thou professest; for is it not said that there is a fire of eternity prepared for the souls of the wicked; and hast not thou incurred its torments?' She, poor girl, heard not, heeded not the shouts of the blasphemer. Her delicate form bounded from rock to rock, over billow, and over foam; as she fell, the ocean lashed itself as it were in triumph to receive her soul, and as she sunk deep in the burning pit, ten thousand voices reverberated from the bottomless abyss, 'Spirit of evil! here indeed is an eternity of torments prepared for thee; for here the worm never dies, and the fire is never quenched.'

# The Dice

## Thomas De Quincey
### (1785–1859)

At first sight, the name of Thomas De Quincey might seem a strange one to encounter in a book such as this. Yet the author of that remarkable work, *Confessions of an Opium Eater* (1821) contributed a number of outstanding short stories to the genre and was responsible for translating several German *Schauerromane* into English. In her study of tales of terror, Edith Birkhead has commented on De Quincey's Gothic stories and summarized, 'They are of most interest in showing the widespread and long-enduring vogue of the species. It is also noteworthy how many writers like De Quincey, whose main business lay elsewhere, found time to make erratic excursions into the realms of the supernatural.'

Thomas De Quincey, the son of a merchant in the Midlands, was dogged by ill-health in his youth and in desperation ran away from school on one occasion and wandered for some months in Wales. Later he moved to London and there existed on the verge of starvation before being reclaimed by his guardian and set-up in Oxford. It was here that he became addicted to opium, the experience forming the major part of his famous work. In subsequent years he met a number of the famous poets of the day and continued his own literary endeavours in the form of magazine articles and stories. From 1828 until his death he lived in Edinburgh and there enjoyed a reputation as being one of the most important periodical contributors of the period.

*The Dice* which I have selected here from his Gothic tales has its roots in German legend and first appeared in the *London Magazine* for 1823. In it De Quincey takes the old theme of a deal with the Devil and imbues it with a special brand of unease . .

FOR more than 150 years had the family of Schroll been settled at Tanbendorf, and generally respected for knowledge and refinement of manners superior to its station. Its present representative, the bailiff Elias Schroll, had in his youth attached himself to literature, but, later in life, from love of the country, he had returned to his native village, and lived there in great credit and esteem.

During this whole period of 150 years, tradition had recorded only one single Schroll as having borne a doubtful character; he, indeed, as many persons affirmed, had dealt with the devil. Certain it is that there was still preserved in the house a scrutoire fixed in the wall and containing some mysterious manuscripts attributed to him, and the date of the year, 1630, which was carved upon the front, tallied with his era. The key of this scrutoire had been constantly handed down to the eldest son through five generations, with a solemn charge to take care that no other eye or ear should ever become acquainted with its contents. Every precaution had been taken to guard against accidents or oversights: the lock was so constructed that even with the right key it could not be opened without special instructions; and for still greater security the present proprietor had added a padlock of most elaborate workmanship, which presented a sufficient obstacle before the main lock could be approached.

In vain did the curiosity of the whole family direct itself to this scrutoire. Nobody had succeeded in discovering any part of its contents, except Rudolph, the only son of the bailiff; he *had* succeeded: at least his own belief was that the old folio with gilt edges, and bound in black velvet, which he had one day surprised his father anxiously reading, belonged to the mysterious scrutoire; for the door of the scrutoire, though not open, was unlocked, and Elias had hastily closed the book with great agitation, at the same time ordering his son out of the room in no very gentle tone. At the time of this incident Rudolph was about twelve years of age.

Since that time the young man had sustained two great losses in the deaths of his excellent mother and a sister tenderly beloved. His father also had suffered deeply in health and spirits under these afflictions. Every day he grew more fretful and humourless; and Rudolph, upon his final return home from school in his eighteenth year, was shocked to find him greatly altered in mind as well as in person. His flesh had fallen away, and he seemed to be consumed by some internal strife of thought. It was evidently his own opinion that he was standing on the edge of the grave; and employed himself unceasingly in arranging his affairs, and in making his successor acquainted with all such arrangements as regarded his more peculiar interests. One evening, as Rudolph came in suddenly from a neighbour's house, and happened to pass the scrutoire, he found the door wide open, and the inside obviously empty. Looking round, he observed his father standing on the hearth close to a great fire, in the midst of which was consuming the old black book.

Elias entreated his son earnestly to withdraw, but Rudolph could not command himself; and he exclaimed, 'I doubt, I doubt, sir, that this is the book which belongs to the scrutoire.'

His father assented with visible confusion.

'Well, then, allow me to say that I am greatly surprised at your treating in this way an heirloom that for a century and more has always been transmitted to the eldest son.'

'You are in the right, my son,' said the father affectionately, taking him by the hand. 'You are partly in the right; it is not quite defensible, I admit; and I myself have had many scruples about the course I have taken. Yet still I feel myself glad upon the whole that I have destroyed this accursed book. He that wrote it never prospered; all traditions agree in that; why then leave to one's descendants a miserable legacy of unhallowed mysteries?'

This excuse, however, did not satisfy Rudolph. He maintained that his father had made an aggression upon his rights of inheritance; and he argued the point so well that Elias himself began to see that his son's complaint was not altogether groundless. The whole of the next day they behaved to each other not unkindly, but yet with some coolness. At night Elias could bear this no longer, and he said, 'Dear Rudolph, we have lived long together in harmony and love; let us not begin to show an altered countenance to each other during the few days that I have yet to live.'

Rudolph pressed his father's offered hand with a filial warmth; and the latter went on to say, 'I purpose now to communicate to you by word of mouth the contents of the book which I have destroyed. I will do this with good faith and without reserve, unless you yourself can be persuaded to forgo your own right to such a communication.'

Elias paused, flattering himself as it seemed that his son *would* forgo his right. But in this he was mistaken; Rudolph was far too eager for the disclosure, and earnestly pressed his father to proceed.

Again Elias hesitated, and threw a glance of profound love and pity upon his son – a glance that conjured him to think better, and to waive his claim; but, this being at length obviously hopeless, he spoke as follows: 'The book relates chiefly to yourself; it points to you as *to the last of our race*. You turn pale. Surely, Rudolph, it would have been better that you had resolved to trouble yourself no further about it?'

'No,' said Rudolph, recovering his self-possession. 'No; for it still remains a question whether this prophecy be true.'

'It does so; it does, no doubt.'

'And is this all that the book says in regard to me?'

'No, it is *not* all; there is something more. But possibly you will only laugh when you hear it; for at this day nobody believes in such strange stories. However, be *that* as it may, the book goes on to say, plainly and positively, that the Evil One (Heaven protect us!) will make you an offer tending greatly to your worldly advantage.'

Rudolph laughed outright, and replied that, judging by the grave exterior of the book, he had looked to hear of more serious contents.

'Well, well, my son,' said the old man, 'I know not that I myself am disposed to place much confidence in these tales of contracts with the devil. But, true or not, we ought not to laugh at them. Enough for me that under any circumstances I am satisfied you have so much natural piety that you would reject all worldly good fortune that could meet you upon unhallowed paths.'

Here Elias would have broken off, but Rudolph said, 'One thing more I wish to know: What is to be the nature of the good fortune offered to me? And did the book say whether I should accept it or not?'

'Upon the nature of the good fortune the writer has not explained himself; all that he says is that, by a discreet use of it, it is in your power to become a very great man. Whether you will accept it — but God preserve thee, my child, from any thought so criminal! — upon this question there is a profound silence. Nay, it seems even as if this trader in black arts had at that very point been overtaken by death, for he had broken off in the very middle of a word. The Lord have mercy upon his soul!'

Little as Rudolph's faith was in the possibility of such a proposal, yet he was uneasy at his father's communication, and visibly disturbed; so that the latter said to him, 'Had it not been better, Rudolph, that you had left the mystery to be buried with me in the grave?'

Rudolph said 'No': but his restless eye and his agitated air too evidently approved the accuracy of his father's solicitude.

The deep impression upon Rudolph's mind from this conversation — the last he was ever to hold with his father — was rendered still deeper by the solemn event which followed. About the middle of that same night he was awakened suddenly by a summons to his father's bedside; his father was dying, and earnestly asking for him.

'My son!' he exclaimed with an expression of the bitterest anguish; stretched out both his arms in supplication towards him; and in the anguish of the effort he expired.

The levity of youthful spirits soon dispersed the gloom which at first hung over Rudolph's mind. Surrounded by jovial companions at the university which he now visited, he found no room left in his bosom for sorrow or care: and his heaviest affliction was the refusal of his guardian at times to comply with his too frequent importunities for money.

After a residence of one year at the university, some youthful irregularities in which Rudolph was concerned subjected him, jointly with three others, to expulsion. Just at that time the Seven Years' War happened to break out: two of the party, named Theiler and Werl, entered the military service together with Rudolph, – the last very much against the will of a young woman to whom he was engaged. Charlotte herself, however, became reconciled to this arrangement when she saw that her objections availed nothing against Rudolph's resolution, and heard her lover describe in the most flattering colours his own return to her arms in the uniform of an officer; for that his distinguished courage must carry him in the very first campaign to the rank of lieutenant was as evident to his own mind as that he could not possibly fall on the field of battle.

The three friends were fortunate enough to be placed in the same company. But, in the first battle, Werl and Theiler were stretched lifeless by Rudolph's side, – Werl by a musket ball through his heart, and Theiler by a cannon shot which took off his head.

Soon after this event, Rudolph himself returned home; but how? Not, as he had fondly anticipated, in the brilliant decorations of a distinguished officer, but as a prisoner in close custody: in a transport of youthful anger he had been guilty, in company with two others, of insubordination and mutiny.

The court-martial sentenced them to death. The judges, however, were so favourably impressed by their good conduct whilst under confinement that they would certainly have recommended them unconditionally to the royal mercy, if it had not been deemed necessary to make an example. However, the sentence was so far mitigated that only one of the three was to be shot. And which was he? That point was reserved in suspense until the day of execution, when it was to be decided by the cast of the dice.

As the fatal day drew near, a tempest of passionate grief assailed the three prisoners. One of them was agitated by the tears of his father; the second by the sad situation of a sickly wife and two children. The third, Rudolph, in case the lot fell upon him, would be summoned to part not only with his life, but also with a young and blooming bride, that lay nearer to his heart than anything else in the world. 'Ah!' said he on the evening before the day of final decision, 'Ah! if but this once I could secure a lucky throw of the dice!' And scarce was the wish uttered when his comrade Werl, whom he had seen fall by his side in the field of battle, stepped into his cell.

'So, brother Schroll, I suppose you didn't much expect to see me?'

'No, indeed, did I not,' exclaimed Rudolph in consternation; for, in fact, on the next day after the battle he had seen with his own eyes this very Werl committed to the grave.

'Ay, ay, it's strange enough, I allow; but there are not many such surgeons as he is that belongs to our regiment; he had me dug up, and brought me round again, I'll assure you. One would think the man was a conjurer. Indeed, there are many things he can do which I defy any man to explain; and, to say the truth, I'm convinced he can execute impossibilities.'

'Well, so let him, for aught that I care; all this art will scarcely do me any good.'

'Who knows, brother? who knows? The man is in this town at this very time; and for old friendship's sake I've just spoken to him about you; and he has promised me a lucky throw of the dice, that shall deliver you from all danger.'

'Ah!' said the dejected Rudolph, 'but even this would be of little service to me.'

'Why, how so?' asked the other.

'How so? Why, because – even if there were such dice (a matter I very much dispute) – yet I could never allow myself to turn aside, by black arts, any bad luck designed for myself upon the heads of either of my comrades.'

'Now, this, I suppose, is what you call being noble? But excuse me if I think that in such cases one's first duty is to one's-self.'

'Ay, but just consider; one of my comrades has an old father to maintain, the other a sick wife with two children.'

'Schroll, Schroll, if your young bride were to hear you, I

fancy she wouldn't think herself much flattered. Does poor Charlotte deserve that you should not bestow a thought on her and her fate? A dear young creature, that places her whole happiness in you, has nearer claims (I think) upon your consideration that an old dotard with one foot in the grave, or a wife and two children that are nothing at all to you. Ah! what a deal of good might you do in the course of a long life with your Charlotte! So then, you really are determined to reject the course which I point out to you? Take care, Schroll! If you disdain my offer, and the lot should chance to fall upon you, – take care lest the thought of a young bride whom you have betrayed, take care, I say, lest this thought should add to the bitterness of death when you come to kneel down on the sand-hill. However, I've given you advice sufficient, and have discharged my conscience. Look to it yourself: and farewell!'

'Stay, brother; a word or two,' said Rudolph, who was powerfully impressed by the last speech, and the picture of domestic happiness held up before him, which he had often dallied with in thought, both when alone and in company with Charlotte. 'Stay a moment. Undoubtedly, I do not deny that I wish for life, if I could receive it a gift from heaven: and that is not impossible. Only I would not willingly have the guilt upon my conscience of being the cause of misery to another. However, if the man you speak of can tell, I should be glad that you would ask him upon which of us three the lot of death will fall. Or – stay; don't ask him,' said Rudolph, sighing deeply.

'I have already asked him,' was the answer.

'Ah! have you so? *And it is after his reply that you come to me with this counsel*?'

The foretaste of death overspread the blooming face of Rudolph with a livid paleness; thick drops of sweat gathered upon his forehead; and the other exclaimed with a sneer – 'I'm going; you take too much time for consideration. May be you will see and recognize me at the place of execution; and, if so, I shall have the dice with me; and it will not be too late even then to give me a sign; but, take notice, I can't promise to attend.'

Rudolph raised his forehead from the palm of his hand, in

which he had buried it during the last moments of his perturbation, and would have spoken something in reply; but his counsellor was already gone. He felt glad, and yet at the same time sorry. The more he considered the man and his appearance, so much the less seemed his resemblance to his friend whom he had left buried on the field of battle. This friend had been the very soul of affectionate cordiality – a temper that was altogether wanting to his present counsellor. No! the scornful and insulting tone with which he treated the unhappy prisoner, and the unkind manner with which he had left him, convinced Schroll that he and Werl must be two different persons. Just at this moment a thought struck him, like a blast of lightning, of the black book that had perished in the fire and its ominous contents. A lucky cast of the dice! Ay; *that* then was the shape in which the tempter had presented himself; and heartily glad he felt that he had not availed himself of his suggestions.

But this temper of mind was speedily changed by his young bride, who hurried in soon after, sobbing, and flung her arms about his neck. He told her of the proposal which had been made to him; and she was shocked that he had not immediately accepted it.

With a bleeding heart, Rudolph objected that so charming and lovely a creature could not miss of a happy fate, even if he should be forced to quit her. But she protested vehemently that he or nobody should enjoy her love.

The clergyman, who visited the prisoner immediately after her departure, restored some composure to his mind, which had been altogether banished by the presence of his bride. 'Blessed are they who die in the Lord!' said the grey-haired divine; and with so much earnestness and devotion, that this single speech had the happiest effect upon the prisoner's mind.

On the morning after this night of agitation, the morning of the fatal day, the three criminals saw each other for the first time since their arrest. Community of fate, and long separation from each other, contributed to draw still closer the bond of friendship that had been first knit on the field of battle. Each of the three testified a lively abhorrence for the wretched necessity of throwing death to some one of his comrades by any cast of the dice which should bring life to himself. Dear as their several friends were to all, yet at this moment the brotherly league which had been tried and proved in the furnace of battle, was triumphant over all opposing considerations. Each would have preferred death himself, rather than escape at the expense of his comrade.

The worthy clergyman, who possessed their entire confidence, found them loudly giving utterance to this heroic determination. Shaking his head, he pointed their attention to those who had claims upon them whilst living, and for whom it was their duty to wish to live as long as possible. 'Place your trust in God!' said he: 'resign yourselves to Him! He it is that will bring about the decision through your hands; and think not of ascribing that power to yourselves, or to his lifeless instruments – the dice. He, without whose permission no sparrow falls to the ground, and who has numbered every hair upon your head – He it is that knows best what is good for you; and He only.'

The prisoners assented by squeezing his hand, embraced each other, and received the sacrament in the best disposition of mind. After this ceremony they breakfasted together, in as resigned, nay, almost in as joyous a mood as if the gloomy and bloody morning which lay before them were ushering in some gladsome festival.

When, however, the procession was marshalled from the outer gate, and their beloved friends were admitted to utter their last farewells, then again the sternness of their courage sank beneath the burden of their melancholy fate. 'Rudolph!' whispered amongst the rest his despairing bride, 'Rudolph! why did you reject the help that was offered to you?' He adjured her not to add to the bitterness of parting; and she in turn adjured him, a little before the word of command was given to march – which robbed her of all consciousness – to make a sign to the stranger who had volunteered his offer of deliverance, provided he should anywhere observe him in the crowd.

The streets and the windows were lined with spectators. Vainly did each of the criminals seek, by accompanying the

clergyman in his prayers, to shelter himself from the thought
that all return, perhaps, was cut off from him. The large house
of his bride's father reminded Schroll of a happiness that was
now lost to him for ever, if any faith were to be put in the words
of his yesterday's monitor; and a very remarkable faintness came
over him. The clergyman, who was acquainted with the circumstances of his case, and therefore guessed the occasion of his sudden agitation, laid hold of his arm, and said, with a powerful
voice, that he who trusted in God would assuredly see all his
*righteous* hopes accomplished – in this world, if it were God's
pleasure, but, if not, in a better.

These were words of comfort: but their effect lasted only for
a few moments. Outside the city gate his eyes were met by the
sand-hill already thrown up; a spectacle which renewed his
earthly hopes and fears. He threw a hurried glance about him:
but nowhere could he see his last night's visitor.

Every moment the decision came nearer and nearer. It has
begun. One of the three has already shaken the box; the die is
cast; he has thrown a six. This throw was now registered amidst
the solemn silence of the crowd. The bystanders regarded him
with silent congratulations in their eyes; for this man and Rudolph were the two special objects of the general compassion:
this man, as the husband and father; Rudolph, as the youngest
and handsomest, and because some report had gone abroad of
his superior education and attainments.

Rudolph was youngest in a double sense; youngest in years,
and youngest in the service: for both reasons he was to throw
last. It may be supposed, therefore, how much all present trembled for the poor delinquent, when the second of his comrades
likewise flung a six.

Prostrated in spirit, Rudolph stared at the unpropitious die.
Then a second time he threw a horrid glance around him, and
that so full of despair that from horrid sympathy a violent shuddering ran through the bystanders. 'Here is no deliverer,'
thought Rudolph; 'none to see me, or to hear me! And, if there
were, it is now too late; for no change of the die is any longer
possible.' So saying, he seized the fatal die; convulsively his

hand clutches it; and before the throw is made he feels that the
die is broken in two.

During the universal thrill of astonishment which succeeded
to this strange accident, he looked round again. A sudden shock
and a sudden joy fled through his countenance. Not far from
him, in the dress of a pedlar, stands Theiler without a wound,
the comrade whose head had been carried off on the field of
battle by a cannon-ball. Rudolph made an under-sign to him
with his eye; for, clear as it now was to his mind with whom he
was dealing, yet the dreadful trial of the moment overpowered
his better resolutions.

The military commission were in some confusion. No provision having been thought of against so strange an accident,
there was no second die at hand. They were just on the point of
despatching a messenger to fetch one, when the pedlar presented
himself with the offer of supplying the loss. The new die is
examined by the auditor, and delivered to the unfortunate Rudolph. He throws; the die is lying on the drum, and again it is a
six! The amazement is universal; nothing is decided; the
throws must be repeated. They *are*; and Weber, the husband of
the sick wife, the father of the two half-naked children, flings
the lowest throw.

Immediately the officer's voice was heard wheeling his men
into their position. On the part of Weber there was as little
delay. The overwhelming injury to his wife and children, inflicted by his own act, was too mighty to contemplate. He shook
hands rapidly with his two comrades; stepped nimbly into his
place; kneeled down. The word of command was heard, 'Lower
your muskets'; instantly he dropped the fatal handkerchief with
the gesture of one who prays for some incalculable blessing;
and, in the twinkling of an eye, sixteen bullets had lightened the
heart of the poor mutineer from its whole immeasurable freight
of anguish.

All the congratulations with which they were welcomed on
their return into the city fell powerless on Rudolph's ear. Scarcely could even Charlotte's caresses affect with any pleasure the

man who believed himself to have sacrificed his comrade
through collusion with a fiend.

The importunities of Charlotte prevailed over all objections
which the pride of her aged father suggested against a son-in-
law who had been capitally convicted. The marriage was solemnized; but at the wedding-festival, amidst the uproar of mer-
riment, the parties chiefly concerned were not happy or tranquil.
In no long time the father-in-law died, and by his death placed
the young couple in a state of complete independence; but
Charlotte's fortune, and the remainder of what Rudolph had
inherited from his father, were speedily swallowed up by an
idle and luxurious mode of living. Rudolph now began to ill-use
his wife. To escape from his own conscience, he plunged into
all sorts of dissolute courses; and very remarkable it was that,
from manifesting the most violent abhorrence for everything
which could lead his thoughts to his own fortunate cast of the
die, he gradually came to entertain so uncontrollable a passion
for playing at dice that he spent all his time in the company of
those with whom he could turn this passion to account. His
house had long since passed out of his own hands; not a soul
could be found anywhere to lend him a shilling. The sickly
widow of Weber, and her two children, whom he had hitherto
supported, lost their home and means of livelihood, and in no
long space of time the same fate fell upon himself, his wife, and
his child.

Too little used to labour to have any hope of improving
his condition in that way, one day he bethought himself that
the Medical Institute was in the habit of purchasing from
poor people, during their lifetime, the reversion of their bodies.
To this establishment he addressed himself; and the ravages
in his personal appearance and health, caused by his dissolute life, induced them the more readily to lend an ear to his
proposal.

But the money thus obtained, which had been designed for
the support of his wife and half-famished child, was squandered
at the gaming-table. As the last dollar vanished, Schroll bit one

of the dice furiously between his teeth. Just then he heard these words whispered at his ear, — 'Gently, brother, gently; all dice do not split in two like that on the sand-hill.' He looked round in agitation, but saw no trace of any one who could have uttered the words.

With dreadful imprecations on himself and those with whom he had played, he flung out of the gaming-house homewards on his road to the wretched garret where his wife and child were awaiting his return and his succour; but here the poor creatures, tormented by hunger and cold, pressed upon him so importunately that he had no way to deliver himself from misery but by flying from the spectacle. But whither could he go thus late at night, when his utter poverty was known in every alehouse? Roaming he knew not whither, he found himself at length in the churchyard. The moon was shining solemnly upon the quiet clouds. Rudolph shuddered at nothing but at himself and his own existence. He strode with bursts of laughter over the dwellings of the departed, and entered a vault which gave him shelter from the icy blasts of wind which now began to bluster more loudly than before. The moon threw her rays into the vault full upon the golden legend inscribed in the wall, — *'Blessed are the dead that die in the Lord* !' Schroll took up a spade that was sticking in the ground, and struck with it furiously against the gilt letters on the wall, but they seemed indestructible; and he was going to assault them with a mattock, when suddenly a hand touched him on the shoulder, and said to him, 'Gently, comrade; thy pains are all thrown away.' Schroll uttered a loud exclamation of terror, for in these words he heard the voice of Weber, and, on turning round, recognized his whole person.

'What wouldst thou have?' asked Rudolph. 'What art thou come for ?'

'To comfort thee,' replied the figure, which now suddenly assumed the form and voice of the pedlar to whom Schroll was indebted for the fortunate die. 'Thou hast forgotten me; and thence it is that thou art fallen into misfortune. Look up and acknowledge thy friend in need that comes only to make thee happy again.'

'If *that* be thy purpose, wherefore is it that thou wearest a shape before which, of all others that have been on earth, I have most reason to shudder?'

'The reason is because I must not allow to any man my help of my converse on too easy terms. Before ever my die was allowed to turn thy fate, I was compelled to give thee certain intimations from which thou knewest with whom it was that thou wert dealing.'

'With whom, then, was it that I was dealing?' cried Schroll, staring with his eyes wide open, and his hair standing erect.

'Thou knewest, comrade, at that time; thou knowest at this moment,' said the pedlar, laughing, and tapping him on the shoulder. 'But what is it that thou desirest?'

Schroll struggled internally; but, overcome by his desolate condition, he said immediately, 'Dice: I would have dice that shall win whenever I wish.'

'Very well; but first of all stand out of the blaze of this golden writing on the wall; it is a writing that has nothing to do with thee. Here are dice; never allow them to go out of thy own possession; for *that* might bring thee into great trouble. When thou needest me, light a fire at the last stroke of the midnight hour; throw in my dice, and give a loud laugh. They will crack once or twice, and then split. At that moment catch at them in the flames; but let not the moment slip, or thou art lost. And let not thy courage be daunted by the sights that I cannot but send before me whensoever I appear. Lastly, avoid choosing any holy day for this work: and beware of the priest's benediction. Here, take the dice.'

Schroll caught at the dice with one hand, whilst with the other he covered his eyes. When he next looked up, he was standing alone.

He now quitted the burying-ground to return as hastily as possible to the gaming-house, where the light of candles was still visible. But it was with the greatest difficulty that he obtained money enough from a 'friend' to enable him to make the lowest stake which the rules allowed. He found it a much easier task to persuade the company to use the dice which he had brought with him. They saw in this nothing but a very common superstition, and no possibility of any imposture, as they and he should naturally have benefited alike by the good luck supposed to accompany the dice. But the nature of the charm was that only the possessor of the dice enjoyed their supernatural powers; and hence it was that towards morning Schroll reeled home intoxicated with the money of all present, to the garret where his family was lying half frozen and famished.

Their outward condition was immediately improved. The money which Schroll had won was sufficient not only for their immediate and most pressing wants: it was enough also to pay for a front apartment, and to leave a sum sufficient for a very considerable stake.

With this sum, and in better attire, Rudolph repaired to a gaming-house of more fashionable resort, and came home in the evening laden with gold.

He now opened a gaming establishment himself; and so much did his family improve in external appearance within a very few weeks that the police began to keep a watchful eye over him.

This induced him to quit the city, and to change his residence continually. All the different baths of Germany he resorted to beyond other towns: but, though his dice perseveringly maintained their luck, he yet never accumulated any money. Everything was squandered upon the dissipated life which he and his family pursued.

At length, at the Baths of –, the matter began to take an unfortunate turn. A violent passion for a beautiful young lady whom Rudolph had attached himself to in vain at balls, concerts, and even at church, suddenly bereft him of all sense and direction. One night, when Schroll (who now styled himself Captain von Schrollshausen) was anticipating a master-stroke from his dice, probably for the purpose of winning the lady by the display of overflowing wealth and splendour, suddenly they lost their virtue, and failed him without warning. Hitherto, they had lost only when he willed them to lose: but, on this occasion, they failed at so crucial a moment as to lose him not only all his own money, but a good deal beside that he had borrowed.

Foaming with rage, he came home. He asked furiously after his wife: she was from home. He examined the dice attentively; and it appeared to him that they were not his own. A powerful suspicion seized upon him. Madame von Schrollshausen had her own gaming circle as well as himself. Without betraying its origin, he had occasionally given her a few specimens of the privilege attached to his dice: and she had pressed him earnestly to allow her the use of them for a single evening. It was true he never parted with them even on going to bed: but it was possible that they might have been changed whilst he was sleeping. The more he brooded upon this suspicion, the more it strengthened: from being barely possible, it became probable: from a probability it ripened into a certainty; and this certainly received the fullest confirmation at this moment when she returned home in the gayest temper, and announced to him that she had been this night overwhelmed with good luck; in proof of which, she poured out upon the table a considerable sum in gold coin. 'And now,' she added laughingly, 'I care no longer for your dice; nay, to tell you the truth, I would not exchange my own for them.'

Rudolph, now confirmed in his suspicions, demanded the dice, as his property that had been purloined from him. She laughed and refused. He insisted with more vehemence; she retorted with warmth; both parties were irritated: and, at length in the extremity of his wrath, Rudolph snatched up a knife and stabbed her; the knife pierced her heart; she uttered a single sob, was convulsed for a moment, and expired. 'Cursed accident!' he exclaimed, when it clearly appeared, on examination, that the dice which she had in her purse were not those he suspected himself to have lost.

No eye but Rudolph's had witnessed the murder: the child had slept on undisturbed: but circumstances betrayed it to the knowledge of the landlord; and, in the morning, he was preparing to make it public. By great offers, however, Rudolph succeeded in purchasing the man's silence: he engaged in substance to make over to the landlord a large sum of money, and to marry his daughter, with whom he had long pursued a clandestine intrigue. Agreeable to this arrangement, it was publicly notified that Madame von Schollshausen had destroyed herself under a sudden attack of hypochondriasis, to which she had been long subject. Some there were undoubtedly who chose to be sceptics on this matter; but nobody had an interest sufficiently deep in the murdered person to prompt him to a legal inquiry.

A fact which at this time gave Rudolph far more disturbance of mind than the murder of his once beloved wife was the full confirmation, upon repeated experience, that his dice had forfeited their power. For he had now been a loser two days running to so great an extent that he was obliged to abscond on a misty night. His child, towards whom his affection increased daily, he was under the necessity of leaving with his host, as a pledge for his return and fulfilment of his promises. He would not have absconded if it had been in his power to summon his dark counsellor forthwith; but on account of the great festival of Pentecost, which fell on the very next day, this summons was necessarily delayed for a short time. By staying, he would have reduced himself to the necessity of inventing various pretexts for delay, in order to keep up his character with his creditors; whereas, when he returned with a sum of money sufficient to meet his debts, all suspicions would be silenced at once.

In the metropolis of an adjacent territory, to which he resorted so often that he kept lodgings there constantly, he passed Whitsunday with impatience, and resolved on the succeeding night to summon and converse with his counsellor. Impatient, however, as he was of any delay, he did not on that account feel the less anxiety as the hour of midnight approached. Though he was quite alone in his apartments, and had left his servant behind at the baths, yet long before midnight he fancied that he heard footsteps and whisperings round about him. The purpose he was meditating, that he had regarded till now as a matter of indifference, now displayed itself in its whole monstrous shape. Moreover, he remembered that his wicked counsellor had himself thought it necessary to exhort him to courage, which at present he felt greatly shaken. However, he had no choice. As he

was enjoined, therefore, with the last stroke of twelve, he set on
fire the wood which lay ready split upon the hearth, and threw
the dice into the flames, with a loud laughter that echoed frightfully from the empty hall and staircase. Confused and half stifled by the smoke which accompanied the roaring flames, he
stood still for a few minutes, when suddenly all the surrounding
objects seemed changed, and he found himself transported to
his father's house. His father was lying on his deathbed just as
he had actually beheld him. He had upon his lips the very same
expression of supplication and anguish with which he had at
that time striven to address him. Once again he stretched out
his arms in love and pity to his son; and once again he seemed
to expire in the act.

Schroll was agitated by the picture, which called up and re-
animated in his memory, with the power of a mighty tormentor, all his honourable plans and prospect from that innocent
period of his life. At this moment the dice cracked for the first
time; and Schroll turned his face towards the flames. A second
time the smoke stifled the light in order to reveal a second picture. He saw himself on the day before the scene on the sand-
hill, sitting in his dungeon. The clergyman was with him. From
the expression of his countenance, he appeared to be just saying
– 'Blessed are the dead that die in the Lord.' Rudolph thought
of the disposition in which he then was, of the hopes which
the clergyman had raised in him, and of the feeling which he
then had that he was still worthy to be reunited to his father, or
had become worthy by bitter penitence. The next fracture of the
die disturbed the scene – but to substitute one that was not at all
more consolatory. For now appeared a den of thieves, in which
the unhappy widow of Weber was cursing her children, who –
left without support, without counsel, without protection – had
taken to evil courses. In the background stood the bleeding
father of these ruined children, one hand stretched out towards
Schroll with a menacing gesture, and the other lifted towards
heaven with a record of impeachment against him.

At the third splitting of the dice, out of the bosom of the
smoke arose the figure of his murdered wife, who seemed to

chase him from one corner of the room to another, until at length she came and took a seat at the fireplace; by the side of which, as Rudolph now observed with horror, his buried father and the unhappy Weber had stretched themselves; and they carried on together a low and noiseless whispering and moaning that agitated him with a mysterious horror.

After long and hideous visions, Rudolph beheld the flames grow weaker and weaker. He approached. The figures that stood round about held up their hands in a threatening attitude. A moment later and the time was gone for ever, and Rudolph, as his false friend had asserted, was a lost man! With the courage of despair he plunged through the midst of the threatening figures, and snatched at the glowing dice – which were no sooner touched than they split asunder with a dreadful sound, before which the apparitions vanished in a body.

The evil counsellor appeared on this occasion in the dress of a gravedigger, and asked, with a snorting sound, – 'What wouldst thou from me?'

'I would remind you of your promise,' answered Schroll, stepping back with awe; 'your dice have lost their power.'

'Through whose fault?'

Rudolph was silent, and covered his eyes fom the withering glances of the fiendish being who was gazing upon him.

'Thy foolish desires led thee in chase of the beautiful maiden into the church; my words were forgotten; and the benediction, against which I warned thee, disarmed the dice of their power. In future observe my directions better.'

So saying, he vanished; and Schroll found three new dice upon the hearth.

After such scenes sleep was not to be thought of; and Rudolph resolved, if possible, to make trial of his dice this very night. The ball at the hotel over the way, to which he had been invited, and from which the steps of the waltzers were still audible, appeared to present a fair opportunity. Thither he repaired; but not without some anxiety, lest some of the noises in his own lodgings should have reached the houses over the way. He was happy to find this fear unfounded. Everything appeared as if calculated only for *his* senses; for, when he inquired, with assumed carelessness, what great explosion *that* was which occurred about midnight, nobody acknowledged to having heard it.

The dice also he was happy to find, answered his expectations. He found a company engaged at play, and, by the break of day, he had met with so much luck that he was immediately able to travel back to the baths, and to redeem his child and his word of honour.

In the baths he now made as many new acquaintances as the losses were important which he had lately sustained. He was reputed one of the wealthiest cavaliers in the place; and many who had designs upon him in consequence of this reputed wealth willingly lost money to him to favour their own scheme so that in a single month he gained sums which would have established him as a man of fortune. Under countenance of this repute, and as a widower, no doubt he might now have made successful advances to the young lady whom he had formerly pursued, for her father had an exclusive regard to property, and would have overlooked morals and respectability of that sort in any candidate for his daughter's hand; but, with the largest offers of money, he could not purchase his freedom from the contract made with his landlord's daughter – a woman of very disreputable character. In fact, six months after the death of his first wife he was married to her.

By the unlimited profusion of money with which his second wife sought to wash out the stains upon her honour, Rudolph's new-raised property was as speedily squandered. To part from her was one of the wishes which lay nearest his heart. He had, however, never ventured to express it a second time, before his father-in-law, for, on the single occasion when he had hinted at such an intention, that person had immediately broken out into the most dreadful threats. The murder of his first wife was the chain which bound him to his second. The boy whom his first wife had left him, closely as he resembled her in features and in the bad traits of her character, was his only comfort, if indeed his gloomy and perturbed mind would allow him at any time to taste of comfort.

To preserve this boy from the evil influences of the many bad examples about him, he had already made an agreement with a man of distinguished abilities, who was to have superintended his education in his own family. But all was frustrated. Madame von Schrollshausen, whose love of pomp and display led her eagerly to catch at every pretext for creating a *fête*, had invited a party on the evening before the young boy's intended departure. The time which was not occupied in the eating-room was spent at the gaming-table, and dedicated to the dice, of whose extraordinary powers the owner was at this time availing himself with more zeal than usual, having just invested all his disposable money in the purchase of a landed estate. One of the guests, having lost very considerable sums in an uninterrupted train of ill luck, threw the dice, in his vexation, with such force upon the table that one of them fell down. The attendants searched for it on the floor, and the child also crept about in quest of it. Not finding it, he rose, and in rising stept upon it, lost his balance, and fell with such violence against the edge of the stove that he died in a few hours of the injury inflicted on the head.

This accident made the most powerful impression upon the father. He recapitulated the whole of his life from the first trial he had made of the dice; from them had arisen all his misfortunes, in what way could he liberate himself from their accursed influence? Revolving this point, and in the deepest distress of mind, Schroll wandered out towards nightfall and strolled through the town. Coming to a solitary bridge in the outskirts, he looked down from the battlements upon the gloomy depths of the waters below, which seemed to regard him with looks of sympathy and strong fascination. 'So be it, then!' he exclaimed, and sprang over the railing; but, instead of finding his grave in the waters, he felt himself below seized powerfully by the grasp of a man, whom, from his scornful laugh, he recognized as his evil counsellor. The man bore him to the shore, and said, 'No, no! my good friend; he that once enters into a league with me, him I shall deliver from death even in his own despite.'

Half crazy with despair, the next morning Schroll crept out

of the town with a loaded pistol. Spring was abroad; spring flowers, spring breezes, and nightingales.* They were all abroad, but not for *him* or *his* delight. A crowd of itinerant tradesmen passed him, who were on the road to a neighbouring fair. One of them, observing his dejected countenance with pity, attached himself to his side, and asked in a tone of sympathy what was the matter. Two others of the passers-by Schroll heard distinctly saying, 'Faith, I should not like, for my part, to walk alone with such an ill-looking fellow.' He darted a furious glance at the men, separated from his pitying companion with a fervent pressure of his hand, and struck off into a solitary track of the forest. In the first retired spot he fired the pistol; and behold! the man who had spoken to him with so much kindness lies stretched in his blood, and he himself is without a wound. At this moment, while staring half-unconsciously at the face of the murdered man, he feels himself seized from behind. Already he seems to himself in the hands of the public executioner. Turning round, however, he hardly knows whether to feel pleasure or pain on seeing his evil suggester in the dress of a gravedigger. 'My friend,' said the gravedigger, 'if you cannot be content to wait for death until I send it, I must be forced to end with dragging you to *that* from which I began by saving you – a public execution. But think not thus, or by any other way, to escape me. After death, thou wilt assuredly be mine again.'

'Who, then,' said the unhappy man, 'who is the murderer of the poor traveller?'

'Who? why, who but yourself? Was it not yourself that fired the pistol?'

'Ay, but at my own head.'

The fiend laughed in a way that made Schroll's flesh creep on his bones. 'Understand this, friend, that he whose fate I hold in my hands cannot anticipate it by his own act. For the present, begone, if you would escape the scaffold. To oblige you once more, I shall throw a veil over this murder.'

---

*It may be necessary to inform some readers, who have never lived far enough to the south to have any personal knowledge of the nightingale, that this bird sings in the day time as well as the night.

Thereupon the gravedigger set about making a grave for the corpse, whilst Schroll wandered away – more for the sake of escaping the hideous presence in which he stood than with any view to his own security from punishment.

Seeing by accident a prisoner under arrest at the guardhouse, Schroll's thoughts reverted to his own confinement. 'How happy,' said he, 'for me and for Charlotte, had I then refused to purchase life on such terms, and had better laid to heart the counsel of my good spiritual adviser!' Upon this a sudden thought struck him, – that he would go and find out the old clergyman, and would unfold to him his wretched history and situation. He told his wife that some private affairs required his attendance for a few days at the town of –. But, say what he would, he could not prevail on her to desist from accompanying him.

On the journey his chief anxiety was lest the clergyman, who was already advanced in years at the memorable scene of the sand-hill, might now be dead. But at the very entrance of the town he saw him walking in the street, and immediately felt himself more composed in mind than he had done for years. The venerable appearance of the old man confirmed him still more in his resolution of making a full disclosure to him of his whole past life: one only transaction, the murder of his first wife, he thought himself justified in concealing; since, with all his penitence for it, the act was now beyond the possibility of reparation.

For a long time the pious clergyman refused all belief to Schroll's narrative; but, being at length convinced that he had a wounded spirit to deal with, and not a disordered intellect, he exerted himself to present all those views of religious consolation which his philanthropic character and his long experience suggested to him as likely to be effectual. Eight days' conversation with the clergyman restored Schroll to the hopes of a less miserable future. But the good man admonished him at parting to put away from himself whatsoever could in any way tend to support his unhallowed connection.

In this direction Schroll was aware that the dice were included: and he resolved firmly that his first measure on returning home should be to bury in an inaccessible place these accursed implements that could not but bring mischief to every possessor. On entering the inn, he was met by his wife, who was in the highest spirits, and laughing profusely. He inquired the cause. 'No,' said she: 'you refused to communicate your motive for coming hither, and the nature of your business for the last week: I, too, shall have my mysteries. As to your leaving me in solitude at an inn, *that* is a sort of courtesy which marriage naturally brings with it; but that you should have travelled hither for no other purpose than that of trifling away your time in the company of an old tedious parson, *that* (you will allow me to say) is a caprice which seems scarcely worth the money it will cost.'

'Who, then, has told you that I have passed my time with an old parson?' said the astonished Schroll.

'Who told me? Why, just let me know what your business was with the parson, and I'll let you know in turn who it was that told me. So much I will assure you, however, now – that the cavalier who was my informant is a thousand times handsomer, and a more interesting companion, than an old dotard who is standing at the edge of the grave.'

All the efforts of Madame von Schrollshausen to irritate the curiosity of her husband proved ineffectual to draw from him his secret. The next day, on their return homewards, she repeated her attempts. But he parried them all with firmness. A more severe trial to his firmness was prepared for him in the heavy bills which his wife presented him on his reaching home. Her expenses in cloths and in jewels had been so profuse that no expedient remained to Schroll but that of selling without delay the landed estate he had so lately purchased. A declaration to this effect was very ill received by his wife. 'Sell the estate?' said she; 'what? sell the sole resource I shall have to rely on when you are dead? And for what reason, I should be glad to know; when a very little of the customary luck of your dice will enable you to pay off these trifles? And whether the bills be paid today or tomorrow cannot be of any very great importance.'

Upon this, Schroll declared with firmness that he never meant
to play again. 'Not play again!' exclaimed his wife; 'pooh!
pooh! you make me blush for you! So, then, I suppose it's all
true, as was said, that scruples of conscience drove you to the old
rusty parson; and that he enjoined as a penance that you should
abstain from gaming? I was told as much: but I refused to
believe it; for in your circumstances the thing seemed too senseless and irrational.'

'My dear girl,' said Schroll, 'consider –'

'Consider! what's the use of considering? what is there to
consider about?' interrupted Madame von Schrollshausen; and,
recollecting the gay cavalier whom she had met at the inn, she
now, for the first time, proposed a separation herself. 'Very
well,' said her husband, 'I am content.' 'So am I,' said his
father-in-law, who joined them at that moment. 'But take
notice that first of all I must have paid over to me an adequate
sum of money for the creditable support of my daughter: else –'

Here he took Schroll aside, and the old threat of revealing the
murder so utterly disheartening him that at length in despair
he consented to his terms.

Once more, therefore, the dice were to be tried; but only for
the purpose of accomplishing the separation: *that* over, Schroll
resolved to seek a livelihood in any other way, even if it were
as a day-labourer. The stipulated sum was at length all collected
within a few hundred dollars; and Schroll was already looking
out for some old disused well into which he might throw the
dice, and then have it filled up; for even a river seemed to him
a hiding-place not sufficiently secure for such instruments of
misery.

Remarkable it was on the very night when the last arrears
were to be obtained of his father-in-law's demand – a night
when Schroll had anticipated with so much bitter anxiety – that
he became unusually gloomy and dejected. He was particularly
disturbed by the countenance of a stranger, who for several days
running had lost considerable sums. The man called himself
Stutz; but he had a most striking resemblance to his old comrade Weber, who had been shot at the sand-hill, and differed

indeed in nothing but in the advantage of blooming youth. Scarce had he leisure to recover from the shock which this spectacle occasioned when a second occurred. About midnight another man, whom nobody knew, came up to the gaming-table, and interrupted the play by recounting an event which he represented as having just happened. A certain man, he said, had made a covenant with some person or other that they call the Evil One — or what is it you call him? and by means of this covenant he had obtained a steady run of good luck at play. 'Well, sir,' he went on, 'and would you believe it? the other he began to repent of this covenant; my gentleman wanted to rat, he wanted to rat, sir. Only, first of all, he resolved privately to make up a certain sum of money. Ah, the poor idiot! he little knew whom he had to deal with: the Evil One, as they choose to call him, was not a man to let himself be swindled in that manner. No, no, my good friend. I saw — I mean, the Evil One saw — what was going on betimes; and he secured the swindler just as he fancied himself on the point of pocketing the last arrears of the sum wanted.'

The company began to laugh so loudly at this pleasant fiction, as they conceived it, that Madame von Schrollshausen was attracted from the adjoining room. The story was repeated to her; and she was the more delighted with it because in the relater she recognized the gay cavalier whom she had met at the inn. Everybody laughed again, excepting two persons — Stutz and Schroll. The first had again lost all the money in his purse; and the second was so confounded by the story that he could not forbear staring with fixed eyes on the stranger, who stood over against him. His consternation increased when he perceived that the stranger's countenance seemed to alter at every moment, and that nothing remained unchanged in it except the cold expression of inhuman scorn with which he perseveringly regarded himself.

At length he could endure this no longer: and he remarked, therefore, upon Stutz again losing a bet, that it was now late; that Mr Stutz was too much in a run of bad luck; and that on these accounts he would defer the further pursuit of their play until another day. And thereupon he put the dice into his pocket.

'Stop!' said the strange cavalier; and the voice froze Schroll with horror; for he knew too well to whom that dreadful tone and those fiery eyes belonged.

'Stop!' said he again; 'produce your dice!' And tremblingly Schroll threw them upon the table.

'Ah! I thought as much,' said the stranger; 'they are loaded dice!' So saying, he called for a hammer, and struck one of them in two. 'See!' said he to Stutz, holding out to him the broken dice, which in fact seemed loaded with lead. 'Stop, vile impostor!' exclaimed the young man, as Schroll was preparing to quit the room in the greatest confusion; and he threw the dice at him, one of which lodged in his right eye. The tumult increased; the police came in; and Stutz was apprehended, as Schroll's wound assumed a very dangerous appearance.

Next day Schroll was in a violent fever. He asked repeatedly for Stutz. But Stutz had been committed to close confinement; it having been found that he had travelled with false passes. He now confessed that he was one of the sons of the mutineer Weber; that his sickly mother had died soon after his father's execution; and that himself and his brother, left without the control of guardians, and without support, had taken to bad course.

On hearing this report, Schroll rapidly worsened; and he unfolded to a young clergyman his whole unfortunate history. About midnight he sent again in great haste for the clergyman. He came. But at sight of him Schroll stretched out his hands in extremity of horror, and waved him away from his presence; but before his signals were complied with the wretched man had expired in convulsions.

From his horror at the sight of the young clergyman, and from the astonishment of the clergyman himself on arriving and hearing that he had already been seen in the sick-room, it was inferred that his figure had been assumed for fiendish purposes. The dice and the strange cavalier disappeared at the same time with their wretched victim, and were seen no more.

# The Astrologer's Prediction

*or*

## The Maniac's Fate

### Anonymous

### (1826)

Secret sects and brotherhoods have intrigued the minds of ordinary people ever since they first existed, and to those not initiated, even the most harmless order can be imagined to practise the most abominable rites and ceremonies. The folk of the nineteenth century were in no way different from any other in this interest and, in consequence, it is hardly surprising that these secret groups provided ideal subject matter for the more adventurous writers of Gothic terror tales.

This story about a member of the Illuminati is taken from an anonymous collection of tales and stories entitled *Legends of Terror* published by Sherwood, Gilbert and Piper of Paternoster Row in 1826. In introducing the story, the compiler chose to give some background notes on the sect and it is perhaps as well to repeat them here: 'At the commencement of the eighteenth century, the Illuminati, or sect of Astrologers, had excited considerable sensation on the Continent. Blending philosophy with enthusiasm, and uniting to a knowledge of every chemical process a profound acquaintance with astronomy, their influence over the superstitious feelings of their countrymen was prodigious. In one or two instances the infatuation was attended with fatal consequences; but in no case was the result so dreadful as in the subsequent narrative.'

REGINALD, sole heir of the illustrious family of Di Venoni, was remarkable, from his earliest infancy, for a wild enthusiastic disposition. His father, it was currently reported, had died of an hereditary insanity; and his friends, when they marked the wild

mysterious intelligency of his eye, and the determined energy of
his aspect, would often assert that the dreadful malady still lingered in the veins of young Reginald. Whether such was the
case or not, certain it is, that his mode of existence was but ill
calculated to eradicate any symptoms of insanity. Left at an early
age to the guidance of his mother, who since the death of her
husband had lived in the strictest seclusion, he experienced but
little variety to divert or enliven his attention. The gloomy chateau in which he resided was situated in Swabia on the borders
of the Black Forest. It was a wild isolated mansion, built after
the fashion of the day in the gloomiest style of Gothic architecture. At a distance rose the ruins of the once celebrated Castle
of Rudstein, of which at present but a mouldering tower remained; and, beyond, the landscape was terminated by the deep
shades and impenetrable recesses of the Black Forest.

Such was the spot in which the youth of Reginald was immured. But his solitude was soon to be relieved by the arrival
of an unexpected resident. On the anniversary of his eighteenth
year, an old man, apparently worn down with age and infirmity,
took up his abode at the ruined tower of Rudstein. He seldom
stirred out during the day; and from the singular circumstance
of his perpetually burning a lamp in the tower, the villagers naturally enough concluded that he was an emissary of the devil.
This report soon acquired considerable notoriety; and having at
last reached the ears of Reginald through the medium of a gos-
siping gardener, his curiosity was awakened, and he resolved
to introduce himself into the presence of the sage, and ascertain
the motives of his singular seclusion. Impressed with this resolution he abruptly quitted the chateau of his mother, and bent
his steps towards the ruined tower, which was situated at a trifling distance from his estate. It was a gloomy night, and the
spirit of the storm seemed abroad on the wings of the wind. As
the clock from the village church struck twelve, he gained the
ruin; and ascending the time-worn stair-case, that tottered at
each step he took, reached with some labour the apartment of
the philosopher. The door was thrown open, and the old man
was seated by the grated casement. His appearance was awfully

impressive. A long white beard depended from his chin, and his feeble frame with difficulty sustained a horoscope that was directed to the heavens. Books, written in unknown characters of cabalism, were promiscuously strewed about the floor; and an alabaster vase, engraved with the signs of the Zodiac, and circled by mysterious letters, was stationed on the table. The appearance of the Astrologer himself was equally impressive. He was habited in a suit of black velvet, fancifully embroidered with gold, and belted with a band of silver. His thin locks hung steaming in the wind, and his right hand grasped a wand of ebony. On the entrance of a stranger he rose from his seat, and bent a scrutinizing glance on the anxious countenance of Reginald.

'Child of ill-starred fortunes!' he exclaimed in a hollow tone, 'dost thou come to pry into the secrets of futurity? Avoid me, for thy life, or, what is dearer still, thine eternal happiness! for I say unto thee, Reginald Di Venoni, it is better that thou hadst never been born, than permitted to seal thy ruin in a spot which, in after years, shall be the witness of thy fall.'

The countenance of the Astrologer as he uttered these words was singularly terrific, and rung in the ears of Reginald like his death-knell. 'I am innocent, father!' he falteringly replied, 'nor will my disposition suffer me to perpetrate the sins you speak of.' – 'Hah!' resumed the prophet, 'man is indeed innocent, till the express moment of his damnation; but the star of thy destiny already wanes in the heaven, and the fortunes of the proud family of Venoni must decline with it. Look to the west! Yon planet that shines so brightly in the night-sky, is the star of thy nativity. When next thou shalt behold it, shooting downward like a meteor though the hemisphere, think on the words of the prophet and tremble. A deed of blood will be done, and thou art he that shall perpetrate it!'

At this instant the moon peeped forth from the dun clouds that lagged slowly in the firmament, and shed a mild radiance upon the earth. To the west, a single bright star was visible. It was the star of Reginald's nativity. He gazed with eyes fixed in the breathless intensity of expectation, and watched it till the

passing clouds concealed its radiance from his view. The Astrologer, in the meantime, had resumed his station at the window.
He raised the horoscope to heaven. His frame seemed trembling
with convulsion. Twice he passed his hand across his brow, and
shuddered as he beheld the aspect of the heavens. 'But a few
days,' he said, 'are yet left me on earth, and then shall my spirit
know the eternal repose of the grave. The star of my nativity
is dim and pale. It will never be bright again, and the aged one
will never know comfort more. Away!' he continued, motion-
ing Reginald from his sight, 'disturb not the last moments of a
dying man; in three days return, and under the base of this ruin
inter the corpse that you will find mouldering within. Away!'

Impressed with a strange awe, Reginald could make no reply. He remained as it were entranced; and after the lapse of a
few minutes rushed from the tower, and returned in a state of
disquietude to the gloomy chateau of his mother.

The three days had now elapsed, and, faithful to his promise,
Reginald pursued his route back to the tower. He reached it at
nightfall, and tremblingly entered the fatal apartment. All within was silent, but his steps returned a hollow echo as he passed.
The wind sighed around the ruin, and the raven from the roofless turrets had already commenced his death-song. He entered.
The Astrologer, as before, was seated by the window, apparently
in profound abstraction, and the horoscope was placed by his
side. Fearful of disturbing his repose, Reginald approached with
caution. The old man stirred not. Emboldened by so unexpected a silence, he advanced and looked at the face of the Astrologer. It was a corpse he gazed on, – the relic of what had once
been life. Petrified with horror at the sight, the memory of his
former promise escaped him, and he rushed in agony from the
apartment.

For many days the fever of his mind continued unabated. He
frequently became delirious, and in the hour of his lunacy was
accustomed to talk of an evil spirit that had visited him in his
slumbers. His mother was shocked at such evident symptoms
of derangement. She remembered the fate of her husband; and
implored Reginald, as he valued her affection, to recruit the

agitation of his spirits by travel. With some difficulty he was induced to quit the home of his infancy. The expostulations of the countess at last prevailed, and he left the Chateau Di Venoni for the sunny climes of Italy.

Time rolled on; and a constant succession of novelty had produced so beneficial an effect, that scarcely any traces remained of the once mysterious and enthusiastic Venoni. Occasionally his mind was disturbed and gloomy, but a perpetual recurrence of amusement diverted the influence of past recollection, and rendered him at least as tranquil as it was in the power of his nature to permit. He continued for years abroad, during which time he wrote frequently to his mother, who still continued at the Chateau Di Venoni, and at last announced his intention of settling finally at Venice. He had remained but a few months in the city, when, at the gay period of the Carnival, he was introduced, as a foreign nobleman, to the beautiful daughter of the Doge. She was amiable, accomplished, and endowed with every requisite to ensure permanent felicity. Reginald was charmed with her beauty, and infatuated with the excelling qualities of her mind. He confessed his attachment, and was informed with a blush that the affection was mutual. Nothing, therefore, remained but application to the Doge; who was instantly addressed on the subject, and implored to consummate the felicity of the young couple. The request was attended with success, and the happiness of the lovers was complete.

On the day fixed for the wedding, a brilliant assemblage of beauty thronged the ducal palace of St Mark. All Venice crowded to the festival; and, in the presence of the gayest noblemen of Italy, Reginald Count Di Venoni received the hand of Marcelia, the envied daughter of the Doge. In the evening, a masqued festival was given at the palace; but the young couple, anxious to be alone, escaped the scene of revelry, and hurried in their gondola to the chateau that was prepared for their reception.

It was a fine moonlight night. The mild beams of the planets sparkled on the silver bosom of the Adriatic, and the light tones of music, 'by distance made more sweet,' came wafted on the western gale. A thousand lamps, from the illuminated squares of the city, reflected their burnished hues along the wave, and the mellow chaunt of the gondoliers kept time to the gentle splashing of their oars. The hearts of the lovers were full, and the witching spirit of the hour passed with all its loveliness into their souls. On a sudden a deep groan escaped the overcharged heart of Reginald. He had looked to the western hemisphere, and the star which, at that moment, flashed brightly in the horizon, reminded him of the awful scene which he had witnessed at the tower of Rudstein. His eye sparkled with delirious brilliancy; and had not a shower of tears come opportunely to his relief, the consequence might have been fatal. But the affectionate caresses of his young bride succeeded for the present in soothing his agitation, and restoring his mind to its former tranquil temperament.

A few months had now elapsed from the period of his marriage, and the heart of Reginald was happy. He loved Marcelia, and was tenderly beloved in return. Nothing, therefore, remained to complete his felicity but the presence of his mother, the Countess. He wrote accordingly to intreat that she would come and reside with him at Venice, but was informed by her confessor in reply, that she was dangerously ill, and requested the immediate attendance of her son. On the receipt of this afflicting intelligence he hurried with Marcelia to the Chateau Di Venoni. The countess was still alive when he entered, and received him with an affectionate embrace. But the exertion of so unexpected an interview with her son, was too great for the agitated spirits of the parent, and she expired in the act of folding him to her arms.

From this moment the mind of Reginald assumed a tone of the most confirmed dejection. He followed his mother to the grave, and was observed to smile with unutterable meaning as he returned home from the funeral. The Chateau Di Venoni increased the native depression of his spirits, and the appearance of the ruined tower never failed to imprint a dark frown upon his brow. He would wander for days from his home, and when he returned, the moody expression of his countenance alarmed the affection of his wife. She did all in her power to assuage his anguish, but his melancholy remained unabated. Sometimes, when the fit was on him, he would repulse her with fury; but, in his gentler moments, would gaze on her as on a sweet vision of vanished happiness.

He was one evening wandering with her through the village, when his conversation assumed a more dejected tone than usual. The sun was slowly setting, and their route back to the chateau lay through the churchyard where the ashes of the countess reposed. Reginald seated himself with Marcelia by the grave, and plucking a few wild flowers from the turf, exclaimed, 'Are you not anxious to join my mother, sweet girl? She has gone to the land of the blest – to the land of love and sunshine! If we are happy in this world, what will be our state of happiness in the next? Let us fly to unite our bliss with hers, and the measure of our joy will be full.' As he uttered these words his eye glared with delirium, and his hand seemed searching for a weapon. Marcelia, alarmed at his appearance, hurried him from the spot, and clasping his hand in hers, drew him gently onward.

The sun in the meantime had sunk, and the stars of evening came out in their glory. Brilliant above all shone the fatal western planet, the star of Reginald's nativity. He observed it with horror, and pointed it out to the notice of Marcelia. 'The hand of heaven is in it!' he mentally exclaimed, 'and the proud fortunes of Venoni hasten to a close.' At this instant the ruined tower of Rudstein appeared in sight, with the moon shining full upon it. 'It is the place,' resumed the maniac, 'where a deed of blood must be done, and I am he that must perpetrate it! But fear not, my poor girl,' he added, in a milder tone, while the tears sprang to his eyes, 'thy Reginald cannot harm thee; he may be wretched, but he never shall be guilty!' With these words he reached the chateau, and threw himself on his couch in restless anxiety of mind.

Night waned, morning dawned on the upland hills of the scenery, and with it came a renewal of Reginald's disorder. The day was stormy, and in unison with the troubled feeling of his spirit. He had been absent from Marcelia since day break, and had given her no promise of return. But as she was seated at twilight near the lattice, playing on her harp a favourite Venetian canzonet, the folding doors flew open, and Reginald made his appearance. His eye was red, with the deepest – the deadliest madness, and his whole frame seemed unusually convulsed. ''Twas not a dream,' he exclaimed, 'I have seen her and she has beckoned us to follow.' 'Seen her, seen who?' said Marcelia, alarmed at his phrenzy. 'My mother,' replied the maniac. 'Listen while I repeat the horrid narrative. Methought as I was wandering in the forest, a sylph of heaven approached, and revealed the countenance of my mother, I flew to join her but was withheld by a sage who pointed to the western star. On a sudden loud shrieks were heard, and the sylph assumed the guise of a demon. Her figure towered to an awful height, and she pointed in scornful derision to thee; yes, to thee, my Marcelia. With rage she drew thee towards me. I seized – I murdered thee; and hollow groans broke on the midnight gale. The voice of the fiendish Astrologer was heard shouting as from a charnel house, "The destiny is accomplished, and the victim may retire with honour." Then, methought, the fair front of heaven was obscured, and thick gouts of clotted, clammy blood showered down in torrents from the blackened clouds of the west. The star shot through the air, and – the phantom of my mother again beckoned me to follow.'

The maniac ceased, and rushed in agony from the apartment. Marcelia followed and discovered him leaning in a trance against the wainscot of the library. With gentlest motion she drew his hand in hers, and led him into the open air. They rambled on, heedless of the gathering storm, until they discovered themselves at the base of the tower of Rudstein. Suddenly the maniac paused. A horrid thought seemed flashing across his brain, as with giant grasp he seized Marcelia in his arms, and bore her to the fatal apartment. In vain she shrieked for help, for pity. 'Dear Reginald, it is Marcelia who speaks, you cannot surely harm her.' He heard – he heeded not, nor once staid his steps, till he reached the room of death. On a sudden his countenance lost its wildness, and assumed a more fearful, but composed look of determined madness. He advanced to the

window, and gazed on the stormy face of heaven. Dark clouds
flitted across the horizon, and hollow thunder echoed awfully
in the distance. To the west the fatal star was still visible, but
shone with sickly lustre. At this instant a flash of lightning re-
illuminated the whole apartment, and threw a broad red glare
upon a skeleton, that mouldered upon the floor. Reginald observed it with affright, and remembered the unburied Astrologer. He advanced to Marcelia, and pointing to the rising moon,
'A dark cloud is sailing by,' he shudderingly exclaimed, 'but
ere the full orb again shines forth, thou shalt die, I will accompany thee in death, and hand in hand will we pass into the
presence of our mother.' The poor girl shrieked for pity, but her
voice was lost in the angry ravings of the storm. The cloud in
the meantime sailed on, – it approached – the moon was dimmed,
darkened, and finally buried in its gloom. The maniac marked
the hour, and rushed with a fearful cry towards his victim.
With murderous resolution he grasped her throat, while the
helpless hand and half strangled articulation, implored his compassion. After one final struggle the hollow death rattle announced that life was extinct, and that the murderer held a
corpse in his arms. An interval of reason now occurred, and on
the partial restoration of his mind, Reginald discovered himself
the unconscious murderer of Marcelia. Madness – deepest madness again took possession of his faculties. He laughed – he
shouted aloud with the unearthly yellings of a fiend, and in the
raging violence of his delirium, hurled himself headlong from
the summit of the tower.

In the morning the bodies of the young couple were discovered, and buried in the same tomb. The fatal ruin of Rudstein
still exists; but is now commonly avoided as the residence of the
spirits of the departed. Day by day it slowly crumbles to earth,
and affords a shelter for the night raven, or the wild beasts of
the forests. Superstition has consecrated it to herself, and the tradition of the country has invested it with all the awful appendages
of a charnel house. The wanderer who passes at night-fall, shudders while he surveys its utter desolation, and exclaims as he
journies on, 'Surely this is a spot where guilt may thrive in safety,
or bigotry weave a spell to enthrall her misguided votaries.'

# *Glenallan*

## Lord Lytton

## (1803–1873)

'The story of terror, with all its faults, had seldom been guilty of demanding intellectual strain or overburdening itself with erudition. It was the dignified task of Lord Lytton to rationalize and elevate the novel of terror, to evolve the "man of reason" from the "child of nature'. (Edith Birkhead, *The Tale of Terror*.)

Although today the work of Edward George Lytton Bulwer, Lord Lytton, is almost completely unknown – the possible exception being his short story, *The Haunted and the Haunters* which by contrast is endlessly reprinted in macabre anthologies – there is little dispute among authorities that he was one of the most important literary figures of his age. Montague Summers considered him with W. Harrison Ainsworth and G. P. R. James 'the greatest romanticist of the last Golden Age of Literature, the palmier days of good Queen Victoria'. Indeed from his accomplished pen came essays, translations, verse, plays and novels – all of which were attuned to the tastes of their time and displayed a resourceful, agile mind.

Bulwer Lytton came early into contact with the world of the supernatural in a haunted chamber at Knebworth House where he 'peeped with bristling hair into the shadowy abysses of hell'. He also had an ancestor who had reputedly dabbled in Black Magic and this is said to have inspired him to make a number of magical experiments himself. His first compositions, however, were some heroic poems written while at Cambridge and in fact his serious writing did not begin until after an unhappy marriage had thrown him completely on his own resources. His most popular novels were probably *Eugene Aram* (1832), *The Last Days of Pompeii* (1834) and *Zanoni* (1842) a superlative occult tale, while his poem, *King Arthur* (1849) is a classic. In later life he served as a member of Parliament and was for a time Colonial Secretary.

The story here is an early example of Lord Lytton's work (1826) and according to his son (writing in a posthumous collection of his father's miscellaneous writings) is notable for 'the traces it contains of that love of the supernatural which is conspicuous in so many of the later creations of his fancy'. The narrator of the tale has some of Lytton's own temperament and disposition and indeed the whole story may well be founded on memories of his maternal grandfather. I am sure all readers who only know Bulwer Lytton through one or two stories will welcome the opportunity of reading this long unobtainable novella.

# I

I WAS born in the county of —. After my mother's death my father, who deeply lamented her loss, resolved to spend the remainder of his life in Ireland. He was the representative, and, with the exception of an only brother, the last of a long line of ancestry; and, unlike most ancient families still existing, the wealth of my father's family was equal to its antiquity. At an early period of life he had established a high reputation in that public career which is the proper sphere of distinction to the rich and the highborn. Men of eager minds, however, should not enter too soon into the world. The more it charms them at first, the more it wearies them at last; hope is chilled by disappointment, magnanimity depressed by a social perspective which artificially lessens even great characters and objects, tedium succeeds to energy, and delight is followed by disgust. At least so thought, and so found, my father before he was thirty; when, at the very zenith of his popular esteem, he retired from public life, to one of his estates in the West of England. It was there, at a neighbouring gentleman's, that he first saw and loved my mother, and it was there that all the patent softness of his nature was called forth.

Men of powerful passions who have passed the spring-time of youth without the excitement of that passion which is the most powerful of all, feel love perhaps with greater tenderness and force when at last it comes upon them. My father and mother had been married for several years; their happiness was only equalled by their affection, and, if anything could weaken the warmth of the thanksgiving my father daily offered to Heaven for the blessings he enjoyed, it was the reflection that there had been born no pledge to their attachment, and no heir to the name and honours of his forefathers. Justly proud of his descent from some of the most illustrious warriors and statesmen of his country, such a reflection might well cast a shade on the otherwise unbroken brightness of his married life. At last, however, in the eighth year of that life, my mother found herself pregnant, and the measure of my father's felicity was complete, as the time of her confinement approached. But on the day when I came into this world to continue the race of the Glenallans, my mother left it, for ever. This stroke fell the heavier on my father, because in the natural buoyancy of his character, he had never contemplated the possibility of such a calamity. He left England for six years, and travelled over the greater part of Europe. At the end of that time he returned, with the determination to withdraw himself completely from society, and devote all his time and intellect to the education of the son he had so dearly acquired. But as it was impossible for one so distinguished to maintain in his own country the rigid seclusion on which he was resolved, my father decided to fix his future abode in Ireland, upon the estate where his mother was born, and which in her right he inherited.

Though so young at the time of our departure from England, I can well remember many of the incidents of the journey, and never can I forget the evening when our travelling carriage stopped before those moss-grown and gigantic ruins which were the only remnants of the ancient power of the Tyrones.

It needed but a slight portion of my father's wealth to repair the ravages made by time and neglect in this ruined but still massive structure, and my future home soon assumed a more lively appearance. Although my father civilly but coldly declined all intercourse with the neighbouring gentry, the lower orders were always sure of finding a warm hearth and a bounteous board in the princely halls he had restored. His beneficence secured to him the affection of his peasantry, even amidst the perpetual disorders of one of the wildest parts of that unhappy country, and notwithstanding the abhorrence with which the existing Government was regarded by the surrounding population. My father's sole occupation was the management of my education. It was both the employment of his severer hours and the recreation of his lighter moments. He was not satisfied with making me a thorough classical scholar, but was particularly anxious to give me a perfect knowledge of the history and literature of my own country; to enlarge my views by habitual meditation; to make me familiar with the sciences of philosophy and political economy; and, in short, to bring me, as nearly as my abilities would permit, upon a par with himself.

Perhaps in his ardour to make me great, he forgot how necessary it was for my happiness to make me amiable. He suffered me to pay too little attention to the courtesies of society; and, thinking that it was impossible for a gentleman to be anything but a gentleman, he remembered not how many trifles, small in themselves but large in the aggregate, were required to lay a just claim to that distinction.

From the lessons of my father I used to turn to my private and lonely amusements. I in some degree inherited his aristocratic pride, and preferred even solitude to the intrusive familiarity of the servants and dependents, who were accustomed to join in the rural sports for which I felt no inclination. It was in solitary wanderings over wide and dreary plains, by rapid streams, amongst the ruins of ancient power, beneath the lofty cliffs, and beside the green and solemn waters of the Atlantic, that my mind insensibly assumed its habitual bias, and that my character was first coloured by the sombre hues which ever afterwards imbued it. As there were none to associate with me, my loneliness became my natural companion; my father I seldom saw, except at meals and during the time I was engaged with him in the studies he had appointed for me.

The effect of one great misfortune upon a mind so powerful as his was indeed extraordinary. Although during my mother's life he had given up all political activity, and lived in comparative retirement, yet he was then proud of preserving the ancient and splendid hospitality of the family, and whilst his house was

the magnificent resort of all who were distinguished by their
rank, their talents or their virtues, I have been told by those who
then frequented it, that his own convivial qualities, his wit, his
urbanity, his graceful and winning charm of manner were no
less admired by his friends than his intellectual powers were
respected by his rivals. But during the whole time that I can
remember him, his habits were so reserved and unsocial that,
but for his unbounded benevolence, he might have passed for
an inveterate misanthropist. Although his love for me was certainly the strongest feeling of his heart, yet he never evinced it
by an affectionate word or look. His manner was uniformly
cold, and somewhat stern, but never harsh. From my earliest
infancy I never received from him an unkind word or a re-
proach; nor did I ever receive from him a caress. In his gifts to
me he was liberal to profusion, and as I grew up to manhood
a separate suite of rooms and servants were allotted to me, far
more numerous and splendid than those with which he himself
was contented.

The only servant I ever admitted to familiar intercourse with
me was an old man whose character was of a kind to deepen the
gloom of those impressions I had already derived from other
sources. He was a sort of living chronicle of horrors. He knew
about every species of apparition and every kind of supernatural
being, whether of Irish, English, or Scottish origin. The wildest
tales constructed by the luxuriant genius of German romancers
would have been tame in comparison with those of old Phelim.
But of all the fictions he used to narrate, and I to revere as sacred
and incontrovertible truths, none delighted me so much as those
relating to my own ancestor, Morshed Tyrone, a wizard of such
awful power that the spirits of earth, air, and ocean ministered
to him as his slaves, and the dead walked restless rounds to perform his bidding. I can remember well how the long winter
evenings were spent, by the flickering light of the turf fire, in
descriptions of the midnight orgies and revels, held perhaps in
the very room where Phelim and I were then sitting. I can remember well the thrilling delight with which I used to watch
for the hour when I laid aside what seemed to me the cold and

airy beauties of Virgil, or the dry and magisterial philosophy of Seneca (the two books my father at this time most wished me to study), that I might listen to those terrific legends. Well, too, can I remember the not all undelightful fear which crept upon me when they were over, and I was left to the dreary magnificence of my solitary apartment.

As I grew up, so far from discarding or wearing out these impressions, so inconsistent with the ideas of the eighteenth century, they grew with my growth, and strengthened with my strength. In the old library I discovered many treatises on the existence of witchcraft. Some of them went so far as to hint at the means of acquiring that dreadful art without the penalties which superstition has attached to it; others were filled with astrological speculations, and to these treasures, which I carefully removed to my own rooms, I was continually adding every work I could procure upon the subject of my favourite pursuits. Still as I read, the ardour of penetrating further into the mysteries hidden from human eyes so powerfully increased, that at last I used to steal forth on certain nights to the lonesome abodes of the dead; and, amidst the corruption of mortality and the horrors of the charnel, I have sometimes watched till morning for the attainment of frightful secrets from which my mind in its ordinary healthful condition would have shrunk with repugnance.

This unnatural state of mind, however, could not last when nothing sustained it but the chimeras of a disordered imagination; and what perhaps conduced more than anything else to restore me to my senses was a long and violent illness, caused by a severe cold caught in one of my midnight expeditions. During several weeks I was confined to my bed, and then the long dormant kindness of my father's nature seemed to revive. A mother's fondest care could not have surpassed the unceasing vigilance, the anxious tenderness, with which he watched and soothed me. He poured forth, for my amusement, the varied stores of a mind rich in the knowledge of men as well as books; and the astonishing fund of information thus lavished for my enjoyment made me conscious of my own mental defects, and anxious to recover the time I had squandered in eccentric reverie. As soon as I was convalescent I fell into a more regular and instructive course of reading: I discarded old Phelim from my confidence, cleared my shelves of their unhallowed lumber, and seemed in a fair way to flow on with the rest of the world's stream in the calm current of ordinary life. Alas, it was not to be!

I have been thus diffuse in the narrative of my earliest years, because it is in that period of life that the character is stamped. It is then we sow the seeds we are to reap hereafter.

## II

I had attained my eighteenth year, and was beginning to think it time to mix somewhat more with my equals, when my father sent for me one morning at an hour which was not the usual time for our daily meeting. Since my recovery he had gradually relapsed into his former habits of reserve, although when we were alone his manner was warmer and his conversation more familiar. I was somewhat surprised at the message, but more surprised by the extraordinary agitation in which I found him when I entered his study.

'Redmond,' said he, 'I believe you have never heard me mention my brother. Perhaps you did not know that I had so near a relation. I have learnt today that he is dead.' Here my father paused, evidently much affected, and I gained time to recover from my surprise at hearing in the same breath of the existence and death of so close a connection.

'In very early youth,' continued my father, 'an unfortunate quarrel arose between us, partly caused by my brother's change of political party for reasons which I thought either frivolous or mercenary. The breach was widened, however, by a very imprudent marriage on his part, at which my family pride revolted; and he, disgusted at what he deemed (not perhaps unjustly, as I have since imagined) my heartless arrogance, resented so warmly some expressions I had used in the first moment of mortification that he forswore for ever my friendship and alliance.

Thus we parted, never to meet again. He withdrew to France; and from that time to this my information respecting him has been slight and trivial. Today I received an official letter informing me of his death and enclosing one from himself, in which, after lamenting our long separation, he recommends (and in terms I dare not refuse to comply with) his only son to my care and affection. I shall therefore write at once to this young man, inviting him to Castle Tyrone, and assuring him of my future solicitude. I have sent for you, Redmond, to acquaint you with this decision and to prepare you for a companion about your own age, who will, I trust, relieve the tedium you must often have felt in the unbroken solitude of our lonely life here.' With these words my father dismissed me.

I will pass over my reflections and anticipations, my fears and hopes, in reference to the prospect of this addition to our home life. During the whole morning of the day when our guest was expected, my father was in a state of silent agitation, as unusual to him as it was surprising to me, although I largely shared it. At length the carriage was seen at a distance; it approached, and a young man leapt lightly down from it. My father received him with a warmth quite foreign to the usual coldness of his manner, and entered into a long conversation with him about his own father. During this conversation I employed myself in taking a minute survey of my new acquaintance.

Ruthven Glenallan was in person small, but the proportions of his figure were perfectly symmetrical. He could scarcely be called handsome, but in his dark and dazzling eye, and in his brilliant smile, there was a power greater perhaps than that of beauty. He had been brought up from childhood in the most polished societies of Italy, and the winning grace of Continental manners was visible in all his gestures and expressions. Except my father, I have never known any person with such varied powers of conversation, or so able to charm and dazzle without apparent effort. Yet at times there was in his countenance a strange and sinister expression, which assumed a more suspicious appearance from the sudden and sparkling smiles immediately succeeding it if he thought himself observed. This peculiarity, however, I did not immediately perceive. For the next week we were inseparable. We walked and talked together, we accommodated our dissimilar habits to each other's inclinations, and we seemed to be laying the foundation of a lasting intimacy. Little as my father was accustomed to observe how those around him passed their time, he was evidently pleased with our friendship; and one morning, when I went to ask his advice about a course of reading on the commerce and politics of America, he said to me: 'I am much gratified by the affection which you and Ruthven feel for each other; the more so, as I am now convinced of what I have always hoped, that you would be but little affected by the loss of a part of that overflowing wealth which will be yours when I am gone. You are aware that a very small portion of my estate is entailed, and I can therefore, without injury to you, bequeath to Ruthven enough for his future independence. Though his father's fortune was not large, his expenditure almost rivalled that of the foreign princes with whom he associated, and at his death little or nothing could be saved from the wreck of his fortune. The least I can do, therefore, to compensate for any fault I have committed towards my brother will be to give to his son a small moiety from the superfluous riches of my own.' I need not say what was my answer; it was, I hope, what it ought to have been.

## III

After the first novelty of companionship was over, I began to find in my cousin's character much that widely differed from my own ideas of excellence. If I spoke of superior worth, if I praised a lofty thought or a noble action, his usual reply was a smile of contempt, or a cold calculation of its probable motives, which he invariably sought to prove selfish or unworthy. Sometimes he laughed at my notions, as the inexperienced absurdities of a romantic visionary; at other times he startled me with a bold avowal of his own, and they were mostly those I had been taught to abhor in the most cynical literature of France and Italy. I must own, moreover, that I had sometimes the meanness to feel jealous of him. My own character was not formed to be popular. Naturally proud and reserved, and cold in my manners though warm in my feelings, there was in me something repellent, which chilled affection and repressed confidence. But Ruthven was precisely the reverse. Really wrapped in himself, yet by the perpetual courtesy of his manners always appearing to think only of others, he was loved as soon as seen. The largest part of my munificent allowance I gave away in charity; but my charity was always silently and oftenest secretly bestowed, nor did my manner of giving it ever heighten the value of the gift. Ruthven seldom or never gave, but when he did give, he so managed it that his gift was sure to be known, and the value of it exaggerated, set off as it was by that winning grace so peculiarly his own, and so particularly seductive to our Irish neighbours. His habits also, both of reading and of recreation, widely differed from my own. He was devoted to politics, which to me seemed neither interesting nor amiable, and his amusements were either the sports of the field or the society of the promiscuous admirers, mostly his social inferiors, whom his conviviality of spirit perpetually gathered round him.

I have said that I was jealous of my cousin. Yes, I was jealous of him; but this was perhaps not altogether so unworthy a feeling as it might appear. I could have recognized without irritation the solid superiority of another; I could have admired such superiority even in a declared rival, with feelings, not of jealousy but of generous emulation; but I could not acknowledge Ruthven as my superior in any quality my character had been trained to admire. I could not but feel that in personal advantages, in depth of information, in abilities natural and acquired, and above all in that region of character which is governed by the heart, any just comparison between us would have been greatly in my favour. Yet he was loved and admired; I was disliked and feared. To a mind ardent in all its emotions, and hearty in all its thoughts, such a reflection could not be but bitterly mortifying. It was a reflection constantly and painfully renewed by the most ordinary events of every day; and the pain of it, which was not wholly selfish, may palliate perhaps, though it cannot condone, the fault I have confessed.

The gradual separation now began to take place in our pursuits was hastened by Ruthven's adoption of a profession. My father had given him his choice, and promised him assistance in any career he might select; and after a short wavering between a commission in the army and a seat in Parliament, he finally decided upon the latter. My father had three boroughs at his disposal: two of them had been lately given to men of high reputation, and at this time, all of them were filled; but the member for one of them was very old, and labouring under all the infirmities of advanced age. There was therefore every probability that it would soon be vacant, and the expected vacancy was promised to my cousin. After this decision, Ruthven applied himself more ardently than ever to the study of politics. Every branch of law and history connected with this great object he pursued with an unwearied attention which scarcely left him an hour at leisure. This intense desire of distinction was decidedly the highest point in his character. In youth, to desire honours is to gain them.

## IV

I resumed my former habits of solitude. I had always been more fond of walking than of any other kind of exercise. Accustomed to it from my earliest childhood, and blest by nature with a more than common activity and strength, I would often wander forth, in all varieties of weather, over those dreary and almost uninhabited wastes which tell so sad a tale of the internal condition of Ireland. Unhappy country! whose sons have in all ages, and more especially in ours, been among the brightest ornaments and best supporters of other lands, whilst their own, formed by nature to be so prosperous, has remained in a condition mourned even by the stranger who beholds it.

One morning, tempted by an unusual flow of animal spirits and the beauty of the advancing spring, I prolonged my excursion far beyond its customary limits. I was greatly attracted by the novelty of the scenery which opened around me, and finding myself at the foot of a small hill, I climbed it, for the pleasure of a wider prospect. There was one object in the foreground of the landscape on which I then looked down which immediately and strangely impressed me; but little did I then anticipate the influence it was destined to exert over my future life. This object was a rather large and very ruinous building, which stood utterly alone, upon a dull and shrubless plain. The oasis of desert, islanded in the loveliness of a landscape with which it had no visible relation, looked as though a wicked enchanter had stolen it by night from another and more dismal land, and dropped it where I saw it, to sadden and deform the beauty of the scenery around it; so foreign did it look to the character of the neighbouring country, and so coldly did it seem to cower in the desolation of its own sterility. My imagination tempted me to approach it.

I found the house in a state of even greater dilapidation than had been apparent to my first and more distant view of it. There was no wall or fence to protect it from the encroachment of man or beast. The rank ivy rioted in its broken windows, and troops of wild thistles crowded its doorless thresholds. At first it seemed to me impossible that such a place could have a human tenant, but presently I perceived a faint smoke rising from a rickety chimney in the shattered roof; and soon afterwards a woman, whose dress and air were evidently not those of a peasant or a pauper, emerged from the crumbling aperture which served as main doorway to the interior of the ruin. She slowly approached the place where I was standing. As she walked, her head was stooped apparently in deep thought, and we were close to each other before she noticed my intrusion. With a respectful gesture I stepped aside to let her pass. She heard my footsteps and looked up. Our eyes immediately and involuntarily met.

Could I devote the unremitting labour of a hundred years to the description of the feelings which that momentary look awakened within me, I should fail to express them. Philosphers may deride, and pedants dispute, the magic of those rare moments which reveal to the heart the capacity and the destiny of emotions it has never felt before; but from the first glance of that woman's eye my soul drank inspirations of passion which have influenced my whole life.

The stranger blushed deeply beneath my riveted and ardent gaze; and, slightly returning the involuntary bow which my ignorance of modern etiquette could alone excuse, she passed on with a quickened step. How often have the most momentous events of our future life originated in the most casual and trifling incidents of the passing moment! Ruthven's favourite dog had that day accompanied me in my lonely excursion. He was one of the fiercest of the fierce breed of English terriers; and his indignation being kindled by some mark of disrespect in the behaviour of a small spaniel which was the lady's only companion, he suddenly flew upon the little creature with a force and ferocity from which it was wholly unable to defend itself. My interference with this unequal combat was successfully exerted at the most opportune moment; and I had the happiness of being rewarded for it by a smile, and a voice, of which the memory almost repays me even now for the terrible sufferings I have since undergone.

To those who read the history of my eventful life, I would fain describe, if I could, the surpassing loveliness of that face which has been the star of its fairest hopes, and even in its darkest moments a guiding light, a glory, and a blessing. But the best part of beauty is what no picture can ever express; and if I attempted to portray the beauty of Ellen St Aubyn, the attempt would be as eternal as my love.

## V

I took advantage of an opportunity so favourable, to enter into conversation with the fair stranger: a conversation embarrassed only by my habitual reserve. She was too high bred, and too genuinely modest, to repulse my respectful advances. Half an hour's walk brought us to the entrance of a large modern mansion, so completely embosomed in the surrounding woodlands that till then I had not perceived it. By this time I had learned that my fair acquaintance was the daughter of Lord St Aubyn;

that her father was dead; that since his death her mother had settled almost entirely in Ireland, which was her native country; and that Lady St Aubyn was accustomed to pass half the year in Dublin, and the rest of it at 'Rose Cliff', the beautiful retreat which then bust into view from the depth of the embowering foliage around it, bright in all the sweetness of the noontide sun. Here I received from my companion a slight but graceful invitation to accompany her into the house, and I gladly accepted it. 'I have brought you,' said Miss St Aubyn to her mother, 'a treasure from an unknown shore. Let me introduce Mr Glenallan.' Lady St Aubyn received me with a charming courtesy which was a pleasant combination of English dignity and Irish cordiality; and in a few moments I found myself in animated conversation with her on the state of the neighbouring country. When at last I rose to take my leave, I was so warmly pressed to stay for dinner, that I felt too pleased and flattered to refuse. Shortly afterwards, some friends who were staying at the house returned from their morning walk, and I was formally introduced to Mrs M—, Lord and Lady C—, Miss P— and Lady L—. In the manner of all these new acquaintances I noticed how instantaneously their first scrutinizing and somewhat supercilious look at me was changed, on the mention of my name, to one of respectful politeness: so great is the magic of a name, when that name is associated with the importance which society accords to birth and wealth. At dinner I was seated between Miss P— and Lady C—. To me these ladies then appeared the most uncommon, though I have since discovered that they were the most common, specimens of womankind. Miss P— was an enthusiastic musician and admirer of poetry, especially the poetry of Scott and Moore. It is a pity that Byron had not then become famous. How she would have adored him! What her family and fortune were, I cannot exactly say. Both were, I believe, respectable. As for her personal and natural qualities, she was rather pretty, if blue eyes, good teeth, a perpetual smile, and a never-varying red and white could make her so, in spite of red hair, a short clumsy figure, a broad hand, and a voice which had not a single tone free from affectation. Lady C— was a fine large woman, highly rouged, and dressed rather more *à la Grecque* than ladies of fifty generally think correct. She spoke with remarkable self-possession; and whether compliments or sarcasm, wit or wisdom, politics or poetry, it was with a voice perfectly unchanging, accompanied by a fixed stare, which, according to the subject discussed, appeared sometimes indecent, sometimes supercilious, always displeasing, and always unfeminine.

These two ladies, however, were just the sort of women best fitted to diminish the embarrassment of a shy and inexperienced young man. They were eternal talkers and loose observers, and my little blunders in established etiquette escaped unheeded. They were not serious blunders. Although no guests ever joined our family meals at home, the refinement of my father's tastes and habits scrupulously maintained, even in the most careless privacy, all those little forms and customs which exist in well-bred families. Moreover, I was a most miscellaneous reader, and not less familiar with all that class of fiction which paints the manners and habits of society than with the more serious literature of ethics. A good novel should be, and generally is, a magnifying or diminishing glass of life. It may lessen or enlarge what it reflects, but the general features of society are faithfully reproduced by it. If a man reads such works with intelligent interest, he may learn almost as much of the world from his library as from the clubs and drawing-rooms of St James's.

How often during dinner my eyes wandered to that part of the table where Ellen St Aubyn was sitting! How intently were they riveted upon her, when her bright cheek was turned away from me, and yet how swiftly were my looks averted when they encountered hers! After the ladies had withdrawn, the conversation was as uninteresting as after-dinner conversation generally is. I took an early opportunity of retreating to the drawing-room to make my adieux, but, with a hospitality truly Irish, I was again pressed to prolong my stay, at least for that night, and to send a servant to Castle Tyrone, with a message informing my father of the cause of my absence.

'Do pray stay,' said Miss P—, 'for I have a great favour to ask of you.'

'Why should you go?' cried Lady C—.

'What's the matter?' added Lady L—, who was somewhat deaf. 'Surely Mr Glenallan is not going; the evening is setting in, and see how hard it rains.'

'It will be quite an insult to Rose Cliff,' chimed in Lady St Aubyn.

To this I could answer nothing, but I looked at Ellen, who blushed as my gaze met hers, and I bowed a delighted assent. The servant was sent, and I remained. The whole of that evening I sat by Ellen, and that evening was therefore one of the happiest of my life.

In the course of our conversation, I asked her who lived in that deserted and ruinous building which had so fortunately attracted my attention.

'It is,' said Ellen, 'the last descendant of one of the oldest and once most powerful families in Ireland; and that house, the only one left of all her ancestral possessions, gives you a good idea of its inmate. She is very old, and apparently very poor; yet she never appears to want, and with all the noble but mistaken pride of high lineage, she would starve rather than accept assistance from anyone not of her own kindred. Her age, her poverty, her loneliness, and something certainly mysterious in her manners and habits, have gained her the reputation of a witch throughout the neighbourhood. When I was quite a child, I found her one morning stretched in a fit, by a well near her house, where I suppose she had gone to draw water. I was fortunate enough to procure assistance in removing her to her own home, where she soon recovered, and ever since that time she has regarded me as an acquaintance, though she is averse to frequent visits, and will never permit me to contribute to her scanty comforts. Today I visited her for the first time since many weeks, but every time I see her she leaves upon my mind a remarkable and I may almost say a fearful impression.'

I was just going to ask some further questions, for I felt deeply interested in what I had just heard from Miss St Aubyn, when to my vexation that provoking Miss P— came up to us and said, 'Dear Mr Glenallan, now it was so good to stay, because I wished it. Don't be vain at my wishing it, for I am going to tell you why I did. You have read, of course, Scott's beautiful poem of "Rokeby". Well, I am making some drawings descriptive of the most striking scenes in it, but I never can draw figures out of my own head. I must have a model, and I want to paint Bertram and Redmond. Well, I have been everywhere and looked at everybody to find an appropriate model, and all to no purpose, but when I first saw you, I said to myself, "Oh, he will just do for Bertram," and so, ... la, thank you, that look is just the thing. Pray keep so. Now don't move a muscle till I get my pencil. Dear, how provoking, if you ain't laughing! Well now, since I saw you talking and laughing so cheerfully with Miss St Aubyn, I thought you would do for Redmond too, so will you let me have your profile for Bertram, and your front face for Redmond? Thank you! I knew you would. I feared at first it might be rude to ask you, but –

Despair
Made us dare,

and I have tried everywhere. First I thought Lord C— would do, but he is so very pale and thin, and then I thought of Mr M—, but he is so very red and fat, and then I looked at Colonel B.-E—, but he wears his collars so high that I could see nothing but his nose and eyes, and if I was to take them with that immensity of black hair round them, people would think I had drawn an owl in an ivy bush. Well, you will do very well. With a little management, that is. You must throw your hair off your forehead, and take off your neckcloth for Redmond, and ... la, if here ain't Lady St Aubyn coming to ask me to sing. What *shall* I sing? "Young Lochinvar" or "When in death I shall calm recline"?'

I stayed a week at 'Rose Cliff', and that time was sufficient to attach my heart to Ellen St Aubyn by the finest and firmest ties of love. She was, indeed, all that was fitted to command the worship of a youthful and ardent enthusiast. Her face, her figure, her temper, her heart, – all were formed in the perfect purity of female loveliness.

## VI

It was in the middle of the day that I took leave of 'Rose Cliff'.

The morning had been wet, but the weather had cleared up by noon, though dark clouds in the distant horizon foreboded a return of storm before night. One of my servants had come with my horses from Castle Tyrone, but I had sent him on before me. Lovers know how sweet is the charm of a solitary ride when solitude is peopled with delicious hopes and remembrances that convert it into a paradise. I had not ridden more than three or four miles upon my way when a very heavy shower coming on drove me for refuge to a neighbouring farmhouse. Here I stayed so long that the evening was already far advanced before I recommenced my journey; but the rain had ceased, and the way was too short to make the lateness of the hour a cause of any inconvenience. I was little more than seven miles from home, when my course was crossed and again stopped by a stream which the recent rain had so swollen as to render it perfectly impassable. I knew of a different road, but it was much longer and rather intricate, and the increasing darkness made me very doubtful whether I should succeed in tracing it out. However, there was no alternative. I must proceed or recede, and of course I chose the former. I had gone some distance when the road branched off in three directions, and I left the choice between them to the discretion of my horse. The event proved how mistaken is the notion entertained by some people about the superior sagacity of those animals. Although I put my horse to his fastest speed, the night came upon me, still completely ignorant of my course, and evidently no nearer home than before. Suddenly I heard a noise behind me, and two horsemen dashed by me, without heeding or answering my loud inquiries as to time and place. I felt all my Irish blood boiling in a moment, and resolving to have some more courteous response from these strangers I galloped after them as fast as my horse's weariness would permit.

They had not gone above a hundred yards before they abruptly turned down a narrow lane, the winding of which completely hid them from sight; and while I was deliberating whether I should follow them, down a road evidently out of my way home, I saw a light which, from its bright and steady beam appeared to proceed from some house, about a mile distant. There I am sure, thought I, of finding either a guide or a lodging, with perhaps the chance of catching those ungallant gentry into the bargain. So, keeping my eye upon the light, and my horse still at a rapid pace, I reached in about ten minutes the door of a small house. The sign-board, hanging over it, indicated that the place was meant for the entertainment of man and beast. I had a faint idea of having seen it before, in my rides and walks, but I took short time to examine its exterior. The door was fast. I could, however, distinctly hear low voices within, but my loud knock was only answered by an instantaneous and profound silence. I twice repeated it without any other result. My third effort was answered by a voice which asked, 'Who is there?'

'I want,' said I, 'a guide and a lodging; open the door immediately.'

Another silence was followed by a gruff command to go away, and not to disturb honest men, at that time of night.

'Hark you,' said I, 'this house is a public one, for the reception of strangers, and I know there are some in it at this moment. Open the door therefore, or refuse at your peril.'

Another voice now replied with a deep curse, and a third added,

'Let him come in and take the consequences.'

'No,' cried the one who has first spoken, 'he shall not come in.'

Then I cried, 'I will break open the door.' And suiting the action to the word, I placed my shoulder against it with some force.

It immediately gave way. There was a narrow passage between the threshold and the room whence the voices had proceeded.

Immediately on my entrance, a man strode out before the door of this room, and eyed me with a menacing attitude.

'Are you,' said I, quietly, 'the master of the house? If so, I will trouble you to take care of my horse.'

There was an appearance of surprise in the man's countenance. Of this I immediately took advantage, and gently putting him aside, I walked into the room.

I must own that I repented of my temerity on the first view of its interior. In the centre of the apartment there was a large oaken table, around which were seated about twelve or fourteen men. The greater number of them were wrapped up in large cloaks, which, with the addition of slouched hats and muffling handkerchiefs, effectually concealed each man's person. At the head of the table stood, in an angry attitude, one man more closely disguised than the rest, for he wore a black mask; and by his right side sat a woman of advanced age. Her features were the most strikingly commanding I ever saw, and her style of dress, which was somewhat in the Moorish fashion, enhanced their imposing effect. The table was spread with papers, which appeared to have been thrown together in great haste and disorder, probably at the moment of my unexpected intrusion; and before each man was placed a brace of pistols, ready cocked, and a drawn sword.

There was a momentary pause. But the dark disguises of the forms around me, the weapons before them, and the lateness of the hour fully proclaimed the unlawful character of their meeting. I felt a strong inclination to retreat from a house where I was evidently no welcome comer. Whether this design appeared in my looks or motion, I cannot say; but, on a sign from him who appeared to be the chief in this unhallowed assembly, a man rose from the table, advanced to the door, bolted and locked it, and quietly returning to his place, laid the key beside his pistols. This I looked upon as a very unfavourable omen; but, resolved, if possible, not to betray my alarm, I turned to the large turf fire, and made some remark on the coldness of the night.

'Was the weather,' said the man at the head of the table, 'the only cause of your trespass upon our society?'

'Sir,' said I, 'if I have intruded upon you and the company

of these gentlemen, you will, I trust, excuse me, and believe that my motive was really and solely the wish I expressed before I entered, to obtain a guide to the nearest town. If I am not mistaken, this house is intended to receive all who seek its shelter, but as I cannot conceive that anyone among you is the landlord, will you allow me to look for him, and accept my repeated apologies for having so unintentionally disturbed you? Sir,' I added (turning to the man who had secured the door), 'will you have the goodness to let me through?' And so saying, I walked, with a sort of despair, to the entrance.

'Stay,' cried the chief in a voice of thunder, and pointing one of his pistols towards me, 'if you move one foot further, your blood be on your own head.'

I felt my indignation rise, and not caring to suppress it, 'By what right,' I cried, 'will you or any man detain me? If, as you say, I have intruded on your company, can you with any reason object to my withdrawing from it?'

Before the chief could reply another man rose suddenly from the table. 'Stranger,' said he, 'look around you. Is not one glance sufficient to convince you that you are among those to whom concealment is necessary, and do you think that we will permit you, not only to endanger our lives, but also imperil the salvation of our country? No! I repeat it, no; it is not our lives that we regard, and as for myself, I scorn this vain meanness, of meeting in darkness and disguise, to concert and execute schemes for so noble a purpose as the liberation of our country. Know us for men in whose ears the groans of Ireland have not fallen in vain. In silence we have seen our constitution insidiously attacked and betrayed. In silence we have submitted to the laws and commands of a tyrannical Government, which grinds us to the dust, while it mocks us with the pretence of friendship and union. In silence we have heard our religion traduced, and seen our nobles robbed of their rights, whilst yet meanly crouching at the court of their conqueror. In the senate of a land not ours, we have no voice to complain, no force to cry for justice. Whilst our rulers boast of tolerance, we are crushed beneath the weight of their bigotry. More than victorious Rome ever imposed upon our tyrants they have inflicted upon us, and all this we have borne, writhing but unresisting. But endurance is exhausted; we can no longer sit helpless in our ruined homes, whilst our dependents, our parents, our wives, our children, are daily and hourly sinking around us, beneath the horrors of famine. They ask us for bread and we have it not to give them; yet though they are perishing beneath our eyes, we will no longer uplift, in the vanity of supplication to our oppressors, hands to which the sword can alone restore the liberties we have lost, and the lives we are losing. There is not one of us here assembled who has not sworn an oath which, if maintained, will liberate his land, but if broken turn against the bosom of its betrayer the swords of his comrades. There is not one of us whose life is not consecrated to the freedom of his country, not one of us who is not ready to shed his blood in that sacred cause. But think not, stranger, that our strength is but the frenzied paroxysm of despair. It is a deeply established and elaborately organized power. At the slightest sign from each one of the men before you, as many thousands are prepared to flock to the standard of Ireland, and when that standard is unfurled, there is not throughout the whole people of this land an honest man whose name will not be enrolled in the ranks that follow it. Our councils are secret, but our cause is sacred. It is sacred because God is the God of mercy and justice, and for justice and for mercy we contend. Yes, although now we assemble in darkness and disguise, ere long the sun of a reviving nation will rise upon the hosts that are gathering in the watches of the night, and the clouds that still obscure its brightness shall be scattered upon the wings of the morning. Such, stranger, are the men in whose presence you stand, and with their fate linked the fate of Ireland. Judge, then, whether we can suffer you to leave us at the risk of our destruction.'

'No, let him die,' shouted the chief. 'Let him die,' echoed the voice of every man in the room, and their swords gleamed in the dim light of it.

'Hear me,' I cried, 'hear me first, and then murder me if you will, for I am in your power.'

'Hear him,' said the man, who a few moments before had turned their wrath against me. And at his word every sound died away into silence.

(End of the manuscript of *Glenallan* – Editor's note.)

# The Tale of the Mysterious Mirror

## Sir Walter Scott

## (1771–1832)

By the time we reach the late 1820s we find a most distinctive trend making itself evident in the Gothic story – it has become even more strongly historical in flavour. And if we pursue our enquiries into the reason for this the cause can be laid almost entirely to the influence of one man, Sir Walter Scott, who, with his Waverley novels, gave literature some of its brightest gems.

The position of Scott and his work is assured and it is therefore interesting to find that Gothic novels and the German romantic writers were among his earliest influences. He was also a friend of Matthew Lewis and indeed contributed to his *Tales of Wonder* in 1801. Eventually, though, he did become disillusioned with the genre 'because the wonders put each other out of countenance' but not before he had translated a number of the popular German stories and composed several tales of his own which are clearly to be categorized as Gothic.

The life of Walter Scott, his early struggles against ill-health and the frustrating years as a law clerk, has, along with the later triumphs, been so adequately documented as to need no more than passing mention here. The financial difficulties which so blighted his fortunes are also to be regretted as they undoubtedly caused him to embark on projects which were not to his taste and to the detriment of his reputation. It is nonetheless remarkable that he should have written so much that is both literate and entertaining.

While, as I have intimated, Scott in time fell out of love with the Gothic story, he did retain a healthy regard for the ghost tale and even recorded having seen an apparition one night when walking home in the twilight. A number of his novels also contained supernatural episodes, most of which have been extracted and anthologized with some regularity. Of all his self-contained short terror stories, *The Tale of the Mysterious Mirror* (or *My Aunt Margaret's Mirror* as it first appeared in *Keepsake* magazine in 1828) is perhaps the least known and certainly the only one to depend on the power of magic. It had apparently been related to Scott as a boy by his great aunt, an extraordinary old spinster who delighted in reading alone in her chamber by the light of a candle fixed in a human skull! The old lady also insisted that the story was true and had happened to Scott's great-grandmother.

The poet Alfred, Lord Tennyson considered *The Tale of the Mysterious Mirror* as 'the finest of all ghost or magical stories' and in writing of Scott's contribution to the Gothic genre, Eino Railo summarized, 'He adopted the whole world of Walpole, Mrs Radcliffe and Lewis, and with bounteous hand proceeded to enrich it from his own treasures of folklore and history.'

# I

You are fond (said my aunt) of sketches of the society which has passed away. I wish I could describe to you Sir Philip Forester, the 'chartered libertine' of Scottish good company, about the end of the last century. I never saw him indeed; but my mother's traditions were full of his wit, gallantry, and dissipation. This gay knight flourished about the end of the seventeenth and beginning of the eighteenth century. He was the Sir Charles Easy and the Lovelace of his day and country: renowned for the number of duels he had fought, and the successful intrigues which he had carried on. The supremacy which he had attained in the fashionable world was absolute; and when we combine it with one or two anecdotes, for which, 'if laws were made for every degree,' he ought certainly to have been hanged, the popularity of such a person really serves to show, either that the present times are much more decent, if not more virtuous, than they formerly were; or that high breeding then was of more difficult attainment than that which is now so called; and, consequently, entitled the successful professor to a proportionable degree of plenary indulgences and privileges. No beau of this day could have borne out so ugly a story as that of Pretty Peggy Grindstone, the miller's daughter at Sillermills – it had well-nigh made work for the Lord Advocate. But it hurt Sir Philip Forester no more than the hail hurts the hearthstone. He was as well received in society as ever, and dined with the Duke of A – the day the poor girl was buried. She died of heartbreak. But that has nothing to do with my story.

Now, you must listen to a single word upon kith, kin, and ally; I promise you I will not be prolix. But it is necessary to the authenticity of my legend that you should know that Sir Philip Forester, with his handsome person, elegant accomplishments, and fashionable manners, married the younger Miss Falconer of King's Copland. The elder sister of this lady had previously become the wife of my grandfather, Sir Geoffrey Bothwell, and brought into our family a good fortune. Miss Jemima, or Miss Jemmie Falconer, as she was usually called, had also about ten thousand pounds sterling – then thought a very handsome portion indeed.

The two sisters were extremely different, though each had their admirers while they remained single. Lady Bothwell had some touch of the old King's Copland blood about her. She was bold, though not to the degree of audacity; ambitious, and desirous to raise her house and family; and was, as has been said, a considerable spur to my grandfather, who was otherwise an indolent man; but whom, unless he has been slandered, his lady's influence involved in some political matters which had been more wisely let alone. She was a woman of high principle, however, and masculine good sense, as some of her letters testify, which are still in my wainscot cabinet.

Jemmie Falconer was the reverse of her sister in every respect. Her understanding did not reach above the ordinary pitch, if, indeed, she could be said to have attained it. Her beauty, while it lasted, consisted, in a great measure, of delicacy of complexion and regularity of features, without any peculiar force of expression. Even these charms faded under the sufferings attendant on an ill-sorted match. She was passionately attached to her husband, by whom she was treated with a callous, yet polite indifference, which, to one whose heart was as tender as her judgement was weak, was more painful perhaps than absolute ill-usage. Sir Philip was a voluptuary, that is, a completely selfish egotist, whose disposition and character resembled the rapier he wore, polished, keen, and brilliant, but inflexible and unpitying. As he observed carefully all the usual forms towards his lady, he had the art to deprive her even of the compassion of the world; and useless and unavailing as that may be while actually possessed by the sufferer, it is, to a mind like Lady Forester's, most painful to know she has it not.

The tattle of society did its best to place the peccant husband above the suffering wife. Some called her a poor spiritless thing, and declared that, with a little of her sister's spirit, she might have brought to reason any Sir Philip whatsoever, were it the termagant Falconbridge himself. But the greater part of their acquaintance affected candour, and saw faults on both sides; though, in fact, there only existed the oppressor and the oppressed. The tone of such critics was – 'To be sure, no one will justify Sir Philip Forester, but then we all know Sir Philip, and Jemmie Falconer might have known what she had to expect from the beginning. – What made her set her cap at Sir Philip? – He would never have looked at her if she had not thrown herself at his head, with her poor ten thousand pounds. I am sure, if it is money he wanted, she spoiled his market. I know where Sir Philip could have done much better. – And then, if she *would* have the man, could not she try to make him more comfortable at home, and have his friends oftener, and not plague him with the squalling children, and take care all was handsome and in good style about the house? I declare I think Sir Philip would have made a very domestic man, with a woman who knew how to manage him.'

Now these fair critics, in raising their profound edifice of domestic felicity, did not recollect that the corner-stone was wanting; and that to receive good company with good cheer, the means of the banquet ought to have been furnished by Sir Philip; whose income (dilapidated as it was) was not equal to the display of hospitality required, and, at the same time, to the supply of the good knight's *menus plaisirs*. So, in spite of all that was so sagely suggested by female friends, Sir Philip carried his good-humour everywhere abroad, and left at home a solitary mansion and a pining spouse.

At length, inconvenienced in his money affairs, and tired even of the short time which he spent in his own dull house, Sir Philip Forester determined to take a trip to the Continent, in the capacity of a volunteer. It was then common for men of fashion to do so; and our knight perhaps was of opinion that a touch of the military character, just enough to exalt, but not render pedantic, his qualities as a *beau garçon*, was necessary to maintain possession of the elevated situation which he held in the ranks of fashion.

Sir Philip's resolution threw his wife into agonies of terror, by which the worthy baronet was so much annoyed that, contray to his wont, he took some trouble to soothe her apprehensions; and once more brought her to shed tears, in which sorrow was not altogether unmingled with pleasure. Lady Bothwell asked, as a favour, Sir Philip's permission to receive her sister and her family into her own house during his absence on the Continent. Sir Philip readily assented to a proposition which saved expense, silenced the foolish people who might have talked of a deserted wife and family, and gratified Lady Bothwell, for whom he felt some respect, as for one who often spoke to him, always with freedom, and sometimes with severity, without being deterred either by his raillery, or the prestige of his reputation.

A day or two before Sir Philip's departure, Lady Bothwell took the liberty of asking him, in her sister's presence, the direct question, which his timid wife had often desired, but never ventured to put to him.

'Pray Sir Philip what route do you take when you reach the Continent?'

'I go from Leith to Helvoet by a packet with advices.'

'That I comprehend perfectly,' said Lady Bothwell dryly; 'but you do not mean to remain long at Helvoet I presume, and I should like to know what is your next object?'

'You ask me, my dear lady,' answered Sir Philip, 'a question which I have not dared to ask myself. The answer depends on the fate of war. I shall, of course, go to headquarters, wherever they may happen to be for the time; deliver my letters of introduction; learn as much of the noble art of war as may suffice a poor interloping amateur; and then take a glance at the sort of thing which we read so much in the *Gazette*.'

'And I trust, Sir Philip,' said Lady Bothwell, 'that you will remember that you are a husband and a father; and that though you think fit to indulge this military fancy, you will not let it hurry you into dangers which it is certainly unnecessary for any save professional persons to encounter?'

'Lady Bothwell does me too much honour,' replied the adventurous knight, 'in regarding such a circumstance with the slightest interest. But to soothe your flattering anxiety, I trust your ladyship will recollect that I cannot expose to hazard the venerable and paternal character which you so obligingly recommend to my protection, without putting in some peril an honest fellow called Philip Forester, with whom I have kept company for thirty years, and with whom, though some folk consider him a coxcomb, I have not the least desire to part.'

'Well, Sir Philip, you are the best judge of your own affairs; I have little right to interfere – you are not my husband.'

'God forbid!' – said Sir Philip hastily; instantly adding, however, 'God forbid that I should deprive my friend Sir Geoffrey of so inestimable a treasure.'

'But you are my sister's husband,' replied the lady; 'and I suppose you are aware of her present distress of mind –'

'If hearing of nothing else from morning to night can make me aware of it,' said Sir Philip, 'I should know something of the matter.'

'I do not pretend to reply to your wit, Sir Philip,' answered Lady Bothwell; 'but you must be sensible that all this distress is on account of apprehensions for your personal safety.'

'In that case, I am surprised that Lady Bothwell, at least, should give herself so much trouble upon so insignificant a subject.'

'My sister's interest may account for my being anxious to learn something of Sir Philip Forester's motions; about which otherwise, I know, he would not wish me to concern myself. I have a brother's safety, too, to be anxious for.'

'You mean Major Falconer, your brother by the mother's side: – What can he possibly have to do with our present agreeable conversation?'

'You have had words together, Sir Philip,' said Lady Bothwell.

'Naturally; we are connections,' replied Sir Philip, 'and as such have always had the usual intercourse.'

'That is an evasion of the subject,' answered the lady. 'By words, I mean angry words, on the subject of your usage of your wife.'

'If,' replied Sir Philip Forester, 'you suppose Major Falconer simple enough to intrude his advice upon me, Lady Bothwell, in my domestic matters, you are indeed warranted in believing that I might possibly be so far displeased with the interference as to request him to reserve his advice till it was asked.'

'And, being on these terms, you are going to join the very army in which my brother Falconer is now serving?'

'No man knows the path of honour better than Major Falconer,' said Sir Philip. 'An aspirant after fame, like me, cannot choose a better guide than his footsteps.'

Lady Bothwell rose and went to the window, the tears gushing from her eyes.

'And this heartless raillery,' she said, 'is all the consideration that is to be given to our apprehensions of a quarrel which may bring on the most terrible consequences? Good God! of what can men's hearts be made, who can thus dally with the agony of others?'

Sir Philip Forester was moved; he laid aside the mocking tone in which he had hitherto spoken.

'Dear Lady Bothwell,' he said, taking her reluctant hand, 'we are both wrong: – you are too deeply serious; I, perhaps, too little so. The dispute I had with Major Falconer was of no earthly consequence. Had anything occurred betwixt us that ought to have been settled *par voie du fait*, as we say in France, neither of us are persons that are likely to postpone such a meeting. Permit me to say that were it generally known that you or my Lady Forester are apprehensive of such a catastrophe, it might be the very means of bringing about what would not otherwise be likely to happen. I know your good sense, Lady Bothwell, and that you will understand me when I say that really my affairs require my absence for some months; – this Jemima cannot understand; it is a perpetual recurrence of questions, why can you not do this, or that, or the third thing; and when you have proved to her that her expedients are totally ineffectual you have just to begin the whole round again. Now, do you tell her, dear Lady Bothwell, that *you* are satisfied. She is, you must confess, one of those persons with whom authority goes further than reasoning. Do but repose a little confidence in me, and you shall see how amply I will repay it.'

Lady Bothwell shook her head, as one but half satisfied. 'How difficult it is to extend confidence, when the basis on which it ought to rest has been so much shaken! But I will do my best to make Jemima easy; and further, I can only say that for keeping your present purpose, I hold you responsible both to God and man.'

'Do not fear that I will deceive you,' said Sir Philip; 'the safest conveyance to me will be through the general post-office, Helvoetsluys, where I will take care to leave orders for forwarding my letters. As for Falconer, our only encounter will be over a bottle of Burgundy! so make yourself perfectly easy on his score.'

Lady Bothwell could *not* make herself easy; yet she was sensible that her sister hurt her own cause by *taking on*, as the maid-servants call it, too vehemently; and by showing before every stranger, by manner and sometimes by words also, a dissatisfaction with her husband's journey, that was sure to come to his ears and equally certain to displease him. But there was no help for this domestic dissension, which ended only with the day of separation.

I am sorry I cannot tell, with precision, the year in which Sir Philip Forester went over to Flanders; but it was one of those in which the campaign opened with extraordinary fury; and many bloody, though indecisive, skirmishes were fought between the French on the one side, and the Allies on the other. In all our modern improvements, there are none, perhaps, greater than in the accuracy and speed with which intelligence is transmitted from any scene of action to those in this country whom it may concern. During Marlborough's campaigns, the sufferings of the many who had relations in, or along with, the army, were greatly augmented by the suspense in which they were detained for weeks, after they had heard of bloody battles in which, in all probability, those for whom their bosoms throbbed with anxiety had been personally engaged. Amongst those who were most agonized by this state of uncertainty, was the – I had almost said deserted – wife of the gay Sir Philip Forester. A single letter had informed her of his arrival on the Continent – no others were received. One notice occurred in the newspapers, in which Volunteer Sir Philip Forester was mentioned as having been entrusted with a dangerous reconnoissance, which he had executed with the greatest courage, dexterity, and intelligence, and received the thanks of the commanding officer. The sense of his having acquired distinction brought a momentary glow into the lady's pale cheek; but it was instantly lost in ashen whiteness at the recollection of his danger. After this, they had no news whatever, neither from Sir Philip, nor even from their brother Falconer. The case of Lady Forester was not indeed different from that of hundreds in the same situation; but a feeble mind is necessarily an irritable one, and the suspense which some bear with constitutional indifference or philosophical resignation, and some with a disposition to believe and hope the best, was intolerable to Lady Forester, at once solitary and sensitive, low-spirited, and devoid of strength of mind, whether natural or acquired.

## II

As she received no further news of Sir Philip, whether directly or indirectly, his unfortunate lady began now to feel a sort of consolation, even in those careless habits which had so often given her pain. 'He is so thoughtless,' she repeated a hundred times a day to her sister, 'he never writes when things are going on smoothly; it is his way: had anything happened he would have informed us.'

Lady Bothwell listened to her sister without attempting to console her. Probably she might be of opinion that even the worst intelligence which could be received from Flanders might not be without some touch of consolation; and that the Dowager Lady Forester, if so she was doomed to be called, might have a source of happiness unknown to the wife of the gayest and finest gentleman in Scotland. This conviction became stronger as they learned from inquiries made at head-quarters, that Sir Philip was no longer with the army; though whether he had been taken or slain in some of those skirmishes which were perpetually occurring, and in which he loved to distinguish himself, or whether he had, for some unknown reason or capricious change of mind, voluntarily left the service, none of his countrymen in the camp of the Allies could form even a conjecture. Meantime his creditors at home became clamorous, entered into possession of his property, and threatened his person, should he be rash enough to return to Scotland. These additional disadvantages aggravated Lady Bothwell's displeasure against the fugitive husband; while her sister saw nothing in any of them, save what tended to increase her grief for the absence of him whom her imagination now represented, — as it had before marriage — gallant, gay, and affectionate.

About this period there appeared in Edinburgh a man of singular appearance and pretensions. He was commonly called the Paduan doctor, from having received his education at that famous university. He was supposed to possess some rare receipts in medicine, with which, it was affirmed, he had wrought remarkable cures. But though, on the one hand, the physicians of Edinburgh termed him an empiric, there were many persons, and among them some of the clergy, who, while they admitted the truth of the cures and the force of his remedies, alleged that Doctor Baptista Damiotti made use of charms and unlawful arts in order to obtain success in his practice. The resorting to him was even solemnly preached against, as a seeking of health from idols, and a trusting to the help which was to come from Egypt. But the protection which the Paduan doctor received from some friends of interest and consequence, enabled him to set these imputations at defiance, and to assume, even in the city of Edinburgh, famed as it was for abhorrence of witches and necromancers, the dangerous character of an expounder of futurity. It was at length rumoured, that for a certain gratification, which, of course, was not an inconsiderable one, Doctor Baptista Damiotti could tell the fate of the absent friends, and show his visitors the personal form of their absent friends, and the action in which they were engaged at the moment. This rumour came to the ears of Lady Forester, who had reached that pitch of mental agony in which the sufferer will do anything, or endure anything, that suspense may be converted into certainty.

Gentle and timid in most cases, her state of mind made her equally obstinate and reckless, and it was with no small surprise and alarm that her sister, Lady Bothwell, heard her express a resolution to visit this man of art, and learn from him the fate of her husband. Lady Bothwell remonstrated on the improbability that such pretensions as those of this foreigner could be founded in anything but imposture.

'I care not,' said the deserted wife, 'what degree of ridicule I may incur; if there be any one chance out of a hundred that I may obtain some certainty of my husband's fate, I would not miss that chance for whatever else the world can offer me.'

Lady Bothwell next urged the unlawfulness of resorting to such sources of forbidden knowledge.

'Sister,' replied the sufferer, 'he who is dying of thirst cannot refrain from drinking even poisoned water. She who suffers under suspense must seek information, even were the powers which offer it unhallowed and infernal. I go to learn my fate alone; and this very evening will I know it: the sun that rises tomorrow shall find me, if not more happy, at least more resigned.'

'Sister,' said Lady Bothwell, 'if you are determined upon this wild step, you shall not go alone. If this man be an impostor, you may be too much agitated by your feelings to detect his villainy. If, which I cannot believe, there be any truth in what he pretends, you shall not be exposed alone to a communication of so extraordinary a nature. I will go with you, if indeed you determine to go. But yet reconsider your project, and renounce inquiries which cannot be prosecuted without guilt, and perhaps without danger.'

Lady Forester threw herself into her sister's arms, and, clasping her to her bosom, thanked her a hundred times for the offer of her company; while she declined with a melancholy gesture the friendly advice with which it was accompanied.

When the hour of twilight arrived, – which was the period when the Paduan doctor was understood to receive the visits of those who came to consult with him, – the two ladies left their apartments in the Canongate of Edinburgh, having their dress arranged like that of women of an inferior description, and their plaids disposed around their faces as they were worn by the same class; for, in those days of aristocracy, the quality of the wearer was generally indicated by the manner in which her plaid was disposed, as well as by the fineness of its texture. It was Lady Bothwell who had suggested this species of disguise, partly to avoid observation as they should go to the conjurer's house, and partly in order to make trial of his penetration by appearing before him in a feigned character. Lady Forester's servant, of tried fidelity, had been employed by her to propitiate the doctor by a suitable fee, and a story intimating that a soldier's wife desired to know the fate of her husband; a subject upon which, in all probability, the sage was very frequently consulted.

To the last moment, when the palace clock struck eight, Lady Bothwell earnestly watched her sister, in hopes that she might retreat from her rash undertaking; but as mildness, and even timidity, is capable at times of vehement and fixed purposes, she found Lady Forester resolutely unmoved and determined when the moment of departure arrived. Ill satisfied with the expedition, but determined not to leave her sister at such a crisis, Lady Bothwell accompanied Lady Forester through more than one obscure street and lane, the servant walking before, and acting as their guide. At length he suddenly turned into a narrow court, and knocked at an arched door, which seemed to belong to a building of some antiquity. It opened, though no one appeared to act as porter; and the servant, stepping aside from the entrance, motioned the ladies to enter. They had no sooner done so, than it shut, and excluded their guide. The two ladies found themselves in a small vestibule, illuminated by a dim lamp, and having, when the door was closed, no communication with the external light of air. The door of an inner apartment, partly open, was at the further side of the vestibule.

'We must not hesitate now, Jemima,' said Lady Bothwell, and walked forwards into the inner room, where, surrounded by books, maps, philosophical utensils, and other implements of peculiar shape and appearance, they found the man of art.

There was nothing very peculiar in the Italian's appearance. He had the dark complexion and marked features of his country, seemed about fifty years old, and was handsomely, but plainly, dressed in a full suit of black clothes, which was then the universal costume of the medical profession. Large waxlights, in silver sconces, illuminated the apartment, which was reasonably furnished. He rose as the ladies entered; and, notwithstanding the inferiority of their dress, received them with the marked respect due to their quality, and which foreigners are usually punctilious in rendering to those to whom such honours are due.

Lady Bothwell endeavoured to maintain her proposed incognito; and, as the doctor ushered them to the upper end of the room, made a motion declining his courtesy, as unfitted for their condition. 'We are poor people, sir,' she said; 'only my sister's distress has brought us to consult your worship whether —'

He smiled as he interrupted her — 'I am aware, madam, of your sister's distress, and its cause; I am aware, also, that I am honoured with a visit from two ladies of the highest consideration — Lady Bothwell and Lady Forester. If I could not distinguish them from the class of society which their present dress would indicate, there would be small possibility of my being able to gratify them by giving the information which they come to seek.'

'I can easily understand —' said Lady Bothwell.

'Pardon my boldness to interrupt you, milady,' cried the Italian; 'your ladyship was about to say that you could easily understand that I had got possession of your names by means of your domestic. But in thinking so, you do injustice to the fidelity of your servant, and, I may add, to the skill of one who is also not less your humble servant — Baptista Damiotti.'

'I have no intention to do either, sir,' said Lady Bothwell, maintaining a tone of composure, though somewhat surprised, 'but the situation is something new to me. If you knew who we are, you also know, sir, what brought us here.'

'Curiosity to know the fate of a Scottish gentleman of rank, now, or lately upon the Continent,' answered the seer; 'his name is Il Cavaliero Philippo Forester; a gentleman who has the honour to be husband to this lady, and, with your ladyship's permission for using plain language, the misfortune not to value as it deserves that inestimable advantage.'

Lady Forester sighed deeply, and Lady Bothwell replied:

'Since you know our object without our telling it, the only question that remains is, whether you have the power to relieve my sister's anxiety?'

'I have, madam,' answered the Paduan scholar; 'but there is still a previous inquiry. Have you the courage to behold with your own eyes what the Cavaliero Philippo Forester is now doing? or will you take it on my report?'

'That question my sister must answer for herself,' said Lady Bothwell.

'With my own eyes will I endure to see whatever you have power to show me,' said Lady Forester, with the same determined spirit which had stimulated her since her resolution was taken upon this subject.

'There maybe danger in it.'

'If gold can compensate the risk,' said Lady Forester, taking out her purse.

'I do not such things for the purpose of gain,' answered the foreigner. 'I dare not turn my art to such a purpose. If I take the gold of the wealthy, it is but to bestow it on the poor; nor do I ever accept more than the sum I have already received from your servant. Put up your purse, madam; an adept needs not your gold.'

Lady Bothwell, considering this rejection of her sister's offer as a mere trick of an empiric, to induce her to press a larger sum upon him, and willing that the scene should be commenced and ended, offered some gold in turn, observing that it was only to enlarge the sphere of his charity.

'Let Lady Bothwell enlarge the sphere of her own charity,' said the Paduan, 'not merely in giving of alms, in which I know she is not deficient, but in judging the character of others; and let her oblige Baptista Damiotti by believing him honest, till she shall discover him to be a knave. Do not be surprised, madam, if I speak in answer to your thoughts rather than your expressions, and tell me once more whether you have courage to look on what I am prepared to show?'

'I own, sir,' said Lady Bothwell, 'that your words strike me with some sense of fear; but whatever my sister desires to witness, I will not shrink from witnessing along with her.'

'Nay, the danger only consists in the risk of your resolution failing you. The sight can only last for the space of seven minutes; and should you interrupt the vision by speaking a single word, not only would the charm be broken, but some danger might result to the spectators. But if you can remain steadily silent for the seven minutes, your curiosity will be gratified without the slightest risk; and for this I will engage my honour.'

Internally Lady Bothwell thought the security was but an indifferent one; but she suppressed the suspicion, as if she had believed that the adept, whose dark features wore a half-formed smile, could in reality read even her most secret reflections. A solemn pause then ensued, until Lady Forester gathered courage enough to reply to the physician, as he termed himself, that she would abide with firmness and silence the sight which he had promised to exhibit to them. Upon this, he made them a low obeisance, and saying he went to prepare matters to meet their wish, left the apartment. The two sisters, hand in hand, as if seeking by that close union to divert any danger which might threaten them, sat down on two seats in immediate contact with each other: Jemima seeking support in the manly and habitual courage of Lady Bothwell; and she, on the other hand, more agitated than she had expected, endeavouring to fortify herself by the desperate resolution which circumstances had forced her sister to assume. The one perhaps said to herself, that her sister never feared anything; and the other might reflect, that what so feeble a minded woman as Jemima did not fear, could not properly be a subject of apprehension to a person of firmness and resolution like herself.

In a few moments the thoughts of both were diverted from their own situation by a strain of music so singularly sweet and solemn, that, while it seemed calculated to avert or dispel any feeling unconnected with its harmony, increased, at the same time, the solemn excitation which the preceding interview was calculated to produce. The music was that of some instrument with which they were unacquainted; but circumstances afterwards led my ancestress to believe that it was that of the harmonica, which she heard at a much later period in life.

When these heaven-born sounds had ceased, a door opened in the upper end of the apartment, and they saw Damiotti, standing at the head of two or three steps, sign to them to advance. His dress was so different from that which he had worn a few minutes before, that they could hardly recognize him; and the deadly paleness of his countenance, and a certain stern rigidity of muscles, like that of one whose mind is made up to some strange and daring action, had totally changed the somewhat sarcastic expression with which he had previously regarded them both, and particularly Lady Bothwell. He was barefooted, excepting a species of sandals in the antique fashion; his legs were naked beneath the knees; above them he wore hose, and a doublet of dark crimson silk close to his body; and over that a flowing loose robe, something resembling a surplice, of snow-white line; his throat and neck were uncovered, and his long, straight hair was carefully combed down at full length.

As the ladies approached at his bidding, he showed no gesture of that ceremonious courtesy of which he had been formerly
lavish. On the contrary, he made the signal of advance with an
air of command; and when, arm in arm, and with insecure steps,
the sisters approached the spot where he stood, it was with a
warning frown that he pressed his finger to his lips, as if reiter-
ating his condition of absolute silence, while, stalking before
them, he led the way into the next apartment.

This was a large room, hung with black, as if for a funeral.
At the upper end was a table, or rather a species of altar, covered
with the same lugubrious colour, on which lay divers objects
resembling the usual implements of sorcery. These objects were
not indeed visible as they advanced into the apartment; for the
light which displayed them, being only that of two expiring
lamps, was extremely faint. The master – to use the Italian
phrase for persons of this description – approached the upper
end of the room with a genuflexion like that of a Catholic to the
crucifix, and at the same time crossed himself. The ladies followed in silence, and arm in arm. Two or three low broad steps
led to a platform in front of the altar, or what resembled such.
Here the sage took his stand, and placed the ladies beside him,
once more earnestly repeating by signs his injunctions of silence.
The Italian then, extending his bare arm from under his linen
vestment, pointed with his forefinger to five large flambeaux,
or torches, placed on each side of the altar. They took fire suc-
cessively at the approach of his hand, or rather of his finger, and
spread a strong light through the room. By this the visitors
could discern that, on the seeming altar, were disposed two
naked swords laid crosswise; a large open book, which they conceived to be a copy of the Holy Scriptures, but in a language to
them unknown; and beside this mysterious volume was placed
a human skull. But what struck the sisters most was a very tall
and broad mirror, which occupied all the space behind the altar,
and, illuminated by the lighted torches, reflected the mysterious
articles which were laid upon it.

The master then placed himself between the two ladies, and,
pointing to the mirror, took each by the hand, without speak-

ing a syllable. They gazed intently on the polished and sable space to which he had directed their attention. Suddenly the surface assumed a new and singular appearance. It no longer simply reflected the objects placed before it, but, as if it had self-contained scenery of its own, objects began to appear within it, at first in a disorderly, indistinct, and miscellaneous manner, like form arranging itself out of chaos; at length, in distinct and defined shape and symmetry. It was thus that, after some shifting of light and darkness over the face of the wonderful glass, a long perspective of arches and columns began to arrange itself on its sides, and a vaulted roof on the upper part of it; till, after many oscillations, the whole vision gained a fixed and stationary appearance, representing the interior of a foreign church. The pillars were stately, and hung with scutcheons; the arches were lofty and magnificent; the floor was lettered with funeral inscriptions. But there were no separate shrines, no images, no display of chalice or crucifix on the altar. It was, therefore, a Protestant church upon the Continent. A clergyman, dressed in the Geneva gown and band, stood by the communion table, and, with the Bible opened before him, and his clerk awaiting in the background, seemed prepared to perform some service of the church to which he belonged.

At length there entered the middle aisle of the building a numerous party, which appeared to be a bridal one, as a lady and gentleman walked first, hand in hand, followed by a large concourse of persons of both sexes, gaily, nay richly, attired. The bride, whose features they could distinctly see, seemed not more than sixteen years old, and extremely beautiful. The bridegroom, for some seconds, moved rather with his shoulder towards them, and his face averted; but his elegance of form and step struck the sisters at once with the same apprehension. As he turned his face suddenly, it was frightfully realized, and they saw, in the gay bridegroom before them, Sir Philip Forester. His wife uttered an imperfect exclamation, at the sound of which the whole scene stirred and seemed to separate.

'I could compare it to nothing,' said Lady Bothwell, while recounting the wonderful tale, 'but to the dispersion of the reflection offered by a deep and calm pool, when a stone is suddenly cast into it, and the shadows become dissipated and broken.' The master pressed both the ladies' hands severely, as if to remind them of their promise, and of the danger which they incurred. The exclamation died away on Lady Forester's tongue, without attaining perfect utterance, and the scene in the glass, after the fluctuation of a minute, again resumed to the eye its former appearance of a real scene, existing within the mirror, as if represented in a picture, save that the figures were movable instead of being stationary.

The representation of Sir Philip Forester, now distinctly visible in form and feature, was seen to lead on towards the clergyman that beautiful girl, who advanced at once with diffidence, and with a species of affectionate pride. In the meantime, and just as the clergyman had arranged the bridal company before him, and seemed about to commence the service, another group of persons, of whom two or three were officers, entered the church. They moved, at first, forward, as though they came to witness the bridal ceremony, but suddenly one of the officers, whose back was towards the spectators, detached himself from his companions, and rushed hastily towards the marriage party, when the whole of them turned towards him, as if attracted by some exclamation which had accompanied his advance. Suddenly the intruder drew his sword; the bridegroom unsheathed his own, and made towards him; swords were also drawn by other individuals, both of the marriage party and of those who had last entered. They fell into a sort of confusion, the clergyman, and some elder and graver persons, labouring apparently to keep the peace, while the hotter spirits on both sides brandished their weapons. But now the period of brief space during which the soothsayer, as he pretended, was permitted to exhibit his art, was arrived. The fumes again mixed together, and dissolved gradually from observation; the vaults and columns of the church rolled asunder and disappeared; and the front of the mirror reflected nothing save the blazing torches, and the melancholy apparatus placed on the altar or table before it.

The doctor led the ladies, who greatly required his support, into the apartment from whence they came; where wine, essences, and other means of restoring suspended animation, had been provided during his absence. He motioned them to chairs, which they occupied in silence; Lady Forester, in particular, wringing her hands, and casting her eyes up to heaven, but without speaking a word, as if the spell had been still before her eyes.

'And what we have seen is even now acting?' said Lady Bothwell, collecting herself with difficulty.

'That,' answered Baptista Damiotti, 'I cannot justly, or with certainty, say. But it is either now acting, or has been acted, during a short space before this. It is the last remarkable transaction in which the Cavalier Forester has been engaged.'

Lady Bothwell then expressed anxiety concerning her sister, whose altered countenance, and apparent unconsciousness of what passed around her, excited her apprehensions how it might be possible to convey her home.

'I have prepared for that,' answered the adept; 'I have directed the servant to bring your equipage as near to this place as the narrowness of the street will permit. Fear not for your sister; but give her, when you return home, this composing draught, and she will be better tomorrow morning. Few,' he added, in a melancholy tone, 'leave this house as well in health as they entered it. Such being the consequence of seeking knowledge by mysterious means, I leave you to judge the condition of those who have the power of gratifying such irregular curiosity. Farewell, and forget not the potion.'

'I will give her nothing that comes from you,' said Lady Bothwell; 'I have seen enough of your art already. Perhaps you would poison us both to conceal your own necromancy. But we are persons who want neither the means of making our wrongs known, nor the assistance of friends to right them.'

'You have had no wrongs from me, madam,' said the adept. 'You sought one who is little grateful for such honour. He seeks no one, and only gives responses to those who invite and call upon him. After all, you have but learned a little sooner the evil which you must still be doomed to endure. I hear your servant's step at the door, and will detain your ladyship and Lady Forester no longer. The next packet from the Continent will explain what you have already partly witnessed. Let it not, if I may advise, pass too suddenly into your sister's hands.'

So saying, he bid Lady Bothwell good night. She went, lighted by the adept, to the vestibule, where he hastily threw a black cloak over his singular dress, and opening the door entrusted his visitors to the care of the servant. It was with difficulty that Lady Bothwell sustained her sister to the carriage, though it was only twenty steps distant. When they arrived at home, Lady Forester required medical assistance. The physician of the family attended, and shook his head on feeling her pulse.

'Here has been,' he said, 'a violent and sudden shock on the nerves. I must know how it has happened.'

Lady Bothwell admitted they had visited the conjurer, and that Lady Forester had received some bad news respecting her husband, Sir Philip.

'That rascally quack would make my fortune were he to stay in Edinburgh,' said the graduate; 'this is the seventh nervous case I have heard of his making for me, and all by effect of terror.' He next examined the composing draught Lady Bothwell had unconsciously brought in hand, tasted it, and pronounced it very germane to the matter, and what would save an application to the apothecary. He then paused, and looking at Lady Bothwell very significantly, at length added, 'I suppose I must not ask your ladyship anything about this Italian warlock's proceedings?'

'Indeed, Doctor,' answered Lady Bothwell, 'I consider what passed as confidential; and though the man may be a rogue, yet, as we were fools enough to consult him, we should, I think, be honest to keep his counsel.'

'*May* be a knave – come,' said the doctor, 'I am glad to hear your ladyship allows such a possibility in anything that comes from Italy.'

'What comes from Italy may be as good as what comes from Hanover, Doctor. But you and I will remain good friends, and that it may be so, we will say nothing of Whig and Tory.'

'Not I,' said the doctor, receiving his fee and taking his hat; 'a Carolus serves my purpose as well as a Willielmus. But I should like to know why old Lady Saint Ringan's, and all that set, go about wasting their decayed lungs in puffing this foreign fellow.'

'Aye – you had best set him down a Jesuit, as Scrub says.' On these terms they parted.

The poor patient – whose nerves, from an extraordinary state of tension, had at length become relaxed in as extraordinary a degree – continued to struggle with a sort of imbecility, the growth of superstitious terror, when the shocking tidings were brought from Holland, which fulfilled even her worst expectations.

They were sent by the celebrated Earl of Stair, and contained the melancholy event of a duel betwixt Sir Philip Forester and his wife's half-brother, Captain Falconer, of the Scotch-Dutch, as they were then called, in which the latter had been killed. The cause of quarrel rendered the incident still more shocking. It seemed that Sir Philip had left the army suddenly, in consequence of being unable to pay a very considerable sum which he had lost to another volunteer at play. He had changed his name, and taken up his residence at Rotterdam, where he had insinuated himself into the good graces of an ancient and rich burgomaster, and, by his handsome person and graceful manners, captivated the affections of his only child, a very young person, of great beauty, and the heiress of much wealth. Delighted with the specious attractions of his proposed son-in-law, the wealthy merchant – whose idea of the British character was too high to admit of his taking any precaution to acquire evidence of his condition and circumstances – gave his consent to the marriage. It was about to be celebrated in the principal church of the city, when it was interrupted by a singular occurrence.

Captain Falconer having been detached to Rotterdam to bring up a part of the brigade of Scottish auxiliaries who were in quarters there, a person of consideration in the town, to whom he had been formerly known, proposed to him for amusement to go to the high church, to see a countryman of his own married to the daughter of a wealthy burgomaster. Captain Falconer went accordingly, accompanied by his Dutch acquaintance with a party of his friends, and two or three officers of the Scotch brigade. His astonishment may be conceived when he saw his own brother-in-law, a married man, on the point of leading to the altar the innocent and beautiful creature, upon whom he was about to practise a base and unmanly deceit. He proclaimed his villainy on the spot, and the marriage was interrupted of course. But against the opinion of more thinking men, who considered Sir Philip Forester as having thrown himself out of the rank of men of honour, Captain Falconer admitted him to the privilege of such, accepted a challenge from him, and in the encounter received a mortal wound. Such are the ways of Heaven, mysterious in our eyes. Lady Forester never recovered from the shock of this dismal intelligence.

'And did this tragedy,' said I, 'take place exactly at the time when the scene in the mirror was exhibited?'

'It is hard to be obliged to maim one's story,' answered my aunt; 'but, to speak the truth, it happened some days sooner than the apparition was exhibited.'

'And so there remained a possibility,' said I, 'that by some secret and speedy communication the artist might have received early intelligence of that incident.'

'The incredulous pretended so,' replied my aunt.

'What became of the adept?' demanded I.

'Why, a warrant came down shortly afterwards to arrest him for high treason, as an agent of the Chevalier St George; and Lady Bothwell, recollecting the hints which had escaped the doctor, an ardent friend of the Protestant succession, did then call to remembrance, that this man was chiefly *prôné* among the ancient matrons of her own political persuasion. It certainly seemed probable that intelligence from the Continent, which could easily have been transmitted by an active and powerful agent, might have enabled him to prepare such a scene of phantasmagoria as she had herself witnessed. Yet there were so many difficulties in assigning a natural explanation that, to the day of her death, she remained in great doubt on the subject, and much disposed to cut the Gordian knot by admitting the existence of supernatural agency.'

'But, my dear aunt,' said I, 'what became of the man of skill?'

Oh, he was too good a fortune-teller not to be able to foresee that his own destiny would be tragical if he waited the arrival of the man with the silver greyhound upon his sleeve. He made, as we say, a moonlight flitting, and was nowhere to be seen or heard of. Some noise there was about papers or letters found in the house, but it died away, and Doctor Baptista Damiotti was soon as little talked of as Galen or Hippocrates.'

'And Sir Philip Forester,' said I, 'did he too vanish for ever from the public scene?'

'No,' replied my kind informer. 'He was heard of once more, and it was upon a remarkable occasion. It is said that we Scots, when there was such a nation in existence, have, among our full peck of virtues, one or two little barleycorns of vice. In particular, it is alleged that we rarely forgive, and never forget, any injuries received; that we used to make an idol of our resentment, as poor Lady Constance did of her grief; and are addicted, as Burns says, to "nursing our wrath to keep it warm". Lady Bothwell was not without this feeling; and, I believe, nothing whatever, scarce the restoration of the Stuart line, could have happened so delicious to her feelings as an opportunity of being revenged on Sir Philip Forester, for the deep and double injury which had deprived her of a sister and of a brother. But nothing of him was heard or known till many a year had passed away.

'At length – it was on a Fastern's E'en (Shrovetide) assembly, at which the whole fashion of Edinburgh attended, full and frequent, and when Lady Bothwell had a seat amongst the lady patronesses, that one of the attendants on the company whispered into her ear that a gentleman wished to speak with her in private.

'In private? and in an assembly-room? – he must be mad. – Tell him to call upon me tomorrow morning.'

'I said so, my lady,' answered the man; 'but he desired me to give you this paper.'

She undid the billet, which was curiously folded and sealed. It only bore the words, '*On business of life and death*,' written in a hand which she had never seen before. Suddenly it occurred to her that it might concern the safety of some of her political friends; she therefore followed the messenger to a small apartment where the refreshments were prepared, and from which the general company was excluded. She found an old man, who, at her approach, rose up and bowed profoundly. His appearance indicated a broken constitution; and his dress, though sedulously rendered conforming to the etiquette of a ballroom, was worn and tarnished, and hung in folds about his emaciated person. Lady Bothwell was about to feel for her purse, expecting to get rid of the supplicant at the expense of a little money, but some fear of a mistake arrested her purpose. She therefore gave the man leisure to explain himself.

'I have the honour to speak with the Lady Bothwell?'

'I am Lady Bothwell: allow me to say that this is no time or place for long explanations. – What are your commands with me?'

'Your ladyship,' said the old man, 'had once a sister.'

'True; whom I loved as my own soul.'

'And a brother.'

'The bravest, the kindest, the most affectionate!' said Lady Bothwell.

'Both these beloved relatives you lost by the fault of an unfortunate man,' continued the stranger.

'By the crime of an unnatural bloody-minded murderer,' said the lady.

'I am answered,' replied the old man, bowing, as if to withdraw.

'Stop, sir, I command you,' said Lady Bothwell. – 'Who are you that, at such a place and time, come to recall these horrible recollections? I insist upon knowing?'

'I am one who intends Lady Bothwell no injury; but, on the contrary, to offer her the means of doing a deed of Christian charity which the world would wonder at, and which Heaven would reward; but I find her in no temper for such a sacrifice as I was prepared to ask.'

'Speak out, sir; what is your meaning,' said Lady Bothwell.

'The wretch that has wronged you so deeply,' rejoined the stranger, 'is now on his death-bed. His days have been days of misery, his nights have been sleepless hours of anguish – yet he cannot die without your forgiveness. His life has been an unremitting penance – yet he dares not part from his burden while your curses load his soul.'

'Tell him,' said Lady Bothwell sternly, 'to ask pardon of that Being whom he has so greatly offended; not of an erring mortal like himself. What could my forgiveness avail him?'

'Much,' answered the old man. 'It will be an earnest of that which he may then venture to ask from his Creator, lady, and from yours. Remember, Lady Bothwell, you too have a death-bed to look forward to; your soul may, all human souls must, feel the awe of facing the judgment-seat, with the wounds of an untented conscience, raw, and rankling – what thought would it be then that should whisper, "I have given no mercy, how then shall I ask for it"?'

'Man, whatsoever thou mayest be,' replied Lady Bothwell, 'urge me not so cruelly. It would be but blasphemous hypocrisy to utter with my lips the words which every throb of my heart protests against. They would open the earth and give to light the wasted form of my sister – the bloody form of my murdered brother – forgive him – Never, never!'

'Great God!' cried the old man, holding up his hands, 'is it thus the worms which Thou hast called out of dust obey the commands of their Maker? Farewell, proud and unforgiving woman. Exult that thou hast added to a death in want and pain the agonies of religious despair; but never again mock Heaven by petitioning for the pardon which thou hast refused to grant.'

He was turning from her.

'Stop,' she exclaimed; 'I will try; yes, I will try to pardon him.'

'Gracious lady,' said the old man, 'you will relieve the overburdened soul, which dare not sever itself from its sinful companion of earth, without being at peace with you. What do I know – your forgiveness may perhaps preserve for penitence the dregs of a wretched life.'

'Ha!' said the lady, as a sudden light broke on her, 'it is the villain himself!' And grasping Sir Philip Forester – for it was he, and no other – by the collar, she raised a cry of 'Murder murder! Seize the murderer!'

At an exclamation so singular, in such a place, the company thronged into the apartment, but Sir Philip Forester was no longer there. He had forcibly extricated himself from Lady Bothwell's hold, and had run out of the apartment which opened on the landing-place of the stair. There seemed no escape in that direction, for there were several persons coming up the steps, and others descending. But the unfortunate man was desperate. He threw himself over the balustrade, and alighted safely in the lobby, though a leap of fifteen feet at least, then dashed into the street and was lost in darkness. Some of the Bothwell family made pursuit, and, had they come up with the fugitive, they might have perhaps slain him; for in those days men's blood ran warm in their veins. But the police did not interfere; the matter most criminal having happened long since, and in a foreign land. Indeed, it was always thought that this extraordinary scene originated in a hypocritical experiment, by which Sir Philip desired to ascertain whether he might return to his native country in safety from the resentment of a family which he had injured so deeply. As the result fell out so contrary to his wishes, he is believed to have returned to the Continent, and there died in exile.

# The Magic Watch

## Raphael

### (1833)

Like any successful public vogue, the Gothic novel had a number of side-effects, and one of these (perhaps the only one to concern us in a collection such as this) was the sudden increased popularity of books about astrology and fortune telling. Several of the leading publishers of terror tales were quick to spot this and by 1830 we find their catalogues listing a great many volumes devoted to 'revealing all the secrets of the future that gentlemen or ladies could wish.'

Although this sub-strata of literature is not well documented, it seems apparent that one of the most popular of these astrologer-authors was a certain Raphael whose books were published by John Bennett at Three-Tun Passage in Paternoster Row. Raphael's *Lady's Witch,* an annual publication, was full of tables and signs which the owner applied to the circumstances of his or her life to see what the future held. A more comprehensive volume was the *Familiar Astrologer* which was written by Raphael in 1833. Apart from being 'an easy guide to fate, destiny and foreknowledge' it also contained several 'strange and marvellous tales, legends and traditions' relating to ghosts, witches, demons and strange occult experiences. One such was *The Magic Watch*, a fine Gothic tale which I believe is well worth a place here. If any reader should come across a volume of this type – though they are now exceedingly rare – study of them will provide not only hours of entertainment, but also an insight into the superstitions of the English populace one hundred and fifty years ago.

IT was a glorious evening in the summer of 1793 – sky and cloud blending in one uniform flood of splendour. The brightness of the heavens was reflected on the broad bosom of the Saale, a river which, passing Jena, falls lower down into the

Elbe, whence the commingled waters roll onward till lost in the Noordt Zee.

On the banks of this stream, not more than a mile from Jena, sat two persons enjoying the delicious coolness of the hour. Their dress was remarkable, and sufficiently indicative of their pursuits. – Their sable garments and caps of black velvet, their long streaming hair, combed down the shoulders and back and the straight swords suspended from their right breasts denoted them to be two of the burschen, or students of the University of Jena.

'Such an evening as this,' said the elder youth, addressing his companion, 'and thou here? Thyrza is much indebted to thee for they attention. Thou a lover!'

'Thyrza is gone with her mother to Carlsbad,' rejoined his companion, 'so thou mayst cease thy wonderment.'

'So far from it, that I wonder the more. A true lover knows not the relations of space. To Carlsbad! why 'tis no more than – but *seht!* who have we here?'

As he spoke, they were approached by a little old man, whose garments of brown serge appeared to have seen considerable service. He wore a conical hat, and carried in his hand an antique gold-headed cane. His features betokened great age; but his frame, though exceedingly spare, was apparently healthy and active. His eyes were singularly large and bright; and his hair, inconsistent in some respects with the rest of his appearance, crowded from under his high-crowned hat in black and grizzly masses.

'A good evening to you, Meine Herren,' said the little old man, with a most polite bow, as he approached the students.

They returned his salutation with the doubtful courtesy usual in intercourse with a stranger, whose appearance induces an anxiety to avoid a more intimate acquaintance with him. The old man did not seem to notice the coolness of his reception, but continued: 'What think you of this?' taking from his pocket a golden watch richly chased, and studded all over with diamonds.

The students were delighted with the splendid jewel, and

admired by turns the beauty of the manufacture and the costliness of the materials. The elder youth, however, found it impossible to refrain from bestowing one or two suspicious glances on the individual whose outward man but little accorded with the possession of so valuable a treasure.

'He must be a thief and have stolen this watch,' thought the sceptical student. 'I will observe him closely.'

But as he bent his eyes again upon the stranger, he met the old man's look, and felt, he knew not why, somewhat daunted by it. He turned aside, and walked from his companion a few paces.

'I would,' thought he, 'give my folio Plato, with all old Blunderdrunck's marginal comments, to know who this old man is, whose look has startled me thus, with his two great hyaena-looking eyes, that shoot through one like a flash of lightning. He looks for all the world like a travelling quack-doctor, with his threadbare cloak and his sugarloaf hat, and yet he possesses a watch fit for an emperor, and talks to two burschen as if they were his boon companions.'

On returning to the spot where he had left his friend, he found him still absorbed in admiration of the watch. The old man stood by, his great eyes still riveted upon the student, and a something, not a smile, playing over his sallow and furrowed countenance.

'You seem pleased with my watch,' said the little old man to Theophan Guscht, the younger student, who continued his fixed and longing gaze on the beautiful bauble: 'Perhaps you would like to become its owner?'

'Its owner!' said Theophan, 'ah, you jest;' – and he thought, 'what a pretty present it would be for Thyrza on our wedding-day.'

'Yes,' replied the old man, 'its owner – I am myself willing to part with it. What offer do you make for it?'

'What offer, indeed; as if I could afford to purchase it. There is not a bursche in our university who would venture to bid a price for so precious a jewel.'

'Well then, you will not purchase my watch?'

Theophan shook his head, half mournfully.

'Nor you Mein Herr?' turning to the other student.

'Nein,' was the brief negative.

'But,' said the old man, again addressing Theophan, 'were I to offer you this watch – a free present – you would not refuse it perhaps?'

'Perhaps I should not: *perhaps,* which is yet more likely – you will not put it in my power. But we love not jesting with strangers.'

'It is rarely that *I* jest,' returned the old man; 'those with whom I do, seldom retort. But say the word, and the watch is yours.'

'Do you really,' exclaimed Theophan, his voice trembling with joyful surprise – 'do you really say so! Ach Gott! – Himmell! what shall I – how can I sufficiently thank you?'

'It matters not,' said the old man, 'you are welcome to it. There is however, one condition annexed to the gift.'

'A condition – what is it?'

The elder student pulled Theophan by the sleeve: 'accept not his gifts,' he whispered; 'come away, I doubt him much.' And he walked on.

'Stay a moment, Jans,' said Theophan; but his companion continued his steps. Theophan was undecided whether or not he should follow him; but he looked at the watch, thought of Thyrza, and remained.

'The condition on which you accept this bauble – the condition on which others have accepted it – is, that you wind it up every night, for a year, before sunset.'

The student laughed. 'A mighty condition, truly – give me the watch.'

'Or,' continued the old man, without heeding the interruption *'if you fail in fulfilling the condition, you die within six hours after the stopping of the watch.* It will stop at sunset if not wound up before.'

'I like not that condition,' said Theophan. 'Be patient – I must consider your offer.'

He did so; he thought of the easiness of avoiding the possible calamity; he thought of the beauty of the watch – above all, he thought of Thyrza and his wedding-day.

'Pshaw! why do I hesitate,' said he to himself; then turning to the old man 'Give me the watch – I agree to your condition.'

'You are to wind it up before sunset for a year or die within six hours.'

'So thou hast said, and I am content and thanks for thy gift.'

'Thank me at the year's end, if thou wilt,' replied the old man, 'meanwhile, farewell.'

'Farewell! I doubt not to be able to render my thanks at the end of the term.'

Theophan was surprised, as he pronounced these words, to perceive that the old man was gone.

'Be he who he may, I fear him not,' said he, 'I know the terms on which I have accepted his gift. – What a fool was Jans Herwest to refuse his offer so rudely.'

He quitted the spot on which he stood, and moved homewards. He entered Jena, sought his lodging, put by his watch, and, lighting his lamp, opened his friend's folio Plato, (with Blunderdrunck's marginal comments,) and endeavoured to apply to the Symposion. But in ten minutes he closed the book with impatience, for his excited mind rejected the philosophic feast; and he strolled into the little garden which his chamber window commanded, to think of the events of the evening, and, with a lover's passion, to repeat and bless the name of his Thyrza.

Time waned, and the watch was regularly wound up. Love smiled, for Thyrza was not cruel. Our bursche had resumed his studies, and was in due time considered as one of the most promising students of the whole University of Jena.

But, as we already observed, time flew apace; and the day but one before the happy day that was to give to Theophan his blooming bride, had arrived – which had been looked forward to with such joyful anticipations, and Theophan had bidden adieu to most of his fellow students, and taken leave of the learned professors whose lectures he had attended with so much benefit. It was a fine morning, and, being at leisure, he bethought him in what manner he should pass the day. Any novice can guess how the problem was solved. He would go and visit Thyrza.

He set out accordingly, and was presently before the gate of David Angerstell's garden. A narrow, pebbled walk intersected it, at the top of which stood the house, an old quaint black and white building, with clumsy projecting upper stories, that spread to almost twice the extent of the foundation. A quantity of round, dropsical-looking flower-pots were ranged on either side of the door. The casement of a projecting window was open to receive the light breezes that blew across the flower beds, at which a young female was seated – a beautiful, taper-waisted girl, with a demure, intelligent countenance, light twining hair, and a blue furtively laughing eye. True as fate, that blue eye had caught a glimpse of her approaching lover. In a moment he was by her side, and kissed with eager lips the soft little white hand that seemed to melt in his pressure.

The lovers met in all the confiding tenderness of mutual affection; happy mortals! the moments flew fast – fast – so fast that – But let us take time.

They had strolled out into the garden; for the considerate parents of Thyrza had shown no disposition to interrupt their discourse further than by a mere welcome to their intended son-in-law. The evening was one of deep, full stillness – that rich, tranquil glow, that heightens and purifies happiness, and deprives sorrow of half its bitterness. Thought was all alive within their breasts, and the eloquence of words seemed faint to the tide of feeling that flashed from their eyes.

Theophan and Thyrza rambled, and looked, and whispered – and rambled, looked, and whispered again and again – and time ambled too gently for his motion to be perceived. The maiden looked on the sky: 'How beautiful the sun has set,' said she.

'The sun set!' echoed Theophan, with a violence that terrified his companion – *'the sun set! then I am lost!* We have met for the last time, Thyrza.'

'Dearest Theophan,' replied the trembling girl, 'why do you

terrify me thus? Met for the last time! Oh! no, it cannot be. What! what calls thee hence?'

'*He calls who must be obeyed* – but six short hours – and then, Thyrza, wilt thou bestow one thought on my memory?'

She spoke not – moved not: – senseless and inanimate she lay in his arms, pale and cold as a marble statue, and beautiful as a sculptor's dream. Theophan bore her swiftly to the house, placed her on a couch, and called for assistance. He listened, and heard approaching footsteps obeying the summons – pressed his lips to her cold forehead, and, springing from the casement, crossed the garden, and in ten minutes was buried in the obscurity of a gloomy wood, or rather thicket, some miles or thereabouts from Jena.

Overcome by the passionate affliction that fevered his blood and throbbed in every pulse, Theophan threw himself down on a grassy eminence, and lay for some time in that torpid state of feeling in which the mind, blunted by sudden and overwhelming calamity, ceases to be aware of the horrors of its situation, and, stunned into a mockery of repose, awaits almost unconsciously the consummation of evil that impends it.

Theophan was attracted from this lethargy by the splashing rain, which fell upon him in large thunder-drops. He looked around, and found himself in almost total darkness. The clouded sky, the low, deep voice of the wind, booming through the trees and swaying their high tops, bespoke the approaching storm. It burst upon him at length in all its fury! Theophan hailed the distraction, for the heart loves what assimilates to itself, and his was wrung almost to breaking with agony. He stood up and shouted to the raging elements! He paused, and listened, for he thought some one replied. He shouted again, but it was not this time in mere recklessness. Amid the howling of the tempest he once more heard an answering shout: there was something strange in the voice that could thus render itself audible above the din of the storm. Again and again it was the same; once it seemed to die away into a fiend-like laugh. Theophan's blood curdled as it ran – and his mood of desperation was exchanged for one of deep, fearful, and overstrained attention.

The tempest suddenly ceased; the thunder died away in faint and distant moanings, and the lightning flashes became less frequent and vivid. The last of these showed Theophan that he was not *alone*. Within his arm's reach stood a little old man: he wore a conical hat – leaned on a gold-headed cane – above all, he had a pair of large glaring eyes, that Theophan had no difficulty in instantly recognizing.

When the momentary flash had subsided, the student and his companion were left in darkness, and Theophan could with difficulty discern the form of his companion.

There was a long silence.

'*Do you remember me?*' at length interrogated the mysterious stranger.

'*Perfectly,*' replied the student.

'That is well – I thought you might have forgotten me; wits have short memories. But perhaps you do not aspire to the character.'

'You, at least, must be aware I have no claim to it, otherwise I had not been the dupe I am.'

'That is to say, you have made a compact, broken your part of it, and are now angry that you are likely to be called upon for the penalty. What is the hour?'

'I know not – I shall shortly.'

'Does *she* know of this? you know whom I mean.'

'Old man!' exclaimed Theophan, fiercely, 'begone. I have broken the agreement – that I know. I must pay the penalty – of that too I am aware, and am ready so to do; but my hour is not yet come: torment me not, but leave me. I would await my doom alone.'

'Ah, well – I can make allowances. You are somewhat testy with your friends; but that we will overlook. Suppose now, the penalty you have incurred could be pretermitted.'

The student replied with a look of incredulous scorn.

'Well, I see you are sceptical,' continued the old man; 'but consider. You are young, active, well gifted in body and in mind.'

'What is that to thee? still more, what is it to me *now*?'

'Much: but do not interrupt me. You love, and are beloved.'

'I tell thee again, cease and begone to – *hell* !'

'*Presently* ! You are all of these now – what will you be, what will Thyrza Angerstell be, tomorrow ?'

The student's patience was exhausted; he sprang on the old man, intending to dash him to the earth.

He might as well have tried his strength on one of the stunted oaks that grew beside him. The old man moved not – not the fraction of an inch.

'Thou hast wearied thyself to little purpose, friend,' said he; 'we will now, if it pleases you, proceed to business. You would doubtless be willing to be released from the penalty of your neglect ?'

'Probably I might.'

'You would even be willing that the lot should fall upon another in preference to yourself?'

The student paused.

'No: I am content to bear the punishment of my own folly. And still – oh, Thyrza !' He groaned in the agony of his spirit.

'What! with the advantages you possess! the prospect before you – the life of happiness you might propose to yourself – and more, the happiness you might confer on Thyrza – with all these in your reach, you prefer death to life? How many an old and useless being, upon whom the lot might fall, would hail joyfully the doom which you shudder even to contemplate.'

'Stay – were I to embrace your offer, how must the lot be decided – to whom must I transfer my punishment?'

'Do this – your term will be prolonged twenty-four hours. Send the watch to Adrian Wenzel, the goldsmith, to sell; if, within that time, he dispose of it, the purchaser takes your place and you will be free. But decide quickly – my time is brief, yours also must be so, unless you accede to my terms.'

'But who are you to whom is given the power of life and death – of sentencing and reprieving? '

'Seek not to know of what concerns you not. Once more, do you agree?'

'First, tell me what is your motive in offering me this chance?'

'Motive ? – none. I am naturally compassionate. But decide – there is a leaf trembling on yonder bough, it will fall in a moment. If it reach the ground before you determine – Farewell !'

The leaf dropped from the tree. '*I consent* !' exclaimed the student. He looked for the old man, but found that he was alone. At the same time the toll of the midnight clock sounded on his ear : it ceased – the hour was passed, *and he lived* !

It was about the noon of the following day that the goldsmith, Adrian Wenzel, sold to a customer the most beautiful watch in Jena. Having completed the bargain, he repaired immediately to Theophan Guscht's lodgings.

'Well, have you sold my watch?'

'I have – here is the money, Mein Herr.'

'Very well : there is your share of the proceeds.'

The goldsmith departed, and Theophan shortly afterwards directed his steps towards Angerstell's house, meditating as he went on his probable reception, and what he could offer in extenuation of his behaviour the day before.

Ere he had settled this knotty point to his satisfaction, he arrived at the garden gate. He hesitated – grew cold and hot by turns – his heart throbbed violently. At last, making a strong effort at self command, he entered.

At the same window, in the same posture in which he had seen her the day before, sat Thyrza Angerstell. But the Thyrza of yesterday was blooming, smiling, and cheerful – today she was pale and wan, the image of hopeless sorrow ; even as a rose which some rude hand has severed from its stem. Theophan's blood grew chill; he proceeded, and had almost reached the porch of the house when Thyrza perceived him. With a loud cry she fell from her seat. He rushed into the room, and raised her in his arms.

She recovered – she spoke to him. She reproached him for the evening before. He obtained a hearing, and explained just as much of the history of the watch as related to its purchase, and the condition annexed to it. This he asserted was a mere trick of the donor, he having broken the condition and being yet alive. They wondered, he with affected, and she with real surprise, that any one should have been tempted to part with so valuable a watch for the idle satisfaction of terrifying the recipient. However, love is proverbially credulous; Theophan's explanation was believed, and the reconciliation was complete.

The lovers had conversed about a quarter of an hour, when Thyrza suddenly reverted again to the subject of the watch.

'It is strange,' said she, 'that I too am connected with a watch similar to yours.'

'How – by what means?'

'Last night I lay sleepless – 'twas your unkindness, Theophan –'

Theophan hastened to renew his vows and supplications.

'Ah, well! you know I have forgiven you. But as I lay, the thought of a watch, such as you describe, presented itself to my mind; how, or why I cannot guess. It haunted me the whole night, and when I rose this morning it was before me still.'

'What followed, dear Thyrza?' enquired the anxious student.

'Listen, and you shall hear. Thinking to drive away this troublesome guest, I walked out. I had scarcely left my home two minutes when I saw a watch, the exact counterpart of my ideal one.'

'Where – where did you see it?'

'At our neighbour's, Adrian Wenzel's.'

'And – you – you!' – His words almost choked him.

'I was impelled by some inexplicable motive – not that I wanted or wished for so expensive a jewel – to purchase this watch.'

'No – no!' exclaimed the agonized student, 'you could not do so!' He restrained himself by an exertion more violent than he had believed himself capable of. He rose from his seat and turned away his face.

Not now, as before, did his anguish vent itself in passion and violence. It seemed that the infliction was too heavy, too superhuman a calamity to be accompanied by the expression of ordinary emotions. He was deadly pale – but his eye was firm, and he trembled not.

'Theophan,' said his mistress, 'what ails you? and why should what I have said produce so fearful an effect upon you? I shall –'

'It is nothing – nothing, dearest Thyrza. I will return instantly, and tell you why I have appeared so discomposed. I am not quite myself – I shall return almost immediately. I will walk but into the lane, and catch a breath of the fresh breeze as it comes wafted from the water.'

He left her, passed out of the garden. 'I could not,' said he inwardly, 'tell her that she was murdered – and by me too!'

He hastened on without an object, and scarcely knowing whither he was directing his steps, passed down the path which led by Angerstell's house, in that depth of despair which is sometimes wont to deceive us with the appearance of calmness. He had no distinct idea of the calamity he had brought upon Thyrza – even she was almost forgotten; and nothing but a vague apprehension of death, connected in some unintelligible manner with himself, was present to his mind. So deep was the stupefaction in which he was involved, that it was not until some one on the road had twice spoken to him, that he heard the question.

'*What is the time of day?*'

Theophan looked round, and encountered the large, horribly-laughing eyes of the giver of the fatal watch. He was about to speak, but the old man interrupted him.

'I have no time to listen to reproaches: you know what you have incurred. If you would avoid the evil, and save Thyrza, I will tell you how.'

He whispered in the student's ear. The latter grew pale for a moment, but recovered himself.

'She shall be safe,' said he, 'if I accept your terms? No equivocation now – I have learnt with whom I deal.'

'Agree to what I have said, and fetch hither the watch within half an hour, and she is delivered from her doom. She shall be yours, and –'

'Promise no more, or give thy promises to those who value them. Swear that she shall be safe! I request no more – wish for no more on earth.'

'Swear!' repeated the old man; 'by what shall I *swear*, I pray thee? But I promise – begone and fetch the watch – remember, half an hour; and, hark! thou accedest to my terms?'

'*I do!*'

So saying, Theophan sped back to the house, unchecked even by the loud laugh that seemed to echo after him. He had walked farther than he had any idea of, and swiftly as he sprang over every impediment to his course, one-third of the allotted time had elapsed before he reached the room in which he had left his beloved.

*It was empty!*

'Thyrza! Thyrza!' shouted the student – 'the watch! the watch! for Heaven's sake, the watch!'

The reverberation of his voice from the walls alone replied.

He then rushed from chamber to chamber, in a state of mind little short of desperation. He descended into the garden; the dull ticking of the family clock struck on his ear as he passed it, and he shuddered. At the extremity of the principal walk he beheld Thyrza.

'The watch! the watch! as you value your life and my – but haste, haste – not a word – *a moment's delay is death!*'

Without speaking, Thyrza flew to the house, accompanied by Theophan.

'It is gone,' said she; 'I left it here, and –'

'Then we are lost! forgive thy –'

'Oh! no, no, it is here,' exclaimed she, 'dearest Theophan! but why –'

He listened not even to the voice of Thyrza; one kiss on her forehead, one look of anguish, and he was gone!

He sped! he flew! – he arrived at the spot where he had left the old man. The place was solitary; but on the sand were traced the words – *The time is past!*

The student fell senseless on the earth.

When he recovered he found himself on a couch – affectionate but mournful glances were vent upon him.

'Thyrza! Thyrza!' exclaimed the wretched youth, 'away to

thy prayers! but a soul like thine has nought to repent. Oh! leave me – that look! go, go!'

She turned away, and wept bitterly. Her mother entered the room.

'Thyrza, my love, come with me. The physician is here.'

'What physician, mother? is it –'

'No, he was from home, this is a stranger; but there is no time to lose.' She led her daughter from the apartment. 'Your patient is in that room' she added, to the physician. He entered, and closed the door.

The mother and daughter had scarcely reached the stair-head, when a cry, which was almost a yell of agony, proceeding from the chamber they had left, interrupted their progress. It was followed by a loud and strange laugh, that seemed to shake the building to its foundation.

The mother called, or rather screamed, for her husband; the daughter sprang to the door of the patient's chamber! It was fastened, and defied her feeble efforts to open it. From within rose the noise of a fearful struggle – the brief exclamations of triumph, or of rage – the groan of pain – the strong stamp of heavy feet – all betokening a death-grapple between the inmates. Suddenly, something was dashed upon the ground with violence, which, from the sound, appeared to have been broken into a thousand pieces.

There was a dead silence, more appalling than the brunt of the contest. The door resisted no longer.

Thyrza, with her father and mother, entered the room: it was perfectly desolate. *On the floor were scattered innumerable fragments of the fatal watch. Theophan was heard of no more.*

On the fifth day from this terrible catastrophe, a plain flag of white marble in the church at –, recorded the name, age, and death of Thyrza Angerstell. The inscription is now partly obliterated; so much so as, in all probability, to baffle the curiosity of any gentle stranger who may wish to seek it out, and drop a tear on the grave of her who sleeps beneath.

# The Demon of the Hartz

### or

### The Three Charcoal Burners

## Thomas Peckett Prest

## (1810–1879)

Thomas Peckett Prest was one of the last of the Gothic storytellers in the old tradition, a man of boundless energy who literally turned out dozens of novels to order. Nevertheless he still remains today an important figure in the genre through the skill of his writing which somehow manages to shine through in even the most hurried work and mediocre plotting. The sheer volume of his work (and as he also employed a number of pen-names there may be much more that will never be accounted to him) makes him with William Harrison Ainsworth by far the most prolific writer in a storyform which thrived on proliferation.

Prest began his writing career adapting farces and melodramas from the French, many of which were performed at the famous Britannia Theatre in London. He was also an accomplished composer of popular songs and not a few of his tunes were on the lips of Londoners during his lifetime. A seemingly tireless worker, he began contributing satire to a number of contemporary magazines and in 1835 started a series of Gothic novels and stories which eventually gave rise to the expression 'blood and thunder tales' now still used about certain kinds of lightweight fiction. He was also not above plagiarism and in collaboration with William Bayle Bernard and Morris Barnett, two notorious hacks, wrote the 'Bos' stories which were a successful parody of Charles Dickens published from 1836–1840.

The most popular of Prest's Gothic novels were probably *The Skeleton Clutch or the Goblet of Gore* (1842), *The Black Monk or The Street of the Grey Turret* (which was published in 1844 and 'owed much to *The Monk* as well as Mrs Radcliffe' according to Montague Summers) and *Varney the Vampire or The Feast of Blood* (1847 – an extract from this work is to be found in one of my recent anthologies\*). Prest also edited a highly successful collection of Gothic terror tales – nearly all of which he wrote himself – entitled *The Calendar of Horrors* (1835) and from this *The Demon of the Hartz* has been taken.

THE solitudes of the Hartz forest in Germany, but especially the mountains called Blockberg, or rather Blockenberg, are the chosen scene for tales of witches, demons, and apparitions. The occupation of the inhabitants, who are either miners or foresters, is of a kind that renders them peculiarly prone to superstition, and the natural phenomena which they witness in pursuit of their solitary or subterraneous profession, are often set down by them to the interference of goblins or the power of magic. Among the various legends current in that wild country, there is a favourite one which supposes the Hartz to be haunted by a sort of tutelar demon, in the shape of a wild man, of huge stature, his head wreathed with oak leaves, and his middle tinctured with the same, bearing in his hand a pine torn up by the root. It is certain that many persons profess to have seen such a man traversing, with huge strides, the opposite ridge of a mountain, when divided from it by a narrow glen; and indeed the fact of the apparition is so generally admitted, that modern scepticism has only found refuge by ascribing it to optical deception.

In elder times, the intercourse of the demon with the inhabitants was more familiar, and, according to the traditions of the Hartz, he was wont, with the caprice usually ascribed to these earth-born powers to interfere with the affairs of mortals, sometimes for their welfare. But it was observed, that even his gifts often turned out, in the long run, fatal to those on whom they were bestowed, and it was no uncommon thing for the pastors, in their care for their flock, to compose long sermons the

\* See *The Midnight People*, ed. Peter Haining. Leslie Frewin, (U.K.), 1968; Grosset & Dunlap (U.S.-retitled Vampires at Midnight), 1970.

burthen whereof was a warning against having any intercourse, direct or indirect, with the Hartz demon. The fortunes of Martin Waldeck have been often quoted by the aged to their giddy children, when they were heard to scoff at a danger which appeared visionary.

A travelling capuchin had possessed himself of the pulpit of the thatched church at a little hamlet called Morgenbrodt, lying in the Hartz district, from which he declaimed against the wickedness of the inhabitants, their communication with fiends, witches, and fairies, and particularly with the woodland goblin of the Hartz. The doctrines of Luther had already begun to spread among the peasantry, for the incident is placed under the reign of Charles V, and they laughed to scorn the zeal with which the venerable man insisted upon his topic. At length, as his vehemence increased with opposition, so their opposition rose in proportion to his vehemence. The inhabitants did not like to hear an accustomed demon, who had inhabited the Brockenberg for so many ages, summarily confounded with Baal-peor, Ashtaroth, and Beelzebub himself, and condemned without reprieve to the bottomless Tophet. The apprehensions that the spirit might avenge himself on them for listening to such an illiberal sentence, added to the national interest in his behalf. A travelling friar, they said, that is here today and away tomorrow, may say what he pleases, but it is we the ancient and constant inhabitants of the country, that are left at the mercy of the insulted demon, and must, of course, pay for all. Under the irritation occasioned by these reflections the peasants from injurious language betook themselves to stones, and having pebbled the priest most handsomely, they drove him out of the parish to preach against demons elsewhere.

Three young men, who had been present and assisting in the attack upon the priest, carried on the laborious and mean occupation of preparing charcoal for the smelting furnaces. On their return to their hut, their conversation naturally turned upon the demon of the Hartz and the doctrine of the capuchin. Maximilian and George Waldeck, the two elder brothers, although they allowed the language of the capuchin to have been indiscreet and worthy of censure, as presuming to determine upon the precise character and abode of the spirit, yet contended it was dangerous, in the highest degree, to accept his gifts, or hold any communication with him. He was powerful they allowed, but wayward and capricious, and those who had intercourse with him seldom came to a good end. Did he not give the brave knight, Ecbert of Rabenwald, that famous black steed, by means of which he vanquished all the champions at the great tournament at Bremen? and did not the same steed afterwards precipitate itself with its rider into an abyss so deep and fearful, that neither horse nor man was ever seen more? Had he not given to Dame Gertrude Trodden a curious spell for making butter come? and was she not burnt for a witch by the grand criminal judge of the Electorate, because she availed herself of his gift? But these, and many other instances which they quoted, of mischance and ill-luck ultimately attending upon the apparent benefits conferred by the Hartz spirit, failed to make any impression on Martin Waldeck, the youngest of the brothers.

Martin was youthful, rash, and impetuous; excelling in all the exercises which distinguish a mountaineer, and brave and undaunted from the familiar intercourse with the dangers that attend them. He laughed at the timidity of his brothers. 'Tell me not of such folly,' he said; 'the demon is a good demon – he lives among us as if he were a peasant like ourselves – haunts the lonely crags or recesses of the mountains like a huntsman or goatherd – and he who loves the Hartz-forest and its wild scenes cannot be indifferent to the fate of the hardy children of the soil. But if the demon were as malicious as you make him, how should he derive power over mortals who barely avail themselves of his gifts, without binding themselves to submit to his pleasure? When you carry your charcoal to the furnace, is not the money as good that is paid you by blaspheming Blaize, the old reprobate overseer, as if you got it from the pastor himself? It is not the goblin's gifts which can endanger you then, but it is the use you shall make of them that you must account for.

And were the demon to appear at this moment, and indicate to me a gold or silver mine, I would begin to dig away before his back were turned, and I would consider myself as under protection of a much Greater than he, while I made a good use of the wealth he pointed out to me.'

To this the elder brother replied, that wealth ill won was seldom well spent, while Martin presumptuously declared, that the possession of all the Hartz would not make the slightest alteration on his habits, morals, or character.

His brother entreated Martin to talk less wildly upon this subject, and with some difficulty contrived to withdraw his attention, by calling it to the consideration of an approaching boar-chase. This talk brought them to their hut, a wretched wigwam, situated upon one side of a wild, narrow, and romantic dell in the recesses of the Brockenberg. They released their sister from attending upon the operation of charring the wood, which requires constant attention, and divided among themselves the duty of watching it by night, according to their custom, one always waking while his brothers slept.

Max Waldeck, the eldest, watched during the two first hours of night, and was considerably alarmed, by observing upon the opposite bank of the glen, or valley a huge fire surrounded by some figures that appeared to wheel around it with antic gestures. Max at first bethought him of calling up his brothers; but recollecting the daring character of the youngest, and finding it impossible to wake the elder without also disturbing him – conceiving also what he saw to be an illusion of the demon, sent perhaps in consequence of the venturous expressions used by Martin on the preceding evening, he thought it best to betake himself to the safe-guard of such prayers as he could murmur over, and to watch in great terror and annoyance this strange and alarming apparition. After blazing for some time, the fire faded gradually away into darkness, and the rest of Max's watch was only disturbed by the remembrance of its terrors.

George now occupied the place of Max, who had retired to rest. The phenomenon of a huge blazing fire, upon the opposite bank of the glen, again presented itself to the eye of the watchman. It was surrounded as before by figures, which, distinguished by their opaque forms, being between the spectator and the red glaring light, moved and fluctuated around it as if engaged in some mystical ceremonies. George, though equally cautious, was of a bolder character than his elder brother. He resolved to examine more nearly the object of his wonder; and accordingly, after crossing the rivulet which divided the glen, he climbed up the opposite bank, and approached within an arrow's flight from the fire, which blazed apparently with the same fury as when he first witnessed it.

The appearance of the assistants who surrounded it, resembled those phantoms which are seen in a troubled dream, and at once confirmed the idea he had entertained from the first, that they did not belong to the human world. Amongst the strange unearthly forms, George Waldeck distinguished that of a giant overgrown with hair, holding an uprooted fir in his hand, with which, from time to time, he seemed to stir the blazing fire and having no other clothing than a wreath of oak leaves round his forehead and loins. George's heart sunk within him at recognizing the well-known apparition of the Hartz demon, as he had often been described to him by the ancient shepherds and huntsmen who had seen his form traversing the mountains. He turned, and was about to fly; but, upon second thoughts, blaming his own cowardice, he recited mentally the verse of the Psalmist, 'All good angels praise the Lord!' which is in that country supposed powerful as an exorcism and turned himself once more towards the place where he had seen the fire. But it was no longer visible.

The pale moon alone enlightened the side of the valley, and when George, with trembling steps, a moist brow, and hair bristling upright under his collier's cap, came to the spot where the fire had been so lately visible, marked as it was by a scathed oak tree, there appeared not on the heath the slightest vestiges of what he had seen. The moss and wild flowers were unscorched, and the branches of the oak tree, which had so lately appeared enveloped in wreaths of flame and smoke, were moist with the dews of midnight.

George returned to his hut with trembling steps, and, arguing like his elder brother, resolved to say nothing of what he had seen, lest he should awake in Martin that daring curiosity which he almost deemed to be allied with impiety.

It was now Martin's turn to watch. The household cock had given his first summons, and the night was well nigh spent. On examining the state of the furnace in which the wood was deposited in order to its being coked, or charred, he was surprised to find that the fire had not been sufficiently maintained; for in his excursion and its consequences, George had forgot the principal object of his watch. Martin's first thought was to call up the slumberers, but observing that both his brothers slept unwontedly deep and heavily, he respected their repose, and set himself to supply their furnace with fuel, without requiring their aid. What he heaped upon it was apparently damp and unfit for the purpose, for the fire seemed rather to decay than revive. Martin next went to collect some boughs from a stack which had been carefully cut and dried for this purpose; but, when he returned, he found the fire totally extinguished. This was a serious evil, which threatened them with loss of their trade for more than one day. The vexed and mortified watchman set about to strike a light in order to rekindle the fire, but the tinder was moist, and his labour proved in this respect also ineffectual. He was now about to call up his brothers, for the circumstance seemed to be pressing, when flashes of light glimmered not only through the window, but through every crevice of the rudely built hut, and summoned him to behold the same apparition which had before alarmed the successive watches of his brethren. His first idea was, that the Muhllerhaussers, their rivals in trade, and with whom they had had many quarrels, might have encroached upon their bounds for the purpose of pirating their wood, and he resolved to awake his brothers, and be revenged on them for their audacity. But a short reflection and observation on the gestures and manner of those who seemed 'to work in the fire', induced him to dismiss this belief, and although rather sceptical in these matters, to conclude that what he saw was a supernatural phenomenon. 'But be they

men or fiends,' said the undaunted forester, 'that busy themselves yonder with such fantastical rites and gestures, I will go
and demand a light to rekindle our furnace.' He relinquished,
at the same time, the idea of waking his brethren. There was a
belief that such adventures as he was about to undertake were
accessible only to one person at a time; he feared also that
his brothers in their scrupulous timidity, might interfere to
prevent his pursuing the investigation he had resolved to commence; and therefore, snatching his boar-spear from the wall,
the undaunted Martin Waldeck set forth on the adventure
alone.

With the same success as his brother George, but with courage far superior, Martin crossed the brook, ascended the hill,
and approached so near the ghostly assembly, that he could
recognize, in the presiding figure, the attributes of the Hartz
demon. A cold shuddering assailed him for the first time in his
life, but the recollection that he had at a distance dared and even
courted the intercourse which was now about to take place,
confirmed his staggering courage, and pride supplying what he
wanted in resolution, he advanced with tolerable firmness towards the fire, the figures which surrounded it appeared still
more phantastical, and supernatural, the nearer he approached
to the assembly. He was received with a loud shout of discordant and unnatural laughter, which, to his stunned ears, seemed
more alarming than a combination of the most dismal and
melancholy sounds which could be imagined. – 'Who art thou?'
said the giant compressing his savage and exaggerated features
into a sort of forced gravity, while they were occasionally agitated by the convulsion of the laughter which he seemed to suppress.

'Martin Waldeck the forester,' answered the hardy youth; –
'And who are you?'

'The king of the waste and of the mine,' answered the
spectre; –'And why hast thou dared to encroach on my mysteries?'

'I came in search of light to rekindle my fire,' answer Martin hardily, and then resolutely asked in his turn, 'What mys-

teries are these that you celebrate here?'

'We celebrate,' answered the demoniac being, 'the wedding of Hërmes with the Black Dragon. – But take thy fire that thou camest to seek, and begone – No mortal may long look upon us and live.'

The peasant stuck his spear point into a large piece of blazing wood, which he heaved with some difficulty, and then turned round to regain his hut, the shouts of laughter being renewed behind him with treble violence, and ringing far down the narrow valley. When Martin returned to the hut, his first care, however much astonished with what he had seen, was to dispose the kindled coal among the fuel so as might best light the fire of his furnace, but after many efforts, and all exertions of bellows and fire-prong, the coal he had brought from the demon's fire became totally extinct, without kindling any of the others. He turned about and observed the fire still blazing on the hill, although those who had been busied around it had disappeared. As he conceived the spectre had been jesting with him, he gave way to the natural hardihood of his temper, and determining to see the adventure to the end, resumed the road to the fire, from which, unopposed by the demon, he brought off in the same manner a blazing piece of charcoal but still without being able to succeed in lighting his fire. Impunity having increased his rashness, he resolved upon a third experiment, and was as successful as before in reaching the fire; but, when he had again appropriated a piece of burning coal, and had turned to depart, he heard the harsh and supernatural voice which had before accosted him, pronounce these words, 'Dare not to return hither a fourth time!'

The attempt to rekindle the fire with this last coal having proved as ineffectual as on the former occasions, Martin relinquished the hopeless attempt, and flung himself on his bed of leaves, resolving to delay till the next morning the communication of his supernatural adventure to his brothers. He was awakened from a heavy sleep into which he had sunk, from fatigue of body and agitation of mind, by loud exclamations of joy and surprise. His brothers, astonished at finding the fire extinguished when they awoke, had proceeded to arrange the fuel in order to renew it, when they found in the ashes three huge metallic masses, which their skill, (for most of the peasants in the Hartz are practised mineralogists,) immediately ascertained to be pure gold.

It was some damp upon their joyful congratulations when they learned from Martin the mode in which he had obtained this treasure, to which their own experience of the nocturnal vision induced them to give full credit. But they were unable to resist the temptation of sharing their brother's wealth. Taking now upon him as head of the house, Martin Waldeck bought lands and forests, built a castle, obtained a patent of nobility, and greatly to the scorn of the ancient nobility of the neighbourhood, was invested with all the privileges of a man of family. His courage in public war, as well as in private feuds, together with the number of retainers whom he kept in pay, sustained him for some time against the odium which was excited by his sudden elevation, and the arrogance of his pretensions. And now it was seen in the instance of Martin Waldeck, as it has been in that of many others, how little mortals can foresee the effect of sudden prosperity on their own disposition. The evil dispositions in his nature, which poverty had checked and repressed, ripened and bore their un-allowed fruit under the influence of temptation and the means of indulgence. As Deep calls unto Deep, one bad passion awakened another : — the fiend of avarice invoked that of pride, and pride was to be supported by cruelty and oppression. Waldeck's character, always bold and daring, but rendered more harsh and assuming by prosperity, soon made him odious, not to nobles only, but likewise to the lower ranks, who saw, with double dislike, the oppressive rights of the feudal nobility of the empire so remorselessly exercised by one who had risen from the very dregs of the people. His adventure, although carefully concealed, began likewise to be whispered, and the clergy already stigmatized as a wizard and accomplice of fiends, the wretch, who, having acquired so huge a treasure in so strange a manner had not sought to sanctify it by dedicating a considerable portion to the use of the church. Surrounded by enemies, public and private, tormented by a thousand feuds, and threatened by the church with excommunication, Martin Waldeck, or, as we must now call him the Baron Von Waldeck, often regretted bitterly the labours and sports of unenvied poverty. But his courage failed him not under all these difficulties and seemed rather to augment in proportion to the danger which darkened around him, until an accident precipitated his fall.

A proclamation by the reigning Duke of Brunswick had invited to a solemn tournament all German nobles of free and honourable descent, and Martin Waldeck, splendidly armed, accompanied by his two brothers, and a gallantly equipped retinue, had the arrogance to appear among the chivalry of the province and demand permission to enter the lists. This was considered as filling up the measure of his presumption. A thousand voices exclaimed, 'we will have no cinder-sifter mingle in our games of chivalry.' Irritated to frenzy, Martin drew his sword, and hewed down the herald who, in compliance with the general outcry, opposed his entrance into the list. A hundred swords were unsheathed to avenge what was, in those days, regarded as a crime only inferior to sacrilege, or regicide. Waldeck, after defending himself with the fury of a lion, was seized, tried on the spot by the judges of the lists, and condemned, as the appropriate punishment for breaking the peace of his sovereign and violating the sacred person of a herald-at-arms, to have his right hand struck from his body, to be ignominiously deprived of the honour of nobility, of which he was unworthy, and be expelled from the city. When he had been stripped of his arms, and sustained the mutilation imposed by this severe sentence, the unhappy victim of ambition was abandoned to the rabble, who followed him with threats and outcries, levelled alternately against the necromancer and oppressor, which at length ended in violence. His brothers, (for his retinue had fled and dispersed) at length succeeded in rescuing him from the hands of the populace, when, satiated with cruelty, they had left him half dead through loss of blood, through the outrages he had sustained. They were not permitted, such was the ingenious cruelty of their enemies, to make use of any other means of removing him, excepting such a collier's cart as they had themselves formerly used, in which they deposited their brother on a truss of straw, scarcely expecting to reach any place of shelter ere death should release him from his misery.

When the Waldecks, journeying in this miserable manner, had approached the verge of their native country, in a hollow way, between two mountains, they perceived a figure advancing towards them, which at first sight seemed to be an aged man. But as he approached, his limbs and stature increased, the cloak fell from his shoulders, his pilgrim's staff was changed into an uprooted pine tree, and the gigantic figure of the Hartz demon passed before them in his terrors. When he came opposite to the cart which contained the miserable Waldeck, his huge features dilated into a grin of unutterable contempt and malignity, as he asked the sufferer, 'How like you the fire MY coals have kindled?' The power of motion, which terror suspended in his two brothers, seemed to be restored to Martin by the energy of his courage. He raised himself on the cart, bent his brows, and, clenching his fist, shook it at the spectre with a ghastly look of hate and defiance. The goblin vanished with his usual tremendous and explosive laugh and left Waldeck exhausted with the effort of expiring nature.

The terrified brethren turned their vehicle towards the towers of a convent which arose in a wood of pine trees beside the road. They were charitably received by a bare-footed and long-bearded capuchin, and Martin survived only to complete the first confession he had made since the day of his sudden prosperity, and to receive absolution from the very priest, whom, precisely that day three years, he had assisted to pelt out of the hamlet of Morgenbrodt. The three years of precarious prosperity were supposed to have a mysterious correspondence with the number of his visits to the spectral fire upon the hill.

The body of Martin Waldeck was interred in the convent where he expired, in which his brothers, having assumed the habit of the order, lived and died in the performance of acts of charity and devotion. His lands, to which no one asserted any claim, lay waste until they were reassumed by the emperor as a lapsed fief, and the ruins of the castle, which Waldeck had called by his own name, are still shunned by the miner and forester as haunted by evil spirits. Thus were the evils attendant upon wealth, hastily attained and ill-employed, exemplified in the fortunes of Martin Waldeck.

# The Devil's Wager

## William Makepeace Thackeray
## (1811–1863)

William Thackeray, like one or two earlier writers represented in this book, is not primarily remembered for his contibutions to the Gothic genre, yet he grew up surrounded by the multi-volumed tales of terror and sixpenny chapbooks and indeed found considerable inspiration from Charles Maturin's *Melmoth the Wanderer,* of which he wrote admiringly to several friends.

After an unsuccessful schooling at Cambridge and the dissipation of what money he had in travelling abroad, Thackeray married and settled for a life of journalism in London. His first contributions appeared in *The Times,* the *New Monthly* and *Fraser's Magazine* and just when it seemed that his life was comfortable and content, the birth of his third child unhinged his wife's mind and caused the break-up of the family. For some years afterwards his work fell into a trough of mediocrity and it was not until the middle 1840s when he began contributing a column to *Punch* which mocked at English snobbery that his latent talent really flowered. From this period also came his great works, *Vanity Fair* (1847), *Pendennis* (1848) and *Henry Esmond* (1852). Financial security brought relief to the closing years of his life and also enabled him to undertake lecturing tours in England and America.

*The Devil's Wager* is a laconic little Gothic tale which Thackeray contributed to *Fraser's Magazine* in 1836 and in certain respects it can be seen as a fore-runner of the 'black humour' fiction now so popular on both sides of the Atlantic.

IT was the hour of the night when there be none stirring save churchyard ghosts – when all doors are closed except the gates of graves, and all eyes shut but the eyes of wicked men.

When there is no sound on the earth except the ticking of the grasshopper, or the croaking of obscene frogs in the pool.

And no light except that of the blinking stars, and the wicked and devilish wills-o'-the-wisp, as they gambol among the marshes, and lead good men astray.

When there is nothing moving in heaven except the owl, as he flappeth along lazily; or the magician, as he rideth on his infernal broomstick, whistling through the air like the arrows of a Yorkshire archer.

It was at this hour (namely, at twelve o'clock of the night,) that two things went winging through the black clouds, and holding converse with each other.

Now the first was Mercurius, the messenger, not of gods (as the heathens feigned), but of demons; and the second, with whom he held company, was the soul of Sir Roger de Rollo, the brave knight. Sir Roger was Count of Chauchigny, in Champagne; Seigneur of Santerre, Villacerf and autre slieux. But the great die as well as the humble; and nothing remained of brave Roger now, but his coffin and his deathless soul.

And Mercurius, in order to keep fast the soul, his companion, had bound him round the neck with his tail; which, when the soul was stubborn, he would draw so tight as to strangle him wellnigh, sticking into him the barbed point thereof; whereat the poor soul, Sir Rollo, would groan and roar lustily.

Now they two had come together from the gates of purgatory, being bound to those regions of fire and flame where poor sinners fry and roast *in saecula saeculorum*.

'It is hard,' said the poor Sir Rollo, as they went gliding through the clouds, 'that I should thus be condemned for ever, and all for want of a single ave.'

'How, Sir Soul?' said the demon. 'You were on earth so wicked, that not one, or a million of aves, could suffice to keep from hell-flame a creature like thee; but cheer up and be merry; thou wilt be but a subject of our lord the Devil, as am I; and, perhaps, thou wilt be advanced to posts of honour, as am I also:' and to show his authority, he lashed with his tail the ribs of the wretched Rollo.

'Nevertheless, sinner as I am, one more ave would have saved me; for my sister, who was Abbess of St Mary of Chauchigny, did so prevail, by her prayer and good works for my lost and wretched soul, that every day I felt the pains of purgatory decrease; the pitchforks which, on my first entry, had never ceased to vex and torment my poor carcass, were now not applied above once a week; the roasting had ceased, the boiling had discontinued; only a certain warmth was kept up, to remind me of my situation.'

'A gentle stew,' said the demon.

'Yeah, truly, I was but in a stew, and all from the effects of the prayers of my blessed sister. But yesterday, he who watched me in purgatory told me, that yet another prayer from my sister and my bonds should be unloosed, and I, who am now a devil, should have been a blessed angel.'

'And the other ave?' said the demon.

'She died, sir – my sister died – death choked her in the middle of the prayer.' And hereat the wretched spirit began to weep and whine piteously; his salt tears falling over his beard, and scalding the tail of Mercurius the devil.

'It is, in truth, a hard case,' said the demon; 'but I know of no remedy save patience, and for that you will have an excellent opportunity in your lodgings below.'

'But I have relations,' said the Earl; 'my kinsman Randal, who has inherited my lands, will he not say a prayer for his uncle?'

'Thou didst hate and oppress him when living.'

'It is true; but an ave is not much; his sister, my niece, Matilda –'

'You shut her in a convent, and hanged her lover.'

'Had I not reason? besides, has she not others?'

'A dozen, without a doubt.'

'And my brother, the prior?'

'A liege subject of my lord the Devil: he never opens his mouth, except to utter an oath, or to swallow a cup of wine.'

'And yet, if but one of these would but say an ave for me, I should be saved.'

'Aves with them are *rarae* aves,' replied Mercurius, wagging his tail waggishly; 'and, what is more, I will lay thee any wager that no one of these will say a prayer to save thee.'

'I would wager willingly,' responded he of Chauchigny; 'but what has a poor soul like me to stake?'

'Every evening, after the day's roasting, my lord Satan giveth a cup of cold water to his servants; I will bet thee thy water for a year, that none of the three will pray for thee.'

'Done!' said Rollo.

'Done!' said the demon; and here, if I mistake not, is thy castle of Chauchigny.'

Indeed, it was true. The soul, on looking down, perceived the tall towers, the courts, the stables and the fair gardens of the castle. Although it was past midnight there was a blaze of light in the banqueting-hall, and a lamp burning in the open window of the Lady Matilda.

'With whom shall we begin?' said the demon: 'with the baron or the lady?'

'With the lady, if you will.'

'Be it so; her window is open, let us enter.'

So they descended, and entered silently into Matilda's chamber.


The young lady's eyes were fixed so intently on a little clock, that it was no wonder that she did not perceive the entrance of her two visitors. Her fair cheek rested in her white arm, and her white arm on the cushion of a great chair in which she sat, pleasantly supported by sweet thoughts and swan's down; a lute was at her side, and a book of prayers lay under the table (for piety is always modest). Like the amorous Alexander, she sighed and looked (at the clock) – and sighed for ten minutes or more, when she softly breathed the word 'Edward!'

At this the soul of the Baron was wroth. 'The jade is at her old pranks,' said he to the devil; and then addressing Matilda: 'I pray thee, sweet niece, turn thy thoughts for a moment from that villainous page, Edward, and give them to thine affectionate uncle.'

When she heard the voice, and saw the awful apparition of

her uncle (for a year's sojourn in purgatory had not increased the comeliness of his appearance), she started, screamed, and of course fainted.

But the devil Mercurius soon restored her to herself. 'What's o'clock?' said she, as soon as she had recovered from her fit: 'is he come?'

'Not thy lover, Maude, but thine uncle — that is, his soul. For the love of heaven, listen to me: I have been frying in purgatory for a year past, and should have been in heaven but for the want of a single ave.'

'I will say it for thee tomorrow, uncle.'

'Tonight, or never.'

'Well, tonight be it:' and she requested the devil Mercurius to give her the prayer-book, from under the table; but he had no sooner touched the holy book than he dropped it with a shriek and a yell. 'It was hotter,' he said, 'than his master Sir Lucifer's own particular pitchfork.' And the lady was forced to begin her ave without the aid of her missal.

At the commencement of her devotions the demon retired, and carried with him the anxious soul of poor Sir Roger de Rollo.

The lady knelt down — she sighed deeply; she looked again at the clock, and began —

'Ave Maria.'

When a lute was heard under the window, and a sweet voice singing —

'Hark!' said Matilda.

> 'Now the toils of day are over,
>     And the sun hath sunk to rest,
> Seeking, like a fiery lover,
>     The bosom of the blushing west —
>
> 'The faithful night keeps watch and ward,
>     Raising the moon, her silver shield,
> And summoning the stars to guard
>     The slumbers of my fair Mathilde!'

'For mercy's sake!' said Sir Rollo, 'the ave first, and next the song.'

So Matilda again dutifully betook her to her devotions, and began —

'Ave Maria gratia plena!' but the music began again, and the prayer ceased of course.

> 'The faithful night! Now all things lie
>     Hid by her mantle dark and dim,
> In pious hope I hither hie,
>     And humbly chant mine ev'ning hymn.

> 'Thou art my prayer, my saint, my shrine!
>     (For never holy pilgrim knee'd,
> Or wept at feet more pure than mine),
>     My virgin love, my sweet Mathilde!'

'Virgin love!' said the Baron. 'Upon my soul, this is too bad!' and he thought of the lady's lover whom he had caused to be hanged.

But *she* only thought of him who stood singing at her window.

'Niece Matilda!' cried Sir Roger, agonizedly, 'wilt thou listen to the lies of an impudent page, whilst thine uncle is waiting but a dozen words to make him happy?'

At this Matilda grew angry: 'Edward is neither impudent nor a liar, Sir Uncle, and I will listen to the end of the song.'

'Come away,' said Mercurius; 'he hath yet got wield, field, sealed, congealed, and a dozen other rhymes beside; and after the song will come the supper.'

So the poor soul was obliged to go; while the lady listened and the page sung away till morning.

'My virtues have been my ruin,' said poor Sir Rollo, as he and Mercurius slunk silently out of the window. 'Had I hanged that knave Edward, as I did the page his predecessor, my niece would have sung mine ave, and I should have been by this time an angel in heaven.'

'He is reserved for wiser purposes,' responded the devil: 'he will assassinate your successor, the lady Mathilda's brother; and, in consequence, will be hanged. In the love of the lady he will be succeeded by a gardener, who will be replaced by a

monk, who will give way to an ostler, who will be deposed by a
Jew pedlar, who shall, finally yield to a noble earl, the future
husband of the fair Mathilde. So that you see, instead of having
one poor soul a-frying we may now look forward to a goodly
harvest for our lord the Devil.'

The soul of the Baron began to think that his companion
knew too much for one who would make fair bets; but there
was no help for it; he would not, and he could not cry off: and
he prayed inwardly that the brother might be found more pious
than the sister.

But there seemed little chance of this. As they crossed the
court, lackeys, with smoking dishes and full jugs, passed and
repassed continually, although it was long past midnight. On
entering the hall, they found Sir Randal at the head of a vast
table surrounded by a fiercer and more motley collection of
individuals than had congregated there even in the time of Sir
Rollo. The lord of the castle had signified that 'it was his royal
pleasure to be drunk,' and the gentlemen of his train had obse-
quiously followed their master. Mercurius was delighted with
the scene, and relaxed his usually rigid countenance into a bland
and benevolent smile, which became him wonderfully.

The entrance of Sir Roger, who had been dead about a year,
and a person with hoofs, horns, and a tail rather disturbed the
hilarity of the company. Sir Randal dropped his cup of wine;
and Father Peter, the confessor, incontinently paused in the
midst of a profane song, with which he was amusing the society.

'Holy Mother!' cried he, 'it is Sir Roger.'

'Alive!' screamed Sir Randal.

'No, my lord,' Mecurius said; 'Sir Roger is dead, but
cometh on a matter of business; and I have the honour to act
as his counsellor and attendant.'

'Nephew,' said Sir Roger, 'the demon saith justly; I am
come on a trifling affair, in which thy service is essential.'

'I will do anything, uncle, in my power.'

'Thou canst give me life, if thou wilt?' But Sir Randal looked
very blank at this proposition. 'I mean life spiritual, Randal,'
said Sir Roger; and thereupon he explained to him the nature
of the wager.

Whilst he was telling his story, his companion Mercurius was playing all sorts of antics in the hall; and, by his wit and fun, became so popular with this godless crew, that they lost all the fear which his first appearance had given them. The friar was wonderfully taken with him, and used his utmost eloquence and endeavours to convert the devil; the knights stopped drinking to listen to the argument; the men-at-arms forbore brawling; and the wicked little pages crowded round the two strange disputants, to hear their edifying discourse. The ghostly man, however, had little chance in the controversy, and certainly little learning to carry it on. Sir Randal interrupted him. 'Father Peter,' said he, 'our kinsman is condemned for ever, for want of a single ave: wilt thou say it for him?' 'Willingly, my lord,' said the monk 'with my book'; and accordingly he produced his missal to read, without which aid it appeared that the holy father could not manage the desired prayer. But the crafty Mercurius had, by his devilish art, inserted a song in the place of the ave, so that Father Peter, instead of chanting a hymn, sang the following irreverent ditty:

> 'Some love the matin-chimes, which tell
>     The hour of prayer to sinner:
> But better far's the mid-day bell,
>     Which speaks the hour of dinner;
> For when I see a smoking fish,
>     Or capon drowned in gravy,
> Or noble haunch on silver dish,
>
>     Full glad I sing mine ave.
> 'My pulpit is an ale-house bench,
>     Whereon I sit so jolly;
> A smiling rosy country wench
>     My saint and patron holy.
> I kiss her cheek so red and sleek,
>     I press her ringlets wavy.
> And in her willing ear I speak
>     A most religious ave.
>
> 'And if I'm blind, yet heaven is kind,
>     And holy saints forgiving;

> For sure he leads a right good life
>    Who thus admires good living.
> Above they say, our flesh is air,
>    Our blood celestial ichor:
> Oh, grant! mid all the changes there,
>    They may not change our liquor!

And with this pious wish the holy confessor tumbled under the table in an agony of devout drunkenness; whilst the knights, the men-at-arms, and the wicked little pages, rang out the last verse with a most melodious and emphatic glee. 'I am sorry, fair uncle,' hiccupped Sir Randal, 'that, in the matter of the ave, we could not oblige thee in a more orthodox manner; but the holy father has failed, and there is not another man in the hall who hath an idea of a prayer.'

'It is my own fault,' said Sir Rollo; 'for I hanged the last confessor.' And he wished his nephew a surly good night, as he prepared to quit the room.

'Au revoir, gentlemen,' said the devil Mercurius; and once more fixed his tail round the neck of his disappointed companion.

The spirit of poor Rollo was sadly cast down; the devil, on the contrary, was in high good humour. He wagged his tail with the most satisfied air in the world, and cut a hundred jokes at the expense of his poor associate. On they sped, cleaving swiftly through the cold night winds, frightening the birds that were roosting in the woods, and the owls that were watching in the towers.

In the twinkling of an eye, as it is known, devils can fly hundreds of miles: so that almost the same beat of the clock which left these two in Champagne found them hovering over Paris. They dropped into the court of the Lazarist Convent, and winded their way, through passage and cloister, until they reached the door of the prior's cell.

Now the prior, Rollo's brother, was a wicked and malignant sorcerer; his time was spent in conjuring devils and doing wicked deeds, instead of fasting, scourging, and singing holy psalms: this Mercurius knew; and he, therefore, was fully at ease as to the final result of his wager with poor Sir Roger.

'You seem to be well acquainted with the road,' said the knight.

'I have reason,' answered Mercurius, 'having for a long period, had the acquaintance of his reverence, your brother; but you have little chance with him.'

'And why?' said Sir Rollo.

'He is under a bond to my master, never to say a prayer, or else his soul and his body are forfeited at once.'

'Why, thou false and traitorous devil!' said the enraged knight; 'and thou knewest this when we made out wager?'

'Undoubtedly: do you suppose I would have done so had there been any chance of losing?'

And with this they arrived at Father Ignatius's door.

'Thy cursed presence threw a spell on my niece, and stopped the tongue of my nephew's chaplain; I do believe that had I seen either of them alone, my wager had been won.'

'Certainly; therefore, I took good care to go with thee; however, thou mayest see the prior alone, if thou wilt; and lo! his door is open. I will stand without for five minutes when it will be time to commence our journey.'

It was the poor Baron's last chance: and he entered his brother's room more for the five minutes' respite than from any hope of success.

Father Ignatius, the prior, was absorbed in magic calculations: he stood in the middle of a circle of skulls, with no garment except his long white beard, which reached to his knees; he was waving a silver rod, and muttering imprecations in some horrible tongue.

But Sir Rollo came forward and interrupted his incantation. 'I am,' said he, 'the shade of thy brother Roger de Rollo; and have come, from pure brotherly love, to warn thee of thy fate.'

'Whence camest thou?'

'From the abode of the blessed in Paradise,' replied Sir Roger, who was inspired with a sudden thought; 'it was but five minutes ago that that Patron Saint of thy church told me of thy danger, and of thy wicked compact with the fiend. "Go," said he, "to try miserable brother, and kill him there is but one way by which he may escape from paying the awful forfeit of his bond."'

'And how may that be?' said the prior; 'the false fiend hath deceived me; I have given him my soul, but have received no worldly benefit in return. Brother! dear brother! how may I escape?'

'I will tell thee. As soon as I heard the voice of blessed St Mary Lazarus' (the worthy Earl had, at a pinch, coined the name of a saint), 'I left the clouds, where, with other angels, I was seated, and sped hither to save thee. "Thy brother," said the Saint, "hath but one day more to live, when he will become for all eternity the subject of Satan; if he would escape, he must boldly break his bond, by saying an ave."'

'It is the express condition of the agreement,' said the unhappy monk, 'I must say no prayer, or that instant I become Satan's, body and soul.'

'It is the express condition of the Saint,' answered Roger, fiercely; 'pray, brother, pray, or thou art lost for ever.'

So the foolish monk knelt down, and devoutly sung out an ave. 'Amen!' said Sir Roger, devoutly.

'Amen!' said Mercurius, as, suddenly, coming behind, he seized Ignatius by his long beard, and flew up with him to the top of the church-steeple.

The monk roared, and screamed, and swore against his brother; but it was of no avail: Sir Roger smiled kindly on him, and said, 'Do not fret, brother; it must have come to this in a year or two.'

And he flew alongside of Mercurius to the steeple-top; *but this time the devil had not his tail round his neck*. 'I will let thee off thy bet,' said he to the demon; for he could afford, now, to be generous.

'I believe, my lord,' said the demon, politely, 'that our ways separate here.' Sir Roger sailed gaily upwards: while Mercurius having bound the miserable monk faster than ever, he sunk downwards to earth, and perhaps lower. Ignatius was heard roaring and screaming as the devil dashed him against the iron spikes and buttresses of the church.

# The Expedition to Hell

## James Hogg

## (1770–1835)

Scotland, at the time of Sir Walter Scott, was particularly rich in writers of macabre tales* and among the names which still endure like Allan Cunningham, John Galt, John Mackay Wilson and James Hogg, not a few produced work in, or inspired by, the Gothic genre. Certainly, though, to try and include examples by all these men would give rise to accusations of bias in favour of the land of Burns, but there is every justification for the next two Scottish tales in that they are particularly illustrative of what was happening to tales of terror at this time: for apart from the strong historical flavour introduced by Scott, they were becoming much more inventive in plot and dwelling more deeply on the fears of the mind.

The first of these is by Hogg, the 'Ettrick Shepherd' as he was known, who wrote the famous *Private Memoirs and Confessions of a Justified Sinner* (1824). Steeped in supernatural lore from his childhood (his mother was a noted teller of local ballads and legends), he retold many of these tales in prose and verse for popular periodicals of the time. In the story which follows dream and reality are mixed together in a fashion unique at the time of its first publication (1836), but very much a part of the weird storyteller's craft today.

THERE is no phenomenon in nature less understood, and about which greater nonsense is written than dreaming. It is a strange thing. For my part I do not understand it, nor have I any desire to do so; and I firmly believe that no philosopher that ever wrote knows a particle more about it than I do, however elaborate and

* See *The Clans of Darkness* edited by Peter Haining. U.K. Victor Gollancz 1971; U.S. Taplinger Publishing Company 1971.

subtle the theories he may advance concerning it. He knows not even what sleep is, nor can he define its nature, so as to enable any common mind to comprehend him; and how, then, can he define that ethereal part of it, wherein the soul holds intercourse with the external world? – how, in that state of abstraction, some ideas force themselves upon us, in spite of all our efforts to get rid of them; while others, which we have resolved to bear about with us by night as well as by day, refuse us their fellowship, even at periods when we most require their aid?

No, no; the philosopher knows nothing about either; and if he says he does; I entreat you not to believe him. He does not know what mind is; even his own mind, to which one would think he has the most direct access: far less can he estimate the operations and powers of that of any other intelligent being. He does not even know, with all his subtlety, whether it be a power distinct from his body, or essentially the same, and only incidentally and temporarily endowed with different qualities. He sets himself to discover at what period of his existence the union was established. He is baffled; for Consciousness refuses the intelligence, declaring, that she cannot carry him far enough back to ascertain it. He tries to discover the precise moment when it is dissolved, but on this Consciousness is altogether silent; and all is darkness and mystery; for the origin, the manner of continuance, and the time and mode of breaking up of the union between soul and body, are in reality undiscoverable by our natural faculties – are not patent, beyond the possibility of mistake: but whosoever can read his Bible, and solve a dream, can do either, without being subjected to any material error.

It is on this ground that I like to contemplate, not the theory of dreams, but the dreams themselves; because they prove to the unlettered man, in a very forcible manner, a distinct existence of the soul, and its lively and rapid intelligence with external nature, as well as with a world of spirits with which it has no acquaintance, when the body is lying dormant, and the same to the soul as if sleeping in death.

I account nothing of any dream that relates to the actions of the day; the person is not sound asleep who dreams about these things; there is no division between matter and mind, but they are mingled together in a sort of chaos – what a farmer would call compost – fermenting and disturbing one another. I find that in all dreams of that kind, men of every profession have dreams peculiar to their own occupations; and, in the country, at least, their import is generally understood. Every man's body is a barometer. A thing made up of the elements must be affected by their various changes and convulsions; and so the body assuredly is. When I was a shepherd, and all the comforts of my life depended so much on good or bad weather, the first thing I did every morning was strictly to overhaul the dreams of the night; and I found that I could calculate better from them than from the appearance and changes of the sky. I know a keen sportsman who pretends that his dreams never deceive him. If the dream is of angling, or pursuing salmon in deep waters, he is sure of rain; but if fishing on dry ground, or in waters so low that the fish cannot get from him, it forebodes drought; hunting or shooting hares is snow, and moorfowl wind, &c. But the most extraordinary professional dream on record is, without all doubt, that well-known one of George Dobson, coach-driver in Edinburgh, which I shall here relate; for though it did not happen in the shepherd's cot, it has often been recited there.

George was part proprietor and driver of a hackneycoach in Edinburgh, when such vehicles were scarce; and one day a gentleman, whom he knew, came to him and said: – 'George, you must drive me and my son here out to –,' a certain place that he named, somewhere in the vicinity of Edinburgh.

'Sir,' said George, 'I never heard tell of such a place, and I cannot drive you to it unless you give me very particular directions.'

'It is false,' returned the gentleman; 'there is no man in Scotland who knows the road to that place better than you do. You have never driven on any other road all your life; and I insist on you taking us.'

'Very well, sir,' said George, 'I'll drive you to hell, if you have a mind; only you are to direct me on the road.'

'Mount and drive on, then' said the other; 'and no fear of the road.'

George did so, and never in his life did he see his horses go at such a noble rate; they snorted, they pranced, and they flew on; and as the whole road appeared to lie down-hill, he deemed that he should soon come to his journey's end. Still he drove on at the same rate, far, far down-hill, – and so fine an open road he never travelled, – till by degress it grew so dark that he could not see to drive any farther. He called to the gentleman, inquiring what he should do; who answered that this was the place they were bound to, so he might draw up, dismiss them, and return. He did so, alighted fom the dickie, wondered at his foaming horses, and forthwith opened the coach-door, held the rim of his hat with the one hand and with the other demanded his fare.

'You have driven us in fine style, George,' said the elder gentleman, 'and deserve to be remembered; but it is needless for us to settle just now, as you must meet us here again tomorrow precisely at twelve o'clock.'

'Very well, sir,' said George; 'there is likewise an old account, you know, and some toll-money;' which indeed there was.

'It shall be all settled tomorrow, George, and moreover, I fear there will be some toll-money today.'

'I perceived no tolls today, your honour,' said George.

'But I perceived one, and not very far back neither, which I suspect you will have difficulty in repassing without a regular ticket. What a pity I have no change on me!'

'I never saw it otherwise with your honour,' said George, jocularly; 'what a pity it is you should always suffer yourself to run short of change!'

'I will give you that which is as good, George,' said the gentleman; and he gave him a ticket written with red ink, which the honest coachman could not read. He, however, put it into his sleeve, and inquired of his employer where that same toll was which he had not observed, and how it was that they did not ask from him as he came through? The gentleman replied, by informing George that there was no road out of that domain, and that whoever entered it must either remain in it, or return by the same path; so they never asked any toll till the person's return, when they were at times highly capricious; but that the ticket he had given him would answer his turn. And he then asked George if he did not perceive a gate, with a number of men in black standing about it.

'Oho! Is yon the spot?' says George; 'then, I assure your honour, yon is no toll-gate, but a private entrance into a great man's mansion; for do not I know two or three of the persons yonder to be gentlemen of the law, whom I have driven often and often? and as good fellows they are too as any I know – men who never let themselves run short of change! Good day. – Twelve o'clock tomorrow?'

'Yes, twelve o'clock noon, precisely;' and with that, George's employer vanished in the gloom, and left him to wind his way out of that dreary labyrinth the best way he could. He found it no easy matter, for his lamps were not lighted, and he could not see a yard before him – he could not even perceive his horses' ears; and what was worse, there was a rushing sound, like that of a town on fire, all around him, that stunned his senses, so that he could not tell whether his horses were moving or standing still. George was in the greatest distress imaginable, and was glad when he perceived the gate before him, with his two identical friends, men of the law, still standing. George drove boldly up, accosted them by their names, and asked what they were doing there; they made him no answer, but pointed to the gate and the keeper. George was terrified to look at this latter personage, who now came up and seized his horses by the reins, refusing to let him pass. In oder to introduce himself, in some degree, to this austere toll-man, George asked him, in a jocular manner, how he came to employ his two eminent friends as assistant gate-keepers?

'Because they are among the last comers,' replied the ruffian, churlishly. 'You will be an assistant here tomorrow.'

'The devil I will, sir.'

'Yes, the devil you will, sir.'

'I'll be d – d if I do then – that I will !'

'Yes, you'll be d – d if you do – that you will.'

'Let my horses go in the meantime, then, sir, that I may proceed on my journey.'

'Nay.'

'Nay ! – Dare you say nay to me, sir ? My name is George Dobson, of the Pleasance, Edinburgh, coach-driver, and coach-proprietor too; and no man shall say *nay* to me, as long as I can pay my way. I have his Majesty's license, and I'll go and come as I choose – and that I will. Let go my horses there, and tell me what is your demand.'

'Well, then, I'll let your horses go,' said the keeper: 'But I'll keep yourself for a pledge.' And with that he let go the horses, and seized honest George by the throat, who struggled in vain to disengage himself, and swore, and threatened, according to his own confession, most bloodily. His horses flew off like the wind so swift, that the coach seemed flying in the air and scarcely bounding on the earth once in a quarter of a mile. George was in furious wrath, for he saw that his grand coach and harness would all be broken to pieces, and his gallant pair of horses maimed or destroyed; and how was his family's bread now to be won ! – He struggled, threatened, and prayed in vain; – the intolerable toll-man was deaf to all remonstrances. He once more appealed to his two genteel acquaintances of the law, reminding them how he had of late driven them to Roslin on a Sunday, along with two ladies, who, he supposed, were their sisters, from their familiarity, when not another coachman in town would engage with them. But the gentlemen, very ungenerously, only shook their heads, and pointed to the gate. George's circumstances now became desperate, and again he asked the hideous tollman what right he had to detain him, and what were his charges.

'What right have I to detain you, sir, say you? Who are you that make such a demand here? Do you know where you are, sir?'

'No, faith, I do not,' returned George; 'I wish I did. But I *shall* know, and make you repent your insolence too. My name, I told you, is George Dobson, licensed coach-hirer in Pleasance,

Edinburgh; and to get full redress of you for this unlawful interruption, I only desire to know where I am.'

'Then, sir, if it can give you so much satisfaction to know where you are,' said the keeper, with a malicious grin, 'you *shall* know, and you may take instruments by the hands of your two friends there instituting a legal prosecution. Your redress, you may be assured, will be most ample, when I inform you that you are in HELL! and out at this gate you pass no more.'

This was rather a damper to George, and he began to perceive that nothing would be gained in such a place by the strong hand, so he addressed the inexorable toll-man, whom he now dreaded more than ever, in the following terms: 'But I must go home at all events, you know, sir, to unyoke my two horses, and put them up, and to inform Chirsty Halliday my wife, of my engagement. And, bless me! I never recollected till this moment, that I am engaged to be back here tomorrow at twelve o'clock, and see, here is a free ticket for my passage this way.'

The keeper took the ticket with one hand, but still held George with the other. 'Oho! were you in with our honourable friend, Mr R – of L – y?' said he. 'He has been on our books for a long while; – however, this will do, only you must put your name to it likewise; and the engagement is this – You, by this instrument, engage your soul, that you will return here by tomorrow at noon.'

'Catch me there, billy!' says George. 'I'll engage no such thing, depend on it; – that I will not.'

'Then remain where you are,' said the keeper, 'for there is no other alternative. We like best for people to come here in their own way, – in the way of their business;' and with that he flung George backwards, heels-over-head down hill, and closed the gate.

George finding all remonstrance vain, and being desirous once more to see the open day, and breathe the fresh air, and likewise to see Christy Halliday, his wife, and set his house and stable in some order, came up again, and in utter desperation, signed the bond, and was suffered to depart. He then bounded away on the track of his horses with more than ordinary swiftness, in hopes to overtake them; and always now and then uttered a loud Wo! in hopes they might hear and obey, though he could not come in sight of them. But George's grief was but beginning; for at a well-known and dangerous spot, where there was a tan-yard on the one hand, and a quarry on the other, he came to his gallant steeds overturned, the coach smashed to pieces, Dawtie with two of her legs broken, and Duncan dead. This was more than the worthy coachman could bear, and many degrees worse than being in hell. There, his pride and manly spirit bore him up against the worst of treatment; but here his heart entirely failed him, and he laid himself down, with his face on his two hands, and wept bitterly, bewailing, in the most deplorable terms, his two gallant horses, Dawtie and Duncan.

While lying in this inconsolable state, some one took hold of his shoulder, and shook it; and a well-known voice said to him, 'Geordie! what is the matter wi' ye, Geordie?' George was provoked beyond measure at the insolence of the question, for he knew the voice to be that of Chirsty Halliday, his wife. 'I think you needna ask that, seeing what you see,' said George. 'O, my poor Dawtie, where are a' your jinkings and prancings now, your moopings and your wincings? I'll ne'er be a proud man again – bereaved o' my bonny pair!'

'Get up, George; get up, and bestir yourself,' said Chirsty Halliday, his wife. 'You are wanted directly to bring the Lord President to the Parliament House. It is a great storm, and he must be there by nine o'clock. – Get up – rouse yourself, and make ready – his servant is waiting for you.'

'Woman, you are demented!' cried George. 'How can I go and bring in the Lord President, when my coach is broken in pieces, my poor Dawtie lying with twa of her legs broken, and Duncan dead? And, moreover, I have a previous engagement, for I am obliged to be in hell before twelve o'clock.'

Chirsty Halliday now laughed outright, and continued long in a fit of laughter; but George never moved his head from the pillow, but lay and groaned, – for, in fact, he was all this while lying snug in his bed; while the tempest without was roaring with great violence, and which circumstance may perhaps account for the rushing and deafening sound which astounded him so much in hell. But so deeply was he impressed with the idea of the reality of his dream, that he would do nothing but lie and moan, persisting and believing in the truth of all he had seen. His wife now went and informed her neighbours of her husband's plight, and of his singular engagement with Mr R – of L – y at twelve o'clock. She persuaded one friend to harness the horses, and go for the Lord President; but all the rest laughed immoderately at poor coachy's predicament. It was, however, no laughing matter to him; he never raised his head, and his wife becoming uneasy about the frenzied state of his mind, made him repeat every circumstance of his adventure to her, (for he would never believe or admit that it was a dream,) which he did in the terms above narrated; and she perceived or dreaded that he was becoming somewhat feverish. She went out, and told Dr Wood of her husband's malady, and of his solemn engagement to be in hell at twelve o'clock.

'He maunna keep it, dearie. He maunna keep that engagement at no rate,' said Dr Wood. 'Set back the clock an hour or twa, to drive him past the time, and I'll ca' in the course of my rounds. Are ye sure he hasna been drinking hard?' – She assured him he had not. – 'Weel, weel, ye maun tell him that he mauna keep that engagement at no rate. Set back the clock, and I'll come and see him. It is a frenzy that maunna be trifled with. Ye maunna laugh at it, dearie, – maunna laugh at it. Maybe a nervish fever, wha kens.'

The Doctor and Chirsty left the house together, and as their road lay the same way for a space, she fell a telling him of the two young lawyers whom George saw standing at the gate of hell, and whom the porter had described as two of the last comers. When the Doctor heard this, he stayed his hurried, stooping pace in one moment, turned full round on the woman, and fixing his eyes on her, that gleamed with a deep unstable lustre, he said, 'What's that ye were saying, dearie? What's that ye were saying? Repeat it again to me, every word.' She did so. On which the Doctor held up his hands, as if palsied with astonishment, and uttered some fervent ejaculations. 'I'll go with you straight,' said he, 'Before I visit another patient.' This is wonderfu'! it is terrible! The young gentlemen are both at rest — both lying corpses at this time! Fine young men — I attended them both — died of the same exterminating disease — Oh, this is wonderful; this is wonderful!'

The Doctor kept Chirsty half running all the way down the High Street and St Mary's Wynd, at such a pace did he walk, never lifting his eyes from the pavement, but always exclaiming now and then, 'It is wonderfu' most wonderfu'!' At length, prompted by woman's natural curiosity, Chirsty inquired at the Doctor if he knew any thing of their friend Mr R — of L — y. But he shook his head, and replied, 'Na, na, dearie, — ken naething about him. He and his son are baith in London — ken naething about him; but the tither is awfu' — it is perfectly awfu'!'

When Dr Wood reached his patient he found him very low, but only a little feverish; so he made all haste to wash his head with vinegar and cold water, and then he covered the crown with a treacle plaster, and made the same application to the soles of his feet, awaiting the issue. George revived a little, when the Doctor tried to cheer him up by joking him about his dream; but on mention of that he groaned, and shook his head. 'So you are convinced, dearie, that it is nae dream?' said the Doctor.

'Dear sir, how could it be a dream?' said the patient. 'I was there in person, with Mr R — and his son; and see, here are the marks of the porter's fingers on my throat.' — Dr Wood looked, and distinctly saw two or three red spots on one side of his throat, which confounded him not a little. — 'I assure you, sir,' continued George, 'it was no dream, which I know to my sad experience. I have lost my coach and horses, — and what more have I? — signed the bond with my own hand, and in person entered into the most solemn and terrible engagement.'

'But ye're no to keep it, I tell ye,' said Dr Wood; 'ye're no to keep it at no rate. It is a sin to enter into a compact wi' the deil, but it is a far greater ane to keep it. Sae let Mr R — and his son bide where they are yonder, for ye sanna stir a foot to bring them out the day.'

'Oh, oh, Doctor!' groaned the poor fellow, 'this is not a

thing to be made a jest o' ! I feel that it is an engagement that I cannot break. Go I must, and that very shortly. Yes, yes, go I must, and go I will, although I should borrow David Barclay's pair.' With that he turned his face towards the wall, groaned deeply, and fell into a lethargy, while Dr Wood caused them to let him alone, thinking if he would sleep out the appointed time, which was at hand, he would be safe; but all the time he kept feeling his pulse and by degrees showed symptoms of uneasiness. His wife ran for a clergyman of famed abilities, to pray and converse with her husband, in hopes by that means to bring him to his senses; but after his arrival, George never spoke more, save calling to his horses, as if encouraging them to run with great speed; and thus in imagination driving at full career to keep his appointment, he went off in a paroxysm, after a terrible struggle, precisely within a few minutes of twelve o'clock.

A circumstance not known at the time of George's death made this singular professional dream the more remarkable and unique in all its parts. It was a terrible storm on the night of the dream, as has been already mentioned, and during the time of the hurricane, a London smack went down off Wearmouth about three in the morning. Among the sufferers were the Hon. Mr R — of L – y, and his son ! George could not know aught of this at break of day, for it was not known in Scotland till the day of his interment; and as little knew he of the deaths of the two young lawyers, who both died of the small-pox the evening before.

# The Iron Shroud

## Anonymous

## (1832)

This second story from Scotland, apart from showing another facet of the 'old style' Gothic tale developing into what we now call the horror story, is also of note in being typical of the short fiction at last finding its way in quantity into literary magazines and periodicals.

It had taken the editors of the day a long time to accept the undeniable and continuing success of the Gothic story and admit it to their columns. Undoubtedly the early trouble of *The Monk* and the notorious sixpenny chapbooks had caused them to be wary of introducing such material to their genteel readers – but popularity was popularity and by the early 1830s hardly a magazine in Britain or Europe did not carry a macabre story or two, especially at Christmas! Edith Birkhead, writing on this aspect of the Gothic development, has said, 'In these periodicals the grave and the gay are now intermingled, and when we are weary of dark intrigues and impenetrable secrets we may turn to lighter reading.'

*The Iron Shroud* has been selected from that most popular of Scottish magazines, *Blackwood's*, and although it appeared anonymously in the autumn of 1832, it has been established that the author was William Mudford, a writer who Sir Walter Scott noted in his journal, 'loves to play at cherrypit with Satan.' The setting and plot are very much in the same mould as Edgar Allan Poe (at the time just beginning to create his unique poems and tales of horror) and it is one story that I have particular pleasure in rescuing from obscurity.

THE castle of the Prince of Tolfi was built on the summit of the towering and precipitous rock of Scylle, and commanded a magnificent view of Sicily in all its grandeur. Here during the wars of the Middle Ages, when the fertile plains of Italy were devastated by hostile factions, those prisoners were confined for whose ransom a costly price was demanded. Here, too, in a dungeon, excavated deep in the solid rock, the miserable victim was immured, whom revenge pursued – the dark, fierce, and unpitying revenge of an Italian heart.

Vivenzio – the noble and the generous, the fearless in battle, and the pride of Naples in her sunny hours of peace – the young, the brave, the proud Vivenzio fell beneath this subtle and remorseless spirit. He was the prisoner of Tolfi, and he languished in that rock-encircled dungeon, which stood alone, and whose portals never opened twice upon a living captive.

It had the semblance of a vast cage, for the roof and floor and sides were of iron, solidly wrought and spaciously constructed. High above there ran a range of seven grated windows, guarded with massive oars of the same metal, which admitted light and air. Save these, and the tall folding doors beneath them, which occupied the centre, no chink, or chasm, or projection broke the smooth black surface of the walls. An iron bedstead, littered with straw, stood in one corner; and beside it a vessel with water and a coarse dish filled with coarser food.

Even the intrepid soul of Vivenzio shrank with dismay as he entered this abode, and heard the ponderous doors triple-locked by the silent ruffians who conducted him to it. Their silence seemed prophetic of his fate, of the living grave that had been prepared for him. His menaces and his entreaties, his indignant appeals for justice, and his impatient questioning of their intentions, were alike vain. They listened, but spoke not. Fit ministers of a crime that should have no tongue!

How dismal was the sound of their retiring steps! And, as their faint echoes died along the winding passages, a fearful presage grew within him, that never more the face, or voice, or tread of man would greet his senses. He had seen human beings for the last time! And he had looked his last upon the bright sky, and upon the smiling earth, and upon a beautiful world he loved, and whose minion he had been! Here he was to end his life – a life he had just begun to revel in. And by what means? By secret poison? or by murderous assault? No – for then it had been needless to bring him thither. Famine perhaps – a thousand deaths in one! It was terrible to think of it – but it was yet more terrible to picture long, long years of captivity in a solitude so appalling, a loneliness so dreary, that thought, for want of fellowship, would lose itself in madness or stagnate into idiocy.

He could not hope to escape, unless he had the power, with his bare hands, of rending asunder the solid iron walls of his prison. He could not hope for liberty from the relenting mercies of his enemy. His instant death under any form of refined cruelty, was not the object of Tolfi, for he might have inflicted it, and he had not. It was too evident, therefore, he was reserved for some premeditated scheme of subtile vengeance; and what vengeance could transcend in fiendish malice either the slow death of famine or the still slower one of solitary incarceration till the last lingering spark of life expired, or till reason fled, and nothing should remain to perish but the brute functions of the body?

It was evening when Vivenzio entered his dungeon, and the approaching shades of night wrapped it in total darkness, as he paced up and down, revolving in his mind these horrible forebodings. No tolling bell from the castle or from any neighbouring church or convent struck upon his ear to tell how the hours passed. Frequently he would stop and listen for some sound that might betoken the vicinity of man; but the solitude of the desert, the silence of the tomb are not so still and deep as the oppressive desolation by which he was encompassed. His heart sank within him, and he threw himself dejectedly upon his couch of straw. Here sleep gradually obliterated the consciousness of misery, and bland dreams wafted his delighted spirit to scenes which were once glowing realities for him, in whose ravishing illusions he soon lost the remembrance that he was Tolfi's prisoner.

When he awoke it was daylight; but how long he had slept he knew not. It might be early morning or it might be sultry noon, for he could measure time by no other note of its progress than light and darkness. He had been so happy in his sleep, amid friends who loved him, and the sweeter endearments of those who loved him as friends could not, that in the first moments of waking his startled mind seemed to admit the knowledge of his situation, as if it had burst upon it for the first time, fresh in all its appalling horrors. He gazed round with an air of doubt and amazement, and took up a handful of the straw upon which he lay, as though he would ask himself what it meant. But memory, too faithful to her office, soon unveiled the melancholy past, while reason, shuddering at the task, flashed before his eyes the tremendous future. The contrast overpowered him. He remained for some time lamenting, like a truth, the bright visions that had vanished; and recoiling from the present, which clung to him as a poisoned garment.

When he grew more calm, he surveyed his gloomy dungeon. Alas! the stronger light of day only served to confirm what the gloomy indistinctness of the preceding evening had partially disclosed, the utter impossibility of escape. As, however, his eyes wandered round and round, and from place to place, he noticed two circumstances which excited his surprise and curiosity. The one, he thought, might be fancy; but the other was positive. His pitcher of water and the dish which contained his food had been removed from his side while he slept, and now stood near the door.

Were he even inclined to doubt this, by supposing he had mistaken the spot where he saw them over night, he could not, for the pitcher now in his dungeon was neither of the same form nor colour as the other, while the food was changed for some other of better quality. He had been visited therefore during the night. But how had the person obtained entrance? Could he have slept so soundly that the unlocking and opening of those ponderous portals were effected without waking him? He would have said this was not possible, but that in doing so he must admit a greater difficulty, an entrance by other means, of which he was convinced there existed none. It was not intended, then, that he should be left to perish from hunger. But the secret and mysterious mode of supplying him with food seemed to indicate he was to have no opportunity of communicating with a human being.

The other circumstance which had attracted his notice was the disappearance, as he believed, of one of the seven grated windows that ran along the top of his prison. He felt confident that he had observed and counted them; for he was rather surprised at their number, and there was something peculiar in their form, as well as in the manner of their arrangement, at unequal distances. It was so much easier, however, to suppose he was mistaken, than that a portion of the solid iron which formed the walls could have escaped from its position, that he soon dismissed the thought from his mind.

Vivenzio partook of the food that was before him without apprehension. It might be poisoned; but if it were, he knew he could not escape death should such be the design of Tolfi; and the quickest death would be the speediest release.

The day passed wearily and gloomily, though not without a faint hope that by keeping watch at night he might observe when the person came again to bring him food, which he supposed he would do in the same way as before. The mere thought of being approached by a living creature, and the opportunity it might present of learning the doom prepared, or preparing, for him, imparted some comfort. Besides, if he came alone, might he not in a furious onset overpower him? Or he might be accessible to pity, or the influence of such munificent rewards as he could bestow, if once more at liberty and master of himself. Say he were armed. The worst that could befall, if nor bribe, nor prayers, nor force prevailed, was a desired blow which, though dealt in a damned cause, might work a desired end. There was no chance so desperate, but it looked lovely in Vivenzio's eyes compared with the idea of being totally abandoned.

The night came, and Vivenzio watched. Morning came, and Vivenzio was confounded! He must have slumbered without knowing it. Sleep must have stolen over him when exhausted by fatigue, and in that interval of feverish repose he had been baffled; for there stood his replenished pitcher of water, and there his day's meal!

Nor was this all. Casting his looks towards the windows of his dungeon, he counted but FIVE! Here was no deception; and he was now convinced there had been none the day before. But what did all this portend? Into what strange and mysterious den had he been cast? He gazed till his eyes ached; he could discover nothing to explain the mystery. That it was so, he knew. Why it was so, he racked his imagination in vain to conjecture. He examined the doors. A single circumstance convinced him they had not been opened.

A wisp of straw which he had carelessly thrown against them the preceding day, as he paced to and fro, remained where he had cast it, though it must have been displaced by the slightest motion of either of the doors. This was evidence that could not be disputed; and it followed there must be some secret machinery in the walls by which a person could enter. He inspected them closely. They appeared to him one solid and compact mass of iron; or joined, if joined they were, with such nice art that no mark of division was perceptible. Again and again he surveyed them – and the floor – and the roof – and that range of visionary windows, as he was now almost tempted to consider them: he could discover nothing, absolutely nothing, to relieve his doubts or satisfy his curiosity. Sometimes he fancied that altogether the dungeon had a more contracted appearance – that it looked smaller; but this he ascribed to fancy, and the impression naturally produced upon his mind by the undeniable disappearance of two of the windows.

With intense anxiety, Vivenzio looked forward to the return of night; and as it approached he resolved that no treacherous sleep should again betray him. Instead of seeking his bed of straw, he continued to walk up and down his dungeon till daylight, straining his eyes in every direction through the darkness to watch for any appearances that might explain these mysteries. While thus engaged, and as nearly as he could judge (by the time that afterwards elapsed before the morning came in) about two o'clock, there was a slight tremulous motion of the floor.

He stooped. The motion lasted nearly a minute; but it was so extremely gentle that he almost doubted whether it was real or only imaginary.

He listened. Not a sound could be heard. Presently, however, he felt a rush of cold air blow upon him; and dashing towards the quarter whence it seemed to proceed, he stumbled over something which he judged to be the water ewer. The rush of cold air was no longer perceptible; and as Vivenzio stretched out his hands he found himself close to the walls. He remained motionless for a considerable time, but nothing occurred during the remainder of the night to excite his attention, though he continued to watch with unabated vigilance.

The first approaches of the morning were visible through the grated windows, breaking, with faint divisions of light, the darkness that still pervaded every other part, long before Vivenzio was enabled to distinguish any object in his dungeon. Instinctively and fearfully he turned his eyes, hot and inflamed with watching, towards them.

There were FOUR! He could see only four; but it might be that some intervening object prevented the fifth from becoming perceptible; and he waited impatiently to ascertain if it were so. As the light strengthened, however, and penetrated every corner of the cell, other objects of amazement struck his sight. On the ground lay the broken fragments of the pitcher he had used the day before, and at a small distance from them, nearer to the wall, stood the one he had noticed the first night. It was filled with water, and beside it was his food.

He was now certain that by some mechanical contrivance an opening was obtained through the iron wall, and that through this opening the current of air had found entrance. But how noiseless! For had a feather almost waved at the time, he must have heard it. Again he examined that part of the wall; but both to sight and touch it appeared one even and uniform surface, while to repeated and violent blows there was no reverberating sound indicative of hollowness.

This perplexing mystery had for a time withdrawn his

thoughts from the windows; but now, directing his eyes again towards them, he saw that the fifth had disappeared in the same manner as the preceding two, without the least distinguishable alteration of external appearances. The remaining four looked as the seven had originally looked; that is, occupying at irregular distances the top of the wall on that side of the dungeon. The tall folding door, too, still seemed to stand beneath, in the centre of these four, as it had at first stood in the centre of the seven. But he could no longer doubt what on the preceding day he fancied might be the effect of visual deception.

The dungeon was smaller. The roof had lowered, and the opposite ends had contracted the intermediate distance by a space equal, he thought, to that over which the three windows had extended. He was bewildered in vain imaginings to account for these things. Some frightful purpose – some devilish torture of mind or body – some unheard-of-device for producing exquisite misery, lurked, he was sure, in what had taken place.

Oppressed with this belief, and distracted more by the dreadful uncertainty of whatever fate impended, than he could be dismayed, he thought, by the knowledge of the worst, he sat ruminating, hour after hour yielding his fears in succession to ever haggard fancy. At last a horrible suspicion flashed suddenly across his mind and he started up with a frantic air.

'Yes !' he exclaimed, looking wildly round his dungeon, and shuddering as he spoke – 'Yes! it must be so! I see it! – I feel the maddening truth like scorching flames upon my brain! Eternal God! – support me! It must be so! Yes, yes, that is to be my fate! Yon roof will descend! – these walls will hem me round – and slowly, slowly, crush me in their iron arms! Lord God! look down upon me, and in mercy strike me with instant death! Oh, fiend – oh, devil – is this your revenge?'

He dashed himself upon the ground in agony; tears burst from him, and the sweat stood in large drops upon his face; he sobbed aloud; he tore his hair; he rolled about like one suffering intolerable anguish of body, and would have bitten the iron floor beneath him; he breathed fearful curses upon Tolfi, and the next moment passionate prayers to heaven for immediate death. Then the violence of his grief became exhausted, and he lay still, weeping as a child would weep.

The twilight of departing day shed its gloom around him ere he arose from that posture of utter and hopeless sorrow. He had taken no food. Not one drop of water had cooled the fever of his parched lips. Sleep had not visited his eyes for six-and-thirty hours. He was faint with hunger, weary with watching and with the excess of his emotions. He tasted of his food; he drank with avidity of the water; and reeling like a drunken man to his straw, cast himself upon it to brood again over the appalling image that had fastened itself upon his almost frenzied thoughts.

He slept. But his slumbers were not tranquil. He resisted, as long as he could, their approach; and when, at last, enfeebled nature yielded to their influence, he found no oblivion from his cares. Terrible dreams haunted him – ghastly visions harrowed up his imagination – he shouted and screamed, as if he already felt the dungeon's ponderous roof descending on him – he breathed hard and thick, as though writhing between its iron walls. Then would he spring up – stare wildly about him – stretch forth his hands to be sure he yet had space enough to live – and, muttering some incoherent words, sink down again, to pass through the same fierce vicissitudes of delirious sleep.

The morning of the fourth day dawned upon Vivenzio. But it was high noon before his mind shook off its stupor, or he awoke to a full consciousness of his situation. And what a fixed energy of despair sat upon his pale features, as he cast his eyes upwards, and gazed upon the THREE windows that now alone remained! The three! – there were no more! – and they seemed to number his own allotted days. Slowly and calmly he next surveyed the top and sides, and comprehended all the meaning of the diminished height of the former, as well as of the gradual approximation of the latter.

The contracted dimensions of his mysterious prison were now too gross and palpable to be the juggle of his heated imagination. Still lost in wonder at the means, Vivenzio could put no cheat upon his reason as to the end. By what horrible ingenuity it was contrived that walls, and roof, and windows, should thus silently and imperceptibly, without noise, and without motion almost, fold, as it were, within each other, he knew not. He only knew they did so; and he vainly strove to persuade himself it was the intention of the contriver to rack the miserable wretch who might be immured there with anticipation, merely, of a fate from which in the very crisis of his agony he was to be reprieved.

Gladly would he have clung even to this possibility if his heart would have let him; but he felt a dreadful assurance of its fallacy. And what matchless inhumanity it was to doom the sufferer to such lingering torments — to lead him day by day to so appalling a death, unsupported by the consolations of religion, unvisited by any human being, abandoned to himself, deserted of all, and denied even the sad privilege of knowing that his cruel destiny would awaken pity! Alone he was to perish! — alone he was to wait a slow coming torture, whose most exquisite pangs would be inflicted by that very solitude and that tardy coming!

'It is not death I fear,' he exclaimed, 'but the death I must prepare for! Methinks, too, I could meet even that — all horrible and revolting as it is — if it might overtake me now. But where shall I find fortitude to tarry till it come! How can I outlive the three long days and nights I have to live? There is no power within me to bid the hideous spectre hence — none to make it familiar to my thoughts, or myself patient to its errand. My thoughts, rather, will flee from me, and I grow mad in looking at it. Oh! for a deep sleep to fall upon me! That so, in death's likeness, I might embrace death itself, and drink no more of the cup that is presented to me than my fainting spirit has already tasted!'

In the midst of these lamentations Vivenzio noticed that his accustomed meal, with the pitcher of water, had been conveyed, as before, into his dungeon. But this circumstance no longer excited his surprise. His mind was overwhelmed with others of a far greater magnitude. It suggested, however, a feeble hope of deliverance; and there is no hope so feeble as not to yield some support to a heart bending under despair.

He resolved to watch during the ensuing night for the signs he had before observed; and, should he again feel the gentle, tremulous motion of the floor or the current of air, to seize that moment for giving audible expression to his misery. Some person must be near him and within reach of his voice at the instant when his food was supplied; some one, perhaps, susceptible of pity. Or if not, to be told even that his apprehensions were just, and that his fate was to be what he foreboded, would be preferable to a suspense which hung upon the possibility of his worst fears being visionary.

The night came; and as the hour approached when Vivenzio imagined he might expect the signs, he stood fixed and silent as a statue. He feared to breathe, almost, lest he might lose any sound which would warn him of their coming. While thus listening, with every faculty of mind and body strained to an agony of attention, it occurred to him he should be more sensible of the motion, probably, if he stretched himself along the iron floor.

He according laid himself softly down, and had not been long in that position when – yes – he was certain of it – the floor moved under him! He sprang up, and in a voice suffocated nearly with emotion, called aloud. He paused – the motion ceased – he felt no stream of air – all was hushed – no voice answered to his – he burst into tears; and as he sank to the ground, in renewed anguish, exclaimed: 'Oh, my God! You alone have power to save me now, or strengthen me for the trial you permit.'

Another morning dawned upon the wretched captive, and the fatal index of his doom met his eyes. Two windows! – and *two* days – and all would be over! Fresh food – fresh water! The mysterious visit had been paid, though he had implored it in vain. But how awfully was his prayer answered in what he now saw! The roof of the dungeon was within a foot of his head. The two ends were so near, that in six paces he trod the space between them. Vivenzio shuddered as he gazed, and as his steps traversed the narrowed area.

But his feelings no longer vented themselves in frantic wailings. With folded arms, and clenched teeth, with eyes that were bloodshot from much watching, and fixed with a vacant glare upon the ground, with a hard quick breathing, and a hurried walk, he strode backwards and forwards in silent musing for several hours. What mind shall conceive, what tongue utter, or what pen describe the dark and terrible character of his thoughts! Like the fate that moulded them, they had no similitude in the wide range of this world's agony for man. Suddenly he stopped, and his eyes were riveted upon that part of the wall which was over his bed of straw. Words are inscribed here! A human language, traced by a human hand! He rushes forwards them; but his blood freezes as he reads:

'I, Ludovica Sforza, tempted by the gold of the Prince of Tolfi, spent three years in contriving and executing this accursed triumph of my art. When it was completed, the perfidious Tolfi, more devil than man, who conducted me hither one morning, to be witness, as he said, of its perfection, doomed *me* to be the first victim of my own pernicious skill; lest, as he declared, I should divulge the secret, or repeat the effort of my ingenuity. May God pardon him, as I hope he will me, that ministered to his unhallowed purpose! Miserable wretch, whoe'er thou art, that readest these lines, fall on thy knees, and invoke as I have done, His sustaining mercy who alone can nerve thee to meet the vengeance of Tolfi, armed with his tremendous engine, which in a few hours must crush *you*, as it will the needy wretch who made it.'

A deep groan burst from Vivenzio. He stood like one transfixed, with dilated eyes, expanded nostrils, and quivering lips, gazing at this fatal inscription. It was as if a voice from the sepulchre had sounded in his ears, 'Prepare!'

Hope forsook him. There was his sentence, recorded in those dismal words. The future stood unveiled before him, ghastly and appalling. His brain already feels the descending horror, – his bones seem to crack and crumble in the mighty grasp of the iron walls! Unknowing what it is he does, he fumbles in his garment for some weapon of self-destruction. He clenches his throat in his convulsive gripe, as though he would strangle himself at once. He stares upon the walls, and his warring spirit demands, 'Will they not anticipate their office if I dash my head against them?'

An hysterical laugh chokes him as he exclaims, 'Why should I? He was but a man who died first in their fierce embrace; and I should be less than man not to do as much!'

The evening sun was descending, and Vivenzio beheld its golden beams streaming through one of the windows. What a thrill of joy shot through his soul at the sight! It was a precious link that united him, for the moment, with the world beyond. There was ecstasy in the thought. As he gazed, long and earnestly, it seemed as if the windows had lowered sufficiently for him to reach them.

With one bound he was beneath them – with one wild spring he clung to the bars. Whether it was so contrived, purposely to madden with delight the wretch who looked, he knew not; but, at the extremity of a long vista, cut through the solid rocks, the ocean, the sky, the setting sun, olive groves, shady walks, and, in the farthest distance, delicious glimpses of magnificent Sicily, burst upon his sight. How exquisite was the cool breeze as it swept across his cheek, loaded with fragrance! He inhaled it as though it were the breath of continued life. And there was a freshness in the landscape, and in the rippling of the calm green sea, that fell upon his withering heart like dew upon the parched earth.

How he gazed, and panted, and still clung to his hold! sometimes hanging by one hand, sometimes by the other, and then grasping the bars with both, as loth to quit the smiling paradise outstretched before him; till exhausted, and his hands swollen and benumbed, he dropped helpless down, and lay stunned for a considerable time by the fall.

When he recovered, the glorious vision had vanished. He was in darkness. He doubted whether it was not a dream that had passed before his sleeping fancy; but gradually his scattered thoughts returned, and with them came remembrance. Yes! he had looked once again upon the gorgeous splendour of nature!

Once again his eyes had trembled beneath their veiled lids

at the sun's radiance, and sought repose in the soft verdure of the olive tree, or the gentle swell of undulating waves. Oh, that he were a mariner, exposed upon those waves to the worst fury of storm and tempest; or a very wretch, loathsome with disease, plague-stricken, and his body one leprous contagion from crown to sole, hunted forth to gasp out the remnant of infectious life beneath those verdant trees, so he might shun the destiny upon whose edge he tottered!

Vain thoughts like these would steal over his mind from time to time in spite of himself; but they scarcely moved it from that stupor into which it had sunk, and which kept him, during the whole night, like one who had been drugged with opium. He was equally insensible to the calls of hunger and of thirst, though the third day was now commencing since even a drop of water had passed his lips. He remained on the ground, sometimes sitting, sometimes lying; at intervals, sleeping heavily; and when not sleeping, silently brooding over what was to come, or talking aloud, in disordered speech, of his wrongs, of his friends, of his home, and of those he loved, with a confused mingling of all.

In this pitiable condition the sixth and last morning dawned upon Vivenzio, if dawn it might be called – the dim obscure light which faintly struggled through the ONE SOLITARY window of his dungeon. He could hardly be said to notice the melancholy token. And yet he did notice it; for as he raised his eyes and saw the portentous sign, there was a slight convulsive distortion of his countenance.

But what did attract his notice, and at the sight of which his agitation was excessive, was the change his iron bed had undergone. It was a bed no longer. It stood before him, the visible semblance of a funeral couch or bier! When he beheld this, he started from the ground, and, in raising himself suddenly struck his head against the roof, which was now so low that he could no longer stand upright. 'God's will be done!' was all he said, as he crouched his body, and placed his hand upon the bier; for such it was.

The iron bedstead had been so contrived, by the mechanical

art of Ludovico Sforza, that as the advancing walls came in contact with its head and feet, a pressure was produced upon concealed springs, which, when made to play, set in motion a very simple though ingeniously contrived machinery that effected the transformation. The object was, of course, to heighten, in the closing scene of this horrible drama, all the feelings of despair and anguish which the preceding ones had aroused. For the same reason the last window was so made as to admit only a shadowy kind of gloom rather than light, that the wretched captive might be surrounded, as it were, with every seeming preparation for approaching death.

Vivenzio seated himself on his bier. Then he knelt and prayed fervently; and sometimes tears would gush from him. The air seemed thick, and he breathed with difficulty; or it might be that he fancied it was so, from the hot and narrow limits of his dungeon, which were now so diminished that he could neither stand up nor lie down at his full length.

But his wasted spirits and oppressed mind no longer struggled within him. He was past hope, and fear shook him no more. Happy if thus revenge had struck its final blow; for he would have fallen beneath it almost unconscious of a pang. But such a lethargy of the soul, after such an excitement of its fiercest passions, had entered into the diabolical calculations of Tolfi; and the fell artificer of his designs had imagined a counter-acting device.

The tolling of an enormous bell struck upon the ears of Vivenzio! He started. It beat but once. The sound was so close and stunning that it seemed to shatter his very brain, while it echoed through the rocky passages like reverberating peals of thunder. This was followed by a sudden crash of the roof and walls, as if they were about to fall upon and close around him at once. Vivenzio screamed, and instinctively spread forth his arms, as though he had a giant's strength to hold them back. They had moved nearer to him, and were now motionless.

Vivenzio looked up and saw the roof almost touching his head, even as he sat cowering beneath it; and he felt that a further contraction of but a few inches only must commence the frightful operation. Roused as he had been, he now gasped for breath. His body shook violently — he was bent nearly double. His hands rested upon either wall, and his feet were drawn under him to avoid the pressure in front. Thus he remained for more than an hour, when that deafening bell beat again, and again there came the crash of horrid death. But the concussion was now so great that it struck Vivenzio down.

As he lay gathered up in lessened bulk, the bell beat loud and frequent — crash succeeded crash — and on, and on, and on came the mysterious engine of death, till Vivenzio's smothered groans were heard no more! He was horribly crushed by the ponderous roof and collapsing sides — and the flattened bier was his *Iron Shroud*.

# The Ghost and the Bone-Setter

## Joseph Sheridan Le Fanu
## (1814–1873)

If any single British writer played a leading role in the evolvement of the old Gothic tale of terror into what we now know as the modern macabre story, it must surely have been Joseph Sheridan Le Fanu – acclaimed by many as the finest ghost story writer of all. Montague Summers, for one, felt that Le Fanu 'inherited the literary mantle of Mrs Radcliffe' (she died some nine years after his birth) while M. R. James considered him 'one of the best storytellers of the last age.'

Joseph Sheridan Le Fanu was the grand-nephew of the famous playwright, Richard Brinsley Sheridan, and himself embraced the 'profession of the pen' after an unsuccessful attempt to take up the law. He began by writing for the *Dublin University Magazine*, of which periodical he later became editor and finally proprietor. His obsession with the supernatural, and indeed his very real interest in the Gothic novels of the period, made him readily admit such work to his publication and also embark on the retelling of famous Irish ghost legends himself. Le Fanu's very first contribution in this style was *The Ghost and the Bone-Setter* which appeared in the magazine in 1838 and which has not, to my knowledge, been reprinted more than once since.

Probably Le Fanu's best works are the novels, *The House by the Churchyard* (1863) and *Uncle Silas* (1864) and the several collections of his stories. His intense interest in the macabre is said to have resulted in his becoming increasingly gloomy and withdrawn and he was a virtual recluse when he died in Dublin in 1873. Nonetheless, his work in the very twilight of the old Gothic genre is of the first importance and his place as a teller of superb *outré* stories assured for all time.

In looking over the papers of my late valued and respected friend, Francis Purcell, who for nearly fifty years discharged the arduous duties of a parish priest in the south of Ireland, I met with the following document. It is one of many such; for he was a curious and industrious collector of old local traditions – a commodity in which the quarter where he resided mightily abounded. The collection and arrangement of such legends was, as long as I can remember him, his hobby; but I had never learned that his love of the marvellous and whimsical had carried him so far as to prompt him to commit the results of his inquiries to writing, until, in the character of residuary legatee, his will put me in possession of all his manuscript papers. To such as may think the composing of such productions as these inconsistent with the character and habits of a country priest, it is necessary to observe, that there did exist a race of priests – those of the old school, a race now nearly extinct – whose education abroad tended to produce in them tastes more literary than have yet been evinced by the *alumni* of Maynooth.

It is perhaps necessary to add that the superstition illustrated by the following story, namely, that the corpse last buried is obliged, during his juniority of internment, to supply his brother tenants of the churchyard in which he lies, with fresh water to allay the burning thirst of purgatory, is prevalent throughout the south of Ireland.

The writer can vouch for a case in which a respectable and wealthy farmer, on the borders of Tipperary, in tenderness to the corns of his departed helpmate, enclosed in her coffin two pair of brogues, a light and a heavy, the one for dry, the other for sloppy weather; seeking thus to mitigate the fatigues of her inevitable perambulations in procuring water and administering it to the thirsty souls of purgatory. Fierce and desperate conflicts have ensued in the case of two funeral parties approaching the same churchyard together, each endeavouring to secure to his own dead priority of sepulture, and a consequent immunity from the tax levied upon the pedestrian powers of the lastcomer. An instance not long since occurred, in which one of two such parties, through fear of losing to their deceased friend this inestimable advantage, made their way to the churchyard by a short cut, and, in violation of one of their strongest prejudices, actually threw the coffin over the wall, lest time should be lost in making their entrance through the gate. Innumerable instances of the same kind might be quoted, all tending to show how strongly among the peasantry of the south this superstition is entertained. However, I shall not detain the reader further by any prefatory remarks, but shall proceed to lay before him the following:

*Extracts from the MS. Papers of the late Rev. Francis Purcell, of Drumcoolagh.*

I tell the following particulars, as nearly as I can recollect them, in the words of the narrator. It may be necessary to observe that he was what is termed a well-spoken man, having for a considerable time instructed the ingenious youth of his native parish in such of the liberal arts and sciences as he found it convenient to profess – a circumstance which may account for the occurrence of several big words in the course of this narrative, more distinguished for euphonious effect than for correctness of application. I proceed then, without further preface, to lay before you the wonderful adventures of Terry Neil.

'Why, thin, 'tis a quare story, an' as thrue as you're sittin' there; and I'd make bould to say there isn't a boy in the seven parishes could tell it better nor crickther than myself, for 'twas my father himself it happened to, an' many's the time I heerd it out iv his own mouth; an' I can say, an' I'm proud av that same, my father's word was as incredible as any squire's oath in the counthry; and so signs an' if a poor man got into any unlucky throuble, he was the boy id go into the court an' prove; but that doesn't signify – he was as honest and as sober a man, barrin' he was a little bit too partial to the glass, as you'd find in a day's walk; an' there wasn't the likes of him in the counthry round for nate labourin' an' *baan* diggin'; and he was mighty handy entirely for carpenther's work, and mendin' ould spude-threes, an' the likes i' that. An' so he tuk up with bone-setting', as was most nathural, for none of them could come up to him in mendin' the leg iv a stool or a table; an' sure, there never was a bonesetter got so much custom – man an' child, young an' ould – there never was such breakin' and mendin' of bones known in the memory of man. Well, Terry Neil – for that was my father's name – began to feel his heart growin' light, and his purse heavy; an' he took a bit iv a farm in Squire Phelim's ground, just undher the ould castle, an' a pleasant little spot it was; an' day an' mornin' poor crathurs not able to put a foot to the ground, with broken arms and broken legs, id be comin' ramblin' in from all quarters to have their bones spliced up. Well, yer honour, all this was as well as well could be; but it was customary when Sir Phelim id go anywhere out iv the country, for some iv the tinants to sit up to watch in the ould castle, just for a kind of compliment to the ould family – an' a mighty unplisant compliment it was for the tinants, for there wasn't a man of them but knew there was something quare about the ould castle. The neighbours had it, that the squire's ould grand-father, as good a gintleman – God be with him – as I heer'd, as ever stood in shoe-leathern use to keep walkin' about in the middle iv the night, ever sinst he bursted a bloodvessel pullin' out a cork out iv a bottle, as you or I might be doin', and will too, plase God – but that doesn't signify. So, as I was sayin', the ould squire used to come down out of the frame, where his picthur was hung up, and to break the bottles and glasses – God be marciful to us all – an' dthrink all he could come at – an' small blame to him for that same; and then if any of the family id be comin' in, he id be up again in his place, looking as quite an' as innocent as if he didn't know anything about it – the mischievous ould chap.

'Well, your honour, as I was sayin', one time the family up at the castle was stayin' in Dublin for a week or two; and so, as usual, some of the tinants had to sit up in the castle, and the third night it kem to my father's turn. "Oh, tare an' ouns!" says he unto himself, "an' must I sit up all night, and that ould vagabone of a sperit, glory be to God,' says he, 'serenadin' through the house, an' doin' all sorts iv mischief?" However, there was no gettin' aff, and so he put a bould face on it, an' he went up at nightfall with a bottle of pottieen, and another of holy wather.

'It was rainin' smart enough, an' the evenin' was darksome and gloomy, when my father got in; and what with the rain he got, and the holy wather he sprinkled on himself, it wasn't long till he had to swally a cup iv the pottieen, to keep the cowld out iv his heart. It was the ould steward, Lawrence Connor, that opened the door – and he an' my father wor always very great. So when he seen who it was, an' my father tould him how it was his turn to watch in the castle, he offered to sit up along with him; and you may be sure my father wasn't sorry for that same. So says Larry:

'"We'll have a bit iv fire in the parlour," says he.

'"An' why not in the hall?' says my father, for he knew that the squire's picthur was hung in the parlour.

'"No fire can be lit in the hall," says Lawrence, "for there's an ould jackdaw's nest in the chimney."

'"Oh thin," says my father, "let us stop in the kitchen, for it's very unproper for the likes iv me to be sittin' in the parlour," says he.

'"Oh, Terry, that can't be," says Lawrence; "if we keep up the ould custom at all, we may as well keep it up properly," says he.

'"Divil sweep the ould custom!" says my father – to himself, do ye mind, for he didn't like to let Lawrence see that he was more afeard himself.

'"Oh, very well," says he. "I'm agreeable, Lawrence," says he; and so down they both wint to the kitchen, until the fire id be lit in the parlour – an' that same wasn't long doing'.

'Well, your honour, they soon wint up again, an' sat down mighty comfortable by the parlour fire, and they beginned to talk, an' to smoke, an' to dhrink a small taste iv the pottieen; and, moreover, they had a good rousin' fire o' bogwood and turf, to warm their shins over.

'Well, sir, as I was sayin' they kep' convarsin' and smokin' together most agreeable, until Lawrence beginn'd to get sleepy, as was but nathural for him, for he was an ould sarvint man, and was used to a great dale iv sleep.

'"Sure it's impossible," says my father, "it's gettin' sleepy you are?"

'"Oh, divil a tasten" says Larry; "I'm only shuttin' my eyes," says he, to keep out the parfume o' the tibacky smoke, that's makin' them wather," says he. "So don't you mind other people's business," says he, stiff enough, for he had a mighty high stomach av his own (rest his sowl), "and go on," says he, "with your story, for I'm listening", says he, shuttin' down his eyes.

'Well, when my father seen spakin' was no use, he went on with his story. By the same token, it was the story of Jim Soolivan and his ould goat he was tellin' —an' a plisant story it is — an' there was so much divarsion in it, that it was enough to waken a dormouse, let alone to prevint a Christian goin' asleep. But, faix, the way my father tould it, I believe there never was the likes heerd sinst nor before, for he bawled out every word av it, as if the life was fairly lavin' him, thrying to keep ould Larry awake; but, faix, it was no use, for the hoorsness came an him, an' before he kem to the end of his story Larry O'Connor beginned to snore like a bagpipes.

'"Oh, blur an' agres," says my father, "isn't this a hard case," says he, "that ould villain, lettin' on to be my friend, and to go asleep this way, an' us both in the very room with a sperit," says he. "The crass o' Christ about us!" says he; and with that he was goin' to shake Lawrence to waken him, but he just remimbered if he roused him, that he'd surely go off to his bed, an' lave him complately alone, an' that id be by far worse.

'"Oh thin," says my father, "I'll not disturb the poor boy. It id be neither friendly nor good-nathured," says he, "to tormint him while he is asleep," says he; "only I wish I was the same way, myself," says he.

'An' with that he beginned to walk up an' down, an' sayin' his prayers, until he worked himself into a sweat, savin' your presence. But it was all no good; so he dthrunk about a pint of sperits, to compose his mind.

'"Oh," says he, "I wish to the Lord I was as asy in my mind as Larry there, Maybe," says he, "if I thried I could go asleep"; an' with that he pulled a big armchair close beside Lawrence, an' settled himself in it as well as he could.

'But there was one quare thing I forgot to tell you. He couldn't help, in spite av himself, lookin' now an' thin at the picthur, an' he immediately obsarved that the eyes av it was follyin' him about, an' starin' at him, an' winkin' at him, wheriver he wint. "Oh," says he, when he seen that, "it's a poor chance I have," says he; "an' bad luck was with me that day I kem into this unforthunate place," says he. "But any way there's no use in bein' freckened now," says he; "for if I am to die, I may as well parspire undaunted," says he.

'Well, your honour, he thried to keep himself quite an' asy, an' he thought two or three times he might have wint asleep, but for the way the storm was groanin' and creakin' through the great heavy branches outside, an' whistlin' through the ould chimleys iv the castle. Well, afther one great roarin' blast iv the wind, you'd think the walls iv the castle was just goin' to fall, quite an' clane, with the shakin' iv it. All av a suddint the storm stopt, as silent an' as quite as if it was a July evenin'. Well, your honour, it wasn't stopped blowin' for three minnites, before he thought he hard a sort iv a noise over the chimley-piece; an' with that my father just opened his eyes the smallest taste in life, an' sure enough he seen the ould square gettin' out iv the picthur, for all the world as if he was throwin' aff his ridin' coat, until he stept out clane an' complate, out av the chimley-piece, an' thrun himself down an the floor. Well, the slieveen ould chap – an' my father thought it was the dirtiest turn iv all – before he beginned to do anything out iv the way, he stopped for a while to listen wor they both asleep; an' as soon as he thought all was quite, he put out his hand and tuk hould iv the whisky bottle, an' dthrank at laste a pint iv it. Well, your honour, when he tuk his turn out iv it, he settled it back mighty cute entirely, in the very same spot it was in before. An' he beginned to walk up an' down the room, lookin' as sober an' as solid as if he never done the likes at all. An' whinever he went apast my father, he thought he felt a great scent of brimstone, an' it was that that freckened him entirely; for he knew it was brimstone that was burned in hell, savin' your presence. At any rate, he often heerd it from Father Murphy, an' he had a right to know what belonged to it – he's dead since, God rest him. Well, your honour, my father was asy enough until the sperit kem past him; so close, God be marciful to us all, that the smell iv the sulphur tuk the breath clane out iv him; an' with that he tuk such a fit iv coughin', that it al-a-most shuk him out iv the chair he was sittin' in.

'"Ho, ho!" says the squire, stoppin' short about two steps aff, and turnin' round facin' my father, "is it you that's in it? – an' how's all with you, Terry Neil?"

'"At your honour's service," says my father (as well as the fright id let him, for he was more dead than alive), "an' it's proud I am to see your honour tonight," says he.

'"Terence," says the squire, "you're a respectable man" (an' it was thrue for him), "an industhrious, sober man, an' an example of inebriety to the whole parish," says he.

'"Thank your honour," says my father, gettin' courage, "you were always a civil spoken gintleman. God rest your honour."

'"*Rest* my honour?" says the sperit (fairly gettin' red in the face with the madness), "Rest my honour?" says he. "Why, you ignorant spalpeen," says he, "you mane, niggarly igno-ramush," says he, "where did you leave your manners?" says he. "If I *am* dead, it's no fault iv mine," says he; "an' it's not to be thrun in my teeth at every hand's turn, by the likes iv you," says he, stampin' his foot an the flure, that you'd think the boords id smash undher him.

'"Oh," says my father, "I'm only a foolish, ignorant poor man," says he.

'"You're nothing else," says the squire: "but any way," says he, "it's not to be listenin' to your gosther, nor convarsin' with the likes iv you, that I came *up* – down I mane," says he – (an' as little as the mistake was, my father tuk notice iv it). "Listen to me now, Terence Neil," says he: "I was always a good masther to Pathrick Neil, your grandfather," says he.

"''Tis thrue for your honour," says my father.

"'And, moreover, I think I was always a sober, riglar gintleman," says the squire.

"'That's your name, sure enough," says my father (though it was a big lie for him, but he could not help it).

"'Well," says the sperit, "although I was as sober as most men – at laste as most gintlemin," says he; "an' though I was at different pariods a most extempory Christian, and most charitable and inhuman to the poor," says he; "for all that I'm not as asy where I am now," says he, "as I had a right to expect," says he.

"'An' more's the pity," says my father. Maybe your honour id wish to have a word with Father Murphy?"

"'Hould your tongue, you misherable bliggard," says the squire, "it's not iv my sowl I'm thinkin' – an' I wondther you'd have the impitence to talk to a gintleman consarnin' his sowl; and when I want *that* fixed," says he, slappin' his thigh, "I'll go to them that knows what belongs to the likes," says he. "It's not my sowl," says he, sittin' down opposite my father; "it's not my sowl that's annoyin' me most – I'm unasy on my right leg," says he, "that I bruk at Glenvarloch cover the day I killed black Barney."

'My father found out afther, it was a favourite horse that fell undher him, afther leapin' the big fence that runs along by the glin.

"'I hope," says my father, "your honour's not unasy about the killin' iv him?"

"'Hould your tongue, ye fool," said the squire, "an' I'll tell you why I'm unasy on my leg," says he. "In the place, where I spend most iv my time," says he, "except the little leisure I have for lookin' about me here," says he, "I have to walk a great dale more than I was ever used to," says he, "and by far more than is good for me either," says he; "for I must tell you," says he, "the people where I am is ancommonly fond iv cowld

wather, for there is nothin' betther to be had; an', moreover, the
weather is hotter than is altogether plisant," says he; "and I'm
appinted," says he, "to assist in carrin' the wather, an' gets a
mighty poor share iv it myself," says he, "an' a mighty
throublesome, wearin' job it is, I can tell you," says he; "for
they're all iv them surprisingly dthry, an' dthrinks it as fast
as my legs can carry it," says he; "but what kills me entirely,"
says he, "is the wakeness in my leg," says he, "an' I want you
to give it a pull or two to bring it to shape," says he, "and that's
the long an' the short iv it," says he.

'"Oh, plase your honour," says my father (for he didn't
like to handle the sperit at all), "I wouldn't have the impi-
dence to do the likes to your honour," says he; "It's only to
poor crathurs like myself I'd do it to," says he.

'"None iv your blarney," says the square. "Here's my leg,"
says he, cockin' it up to him — "pull it for the bare life," says
he; "an' if you don't, by the immortial powers I'll not lave a
bone in your carcish I'll not powdher," says he.

'When my father heerd that, he seen there was no use in
purtendin', so he tuk hould iv the leg, an' he kep' pullin'
an' pullin', till the sweat, God bless us, beginned to pour down
his face.

'"Pull, you devil" says the squire.

'"At your sarvice, your honour," says my father.

'"Pull harder," says the squire.

'My father pulled like the divil.

'"I'll take a little sup," says the squire, rachin' over his hand
to the bottle, "to keep up my courage," says he, lettin' an to be
very wake in himself intirely. But, as cute as he was, he was
out here, for he tuk the wrong one. "Here's to your good health,
Terence," says he; "an' now pull like the very divil." An' with
that he lifted the bottle of holy wather, but it was hardly to his
mouth, whin he let a screech out, you'd think the room id
fairly split with it, an' made one chuck that sent the leg clane
aff his body in my father's hands. Down wint the squire over
the table, an' bang wint my father half-way across the room on
his back, upon the flure. Whin he kem to himself the cheerful

mornin' sun was shinin' through the windy shutthers, an' he was lying flat an his back, with the leg iv one of the great ould chairs pulled clane out iv the socket an' tight in his hand, pintin' up to the ceilin', an' ould Larry fast asleep, an' snorin' as loud as ever. My father wint that mornin' to Father Murphy, an' from that to the day of his death, he never neglected confission nor mass, an' what he tould was betther believed that he spake av it but seldom. An', as for the squire, that is the sperit, whether it was that he did not like his liquor, or by rason iv the loss iv his leg, he was never known to walk agin.'

# The Tribunal of the Inquisition

## G. W. M. Reynolds
### (1814–1879)

As a final selection from the work of the British Gothic storytellers I have chosen a man considered by several scholars of the genre to be both greatly underestimated and unjustly overlooked in most studies of English literature: George William Macarthur Reynolds. What little fame is accredited to him is usually for having founded the Sunday newspaper, *Reynold's Weekly* (later retitled *Reynold's News* and now defunct) and a series of linked stories which appeared first in weekly penny numbers and then in volume form as *The Mysteries of London* (1845–1850).

G. W. M. Reynolds was the son of a Royal Navy captain who left him a fortune on his death. Failing to complete the academic course which his father had compelled him to undertake, young Reynolds went to Europe and settled in Paris. Here he commenced his life-long involvement with newspapers by starting *The London and Paris Courier* – a disastrous venture which absorbed much of his legacy. Returning to London he became a magazine editor and also began writing for the Fleet Street publisher, Edward Lloyd, who numbered among his many contributors Thomas Peckett Prest. In the succeeding years he began his *Mysteries*, became involved in politics and – with the continuing popularity of his novels – established *Reynold's Weekly*. At the height of his fame he was certainly among the two or three most widely read authors of the time.

Due to the response to the *Mysteries of London*, Reynolds wrote a number of sequels including *Mysteries of the Court of Naples* and *Mysteries of the Inquisition*. From the later work comes the following grim story which contains much of that chilling atmosphere which made the Gothic terror-romance so widely popular in its time and the idea on which it was founded of reading terror-for-pleasure so enduring.

THE great hall, in which the court sat, was hung with black cloth. At one end was an ample semicircular table, behind which was a high dais supporting a large arm chair of black velvet. The table and the floor of the dais was covered with coarse black baize.

On the species of throne sat the Grand Inquisidor, Peter Arbuez. Above his seat, and hanging to the wall was a great crucifix of ivory upon a black ground. Two other seats, of the same sombre hue as that of the presiding judge, stood on each side of the inquisitorial throne. These were destined for the inquisidors, who acted as puisne or assistant judges. Upon the table, at the right hand of the Inquisidor, stood a bell: on the other side was a large bible spread open. In the middle of the table, opposite the president, were writing materials, flanked by an hour-glass.

On the other side of the table was a rude bench, or rather a triangle of coarse wood, supported upon four legs, and intended to serve as a seat for the accused. At the right hand of the Grand Inquisidor stood the sbirri and four men masked, and clothed in long black garments, their heads covered with a species of hood, with holes prepared for the use of the eyes, mouth, and nose, – four men of an appearance horrible to behold! On the left of the Grand Inquisidor were two clerks or secretaries, who wrote to the dictation of the president, or took down the testimony of witnesses.

Peter Arbuez, attired in his grand ecclesiastical costume, and wearing round his neck the white cross which distinguished the votaries of Saint Dominicus, sat upon the presidential throne, and cast around him a sinister glance. The four assistant judges, not sharing the passions which agitated the soul of that terrible man, but animated by the same spirit of domination, awaited the entrance of the prisoner with feigned anxiety. But no interior emotion agitated their brazen countenances: they were strangers to those struggles and doubts which usually agitate every upright judge, who is aware of his duty to punish offenders, and yet trembles for fear he should strike an innocent person. *Their* decrees were decided before-hand. To crush – to overwhelm, without compunction, such was their motto. They only feared the necessity of declaring an acquittal – and never pronounced one willingly.

At the opposite end of the apartment stood priests and monks of different orders – the usual witnesses of those solemnities, – and a few grandees of Spain, who were devoted to the Inquisition, and whom Peter Arbuez had invited by notes; for it was not a common offender who was now about to appear before the inquisitorial judges: it was a great and powerful nobleman – an excellent Catholic accused of heresy – and whom his peers would see condemned to horrible tortures without daring to utter a word in his defence.

A terrible silence pervaded that mournful assembly. One would have thought that it was a congregation of mutes and funereal votaries, so deeply did those present wear an expression of sorrow and of death. But in a few moments a slight movement took place on the part of the spectators: their eyes were slowly turned towards the door; and the accused, conducted between two sbirri, entered the judgment hall.

He was a tall man, deadly pale, and apparently about fifty years of age. His hair, of a jet black dye naturally, but now chequered with grey, spread over an open forehead, expressive of loftiness rather than of intellect; his eyes beamed with the honourable and chivalrous fire of a true son of Castille; and a profound religious resignation, the distinctive characteristic of the Christians of Spain, attempered the expression of bitterness and grief which veiled the countenance of that individual. He was, moreover, enervated and enfeebled by the privations he had undergone during two days of confinement and solitary reflections in the dungeons of the inquisition.

He advanced with slow steps in the midst of his guards, and, when he came in front of the president, he looked around for a seat whereon to rest himself; but perceiving only the triangular bench behind him, a smile of bitter contempt curled his lips. He however seated himself, as well as he could on that stool of strange inquisitorial invention. Then, raising his head without audacity, but with inconceivable dignity he fixed upon Peter

Arbuez a glance so full of meaning that it would have put to the blush any one save the Inquisidor.

Peter Arbuez sustained that glance without apparent emotion, and, addressing the prisoner, said, 'Accused, rise, and swear upon the Bible to tell the truth.' The prisoner arose slowly, approached the table, and, placing his hand upon the sacred volume, exclaimed in a firm and penetrating tone, 'I swear in the name of the Saviour and his Holy Gospel, to tell the whole truth.'

'What is your name?' demanded the Grand Inquisidor.

'Paul Joachim Manuel Argoso, Count of Cervallos, grandee of Spain of the second class, and governor of the city of Seville, by the will of our well-beloved King Charles the Fifth!'

'Pass over your titles,' said the Inquisidor: 'they belong to you no more. Every one who is arrested by the holy office loses his distinctions and his property.'

Manuel Argoso answered not a word; but his lower lip painfully quivered: the pure blood of Castille had revolted within him.

'Your age?' demanded the Inquisidor.

'Fifty years,' answered the governor.

'Manuel Argoso,' continued the Inquisidor, in a slow, harmonious, but implacable tone, 'you are accused of having received at your house, a young man of an heretical race – a young man who professes sentiments opposed to the doctrines of the Holy Catholic Church, and whom you did not denounce.'

'My lord I know not what you mean,' answered Manuel Argoso, gravely.

'Not to denounce heresy, is to encourage heresy,' proceeded the Inquisidor. 'You could not be ignorant that Don Stephen de Vargas, descended from a Moorish family, is far from being a pure Catholic; and not only have you received him at your house, but you have betrothed him to your only daughter.'

At these words a melancholy sigh rent the bosom of the unfortunate man; and a tear was seen stealing down his countenance: – but, recovering himself immediately, he said, 'My lord, the youthful Stephen de Vargas, is descended from one of those noble Abencerrage families who submitted voluntarily to the religion of Jesus Christ, and who recognized Ferdinand and Isabella as their sovereigns. Those families received from our monarchs the same privileges that are enjoyed by our Castilian nobles; and I cannot see how we can deny them those rights which they legitimately acquired a century ago.'

'He who obtains a privilege, has a duty to perform,' answered the Grand Inquisidor; 'and when he forgets that duty, his privilege is forfeited. Don Stephen de Vargas, professing doctrines contrary to the holy canons of the church, loses his safeguard as a good Catholic: he is stained with heresy; and whoever forms an alliance with him, is reputed a heretic, and becomes liable to the penalties attached to that crime.'

'My lord,' said Argoso, solemnly, 'I swear to you upon my honour as a nobleman and a knight, that Don Stephen de Vargas has never pronounced in my presence a word which a pious Christian and a loyal subject might not hear.'

'He denies his faults!' ejaculated the Grand Inquisidor, with an air of compassion, turning at the same time towards the assistant judges as if to consult them with a glance. The judges answered with gestures of horror, and hypocritically raised their eyes to heaven. This pantomime was familiar to them, and supplied with them the place of that rectitude and logical discrimination which characterize honourable judges. The clerks took down the above dialogue; and while they finished their notes, Peter Arbuez seemed to reflect profoundly.

At length regarding the governor of Seville with an air of profound melancholy – so well assumed that it deceived many present – he said, 'My son, you behold me sincerely afflicted at your obstinacy. I have loved you as a friend; and in my zeal in favour of christianity and the sincerity of my friendship, I pray that heaven will endow you with the spirit of repentance and contrition.'

'My lord,' said Don Manuel Argoso, 'God is my judge that I never entertained a thought contrary to the laws of the holy gospel.'

'But you confess your relations with the young semi-Moorish heretic?' said the Inquisidor insidiously.

'Don Stephen de Vargas is no heretic, my lord,' returned the governor firmly, 'he is as good a Catholic as you or I.'

'Heavens!' cried the Inquisidor; 'the Evil Spirit blinds him, and he insults our holy religion!'

'My lord,' said one of the judges, 'he avows his relations with Don Stephen de Vargas.'

'He does,' answered the Inquisidor. 'Prisoner, can you deny that you have educated your daughter in the same anti-Catholic sentiments which you profess?'

'My lord, I leave you to answer that question yourself, for your lordship was a daily visitor at my house,' said Argoso.

'I was not her confessor,' replied the Inquisidor drily.

'Oh! my lord, is Dolorez accused of that same heresy which is so falsely imputed to me? Is Dolorez a prisoner also?'

'We are not speaking of your daughter at present,' said the Inquisidor: 'it is you who are accused.'

'My daughter! what have you done with my daughter?' cried the wretched father, joining his hands together, in a suppliant tone.

'Silence!' exclaimed the Inquisidor severely. 'I am not here to answer questions, nor you to ask them. Let the witnesses enter.'

The side door of the hall opened and two figures enveloped in long black cloaks, and wearing white wax masks upon their countenances moved slowly into the room. A shudder passed through the frame of Don Manuel Argoso; for it seemed as if the very dead had risen up against him – so much did those mysterious beings resemble two moving corpses, swathed in funereal gowns!

The Grand Inquisidor directed them to swear that they would tell the truth. They took the oath; and then the first, who was no other than Henriques, delivered his testimony which was to the effect that Don Stephen de Vargas was notoriously a heretic, and that he was a frequent visitor at the palace of Don Manuel Argoso.

The other witness was then ordered to stand forward; and the Inquisidor began to question him. In those examinations the witnesses merely deposed to facts, or to inventions which passed for facts, their names never being divulged in the public court; and hence their strange and appalling disguise. The officers of the Inquisition usually provided the attendance of the witnesses; and in this case Peter Arbuez had directed his favourite Joseph to prepare two for the first examination of the noble prisoner.

'Dost thou know the accused?' said the Grand Inquisidor to the second witness.

'I do,' was the reply, given in a tone which seemed familiar to the Inquisidor, and which he nevertheless could not altogether recollect.

'What do you know of him?'

'That he is as good a Catholic as you or any one here,' was the calm and intrepid answer.

'What!' cried the Grand Inquisidor, thrown off his guard by this unexpected reply, which also produced a lively emotion in the minds of all present; 'you are here to take the part of a heretic?'

'I am here to tell the truth,' was the answer.

'And do you know the consequences of defending a heretic?' demanded the enraged Arbuez.

'I know that the person of a witness is sacred and inviolable, and that I have nothing to fear from you, all-powerful though you be,' returned the witness in a mild, slow, and yet firm tone.

'Enough – depart,' cried the Grand Inquisidor: 'you are a witness unworthy of belief; for all Seville knows that Don Stephen is a heretic, and the accused himself had admitted his relations with him.'

'Then why call witnesses at all?' asked the mysterious masque.

'Away with him – he insults the tribunal!' exclaimed Arbuez, scarcely able to restrain his rage. 'Let him at once be unmasked in the privaet hall, and suffered to depart by the wicket of the donjon.'

The masked witness was hurried away by the sbirri, and Arbuez murmured to himself –

'This is strange – most strange! Could Joseph have deceived me? No – he must have been himself deceived! And that voice – methinks its tones are not strange to me!'

'My lord,' whispered an assistant judge, 'we are satisfied that the prisoner merits the cord.'

'Now then let the will of God be done,' exclaimed the Grand Inquisidor aloud. 'Away with the accused to the torture room!' The sbirri and masked executioners before described, precipitated themselves upon Don Manuel Argoso and hurried him into an adjacent hall – or rather large vault.

This was the torture room.

Cold, cheerless, and horrible was the aspect of that ominous place. Instruments of torture met the eye on every side. Cords, thumb-screws, steel rods, pinchers, knives, scissors, long nails, and iron boots, were suspended to the walls, or heaped upon the shelves; and in one corner a charcoal furnace sent forth its lurid light, the flames playing backwards and forwards in the obscure angle in which it stood.

Two men in masks held torches in their hands, and two others took their station close to the unfortunate governor who was placed beneath a pulley attached to the ceiling, and from which depended a long cord.

For a moment the governor fancied he had quitted this world, and reached the other, where he had been consigned to that terrible place of which Scripture speaks as being the scene of 'weeping and gnashing of teeth'.

In a few minutes Peter Arbuez entered the room, accompanied by another inquisidor and by the apostolic notary.

The accused was standing in the middle of that terrible chamber of torment. When his judge appeared before him, a melancholy sense of the reality of the whole scene seized upon his mind; and, raising his eyes to Heaven as if to implore it for mercy, he beheld the pulley above his head. He shuddered involuntarily.

Peter Arbuez and the Inquisidor who accompanied him,

seated themselves upon a bench, in order to behold the melancholy scene; and Don Manuel, although endowed with a strong mind, could not defend himself against the profound terror. He thought of his daughter, who would perhaps be compelled to submit to the same ordeal; and all his courage abandoned him.

'My son,' said Peter Arbuez, advancing towards him, 'confess your crimes, and do not afflict us by persisting in error and heresy: spare us the pain of being compelled to obey the just and severe laws of the Inquisition in treating you with all the rigour which they impose upon the criminal.'

Manuel Argoso did not reply; but he cast upon the Grand Inquisidor a look which seemed to defy the torture.

Arbuez made a sign, and the torturer divested the victim of all his upper garments, leaving him stripped to the shirt.

'Avow and confess everything,' said the Grand Inquisidor once more, but still preserving a soft and persuasive tone. 'We are your fathers in God, and our only desire is to save your soul. Come, my son – a sincere confession can alone save you in the next world, and spare you the just vengeance of God in this.'

'I cannot confess crimes which do not exist.'

'My son,' said the Inquisidor, 'I am truly grieved to behold your impertinence; and I implore the Saviour to touch your soul, which, without his grace, will be infallibly lost; for the demon holds it in his power; and it is he who inspires you with this culpable obstinacy in your evil ways.'

Peter Arbuez fell upon his knees, and murmured a prayer which was unintelligible to those by whom he was surrounded. He then made the sign of the cross several times, struck his breast with apparent contrition and humility, and remained for some moments with his head resting on his two hands.

At that moment the terrible Inquisidor of Seville was only a humble Dominican, praying and weeping for the sins of others!

At length he rose.

'Miserable slave of the demon,' he said addressing himself to the accused, 'has God deigned to listen to my humble prayers, and unsealed your eyes to the light of our holy faith!'

'My belief is still the same,' answered Argoso; 'never has it

varied for a moment; and such as I received it from my fathers, do I hold it now.'

'God is my judge that this is not my fault,' exclaimed the Grand Inquisidor, raising his eyes to heaven. 'Away with him to the rack!'

This horrible torture was immediately applied.

Argoso did not, however, utter a complaint: only his chest, breathless and suffocating, gave forth a hollow sound between a concentrated groan and the rattle of death. His glassy eyes seemed to have no power to close themselves. The cord which confined his hands together, had cut so deeply into his flesh, that the blood spurted over his shirt on the ground: and, as the floor of the cavern was formed of a soft and damp clay, the victim was covered with mingled slime and gore.

He fell upon the ground, an inert mass: his dislocated bones and distended muscles could no longer sustain him.

It was a horrible spectacle to behold that man, strong, robust, and vigorous, crushed by an atrocious torture, and punished before he had been judged!

What might not be expected from a jurisprudence which imposed upon the accused such terrible tests? But the Inquisidors had no pity; they ruled by means of torture – they fed upon the agonies of their victims!